Charles Davies

Elements of Geometry and Trigonometry

SALZWASSER VERLAG

Charles Davies

Elements of Geometry and Trigonometry

Reprint of the original, first published in 1858.

1st Edition 2023 | ISBN: 978-3-37514-885-0

Verlag (Publisher): Salzwasser Verlag GmbH, Zeilweg 44, 60439 Frankfurt, Deutschland
Vertretungsberechtigt (Authorized to represent): E. Roepke, Zeilweg 44, 60439 Frankfurt, Deutschland
Druck (Print): Books on Demand GmbH, In de Tarpen 42, 22848 Norderstedt, Deutschland

ELEMENTS

OF

GEOMETRY AND TRIGONOMETRY,

FROM THE WORKS OF

A. M. LEGENDRE.

REVISED AND ADAPTED TO THE COURSE OF MATHEMATICAL INSTRUCTION IN THE UNITED STATES,

BY CHARLES DAVIES, LL. D.,

AUTHOR OF ARITHMETIC, ALGEBRA, PRACTICAL MATHEMATICS FOR PRACTICAL MEN, ELEMENTS OF DESCRIPTIVE AND OF ANALYTICAL GEOMETRY, ELEMENTS OF DIFFERENTIAL AND INTEGRAL CALCULUS, AND SHADES, SHADOWS, AND PERSPECTIVE.

NEW-YORK:

PUBLISHED BY A. S. BARNES & CO.,

No. 51 JOHN-STREET.

CINCINNATI:—RICKEY, MALLORY & WEBB.

1858.

PREFACE.

In the preparation of the present edition of the Geometry of A. M. Legendre, the original work has been consulted as a model and guide, but not implicitly followed as a standard. The general methods, the language employed, and the arrangement of the arguments in many of the demonstrations, will be found to differ essentially from the original, and also from the English translation by Dr. Brewster.

In the original work, as well as in the translation, the propositions are not enunciated in general terms, but with reference to, and by the aid of, the particular diagrams used for the demonstrations. It is believed that this departure from the method of Euclid has been generally regretted. The propositions of Geometry are general truths, and as such, should be stated in general terms, and without reference to particular figures. The method of enunciating them by the aid of particular diagrams, seems to have been adopted to avoid the difficulty which beginners experience in comprehending abstract propositions. But in avoiding this difficulty, and thus lessening at first, the intellectual labor, the faculty of abstraction, which it is one of the primary objects of the study of Geometry to strengthen, remains, to a certain extent, unimproved.

The methods of demonstration, in several of the Books, have been entirely changed. By regarding the circle as the limit of the inscribed and circumscribed polygons, the demonstrations in Book V. have been much simplified; and the same principle is made the basis of several important demonstrations in Book VIII.

The term *Solid* has heretofore been used in Geometry to denote a limited portion of space. It would seem to have been adopted, and has doubtless been continued in use, because the mind readily apprehends the forms and relations of tangible objects, while it often experiences difficulty in dealing with those which are purely abstract. Geometry, however, has nothing to do with matter, which is always implied by the term *Solid* or *Solidity*. All the definitions, axioms, and demonstrations, relate only to *extent* and *form;* and hence, should not be encumbered with the foreign idea of material things. The term *Volume* has been substituted for *Solid*, and is deemed to be much more appropriate.

In the present, as in the previous Edition, that part of Plane Trigonometry which relates only to the computation of the sides and angles of Triangles, has been separated from that which is purely analytical; this method of treating the subject having been generally approved.

The Treatise on Analytical Plane and Spherical Trigonometry, of the present Edition, was prepared by Professor Church, of the Military Academy, for publication as a separate work; but, under the impression that it would be more useful as a component part of a regular course, he generously offered it as a substitute for the Trigonometry of the previous Editions.

It seems appropriate, that a course of Mathematics which had its origin in the wants of the Military Academy, at an early period of its history, and which lays claim to no higher merit than to keep pace with the growth and development of science in that institution, should be enriched by so valuable a contribution. It is not easy to make suitable acknowledgments for the results of much careful study combined with long experience in teaching, or to express the sense of obligation for so acceptable a token of personal friendship.

The application of Trigonometry to the measurement of Heights and Distances, embracing the use of the Table of Logarithms, and of Logarithmic Sines; and the application of Geometry to the mensuration of planes and volumes, are useful exercises for the Student. Practical examples cannot fail to point out the generality and utility of abstract science.

FISHKILL LANDING,
July, 1857.

CONTENTS.

APPENDIX.

TRIGONOMETRY.

INTRODUCTION.

PLANE TRIGONOMETRY.

TREATED GEOMETRICALLY

ANALYTICAL TRIGONOMETRY.

ANALYTICAL PLANE TRIGONOMETRY.

SPHERICAL TRIGONOMETRY.

MENSURATION OF SURFACES.

MENSURATION OF VOLUMES.

ELEMENTS

OF

GEOMETRY.

INTRODUCTION.

1. SPACE extends indefinitely in every direction, and contains all bodies.

2. EXTENSION is any limited portion of space, and has three dimensions: length, breadth, and thickness.

3. A VOLUME is *any one* of a class of things, falling under the common term, Extension; and when occupied by matter is called a *Body* or *Solid.* The difference between the terms, Extension and Volume, is simply this: the former is a common term denoting *any* and *every* limited portion of space, while the latter is a singular term, denoting but one such portion.

The term, *Solid,* has heretofore been used in Geometry, in preference to Volume, because the mind apprehends readily the forms and relations of tangible objects, while it often experiences much difficulty in dealing with the abstract notions derived from them. It is, however, important to observe, that *the geometrical properties of Volumes have no connection whatever with matter, and that the demonstrations which establish and make known those properties, are based on the attributes of Extension only.*

4. A Volume being a limited portion of space, is necessarily divided from the indefinite space which surrounds it: that which so divides it, is called a *Surface.* Now, since that which bounds a volume is no part of the volume itself, it follows, that a surface has but two dimensions, length and breadth.

5. If we consider a limited portion of a surface, then that which separates such portion from the other parts of the surface, is called a *Line.* This mark of division forms no part of the surfaces which it separates: hence, a line has length only, without breadth or thickness.

6. If we regard a limited portion of a line, that which separates such portion from the part beyond, at either extremity, is called a *Point.* But this mark of division forms no part of the line itself: hence, a point has neither length, breadth, nor thickness, but place, or position, only.

7. Although we use the term *Volume* to denote a given portion of space, the term *surface* to denote the boundary of a volume, the term *line* to denote the boundary of a surface, and the term *point* to designate the limit of a line, still, we may employ either of these terms, in an abstract sense, without any reference to the others.

Thus, we may contemplate a river, as a volume, without considering its boundaries; may look upon the surface and perceive that it has length and breadth without referring to its depth; or, we may regard the distance across, without taking into account either its depth or length. So, likewise, we may consider a point without any reference to the line which it limits.

In the definitions and reasonings of Geometry, these terms are always used in an *abstract sense;* they are mere *signs to the mind of the conceptions for which they stand.*

8. ANGLE is a term which designates the portion of a surface lying between two lines meeting at a common point; and it also denotes a portion of space lying between two or more planes.

9. MAGNITUDE is a general term employed to denote the quantities which arise from considering the dimensions of extension, and is equally applicable to lines, angles, surfaces, and volumes. Geometry is conversant about four kinds of magnitudes:

1. Lines; which have length without breadth or thickness:

2. Angles; bounded by straight lines, by curves, by planes, or by curved surfaces:

3. Surfaces; which have length and breadth without thickness: and,

4. Volumes; which have length, breadth, and thickness.

10. FIGURE is a term applied to a geometrical magnitude, and expresses the idea of shape or form. Thus, "A triangle is a plane *figure* bounded by three straight lines."

11. A PROPERTY of a figure, is a mark or attribute common to all figures of the same class.

12. The portions of extension which constitute the geometrical magnitudes, are indicated to the mind by certain marks, called *lines*.

Thus, we say, the straight line AB, measures the shortest distance between the two points A and B. The mark AB, on the paper, is not the geometrical line AB, but only the *sign* or *representative* of it—the geometrical line itself, having merely a mental existence.

We also say, that the triangle ACB is bounded by the three straight lines AB, AC, CB. Now, the triangle ACB, is but the *sign*, to the mind, of a portion of a plane. That which the eye sees is not the geometrical conception on which the mind acts and reasons: but is, as it were, the word or sign which stands for and expresses the abstract idea.

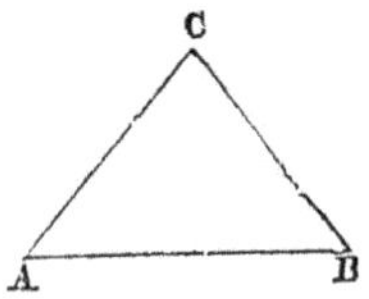

These considerations have induced me to represent the geometrical magnitudes by the fewest possible lines, and to reject altogether the method of shading the figures. It is the conception of extension, in the abstract, with which the mind should be made conversant, and too much pains cannot be taken to exclude the idea that we are dealing with material things.

ELEMENTS OF GEOMETRY.

BOOK I.

DEFINITIONS.*

1. EXTENSION is a limited portion of space. It has three dimensions: length, breadth, and height or thickness.

2. A MAGNITUDE is anything that can be measured. A *geometrical magnitude* is a magnitude which possesses one or more of the attributes of extension.

3. GEOMETRY is the science which treats of the properties and relations of the geometrical magnitudes.

4. A POINT is that which has position, but not magnitude.

5. A LINE is that which has length, but neither breadth nor thickness. Lines are of two kinds, *Straight* and *Curved.*

6. A STRAIGHT LINE is one which lies in the same direction at every point.

7. A BROKEN LINE is one made up of limited straight lines not lying in the same direction.

8. A CURVED LINE is one which changes its direction at every point.

The word *line*, alone, is used to designate a straight line; and the word *curve*, to designate a curved line.

9. A SURFACE is that which has length and breadth, without thickness.

---

* See Davies' Logic and Utility of Mathematics, § 1.

Surfaces are of two kinds, *Plane* and *Curved.*

10. A PLANE is a surface, such, that if any two of its points be joined by a straight line, that line will lie wholly in the surface.

11. A CURVED SURFACE is a surface which is neither a plane nor composed of planes.

12. A VOLUME is that which has length, breadth, and thickness.

13. A PLANE ANGLE is a portion of a plane lying between two straight lines meeting at a point. The straight lines are called the *sides* of the angle, and their common point, the *vertex* of the angle.

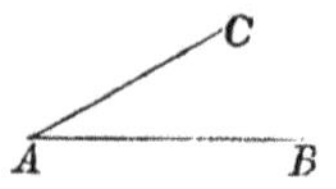

Thus, CAB is a plane angle, BA and CA are its sides, and A is its vertex. An angle is sometimes designated by a single letter written at the vertex, as the angle A. Generally, however, three letters are employed to designate an angle, as the angle CAB, the letter at the vertex being always placed in the middle.

Angles are of two kinds, *right angles* and *oblique angles.*

14. If one straight line meet another, forming two angles on the same side of the second line, they are called *adjacent angles.* When the adjacent angles are equal, each is called a RIGHT ANGLE, and the two lines are said to be *perpendicular* to each other.

15. All angles which are not right angles, are called OBLIQUE ANGLES.

Oblique angles are of two kinds, *acute* and *obtuse.*

An ACUTE ANGLE is an angle less than a right angle.

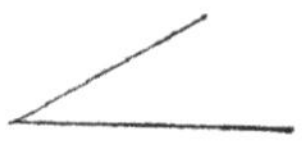

An OBTUSE ANGLE is an angle greater than a right angle.

16. Two straight lines are *parallel*, when lying in the same plane, they cannot meet, how far soever, either way, both of them be produced. They then have the same direction.

17. A POLYGON is a portion of a plane bounded by straight lines.

The broken line which bounds a polygon, is called its *perimeter.*

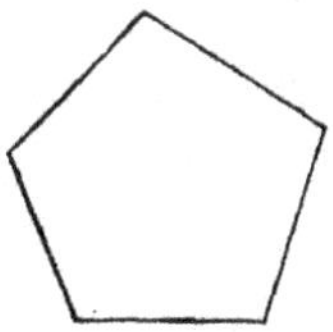

18. Polygons are named from the number of their sides or angles.

A polygon of three sides is called a *triangle;* one of four sides, a *quadrilateral;* one of five sides, a *pentagon;* one of six sides, a *hexagon;* one of seven sides, a *heptagon;* one of eight sides, an *octagon;* one of nine sides, a *nonagon;* one of ten sides, a *decagon;* one of eleven sides, an *undecagon;* one of twelve sides, a *dodecagon;* and so on.

19. An EQUILATERAL polygon is one which has all its sides equal. An *equiangular* polygon is one which has all its angles equal. A *regular* polygon is one which is both equilateral and equiangular.

20. Two polygons are *equilateral*, or *mutually equilateral*, when they have their sides equal each to each, and placed in the same order; that is, when following their perimeters in the same direction, the first side of the one is equal to the first side of the other, the second to the second, the third to the third, and so on.

21. Two polygons are *equiangular*, or *mutually equiangular*, when they have their angles equal each to each, and placed in the same order. In polygons which are mutually equilateral, or mutually equiangular, any two corresponding sides or angles are called *homologous.*

22. Triangles may be classified either with reference to their sides or to their angles.

When classified with reference to their sides, there are three classes:

1st. *Scalene triangles*, those in which no two sides are equal.

2d. *Isosceles triangles*, those in which two sides are equal.

3d. *Equilateral triangles*, those in which all the sides are equal.

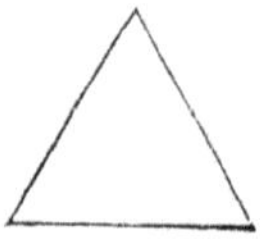

When classified with reference to their angles, there are also three classes:

1st. *Acute angled triangles*, those whose angles are all acute.

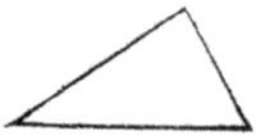

2d. *Right-angled triangles*, those which have one right angle.

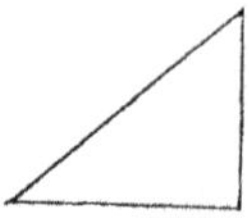

3d. *Obtuse-angled triangles*, those which have one obtuse angle.

23. Quadrilaterals are divided into three classes, according to the relative directions of their sides:

1st. The TRAPEZIUM, which has no two sides parallel.

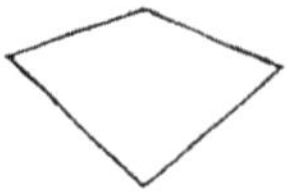

2d. The TRAPEZOID, which has only two of its sides parallel.

3d. The PARALLELOGRAM, which has its opposite sides parallel, two and two.

24. Parallelograms are divided according to the nature of their sides and angles, into four classes:

1st. The RHOMBOID, which is an oblique-angled parallelogram.

2d. The RHOMBUS, which is an equilateral rhomboid.

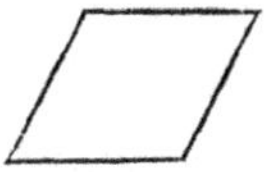

3d. The RECTANGLE, which is a right-angled parallelogram.

4th. The SQUARE, which is an equilateral rectangle.

25. A DIAGONAL is a line joining the vertices of two angles, which are not consecutive.

26. A BASE of a polygon is any side on which the polygon may be supposed to stand.

DEFINITIONS OF TERMS.

1. An *axiom* is a self-evident truth.

2. A *demonstration* is a train of logical arguments brought to a conclusion.

3. A *theorem* is a truth which becomes evident by demonstration.

4. A *problem* is a question which requires a solution.

5. A *lemma* is an auxiliary proposition, employed in the demonstration of a theorem, or the solution of a problem.

6. The common name, *proposition*, is applied indifferently, to axioms, theorems, and problems.

7. A *corollary* is an obvious consequence, of one or more propositions.

8. A *scholium* is a remark made on one or more preceding propositions, which tends to point out their connection, their use, their restriction, or their extension.

9. An *hypothesis* is a supposition, made either in the enunciation of a proposition, or in the course of a demonstration.

10. A *postulate* is a self-evident problem.

EXPLANATION OF SIGNS.

1. The sign $=$ is the sign of equality; thus, the expression $A=B$, signifies that A is equal to B.

2. To signify that A is less than B, the expression $A<B$ is used.

3. To signify that A is greater than B, the expression $A>B$ is used; the less quantity being always at the vertex of the angle.

4. The sign $+$ is called *plus*; it indicates addition.

5. The sign $-$ is called *minus*; it indicates subtraction:

Thus, $A+B$, represents the sum of the quantities A and B; $A-B$ represents their difference, or what remains after B is taken from A; and $A-B+C$, or $A+C-B$, signifies that A and C are to be added together, and that B is to be subtracted from their sum.

6. The sign $\times$ indicates multiplication: thus $A\times B$ represents the product of A and B.

The expression $A\times(B+C-D)$ represents the product of A by the quantity $B+C-D$. If $A+D$ were to be multiplied by $A-B+C$, the product would be indicated thus;

$$(A+D)\times(A-B+C),$$

whatever is enclosed within the curved lines, being considered as a single quantity. The same thing may also be indicated by a bar: thus,

$$\overline{A+B+C}\times D,$$

denotes that the sum of A, B and C, is to be multiplied by D.

7. A figure placed before a quantity, serves as a multiplier to that quantity; thus, $3AB$ signifies that the line AB is taken three times; $\frac{1}{2}A$ signifies the half of the angle A.

8. The square of the line AB is designated by $\overline{AB}^2$; its cube by $\overline{AB}^3$. What is meant by the square and cube of a line, will be explained in its proper place.

9. The sign $\surd$ indicates a root to be extracted; thus $\surd 2$ means the square-root of 2; $\sqrt{A\times B}$ means the square-root of the product of A and B.

AXIOMS.

1. Things which are equal to the same thing, are equal to each other.

2. If equals be added to equals, the sums will be equal.

3. If equals be taken from equals, the remainders will be equal.

4. If equals be added to unequals, the wholes will be unequal.

5. If equals be taken from unequals, the remainders will be unequal.

6. Things which are doubles of equal things, are equal to each other.

7. Things which are halves of equal things, are equal to each other.

8. The whole is greater than any of its parts.

9. The whole is equal to the sum of all its parts.

10 All right angles are equal to each other.

11 From one point to another only one straight line can be drawn.

12. A straight line measures the shortest distance between two points.

13. Through the same point, only one straight line can be drawn which shall be parallel to a given line.

14. Magnitudes, which being applied the one to the other, coincide throughout their whole extent, are equal

POSTULATES.

1. Let it be granted, that a straight line may be drawn from one point to another point.

2. That a terminated straight line may be prolonged, in a straight line, to any length.

3. That if two straight lines are unequal, the length of the less may always be laid off on the greater.

4. That a limited straight line may be bisected: that is, divided into two equal parts.

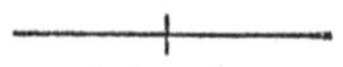

5. That a straight line may bisect a given angle.

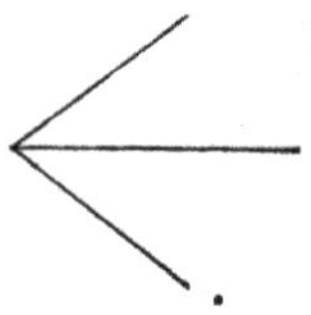

6. That a perpendicular may be drawn to a given straight line, either from a point without the line, or at a point of a line.

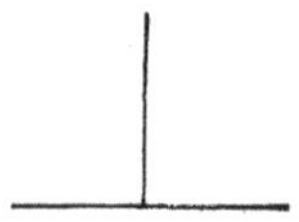

7. That a straight line may be drawn, making with a given straight line, an angle equal to a given angle.

8. That a line may be drawn through a given point, and parallel to a given straight line.

PROPOSITION I. THEOREM.

If one straight line meet another straight line, the sum of the two adjacent angles will be equal to two right angles.

Let the straight line DC meet the straight line AB at C; then will the angle ACD plus the angle DCB, be equal to two right angles.

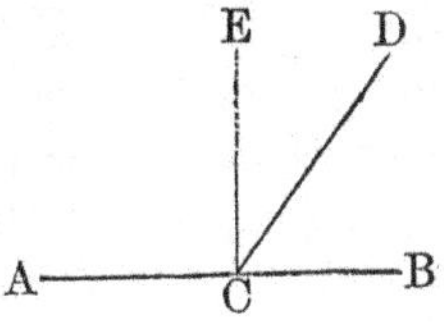

At the point C suppose CE to be drawn perpendicular to AB: then, $ACE + ECB =$ two right angles (D. 13).* But ECB is equal to $ECD + DCB$ (A. 9): hence, $ACE + ECD + DCB =$ two right angles. But $ACE + ECD = ACD$ (A. 9): therefore, $ACD + DCB =$ two right angles.

Cor. 1. If one of the angles ACD or DCB, is a right angle, the other will also be a right angle.

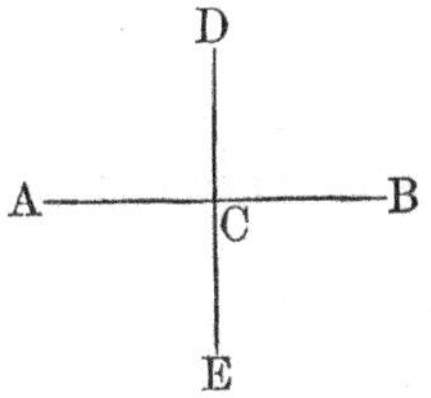

Cor. 2. If a straight line DE is perpendicular to another straight line AB; then, conversely, AB will be perpendicular to DE.

For, since DE is perpendicular to AB, the angle ACD will be a right angle (D. 13). But since AC meets DE at the point C, making one angle ACD a right angle, the adjacent angle ACE will also be a right angle (C. 1). Therefore, AB is perpendicular to DE (D. 13).

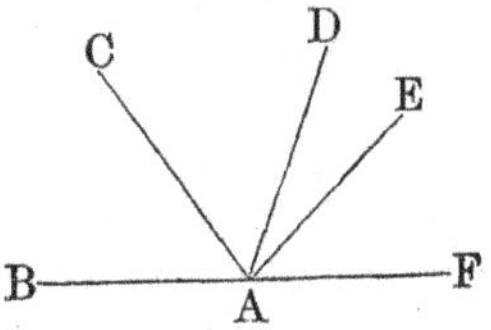

Cor. 3. The sum of the consecutive angles BAC, CAD, DAE, EAF, formed on the same side of the line BF, is equal to two right angles; for, their sum is equal to that of the two adjacent angles BAC and CAF.

---

* In the references, A. stands for Axiom—D. for Definition—B. for Book—P. for Proposition—C. for Corollary—S. for Scholium, and Prob. for Problem.

PROPOSITION II. THEOREM.

Two straight lines, which have two points common, coincide the one with the other, throughout their whole extent, and form one and the same straight line.

Let A and B be the two common points of two straigh lines.

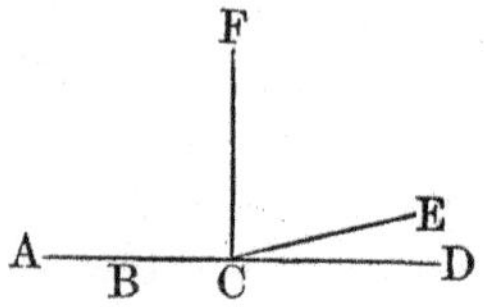

In the first place, the two lines will coincide between the points A and B; for, otherwise there would be two straight lines between A and B, which is impossible (A. 11).

Suppose, however, that in being prolonged, these lines begin to separate at some point, as C, the one becoming CD, the other, CE. At the point C, suppose CF to be drawn, making with AC, the right angle ACF.

Now, since ACD is a straight line, the angle FCD will be a right angle (P. I., C. 1): and since ACE is a straight line, the angle FCE will also be a right angle. Hence, the angle FCD is equal to the angle FCE (A. 10): that is, a whole is equal to one of its parts, which is impossible (A. 8): therefore the two straight lines which have two points, A and B, in common, cannot separate at any point, when prolonged; hence, they form one and the same straight line.*

Cor. Two straight lines cannot intersect in more than one point.

PROPOSITION III. THEOREM.

When a straight line meets two other straight lines at a common point, making the sum of the two contiguous angles equal to two right angles, the two lines form one and the same straight line.

Let the straight line CD meet the two lines AC, CB, at their common point C, and let the sum of the two adjacent angles, DCA, DCB, be equal to two right angles: then,

* See Note A. It is earnestly recommended to every pupil to read and understand this Note. Also, see Logic and Utility of Mathematics, § 262.

will CB be the prolongation of AC; or, AC and CB will form one and the same straight line.

For, if CB is not the prolongation of AC, let CE be that prolongation. Then the line ACE being straight, the sum of the angles ACD, DCE, will be equal to two right angles (P. I). But by hypothesis, the sum of the angles ACD, DCB, is also equal to two right angles: therefore (A. 1),

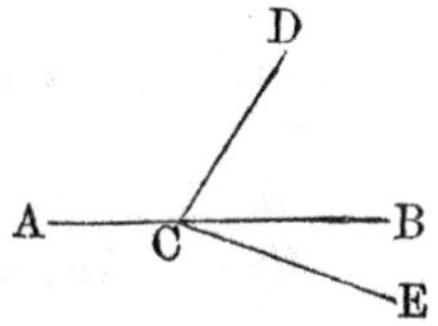

$$ACD+DCE \text{ must be equal to } ACD+DCB.$$

Taking away the angle ACD from each, there remains the angle DCE equal to the angle DCB: that is, a whole equal to a part, which is impossible (A. 8): therefore, AC and CB form one and the same straight line.

PROPOSITION IV. THEOREM.

When two straight lines intersect each other, the opposite or vertical angles, which they form, are equal.

Let AB and DE be two straight lines, intersecting each other at C; then will the angle ECB be equal to the angle ACD, and the angle ACE to the angle DCB.

For, since the straight line DE is met by the straight line AC, the sum of the angles ACE, ACD, is equal to two right angles (P. I.); and since the straight line AB is met by the straight line EC, the sum of the angles ACE, and ECB, is equal to two right angles: hence (A. 1),

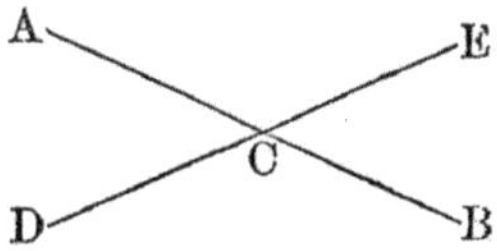

$$ACE+ACD \text{ is equal to } ACE+ECB.$$

Take away from both, the common angle ACE, there remains (A. 3) the angle ACD, equal to its opposite or vertical angle ECB. In a similar manner it may be proved that ACE is equal to DCB.

Scholium. The four angles formed about a point by two straight lines, which intersect each other, are together equal to four right angles. For, the sum of the two angles ACE, ECB, is equal to two right angles (P. I); and the sum of the other two, ACD, DCB, is also equal to two right angles: therefore, the sum of the four, is equal to four right angles.

In general, *if any number of straight lines* CA, CB, CD, &c., meet in a common point C, the sum of all the successive angles, ACB, BCD, DCE, ECF, FCA, will be equal to four right angles. For, if four right angles were formed about the point C, by two lines perpendicular to each other, their sum would be equal to the sum of the consecutive angles ACB, BCD, DCE, ECF, FCA

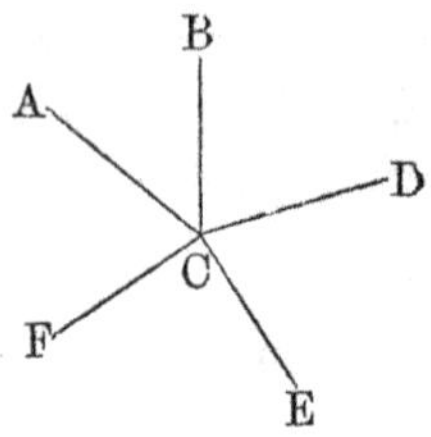

PROPOSITION V. THEOREM.

If two triangles have two sides and the included angle of the one, equal to two sides and the included angle of the other, each to each, the two triangles will be equal.

In the two triangles EDF and BAC, let the side ED be equal to the side BA, the side DF to the side AC, and the angle D to the angle A; then will the triangle EDF be equal to the triangle BAC.

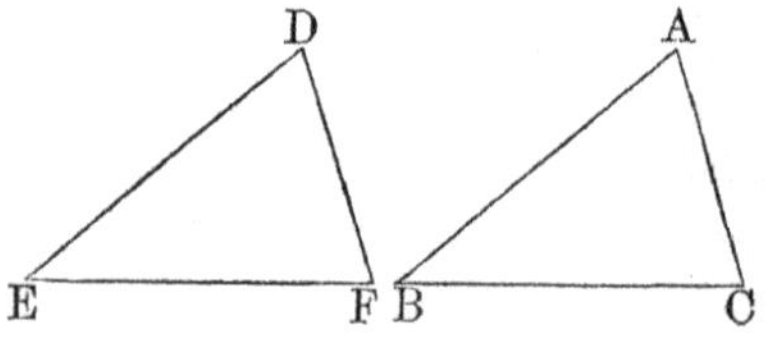

For, if these triangles be applied the one to the other, they will exactly coincide. Let the side ED be placed on the equal side BA; then, since the angle D is equal to the angle A, the side DF will take the direction AC. But DF is equal to AC; therefore the point F will fall on C, and the third side EF, will coincide with the third side BC (A. 11): consequently, the triangle EDF is equal to the triangle BAC (A. 14).

Cor. When two triangles have these three things equal, viz., the side $ED=BA$, the side $DF=AC$, and the angle $D=A$, the remaining three are also respectively equal, viz., the side $EF=BC$, the angle $E=B$, and the angle $F=C$.

PROPOSITION VI. THEOREM.

If two triangles have two angles and the included side of the one, equal to two angles and the included side of the other, each to each, the two triangles will be equal.

Let EDF and BAC be two triangles, having the angle E equal to the angle B, the angle F to the angle C, and the included side EF to the included side BC; then will the triangle EDF be equal to the triangle BAC.

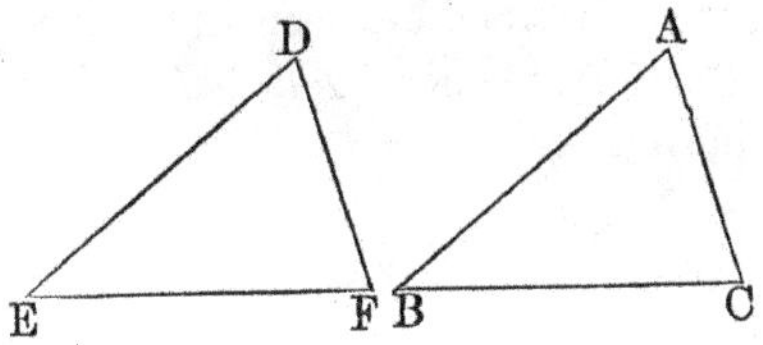

For, let the side EF be placed on its equal BC, the point E falling on B, and the point F on C. Then, since the angle E is equal to the angle B, the side ED will take the direction BA; and hence, the point D will be found somewhere in the line BA. In like manner, since the angle F is equal to the angle C, the line FD will take the direction CA, and the point D will be found somewhere in the line CA. Hence, the point D, falling at the same time in the two straight lines BA and CA, must fall at their intersection A (P. II., COR.): hence, the two triangles EDF, BAC, coincide with each other, and consequently, are equal (A. 14).

Cor. Whenever, in two triangles, these three things are equal, viz.: the angle $E=B$, the angle $F=C$, and the included side EF equal to the included side BC, it may be inferred that the remaining three are also respectively equal, viz.: the angle $D=A$, the side $ED=BA$, and the side $DF=AC$.

Scholium. Two triangles which being applied to each other, coincide in all their parts, are equal (A. 14). The like parts are those which coincide with each other; hence, they are also equal each to each. The converse of this proposition is also true; viz., *if two triangles have all the parts of the one equal to the parts of the other, each to each, the triangles will be equal:* for, when applied to each other, they will mutually coincide.

PROPOSITION VII. THEOREM.

The sum of any two sides of a triangle, is greater than the third side.

Let ABC be a triangle: then will the sum of two of its sides, as AB, BC, be greater than the third side AC

For the straight line AC measures the shortest distance between the points A and C (A. 12); hence, $AB+BC$ is greater than AC.

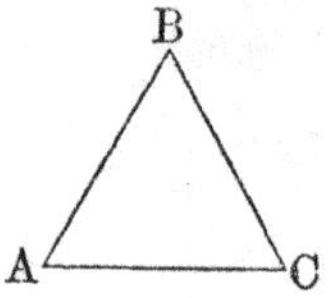

Cor. If from both members of the inequality

$$AC<AB+BC$$

we take away either of the sides, as BC, we shall have (A. 5)

$$AC-BC<AB:$$

that is, *the difference between any two sides of a triangle is less than the third side.*

PROPOSITION VIII. THEOREM.

If from any point within a triangle, two straight lines be drawn to the extremities of either side, their sum will be less than that of the two remaining sides of the triangle.

Let O be any point within the triangle BAC, and let the lines OB, OC, be drawn to the extremities of either side, as BC; then will

$$OB+OC<BA+AC.$$

Let BO be prolonged till it meets the side AC in D then

$$OC<OD+DC \text{ (P. 7)}:$$

add BO to each, and we have

$$BO+OC<BO+OD+DC \text{ (A. 4)}:$$

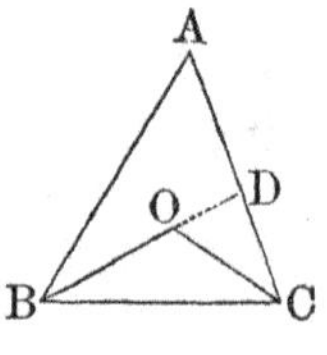

or, $BO+OC<BD+DC.$

But, $BD<BA+AD$:

add DC to each, and we have

$$BD+DC<BA+AC.$$

But it has been shown that

$$BO+OC<BD+DC:$$

therefore, still more is

$$BO+OC<BA+AC.$$

PROPOSITION IX. THEOREM.

If two triangles have two sides of the one equal to two sides of the other, each to each, and the included angles unequal, the third sides will be unequal; and the greater side will belong to the triangle which has the greater included angle.

Let BAC and EDF be two triangles, having the side $AB=DE$, $AC=DF$, and the angle $A>D$; then will the side BC be greater than EF.

Make the angle $CAG=D$; take $AG=DE$, and draw CG.

Then, the triangles GAC and EDF will be equal, since they have two sides and an included angle in each equal, each to each (P. 5); consequently, CG is equal to EF (P. 5, C).

There may be three cases in this proposition.

1st. When the point G falls without the triangle BAC

2d. When it falls on the side BC; and

3d. When it falls within the triangle.

Case I. In the triangles AGC and ABC, we have,

$GI+IC>GC$; and

$AI+IB>AB$;

therefore

$AG+BC>GC+AB.$

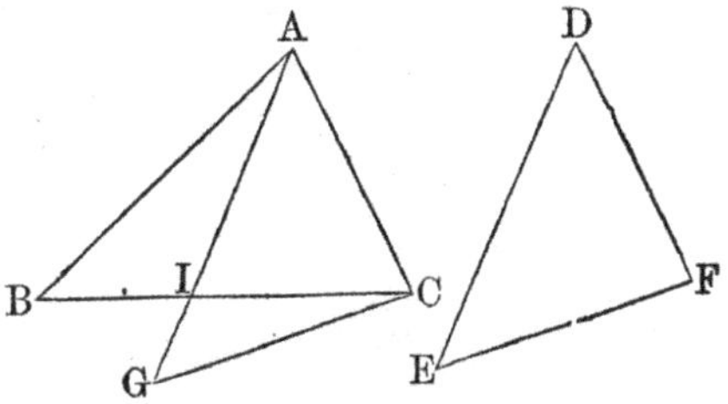

Taking away AG from the one side and its equal AB from the other, and there will remain BC

greater than GC. But we have found that GC is equal to EF; therefore, BC will be greater than EF.

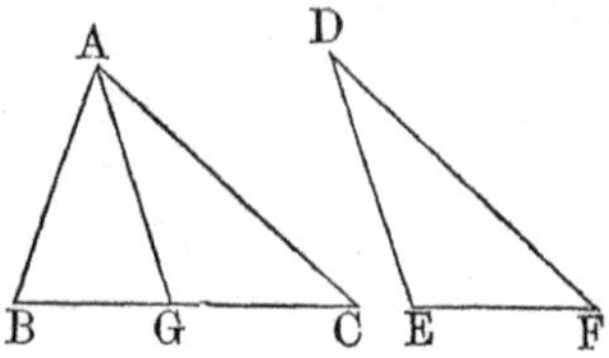

Case II. If the point G fall on the side BC, it is evident that GC, or its equal EF, will be shorter than BC (A. 8).

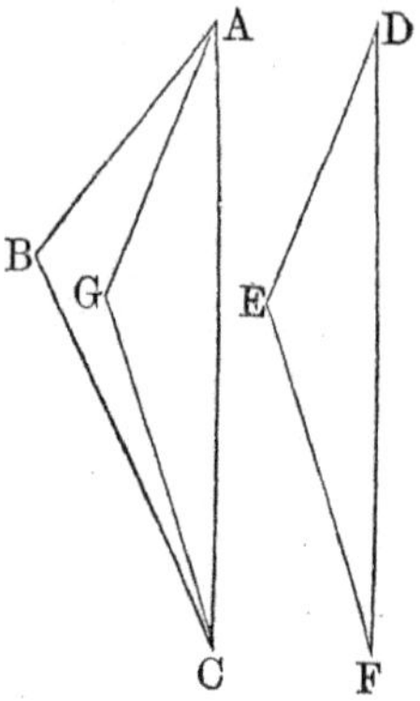

Case III. Lastly, if the point G fall within the triangle BAC, we shall have

$$AG+GC<AB+BC,$$

taking AG from the one, and its equal AB from the other, there will remain

$$GC<BC \text{ or } BC>EF.$$

Cor. Conversely: if two sides BA, AC, of a triangle BAC, are equal to two sides ED, DF, of a triangle EDF, each to each, while the third side BC of the first is greater than the third side EF of the second, then the angle BAC of the first triangle will be greater than the angle EDF of the second.

For, if not greater, the angle BAC must be equal to EDF or less than it. In the first case, the side BC would be equal to EF (P. 5, C), in the second, BC would be less than EF; but either of these results contradicts the hypothesis: therefore, BAC is greater than EDF.

PROPOSITION X. THEOREM.

If two triangles have the three sides of the one equal to the three sides of the other, each to each, the triangles are equal.

Let EDF and BAC be two triangles, having the side $ED=BA$, the side $EF=BC$, and the side $DF=AC$; then will the angle $D=A$, the angle $E=B$, and the angle $F=C$, and consequently the triangle EDF will be equal to the triangle BAC.

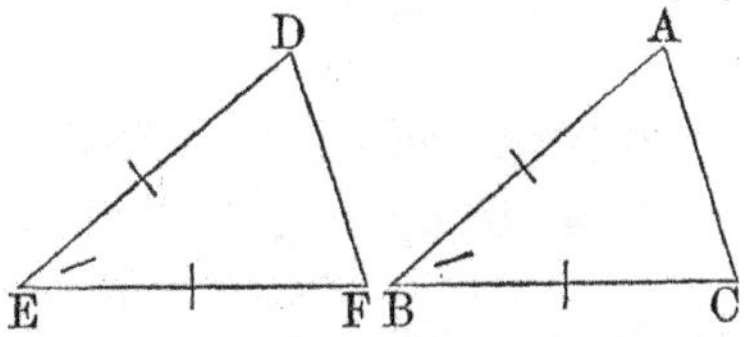

For, since the sides ED, DF, are equal to BA, AC, each to each, if the angle D were greater than A, it would follow, by the last proposition, that the side EF would be greater than BC; and if the angle D were less than A, the side EF would be less than BC. But EF is equal to BC, by hypothesis; therefore, the angle D can neither be greater nor less than A; therefore it must be equal to it. In the same manner it may be shown that the angle E is equal to B, and the angle F to C: hence, the two triangles are equal (P. 6, S).

Scholium. It may be observed, that when two triangles are equal to each other, the equal angles lie opposite the equal sides, and consequently, the equal sides opposite the equal angles: thus, the equal angles D and A, lie opposite the equal sides EF and BC.

PROPOSITION XI. THEOREM.

In an isosceles triangle, the angles opposite the equal sides are equal.

Let BAC be an isosceles triangle, having the side BA equal to the side AC; then will the angle C be equal to the angle B.

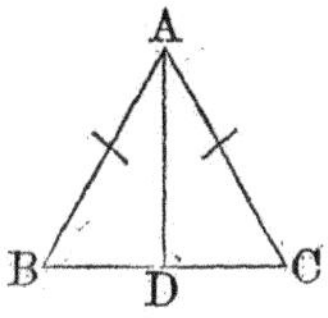

For, join the vertex A, and the middle point D, of the base BC. Then, the triangles BAD, DAC, will have all the sides of the one equal to those of the other, each to each. For, BA is equal to AC, by hypothesis, AD is common, and BD is equal to DC by construction: therefore, by the last proposition, the angle B is equal to the angle C.

Cor. 1. An equilateral triangle is likewise equiangular, that is to say, has all its angles equal.

Cor. 2. The equality of the triangles BAD, DAC, proves also that the angle BAD, is equal to DAC, and BDA to

ADC; hence, the latter two are right angles. *Therefore, the line drawn from the vertex of an isosceles triangle to the middle point of the base, divides the angle at the vertex into two equal parts, and is perpendicular to the base.*

Scholium. In a triangle which is not isosceles, any side may be assumed indifferently as the *base;* and the *vertex* is, in that case, the vertex of the opposite angle. In an isosceles triangle, however, that side is generally assumed as the base, which is not equal to either of the other two.

PROPOSITION XII. THEOREM.

Conversely: If two angles of a triangle are equal, the sides opposite them are also equal, or, the triangle is isosceles.

In the triangle BAC, let the angle B be equal to the angle ACB; then will the side AC be equal to the side AB.

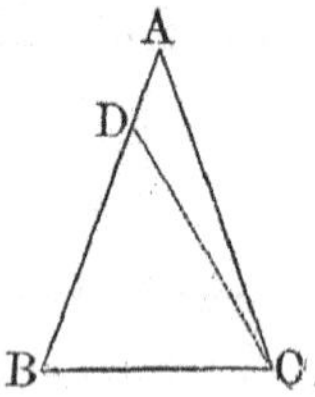

For, if these sides are not equal, suppose AB to be the greater. Then, take BD equal to AC, and draw CD. Now, in the two triangles BDC, BAC, we have $BD=AC$, by construction; the angle B equal to the angle ACB, by hypothesis; and the side BC common: therefore, the two triangles, BDC, BAC, have two sides and the included angle of the one, equal to two sides and the included angle of the other, each to each: hence they are equal (P. 5). But the part cannot be equal to the whole (A. 8); hence, there is no inequality between the sides BA and AC; therefore, the triangle BAC is isosceles.

PROPOSITION XIII. THEOREM.

The greater side of every triangle is opposite to the greater angle; and conversely, the greater angle is opposite to the greater side.

First, In the triangle CAB, let the angle C be greater than the angle B; then will the side AB, opposite C, be greater than AC, opposite B.

For, make the angle $BCD=B$. Then, in the triangle CDB, we shall have $CD=BD$ (P. 12).

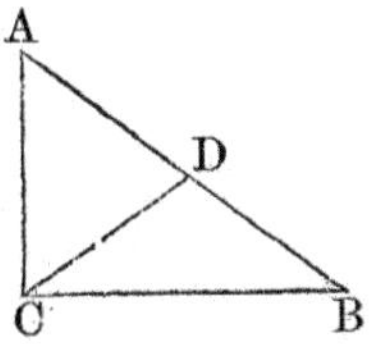

Now, the side $AC<AD+DC$;

but $AD+DC=AD+DB=AB$:

therefore, $AC<AB$, or, $AB>AC$.

Secondly. Suppose the side $AB>AC$; then will the angle C, opposite to AB, be greater than the angle B, opposite to AC.

For, if the angle $C<B$, it follows, from what has just been proved, that $AB<AC$; which is contrary to the hypothesis. If the angle $C=B$, then the side $AB=AC$ (P. 12); which is also contrary to the supposition. Therefore, when $AB>AC$, the angle C cannot be less than B, nor equal to it; therefore, the angle C must be greater than B.

PROPOSITION XIV. THEOREM.

From a given point, without a straight line, only one perpendicular can be drawn to that line.

Let A be the point, and DE the given line.

Let us suppose that we can draw two perpendiculars, AB, AC. Prolong either of them, as AB, till BF is equal to AB, and draw FC. Then the two triangles CAB, CBF, will be equal: for, the angles CBA and CBF are right angles, the side CB is common, and the side AB equal to BF, by construction; therefore, the two triangles are equal, and the angle $ACB=BCF$ (P. 5, C). But the angle ACB is a right angle, by hypothesis; therefore, BCF must likewise be a right angle. Now, if the adjacent angles BCA, BCF, are together equal to two right angles, ACF must be a straight line (P. 3). Whence, it follows, that between the same two points, A and F, two straight lines can be drawn, which is impossible (A. 11): therefore, only one

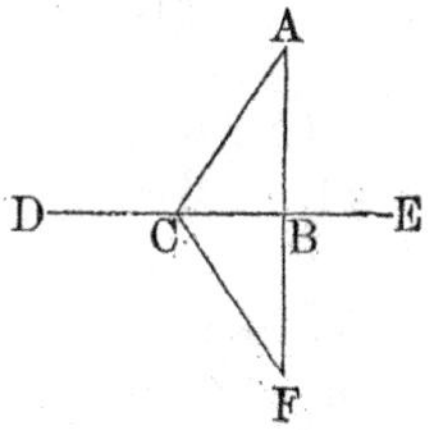

perpendicular can be drawn from the same point to the same straight line.

Cor. At a given point C, in the line AB, it is also impossible to erect more than one perpendicular to that line. For, if CD, CE, were both perpendicular to AB, the angles BCD, BCE, would both be right angles; hence, they would be equal (A. 10), and a part would be equal to the whole, which is impossible.

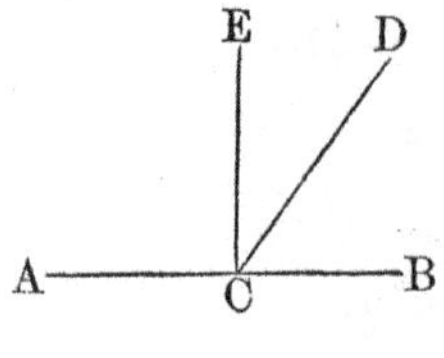

PROPOSITION XV. THEOREM.

If from a point without a straight line, a perpendicular be let fall on the line, and oblique lines be drawn to different points:

1st. *The perpendicular will be shorter than any oblique line.*

2d. *Any two oblique lines which intersect the given line at points equally distant from the foot of the perpendicular, will be equal.*

3d. *Of two oblique lines which intersect the given line at points unequally distant from the perpendicular, the one which cuts off the greater distance will be the longer.*

Let A be the given point, DE the given line, AB the perpendicular, and AD, AC, AE, the oblique lines.

Prolong the perpendicular AB till BF is equal to AB, and draw FC, FD.

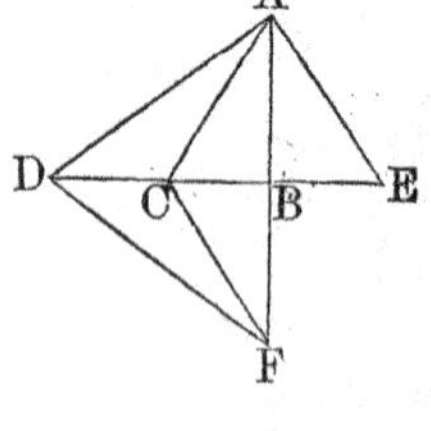

First. The triangle BCF, is equal to the triangle CAB, for they have the right angle $CBF = CBA$, the side CB common, and the side $BF = BA$; hence, the third sides, CF and CA are equal (P. 5, C). But ABF, being a straight line, is shorter than ACF, which is a broken line (A. 12); therefore, AB, the half of ABF, is shorter than AC, the half of ACF; hence, the perpendicular is shorter than any oblique line.

Secondly. Let us suppose $BC=BE$; then the triangle CAB will be equal to the triangle BAE; for $BC=BE$, the side AB is common, and the angle $CBA=ABE$; hence, the sides AC and AE are equal (P. 5, C): therefore, two oblique lines, which meet the given line at equal distances from the perpendicular, are equal.

Thirdly. Since the point C is within the triangle FDA, the sum of the sides FD, DA, is greater than the sum of the lines FC, CA (P. 8): therefore AD, the half of the broken line FDA, is greater than AC, the half of FCA: consequently, the oblique line which cuts off the greater distance, is the longer.

Cor. 1. The perpendicular measures the shortest distance of a point from a line.

Cor. 2. From the same point to the same straight line, only two equal straight lines can be drawn; for, if there could be more, we should have at least two equal oblique lines on the same side of the perpendicular, which is impossible.

PROPOSITION XVI. THEOREM.

If at the middle point of a given straight line, a perpendicular to this line be drawn:

1*st. Any point of the perpendicular will be equally distant from the extremities of the line:*

2*d. Any point, without the perpendicular, will be unequally distant from the extremities.*

Let AB be the given straight line, C its middle point, and ECF the perpendicular.

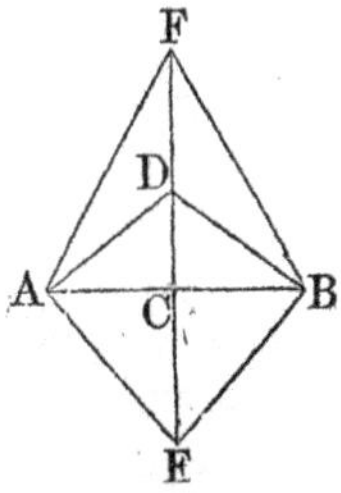

First. Let D be any point of the perpendicular, and draw DA and DB. Then, since $AC=CB$, the two oblique lines AD, DB, are equal (P. 15). So, likewise, are the two oblique lines, AE, EB, the two AF, FB, and so on. Therefore, any point in the perpendicular is equally distant from the extremities A and B.

Secondly. Let I be any point out of the perpendicular. If IA and IB be drawn, one of these lines will cut the perpendicular in some point as D; from this point, drawing DB, we shall have $DB=DA$. But, the straight line IB is less than $ID+DB$, and

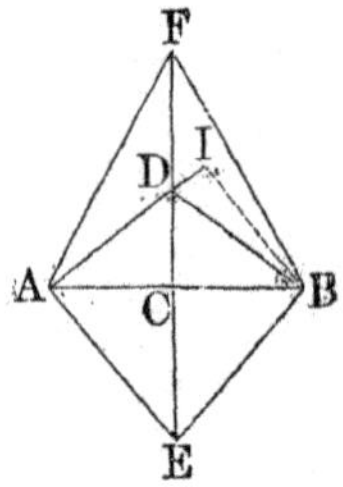

$$ID+DB=ID+DA=IA;$$

therefore, $IB<IA$; consequently, any point out of the perpendicular, is unequally distant from the extremities A and B

Cor. Conversely: if a straight line have two points E and F, each of which is equally distant from the extremities A and B, it will be perpendicular to AB at the middle point C.

PROPOSITION XVII. THEOREM.

If two right-angled triangles have the hypothenuse and a side of the one equal to the hypothenuse and a side of the other, each to each, the triangles are equal.

Let BAC and EDF be two right-angled triangles, having the hypothenuse $AC=DF$, and the side $BA=ED$: then will the triangle BAC be equal to the triangle EDF.

If the sides BC and EF are equal, the triangles are equal (P. 10). Now, suppose these two sides to be unequal, and BC to be the greater.

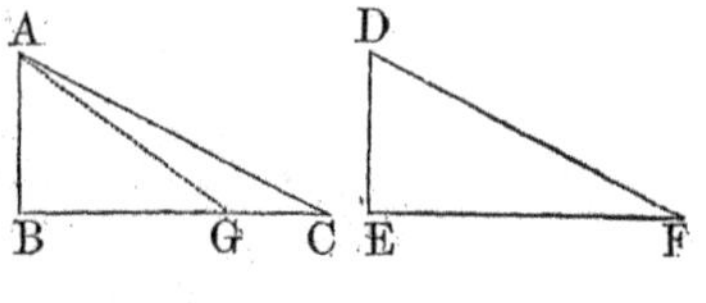

On BC take $BG=EF$, and draw AG. Then, in the two triangles BAG, EDF, the angles B and E are equal, being right angles, the side $BA=ED$ by hypothesis, and the side $BG=EF$ by construction; consequently, $AG=DF$ (P. 5, C). But by hypothesis $AC=DF$; and therefore, $AC=AG$ (A. 1). But the oblique line AC cannot be equal to AG, since BC is greater than BG (P. 15); consequently, BC and EF cannot be unequal, and hence, the triangles are equal (P. 10).

PROPOSITION XVIII. THEOREM.

If two straight lines are perpendicular to a third line, they are parallel to each other.

Let the two lines AC, BD, be perpendicular to AB, then will they be parallel.

For, if they could meet in a point O, on either side of AB, there would be two perpendiculars OA, OB, let fall from the same point on the same straight line; which is impossible (P. 14).

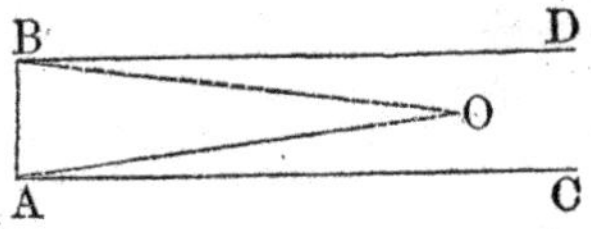

PROPOSITION XIX. THEOREM.

If two straight lines meet a third line, making the sum of the interior angles on the same side equal to two right angles, the two lines are parallel.

Let the two lines KC, HD, meet the line BA, making the angles BAC, ABD, together equal to two right angles: then the lines KC, HD, will be parallel.

Through G, the middle point of BA, draw the straight line EGF, perpendicular to KC: then, it will also be perpendicular to HD. For, the sum $BAC+ABD$ is equal to two right angles, by hypothesis; the sum $ABD+ABE$ is likewise equal to two right angles (P. 1): taking away ABD from both, there will remain the angle $BAC=ABE$.

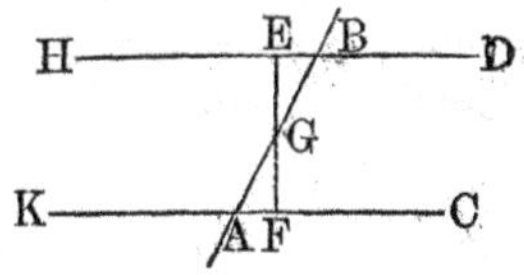

Again, the angles EGB, AGF, are equal (P. 4); therefore, the triangles EGB and AGF, have two angles and the included side equal, each to each; therefore, the triangles are equal, and the angle GEB is equal to GFA (P. 6, C). But GFA is a right angle by construction; therefore, GEB is a right angle; hence, the two lines KC, HD, are perpendicular to the same straight line, and are therefore parallel (P. 18).

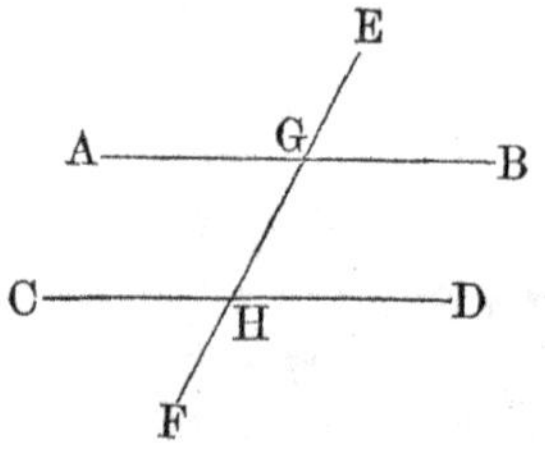

Scholium. When two parallel straight lines *AB*, *CD*, are met by a third line *FE*, the angles which are formed take particular names.

Interior angles on the same side, are those which lie within the parallels, and on the same side of the secant line; thus, *HGB*, *GHD*, are interior angles on the same side; and so also are the angles *HGA*, *GHC*.

Exterior angles on the same side, are those which lie without the parallels, and on the same side of the secant line.

Alternate interior angles lie within the parallels, and on different sides of the secant line, but not adjacent; *AGA*, *GHD*. are alternate angles; and so are the angles *GHC*, *BGH*.

Alternate exterior angles lie without the parallels, and on different sides of the secant line, but not adjacent: *EGB*, *CHF*, are alternate exterior angles; so also are the angles *AGE*, *FHD*.

Opposite exterior and *interior angles* lie on the same side of the secant line, the one without and the other within the parallels, but not adjacent: thus, *EGB*, *GHD*, are opposite exterior and interior angles; and so also, are the angles *AGE*, *GHC*.

Cor. 1. *If two straight lines meet a third line, making the alternate angles equal, the straight lines are parallel.*

Let the straight line *EF* meet the two straight lines *CD*, *AB*, making the alternate angles *AGH*, *GHD*, equal to each other: then will *AB* and *CD* be parallel.

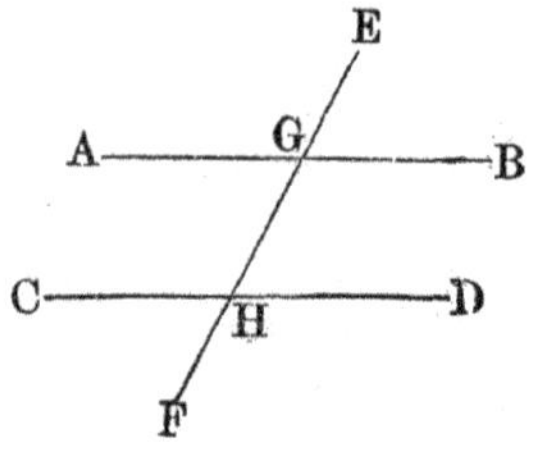

For, to each of the equal angles, add the angle *HGB*; we shall then have

$$AGH+HGB=GHD+HGB.$$

But $AGH+HGB$ is equal to two right angles (P. 1): hence, $GHD+HGB$ is also equal to two right angles (A. 1): then *CD* and *AB* are parallel (P. 19.)

Cor. 2. If a straight line EF, meet two straight lines CD, AB, making the exterior angle EGB, equal to the interior and opposite angle GHD, the two lines will be parallel. For, to each add the angle HGB: we shall then have,

$$EGB+HGB=GHD+HGB:$$

but $EGB+HGB$ is equal to two right angles; hence, $GHD+HGB$ is equal to two right angles; therefore, CD, and AB, are parallel (P. 19).

PROPOSITION XX. THEOREM.

If a straight line meet two parallel straight lines, the sum of the interior angles on the same side will be equal to two right angles.

Let the parallels AB, CD, be met by the secant line FE: then will $HGB+GHD$, or $HGA+GHC$, be equal to two right angles.

For, if $HGB+GHD$ be not equal to two right angles, let IGL be drawn, making the sum $HGL+GHD$ equal to two right angles; then IL and CD will be parallel (P. 19); and hence, we shall have two lines GB, GL, drawn through the same point G and parallel to CD, which is impossible (A. 13): hence, $HGB+GHD$ is equal to two right angles. In the same manner it may be proved that $HGA+GHC$ is equal to two right angles.

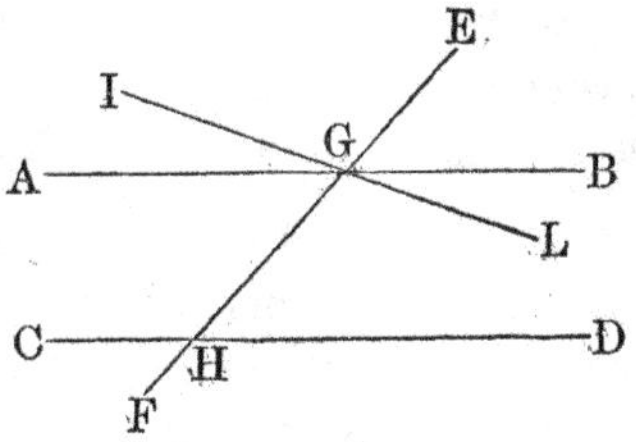

Cor. 1. If HGB is a right angle, GHD will be a right angle also: therefore, *every straight line perpendicular to one of two parallels, is perpendicular to the other.*

Cor. 2. *If a straight line meet two parallel straight lines, the alternate angles will be equal.*

Let AB, CD, be two parallels, and FE the secant line.

The sum $HGB+GHD$ is equal to two right angles. But the sum $HGB+HGA$ is also equal to two right angles (P. 1). Taking from each the angle HGB, and there remains $AGH=GHD$. In the same manner we may prove that $GHC=HGB$.

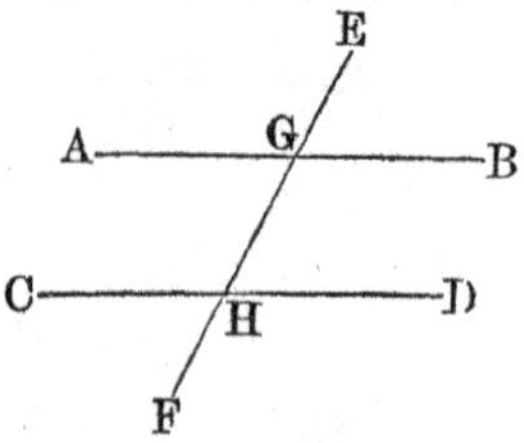

Cor. 3. If a straight line meet two parallel lines, the opposite exterior and interior angles will be equal. For, the sum $HGB+GHD$ is equal to two right angles. But the sum $HGB+EGB$ is also equal to two right angles. Taking from each the angle HGB, and there remains $GHD=EGB$. In the same manner we may prove that $GHC=AGE$.

Scholium. We see that of the eight angles formed by a line cutting two parallel lines obliquely, the four acute angles are equal to each other, and so also are the four obtuse angles.

PROPOSITION XXI. THEOREM.

If two straight lines meet a third line, making the sum of the interior angles on the same side less than two right angles, the two lines will meet if sufficiently produced.

Let the two lines CD, IL, meet the line EF, making the sum of the interior angles HGL, GHD, less than two right angles: then will IL and CD meet if sufficiently produced.

For, if they do not meet they are parallel (D. 16). But they are not parallel, for if they were, the sum of the interior angles LGH, GHD, would be equal to two right angles (P. 20), whereas it is less by hypothesis: hence, the lines IL, CD, will meet if sufficiently produced.

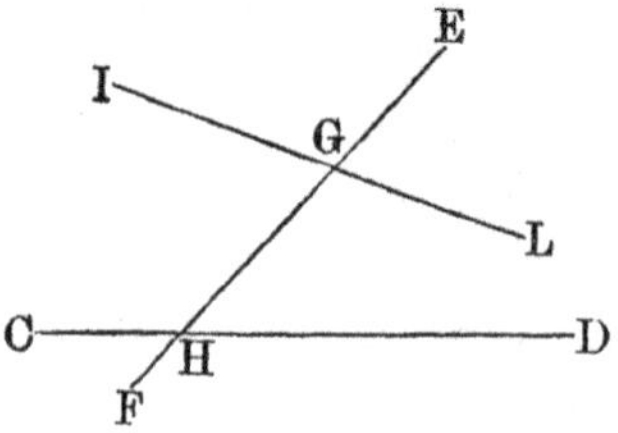

Cor. It is evident that the two lines IL, CD, will meet on that side of EF on which the sum of the two angles HGL, GHD, is less than two right angles.

PROPOSITION XXII. THEOREM.

Two straight lines which are parallel to a third line, are parallel to each other.

Let CD and AB be parallel to the third line EF; then are they parallel to each other.

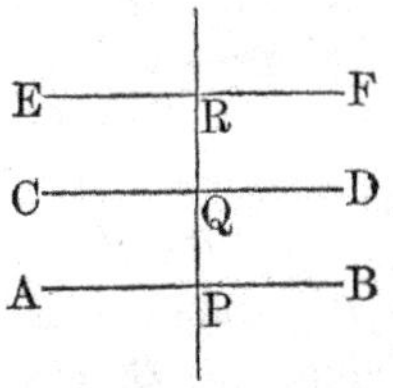

Draw PQR perpendicular to EF, and cutting AB, CD, in the points P and Q. Since AB is parallel to EF, PR will be perpendicular to AB (P. 20, C. 1); and since CD is parallel to EF, PR will for a like reason be perpendicular to CD. Hence, AB and CD are perpendicular to the same straight line; hence, they are parallel (P. 18).

PROPOSITION XXIII. THEOREM.

Two parallels are everywhere equally distant.

Let CD and AB be two parallel straight lines. Through any two points of AB, as F and E, suppose FH and EG to be drawn perpendicular to AB. These lines will also be perpendicular to CD (P. 20, C. 1); and we are now to show that they will be equal to each other.

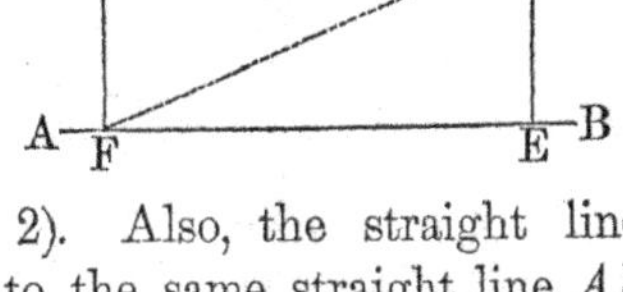

If GF be drawn, the angles GFE, FGH, considered in reference to the parallels AB, CD, will be alternate angles, and therefore, equal to each other (P. 20, C. 2). Also, the straight lines FH, EG, being perpendicular to the same straight line AB, are parallel (P. 18); and the angles EGF, GFH, considered in reference to the parallels FH, EG, will be alternate angles, and therefore equal. Hence, the two triangles EFG, FGH, have a common side, and two adjacent angles in each equal; therefore, the triangles are equal (P. 6); consequently, FH, which measures the distance of the parallels AB and CD at the point F, is equal to EG, which measures the distance of the same parallels at the point E.

PROPOSITION XXIV. THEOREM.

If two angles have their sides parallel and lying in the same direction, they will be equal.

Let BAC and DEF be the two angles, having AB parallel to ED, and AC to EF; then will they be equal.

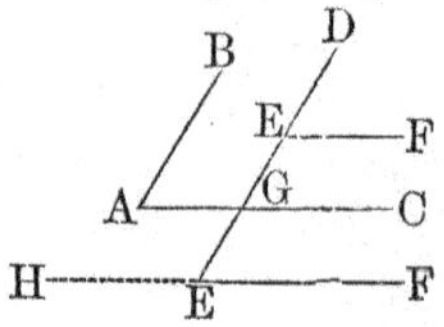

For, produce DE, if necessary, till it meets AC in G. Then, since EF is parallel to GC, the angle DEF is equal to DGC (P. 20, C. 3); and since DG is parallel to AB, the angle DGC is equal to BAC; hence, the angle DEF is equal to BAC (A. 1).

Scholium. The restriction of this proposition to the case where the side EF lies in the same direction with AC, and ED in the same direction with AB, is necessary, because if FE were prolonged towards H, the angle DEH would have its sides parallel to those of the angle BAC, but would not be equal to it. In that case, DEH and BAC would be together equal to two right angles. For, $DEH+DEF$ is equal to two right angles (P. 1); but DEF is equal to BAC: hence, $DEH+BAC$ is equal to two right angles.

PROPOSITION XXV. THEOREM.

In every triangle the sum of the three angles is equal to two right angles.

Let ABC be any triangle: then will the sum of the angles $C+A+B$ be equal to two right angles.

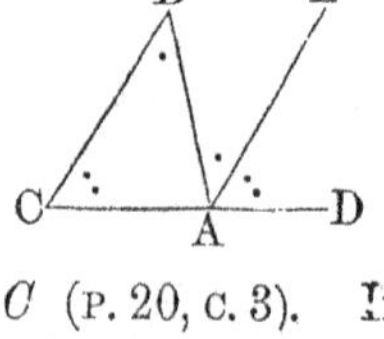

For, prolong the side CA towards D, and at the point A, suppose AE to be drawn, parallel to BC. Then, since AE, CB, are parallel, and CAD cuts them, the exterior angle DAE is equal to its interior opposite angle C (P. 20, C. 3). In like manner, since AE, CB, are parallel, and AB cuts them, the alternate angles B and BAE, are equal; hence, the three angles of the triangle BAC are equal to the three angles CAB, BAE, EAD, each to each; but the sum of these three angles is equal to two right angles (P. 1); consequently, the sum of the three angles of the triangle, is equal to two right angles (A. 1).

Cor. 1. Two angles of a triangle being given, or merely their sum, the third will be found by subtracting that sum from two right angles.

Cor. 2. If two angles of one triangle are respectively equal to two angles of another, the third angles will also be equal, and the two triangles will be mutually equiangular.

Cor. 3. In any triangle there can be but one right angle: for if there were two, the third angle must be zero. Neither can a triangle have more than one obtuse angle.

Cor. 4. In every right-angled triangle, the sum of the two acute angles is equal to one right angle.

Cor. 5. Since every equilateral triangle is also equiangular (P. 11, C. 1), each of its angles will be equal to the third part of two right angles; so, that, if the right angle is expressed by unity, each angle of an equilateral triangle will be expressed by $\frac{2}{3}$.

Cor. 6. In every triangle ABC, the exterior angle BAD is equal to the sum of the two interior opposite angles B and C. For, AE being parallel to BC, the part BAE is equal to the angle B, and the other part DAE is equal to the angle C.

PROPOSITION XXVI. THEOREM.

The sum of all the interior angles of a polygon, is equal to two right angles taken as many times as the figure has sides less two.

Let $ABCDE$ be any polygon: then will the sum of its interior angles

$$A+B+C+D+E$$

be equal to twice as many right angles, less four, as the figure has sides.

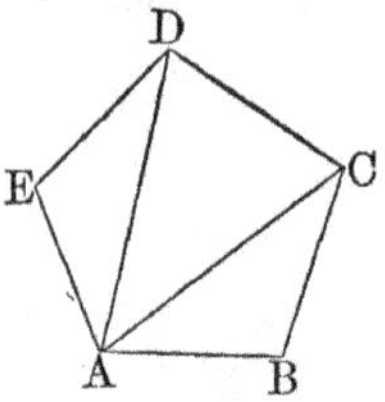

From the vertex of any angle A, draw diagonals AC, AD, to the vertices of the other angles. It is plain that the polygon will be divided into as many triangles, less two, as it has sides; for, these triangles may be considered as having the point A for a common vertex, and for bases, the several sides of the polygon, excepting the two sides which form the angle A. It is evident, also, that the sum of all the angles in these triangles does not differ from the sum of all the angles in the polygon: hence, the sum of all the angles of the polygon is equal to two right angles, taken as many times as there are triangles in the figure; that is, as many times as there are sides, less two. But this product is equal to twice as many right angles as the figure has sides, less four right angles.

Cor. 1. The sum of the interior angles in a quadrilateral is equal to two right angles multiplied by $4-2$, which is equal to four right angles: hence, if all the angles of a quadrilateral are equal, each of them will be a right angle. Hence, each of the angles of a rectangle, and of a square, is a right angle (D. 25).

Cor. 2. The sum of the interior angles of a pentagon is equal to two right angles multiplied by $5-2$, which amounts to six right angles: hence, when a pentagon is equiangular, each angle is equal to the fifth part of six right angles, or to $\frac{6}{5}$ of one right angle.

Cor. 3. The sum of the interior angles of a hexagon is equal to $2\times(6-2,)$ or eight right angles; hence, in the equiangular hexagon, each angle is the sixth part of eight right angles, or $\frac{4}{3}$ of one.

Cor. 4. In any equiangular polygon, any interior angle is equal to twice as many right angles, less four, as the figure has sides, divided by the number of angles.

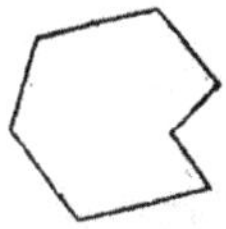

Scholium. When this proposition is applied to polygons which have *re-entrant* angles, each re-entrant angle must be regarded as greater than two right angles. But to avoid all ambiguity, we shall henceforth limit our reasoning to polygons with *salient* angles, which are named *convex polygons.* Every *convex* polygon is such, that a straight line, drawn at pleasure, cannot meet the sides of the polygon in more than two points.

PROPOSITION XXVII. THEOREM.

If the sides of any polygon be prolonged, in the same direction, the sum of the exterior angles will be equal to four right angles.

Let the sides of the polygon $ABCDFG$, be prolonged, in the same direction; then will the sum of the exterior angles

$$a+b+c+d+f+g,$$

be equal to four right angles.

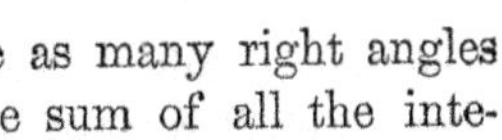

For, each interior angle, plus its exterior angle, as $A+a$, is equal to two right angles (P. 1). But there are as many exterior as interior angles, and as many of each as there are sides of the polygon: hence the sum of all the interior and exterior angles, is equal to twice as many right angles as the polygon has sides. Again, the sum of all the interior angles is equal to twice as many right angles as the figure has sides, less four right angles (P. 26). Hence, the interior angles plus four right angles, is equal to twice as many right angles as the polygon has sides, and consequently, equal to the sum of the interior angles plus the sum of the exterior angles. Taking from each the sum of the interior angles, and there remains the sum of the exterior angles, equal to four right angles.

PROPOSITION XXVIII. THEOREM.

In every parallelogram, the opposite sides and opposite angles are equal each to each.

Let $ABCD$ be a parallelogram: then will $AB=DC$, $AD=BC$, the angle $A=C$, and the angle $ADC=ABC$.

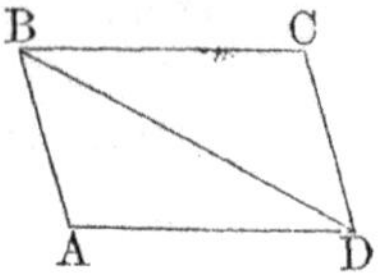

For, draw the diagonal BD, dividing the parallelogram into the two triangles, ABD, DBC. Now, since AD, BC, are parallel, the angle $ADB=DBC$ (P. 20, C. 2); and since AB, CD, are parallel, the angle $ABD=BDC$: and since the side DB is common, the two triangles are equal (P. 6); therefore, the side AB, opposite the angle ADB, is equal to the side DC, opposite the equal angle DBC (P. 10, S.), and the third sides AD, BC, are equal: hence, the opposite sides of a parallelogram are equal.

Again, since the triangles are equal, the angle A is equal to the angle C (P. 10, S.) Also, the angle ADC composed of the two angles, ADB, BDC, is equal to ABC, composed of the corresponding equal angles DBC, ABD (A. 2): hence, the opposite angles of a parallelogram are equal.

Cor. 1. Two parallels AB, CD, included between two other parallels AD, BC, are equal; and the diagonal DB divides the parallelogram into two equal triangles.

Cor. 2. Two parallelograms which have two sides and the included angle in the one equal to two sides and the included angle in the other, each to each, are equal.

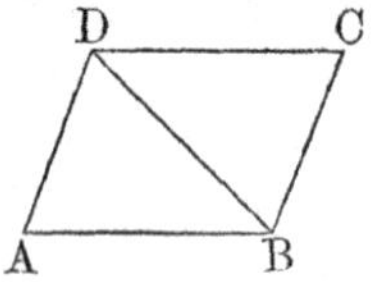

Let the parallelogram $ABCD$, have the sides AB, AD, and the included angle BAD equal to the sides AB, AD, and the included angle BAD, in the next figure; then will they be equal.

For, in each figure, draw the diagonal DB. By the last corollary, the diagonal divides each parallelogram into two equal triangles: but the triangle BAD in one parallelogram, is equal to the triangle BAD in the other (P. 5): hence, the parallelograms are equal (A. 6).

PROPOSITION XXIX. THEOREM.

If the opposite sides of a quadrilateral are equal, each to each, the equal sides are parallel, and the figure is a parallelogram.

Let $ABCD$ be a quadrilateral, having its opposite sides respectively equal, viz.: $AB=DC$, and $AD=BC$; then will these sides be parallel, and the figure a parallelogram.

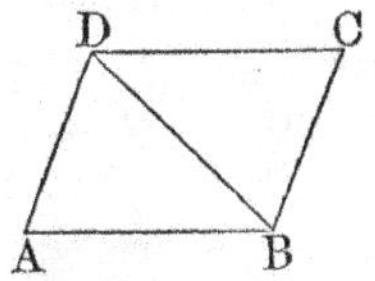

For, having drawn the diagonal BD the two triangles ABD, BDC, have all the sides of the one equal to the corresponding sides of the other; therefore they are equal, and the angle ADB, opposite the side AB, is equal to DBC, opposite CD (P. 10, S.); therefore the side AD is parallel to BC (P. 19, C. 1) For a like reason AB is parallel to CD: therefore, the quadrilateral $ABCD$ is a parallelogram.

PROPOSITION XXX. THEOREM.

If two opposite sides of a quadrilateral are equal and parallel, the other sides are equal and parallel, and the figure is a parallelogram.

Let $ABCD$ be a quadrilateral, having the sides AB, CD, equal and parallel; then will the figure be a parallelogram.

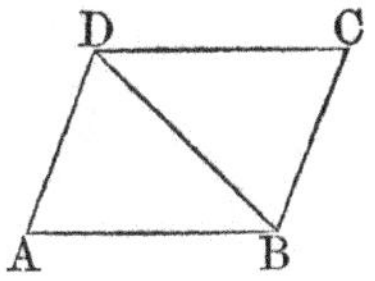

For, draw the diagonal DB, dividing the quadrilateral into two triangles. Then, since AB is parallel to DC, the alternate angles ABD, BDC are equal (P. 20, C. 2); moreover, the side DB is common, and the side $AB=DC$; hence, the triangle ABD is equal to the triangle DBC (P. 5); therefore, the side AD is equal to BC, the angle $ADB=DBC$, and consequently AD is parallel to BC (P. 19, C. 1); hence, the figure $ABCD$ is a parallelogram.

PROPOSITION XXXI. THEOREM.

The two diagonals of a parallelogram divide each other into equal parts, or mutually bisect each other.

Let $ADCB$ be a parallelogram, AC and DB its diagonals, intersecting at E; then will $AE=EC$, and $DE=EB$.

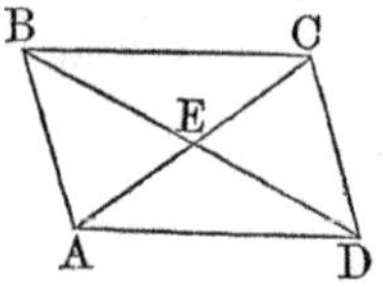

Comparing the triangles AED, BEC, we find the side $AD=CB$ (P. 28), the angle $ADB=CBE$, and the angle $DAE=ECB$ (P. 20, C. 2); hence, these triangles are equal (P. 6); consequently, AE, the side opposite the angle ADE, is equal to EC opposite CBE, and DE opposite DAE is equal to EB opposite ECB.

Cor. Conversely: If the two diagonals of a quadrilatera bisect each other, the figure is a parallelogram.

Scholium. In the case of the rhombus, the sides AB BC, being equal, the triangles AEB, EBC, have all the sides of the one equal to the corresponding sides of the other, and are therefore equal: whence, it follows, that the angles AEB, BEC, are equal, and therefore, the two diagonals of a rhombus bisect each other at right angles.

BOOK II.

OF RATIOS AND PROPORTIONS.

DEFINITIONS.

1. PROPORTION is the relation which one magnitude, regarded as a standard, bears to another magnitude of the same kind.*

2. RATIO is the measure of the proportion which one magnitude bears to another; and is the quotient which arises from dividing the second by the first. Thus, if A and B represent magnitudes of the same kind, the ratio of A to B is expressed by

$$\frac{B}{A};$$

A and B are called the terms of the ratio; the first is called the *antecedent*, and the second, the *consequent.*

3. The ratio of magnitudes may be expressed by numbers, either exactly or approximatively; and in the latter case, the approximation may be brought nearer to the true ratio than any assignable difference.

Thus, of two magnitudes, one may be considered to be divided into some number of equal parts, each of the same kind as the whole, and regarding one of these parts as a unit of measure, the magnitude may be expressed by the number of units it contains. If the other magnitude contain an exact number of these units, it also may

---

* See Davies' Logic of Mathematics: Proportion, § 267.

be expressed by the number of its units, and the two magnitudes are then said to be *commensurable.*

If the second magnitude do not contain the measuring unit an exact number of times, there may perhaps be a smaller unit which will be contained an exact number of times in each of the magnitudes. But if there is no unit of an *assignable* value, which is contained an exact number of times in each of the magnitudes, the magnitudes are said to be *incommensurable.*

It is plain, however, that if the unit of measure be repeated as many times as it is contained in the second magnitude, the result will differ from the second magnitude by a quantity less than the unit of measure, since the remainder is always less than the divisor. Now, since the unit of measure may be made as small as we please, it follows, that magnitudes may be represented by numbers to any degree of exactness, or they will differ from their numerical representatives by less than any assignable magnitude.

4. We will illustrate these principles by finding the ratio between the straight lines CD and AB, which we will suppose commensurable.

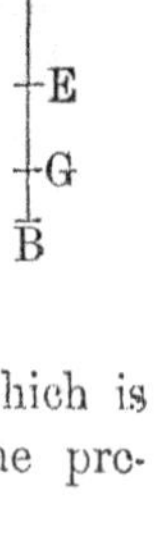

From the greater line AB, cut off a part equal to the less CD, as many times as possible; for example, twice, with the remainder BE.

From the line CD, cut off a part, CF, equal to the remainder BE, as many times as possible; once, for example, with the remainder DF.

From the first remainder BE, cut off a part equal to the second, DF, as many times as possible; once, for example, with the remainder BG.

From the second remainder DF, cut off a part equal to BG, the third remainder, as many times as possible.

Continue this process, till a remainder occurs, which is contained exactly, a certain number of times, in the preceding one.

Then, this last remainder will be the common measure of the proposed lines. Regarding this as unity, we shall easily find the values of the preceding remainders; and at last, those of the two proposed lines, and hence, their ratio in numbers.

Suppose, for instance, we find GB to be contained exactly twice in FD; BG will be the common measure of the two proposed lines. Put $BG=1$; we shall then have, $FD=2$; but EB contains FD once, *plus* GB; therefore, we have $EB=3$: CD contains EB once, *plus* FD; therefore, we have $CD=5$: and lastly, AB contains CD twice, *plus* EB; therefore, we have $AB=13$; hence, the ratio of the lines is that of 5 to 13. If the line CD were taken for unity, the line AB would be $\frac{13}{5}$; if AB were taken for unity, CD would be $\frac{5}{13}$.

5. What has been shown, in respect to the straight lines, CD and AB, is equally true of any two magnitudes, A and B.

For, we may conceive A to be divided into a number M of units, each equal to A': then $A=M\times A'$: let B be divided into a number N of equal units, each equal to A'; then $B=N\times A'$; M and N being integer numbers. Now the ratio of A to B, will be the same as the ratio of $M\times A'$ to $N\times A'$; that is, the same as the ratio of the numerical quantities M and N, since A' is a common unit.

6. If there be four magnitudes, A, B, C, and D, having such values that

$$\frac{B}{A}=\frac{D}{C},$$

then A is said to have the same *ratio* to B, that C has to D; or, the ratio of A to B is said to be equal to the ratio of C to D. When four quantities have this relation to each other, they are said to be in *proportion*.

To indicate that the ratio of A to B is equal to the ratio of C to D, the quantities are usually written thus,

$$A : B :: C : D,$$

and read, A is to B as C is to D. The quantities which are compared together are called the *terms* of the proportion. The first and last terms are called the *two extremes*, and the second and third terms, the *two means*.

7. Of four proportional quantities, the last is said to be *a fourth proportional* to the other three, taken in order. The first and second terms, are called the *first couplet* of the proportion; and the third and fourth terms, the *second couplet:* the first and third terms are called the *antecedents*, and the second and fourth terms, the *consequents.*

8. Three quantities are in proportion, when the first has the same ratio to the second, that the second has to the third; and then the middle term is said to be a *mean proportional* between the other two.

9. Magnitudes are in proportion by *alternation*, or alternately, when antecedent is compared with antecedent, and consequent with consequent.

10. Magnitudes are in proportion by *inversion*, or *inversely*, when the consequents are taken as antecedents, and the antecedents as consequents.

11. Magnitudes are in proportion by *composition*, when the sum of the antecedent and consequent is compared either with antecedent or consequent.

12. Magnitudes are in proportion by *division*, when the difference of the antecedent and consequent is compared either with antecedent or consequent.

13. Equimultiples of two quantities are the products which arise from multiplying the quantities by the same number: thus, $m \times A$, $m \times B$, are equimultiples of A and B, the common multiplier being m.

14. Two varying quantities, A and B, are said to be *reciprocally proportional, or inversely proportional*, when their values are so changed that one is increased as many times as the other is diminished. In such case, either of them is always equal to a constant quantity divided by the other, and their product is constant.

PROPOSITION I. THEOREM.

When four magnitudes are in proportion, the product of the two extremes is equal to the product of the two means.

Let A, B, C, D, be any four magnitudes, and M, N, P, Q, their numerical representatives;

then, if $M : N :: P : Q$,

we shall have $M \times Q = N \times P$.

For, since the magnitudes are in proportion, we have (D. 6),

$$\frac{N}{M} = \frac{Q}{P}; \text{ therefore,}$$

$$N = M \times \frac{Q}{P}; \text{ whence, } N \times P = M \times Q.$$

Cor. If there are three proportional quantities, the product of the extremes will be equal to the square of the mean (D. 8). For, if $N = P$, we have

$$M \times Q = N^2 \text{ or } P^2.$$

PROPOSITION II. THEOREM.

If the product of two magnitudes be equal to the product of two other magnitudes, two of them may be made the extremes and the other two the means of a proportion.

If we have, $M \times Q = N \times P$,

then will $M : N :: P : Q$.

For, by changing the places of the members of the equation,

$$M \times Q = N \times P, \text{ we have}$$

$$N \times P = M \times Q.$$

Then, dividing both members by $M \times P$, we have

$$\frac{N}{M} = \frac{Q}{P}:$$

whence, by Definition 6,

$$M : N :: P : Q.$$

PROPOSITION III. THEOREM.

If four magnitudes are in proportion, they will be in proportion when taken alternately.

Let $M : N :: P : Q$; then will

$M : P :: N : Q$.

For, since $M : N :: P : Q$, we have,

$$\frac{N}{M} = \frac{Q}{P}.$$

Multiplying both members by $\frac{P}{N}$, and we have,

$$\frac{P}{M} = \frac{Q}{N};$$

hence, $M : P :: N : Q$.

PROPOSITION IV. THEOREM.

If there be four proportional magnitudes, and four other proportional magnitudes, having the antecedents the same in both, the consequents will be proportional.

Let $M : N :: P : Q$, giving, $\frac{N}{M} = \frac{P}{Q}$

and $M : R :: P : S$, giving, $\frac{R}{M} = \frac{S}{P}$.

Dividing the first equation by the second, member by member,

$$\frac{N}{R} = \frac{Q}{S}, \text{ or } NS = QR; \text{ whence (P. 2),}$$

$$N : Q :: S : R.$$

Cor. If there be two sets of proportionals, in which the ratio of an antecedent and consequent of the one is equal to the ratio of an antecedent and consequent of the other, the remaining terms will be proportional.

For, if we have the two proportions,

$M : P :: N : Q$ and $R : S :: T : V$,

we shall also have

$$\frac{P}{M} = \frac{Q}{N} \text{ and } \frac{S}{R} = \frac{V}{T}$$

Now, if $\frac{P}{M} = \frac{S}{R}$, then $\frac{Q}{N} = \frac{V}{T}$,

and we shall have $N : Q :: T : V$.

PROPOSITION V. THEOREM.

If four magnitudes are in proportion, they will be in proportion when taken inversely.

If $M : N :: P : Q$, then will $N : M :: Q : P$

For, from the given proportion, we have

$\frac{N}{M}=\frac{Q}{P}$, taking the reciprocals of both members,

$\frac{M}{N}=\frac{P}{Q}$; whence, we have,

$$N : M :: Q : P.$$

PROPOSITION VI. THEOREM.

If four magnitudes are in proportion, they will be in proportion by composition or division.

If we have $M : N :: P : Q$,

we shall also have $M \pm N : M :: P \pm Q : P$.

For, from the given proportion, we have

$$M \times Q = N \times P, \text{ or } N \times P = M \times Q.$$

Add each of the members of the last equation to, and subtract it from $M \times P$, and we shall have,

$$M \times P \pm N \times P = M \times P \pm M \times Q; \text{ or}$$
$$(M \pm N) \times P = (P \pm Q) \times M.$$

But $M \pm N$ and P, may be considered the two extremes, and $P \pm Q$ and M, the two means of a proportion (P. 2): hence,

$$(M \pm N) : M :: (P \pm Q) : P.$$

PROPOSITION VII. THEOREM.

Equimultiples of any two magnitudes, have the same ratio as the magnitudes themselves.

Let M and N be any two magnitudes, and m any number whatever; then will $m \times M$, and $m \times N$, be equal mul tiples of M and N: then $m \times M$ will be to $m \times N$, in the ratio of M to N.

For, $$M \times N = N \times M:$$
multiplying each member by m, and we have
$$m \times M \times N = m \times N \times M: \text{ then (P. 2)},$$
$$m \times M : m \times N :: M : N.$$

PROPOSITION VIII. THEOREM.

Of four proportional magnitudes, if there be taken any equimultiples of the two antecedents, and any equimultiples of the two consequents, such equimultiples will be proportional.

Let M, N, P, Q, be four magnitudes in proportion; and let m and n be any numbers whatever, then will
$$m \times M : n \times N :: m \times P : n \times Q.$$
For, since $$M : N :: P : Q,$$
we have $$M \times Q = N \times P;$$
hence, $$m \times M \times n \times Q = n \times N \times m \times P,$$
by multiplying both members of the equation by $m \times n$. But $m \times M$ and $n \times Q$, may be regarded as the two extremes, and $n \times N$ and $m \times P$, as the means of a proportion; hence,
$$m \times M : n \times N :: m \times P : n \times Q.$$

PROPOSITION IX. THEOREM.

Of four proportional magnitudes, if the two consequents be either augmented or diminished by magnitudes which have the same ratio as the antecedents, the resulting magnitudes and the antecedents will be proportional.

Let $M : N :: P : Q$,
and let $M : P :: m : n$;
then will $M : P :: N \pm m : Q \pm n$.

For, since $M : N :: P : Q$, $M \times Q = N \times P$.
and since $M : P :: m : n$, $M \times n = P \times m$,
therefore, $M \times Q \pm M \times n = N \times P \pm P \times m$,
or $M \times (Q \pm n) = P \times (N \pm m)$:
hence (P. 2), $M : P :: N \pm m : Q \pm n$.

PROPOSITION X. THEOREM.

If any number of magnitudes are proportionals, any one antecedent will be to its consequent, as the sum of all the antecedents to the sum of the consequents.

Let $M : N :: P : Q :: R : S$, &c.

Then since,

$M : N :: P : Q$, we have $M\times Q=N\times P$,

and, $M : N :: R : S$, we have $M\times S=N\times R$,

add to each $M\times N=M\times N$,

then, $M\times N+M\times Q+M\times S=M\times N+N\times P+N\times R$,

or, $M\times(N+Q+S)=N\times(M+P+R)$;

therefore (P. 2), $M : N :: M+P+R : N+Q+S$.

PROPOSITION XI. THEOREM.

If two magnitudes be each increased or diminished by like parts of each, the resulting magnitudes will have the same ratio as the magnitudes themselves.

Let M and N be any two magnitudes and $\frac{M}{m}$ and $\frac{N}{m}$ like parts of each.

We have $M\times N=M\times N$

add to both, or subt. $\frac{M\times N}{m}=\frac{M\times N}{m}$, member by member

and we have (A. 2), $M\times N\pm\frac{M\times N}{m}=M\times N\pm\frac{M\times N}{m}$,

or, $$M\left(N\pm\frac{N}{m}\right)=N\left(M\pm\frac{M}{m}\right),$$

that is (P. 2), $M : N :: M\pm\frac{M}{m} : N\pm\frac{N}{m}$.

PROPOSITION XII. THEOREM

If four magnitudes are proportional, their squares or cubes will also be proportional.

Let $M : N : P : Q$,

Then will, $M\times Q=N\times P$.

By squaring both members, $M^2 \times Q^2 = N^2 \times P^2$,

and by cubing both members, $M^3 \times Q^3 = N^3 \times P^3$;

therefore, $M^2 : N^2 :: P^2 : Q^2$,

and $M^3 : N^3 :: P^3 : Q^3$.

Cor. In a similar way it may be shown that like powers or roots of proportional magnitudes are proportionals.

PROPOSITION XIII. THEOREM.

If there be two sets of proportional magnitudes, the products of the corresponding terms will be proportionals.

Let $M : N :: P : Q$,

and $R : S :: T : V$,

then will $M \times R : N \times S :: P \times T : Q \times V$.

For, since $M \times Q = N \times P$,

and $R \times V = S \times T$,

we shall have $M \times Q \times R \times V = N \times P \times S \times T$,

or, $\overline{M \times R} \times \overline{Q \times V} = \overline{N \times S} \times \overline{P \times T}$;

therefore, $\overline{M \times R} : \overline{N \times S} :: \overline{P \times T} : \overline{Q \times V}$.

PROPOSITION XIV. THEOREM.

If any number of magnitudes are continued proportionals; then, the ratio of the first to the third will be the square of the common ratio; and the ratio of the first to the fourth will be the cube of the common ratio; and so on.

For let A be the first term, and r the common ratio: the proportional magnitudes will then be represented by

$$A, \quad r^1 \times A, \quad r^2 \times A, \quad r^3 \times A, \quad r^4 \times A, \text{ \&c.}:$$

Now, the ratio of the first to any one of the following terms exactly corresponds with the enunciation.

BOOK III.

THE CIRCLE, AND THE MEASUREMENT OF ANGLES.

DEFINITIONS.

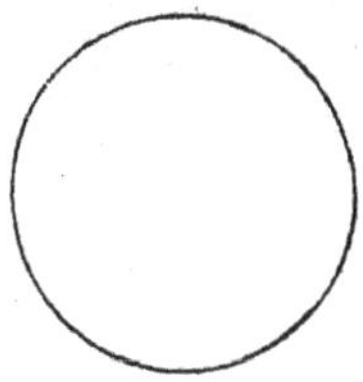

1. A CIRCLE is a portion of a plane bounded by a curved line, every point of which is equidistant from a point within, called the *centre*.

The bounding line is called the *circumference*.

2. A straight line, drawn from the centre to the circumference, is called a *radius*, or *semidiameter*. A line drawn through the centre, and terminating in the circumference, is called a *diameter*.

From the definition of a circle, it follows, that all the radii are equal; all the diameters are also equal, and each double the radius.

3. Any part of a circumference is called an *arc*. A straight line joining the extremities of an arc is called a *chord*, or *subtense* of the arc.*

4. A SEGMENT is the part of a circle included between an arc and its chord.

5. A SECTOR is the part of a circle included between an arc, and the two radii drawn to the extremities of the arc.

---

* In all cases, the same chord belongs to two arcs, and consequently, also to two segments: but the smaller one is always meant, unless the contrary is expressed.

6. A STRAIGHT LINE is said to be *inscribed in a circle*, when its extremities are in the circumference.

An *inscribed angle* is one whose vertex is in the circumference, and whose sides are chords of the circle.

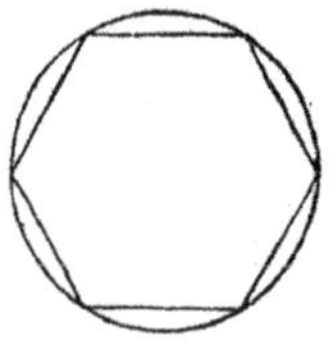

7. An *inscribed triangle* is one which has the vertices of its three angles in the circumference.

And generally, a *polygon* is said to be *inscribed* in a circle, when the vertices of all its angles are in the circumference. The circumference of the circle is then said to *circumscribe* the polygon.

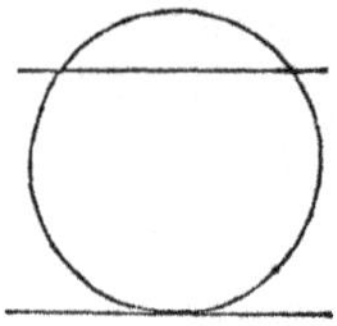

8. A SECANT is a line which intersects the circumference in two points, and lies partly within, and partly without the circle.

9. A TANGENT is a line which has but one point in common with the circumference.

The point where the tangent touches the circumference, is called the *point of contact.*

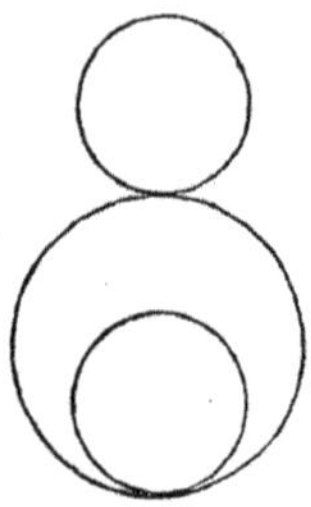

10. Two circumferences *touch* each other when they have but one point in common. The common point is called the point of *tangency.*

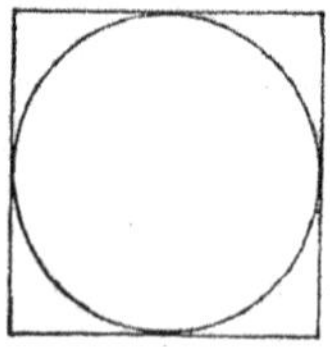

11. A polygon is *circumscribed about a circle*, when each of its sides is tangent to the circumference. In the same case, the circle is said to be *inscribed* in the polygon.

POSTULATE.

12. Let it be granted that the circumference of a circle may be described from any centre, and with any radius.

PROPOSITION I. THEOREM.

Every diameter divides the circle and its circumference each into two equal parts.

Let $AEBF$ be a circle, and AB a diameter. Now, if the figure AEB be applied to AFB, their common base AB retaining its position, the curve line AEB must fall exactly on the curve line AFB, otherwise there would, in the one or the other, be points unequally distant from the centre, which is contrary to the definition of a circle. Hence, the diameter divides the circle and its circumference, each into two equal parts.

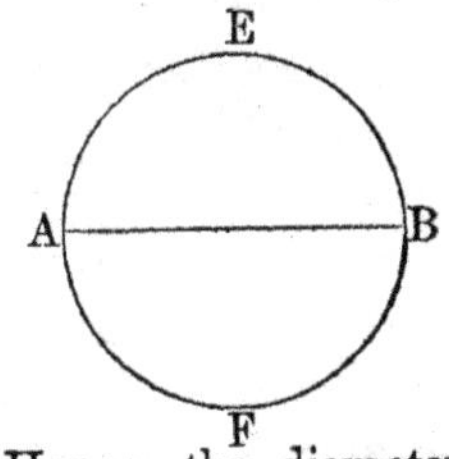

PROPOSITION II. THEOREM.

A diameter is greater than any other chord.

Let AD be any chord, not passing through the centre. Draw the radii CA, CD, to its extremities. We shall then have (B. I., P. 7)*,

$$AD < AC + CD,$$

but AC plus CD is equal to AB; hence, $AD < AB$, or $AB > AD$.

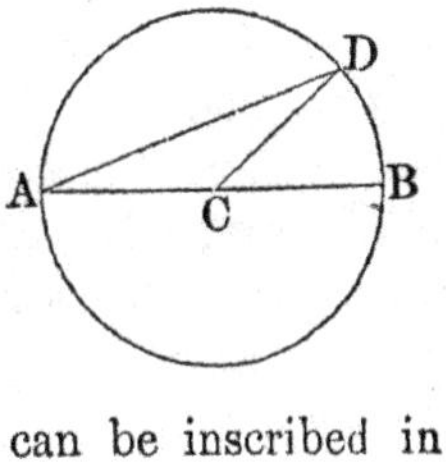

Cor. Hence, the greatest line which can be inscribed in a circle is a diameter.

PROPOSITION III. THEOREM.

A straight line cannot meet the circumference of a circle in more than two points.

For, if it could meet it in three, those three points would be equally distant from the centre; and there would be three equal straight lines drawn from the same point to the same straight line, which is impossible (B. I., P. 15, C. 2).

* When reference is made from one Proposition to another, in the *same Book*, the number of the Proposition referred to is alone given; but when the Proposition is found in a different Book, the number of the Book is also given.

PROPOSITION IV. THEOREM.

In the same circle, or in equal circles, equal arcs are subtended by equal chords: and conversely, equal chords subtend equal arcs.

Let C and O be the centres of two equal circles, and suppose the arc AMD equal to the arc ENG: then will the chord AD be equal to the chord EG.

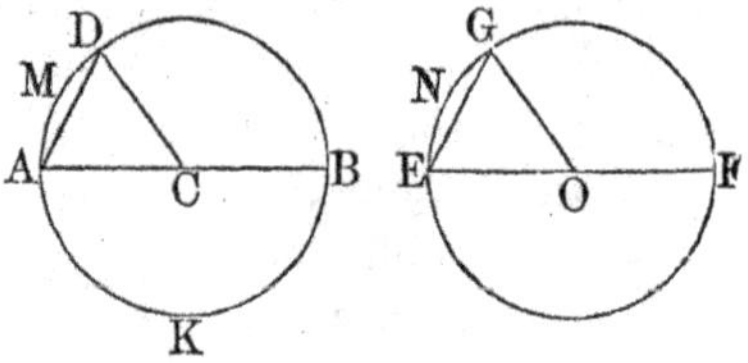

For, since the diameters AB, EF, are equal, the semi-circle $AMDB$ may be applied to the semi-circle $ENGF$, and the curve line $AMDB$ will coincide with the curve line $ENGF$. But the part AMD is equal to the part ENG, by hypothesis; hence, the point D will fall on G; therefore, the chord AD will coincide with EG (B. I., A. 11), and hence, is equal to it (B. I., A. 14).

Conversely: If the chord AD is equal to the chord EG, the subtended arcs AMD, ENG, will also be equal.

For, drawing the radii CD, OG, the triangles ACD, EOG, will have their sides equal, each to each, namely, $AC=EO$, $CD=OG$, and $AD=EG$; hence, the triangles are themselves equal; and, consequently, the angle ACD is equal to EOG (B. I., P. 10.)

Now, place the semi-circle ADB on its equal EGF, so that the radius AC may fall on the equal radius EO. Then, since the angle ACD is equal to the angle EOG, the radius CD will fall on OG, and the sector $AMDC$ will coincide with the sector $ENGO$, and the arc AMD with the arc ENG: therefore, the arc AMD, is equal to the arc ENG (B. I., A. 14).

PROPOSITION V. THEOREM.

In equal circles, or in the same circle, a greater arc is subtended by a greater chord: and conversely, the greater chord subtends the greater arc.

Let C be the common centre of two equal circles: then, if the arc ADH is greater than the arc AD, the chord AH will be greater than the chord AD.

For, draw the radii CA, CD, CH, and the chords AD, AH. Now, the two sides AC, CH, of the triangle ACH are equal to the two sides AC, CD, of the triangle ACD, and the angle ACH, is greater than ACD: hence, the third side AH is greater than the third side AD (B. I., P. 9); therefore the chord which subtends the greater arc is the greater.

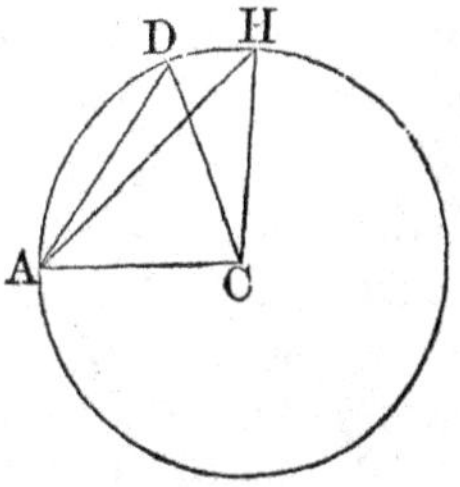

Conversely: If the chord AH is greater than AD, the arc ADH will be greater than the arc AD.

For, if ADH were equal to AD, the chord AH would be equal to the chord AD (P. 4), which is contrary to the hypothesis: and if the arc ADH were less than AD, the chord AH would be less than AD, which is also contrary to the hypothesis. Then, since the arc ADH, subtended by the greater chord, cannot be equal to, nor less than AD, it must be greater.

Scholium. The arcs here treated of are each less than the semi-circumference. If they were greater, the reverse property would have place; for, as the arcs increase, the chords will diminish, and conversely.

PROPOSITION VI. THEOREM.

The radius which is perpendicular to a chord, bisects the chord, and bisects also the subtended arc of the chord.

Let AB be any chord, and CG a radius perpendicular to it: then will AD be equal to DB, and the arc AG to the arc GB.

For, draw the radii CA, CB. Then the two right-angled triangles ADC, CDB, will have AC equal to CB, and CD common; hence, AD is equal to DB (B. I., P. 17).

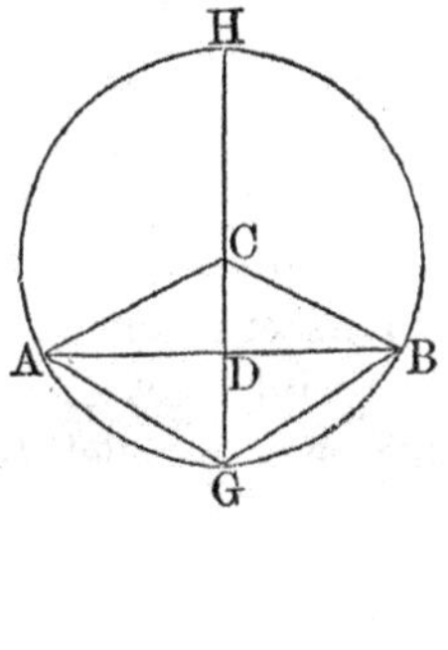

Again, since AD, DB, are equal, CG is a perpendicular

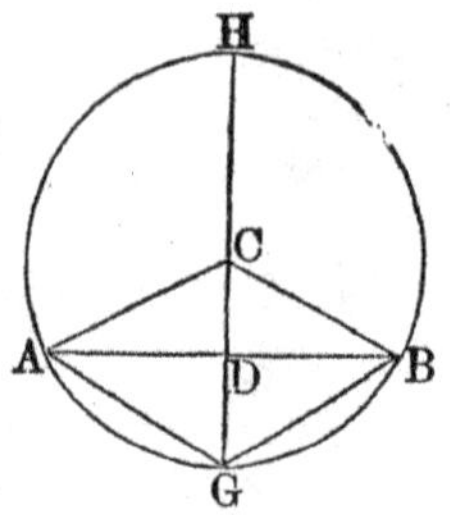

erected from the middle of AB; and since G is a point of this perpendicular, the chords AG and GB are equal (B. I., P. 16). But if the chord AG is equal to the chord GB, the arc AG is equal to the arc GB (P. 4); hence, the radius CG, at right angles to the chord AB, divides the arc subtended by that chord into two equal parts.

Scholium. The centre C, the middle point D of the chord AB, and the middle point G of the subtended arc, are three points of the same straight line perpendicular to the chord. But two points determine the position of a straight line (A. 11); hence, every straight line which passes through two of these points, will necessarily pass through the third, and be perpendicular to the chord.

It follows, also, that *the perpendicular raised at the middle point of a chord passes through the centre of the circle, and through the middle point of the subtended arc.*

For, the perpendicular to the chord, drawn from the centre of the circle, passes through the middle point of the chord, and only one perpendicular can be drawn from the same point to the same straight line (B. I., P. 14, C).

PROPOSITION VII. THEOREM.

Through three given points, not in the same straight line, one circumference may always be made to pass, and but one.

Let A, B, and C, be the given points.

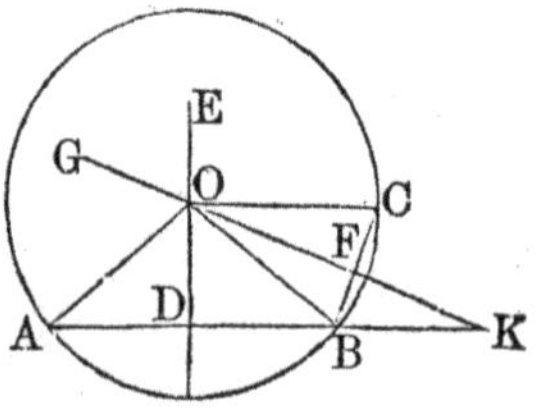

Join the points A and B by the straight line AB, and the points B and C by the straight line BC, and then bisect these lines by the perpendiculars DE FG: we say first, that DE and FG, will intersect in some point O.

For, they intersect each other unless they are parallel (B. I., D. 16). Now, if they are parallel, the line AB which is perpendicular to DE, is also perpendicular to FG, and the angle K is a right angle (B. I., P. 20, C. 1). But BK, the prolongation of AB, is a different line from BF, because the three points A, B, C, are not in the same straight line; hence, there would be two perpendiculars, BF, BK, let fall from the same point B, on the same straight line, which is impossible (B. I., P. 14); hence, DE, FG, are not parallel, and consequently, will intersect in some point O.

Moreover, since the point O lies in the perpendicular DE, it is equally distant from the two points, A and B (B. I., P. 16); and since the same point O lies in the perpendicular FG, it is also equally distant from the two points B and C: hence, the three distances OA, OB, OC, are equal; therefore, the circumference described from the centre O, with the radius OB, will pass through the three given points, A, B, C.

We have now shown that one circumference can always be made to pass through three given points, not in the same straight line: we say farther, that but one can be described through them.

For, if there were a second circumference passing through the three given points A, B, C, its centre could not be out of the line DE, for any point out of this line is unequally distant from A and B (B. I., P. 16); neither could it be out of the line FG, for a like reason; therefore, it would be in both the lines DE, FG. But two straight lines cannot cut each other in more than one point; hence, there is but one circumference which can pass through three given points.

Cor. Two circumferences cannot intersect in more than two points; for, if they have three common points, there will be two circumferences passing through the same three points; which has been shown, by the proposition, to be impossible

PROPOSITION VIII. THEOREM.

In the same, or in equal circles, two equal chords are equally distant from the centre; and of two unequal chords, the less is at the greater distance from the centre.

Suppose the chord AB to be equal to the chord DE. From C the centre of the circle, draw CF, and CG respectively perpendicular to the chords: then will CF be equal to CG.

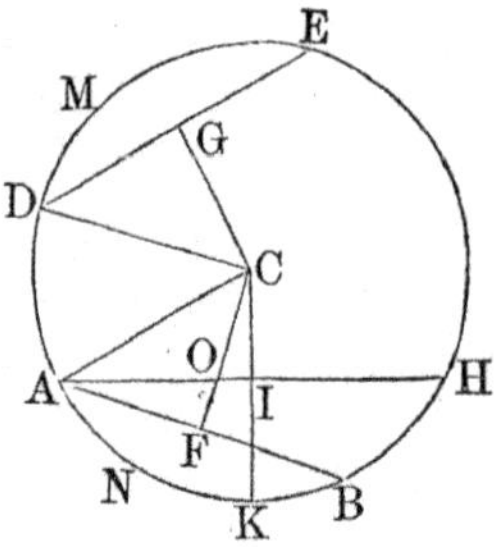

Draw the radii CA, CD; then in the right-angled triangles CAF, DCG, the hypothenuses CA, CD, are equal (D. 2); and the side AF, the half of AB (P. 6), is equal to the side DG, the half of DE: hence, the triangles are equal, and CF is equal to CG (B. I., P. 17); consequently, the two equal chords AB, DE, are equally distant from the centre.

Secondly. Let the chord AH be greater than DE: then will DE be furthest from the centre C. Since the chord AH is greater than DE the arc AKH is greater than DME (P. 5). Cut off from the former, a part ANB, equal to DME; draw the chord AB, and draw CF perpendicular to this chord, and CI perpendicular to AH. It is evident that CF is greater than CO (B. I., A. 8), and CO than CI (B. I., P. 15); therefore, CF is still greater than CI. But CF is equal to CG, because the chords AB, DE, are equal: hence, CG is greater than CI; therefore, of two unequal chords, the less is the farther from the centre of the circle.

PROPOSITION IX. THEOREM.

A straight line perpendicular to a radius, at its extremity, is tangent to the circumference.

Let the line BD be perpendicular to the radius CA at its extremity A; then will it be tangent to the circumference.

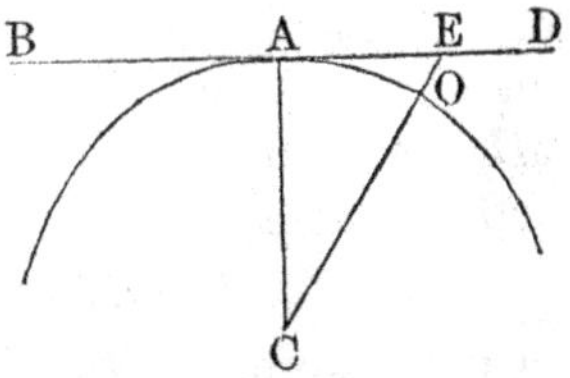

For, every oblique line CE, is longer than the perpendicular CA (B. I., P. 15); hence, the point E is without the circle; therefore, the line BD has no point but A in common with the circumference; consequently, the line BD is a tangent (D. 9).

Cor. 1. Conversely, if a straight line be tangent to a circle, it will be perpendicular to the radius drawn to the point of contact.

Let BAD be a tangent, and CA a radius drawn through the point of contact A: then will BD be perpendicular to CA. For, through the centre C, suppose any other line, as COE, to be drawn. Then, since BD is a tangent, the point E will lie without the circle, and consequently CE will be greater than the radius CO or CA; therefore, the radius CA, measures the shortest distance from the centre C, to the tangent BD: hence, it is perpendicular to the tangent (B. I., P. 15, C. 1).

Cor. 2. At a given point of the circumference only one tangent can be drawn to the circle. For, let A be the given point, BD a tangent, and CA the radius drawn through the point of contact A. Now, if another tangent could be drawn, it would also be perpendicular to CA at the point A, by the last corollary: that is, we should have two lines perpendicular to CA, at the same point; which is impossible (B. I., P. 14, C).

PROPOSITION X. THEOREM.

Two parallels intercept equal arcs of the circumference.

There may be three cases.

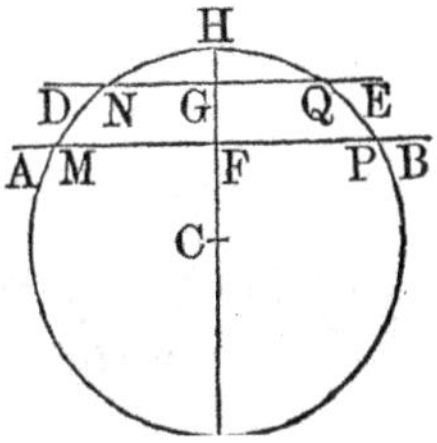

First. When the two parallels are secants. Let AB and DE be two parallels: draw the radius CH perpendicular to the chord MP. It will, at the same time, be perpendicular to NQ (B. I., P. 20, C. 1); therefore, the point H will be at

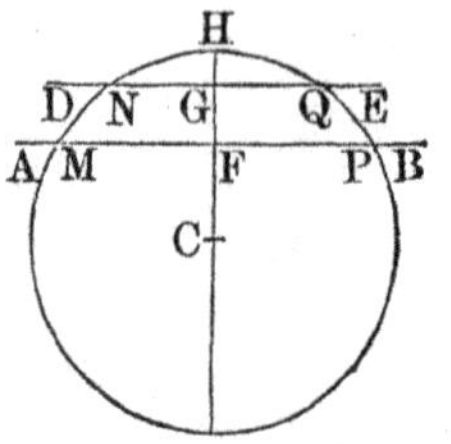

once the middle of the arc MHP, and of the arc NHQ (P. 6); consequently, we shall have the arc $MH=HP$, and the arc $NH=HQ$; and therefore

$$MH-NH=HP-HQ;$$

in other words, $MN=PQ$.

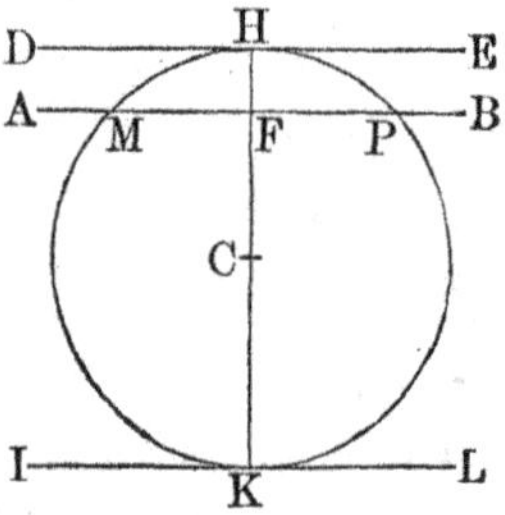

Second. When, of the two parallels AB, DE, one is a secant, and the other a tangent, draw the radius CH to the point of contact H; it will be perpendicular to the tangent DE (P. 9, C. 1), and also to its parallel MP (B. I., P. 20, C. 1). But since CH is perpendicular to the chord MP, the point H must be the middle of the arc MHP (P. 6); therefore, the arcs MH, HP, included between the parallels AB, DE, are equal.

Third. If the two parallels DE, IL, are tangents, the one at H, the other at K, draw the parallel secant AB; and, from what has just been shown, we shall have

$$MH=HP, \ MK=KP:$$

and hence, the whole arc $HMK=HPK$. It is further evident that each of these arcs is a semi-circumference.

Cor. Conversely: If the arc HM is equal to the arc HP, it is plain that the chord MP will be parallel to the tangent DE.

PROPOSITION XI. THEOREM.

If two circumferences have one point common, out of the straight line which joins their centres, they will also have a second point in common; and the two points will be situated in a line perpendicular to the line joining the centres, and at equal distances from it.

Let the two circumferences described about the centres C and D intersect each other at the point A; draw AF

perpendicular to CD, and prolong it till BF is equal to AF; then will the circumferences also intersect each other at B.

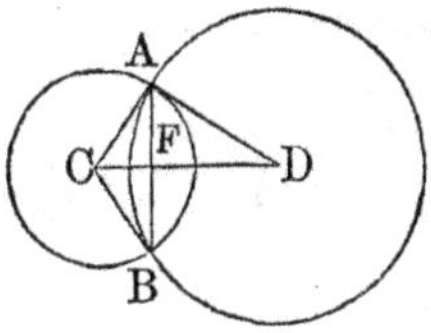

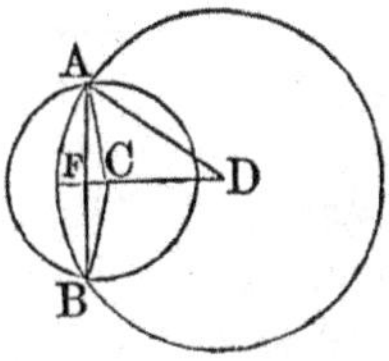

For, since AF is equal to FB, CF common and the angles at F right angles, the hypothenuses CB and CA are equal (B. I., P. 5): hence, the circumference described about the centre C, with the radius CA, will pass through B. In the same manner it may be shown, that the circumference described about the centre D, with the radius DA. will also pass through B.

Cor. If two circumferences intersect each other, they will intersect in two points, and the line which joins the centres will be perpendicular to the common chord at the middle point.

PROPOSITION XII. THEOREM.

If the circumferences of two circles intersect each other, the distance between their centres will be less than the sum of their radii, and greater than the difference.

Let two circumferences be described about the centres C and D, with the radii CA and DA: then, if these circumferences intersect each other, the triangle CAD can always be formed. Now, in this triangle, CAD,

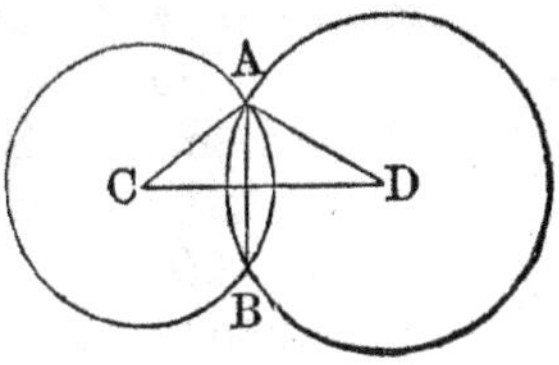

$$CD < CA + AD \quad \text{(B. I., P. 7)},$$

also,
$$CD > DA - AC \quad \text{(B. I., P. 7, C.)}$$

PROPOSITION XIII. THEOREM.

If the distance between the centres of two circles is equal to the sum of their radii, the circumferences will touch each other externally.

Let C and D be the centres of two circles at a distance from each other equal to $CA+AD$.

The circles will evidently have the point A common, and they will have no other; because if they have two points common, the distance between their centres must be less than the sum of their radii, which is contrary to the supposition.

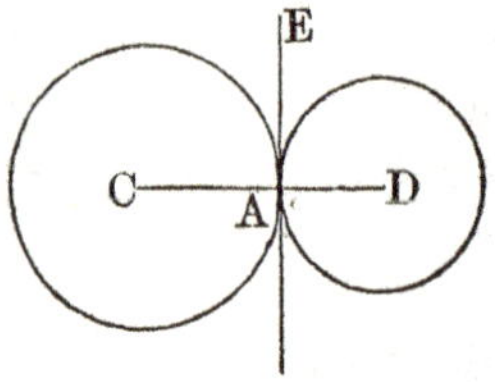

Cor. If the distance between the centres of two circles is greater than the sum of their radii, the two circumferences will be exterior the one to the other.

PROPOSITION XIV. THEOREM.

If the distance between the centres of two circles is equal to the difference of their radii, the two circumferences will touch each other internally.

Let C and D be the centres of two circles at a distance from each other equal to $AD-CA$.

It is evident, as before, that the two circumferences will have the point A common: they can have no other; because if they had, the distance between the centres would be greater than $AD-CA$ (P. 12); which is contrary to the supposition.

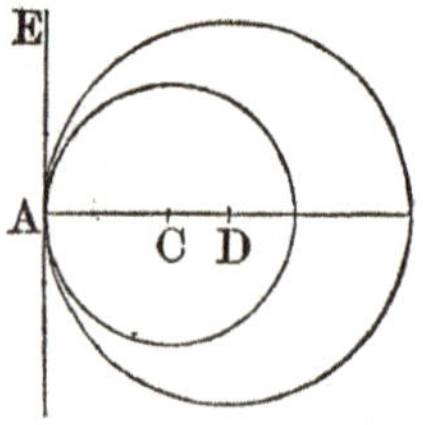

Cor. 1. Hence, if two circles touch each other, either externally or internally, their centres and the point of contact will be in the same straight line.

Cor. 2. If the distance between the centres of two

circles is less than the difference of their radii, one circle will be entirely within the other.

Scholium 1. All circles which have their centres on the right line AD, and which pass through the point A, are tangent to each other at the point A. For, they have only the point A common, and if through A, AE be drawn perpendicular to AD, it will be a common tangent to all the circles.

Scholium. 2. Two circumferences must occupy with respect to each other, one of the five positions above indicated.

1*st.* They may intersect each other in two points:
2*d.* They may touch each other externally:
3*d.* They may be external, the one to the other:
4*th.* They may touch each other internally:
5*th.* The one may be entirely within the other.

PROPOSITION XV. THEOREM.

In the same circle, or in equal circles, radii making equal angles at the centre, intercept equal arcs on the circumference. And conversely: If the arcs intercepted are equal, the angles contained by the radii are also equal.

Let C and C be the centres of equal circles, and the angle $ACB=DCE$.

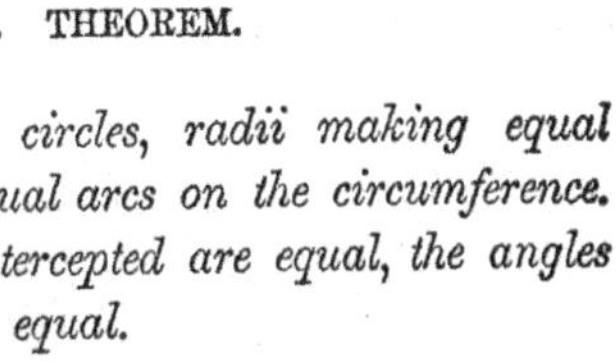

First. Since the angles ACB, DCE, are equal, one of them may be placed upon the other. Let the angle ACB be placed on DCE. Then since their sides are equal, the point A will evidently fall on D, and the point B on E. The arc AB will also fall on the arc DE; for, if the arcs did not exactly coincide, there would, in the one or the other, be points unequally distant from the centre; which is impossible: hence, the arc AB is equal to DE (A. 14).

Second. If the arc $AB=DE$, the angle ACB is equal

to DCE. For, if these angles are not equal, suppose one of them, as ACB, to be the greater, and let ACI be taken equal to DCE. From what has just been shown, we shall then have $AI = DE$; but, by hypothesis, AB is equal to DE; hence, AI must be equal to AB, or a part equal to the whole, which is absurd (A. 8); hence, the angle ACB is equal to DCE.

PROPOSITION XVI. THEOREM.

In the same circle, or in equal circles, if two angles at the centre have to each other the ratio of two whole numbers, the intercepted arcs will have to each other the same ratio: or, we shall have the angle to the angle, as the corresponding arc to the corresponding arc.

Suppose, for example, that the angles ACB, DCE, are to each other as 7 is to 4; or, what is the same thing, suppose that the angle M, which may serve as a common measure, is contained 7 times in the angle ACB, and 4

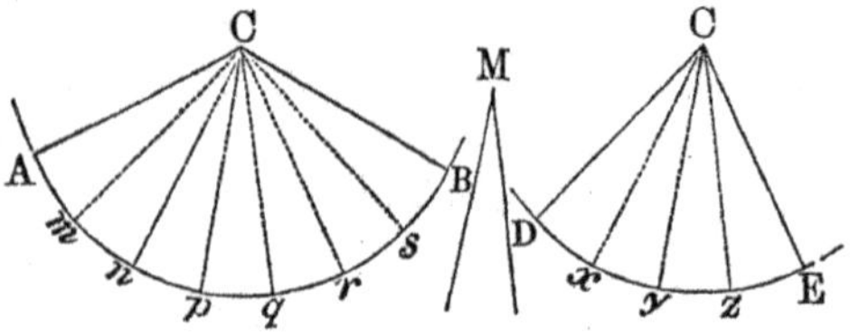

times in DCE. The seven partial angles ACm, mCn, nCp, &c., into which ACB is divided, are each equal to any of the four partial angles into which DCE is divided; and each of the partial arcs, Am, mn, np, &c., is equal to each of the partial arcs Dx, xy, &c. (P. 15). Therefore, the whole arc AB will be to the whole arc DE, as 7 is to 4. But the same reasoning would evidently apply, if in place of 7 and 4 any numbers whatever were employed; hence, if the angles ACB, DCE, are to each other as two whole numbers, they will also be to each other as the arcs AB, DE.

Cor. Conversely: If the arcs AB, DE, are to each other as two whole numbers, the angles ACB, DCE will be to each other as the same whole numbers, and we shall have

$$AB : DE :: ACB : DCE.$$

For, the partial arcs, Am, mn, &c., and Dx, xy, &c., being equal, the partial angles ACm, mCn, &c., and DCx, xCy, &c., will also be equal, and the entire arcs will be to each other as the entire angles.

PROPOSITION XVII. THEOREM.

In the same circle, or in equal circles, any two angles at the centre are to each other as the intercepted arcs.

Let ACB and ACD be two angles at the centres of equal circles: then will

$$ACB : ACD :: AB : AD.$$

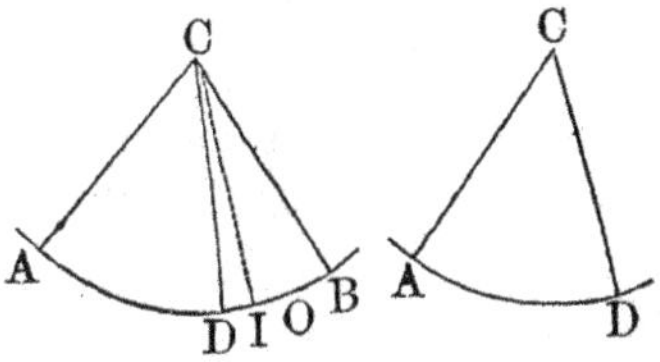

For, if the angles are equal, the arcs will be equal (P. 15). If they are unequal, let the less be placed on the greater. Then, if the proposition is not true, the angle ACB will be to the angle ACD as the arc AB is to an arc greater or less than AD. Suppose such arc to be greater, and let it be represented by AO; we shall thus have,

the angle ACB : angle ACD :: arc AB : arc AO.

Next conceive the arc AB to be divided into equal parts, each of which is less than DO; there will be at least one point of division between D and O; let I be that point; and draw CI. Then the arcs AB, AI, will be to each other as two whole numbers, and by the preceding theorem, we shall have,

angle ACB : angle ACI :: arc AB : arc AI.

Comparing the two proportions with each other, we see that the antecedents in each are the same: hence, the consequents are proportional (B. II., P. 4); and thus we find,

the angle ACD : angle ACI :: arc AO : arc AI.

But the arc AO is greater than the arc AI; hence, if this proportion is true, the angle ACD must be greater than the angle ACI: on the contrary, however, it is less; hence, the angle ACB cannot be to the angle ACD as the arc AB is to an arc greater than AD.

By a process of reasoning entirely similar, it may be shown that the fourth term of the proportion cannot be less than AD; hence, it is AD itself; therefore, we have

$$\text{angle } ACB : \text{angle } ACD :: \text{arc } AB : \text{arc } AD.$$

Scholium 1. Since the angle at the centre of a circle, and the arc intercepted by its sides, have such a connection, that if the one be augmented or diminished, the other will be augmented or diminished in the same ratio, we are authorized to assume the one of these magnitudes as the measure of the other; and we shall henceforth assume the *arc AB as the measure of the angle ACB.* It is only necessary, in the comparison of angles with each other, that the arcs which serve to measure them, be described with equal radii.

Scholium 2. An angle less than a right angle will be measured by an arc less than a quarter of the circumference: a right angle, by a quarter of the circumference: and an obtuse angle by an arc greater than a quarter, and less than half the circumference.

Scholium 3. It appears most natural to measure a quantity by a quantity of the same species; and upon this principle it would be convenient to refer all angles to the right angle. This being made the unit of measure, an acute angle would be expressed by some number between 0 and 1; an obtuse angle by some number between 1 and 2. This mode of expressing angles would not, however, be the most convenient in practice. It has been found more simple to measure them by the arcs of a circle, on account of the facility with which arcs can be made to correspond to angles, and for various other reasons. At all events, if the measurement of angles by the arcs of a circle is in any degree indirect, it is still very easy to obtain the direct and absolute measure by this method; since, by comparing the fourth part of the circumference with the arc which serves as a measure of any angle, we find the ratio of a right angle to the given angle, which is the *absolute measure.*

Scholium 4. All that has been demonstrated in the last three propositions, concerning the comparison of angles with arcs, holds true equally, if applied to the comparison of sectors with arcs. For, sectors are not only equal when their angles are so, but are in all respects proportional to their angles; hence, *two sectors ACB, ACD, taken in the same circle, or in equal circles, are to each other as the arcs AB, AD, the bases of those sectors.* Hence, it is evident that the arcs of equal circles, which serve as a measure of corresponding angles, are proportional to their sectors.

PROPOSITION XVIII. THEOREM.

Any inscribed angle is measured by half the arc included between its sides.

Let *BAD* be an inscribed angle, and let us first suppose the centre of the circle to lie within the angle *BAD*. Draw the diameter *ACE*, and the radii *CB*, *CD*.

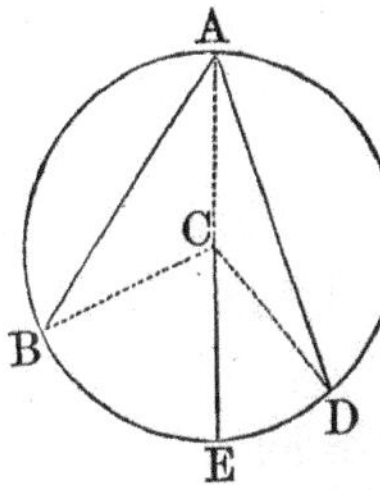

The angle *BCE*, being exterior to the triangle *ABC*, is equal to the sum of the two interior angles *CAB*, *ABC* (B. I., P. 25, C. 6): but the triangle *BAC* being isosceles, the angle *CAB* is equal to *ABC*; hence, the angle *BCE* is double *BAC*. Since *BCE* is at the centre, it is measured by the arc *BE* (P. 17, S. 1); hence, *BAC* will be measured by the half of *BE*. For a like reason, the angle *CAD* will be measured by the half of *ED*; hence, *BAC*+*CAD*, or *BAD* will be measured by half of *BE*+*ED*, or half of *BED*.

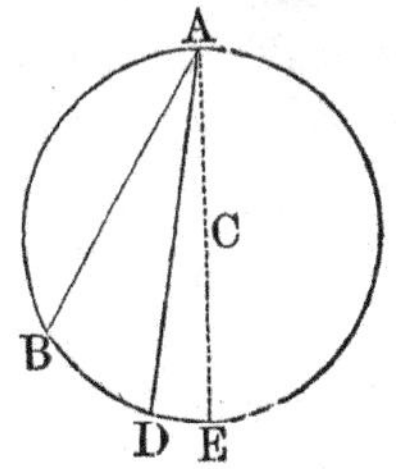

Secondly. Suppose the centre *C* to lie without the angle *BAD*. Then, drawing the diameter *ACE*, the angle *BAE* will be measured by the half of *BE*; the angle *DAE* by the half of *DE*: hence, their difference, *BAD*, will be measured by the half of *BE* *minus* the half of *ED*, or by the half of *BD*. Hence, every inscribed angle is measured by half the arc included between its sides.

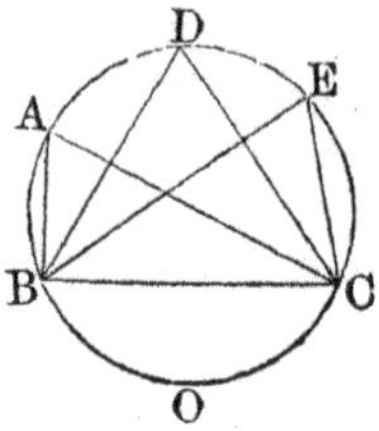

Cor. 1. All the angles *BAC*, *BDC*, *BEC*, inscribed in the same segment are equal; because they are each measured by half of the same arc *BOC*.

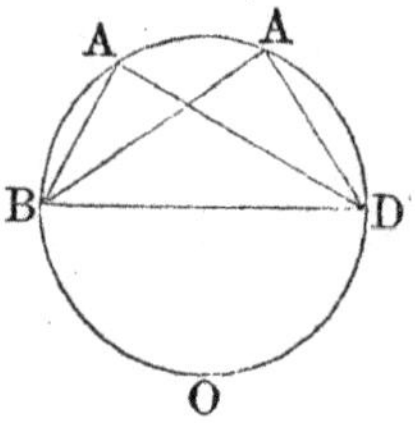

Cor. 2. Every angle *BAD*, inscribed in a semicircle is a right angle; because it is measured by half the semicircumference *BOD*, that is, by the fourth part of the whole circumference (P. 17, s. 2).

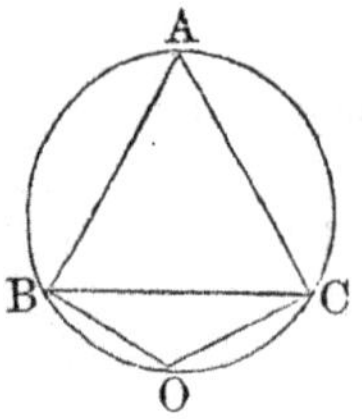

Cor. 3. Every angle *BAC*, inscribed in a segment greater than a semicircle, is an acute angle; for it is measured by half the arc *BOC*, less than a semicircumference (P. 17, s. 2).

And every angle *BOC*, inscribed in a segment less than a semicircle, is an obtuse angle; for it is measured by half the arc *BAC*, greater than a semicircumference.

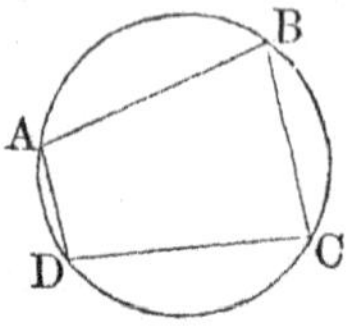

Cor. 4. The opposite angles *A* and *C*, of an inscribed quadrilateral *ABCD*, are together equal to two right angles: for, the angle *BAD* is measured by half the arc *BCD*, the angle *BCD* is measured by half the arc *BAD*; hence, the two angles *BAD*, *BCD*, taken together, are measured by half the circumference; hence, their sum is equal to two right angles (P. 17, s. 2).

PROPOSITION XIX. THEOREM.

The angle formed by two chords, which intersect each other, is measured by half the sum of the included arcs.

Let *AB*, *CD*, be two chords intersecting each other at *E*: then will the angle *AEC*, or *DEB*, be measured by half of $AC+DB$.

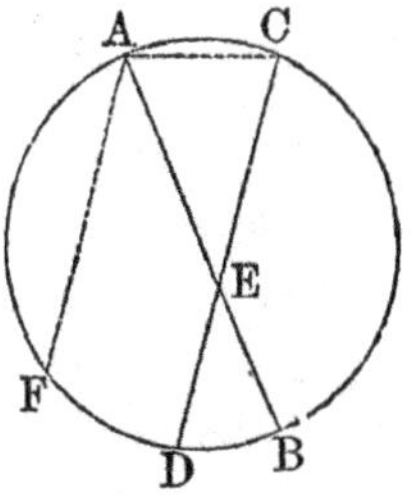

Draw AF parallel to DC: the arc DF will be equal to AC (P. 10), and the angle FAB equal to the angle DEB (B. I., P. 20, C. 3). But the angle FAB is measured by half the arc FDB (P. 18); therefore, DEB is measured by half of FDB; that is, by half of $DB+DF$, or half of $DB+AC$.

To prove the same for the angle DEA, or its equal BEC. Draw the chord AC. Then, the angle DCA will be measured by half the arc DFA; and the angle BAC by half the arc CB (P. 18). But the outward angle AED, of the triangle EAC, is equal to the sum of the angles A and C (B. I., P. 25, C. 6); hence, this angle is measured by one-half of BC plus one-half of AFD; that is, by half the sum of the intercepted arcs. By drawing a chord BC, similar reasoning would apply to the angle AEC or DEB.

PROPOSITION XX. THEOREM.

The angle formed by two secants, is measured by half the difference of the included arcs.

Let AB, AC, be two secants: then will the angle BAC be measured by half the difference of the arcs BEC and DF.

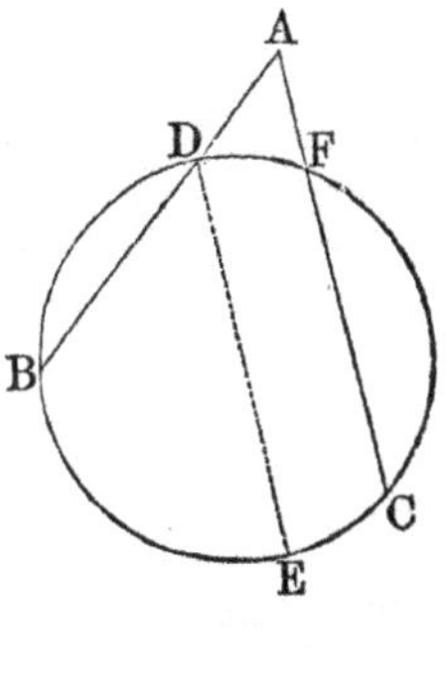

Draw DE parallel to AC: the arc EC will be equal to DF (P. 10), and the angle BDE equal to the angle BAC (B. I., P. 20, C. 3). But BDE is measured by half the arc BE (P. 18); hence, BAC is also measured by half the arc BE; that is, by half the difference of BEC and EC, and consequently, by half the difference of BEC and DF.

PROPOSITION XXI. THEOREM.

Any angle formed by a tangent and a chord passing through the point of contact, is measured by half the arc included between its sides.

Let BE be a tangent, and AC a chord.

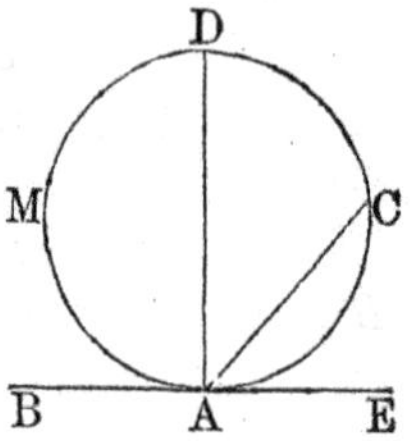

From A, the point of contact, draw the diameter AD. The angle BAD is a right angle (P. 9), and is measured by half the semicircumference AMD (P. 17, s. 2); the angle DAC is measured by the half of DC; hence, $BAD+DAC$, or BAC, is measured by the half of AMD plus the half of DC, or by half the whole arc $AMDC$.

It may be shown, by taking the difference of the angles DAE, DAC, that the angle CAE is measured by half the arc AC, included between its sides.

PROBLEMS

RELATING TO THE FIRST AND THIRD BOOKS

PROBLEM I.

To bisect a given straight line.

Let AB be the given straight line.

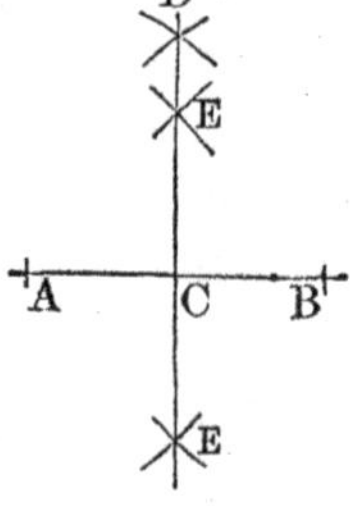

From the points A and B as centres, with a radius greater than the half of AB, describe two arcs cutting each other in D; the point D will be equally distant from A and B. Find, in like manner, above or beneath the line AB, a second point E, equally distant from the points A and B; through the two points D and E, draw the line DE, and the point C, where this line meets AB, will be equally distant from A and B.

For, the two points D and E, being each equally distant from the extremities A and B, must both lie in the perpendicular raised at the middle point of AB (B. I., P. 16, C). But only one straight line can be drawn through two given points (A. 11); hence, the line DE must itself be that perpendicular, which divides AB into two equal parts.

PROBLEM II.

At a given point, of a given straight line, to erect a perpendicular to that line.

Let BC be the given line, and A the given point.

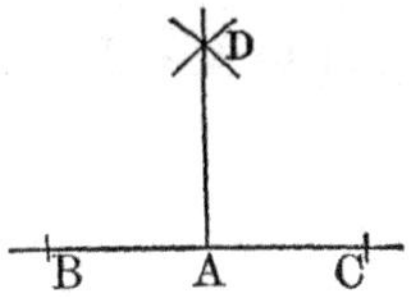

Take the points B and C at equal distances from A; then from the points B and C as centres, with a radius greater than BA, describe two arcs intersecting each other at D; draw AD and it will be the perpendicular required.

For, the point D, being equally distant from B and C, must be in the perpendicular raised at the middle of BC (B. I., P. 16); and since two points determine a line, AD is that perpendicular.

Scholium. The same construction serves for making a right angle BAD, at a given point A, on a given straight line BC.

PROBLEM III.

From a given point, without a straight line, to let fall a perpendicular on that line.

Let A be the point, and BD the given straight line.

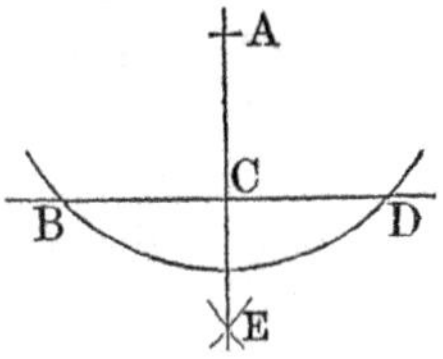

From the point A as a centre, and with a radius sufficiently great, describe an arc cutting the line BD in two points B and D; then find a point E, equally distant from the points B and D, and draw AE: it will be the perpendicular required.

For, the two points A and E are each equally distant from the points B and D; hence, the line AE is a perpendicular passing through the middle of BD (B. I., P. 16, C).

PROBLEM IV.

At a point in a given line, to construct an angle equal to a given angle.

Let A be the given point, AB the given line, and IKL, the given angle.

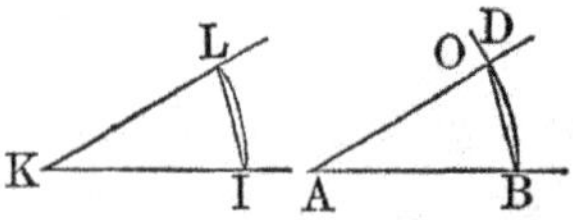

From the vertex K, as a centre, with any radius, KI, describe the arc IL, terminating in the sides of the angle. From the point A as a centre, with a distance AB, equal to KI, describe the indefinite arc BO; then take a radius equal to the chord LI, with which, from the point B as a centre, describe an arc cutting the indefinite arc BO, in D; draw AD; and the angle BAD will be equal to the given angle K.

For, the two arcs BD, LI, have equal radii, and equal chords; hence, they are equal (P. 4); therefore, the angles BAD, IKL, measured by them, are also equal (P. 15).

PROBLEM V.

To bisect a given arc, or a given angle.

First. Let it be required to divide the arc AEB into two equal parts. From the points A and B, as centres, with equal radii, describe two arcs cutting each other in D; through the point D and the centre C, draw CD: it will bisect the arc AB in the point E.

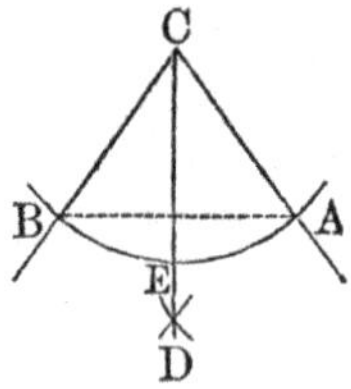

For, the two points C and D are each equally distant from the extremities A and B of the chord AB; hence, the line CD bisects the chord at right angles (B. I., P. 16, C); and consequently, it bisects the arc AEB in the point E (P. 6).

Secondly. Let it be required to divide the angle ACB into two equal parts. We begin by describing, from the vertex C, as a centre, the arc AEB; which is then bisect ed as above. It is plain that the line CD will divide the angle ACB into two equal parts (P. 17, S. 1).

Scholium. By the same construction, each of the halves AE, EB, may be divided into two equal parts; and thus, by successive subdivisions, a given angle, or a given arc, may be divided into four equal parts, into eight, into sixteen, and so on.

PROBLEM VI.

Through a given point, to draw a line parallel to a given straight line.

Let A be the given point, and BC the given line.

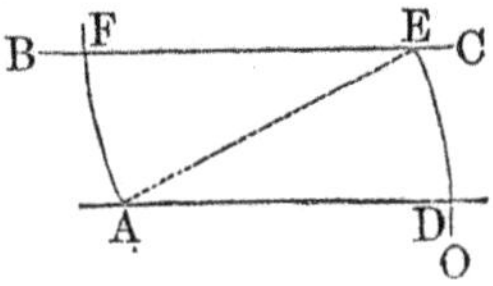

From the point A as a centre, with a radius AE, greater than the shortest distance from A to BC, describe the indefinite arc EO; from the point E as a centre, with the same radius, describe the arc AF; lay off $ED = AF$, and draw AD: this is the parallel required.

For, drawing AE, the angles AEF, EAD, are equal (P. 15); therefore, the lines AD, EF, are parallel (B. I., P. 19, C. 1).

PROBLEM VII.

Two angles of a triangle being given, to find the third.

Let A and B be the given angles.

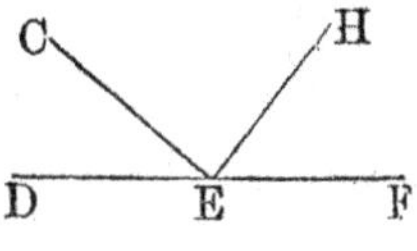

Draw the indefinite line DEF; at any point as E, construct the angle DEC equal to the angle A, and the angle CEH equal to the other angle B: the remaining angle HEF will be the third angle required; because, these three angles are together equal to two right angles (B. I., P. 1, C. 3), and so are the three angles of a triangle (B. I., P. 25); consequently, HEF is equal to the third angle of the triangle

PROBLEM VIII.

Two sides of a triangle, and the angle which they contain, being given, to construct the triangle.

Let the lines B and C be equal to the given sides, and A the given angle.

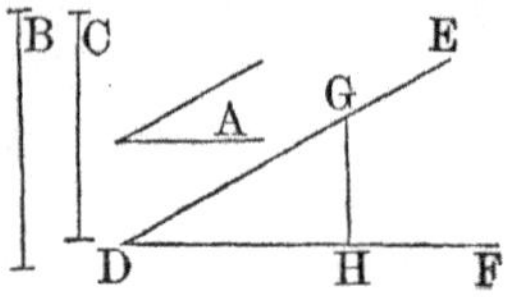

Having drawn the indefinite line DF, make at the point D, the angle FDE equal to the given angle A; then take $DG=B$, $DH=C$, and draw GH: DGH will be the triangle required (B. I., P. 5).

PROBLEM IX.

A side and two angles of a triangle being given, to construct the triangle.

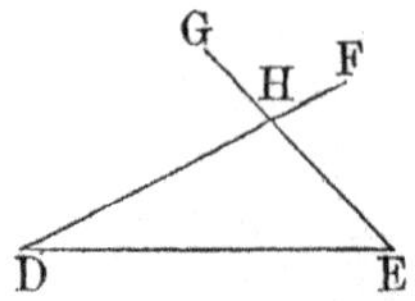

The two angles will either be both adjacent to the given side, or one will be adjacent, and the other opposite: in the latter case find the third angle (PROB. 7), and the two adjacent angles will be known. Then draw the straight line DE, and make it equal to the given side: at the point D, make an angle EDF, equal to one of the adjacent angles, and at E, an angle DEG equal to the other; the two lines DF, EG, will intersect each other in H; and DEH will be the triangle required (B. I., P. 6).

PROBLEM X.

The three sides of a triangle being given, to construct the triangle.

Let A, B, and C, denote the three given sides.

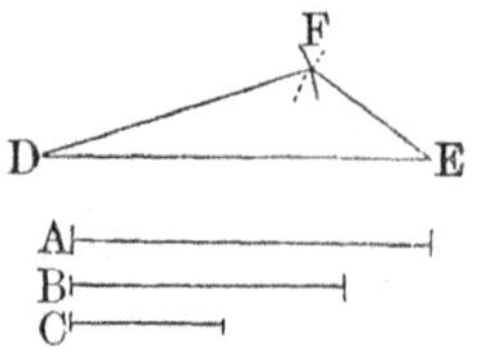

Draw DE, and make it equal to the side A; from the point D as a centre, with a radius equal to the second side B, describe an arc; from E as a centre, with a radius equal to the third side C, describe another arc intersecting the former in F; draw DF, EF; and DEF will be the triangle required (B. I., P. 10).

Scholium. If one of the sides were greater than the sum of the other two, the arcs would not intersect each other, for no such triangle could exist (B. I., P. 7): but the solution will always be possible, when the sum of each two of the lines, is greater than the third.

PROBLEM XI.

Two sides of a triangle, and the angle opposite one of them, being given, to construct the triangle.

Let A and B be the given sides, and C the given angle. There are two cases.

First. When the angle C is a right angle, or when it is obtuse. Draw DF and make the angle $FDE=C$; take $DE=A$: from the point E as a centre, with a radius equal to the given side B, describe an arc cutting DF in F; draw EF; then DEF will be the triangle required.

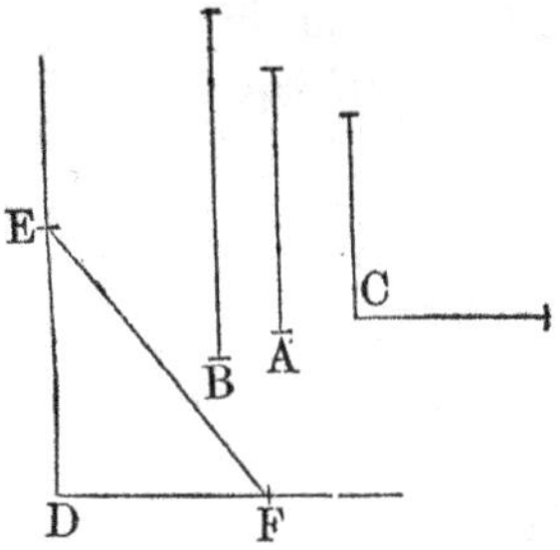

In this case, the side B must be greater than A; for the angle C being a right angle, or an obtuse angle, is the greatest angle of the triangle (B. I., P. 25, C. 3), and the side opposite to it must, therefore, also be the greatest (B. I., P. 13).

Secondly. If the angle C is acute, and B greater than A, the same construction will again apply, and DEF will be the triangle required.

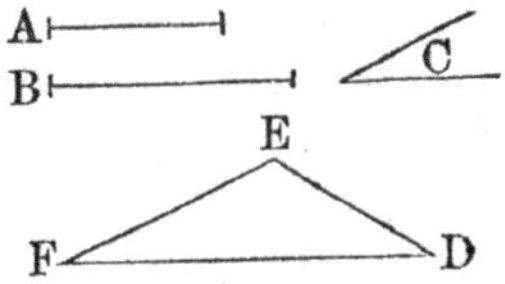

But if the angle C is acute, and the side B less than A, then the arc described from the centre E, with the radius $EF=B$, will cut the side DF in two points F and G, lying on the same side of D: hence, there will be two triangles DEF, DEG, either of which will satisfy all the conditions of the problem.

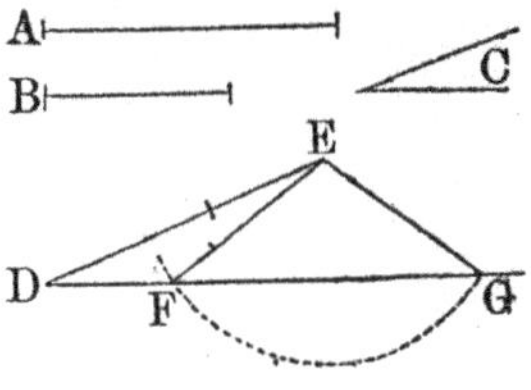

Scholium. If the arc described with E as a centre, should be tangent to the line DG, the triangle would be right angled, and there would be but one solution. The problem will be impossible in all cases, when the side B is less than the perpendicular let fall from E on the line DF.

PROBLEM XII.

The adjacent sides of a parallelogram and their included angle being given, to construct the parallelogram.

Let A and B be the given sides, and C the given angle.

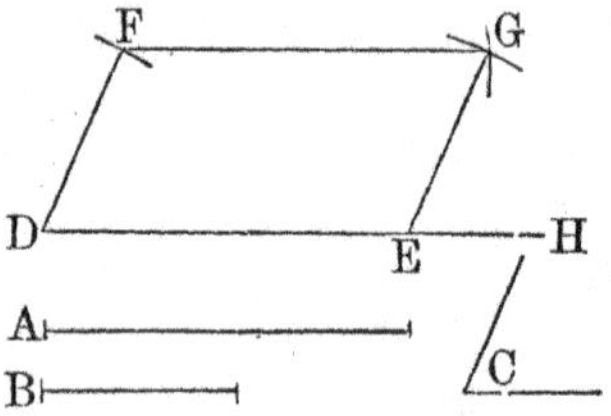

Draw the line DH, and lay off DE equal to A: at the point D, make the angle $EDF=C$; take $DF=B$; describe two arcs, the one from F as a centre, with a radius $FG=DE$, the other from E as a centre, with a radius $EG=DF$; to the point G, where these arcs intersect each other, draw FG, EG; $DEGF$ will be the parallelogram required.

For, the opposite sides are equal, by construction; hence, the figure is a parallelogram (B. I., P. 29); and it is formed with the given sides and the given angle.

Cor. If the given angle is a right angle, the figure will be a rectangle; if, in addition to this, the sides are equal, it will be a square.

PROBLEM XIII.

To find the centre of a given circle or arc.

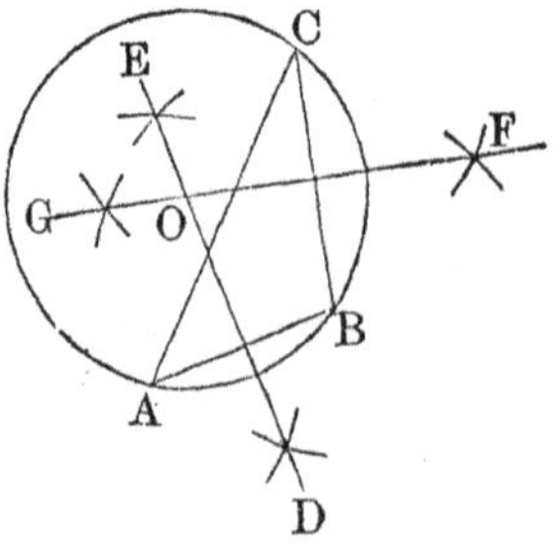

Take three points, A, B, C, anywhere in the circumference, or in the arc; draw AB, BC, or suppose them to be drawn; bisect these two lines by the perpendiculars DE, FG (PROB. 1): the point O, where these perpendiculars meet, will be the centre sought (P. 6, S).

Scholium. The same construction serves for making a circumference pass through three given points A, B, C; and also for describing a circumference, which shall circumscribe a given triangle ABC.

PROBLEM XIV.

Through a given point, to draw a tangent to a given circle.

Let A be the given point, and C the centre of the given circle.

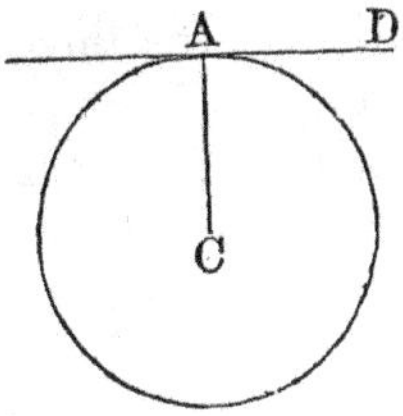

If the given point A lies in the circumference, draw the radius CA, and erect AD perpendicular to it: AD will be the tangent required (P. 9).

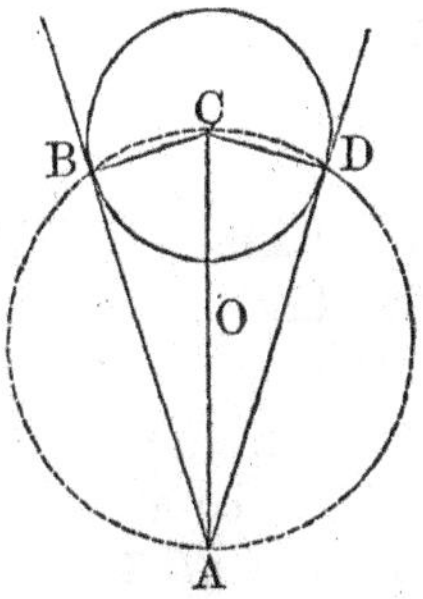

If the point A lies without the circle, join A and the centre, by the straight line CA: bisect CA in O; from O as a centre, with the radius OC, describe a circumference intersecting the given circumference in B; draw AB: this will be the tangent required.

For, drawing CB, the angle CBA being inscribed in a semicircle is a right angle (P. 18, C. 2); therefore, AB is a perpendicular at the extremity of the radius CB; hence, it is a tangent (P. 9).

Scholium 1. When the point A lies without the circle, there will be two equal tangents, AB, AD, passing through the point A: for, there will be two right-angled triangles, CBA, CDA, having the hypothenuse CA common, and the side $CB=CD$; hence, there will be two equal tangents, AB, AD. The angles CAD, CAB, are also equal (B. 1., P. 17).

Scholium 2. As there can be but one line bisecting the angle BAD, it follows, that the line which bisects the angle formed by two tangents, must pass through the centre of the circle.

PROBLEM XV.

To inscribe a circle in a given triangle.

Let ABC be the given triangle.

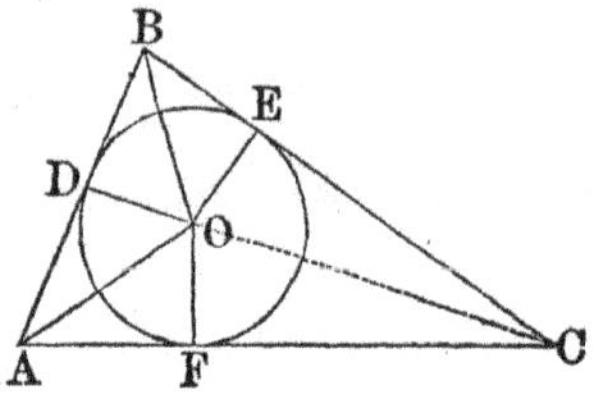

Bisect the angles A and B, by the lines AO and BO, meeting in the point O (PROB. 5); from the point O, let fall the perpendiculars OD, OE, OF (PROB. 3), on the three sides of the triangle: these perpendiculars will all be equal.

For, by construction, we have the angle $DAO=OAF$, the right angle $ADO=AFO$; hence, the third angle AOD is equal to the third AOF (B. I., P. 25, C. 2). Moreover, the side AO is common to the two triangles AOD, AOF; and the angles adjacent to the equal side are equal: hence, the triangles themselves are equal (B. I., P. 6); and DO is equal to OF. In the same manner it may be shown that the two triangles BOD, BOE, are equal; therefore OD is equal to OE; hence, the three perpendiculars OD, OE, OF, are all equal.

Now, if from the point O as a centre, with the radius OD, a circle be described, this circle will be inscribed in the triangle ABC (D. 11); for, the side AB, being perpendicular to the radius at its extremity, is a tangent (P. 9); and the same thing is true of the sides BC, AC.

Scholium. The three lines which bisect the three angles of a triangle meet in the same point.

PROBLEM XVI.

On a given straight line to construct a segment that shall contain a given angle; that is to say, a segment such, that any angle inscribed in it shall be equal to a given angle.

Let AB be the given straight line, and C the given angle.

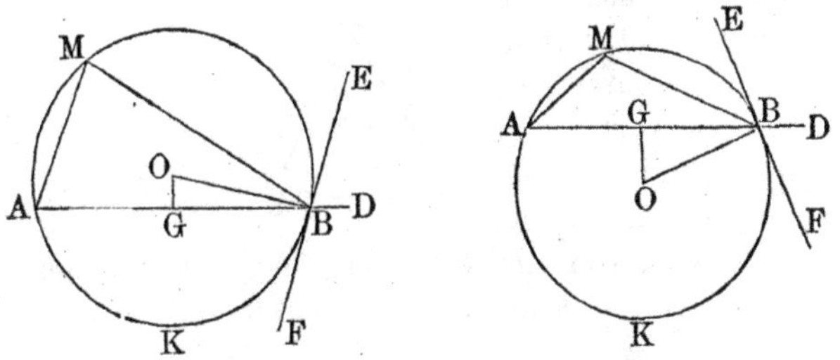

Produce AB towards D. At the point B, make the angle $DBE=C$; draw BO perpendicular to BE, and at the middle point G, draw GO perpendicular to AB: from the point O, where these perpendiculars meet, as a centre, with the distance OB, describe a circumference: the required segment will be AMB.

For, since BF is perpendicular to the radius OB at its extremity, it is a tangent (P. 9), and the angle ABF is measured by half the arc AKB (P. 21). Also, the angle AMB, being an inscribed angle, is measured by half the arc AKB (P. 18): hence, we have $AMB=ABF=EBD=C$: hence, any angle inscribed in the segment AMB is equal to the given angle C.

Scholium. If the given angle were a right angle, the required segment would be a semicircle described on AB as a diameter.

PROBLEM XVII.

Two angles being given, to find their common measure, if they have one, and by means of it, their ratio in numbers.

Let CAD and EBF be the given angles. With A and B as centres, and with equal radii describe the arcs CD, EF, to serve as measures for the angles. Afterwards, proceed in the comparison of the arcs CD, EF, in the same manner as in the comparison of two straight lines (B. II., D. 4); since an arc may be cut off from an arc of the same radius, as a straight

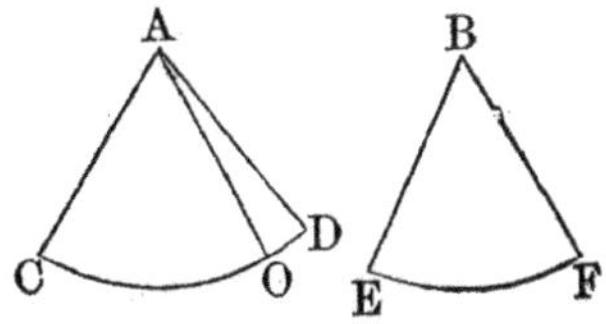

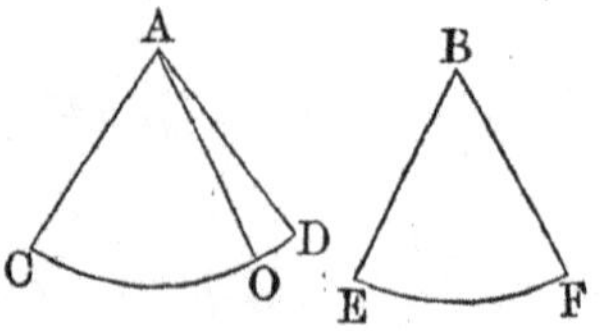

line from a straight line. We shall thus arrive at the common measure of the arcs CD, EF, if they have one, and thereby at their ratio in numbers. This ratio will be the same as that of the given angles (P. 17); and if DO is the common measure of the arcs, the angle DAO will be that of the angles.

Scholium. According to this method, the absolute value of an angle may be found by comparing the arc which measures it, with a quarter circumference. For example, if a quarter circumference is to the arc CD as 3 to 1, then, the angle A will be $\frac{1}{3}$ of one right angle, or $\frac{1}{12}$ of four right angles.

It may happen, that the arcs compared have no common measure; in which case, the numerical ratios of the angles will only be found approximatively with more or less correctness, according as the operation is continued a greater or less number of times.

BOOK IV.

PROPORTIONS OF FIGURES—MEASUREMENT OF AREAS.

DEFINITIONS.

1. SIMILAR POLYGONS are those which are mutually equiangular (B. I., D. 22), and have their sides about the equal angles, taken in the same order, proportional.

2. In polygons which are mutually equiangular, the angles which are equal, each to each, are called *homologous* angles: and the sides which are like situated, in respect to the equal angles, are called *homologous* sides.

3. AREA, denotes the superficial contents of a figure. The area of a figure is expressed numerically by the number of times which the figure contains some other figure regarded as a unit of measure.

4. EQUIVALENT FIGURES are those which have equal areas. The term *equal*, when applied to quantity in general, denotes an equality of measures; but when applied to geometrical figures it denotes an equality in every respect; and such figures when applied the one to the other, coincide in all their parts (A. 14). The term *equivalent*, denotes an equality in one respect only; viz.: an equality between the measures of figures. The sign ⇔, denotes equivalency, and is read, *is equivalent to.*

5. Two sides of a polygon are said to be *reciprocally proportional* to two sides of another, when one of the sides of the first is to one of the sides of the second, as the remaining side of the second is to the remaining side of the first.

6. SIMILAR ARCS, SECTORS, or, SEGMENTS, are those, which in different circles, correspond to equal angles at the centre.

Thus, if the angles A and O are equal, the arc BFC will be similar to DGE, the sector BAC to the sector DOE, and the segment BCF, to the segment DEG.

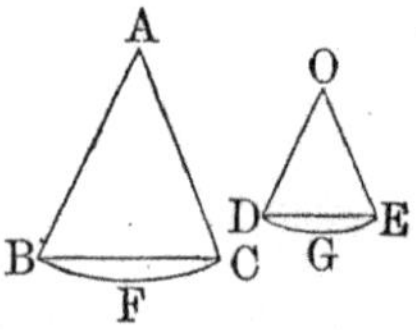

7. The ALTITUDE of a triangle is the perpendicular let fall from the vertex of an angle on the opposite side, or on that side produced: such side is then called a *base*.

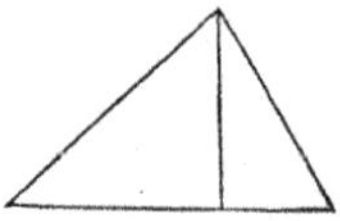

8. The *altitude* of a parallelogram is the perpendicular distance between two opposite sides. These sides are called *bases*.

9. The *altitude* of a trapezoid is the perpendicular distance between its two parallel sides.

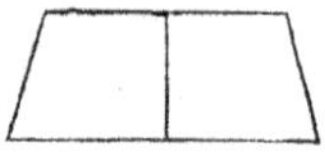

PROPOSITION I. THEOREM.

Parallelograms which have equal bases and equal altitudes, are equivalent.

Since the two parallelograms have equal bases, those bases may be placed the one on the other. Therefore, let AB be the common base of the two parallelograms $ABCD$, $ABEF$, which have the same altitude: then will they be equivalent.

For, in the parallelogram $ABCD$, we have

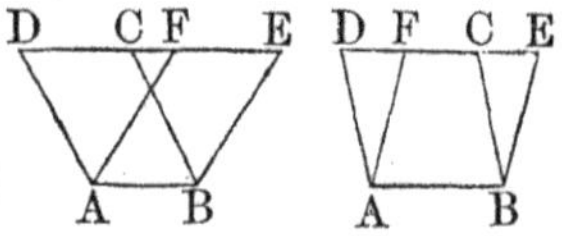

$AB=DC$, and $AD=BC$ (B. I., P. 28);

and in the parallelogram $ABEF$, we have,

$$AB=EF, \text{ and } AF=BE:$$

hence, $$DC=EF \text{ (A. 1).}$$

Now, if from the line DE, we take away DC, there will

remain CE; and if from the same line we take away EF, there will remain DF;

hence, $CE = DF$ (A. 3);

therefore, the triangles ADF and BCE are mutually equilateral, and consequently, equal (B. I., P. 10).

But if from the quadrilateral $ABED$, we take away the triangle ADF, there will remain the parallelogram $ABEF$; and if from the same quadrilateral, we take away the equal triangle BCE, there will remain the parallelogram $ABCD$. Hence, any two parallelograms, which have equal bases and equal altitudes, are equivalent.

Scholium. Since the rectangle and square are parallelograms (B. I., D. 25), it follows that either is equivalent to any parallelogram having an equal base and an equal altitude. And generally, whatever property is proved as belonging to a parallelogram, belongs equally to every variety of parallelogram.

PROPOSITION II. THEOREM.

If a triangle and a parallelogram have equal bases and equal altitudes, the triangle will be equivalent to half the parallelogram.

Place the base of the triangle on that of the parallelogram $ABFD$: then will they have a common base AB.

Now, since the triangle and the parallelogram have equal altitudes, the vertex C, of the triangle, will be in the upper base of the parallelogram, or in that base prolonged (B. I., P. 23). Through A, draw AE parallel to BC, forming the parallelogram $ABCE$.

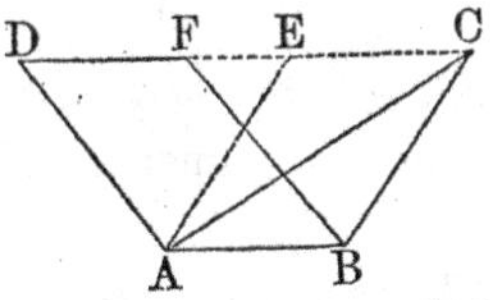

Now, the parallelograms $ABFD$, $ABCE$, are equivalent, having the same base and the same altitude (P. 1). But the triangle ABC is half the parallelogram BE (B. I., P. 28, C. 1): therefore, it is equivalent to half the parallelogram BD (A. 7).

Cor. All triangles which have equal bases and equal altitudes are equivalent, being halves of equivalent parallelograms.

PROPOSITION III. THEOREM.

Two rectangles having equal altitudes are to each other as their bases.

Let *ABCD, AEFD*, be two rectangles having the common altitude *AD*: they are to each other as their bases *AB, AE.*

First. Suppose that the bases are commensurable, and are to each other, for example, as the numbers 7 and 4. If *AB* be divided into 7 equal parts, *AE* will contain 4 of those parts. At each point of division erect a perpendicular to the base; seven partial rectangles will thus be formed, all equal to each other, because they have equal bases and the same altitude (P. 1, S). The rectangle *ABCD* will contain seven partial rectangles, while *AEFD* will contain four: hence, the rectangle

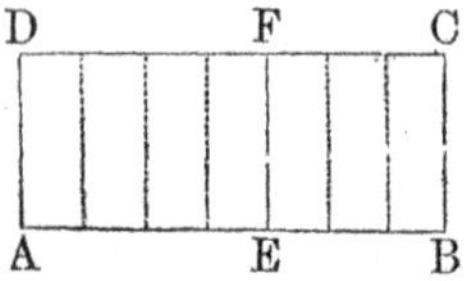

ABCD : *AEFD* :: 7 : 4, or as *AB* : *AE.*

The same reasoning may be applied to any other ratio equally with that of 7 to 4: hence, whatever be the ratio, we have, when its terms are commensurable,

ABCD : *AEFD* :: *AB* : *AE.*

Second. Suppose that the bases *AB, AE*, are incommensurable: we shall still have

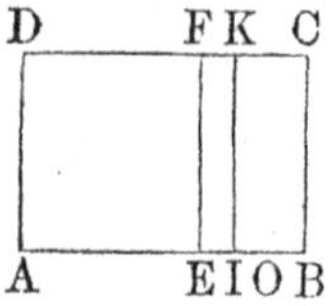

ABCD : *AEFD* :: *AB* : *AE.*

For, if the rectangles are not to each other in the ratio of *AB* to *AE*, they are to each other in a ratio greater or less: that is, the fourth term must be greater or less than *AE.* Suppose it to be greater, and that we have

ABCD : *AEFD* :: *AB* : *AO.*

Suppose *AB* divided into equal parts, each less than *EO.* There will be at least one point *I* of division between *E* and *O*: from this point draw *IK* perpendicular to *AI*, forming the new rectangle AK: then, since the bases AB, AI, are commensurable, we have,

$$ABCD : AIKD :: AB : AI.$$

But by hypothesis we have

$$ABCD : AEFD :: AB : AO.$$

In these two proportions the antecedents are equal; hence, the consequents are proportional (B. II., P. 4), that is,

$$AIKD : AEFD :: AI : AO.$$

But AO is greater than AI; which requires that the rectangle $AEFD$ be greater than $AIKD$: on the contrary, however, it is less (A. 8); hence, the proportion is not true; therefore $ABCD$ cannot be to $AEFD$, as AB is to a line greater than AE.

In the same manner, it may be shown that the fourth term of the proportion cannot be less than AE; therefore, being neither greater nor less, it is equal to AE. Hence, any two rectangles having equal altitudes, are to each other as their bases.

PROPOSITION IV. THEOREM.

Any two rectangles are to each other as the products of their bases and altitudes.

Let $ABCD$, $AEGF$, be two rectangles; then will the rectangle,

$$ABCD : AEGF :: AB \times AD : AE \times AF.$$

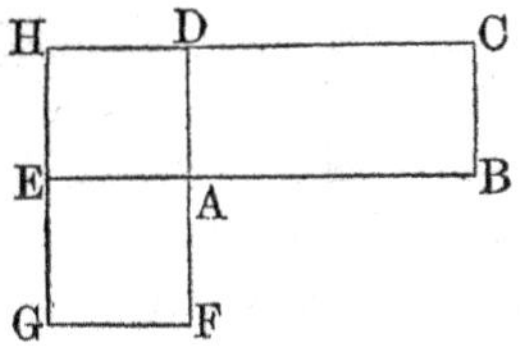

Having placed the two rectangles, so that the angles at A are opposite, produce the sides GE, CD, till they meet in H. Then, the two rectangles $ABCD$, $AEHD$, having the same altitude AD, are to each other as their bases AB, AE: in like manner the two rectangles $AEHD$, $AEGF$, having the same altitude AE, are to each other as their bases AD, AF: thus we have,

$$ABCD : AEHD :: AB : AE,$$

$$AEHD : AEGF :: AD : AF.$$

Multiplying the corresponding terms of these proportions together (B. II., P. 13), and omitting the factor $AEHD$, which is common to both the antecedent and consequent (B. II., P. 7), we have

$$ABCD \; : \; AEGF \; :: \; AB \times AD \; : \; AE \times AF.$$

Scholium 1. If we take a line of a given length, as one inch, one foot, one yard, &c., and regard it as the linear unit of measure, and find how many times this unit is contained in the base of any rectangle, and also, how many times it is contained in the altitude: then, the product of these two ratios may be assumed as the *measure* of the rectangle.

A

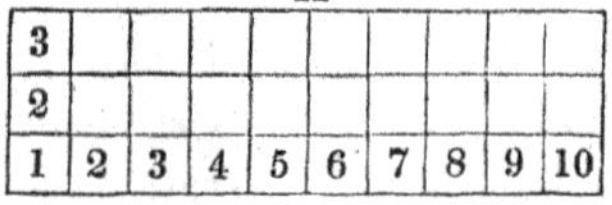

For example, if the base of the rectangle A contains ten units and its altitude three, the rectangle will be represented by the number $10 \times 3 = 30$; a number which is entirely abstract, so long as we regard the numbers 10 and 3 as ratios.

But if we assume the square constructed on the linear unit, as the unit of surface, then, the product will give the number of superficial units in the surface; because, for one unit in height, there are as many superficial units as there are linear units in the base; for two units in height, twice as many; for three units in height, three times as many, &c.

In this case, the measurement which before was merely relative, becomes absolute: the number 30, for example, by which the rectangle was measured, now represents 30 superficial units, or 30 of those equal squares described on the unit of linear measure: this is called the *Area* or *Contents* of the rectangle.

Scholium 2. In geometry, the product of two lines frequently means the same thing as their *rectangle*, and this expression has passed into arithmetic, where it serves to designate the product of two unequal numbers. The term *square* is employed to designate the product of a number multiplied by itself.

The squares of the numbers 1, 2, 3, &c. are 1, 4, 9, &c. So likewise, the geometrical square constructed on a double line is evidently four times as great as the square on a single one; on a triple line it is nine times as great, &c.

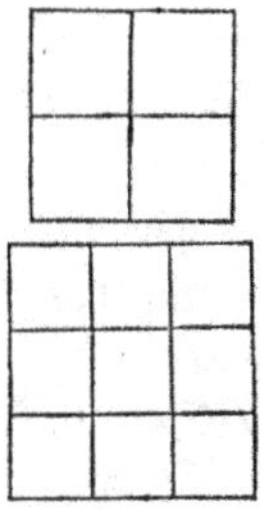

PROPOSITION V. THEOREM.

The area of a parallelogram is equal to the product of its base and altitude.

Let $ABCD$ be any parallelogram, and BE its altitude: then will its area be equal to $AB \times BE$. Draw BE perpendicular to AB, and complete the rectangle $ABEF$.

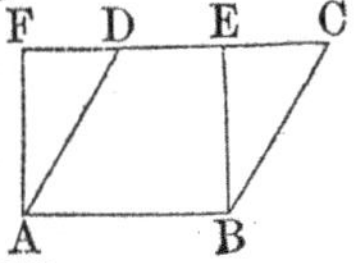

The parallelogram $ABCD$ is equivalent to the rectangle $ABEF$ (P. 1, S.); but this rectangle is measured by $AB \times BE$ (P. 4, S. 1); therefore, $AB \times BE$ is equal to the area of the parallelogram $ABCD$.

Cor. Parallelograms of equal bases are to each other as their altitudes; and parallelograms of equal altitudes are to each other as their bases. For, let C and D denote the altitudes of two parallelograms, and B the base of each:

then, $B \times C : B \times D :: C : D$ (B. II., P. 7).

If A and B are the bases, and C the altitude of each, we shall have,

$$A \times C : B \times C :: A : B:$$

and parallelograms, generally, are to each other as the products of their bases and altitudes.

PROPOSITION VI. THEOREM.

The area of a triangle is equal to half the product of its base and altitude.

Let BAC be a triangle, and AD perpendicular to the base: then will its area be equal to one-half of $BC \times AD$.

For, draw CE parallel to BA, and AE parallel to BC, completing the parallelogram BE. Then, the triangle ABC is half the parallelogram $ABCE$, which has the same base BC, and the same altitude AD (P. 2); but the area of the parallelogram is equal to $BC \times AD$ (P. 5); hence, that of the triangle must be $\frac{1}{2}BC \times AD$, or $BC \times \frac{1}{2}AD$.

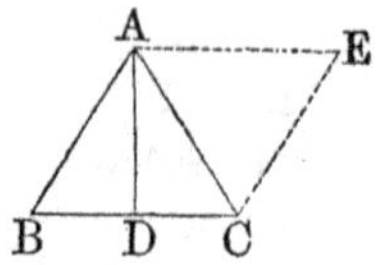

Cor. Two triangles of equal altitudes are to each other as their bases, and two triangles of equal bases are to each other as their altitudes. And triangles generally, are to each other, as the products of their bases and altitudes.

PROPOSITION VII. THEOREM.

The area of a trapezoid is equal to the product of its altitude, by half the sum of its parallel sides.

Let $ABCD$ be a trapezoid, EF its altitude, AB and CD its parallel bases: then will its area be equal to $EF \times \frac{1}{2}(AB+CD)$.

Through I, the middle point of the side BC, draw KL parallel to the opposite side AD; and produce DC till it meets KL.

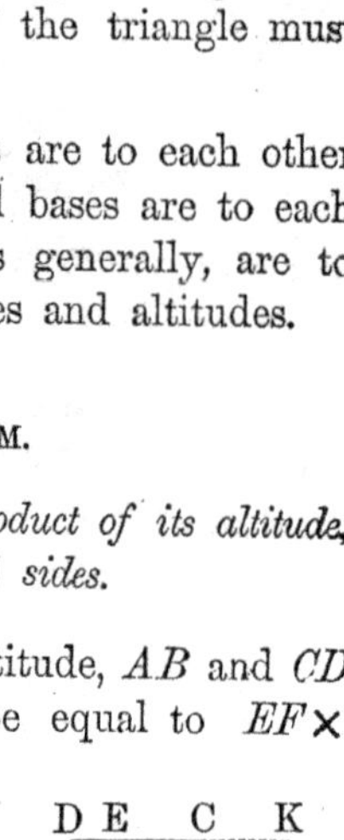

In the triangles IBL, ICK, we have the side $IB=IC$, by construction; the angle $LIB=CIK$ (B. I., P. 4); and since CK and BL are parallel, the angle $IBL=ICK$ (B. I., P. 20, C. 2); hence, the triangles are equal (B. I., P. 6); therefore, the trapezoid $ABCD$ is equivalent to the parallelogram $ALKD$, and consequently, is measured by $EF \times AL$ (P. 5).

But we have $AL=DK$; and since the triangles IBL and KCI are equal, the side $BL=CK$: hence $AB+CD=AL+DK=2AL$; hence, AL is the half sum of the bases AB, CD; hence, the area of the trapezoid $ABCD$, is equal to the altitude EF multiplied by the half sum of the bases AB, CD, a result which is expressed thus:

$$ABCD=EF \times \frac{AB+CD}{2}.$$

Scholium. If through I, the middle point of BC, the line IH be drawn parallel to the base AB, it will bisect AD at H. For, since the figure $ALIH$ is a parallelogram, as also, $HIKD$, their opposite sides are parallel, and we have $AH=IL$, and $DH=IK$; but since the triangles LBI, IKC, are equal, we have $IL=IK$; therefore, $AH=HD$.

But since the line $HI=AL$, it is also equal to $\frac{AB+CD}{2}$; hence, the area of the trapezoid may also be expressed by $EF\times HI$; consequently, *the area of a trapezoid is equal to its altitude multiplied by the line which connects the middle points of its inclined sides.*

PROPOSITION VIII. THEOREM.

The square described on the sum of two lines is equivalent to the sum of the squares described on the lines, together with twice the rectangle contained by the lines.

Let AB, BC, be any two lines, and AC their sum; then

$$\overline{AC}^2 \text{ or } (AB+BC)^2 \Leftrightarrow \overline{AB}^2+\overline{BC}^2+2AB\times BC.$$

On AC describe the square $ACDE$; take $AF=AB$; draw FG parallel to AC, and BH parallel to AE.

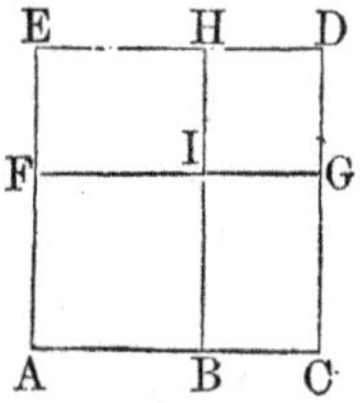

The square $ACDE$ is made up of four parts; the first $ABIF$ is the square described on AB, since we made $AF=AB$: the second $IGDH$ is the square described on IG, or BC; for, since we have $AC=AE$ and $AB=AF$, the difference, $AC-AB$ must be equal to the difference $AE-AF$, which gives $BC=EF$; but IG is equal to BC, and DG to EF, because of the parallels; therefore, $IGDH$ is equal to a square described on BC. Now, if these two squares be taken away from the large square, there will remain the two rectangles $BCGI$, $FIHE$, each of which is measured by $AB\times BC$: hence, the square on the sum of two lines is equivalent to the sum of the squares on the lines, together with twice the rectangle contained by the lines.

Cor. If the line AC were divided into two equal parts, the two rectangles FH, BG, would become squares, and the square described on the whole line would be equivalent to four times the square described on half the line.

Scholium. This property is the same as the property demonstrated in algebra, in obtaining the square of a binomial; which is expressed thus:

$$(a+b)^2=a^2+2ab+b^2.$$

PROPOSITION IX. THEOREM.

The square described on the difference of two lines, is equivalent to the sum of the squares described on the lines, diminished by twice the rectangle contained by the lines.

Let AB, BC, be two lines, and AC their difference; then, $\overline{AC}^2$, or $(AB-BC)^2 \Leftrightarrow \overline{AB}^2+\overline{BC}^2-2AB\times BC$.

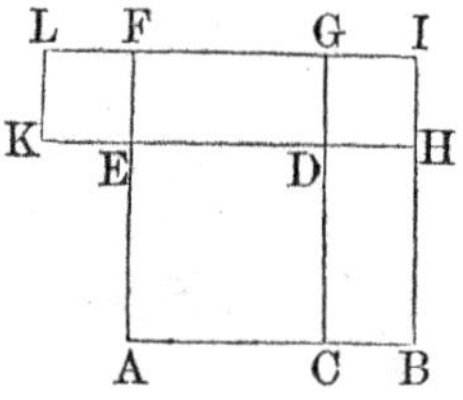

On AB describe the square $ABIF$; take $AE=AC$; through C draw CG parallel to BI, and through E draw EH parallel to AB, and prolong it to K, making $EK=CB$, and then complete the square $KEFL$.

Since $KD=AB$, and $BC=KL$, the two rectangles CI, KG, are each measured by $AB\times BC$: the whole figure $ABILKEA$, is equivalent to $\overline{AB}^2+\overline{BC}^2$; take from each the two rectangles CI, KG, and there will remain the square $ACDE$, equivalent to $\overline{AB}^2+\overline{BC}^2$ diminished by twice the rectangle of $AB\times BC$.

Scholium. This property is expressed by the algebraical formula,

$$(a-b)^2=a^2-2ab+b^2.$$

PROPOSITION X. THEOREM.

The rectangle contained by the sum and the difference of two lines, is equivalent to the difference of their squares.

Let AB, BC, be two lines; then

$$(AB+BC)\times(AB-BC) \simeq \overline{AB}^2-\overline{BC}^2.$$

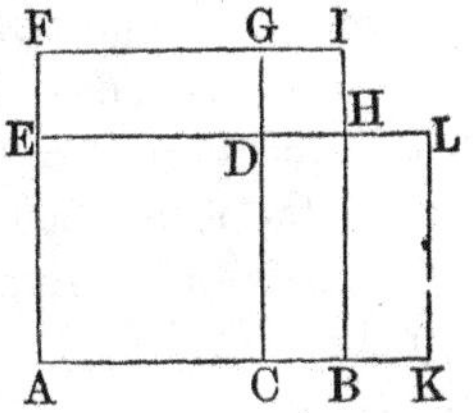

Upon AB and AC, describe the squares $ABIF$, $ACDE$; prolong AB till BK is equal to BC; and complete the rectangle $AKLE$, and prolong CD to G.

The base AK of the rectangle AL is the sum of the two lines AB BC; and its altitude AE is their difference; therefore, the rectangle $AKLE$ is equivalent to

$$(AB+BC)\times(AB-BC).$$

Again, $DHIG$ is equal to a square described on CB; and since BH is equal to ED, and BK to EF, the rectangle BL is equal to the rectangle EG: hence, the rectangle $AKLE$ is equivalent to $ABHE$ plus $EDGF$, which is precisely the difference between the two squares AI and DI described on the lines AB, CB: hence, we have (A. 1.),

$$(AB+BC)\times(AB-BC) \simeq \overline{AB}^2-\overline{BC}^2.$$

Scholium. This property is expressed by the algebraical formula,

$$(a+b)\times(a-b)=a^2-b^2.$$

PROPOSITION XI. THEOREM.

The square described on the hypothenuse of a right-angled triangle is equivalent to the sum of the squares described on the other two sides.

Let BCA be a right-angled triangle, right-angled at A: then will the square described on the hypothenuse BC be equivalent to the sum of the squares described on the other two sides, BA, AC.

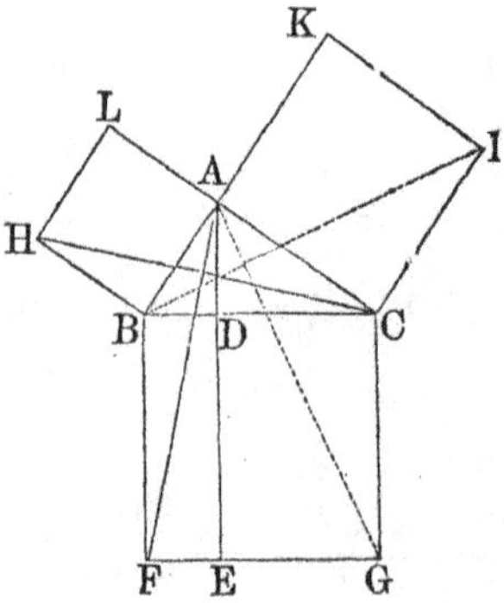

Having described a square on each of the three sides, let fall from A, on the hypothenuse, the perpendicular AD, and prolong it to E; and draw the diagonals AF, CH.

The angle ABF is made up of the angle ABC, together with the right angle CBF; the angle CBH is made up of the same angle ABC, together with the right-angle ABH; hence, the angle ABF is equal to HBC (A. 2). But we have $AB=BH$, being sides of the same square; and $BF=BC$, for the same reason: therefore, the triangles ABF, HBC, have two sides and the included angle equal, each to each; therefore, they are themselves equal (B. I., P. 5).

But the triangle ABF is equivalent to half the rectangle BE, because they have the same base BF, and the same altitude BD (P. 2). The triangle HBC, in like manner is equivalent to half the square AH: for, the angles BAC, BAL, being both right angles, AC and AL form one and the same straight line parallel to HB (B. I., P. 3); hence, the triangle and square have equal altitudes (B. I., P. 23); they also have the common base BH; consequently, the triangle is half the square (P. 2).

The triangle ABF has already been proved equal to the triangle HBC; hence, the rectangle $BDEF$, which is double the triangle ABF, must be equivalent to the square AH, which is double the equal triangle HBC. In the same manner it may be proved, that the rectangle $EGCD$ is equivalent to the square AI. But the two rectangles $FEDB$, $EGCD$, taken together, make up the square $FGCB$: therefore, the square $FGCB$, described on the hypothenuse, is equivalent to the sum of the squares $BALH$, $CIKA$, described on the two other sides; that is,

$$\overline{BC}^2 \simeq \overline{AB}^2 + \overline{AC}^2.$$

Cor. 1. Hence, the square of one of the sides of a right

angled triangle is equivalent to the square of the hypothenuse diminished by the square of the other side; thus,

$$\overline{AB}^2 \simeq \overline{BC}^2 - \overline{AC}^2.$$

Cor. 2. If from the vertex of the right angle, a perpendicular be let fall on the hypothenuse, the parts of the hypothenuse are called *segments:* we shall then have,

The square of the hypothenuse is to the square of either side about the right angle, as the hypothenuse to the segment adjacent to that side.

For, by reason of the common altitude BF, the square BG is to the rectangle BE, as BC to BD (P. 3): but the square BL is equivalent to the rectangle BE: hence

$$\overline{BC}^2 : \overline{BA}^2 :: BC : BD.$$

We may show, in like manner, that

$$\overline{BC}^2 : \overline{AC}^2 :: BC : DC.$$

Cor. 3. *The squares of the two sides containing the right angle, are to each other as the adjacent segments of the hypothenuse.*

For, the rectangles $BDEF$, $DCGE$, having the same altitude, are to each other as their bases BD, CD (P 3). But these rectangles are equivalent to the squares AH, AI: therefore, we have

$$\overline{AB}^2 : \overline{AC}^2 :: BD : DC.$$

Cor. 4. *The square described on the diagonal of a given square is equivalent to double the given square.*

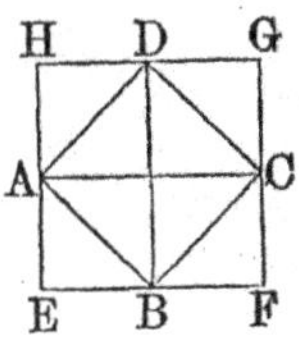

Let $ABCD$ be a square described on AB, and $EFGH$ a square described on the diagonal AC. The triangle ABC being right-angled and isosceles, we shall have

$$\overline{AC}^2 \simeq \overline{AB}^2 + \overline{BC}^2 \simeq 2\overline{AB}^2.$$

Hence, *the square on the diagonal is equivalent to double the square on the side.*

Cor. 5. By the last corollary, we have

$$\overline{AC}^2 : \overline{AB}^2 :: 2 : 1;$$

hence, by extracting the square root (B. II., P. 12, C.),

$$AC : AB \quad \sqrt{2} : 1:$$

that is, *the diagonal of a square is to the side as the square root of two to one:* consequently, *the diagonal and side of a square are incommensurable.*

PROPOSITION XII. THEOREM.

In any triangle, the square of a side opposite an acute angle is equivalent to the sum of the squares of the base and the other side, diminished by twice the rectangle contained by the base and the distance from the vertex of the acute angle to the foot of the perpendicular let fall from the vertex of the opposite angle on the base, or on the base produced.

Let ABC be a triangle, C one of the acute angles, and AD perpendicular to the base BC; then will

$$\overline{AB}^2 \approx \overline{BC}^2 + \overline{AC}^2 - 2BC \times CD.$$

First. When the perpendicular falls within the triangle ABC, we have $BD = BC - CD$, and consequently,

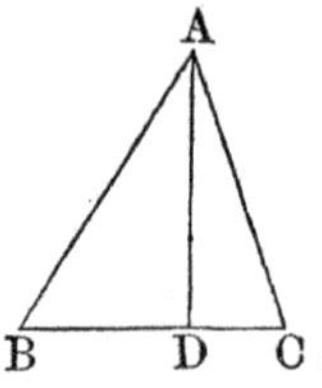

$$\overline{BD}^2 \approx \overline{BC}^2 + \overline{CD}^2 - 2BC \times CD \text{ (P. 9).}$$

Adding $\overline{AD}^2$ to each, and observing that the right-angled triangles ABD, ADC,

give $\overline{AD}^2 + \overline{BD}^2 \approx \overline{AB}^2$, and $\overline{AD}^2 + \overline{CD}^2 \approx \overline{AC}^2$,

we have $\overline{AB}^2 \approx \overline{BC}^2 + \overline{AC}^2 - 2BC \times CD.$

Secondly. When the perpendicular AD falls without the triangle ABC, we have $BD = CD - BC$; and consequently,

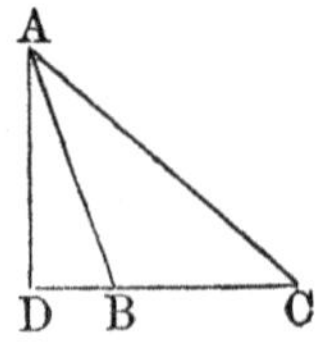

$$\overline{BD}^2 \approx \overline{CD}^2 + \overline{BC}^2 - 2CD \times BC \text{ (P. 9).}$$

Adding $\overline{AD}^2$ to both, we find, as before,

$$\overline{AB}^2 \approx \overline{BC}^2 + \overline{AC}^2 - 2BC \times CD.$$

PROPOSITION XIII. THEOREM.

In any obtuse-angled triangle, the square of the side opposite the obtuse angle is equivalent to the sum of the squares of the base and the other side, augmented by twice the rectangle contained by the base and the distance from the vertex of the obtuse angle to the foot of the perpendicular let fall from the vertex of the opposite angle on the base produced.

Let ACB be a triangle, C the obtuse angle, and AD perpendicular to BC produced; then

$$\overline{AB}^2 \simeq \overline{AC}^2 + \overline{BC}^2 + 2BC \times CD.$$

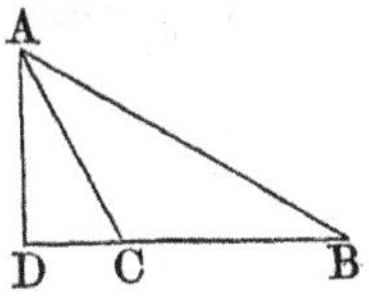

For, we have, $BD = BC + CD$;
consequently (P. 8),

$$\overline{BD}^2 \simeq \overline{BC}^2 + \overline{CD}^2 + 2BC \times CD.$$

Adding $\overline{AD}^2$ to both members, and reducing as in the last theorem, and we have

$$\overline{AB}^2 \simeq \overline{BC}^2 + \overline{AC}^2 + 2BC \times CD.$$

Scholium. The right-angled triangle is the only one in which the sum of the squares described on two sides is equivalent to the square described on the third; for, if the angle contained by the two sides is acute, the sum of their squares is greater than the square of the opposite side; if obtuse, it is less.

PROPOSITION XIV. THEOREM.

In any triangle, the sum of the squares described on two sides is equivalent to twice the square of half the third side, plus twice the square of the line drawn from the middle point of that side to the vertex of the opposite angle.

Let ABC be any triangle, and AE a line drawn to the middle of the base BC; then

$$\overline{AB}^2 + \overline{AC}^2 \simeq 2\overline{BE}^2 + 2\overline{AE}^2.$$

For, on BC, let fall the perpendicular AD. Then,

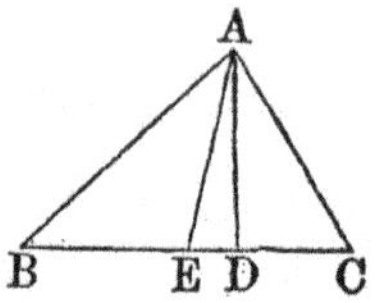

$\overline{AC}^2 \Leftrightarrow \overline{AE}^2+\overline{EC}^2-2EC\times ED$. (P. 12).

And,

$\overline{AB}^2 \Leftrightarrow \overline{AE}^2+\overline{EB}^2+2EB\times ED$ (P. 13).

Hence, by adding and observing that EB and EC are equal, we have

$$\overline{AB}^2+\overline{AC}^2 \Leftrightarrow 2\overline{EB}^2+2\overline{AE}^2.$$

Cor. 1. *In any quadrilateral, the sum of the squares of the four sides is equivalent to the sum of the squares of the two diagonals, plus four times the square of the line joining the middle points of the diagonals.*

Let $ABCD$ be a quadrilateral, AC, BD, the diagonals, and EF a line joining their middle points E and F.

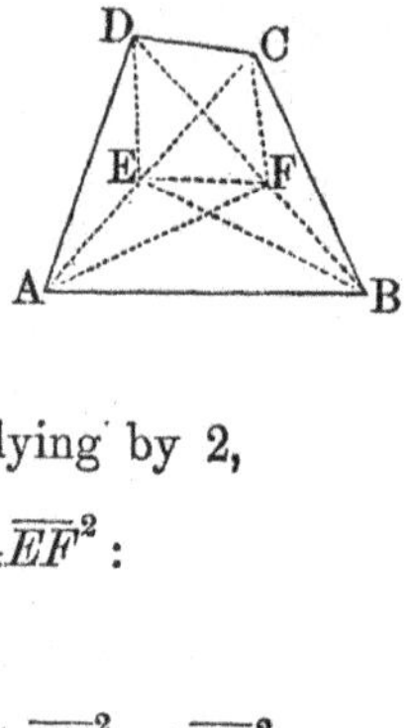

From the theorem, we have

$$\overline{CD}^2+\overline{CB}^2 \Leftrightarrow 2\overline{BF}^2+2\overline{CF}^2,$$

$$\overline{AD}^2+\overline{AB}^2 \Leftrightarrow 2\overline{BF}^2+2\overline{AF}^2:$$

and from the same theorem, by multiplying by 2,

$$2\overline{CF}^2+2\overline{AF}^2 \Leftrightarrow 4\overline{AE}^2+4\overline{EF}^2:$$

hence, by addition,

$$\overline{CD}^2+\overline{CB}^2+\overline{AD}^2+\overline{AB}^2 \Leftrightarrow 4\overline{BF}^2+4\overline{AE}^2+4\overline{EF}^2:$$

whence (P. 8, C.),

$$\overline{CD}^2+\overline{CB}^2+\overline{AD}^2+\overline{AB}^2 \Leftrightarrow \overline{BD}^2+\overline{AC}^2+4\,\overline{EF}^2.$$

Cor. 2. In the case of the parallelogram the points E and F will coincide, and the sum of the squares described on the sides will be equivalent to the sum of the squares described on the diagonals.

PROPOSITION XV. THEOREM.

If, in any triangle, a line be drawn parallel to the base, it will divide the two other sides proportionally.

Let ABC be a triangle, and DE a straight line drawn parallel to the base BC; then

$$AD : DB :: AE : EC.$$

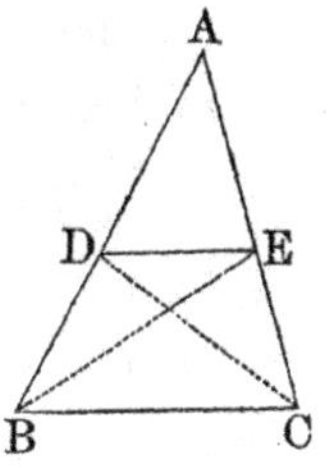

Draw the lines BE and CD. Then, the triangles ADE, BDE, having a common vertex, E, have the same altitude, and are to each other as their bases (P. 6, C.); hence we have

$$ADE : BDE :: AD : DB.$$

The triangles ADE, DEC, with a common vertex D, also have the same altitude, and are to each other as their bases; hence,

$$ADE : DEC :: AE : EC.$$

But the triangles BDE, DEC, are equivalent, having the same base DE, and their vertices B and C in a line parallel to the base: and therefore, we have (B. II., P. 4, C.)

$$AD : DB :: AE : EC.$$

Cor. 1. Hence, by composition, we have (B. II., P. 6),

$AD+DB : AD :: AE+EC : AE$, or $AB : AD :: AC : AE$;

and also, $AB : BD :: AC : CE$.

Cor. 2. If any number of parallels AC, EF, GH, BD, be drawn between two straight lines AB, CD, those straight lines will be cut proportionally, and we shall have

$$AE : CF :: EG : FH : GB : HD.$$

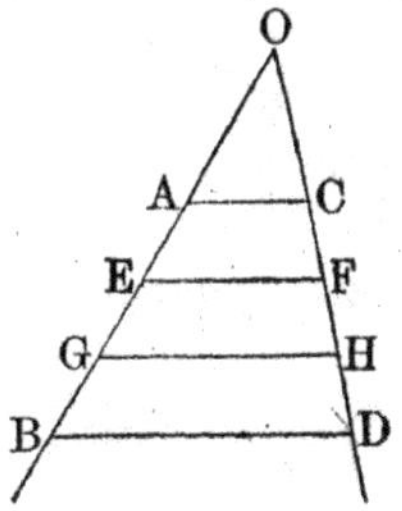

For, let O be the point where AB and CD meet. In the triangle OEF, the line AC being drawn parallel to the base EF, we shall have

$$OE : AE :: OF : CF.$$

In the triangle OGH, we shall likewise have

$$OE : EG :: OF : FH.$$

And, by reason of the common antecedents OE, OF (B. II., P. 4), we have

$$AE : CF :: EG : FH.$$

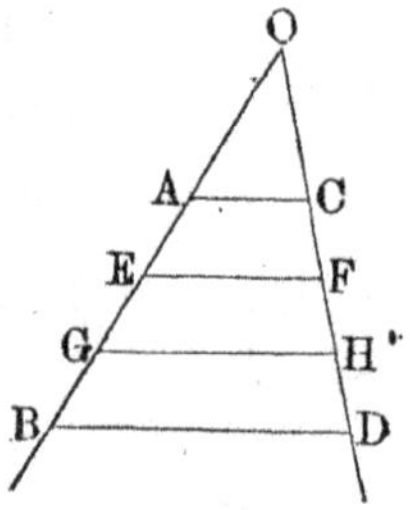

It may be proved in the same manner, that

$$EG : FH :: GB : HD,$$

and so on; hence, the lines AB, CD, are cut proportionally by the parallels AC, EF, GH, &c.

PROPOSITION XVI. THEOREM.

If two sides of a triangle are cut proportionally by a straight line, this straight line will be parallel to the third side.

In the triangle BAC, let the line DE be drawn, cutting the sides BA and CA proportionally in the points D and E; that is, so that

$$BD : DA :: CE : EA :$$

then will DE be parallel to BC.

Having drawn the lines BE and DC, we have (P. 6, C.),

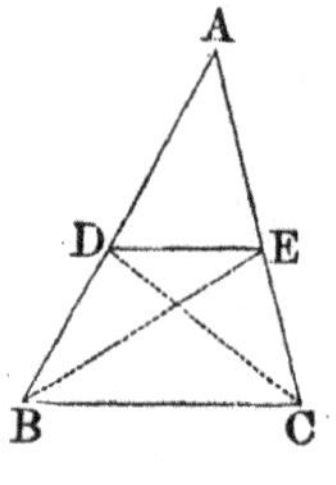

$$BDE : DAE :: BD : DA,$$
$$DEC : DAE :: CE : EA :$$

but, by hypothesis,

$$BD : DA :: CE : EA :$$

hence (B. II., P. 4, C.),

$$BDE : DAE :: DEC : DAE,$$

and since BDE and DEC have the same ratio to DEA, they have the same area, and hence are equivalent (D. 4). They also have a common base DE; hence, they have the same altitude (P. 6, C.); and consequently, their vertices B and C lie in a parallel to the base DE (B. I., P. 23): hence DE is parallel to BC.

PROPOSITION XVII. THEOREM.

The line which bisects the vertical angle of a triangle, divides the base into two segments, which are proportional to the adjacent sides.

In the triangle ACB, let AD be drawn, bisecting the angle CAB; then

$$BD : CD :: AB : AC.$$

Through the point C draw CE parallel to AD, and prolong it till it meets BA produced in E.

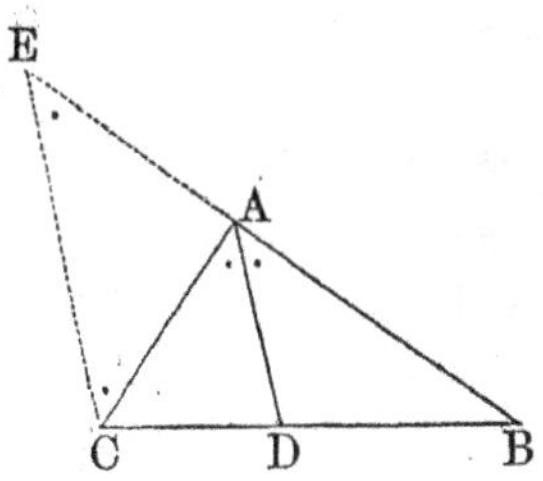

In the triangle BCE, the line AD is parallel to the base CE; hence, we have the proportion (P. 15),

$$BD : DC :: BA : AE.$$

But the triangle ACE is isosceles: for, since AD, CE, are parallel, we have the angle $ACE=DAC$, and the angle $AEC=BAD$ (B. I., P. 20, C. 2, 3); but, by hypothesis, $DAC=DAB$; hence, the angle $ACE=AEC$, and consequently, $AE=AC$ (B. I., P. 12). In place of AE in the above proportion, substitute AC, and we shall have,

$$BD : DC :: AB : AC.$$

Cor. If the line AD bisects the exterior angle CAE of the triangle BAC, we shall have,

$$BD : CD : AB : AC.$$

For, through C draw CF parallel to AD.

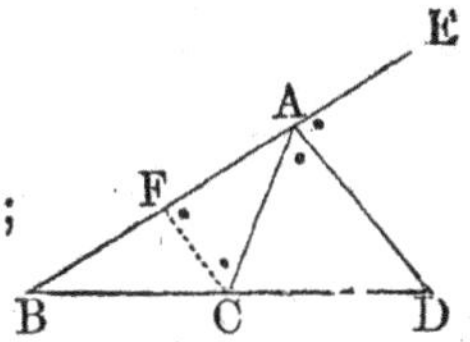

Then, the angle $CAD=ACF$, and, the angle $EAD=AFC$; hence, (A. 1), the angle $ACF=AFC$; consequently, AF is equal to AC.

But, since FC is parallel to the base AD,

$$BD : DC : AB : AF;$$

hence, $$BD : DC : AB : AC.$$

PROPOSITION XVIII. THEOREM.

Equiangular triangles have their homologous sides proportional, and are similar.

Let BCA and CED be two equiangular triangles, having the angle $BAC=CDE$, $ABC=DCE$, and $ACB=DEC$; then, the homologous sides will be proportional, viz.:

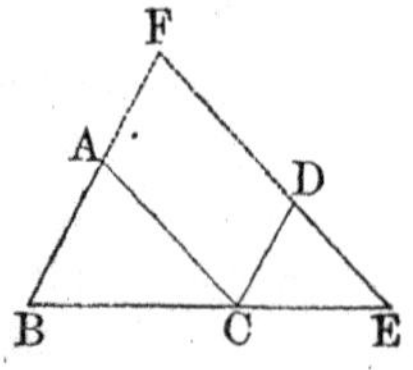

$$BC : CE :: BA : CD :: AC : DE.$$

Place the homologous sides BC, CE in the same straight line; and prolong the sides BA, ED, till they meet in F.

Since BCE is a straight line, and the angle BCA equal to CED, it follows that AC is parallel to DE (B. I., P. 19, C. 2). In like manner, since the angle ABC is equal to DCE, the line AB is parallel to DC. Hence, the figure $ACDF$ is a parallelogram, and has its opposite sides equal (B. I., P. 28).

In the triangle BEF, the line AC is parallel to the base FE; hence, we have (P. 15,)

$$BC : CE :: BA : AF;$$

or putting CD in the place of its equal AF,

$$BC : CE :: BA : CD.$$

In the same triangle BEF, CD is parallel to BF; and hence,

$$BC : CE :: FD : DE;$$

or putting AC in the place of its equal FD,

$$BC : CE :: AC : DE.$$

And finally, since both these proportions have an antecedent and consequent common, we have (B. II., P. 4, C.),

$$BA : CD :: AC : DE.$$

Thus, the equiangular triangles CAB, CED, have their homologous sides proportional. But two figures are similar when they have their angles equal, each to each, and their homologous sides proportional (D. 1, 2); consequently, the two equiangular triangles BAC, CED, are similar figures.

Cor. Two triangles which have two angles of the one equal to two angles of the other, each to each, are similar; for, the third angles are then equal, and the two triangles are equiangular (B. I., P. 25, C. 2).

Scholium. Observe, that in similar triangles, the homologous sides in each are opposite to the equal angles; thus, the angle BCA being equal to CED, the side AB is homologous to DC; in like manner AC and DE are homologous, because opposite to the equal angles ABC, DCE.

PROPOSITION XIX. THEOREM.

Conversely: Triangles which have their homologous sides proportional, are mutually equiangular and similar.

If, in the two triangles BAC, EDF, we have,

$$BC : EF :: BA : ED :: AC : DF;$$

then will the triangles BAC, EDF, have their angles equal each to each, namely,

$$A=D, \ B=E, \ C=F.$$

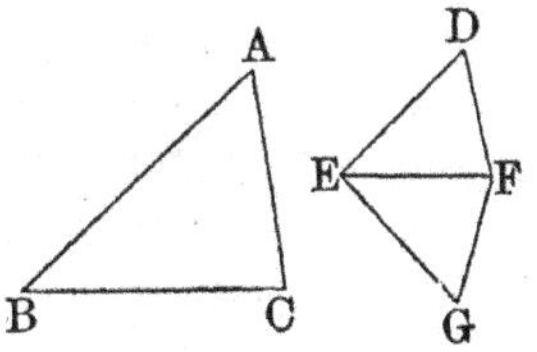

At the point E, make the angle $FEG=B$, and at F, the angle $EFG=C$; the third angle G will then be equal to the third angle A (B. I., P. 25, C. 2). Therefore, by the last theorem, we shall have

$$BC : EF :: AB : EG:$$

but, by hypothesis, we have

$$BC : EF :: AB : DE;$$

hence, $EG=DE$. By the same theorem, we shall also have

$$BC : EF :: AC : FG;$$

and by hypothesis, we have

$$BC : EF :: AC : DF;$$

hence, $FG=DF$. Hence, the triangles EGF, FED, having

their three sides equal, each to each, are themselves equal (B. I., P. 10). But, by construction, the triangles *EGF* and *ABC* are equiangular: hence, *DEF* and *ABC* are also equiangular and similar (A. 1).

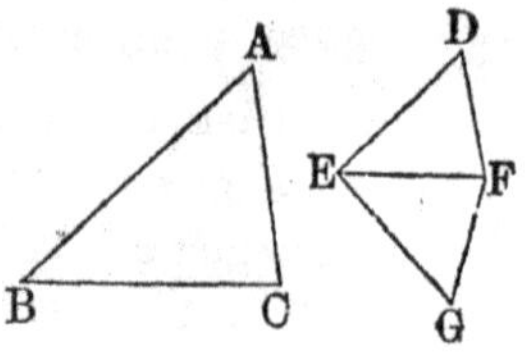

Scholium 1. By the last two propositions, it appears that triangles which are equiangular are similar: and conversely: if triangles have their sides proportional, they are equiangular, and consequently, similar.

The case is different with regard to figures of more than three sides: even in quadrilaterals, the proportion between the sides may be altered without changing the angles, or the angles may be changed without altering the proportion between the sides. Thus, in quadrilaterals, equality between the corresponding angles does not insure proportionality among the sides: and conversely: proportionality among the sides does not insure equality among the corresponding angles. It is evident, for example, that if in the quadrilateral *ABCD*, we draw *EF* parallel to *BC*, the angles of the quadrilateral *AEFD*, are made equal to those of *ABCD*; though the proportion between their sides is different; and in like manner, without changing the four sides *AB*, *BC*, *CD*, *AD*, we can change the angles by making the point *B* approach to *D*, or recede from it

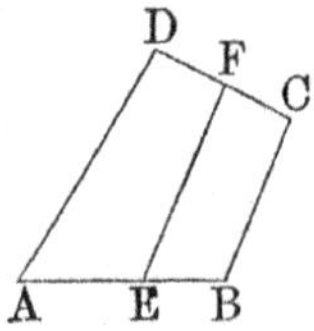

Scholium 2. The two preceding propositions, are in strictness but one, and these, together with that relating to the square of the hypothenuse, are the most important and fertile in results of any in geometry. They are almost sufficient of themselves for every application to subsequent reasoning, and for solving every problem. The reason is, that all figures may be divided into triangles, and any triangle into two right-angled triangles. Thus, the properties of triangles include, by implication, those of all figures

PROPOSITION XX. THEOREM.

Two triangles, which have an angle of the one equal to an angle of the other, and the sides containing those angles proportional, are similar.

Let ABC, DEF, be two triangles, having the angle A equal to D; then, if

$$AB : DE :: AC : DF,$$

the two triangles will be similar.

Make $AG=DE$, and draw GH parallel to BC. The angle AGH will be equal to the angle ABC (B. I., P. 20, C. 3); and the triangles AGH, ABC, will be equiangular: hence, we shall have,

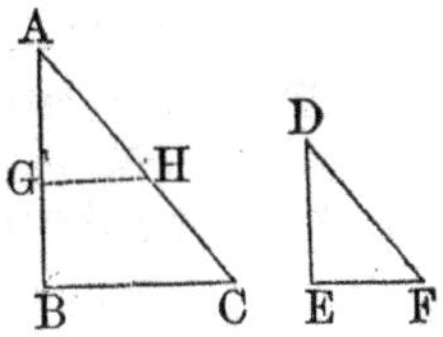

$$AB : AG : AC : AH.$$

But, by hypothesis, we have,

$$AB : DE :: AC : DF;$$

and by construction, $AG=DE$: hence $AH=DF$. Therefore, the two triangles AGH, DEF, have two sides and the included angle of the one equal to two sides and the included angle of the other: hence, they are equal (B. I., P. 5); but the triangle AGH is similar to ABC: therefore, DEF is also similar to ABC.

PROPOSITION XXI. THEOREM.

Two triangles, which have their sides, two and two, either parallel or perpendicular to each other, are similar.

Let BAC, EDF, be two triangles, having their sides respectively parallel to each other; then will they be similar.

First. If the side BA is parallel to ED, and BC to EF, the angle ABC is equal to DEF (B. I., P. 24): if CA is parallel to FD, the angle BCA is equal to EFD, and also, BAC to EDF; hence, the triangles CBA, FED, are equiangular; consequently they are similar (P. 18).

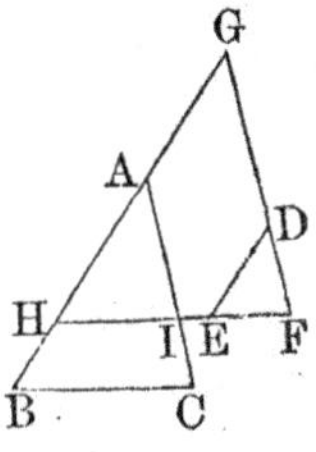

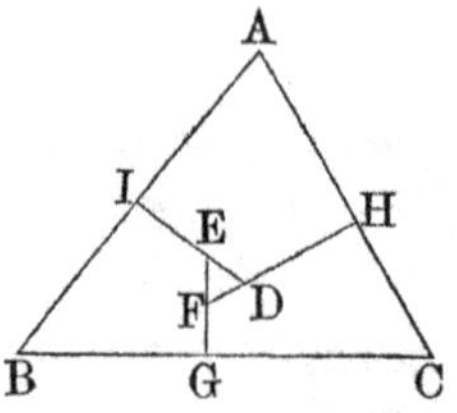

Secondly. If the side *DE* is perpendicular to *BA*, and the side *FD* to *CA*, the two angles *I* and *H* of the quadrilateral *DHAI* are right angles; and since all the four angles are together equal to four right angles (B. I., P. 26, C. 1), the remaining two *IAH*, *IDH*, are together equal to two right angles. But the sum of the angles *EDF*, *IDH*, is also equal to two right angles (B. I., P. 1): hence, the angle *EDF* is equal to *IAH*, or *BAC* (A. 3). In like manner, if the third side *EF* is perpendicular to the third side *BC*, it may be shown that the angle *DFE* is equal to *C*, and *DEF* to *B*: hence, the triangles *ABC*, *DEF*, which have the sides of the one perpendicular to the corresponding sides of the other, are equiangular and similar (P. 18).

Scholium. In the case of the sides being parallel, the homologous sides are the parallel ones: in the case of their being perpendicular, the homologous sides are the perpendicular ones. Thus, in the latter case, *DE* is homologous with *BA*, *DF* with *AC*, and *EF* with *BC*.

The case of the perpendicular sides may present a relative position of the two triangles different from that exhibited in the diagram. But we can always conceive a triangle *FED* to be constructed within the triangle *ABC*, and such that its sides shall be parallel to those of the triangle compared with *BAC*; and then the demonstration given in the text will apply.

PROPOSITION XXII. THEOREM.

In any triangle, if a line be drawn parallel to the base, all lines drawn from the vertex will divide the base and the parallel into proportional parts.

Let *BAC* be a triangle, *DE* parallel to the base *BC*, and the other lines drawn as in the figure; then

$$DI : BF :: IK : FG :: KL : GH.$$

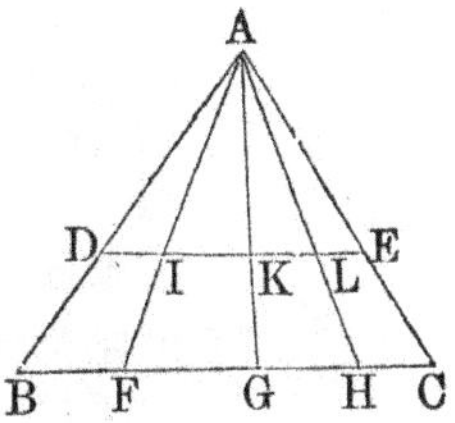

For, since DI is parallel to BF, the triangles IDA and FBA are equiangular; and we have

$$DI : BF :: AI : AF;$$

and, since IK is parallel to FG, we have, in like manner,

$$AI : AF :: IK : FG;$$

hence (B. II., P. 4, C.), $DI : BF :: IK : FG$.

In the same manner, we may prove that

$$IK : FG :: KL : GH;$$

and so with the other segments: hence, the line DE is divided at the points I, K, L, in the same proportion, as the base BC is divided, at the points F, G, H.

Cor. Therefore, if BC were divided into equal parts at the points F, G, H, the parallel DE would be divided also into equal parts at the points I, K, L.

PROPOSITION XXIII. THEOREM.

In a right-angled triangle, if a perpendicular is drawn from the vertex of the right angle to the hypothenuse.

1st. *The triangles on each side of the perpendicular are similar to the given triangle, and to each other:*

2d. *Either side about the right angle is a mean proportional between the hypothenuse and the adjacent segment:*

3d. *The perpendicular is a mean proportional between the segments of the hypothenuse.*

Let BAC be a right-angled triangle, and AD perpendicular to the hypothenuse BC.

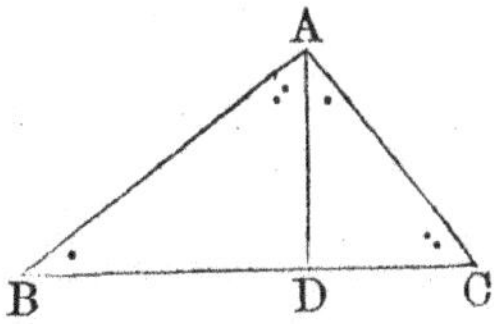

First. The triangles BAD and BAC have the common angle B, the right angle $BDA = BAC$, and therefore, the third angle BAD of the one, equal to the third angle C, of the other (B. I., P. 25, C. 2): hence, these two triangles are similar (P. 18). In the same manner it may be shown that the triangles DAC and BAC are similar; hence, the three triangles are all equiangular and similar.

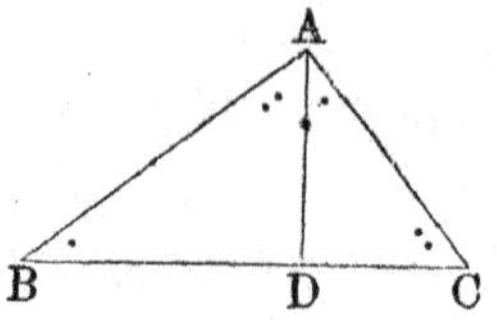

Secondly. The triangles BAD, BAC, being similar, their homologous sides are proportional. But BD in the small triangle, and BA in the large one, are homologous sides, because they lie opposite the equal angles BAD, BCA (P. 18, S.); the hypothenuse BA of the small triangle is homologous with the hypothenuse BC of the large triangle: hence, the proportion,

$$BD : BA :: BA : BC.$$

By the same reasoning we have

$$DC : AC :: AC : BC;$$

hence, each of the sides AB, AC, is a mean proportional between the hypothenuse and the adjacent segment.

Thirdly. Since the triangles DBA, DAC, are similar, we have, by comparing their homologous sides,

$$BD : AD :: AD : DC;$$

hence, the perpendicular AD is a mean proportional between the segments BD, DC, of the hypothenuse.

Scholium. Since $BD : AB :: AB : BC$,

we have (B. II., P. 1, C.), $\overline{AB}^2 \simeq BD \times BC.$

For a like reason, $\overline{AC}^2 \simeq DC \times BC;$

therefore, $\overline{AB}^2 + \overline{AC}^2 \simeq BD \times BC + DC \times BC \simeq (BD + DC) \times$

$$BC \simeq BC \times BC \simeq \overline{BC}^2;$$

that is, *the square described on the hypothenuse BC is equivalent to the sum of the squares described on the two sides BA, AC.* Thus, we again arrive at this property of the right-angled triangle, and by a path very different from that which formerly conducted us to it: and thus it appears that, strictly speaking, this property is a consequence of the more general property, that the sides of equiangular triangles are proportional. Thus, the fundamental propositions of geometry are reduced, as it were, to this single one, that *equiangular triangles have their homologous sides proportional.*

It happens frequently, as in this instance, that by deducing consequences from one or more propositions, we are led back to some proposition already proved. In fact, the chief characteristic of geometrical theorems, and one indubitable proof of their certainty is, that, however we combine them together, provided that our reasoning be correct, the results we obtain always agree with each other. The case would be different, if any proposition were false or only approximately true: it would frequently happen that on combining the propositions together, the error would increase and become perceptible. Examples in which the conclusions do not agree with each other, are to be seen in all the demonstrations, in which the *reductio ad absurdum* is employed. In such demonstrations, if the hypothesis is untrue, a train of accurate reasoning leads to a manifest absurdity: that is, to a conclusion in contradiction to a principle previously established: and from this we conclude that the hypothesis is false.

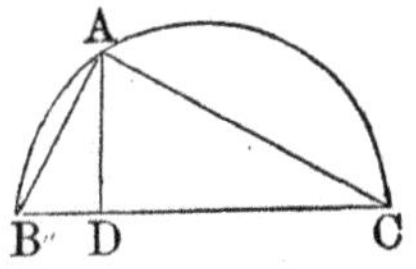

Cor. If from the point A, in the circumference of a circle, two chords BA, AC, be drawn to the extremities of a diameter BC, the triangle BAC will be right-angled at A (B. III., P. 18, C. 2); hence, first, *the perpendicular AD is a mean proportional between the two segments BD, DC, of the diameter*, hence,

$$\overline{AD}^2 \approx BD \times DC.$$

Furthermore, by the proposition, *the chord BA is a mean proportional between the diameter BC, and the adjacent segment BD*, that is,

$$\overline{BA}^2 \approx BC \times BD, \text{ and } \overline{AC}^2 \approx BC \times CD.$$

PROPOSITION XXIV. THEOREM.

Two triangles having an angle in each equal, are to each other as the rectangles of the including sides.

Let ABC, ADE, be two triangles having the equal angles A, placed, the one on the other; then the triangle

$$ABC : ADE :: AB \times AC : AD \times AE.$$

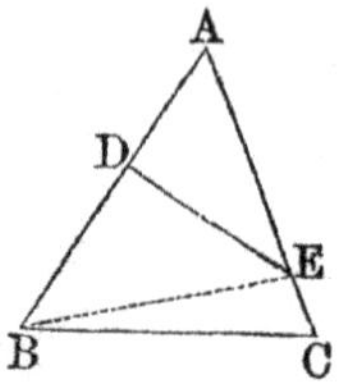

Draw BE. Then, the triangles ABE, ADE, having the common vertex E, and their bases in the same straight line, are to each other as their bases, (P. 6, C.) that is

$$BAE : DAE :: BA : DA.$$

In like manner, since B is a common vertex, the triangle

$$BAC : BAE :: AC : AE.$$

Multiply together the corresponding terms of these proportions, omitting the common factor BAE; and we have (B. II., P. 13),

$$BAC : DAE : BA \times AC : AD \times AE.$$

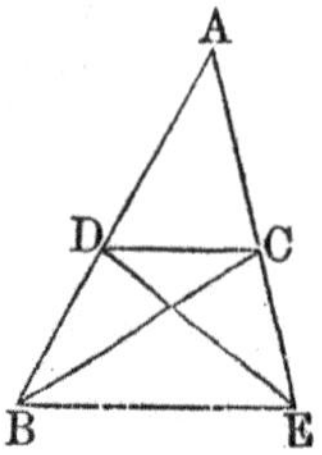

Cor. If the two triangles are equivalent, we have,

$$BA \times AC = DA \times AE:$$

hence (B. II., P. 2),

$$BA : DA : AE : AC:$$

consequently, DC and BE are parallel (P. 16).

PROPOSITION XXV. THEOREM.

Similar triangles are to each other as the squares described on their homologous sides.

Let ABC, DEF, be two similar triangles, having the angle A equal to D, and the angle $B=E$: then will the triangle BAC be to the triangle EDF, as a square described on any side of BAC to a square described on the homologous side of EDF.

First, by reason of the equal angles A and D, we have (P. 24),

$$BAC : DEF :: BA \times AC : DE \times DF.$$

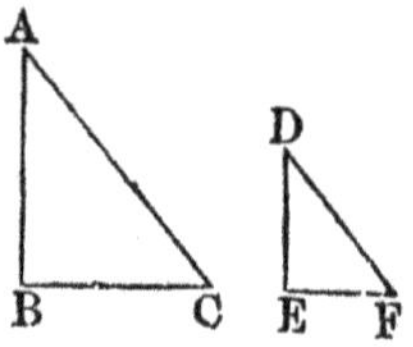

Also, because the triangles are similar (P. 18),

$$BA : DE :: AC : DF,$$

And multiplying the terms of this proportion by the corresponding terms of the identical proportion

$$AC : DF :: AC : DF,$$

there will result

$$BA \times AC : DE \times DF :: \overline{AC}^2 : \overline{DF}^2$$

Consequently (B. II., P. 4, C.),

$$BAC : DEF :: \overline{AC}^2 : \overline{DF}^2.$$

Therefore, the similar triangles *BAC*, *EDF*, are to each other as the squares described on their homologous sides *AC*, *DF*, or as the squares described on any other two homologous sides.

PROPOSITION XXVI. THEOREM.

Two similar polygons may be divided into the same number of triangles, similar each to each, and similarly placed.

Let *AEDCB*, *FKIHG*, be two similar polygons.

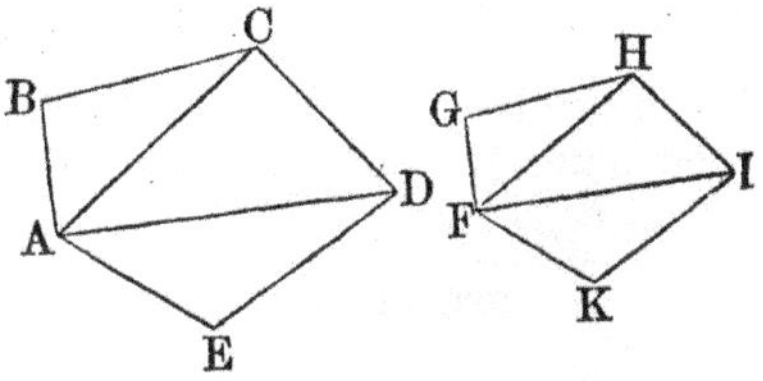

From the vertex of any angle *A*, in the polygon *AEDCB*, draw diagonals, *AD*, *AC*. From the vertex of the homologous angle *F*, in the other polygon, draw the diagonals *FI*, *FH*, to the vertices of the other angles.

The polygons being similar, the homologous angles, *ABC*, *FGH*, are equal, and the sides *AB*, *BC*, proportional to *FG*, *GH*, that is,

$$AB : FG :: BC : GH \text{ (D. 1).}$$

Wherefore, the triangles *ABC*, *FGH*, have an angle in each equal, and the adjacent sides proportional: hence, they are similar (P. 20); consequently, the angle *BCA* is equal to *GHF*. Taking away these equal angles from the equal angles *BCD*, *GHI*, and there remains *ACD*=*FHI*. But since the triangles *ABC*, *FGH*, are similar, we have

$$AC : FH :: BC : GH;$$

and since the polygons are similar,

$$BC : GH :: CD : HI;$$

hence, $AC : FH :: CD : HI.$

The angle ACD, we already know, is equal to FHI; hence, the triangles ACD, FHI, are similar (P. 20). In the same manner, it may be shown that all the remaining tri angles are similar, whatever be the number of sides in the polygons proposed: therefore, two similar polygons may be divided into the same number of triangles, similar, and similarly placed.

Scholium. The converse of the proposition is equally true: *If two polygons are composed of the same number of triangles similar and similarly situated, the two polygons are similar.*

For, the similarity of the respective triangles will give the angles,

$$ABC=FGH,\ BCA=GHF,\ ACD=FHI:$$

hence, $BCD=GHI$, likewise, $CDE=HIK$, &c.

Moreover, we have,

$$AB : FG :: BC : GH :: CD : HI :: DE : IK, \text{ \&c.};$$

hence, the two polygons have their angles equal each to each, and their sides proportional; consequently, they are similar.

PROPOSITION XXVII. THEOREM.

The perimeters of similar polygons are to each other as their homologous sides: and the polygons are to each other as the squares described on these sides.

Let $AEDCB$ and $FKIHG$, be two similar polygons: then

$$\text{per. } AEDCB : \text{per. } FKIHG :: AE : FK.$$

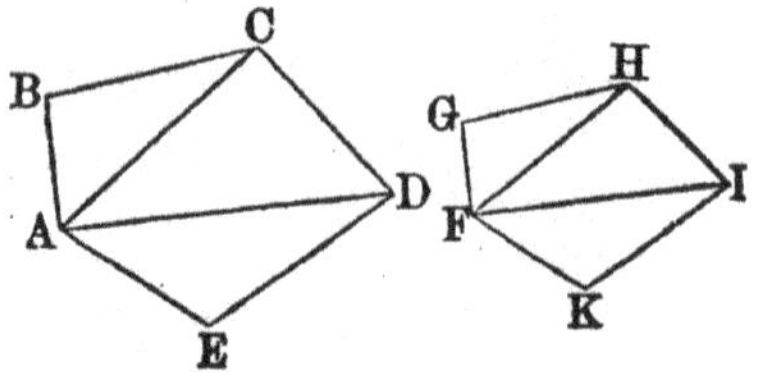

First. Since the figures are similar, we have

$AB : FG :: BC : GH :: CD : HI$, &c., hence, the sum of the antecedents $AB+BC+$

CD, &c., which makes up the perimeter of the first polygon, is to the sum of the consequents $FG+GH+HI$, &c., which makes up the perimeter of the second polygon, as any one antecedent is to its consequent (B. II., P. 10); that is, as AB to FG, or as any other two homologous sides.

Secondly. Since the triangles ABC, FGH, are similar, we have (P. 25),

$$ABC : FGH :: \overline{AC}^2 : \overline{FH}^2;$$

and from the similar triangles ACD, FHI,

$$ACD : FHI :: \overline{AC}^2 : \overline{FH}^2;$$

therefore, by reason of the common ratio, $\overline{AC}^2$ to $\overline{FH}^2$, we have (B. II., P. 4, C.)

$$ABC : FGH :: ACD : FHI.$$

By the same reasoning, we should find

$$ACD : FHI :: ADE : FIK;$$

and so on, if there were more triangles. And from this series of equal ratios, we conclude that the sum of the antecedents $ABC+ACD+ADE$, which makes up the polygon $AEDCB$, is to the sum of the consequents $FGH+FHI+FIK$, which makes up the polygon $FKIHG$, as one antecedent ABC, is to its consequent FGH (B. II., P. 10), or as $\overline{AB}^2$ is to $\overline{FG}^2$ (P. 25); hence, *similar polygons are to each other as the squares described on their homologous sides.*

Cor. If three similar figures are described on the three sides of a right-angled triangle, the figure on the hypothenuse is equivalent to the sum of the other two.

Let A, B, C, denote three similar figures described on the hypothenuse and sides of a right-angled triangle, and a, b, c, the corresponding squares; then,

$$A : B : C :: a : b : c;$$

and, $A : B+C :: a : b+c$ (B. II., P. 9):

but, a is equivalent to $b+c$ (P. 11);

hence, A is equivalent $B+C$.

PROPOSITION XXVIII. THEOREM.

If two chords intersect each other in a circle, the segments are reciprocally proportional.

Let the chords AB and CD intersect at O: then

$$AO : DO :: OC : OB.$$

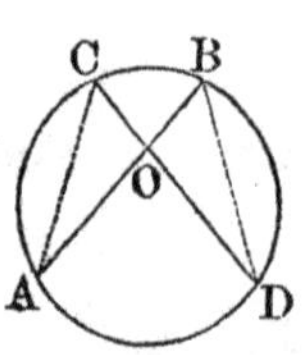

Draw AC and BD. In the triangles AOC, DOB, the angles at O are equal, being vertical angles (B. I., P. 4): the angle A is equal to the angle D, because both are inscribed in the same segment (B. III., P. 18, C. 1); for the same reason the angle $C=B$; the triangles are therefore similar (P. 18), and the homologous sides give the proportion

$$AO : DO :: CO : OB.$$

Cor. Therefore,

$$AO \times OB \approxeq DO \times CO:$$

hence, the rectangle of the two segments of one chord is equivalent to the rectangle of the two segments of the other.

PROPOSITION XXIX. THEOREM.

If from a point without a circle, two secants be drawn terminating in the concave arc, the whole secants will be reciprocally proportional to their external segments.

Let the secants OB, OC, be drawn from the point O: then

$$OB : OC :: OD : OA.$$

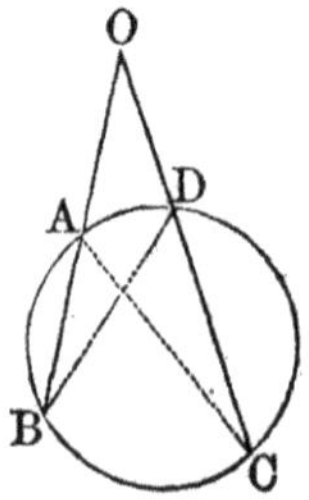

For, drawing AC, BD, the triangles AOC, BOD have the angle O common; likewise the angle $B=C$ (B. III., P. 18, C. 1); these triangles are therefore similar (P. 18), and their homologous sides give the proportion,

$$OB : OC :: OD : OA.$$

Cor. Hence, the rectangle

$$OB \times OA \approxeq OC \times OD.$$

Scholium. This proposition, it may be observed, bears a close analogy to the preceding, and differs from it only as the two chords AB, CD, instead of intersecting each other within, cut each other without the circle. The following proposition may be regarded as a particular case of the proposition just demonstrated.

PROPOSITION XXX. THEOREM.

If from a point without a circle, a tangent and a secant be drawn, the tangent will be a mean proportional between the secant and its external segment.

From the point O, let the tangent OA, and the secant OC be drawn, then

$$OC : OA :: OA : OD,$$

or,

$$\overline{OA}^2 \Leftrightarrow OC \times OD.$$

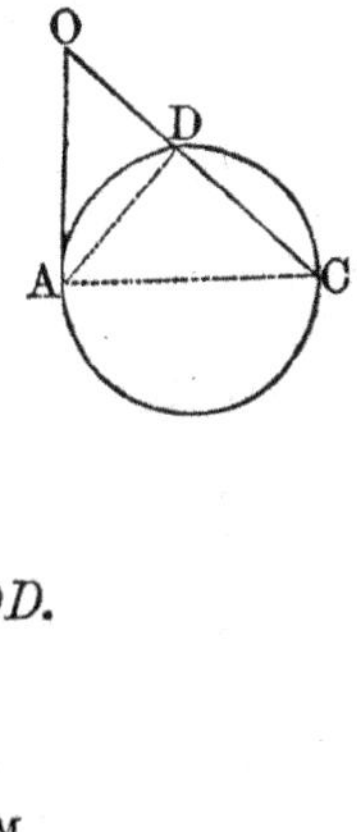

For, drawing AD and AC, the triangles DAO, CAO, have the angle O common; also, the angle OAD, formed by a tangent and a chord, is measured by half the arc AD (B. III., P. 21); and the angle C has the same measure (B. III., P. 18); hence, the angle $OAD = C$ (A. 1): therefore, the two triangles are similar, and we have the proportion

$$OC : OA :: OA : OD.$$

which gives

$$\overline{OA}^2 \Leftrightarrow OC \times OD.$$

PROPOSITION XXXI. THEOREM.

If either angle of a triangle is bisected by a line terminating in the opposite side, the rectangle of the sides about the bisected angle, is equivalent to the square of the bisecting line plus the rectangle of the segments of the third side.

In the triangle BAC, let AD bisect the angle A; then,

$$AB \times AC \Leftrightarrow \overline{AD}^2 + BD \times DC.$$

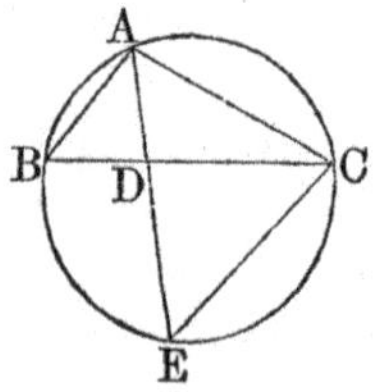

Describe a circle through the three points A, B, C (B. III., PROB. 13, S.); prolong AD till it meets the circumference in E, and draw CE.

The triangle BAD is similar to the triangle EAC; for, by hypothesis, the angle $BAD=EAC$; also, the angle $B=E$, since they are both measured by half the arc AC (B. III., P. 18); hence, these triangles are similar, and the homologous sides give the proportion

$$BA : AE :: AD : AC;$$

hence, $BA \times AC \Leftrightarrow AE \times AD$; but $AE=AD+DE$, and multiplying each of these equals by AD, we have

$$AE \times AD \Leftrightarrow \overline{AD}^2+AD \times DE;$$

now (P. 28, C.), $\quad AD \times DE \Leftrightarrow BD \times DC;$

hence, finally, $BA \times AC \Leftrightarrow \overline{AD}^2+BD \times DC.$

PROPOSITION XXXII. THEOREM.

In any triangle, the rectangle of any two sides is equivalent to the rectangle of the diameter of the circumscribed circle, and the perpendicular let fall from the vertex of the included angle on the third side.

In the triangle BAC, let AD be drawn perpendicular to BC; and let EC be the diameter of the circumscribed circle: then will

$$AB \times AC \Leftrightarrow AD \times CE.$$

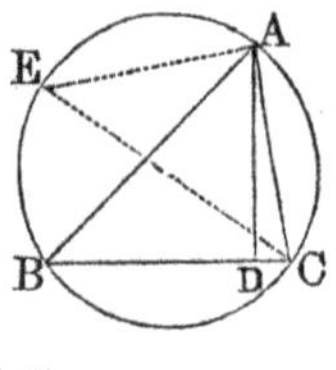

For, drawing AE, the triangles DBA, CAE, are right-angled, the one at D, the other at A: also, the angle $B=E$ (B. III., P. 18, C. 1); these triangles are therefore similar, and we have

$$AB : CE :: AD : AC;$$

and hence, $\quad AB \times AC \Leftrightarrow CE \times AD.$

Cor. If these equal quantities be multiplied by BC, there will result

$$AB \times AC \times BC = CE \times AD \times BC;$$

now, $AD \times BC$ is double the area of the triangle (P. 6); therefore, *the product of the three sides of a triangle is equal to its area multiplied by twice the diameter of the circumscribed circle.*

The product of three lines is sometimes represented by a *solid*, for a reason that will be seen hereafter. Its value is easily conceived, by supposing the lines to be reduced to numbers, and then multiplying these numbers together.

Scholium. It may also be demonstrated, that *the area of a triangle is equal to its perimeter multiplied by half the radius of the inscribed circle.*

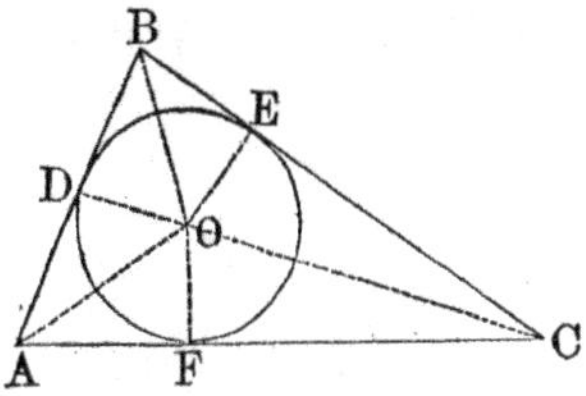

For, the triangles AOB, BOC, AOC, which have a common vertex at O, have for their common altitude the radius of the inscribed circle; hence, the sum of these triangles will be equal to the sum of the bases AB, BC, AC, multiplied by half the radius OD; hence, the area of the triangle ABC *is equal to its perimeter multiplied by half the radius of the inscribed circle.*

PROPOSITION XXXIII. THEOREM.

In every quadrilateral inscribed in a circle, the rectangle of the two diagonals is equivalent to the sum of the rectangles of the opposite sides, taken two and two.

Let $ABCD$ be a quadrilateral inscribed in a circle, and AC, BD, its diagonals: then we shall have

$$AC \times BD \Leftrightarrow AB \times CD + AD \times BC.$$

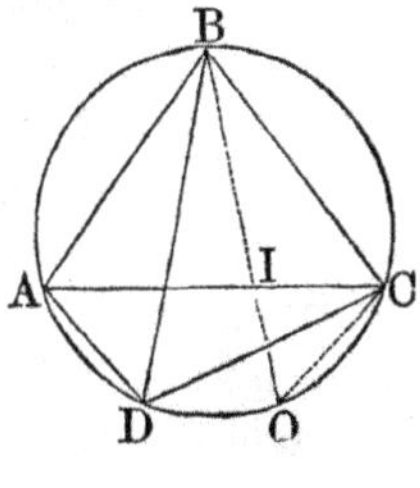

Take the arc $CO = AD$, and draw BO, meeting the diagonal AC in I.

The angle $ABD = CBI$, since the one has for its measure half of the arc AD (B. III., P. 18), and the other, half of CO, equal to AD; the angle $ADB = BCI$, because they are subtended by the same arc; hence, the triangle ABD is similar to the triangle IBC, and we have the proportion

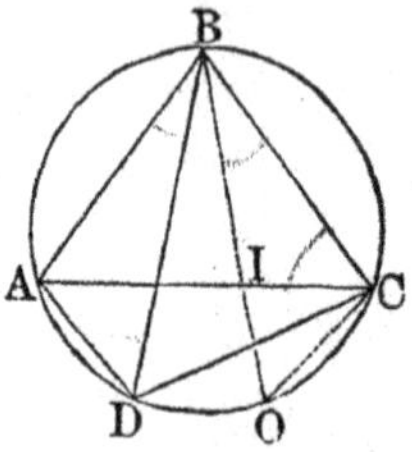

$$AD : CI :: BD : BC;$$

and consequently,

$$AD \times BC = CI \times BD.$$

Again, the triangle ABI is similar to the triangle BDC; for the arc AD being equal to CO, if OD be added to each of them, we shall have the arc $AO = DC$; hence, the angle ABI is equal to DBC; also, the angle BAI to BDC, because they stand on the same arc; hence, the triangles ABI, DBC, are similar, and the homologous sides give the proportion

$$AB : BD :: AI : CD;$$

hence,
$$AB \times CD = AI \times BD.$$

Adding the two results obtained, and observing that

$$AI \times BD + CI \times BD = (AI + CI) \times BD = AC \times BD,$$

we shall have

$$AD \times BC + AB \times CD = AC \times BD.$$

PROBLEMS

RELATING TO THE FOURTH BOOK.

PROBLEM I.

To divide a given straight line into any number of equal parts, or into parts proportional to given lines.

First. Let it be proposed to divide the line AB into five equal parts. Through the extremity A, draw the indefinite straight line AG: take AC of any length, and apply it five times upon AG; join the last point of division G, and the extremity B of the given line, by the straight line GB; then through C, draw CI parallel to GB:

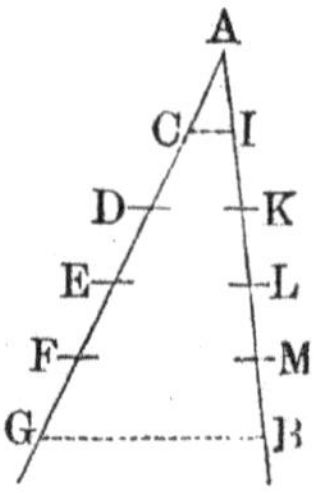

AI will be the fifth part of the line AB; and by applying AI five times upon AB, the line AB will be divided into five equal parts.

For, since CI is parallel to GB, the sides AG, AB, are cut proportionally in C and I (P. 15). But AC is the fifth part of AG, hence, AI is the fifth part of AB.

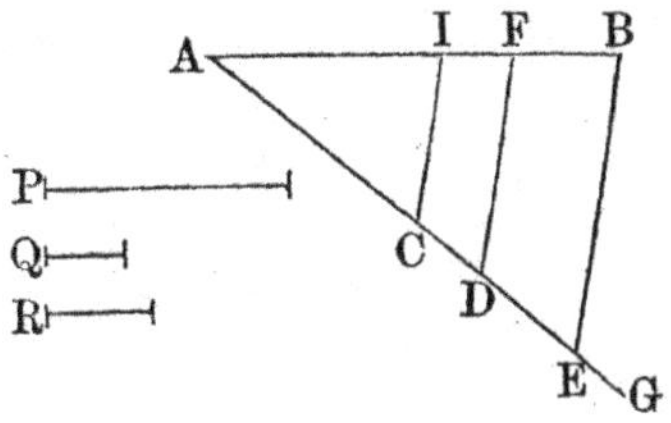

Secondly. Let it be proposed to divide the line AB into parts proportional to the given lines P, Q, R. Through A, draw the indefinite line AG; make $AC=P$, $CD=Q$, $DE=R$; join the extremities E and B; and through the points C and D, draw CI, DF, parallel to EB; the line AB will be divided into parts AI, IF, FB, proportional to the given lines P, Q, R.

For, by reason of the parallels CI, DF, EB, the parts AI, IF, FB, are proportional to the parts AC, CD, DE (P. 15, C. 2); and by construction, these are equal to the given lines P, Q, R.

PROBLEM II.

To find a fourth proportional to three given lines, A, B, C.

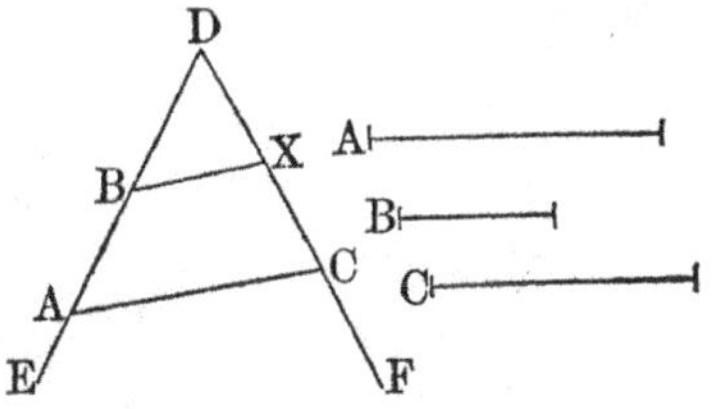

Draw the two indefinite lines DE, DF, forming any angle with each other. Upon DE take $DA=A$, and $DB=B$; upon DF take $DC=C$, draw AC; and through the point B, draw BX parallel to AC; and DX will be the fourth proportional required. For, since BX is parallel to AC, we have the proportion (P. 15, C. 1),

$$DA : DB :: DC : DX;$$

now, the first three terms of this proportion are equal to the three given lines: consequently, DX is the fourth proportional required.

Cor. A third proportional to two given lines, A, B, may be found in the same manner, for it will be the same as a fourth proportional to the three lines, A, B, B.

PROBLEM III.

To find a mean proportional between two given lines A and B

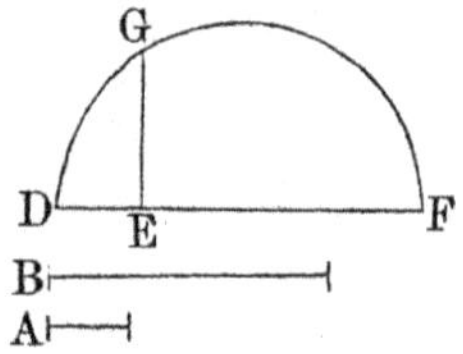

Upon the indefinite line DF, take $DE=A$, and $EF=B$; and upon the whole line DF, as a diameter, describe the semicircumference DGF; at the point E, erect, upon the diameter, the perpendicular EG meeting the semicircumference in G; EG will be the mean proportional required.

For, the perpendicular EG, let fall from a point in the circumference upon the diameter, is a mean proportional between the two segments of the diameter DE, EF (P. 23, C.); and these segments are equal to the given lines A and B.

PROBLEM IV.

To divide a given line into two such parts, that the greater part shall be a mean proportional between the whole line and the other part.

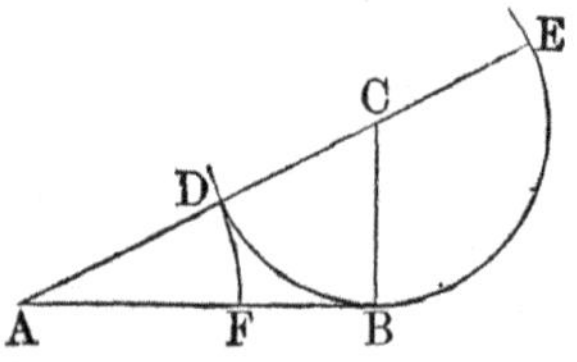

Let AB be the given line.

At the extremity B, erect the perpendicular BC, equal to the half of AB; from the point C, as a centre, with the radius CB, describe a semicircle; draw AC cutting the circumference in D; and take $AF=AD$: then F will be the point of division, and we shall have,

$$AB : AF :: AF : FB.$$

For, AB being perpendicular to the radius at its extremity, is a tangent (B. III., P. 9); and if AC be prolonged till it again meets the circumference, in E, we shall have (P. 30),

$$AE : AB :: AB : AD;$$

hence, by division,

$$AE-AB : AB :: AB-AD : AD.$$

But, since the radius is the half of AB, the diameter DE is equal to AB, and consequently, $AE-AB=AD=AF$; also, because $AF=AD$, we have $AB-AD=FB$: hence,

$$AF : AB :: FB : AD, \text{ or } AF;$$

whence, by inversion,

$$AB : AF :: AF : FB.$$

Scholium. This sort of division of the line AB, viz., *so that the whole line shall be to the greater part as the greater part is to the less,* is called division in *extreme and mean ratio.* It may further be observed, that the secant AE is divided in extreme and mean ratio at the point D; for, since $AB=DE$, we have,

$$AE : DE :: DE : AD.$$

PROBLEM V.

Through a given point, in a given angle, to draw a line so that the segments comprehended between the point and the two sides of the angle, shall be equal.

Let BCD be the given angle, and A the given point.

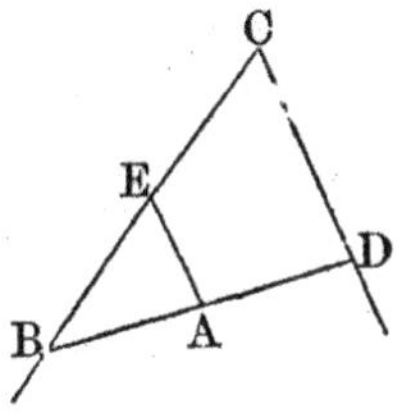

Through the point A, draw AE parallel to CD, make $BE=CE$, and through the points B and A, draw BAD; this will be the line required.

For, AE being parallel to CD, we have,

$$BE : EC :: BA : AD;$$

but $BE=EC$; therefore, $BA=AD$.

PROBLEM VI.

To construct a square that shall be equivalent to a given parallelogram, or to a given triangle.

First. Let $ABCD$ be the given parallelogram, AB its base, and DE its altitude: between AB and DE find a mean proportional XY; then will the square described upon XY be equivalent to the parallelogram $ABCD$.

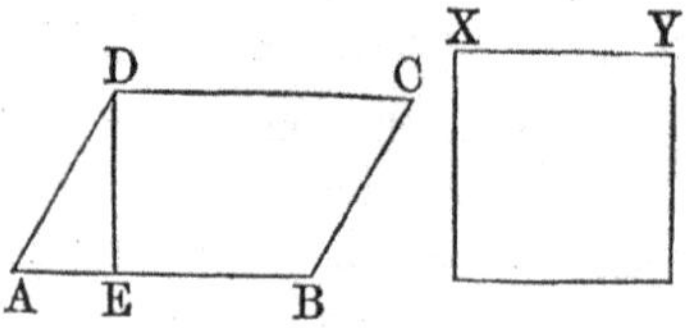

For, by construction,

$$AB : XY :: XY : DE;$$

therefore, $\overline{XY}^2 \Leftrightarrow AB \times DE;$

but $AB \times DE$ is the measure of the parallelogram (P. 5), and $\overline{XY}^2$ that of the square; consequently, they are equivalent.

Secondly. Let BAC be the given triangle, BC its base, AD its altitude: find a mean proportional between BC and the half of AD, and let XY be that mean; the square described upon XY will be equivalent to the triangle ABC.

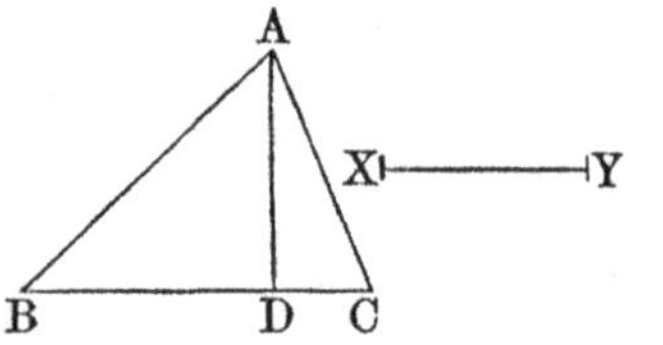

For, since

$$BC : XY :: XY : \tfrac{1}{2}AD,$$

it follows, that

$$\overline{XY}^2 \Leftrightarrow BC \times \tfrac{1}{2}AD;$$

hence, the square described upon XY is equivalent to the triangle BAC.

PROBLEM VII.

Upon a given line, to construct a rectangle that shall be equivalent to a given rectangle.

Let AD be the line, and $ABFC$ the given rectangle.

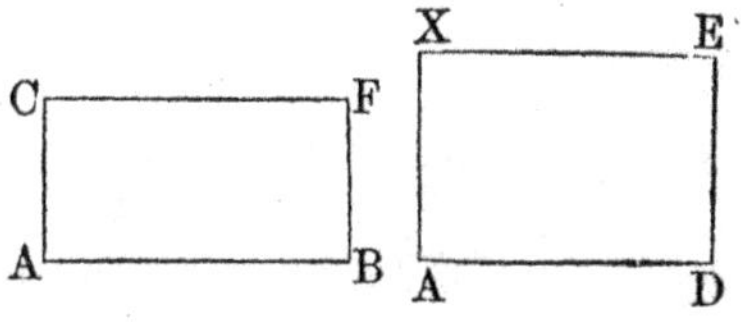

Find a fourth proportional to the three lines, AD, AB, AC, and let AX be that fourth proportional; a rectangle constructed with the sides AD and AX will be equivalent to the rectangle $ABFC$.

For, since

$$AD : AB :: AC : AX,$$

it follows, that $AD \times AX \approx AB \times AC$;

hence, the rectangle $ADEX$ is equivalent to the rectangle $ABFC$.

PROBLEM VIII.

To find two lines whose ratio shall be the same as the ratio of two rectangles contained by given lines.

Let $A \times B$, $C \times D$, be the rectangles contained by the given lines A, B, C, and D.

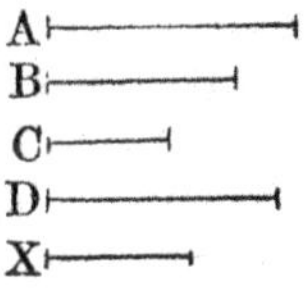

Find X, a fourth proportional to the three lines, B, C, D; then will the two lines A and X have the same ratio to each other as the rectangles $A \times B$ and $C \times D$.

For since,

$$B : C :: D : X,$$

it follows that $C \times D \approx B \times X$; hence,

$$A \times B : C \times D :: A \times B : B \times X :: A : X.$$

Cor. Hence, to obtain the ratio of the squares described upon the given lines A and C, find a third proportional X, to the lines A and C, so that

$$A : C :: C : X;$$

you will then have

$$A \times X \approx C^2, \text{ or } A^2 \times X \approx A \times C^2; \text{ hence,}$$

$$A^2 : C^2 :: A : X.$$

PROBLEM IX.

To find a triangle that shall be equivalent to a given polygon.

Let $AEDCB$ be the given polygon.

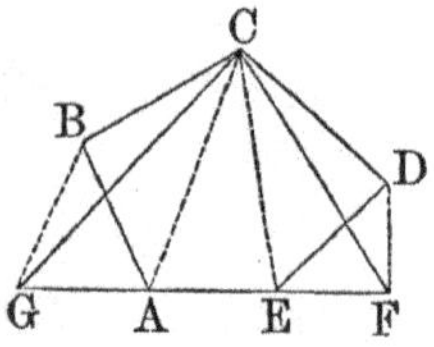

First. Draw the diagonal CE cutting off the triangle CDE; through the point D, draw DF parallel to CE, meeting AE prolonged, in F; draw CF: the polygon $AEDCB$ is equivalent to the polygon $AFCB$, which has one side less than the given polygon.

For the triangles CDE, CFE, have the base CE common, they have also equal altitudes, since their vertices D and F, are situated in a line DF parallel to the base: these triangles are therefore equivalent (P. 2, C.) Add to each of them the figure $AECB$, and there will result the polygon $AEDCB$, equivalent to the polygon $AFCB$.

The angle B may in like manner be cut off, by substituting for the triangle ABC, the equivalent triangle AGC, and thus the pentagon $AEDCB$ will be changed into an equivalent triangle GCF.

The same process may be applied to every other figure; for, by successively diminishing the number of its sides, one being retrenched at each step of the process, the equivalent triangle will at last be found.

Scholium. We have already seen that every triangle may be changed into an equivalent square (PROB. 6); and thus a square may always be found equivalent to a given rectilineal figure, which operation is called *squaring* the rectilineal figure, or the *quadrature* of it.

The problem of *the quadrature of the circle* consists in finding a square equivalent to a circle whose diameter is given.

PROBLEM X.

To find the side of a square which shall be equivalent to the sum or the difference of two given squares.

Let A and B be the sides of the given squares.

First. If it is required to find a square equivalent to the sum of these squares, draw the two indefinite lines, ED, EF, at right angles to each other; take $ED=A$, and $EG=B$; and draw DG: this will be the required side of the square.

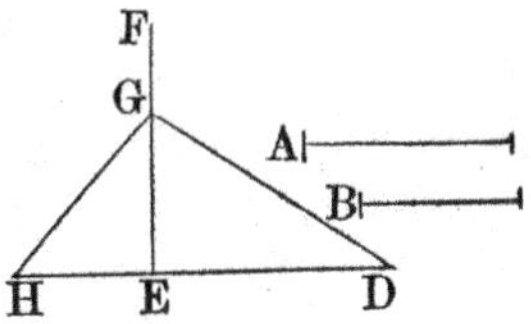

For the triangle DEG being right-angled, the square described upon the hypothenuse DG, is equivalent to the sum of the squares upon ED and EG (P. 11).

Secondly. If it is required to find a square equivalent to the difference of the given squares, form, as before, the right angle FEH; take GE equal to the shorter of the sides A and B; from the point G as a centre, with a radius GH, equal to the other side, describe an arc cutting EH in H: the square described upon EH will be equivalent to the difference of the squares described upon the lines A and B.

For, the triangle GEH is right-angled, the hypothenuse $GH=A$, and the side $GE=B$; hence, the square described upon EH, is equivalent to the difference of the squares A and B (P. 11, C. 1).

Scholium. A square may thus be found, equivalent to the sum of any number of squares; for a construction similar to that which reduces two of them to one, will reduce three of them to two, and these two to one, and so of others. It would be the same, if any of the squares were to be subtracted from the sum of the others.

PROBLEM XI.

To find a square which shall be to a given square as one given line is to another given line.

Let AC be the given square, and M and N the given lines.

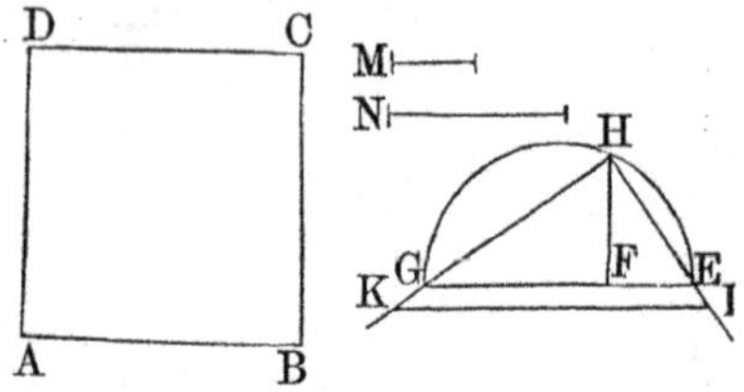

Upon the indefinite line EG, take $EF=M$, and $FG=N$; upon EG as a diameter describe a semicircumference, and at the point F erect the perpendicular FH. From the point H, draw the chords HG HE, which produce indefinitely: upon the first, take HK equal to the side AB of the given square, and through the point K draw KI parallel to EG; HI will be the side of the required square.

For, by reason of the parallels KI, GE, we have

$$HI : HK :: HE : HG;$$

hence,
$$\overline{HI}^2 : \overline{HK}^2 :: \overline{HE}^2 : \overline{HG}^2:$$

but in the right-angled triangle GHE, the square of HE is to the square of HG as the segment EF is to the segment FG (P. 11, C. 3), or as M is to N; hence,

$$\overline{HI}^2 : \overline{HK}^2 :: M : N.$$

But $HK=AB$; therefore, the square described upon HI is to the square described upon AB as M is to N.

Upon a given line, to construct a polygon similar to a given polygon.

Let FG be the given line, and $AEDCB$ the given polygon.

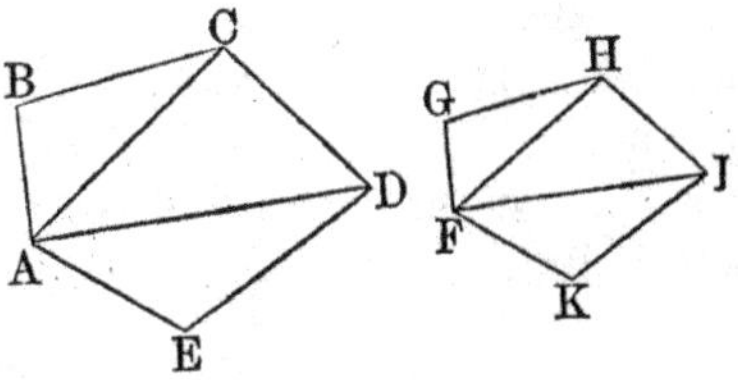

In the given polygon, draw the diagonals AC, AD; at the point F make the angle $GFH=BAC$, and at the point G, the angle $FGH=ABC$; the lines FH, GH will intersect each other in H, and the triangle FGH will be similar to ABC (P. 18). In the same manner upon FH, homologous to AC, construct the triangle FIH similar to ADC; and upon FI, homologous to AD, construct the triangle FIK similar to ADE. The polygon $FGHIK$ will be similar to $ABCDE$, as required.

For, these two polygons are composed of the same number of similar triangles, similarly placed (P. 26, S.)

PROBLEM XIII.

Two similar polygons being given, to construct a similar polygon which shall be equivalent to their sum or difference.

Let A and B be homologous sides of the given figures.

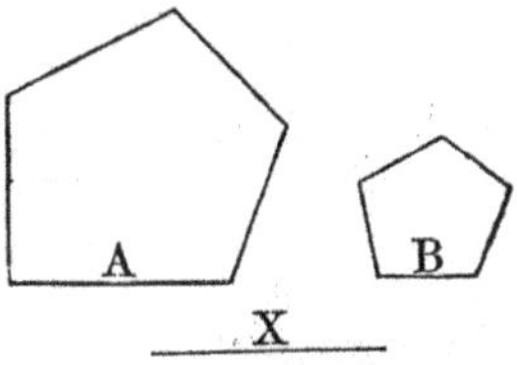

Find a square equivalent to the sum or difference of the squares described upon A and B; let X be the side of that square; then will X be that side in the figure required, which is homologous to the sides A and B in the given figures. Let the figure itself, then, be constructed on the side X, as in the last problem. This figure will be equivalent to the sum or difference of the figures described on A and B (P. 27, C.)

PROBLEM XIV.

To construct a polygon similar to a given polygon, and having to it the given ratio of M to N.

Let A be a side of the given polygon, and X the homologous side of the required polygon.

Find the value of X, such, that its square shall be to the square of A, as M to N (PROB. 11). Then upon X describe a figure similar to the given figure (PROB. 12): this will be the figure required.

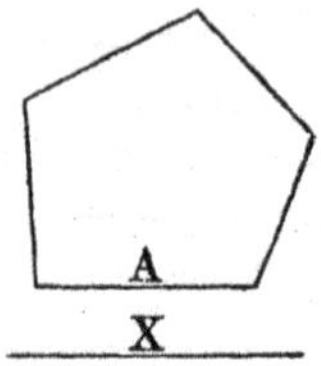

PROBLEM XV.

To construct a figure similar to the figure P, and equivalent to the figure Q.

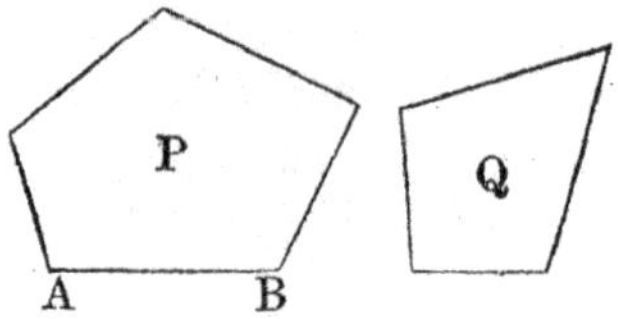

Find M, the side of a square equivalent to the figure P, and N the side of a square equivalent to the figure Q (PROB. 9, S.) Let X be a fourth proportional to the three given lines, M, N, AB; upon the side X, homologous to AB, describe a figure similar to the figure P; it will also be equivalent to the figure Q.

For, calling Y the figure constructed, upon the side X, we have,

$$P : Y :: \overline{AB}^2 : X^2;$$

but by construction,

$$AB : X :: M : N, \text{ or, } \overline{AB}^2 : X^2 :: M^2 : N^2;$$

hence, $\quad P : Y :: M^2 : N^2.$

But, by construction also,

$$M^2 \approx P, \text{ and } N^2 \approx Q \cdot$$

therefore, $\quad P : Y :: P : Q;$

consequently, $Y \approx Q$; hence, the figure Y is similar to the figure P, and equivalent to the figure Q.

PROBLEM XVI.

To construct a rectangle equivalent to a given square, and having the sum of its adjacent sides equal to a given line.

Let C be the square, and the line AB equal to the sum of the sides of the required rectangle.

Upon AB as a diameter, describe a semicircumference; at A, draw AD perpendicular to AB, and make it equal to the side of the square C; then draw the line DE parallel to the diameter AB; from the point E, where the parallel cuts the circumference, draw EF perpendicular to the diameter; AF and FB will be the sides of the required rectangle.

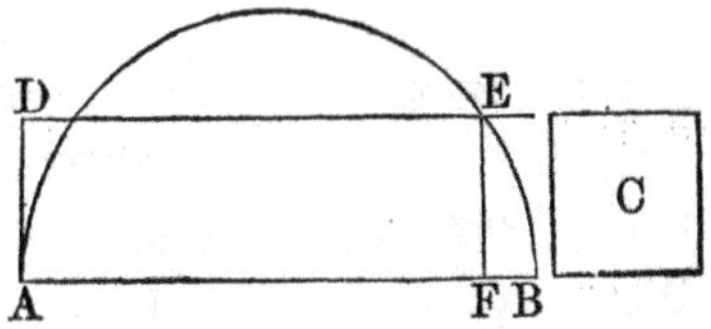

For, their sum is equal to AB; and their rectangle $AF \times FB$ is equivalent to the square of EF, or to the square of AD; hence, this rectangle is equivalent to the given square C.

Scholium. The problem is impossible, if the distance AD exceeds the radius; that is, the side of the square C must not exceed half the line AB.

PROBLEM XVII.

To construct a rectangle that shall be equivalent to a given square, and the difference of whose adjacent sides shall be equal to a given line.

Let C denote the given square, and AB the difference of the sides of the rectangle.

Upon the given line AB, as a diameter, describe a circumference. At the extremity of the diameter, draw the tangent AD, and make it equal to the side of the square C; through the point D and the centre O draw the secant DOF, intersecting the circumference in E and F; then will DE and DF be the adjacent sides of the required rectangle.

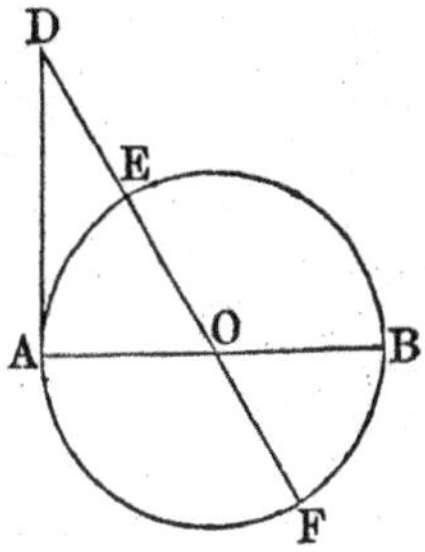

For, the difference of these lines is equal to the diameter EF or AB; and the rectangle DE, DF is equivalent to $\overline{AD}^2$ (P. 30); hence, the rectangle $DF \times DE$, is equivalent to the given square C

PROBLEM XVIII.

To find the common measure, between the side and diagonal of a square.

Let $ABCG$ be any square, and AC its diagonal.

We first apply CB to CA. For this purpose let the semicircumference DBE be described, from the centre C, with the radius CB, and produce AC to E. It is evident that CB is contained once in AC, with the remainder AD. The result of the first operation is, therefore, a quotient 1, with the remainder AD. This remainder must now be compared with BC, or its equal AB.

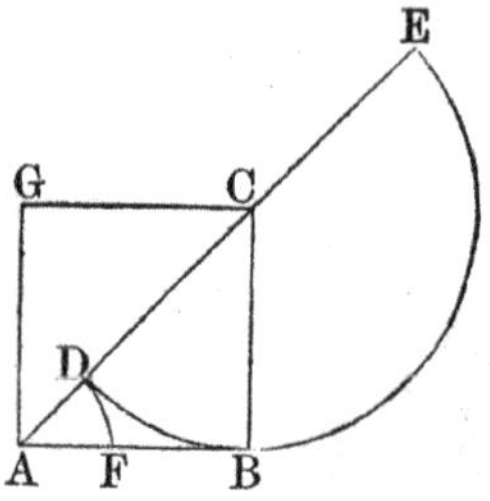

Since the angle ABC is a right angle, AB is a tangent, and since AE is a secant drawn from the same point, we have (P 30),

$$AD : AB :: AB : AE.$$

Hence, in the second operation, where AD is compared with AB, the equal ratio of AB to AE may be taken instead: but AB, or its equal CD, is contained twice in AE, with the remainder AD; the result of the second operation is therefore a quotient 2 with the remainder AD, and this must be again compared with AB.

Thus, the third operation consists in comparing again AD with AB, and may be reduced in the same manner to the comparison of AB or its equal CD with AE; from which there will again be obtained a quotient 2, and the remainder AD.

Hence, it is evident that the process will never terminate, and consequently that no remainder is contained in the preceding divisor an exact number of times; therefore, there is no common measure between the side and the diagonal of a square. This property has already been shown, since (P. 11, C. 5),

$$AB : AC :: 1 : \sqrt{2},$$

but it acquires a greater degree of clearness by the geometrical investigation.

BOOK V.

REGULAR POLYGONS—MEASUREMENT OF THE CIRCLE

DEFINITION.

A REGULAR POLYGON is one which is both equilateral and equiangular.

A regular polygon may have any number of sides. The equilateral triangle is one of three sides; the square, is one of four.

PROPOSITION I. THEOREM.

Regular polygons of the same number of sides are similar figures.

Let $ABCDEF$, $abcedf$, be two such polygons.

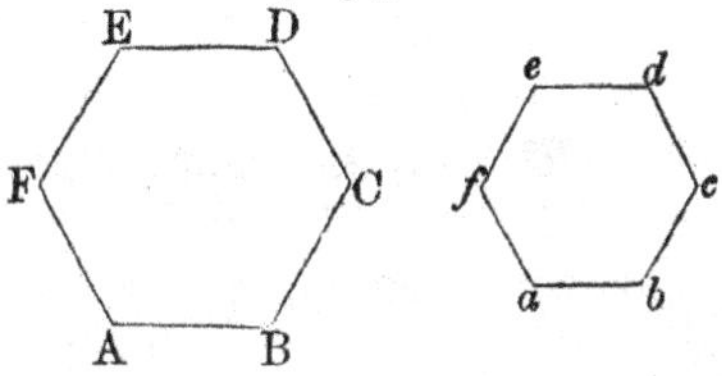

Then, either angle, as A, of the polygon $ABCDEF$, is equal to twice as many right angles less four, as the figure has sides, divided by the number of sides; and the same is true of either angle of the other polygon (B. I., P. 26, C. 4); hence (A. 1), the angles of the polygons are equal.

Again, since the polygons are regular, the sides AB, BC, CD, &c., are equal, and so likewise the sides ab, bc, cd (D.), &c.; hence

$$AB : ab :: BC : bc :: CD : cd, \&c.;$$

therefore, the two polygons have their angles equal, and their sides taken in the same order proportional; consequently, they are similar (B. IV., D. 1).

Cor. 1. The perimeters of two regular polygons of the same number of sides, are to each other as their homologous sides, and their surfaces are to each other as the squares of those sides (B. IV., P. 27).

Cor. 2. The angle of a regular polygon, like the angle of an equiangular polygon, is determined by the number of its sides (B. I., P. 26, C. 4).

PROPOSITION II. THEOREM.

A regular polygon may be circumscribed by the circumference of a circle, and a circle may be inscribed within it.

Let $HGFE$, &c., be any regular polygon.

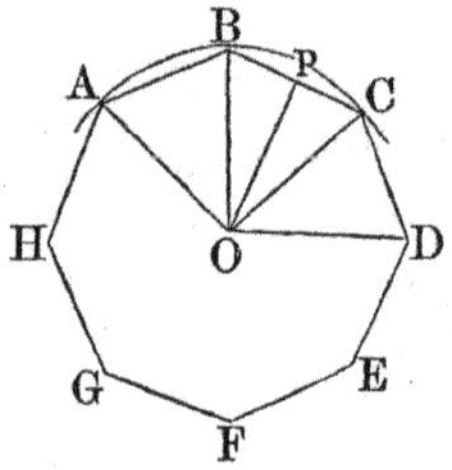

Through the three points A, B, C, describe the circumference of a circle: the centre O will lie in the line OP, drawn perpendicular to BC at the middle point P (B. III., P. 6, S.) Then draw OB and OC.

If the quadrilateral $OPCD$ be placed upon the quadrilateral $OPBA$, they will coincide; for, the side OP is common; the angle $OPC=OPB$, each being a right angle; hence, the side PC will apply to its equal PB, and the point C will fall on B: besides, the polygon being regular, the angle $PCD=PBA$ (D.); hence, CD will take the direction BA; and since $CD=BA$, the point D will fall on A, and the two quadrilaterals will coincide. Hence, OD is equal to AO; and consequently, the circumference which passes through the three points A, B, C, will also pass through the point D. In the same manner it may be shown, that the circumference which passes through the three points B, C, D, will also pass through the point E; and so of all the other vertices; hence, the circumference which passes through the points A, B, C, passes also through the vertices of all the angles of the polygon, consequently, the circumference of the circle circumscribes the polygon (B. III., D. 7).

Again, in reference to this circle, all the sides AB, BC, CD, &c., of the polygon, are equal chords; they are therefore equally distant from the centre (B. III., P. 8): hence, if from the point O as a centre, with the radius OP, a circumference be described, it will touch the side BC, and all the other sides of the polygon, each in its middle point, and the circle will be inscribed in the polygon (B. III., D. 11).

Scholium. The point O, the common centre of the inscribed and circumscribed circles, may also be regarded as the centre of the polygon; and the angle AOB is called *the angle at the centre*, being formed by two lines drawn from the centre to the extremities of the same side AB. The perpendicular OP, is called the *apothem* of the polygon.

Cor. 1. Since all the chords AB, BC, CD, &c., are equal, all the angles at the centre are likewise equal (B. III., P. 4); and therefore, the value of any angle will be found by dividing four right angles by the number of sides of the polygon.

Cor. 2. To inscribe a regular polygon of any number of sides in a given circle, we have only to divide the circumference into as many equal parts as the polygon has sides; for, when the arcs are equal, the chords AB, BC, CD, &c., are also equal (B. III., P. 4); hence, likewise the triangles AOB, BOC, COD, must be equal, because their sides are equal each to each (B. I., P. 10); therefore, by addition, all the angles ABC, BCD, CDE, &c., are equal (A. 2); hence, the figure $ABCDEH$, is a regular polygon.

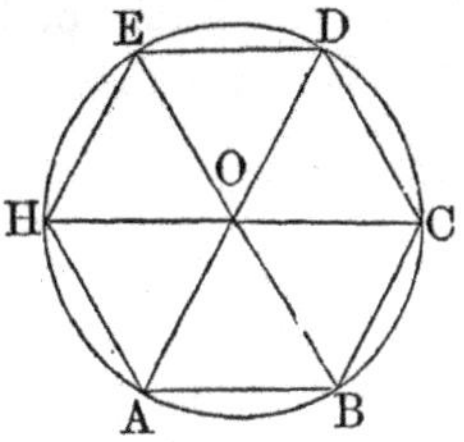

PROPOSITION III. PROBLEM.

To inscribe a square in a given circle.

Draw two diameters AC, BD, intersecting each other at right angles; join their extremities A, B, C, D, the figure $ABCD$ will be a square.

For, the angles AOB, BOC, &c., being equal, the chords AB, BC, &c., are also equal (B. III., P. 4): and the angles ABC, BCD, &c., being inscribed in semicircles, are right angles (B. III., P. 18, C. 2).

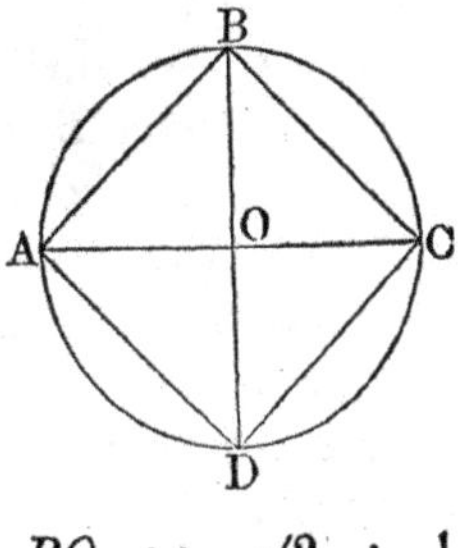

Scholium. Since the triangle BCO is right-angled and isosceles, we have (B. IV., P. 11, C. 5), $BC : BO :: \sqrt{2} : 1$; hence, *the side of the inscribed square is to the radius, as the square root of two, to unity.*

PROPOSITION IV. THEOREM.

If a regular hexagon be inscribed in a circle, its side will be equal to the radius.

Let $ABCDEH$, be a regular hexagon, inscribed in a circle: then will its side AB be equal to the radius OA.

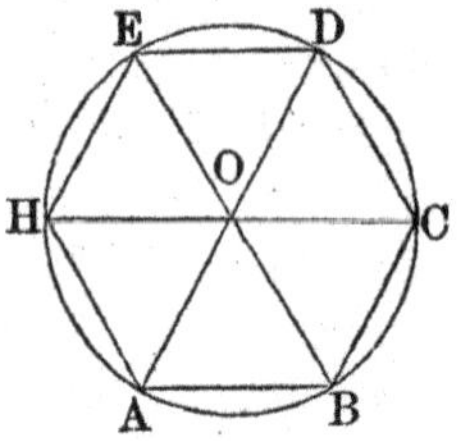

For, the angle AOB is equal to one-sixth of four right angles, (P. 2, C. 1), or one-third of two right angles: hence, the sum of the remaining angles OAB, OBA, is equal to two-thirds of two right angles (B. I., P. 25). But the triangle AOB is isosceles, hence, the angles at the base are equal (B. I., P. 11): therefore each is one-third of two right angles: hence, the triangle AOB is equiangular: hence, $AB = AO$ (B. I., P. 12).

PROPOSITION V. PROBLEM.

To inscribe in a given circle, a regular hexagon.

Let O be the centre, and OB the radius of the given circle.

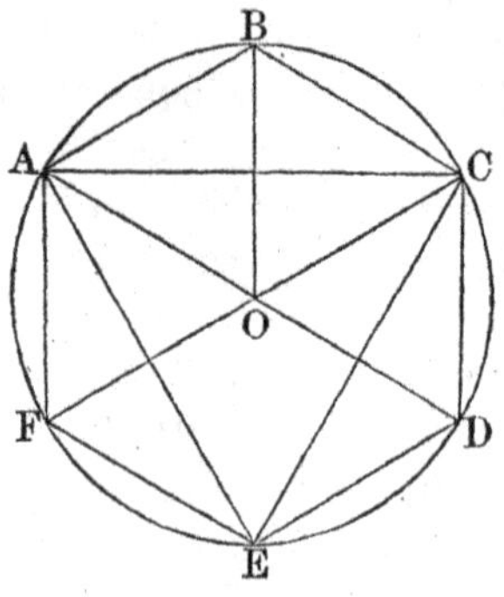

Beginning at any point, as B, apply the radius BO, six times as a chord to the circumference, and we shall form the regular hexagon $BCDEFA$ (P. 4). Hence, to inscribe a regular hexagon in a given circle, the radius must be applied six times as a chord, to the circumference; which will bring us round to the point of beginning.

Cor. 1. If the vertices of the alternate angles be joined

by the lines AC, CE, EA, there will be inscribed in the circle an equilateral triangle ACE, since each of its angles will be measured by one-sixth of four right angles, or one-third of two (B. I., P. 25, C. 5).

Cor. 2. If we draw the radii OA, OC, the figure $OCBA$ will be a rhombus: for, we have

$$OC = CB = BA = AO.$$

Hence, the sum of the squares of the diagonals is equivalent to the sum of the squares of the sides (B. IV., P. 14, C. 2):

that is, $\overline{AC}^2 + \overline{OB}^2 \simeq 4\overline{AB}^2 \simeq 4\overline{OB}^2$;

and by taking away $\overline{OB}^2$, we have,

$$\overline{AC}^2 \simeq 3\overline{OB}^2; \text{ hence,}$$

$$\overline{AC}^2 : \overline{OB}^2 : 3 : 1; \text{ or,}$$

$$AC : OB :: \sqrt{3} : 1:$$

hence, *the side of the inscribed equilateral triangle is to the radius, as the square root of three, to one.*

PROPOSITION VI. PROBLEM.

In a given circle to inscribe a regular decagon.

Let O be the centre, and OA the radius of the given circle.

Divide the radius OA in extreme and mean ratio at the point M (B. IV., PROB. 4): Take OM, the greater segment, and lay it off from A to B; the chord AB will be the side of the regular decagon, and by applying it ten times to the circumference, the decagon will be inscribed in the circle.

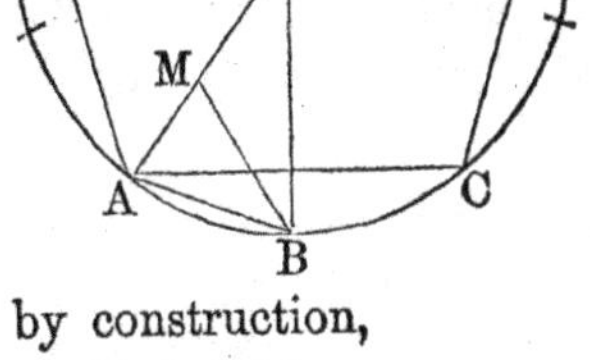

For, drawing MB, we have by construction,

$$AO : OM :: OM : AM;$$

or, since $AB = OM$,

$$AO : AB :: AB : AM.$$

But since the triangles *ABO*, *AMB*, have a common angle *A*, included between proportional sides, they are similar (B. IV., P. 20). Now the triangle *BAO* being isosceles, *AMB* must be isosceles also, and *AB*=*BM*; but *AB* = *OM*; hence, also *MB*=*MO*; hence, the triangle *BMO* is isosceles.

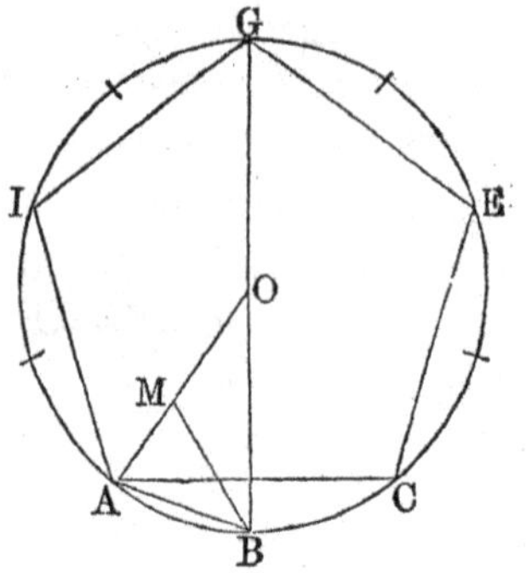

Again, in the isosceles triangle *BMO*, the angle *AMB* being exterior, is double the interior angle *O* (B. I., P. 25, C. 6): but the angle *AMB*=*MAB*; hence, the triangle *OAB* is such, that each of the angles *OAB* or *OBA*, at its base, is double the angle *O*, at its vertex; hence, the three angles of the triangle are together equal to five times the angle *O*, which consequently, is the fifth part of two right angles, or the tenth part of four; hence, the arc *AB* is the tenth part of the circumference, and the chord *AB* is the side of the regular decagon.

Cor. 1. By joining the vertices of the alternate angles of the decagon, a regular pentagon *ACEGI* will be inscribed.

Cor. 2. Any regular polygon being inscribed, if the arcs which the sides subtend be severally bisected, the chords of those semi-arcs will form a new regular polygon of double the number of sides: thus it is plain, that the square will enable us to inscribe, successively, regular polygons of 8, 16, 32, &c., sides. And in like manner, by means of the hexagon, regular polygons of 12, 24, 48, &c., sides may be inscribed; and by means of the decagon, polygons of 20, 40, 80, &c., sides.

Cor. 3. It is further evident, that any of the inscribed polygons will be less than the inscribed polygon of double the number of sides, since a part is less than the whole.

PROPOSITION VII. PROBLEM.

A regular inscribed polygon being given, to circumscribe a similar polygon about the same circle.

Let O be the centre of the circle, and $CDEFAB$ a regular inscribed polygon.

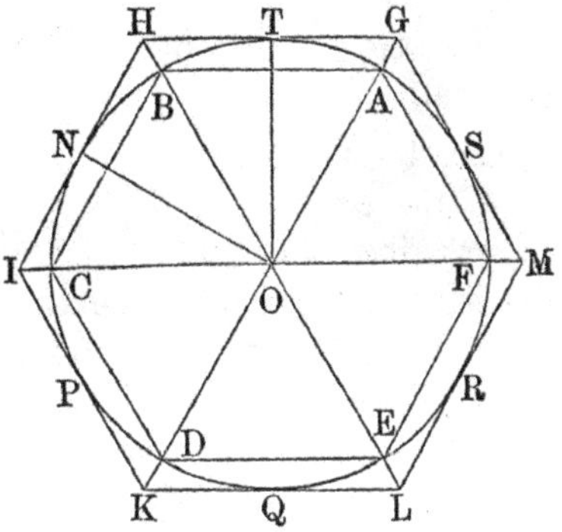

At T, the middle point of the arc AB, draw a tangent GH, and do the same at the middle point of each of the arcs BC, CD, &c.; these tangents will be parallel to the chords AB, BC, CD, &c. (B. III., P. 10, C.); and will, by their intersections, form the regular circumscribed polygon $GHIK$ &c., similar to the one inscribed.

For, since T is the middle point of the arc BTA, and N the middle point of the equal arc BNC, it follows, that $BT=BN$; or that the vertex B of the inscribed polygon, is at the middle point of the arc NBT. Draw OH. The line OH will pass through the point B.

For, the right-angled triangles OTH, NOH, having the common hypothenuse OH, and the side $OT=ON$, are equal (B. I., P. 17), and consequently the angle $TOH=HON$, wherefore the line OH passes through the middle point B of the arc TN (B. III., P. 15). In the same manner it may be shown that OI passes through C; and similarly for the other vertices.

But since GH is parallel to AB, and HI to BC, the angle $GHI=ABC$ (B. I., P. 24); in like manner, $HIK=BCD$; and so for the other angles: hence, the angles of the circumscribed polygon are equal to those of the inscribed. And further, by reason of these same parallels, we have

$$GH : AB :: OH : OB, \text{ and } HI : BC :: OH : OB;$$

therefore, $$GH : AB :: HI : BC.$$

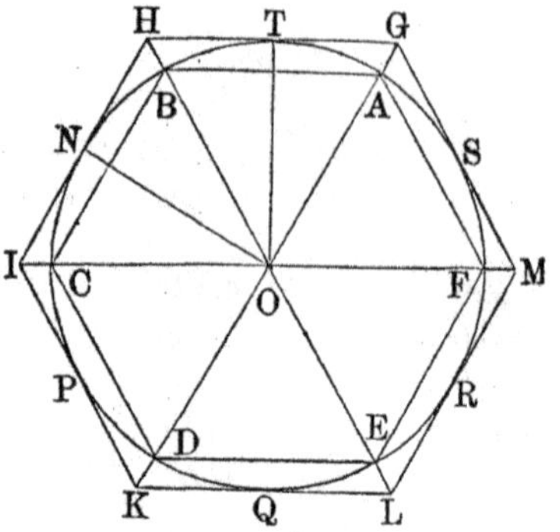

But $AB=BC$, therefore $GH=HI$. For a like reason, $HI=IK$, &c.; hence, the sides of the circumscribed polygon are all equal; hence, this polygon is regular and similar to the inscribed polygon.

Cor. 1. Reciprocally: if the circumscribed polygon $GHIK$ &c., be given, and the inscribed one ABC &c., be required, it will only be necessary to draw from the vertices of the angles G, H, I, &c., of the given polygon, straight lines OG, OH, &c., meeting the circumference in the points A, B, C, &c.; then to join these points by the chords AB, BC, &c.; this will form the inscribed polygon. An easier solution of this problem would be, simply to join the points of contact T, N, P, &c., by chords TN, NP, &c., which likewise would form an inscribed polygon similar to the circumscribed one.

Cor. 2. Hence, we may circumscribe about a circle any regular polygon similar to an inscribed one, and conversely.

Cor. 3. It is plain that $NH+HT=HT+TG=HG$, one of the equal sides of the polygon.

Cor. 4. If through B, A, F, &c., the middle points of the arcs NBT, TAS, SFR, &c., we draw tangent lines, we shall thus form a new regular circumscribed polygon having double the number of sides: and this process may be repeated as often as we please. The new polygon will be regular, because it will be similar to a new inscribed polygon which may be formed (P. 6, C. 2) of double the number of sides of the first. It is plain, that each new circumscribed polygon will be less than the one from which it was derived, since a part is less than the whole.

PROPOSITION VIII. THEOREM.

The area of a regular polygon is equal to its perimeter multiplied by half the radius of the inscribed circle.

Let there be the regular polygon $GHIK$, and ON, OT, radii of the inscribed circle drawn to the points of tangency: then will its area be equal to the perimeter multiplied by one-half of OT.

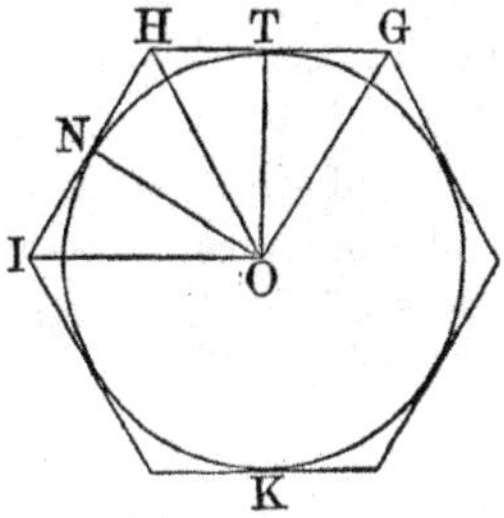

For, the triangle GOH is measured by $GH\times\frac{1}{2}OT$; the triangle OHI, by $HI\times\frac{1}{2}ON$: but $ON=OT$; hence, the two triangles taken together are measured by

$$(GH+HI)\times\tfrac{1}{2}OT.$$

And, by finding the measures of the other triangles, it will appear that the sum of them all, or the whole polygon, is measured by the sum of the bases GH, HI, &c., or, the perimeter of the polygon, multiplied by one-half of OT; that is, the area of the polygon is equal to its perimeter multiplied by half the radius of the inscribed circle.

PROPOSITION IX. THEOREM.

The perimeters of regular polygons, having the same number of sides, are to each other as the radii of the circumscribed circles; and also, as the radii of the inscribed circles; and their areas are to each other as the squares of those radii.

Let AB be the side of one polygon, O the centre, and consequently OA the radius of the circumscribed circle, and OD, perpendicular to AB, the radius of the inscribed circle. Let ab, be a side of the other polygon, o the centre, oa and od, the radii of the circumscribed and the inscribed circles.

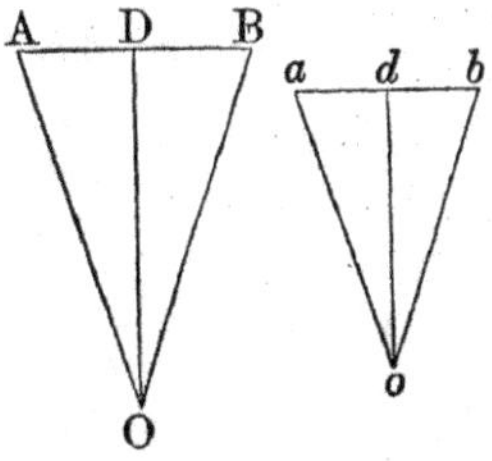

Then, the perimeters of the two polygons are to each other as the sides AB and ab (B. IV., P. 27): but the angles A and a are equal, being each half of the angle of the polygon; so also are the angles B and b; hence, the triangles ABO, abo, are similar, as are, likewise, the right-angled triangles ADO, ado; therefore,

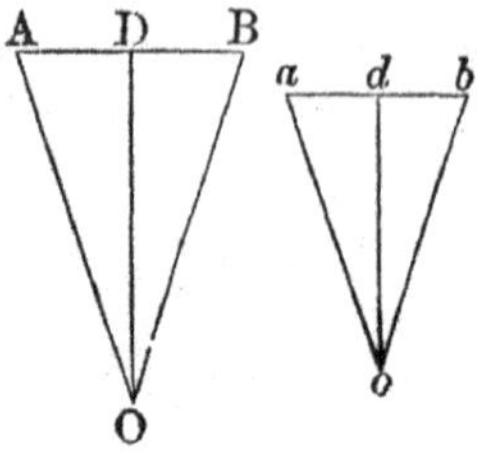

$$AB : ab :: AO : ao :: DO : do;$$

hence, the perimeters of the polygons are to each other as the radii AO, ao, of the circumscribed circles, and also, as the radii DO, do, of the inscribed circles.

The surfaces of these polygons are to each other as the squares of the homologous sides AB, ab (B. IV., P. 27); they are therefore likewise to each other as the squares of AO, ao, the radii of the circumscribed circles, or as the squares of OD, od, the radii of the inscribed circles.

PROPOSITION X. THEOREM.

Two regular polygons, of the same number of sides, can always be formed, the one circumscribed about a circle, the other inscribed in it, which shall differ from each other by less than any given surface.

Let Q be the side of a square less than the given surface. Bisect AC, a fourth part of the circumference, and then bisect the half of this fourth, and proceed in this manner, always bisecting one of the arcs formed by the last bisection, until an arc is found whose chord AB is less than Q. As this arc will be an exact part of the circumference, if we apply the chords AB, BC, CD, &c., each equal to AB, the last will terminate at A, and there will be formed a regular polygon $ABCDE$ &c., inscribed in the circle.

Next, describe about the circle a similar polygon $abcde$ &c. (P. 7): the difference of these two polygons will be less than the square of Q.

For, from the points a and b, draw the lines aO, bO, to the centre O: they will pass through the points A and B (P. 7). Draw also OK to the point of contact K: it will bisect AB in I, and be perpendicular to it (B. III., P. 6, S.) Prolong AO to E, and draw BE.

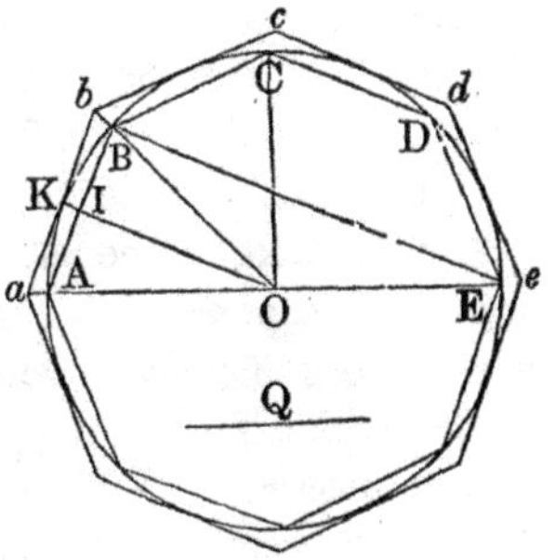

Let p represent the circumscribed polygon, and P the inscribed polygon: then since the triangles aOb, AOB, are like parts of p and P, we have (B. II., P. 11),

$$p : P :: aOb :: AOB.$$

But, since the triangles are similar (B. IV., P. 25),

$$p : P :: \overline{Oa}^2 : \overline{OA}^2 :: \overline{OK}^2 \text{ or } \overline{OA}^2 : \overline{OI}^2$$

Hence, by division,

$$p : p-P :: \overline{OA}^2 : \overline{OA}^2 - \overline{OI}^2 :: \overline{OA}^2 : \overline{AI}^2.$$

Multiplying both members of the second couplet by 4,

$$p : p-P :: 4\overline{OA}^2 : 4\overline{AI}^2;$$

hence, $p : p-P :: \overline{AE}^2 : \overline{AB}^2$ (B. 10, P. 8, COR.)

But p is less than the square described on the diameter AE (P. 7, C. 4); therefore, $p-P$ is less than the square described on AB: that is, less than the given square on Q: hence, the difference between the circumscribed and inscribed polygons may, by increasing the number of sides, always be made less than any given surface.

PROPOSITION XI. PROBLEM.

The surface of a regular inscribed polygon, and that of a similar circumscribed polygon, being given; to find the surfaces of the regular inscribed and circumscribed polygons having double the number of sides.

Let AB be a side of the given inscribed polygon; EF, parallel to AB, a side of the circumscribed polygon, and C the centre of the circle. If the chord AM and the tangents AP, BQ, be drawn, AM will be a side of an inscribed polygon, having twice the number of sides, and $AP+PM=2PM$ or PQ, will be a side of the similar circumscribed polygon (P. 7, C. 3).

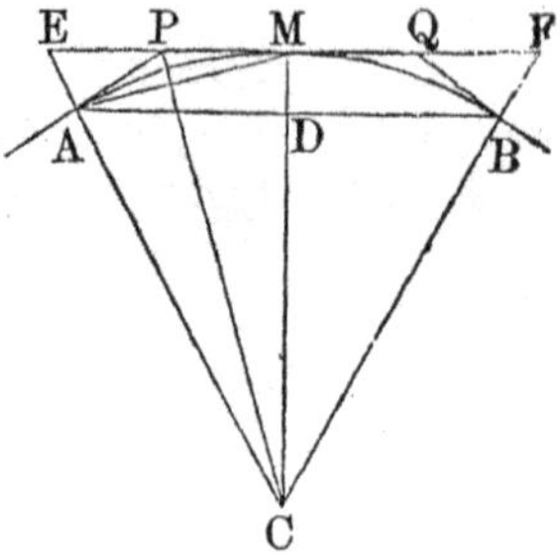

Now, as the same construction will take place at each angle corresponding to ACM, it will be sufficient to consider ACM by itself; for the triangles connected with it are evidently to each other as the whole polygons of which they form part. Let P, then, be the surface of the inscribed polygon whose side is AB, p, that of the similar circumscribed polygon; P' the surface of the polygon whose side is AM, p' that of the similar circumscribed polygon: P and p are given; we have to find P' and p'.

First. Now the triangles ACD, ACM, having the common vertex A, are to each other as their bases CD, CM (B. IV., P. 6, C.); they are likewise to each other as the polygons P and P', of which they form part (B. II., P. 11): hence,

$$P : P' :: CD : CM.$$

Again, the triangles CAM, CME, having the common vertex M, are to each other as their bases CA, CE; they are likewise to each other as the polygons P' and p of which they form part; hence,

$$P' : p :: CA : CE.$$

But since AD and ME are parallel, we have,

$$CD : CM :: CA : CE;$$

hence, $$P : P' :: P' : p;$$

hence, the polygon P' is a mean proportional between the two given polygons P and p, and consequently,

$$P' = \sqrt{P \times p}.$$

Secondly. The altitude CM being common, the triangle CPM is to the triangle CPE, as PM is to PE; but since CP bisects the angle MCE, we have (B. IV., P. 17),

$$PM : PE :: CM : CE :: CD : CA :: P : P';$$

hence, $$CPM : CPE :: P : P';$$

and consequently,

$$CPM : CPM+CPE, \text{ or } CME :: P : P+P';$$

and hence, $2CPM$, or $CMPA : CME :: 2P : P+P'$.

But $CMPA$ is to CME as the polygons p' and p, of which they form part: hence,

$$p' : p :: 2P : P+P'.$$

Now as P' has been already determined; this new proportion will serve to determine p', and give us

$$p' = \frac{2P \times p}{P+P'};$$

and thus by means of the polygons P and p it is easy to find the polygons P' and p', which have double the number of sides.

PROPOSITION XII. PROBLEM.

To find the approximate area of a circle whose radius is unity.

Let the radius of the circle be 1; the side of the inscribed square will be $\sqrt{2}$ (P. 3, s.); that of the circumscribed square will be equal to the diameter 2; hence, the surface of the inscribed square will be two, and that of the circumscribed square will be 4. Hence, $P=2$, and $p=4$; by the last proposition we shall find the

inscribed octagon $P'=\sqrt{8}=2.8284271$,

circumscribed octagon $p'=\dfrac{16}{2+\sqrt{8}}=3.3137085$.

The inscribed and the circumscribed octagons being thus determined, we shall easily, by means of them, determine the polygons having twice the number of sides. We have only in this case to put $P=2.8284271$, $p=3.3137085$; we shall find

$$P'=\sqrt{P \times p}=3.0614674,$$

$$p'=\frac{2P \times p}{P+P'}=3.1825979.$$

These polygons of 16 sides will enable us to find the polygons of 32 sides; and the processes may be continued until the difference between the inscribed and circumscribed polygons is less than any given surface (P. 10). Since the circle lies between the polygons, it will differ from either polygon by less than the polygons differ from each other: and hence, in so far as the figures which express the areas of the two polygons agree, they will be the true figures to express the area of the circle.

We have subjoined the computation of these polygons, carried on till they agree as far as the seventh place of decimals.

Number of Sides.	Inscribed Polygons.	Circumscribed Polygons
4	2.0000000	4.0000000
8	2.8284271	3.3137085
16	3.0614674	3.1825979
32	3.1214451	3.1517249
64	3.1365485	3.1441184
128	3.1403311	3.1422236
256	3.1412772	3.1417504
512	3.1415138	3.1416321
1024	3.1415729	3.1416025
2048	3.1415877	3.1415951
4096	3.1415914	3.1415933
8192	3.1415923	3.1415928
16384	3.1415925	3.1415927
32768	3.1415926	3.1415926

The approximate area of the circle, we infer, therefore, is equal to 3.1415926. Some doubt may exist perhaps about the last decimal figure, owing to errors proceeding from the parts omitted; but the calculation has been carried on with an additional figure, that the final result here given might be absolutely correct even to the last decimal place. The number generally used, for computation, is 3.1416, a number very near the true area.

Scholium 1. Since the inscribed polygon has the same number of sides as the circumscribed polygon, and since the two polygons are regular, they will be similar (P. 1): and, therefore, when their areas approach to an equality with the circle, their perimeters will approach to an equality with the circumference.

Scholium 2. That magnitude to which a varying magnitude approaches continually, and which it cannot pass, is called a *limit.*

Having shown that the inscribed and circumscribed polygons may be made to differ from each other by less than any given surface (P. 10), and since each differs from the circle less than from the other polygon, it follows that the circle is the limit of all inscribed and circumscribed polygons, formed by continually doubling the number of sides, and that the circumference is the limit of their perimeters. Hence, no sensible error can arise in supposing that what is true of such a polygon is also true of its limit, the circle. Indeed, the circle is but a regular polygon of an infinite number of sides.

PROPOSITION XIII. THEOREM.

The circumferences of circles are to each other as their radii, and the areas are to each other as the squares of their radii.

Let us designate the circumference of the circle whose radius is CA by *circ.* CA; and its area, by *area* CA: it is then to be shown that

$$circ.\ CA : circ.\ OB :: CA : OB, \text{ and that}$$
$$area\ CA : area\ OB :: \overline{CA}^2 : \overline{OB}^2.$$

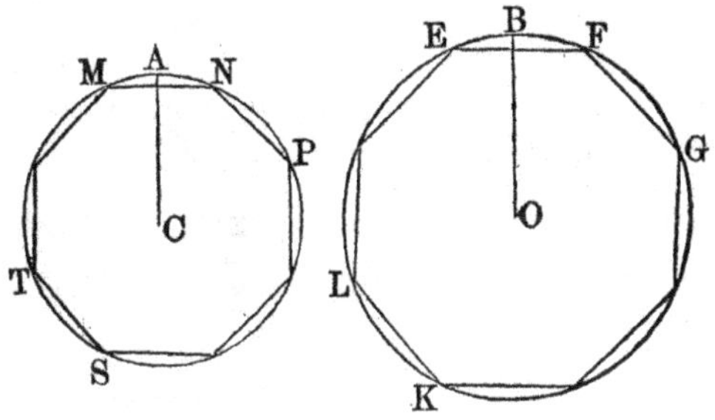

Inscribe within the circles two regular polygons of the same number of sides. Then, whatever be the number of sides, their perimeters will be to each other as the radii CA and OB (P. 9). Now, if the arcs subtended by the sides

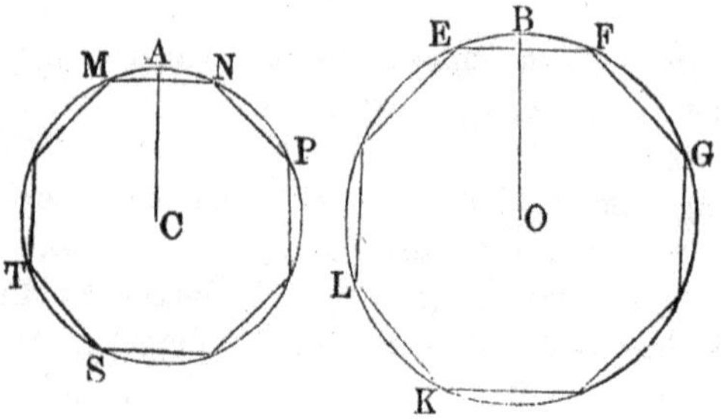

of the polygons be continually bisected, and corresponding polygons formed, the perimeter of each new polygon will approach the circumference of the circumscribed circle, and at the limit (P. 12, s. 2), we shall have

$$\textit{circ. } CA \;:\; \textit{circ. } OB \;::\; CA \;:\; OB.$$

Again, the areas of the inscribed polygons are to each other as $\overline{CA}^2$ to $\overline{OB}^2$ (P. 9). But when the number of sides of the polygons is increased, as before, at the limit we shall have

$$\textit{area } CA \;:\; \textit{area } OB \;::\; \overline{CA}^2 \;:\; \overline{OB}^2.$$

Cor. 1. It is plain that the limit of any portion of the perimeter of an inscribed regular polygon lying between the vertices of two angles, is the corresponding arc of the circumscribed circle. Thus, the limit of the portion of the perimeter intercepted between G and E is the arc GFE.

Cor. 2. If we multiply the antecedent and consequent of the second couplet of the first proportion by 2, and of the second by 4, we shall have

$$\textit{circ. } CA \;:\; \textit{circ. } OB \;::\; 2CA \;:\; 2OB;$$

and $$\textit{area } CA \;:\; \textit{area } OB \;::\; \overline{4CA}^2 \;:\; \overline{4OB}^2;$$

that is, *the circumferences of circles are to each other as their diameters, and their areas are to each other as the squares of their diameters.*

PROPOSITION XIV. THEOREM.

Similar arcs are to each other as their radii. and similar sectors are to each other as the squares of their radii.

Let AB, DE, be similar arcs, and ACB, DOE, similar sectors: then

$$AB : DE :: CA : OD;$$

and $$ACB : DOE :: \overline{CA}^2 : \overline{OD}^2.$$

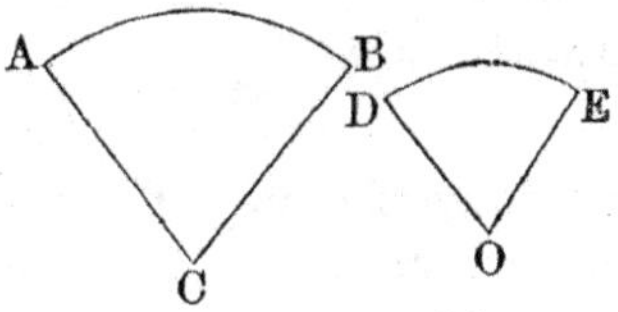

For, since the arcs are similar, the angle C is equal to the angle O (B. IV., D. 6). But we have (B. III., P. 17),

angle C : 4 right angles :: AB : *circ.* CA,

and, angle O : 4 right angles :: DE : *circ.* OD;

hence (B. II., P. 4, C.),

$$AB : DE :: circ.\ CA : circ.\ OD;$$

but these circumferences are as the radii AC, DO (P. 13); hence,

$$AB : DE :: CA : OD.$$

For a like reason, the sectors ACB, DOE, are to each other as the whole circles: which again are as the squares of their radii (P. 13); therefore,

$$sect.\ ACB : sect.\ DOE :: \overline{CA}^2 : \overline{OD}^2.$$

PROPOSITION XV. THEOREM.

The area of a circle is equal to the product of half the radius by the circumference.

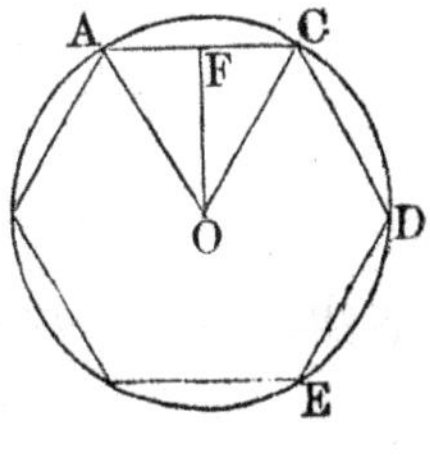

Let $ACDE$ be a circle whose centre is O and radius OA: then will

$$area\ OA = \tfrac{1}{2}OA \times circ.\ OA.$$

For, inscribe in the circle any regular polygon, and draw OF perpendicular to one of its sides. The area of

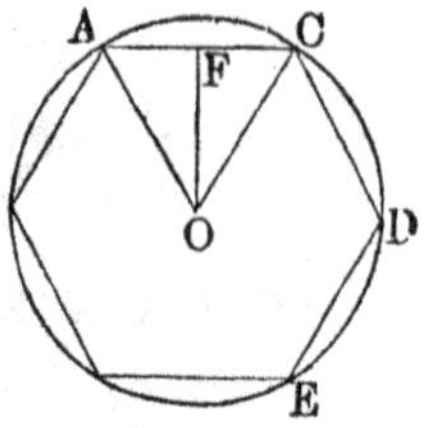

the polygon is equal to $\frac{1}{2}OF$, multiplied by the perimeter (P. 8). Now, let the arcs which are subtended by the sides of the polygon be bisected and new polygons formed as before: the limit of the perimeter is the circumference of the circle; the limit of the apothem is the radius OA, and the limit of the area of the polygon is the area of the circle (P. 12, s. 2). Passing to the limit, the expression for the area becomes

$$\textit{area } OA = \tfrac{1}{2}OA \times \textit{circ. } OA\,;$$

consequently, the area of a circle is equal to the product of half the radius by the circumference.

Cor. The area of a sector is equal to the arc of the sector multiplied by half the radius.

For, we have (B. III., P. 17, S. 4),

$$\textit{sect. } ACB : \textit{area } CA :: AMB : \textit{circ. } CA\,;$$

or, $\textit{sect. } ACB : \textit{area } CA :: AMB \times \frac{1}{2}CA : \textit{circ. } CA \times \frac{1}{2}CA$.

But, $\textit{circ. } CA \times \frac{1}{2}CA$ is equal to the area CA; hence, $AMB \times \frac{1}{2}CA$ is equal to the area of the sector.

PROPOSITION XVI. THEOREM.

The area of a circle is equal to the square of the radius multiplied by the ratio of the diameter to the circumference.

Let the circumference of the circle whose diameter is unity be denoted by π: then, since the diameters of circles are to each other as their circumferences (P. 13, C. 2), π will denote the ratio of any diameter to its circumference. We shall then have

$$1 : \pi :: 2CA : \textit{circ. } CA :$$

therefore, $\textit{circ. } CA = \pi \times 2CA$.

Multiplying both members by $\frac{1}{2}CA$, we have

$$\tfrac{1}{2}CA \times \textit{circ. } CA = \pi \times \overline{CA}^2,$$

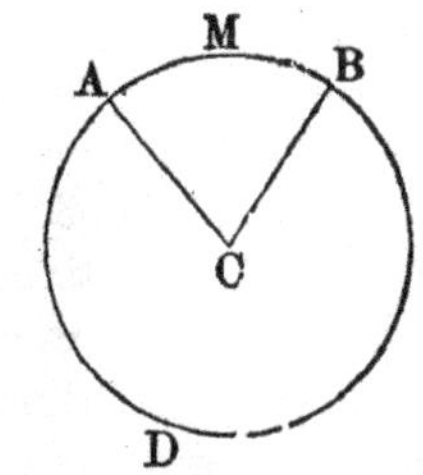

or (P. 15) *area* $CA = \pi \times \overline{CA}^2$, that is, *the area of a circle is equal to π into the square of the radius.*

Scholium 1. Let $CA = R$, and *area* $CA = A$: then, $A = \pi R^2$, making $CA = 1$; we shall have

$$\text{area } CA = \pi.$$

But we have found the area of the circle whose radius is 1 to be 3.1415926 (P. 12): therefore, we have

$$\pi = 3.1415926.$$

In common calculations, we take $\pi = 3.1416$.

Scholium 2. The problem of the quadrature of the circle, as it is called, consists in finding a square equivalent in surface to a circle, the radius of which is known. Now it has just been proved, that a circle is equivalent to the rectangle contained by its circumference and half its radius (P. 15); and this rectangle may be changed into an equivalent square, by finding a mean proportional between its length and its breadth (B. IV., PROB. 3). To square the circle, therefore, is to find the circumference when the radius is given; and for effecting this, it is enough to know the ratio of the diameter to the circumference.

Hitherto the ratio in question has never been determined except approximatively; but the approximation has been carried so far, that a knowledge of the exact ratio would afford no real advantage whatever beyond that of the approximate ratio. Accordingly, this problem, which engaged geometers so deeply, when their methods of approximation were less perfect, is now degraded to the rank of those idle questions, with which no one possessing the slightest tincture of geometrical science, will occupy any portion of his time.

Archimedes showed that the ratio of the diameter to the circumference is included between $3\frac{10}{70}$ and $3\frac{10}{71}$; hence, $3\frac{1}{7}$ or $\frac{22}{7}$ affords at once a pretty accurate approximation to the number above designated by π; and the simplicity of this first approximation has brought it into very general use. *Metius*, for the same quantity, found the much more accurate value $\frac{355}{113}$. At last, the value of π, developed to a certain order of decimals, was found by other calculators to be 3.1415926535897932 &c.: and some have had patience enough to continue these decimals to the hundred and twenty-seventh, or even to the hundred and fortieth place. Such an approximation is practically equivalent to perfect accuracy: the root of an imperfect power is in no case more accurately known.

PROPOSITION XVII. THEOREM.

*If the circumferences of two circles intersect each other, the arc of the common chord in the less circle will be longer than the corresponding arc of the greater.**

Let A and B be the centres of two circles, AC, BC, their radii, C and D the points in which their circumferences intersect and CD their common chord: then will the arc DEC described with the radius BC, be longer than the arc DFC described with the greater radius AC.

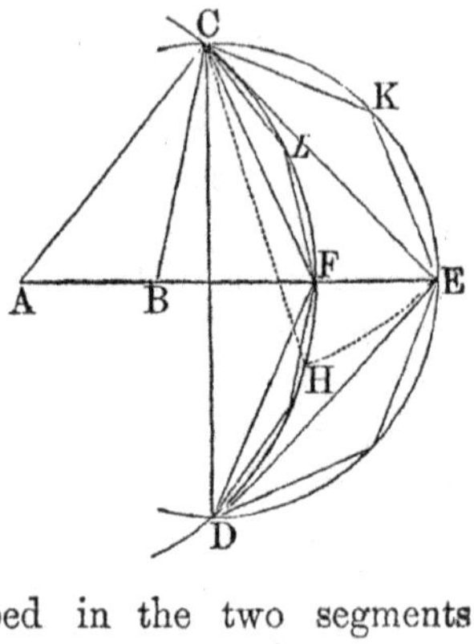

Join the centres A and B, and prolong AB to E. Then, since AB bisects the chord CD at right angles (B. III., P. 11); it also bisects the arcs at the points F and E (B. III., P. 6). Draw CE and DE which will be equal to each other (B. III., P. 4); also CF and DF.

Bisect the arcs CE, ED, and also the arcs CF, FD, and draw chords subtending the new arcs: there will thus be inscribed in the two segments DEC, DFC, regular portions of two polygons, having the same number of sides in each.

Now, since the point F is within the triangle DEC,

* The arc considered in this demonstration is the one which is less than a semicircle.

EC plus *ED* is greater than *CF* plus *FD* (B. I., P. 8): hence, the half, *CE* is greater than the half, *CF*. If now, with *C* as a centre, and *CE* as a radius, we describe an arc *EH*, the chord *CE* being greater than *CF*, the arc *CFH* will be greater than the arc *CF* (B. III., P. 5). If we suppose the arc *CKE* to move with the chord *CE* then, when the chord *CE* becomes the chord *CH*, the arc *CKE* will pass through the points *C* and *H*, and will have with *CFH*, the common chord *CH*.

If, now, we bisect the arc which is equal to *CKE*, and also the arc *CFH*, we know from what has already been shown, that the chord of half the outer arc will be greater than the chord of half the inner arc *CFH*, much more will it be greater than the chord of *CL*, which is half the arc *CF*; that is, the chord of the arc *CK*, one-half of *CE*, will always be greater than the chord of the arc *CL*, one-half of *CF*. Hence, the perimeter of that portion of the polygon inscribed in the segment *CED*, will be greater than the perimeter of the corresponding polygon inscribed in the segment *CFD*. If, then, we continue the operations indefinitely, the limit of the outer perimeter will be the arc *CED*, and of the inner, the arc *CFD*: hence, the arc *CED* is greater than the arc *CFD*.

Cor. If equal chords be taken in unequal circles, the arc of the chord in the greatest circle will be the shortest; for, the circles may always be placed as in the figure.

BOOK VI.

PLANES AND POLYEDRAL ANGLES.

DEFINITIONS.

1. A straight line is *perpendicular to a plane*, when it is perpendicular to every straight line of the plane which passes through its foot: conversely, the plane is perpendicular to the line. The point at which the perpendicular meets the plane, is called the *foot* of the perpendicular.

2. A line *is parallel to a plane*, when it cannot meet that plane, to what distance soever both be produced. Conversely, the plane is parallel to the line.

3. Two *planes* are *parallel* when they cannot meet, to what distance soever both be produced.

4. The indefinite space lying between two planes which intersect each other, is called a *diedral angle:* the planes are called the *faces* of the angle, and their line of common intersection, the *edge* of the angle.

The *measure* of a *diedral angle* is the same as that of the plane angle contained between two lines, one drawn in each face, and both perpendicular to the common intersection at the same point. This angle may be acute, obtuse, or a right angle. If it is a right angle, the two *faces* are perpendicular to each other.

5. A POLYEDRAL angle is the indefinite space included by several plane angles meeting at a common point. Each plane angle is called a *face:* the line in which any two faces intersect, is called an *edge:* and the common point of meeting of all the plane angles, is called the *vertex* of the polyedral angle.

Thus, the polyedral angle whose vertex is S, is bounded by the four faces, ASB, BSC, CSD, DSA. Three planes, at least, are necessary to form a polyedral angle.

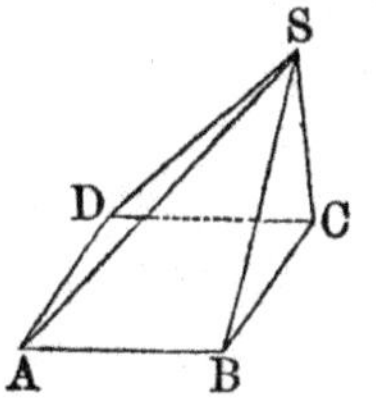

A polyedral angle bounded by three planes, is called a *triedral angle.*

POSTULATES.

1. Let it be granted, that from a given point of a plane, a line may be drawn perpendicular to that plane.

2. Let it be granted, that from a given point without a plane, a perpendicular may be let fall on the plane.

PROPOSITION I. THEOREM.

A straight line cannot be partly in a plane, and partly out of it.

For, by the definition of a plane (B. I., D. 9), when a straight line has two points common with it, the line lies wholly in the plane.

Scholium. To discover whether a surface is plane, apply a straight line in different ways to that surface, and ascertain if it coincides with the surface throughout its whole extent.

PROPOSITION II. THEOREM.

Two straight lines which intersect each other, lie in the same plane, and determine its position.

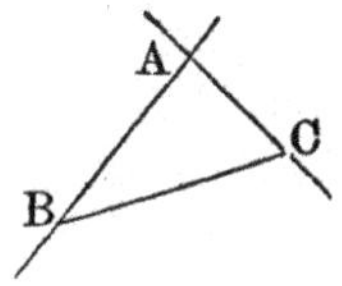

Let AB, AC, be two straight lines which intersect each other in A; a plane may be conceived in which the straight line AB is found; if this plane be turned round AB, until it pass through the point C, then the line AC, which has two of its points A and C, in this plane, lies wholly in it; hence, the position of the plane is determined by the single condition of containing the two straight lines AB, AC.

Cor. 1. Any three points *A*, *B*, *C*, not in a straight line, determine the position of a plane. Hence, a triangle *BAC*, determines the position of a plane.

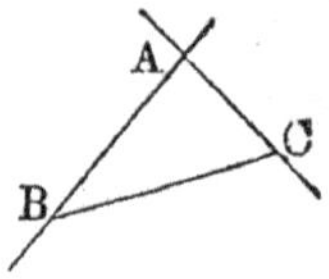

Cor. 2. Hence, also, two parallels *AB*, *CD*, determine the position of a plane; for, drawing the secant *EF*, the plane of the two straight lines *AE*, *EF*, is that of the parallels *AB*, *CD*. But the lines *AE*, *EF*, determine this plane; therefore, so do the parallels, *AB*, *CD*.

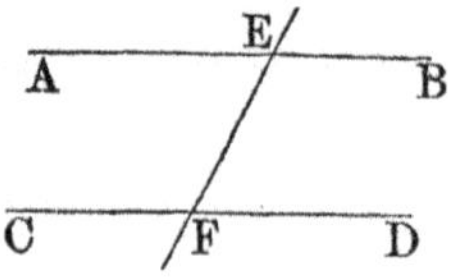

PROPOSITION III. THEOREM.

If two planes meet one another, their common intersection will be a straight line.

Let the two planes *AB*, *CD*, cut one another, and let *E* and *F* be two points of their common section. Draw the straight line *EF*. This line lies wholly in the plane *AB*, and also, wholly in the plane *CD* (B. I., D. 9): therefore, it is in both planes at once. But since a straight line and a point out of it cannot lie in two planes at the same time (P. II., C. 1), *EF* contains all the points common to both planes, and consequently, is their common intersection.

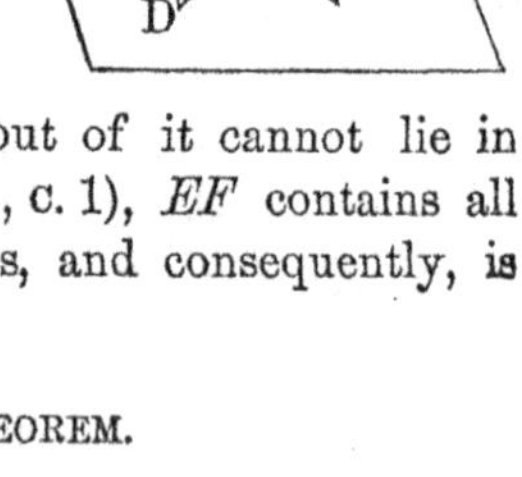

PROPOSITION IV. THEOREM.

If a straight line be perpendicular to two straight lines at their point of intersection, it will be perpendicular to the plane of those lines.

Let *MN* be the plane of the two lines *BB*, *CC*, and let *AP* be perpendicular to each of them at their point of intersection *P*; then will *AP* be perpendicular to every line of the plane passing through *P*, and consequently to the plane itself (D. 1).

For, through P draw in the plane MN, any straight line as PQ. Through any point of this line, as Q, draw BQC, so that BQ shall be equal to QC (B. IV., PROB. 5); draw AB, AQ, AC.

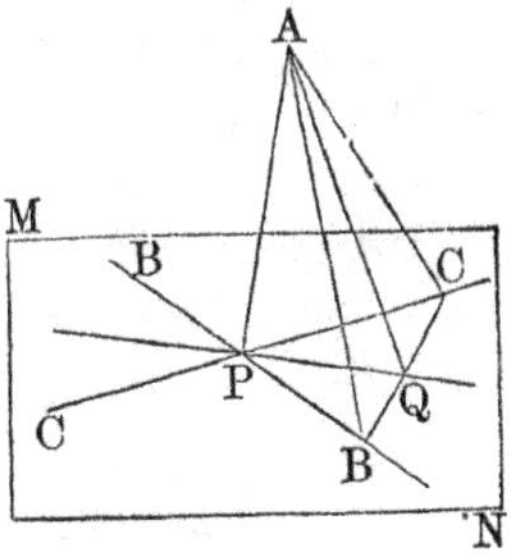

The base BC being divided into two equal parts at the point Q, the triangle BPC gives (B. IV., P. 14).

$$\overline{PC}^2+\overline{PB}^2 \asymp 2\overline{PQ}^2+2\overline{QC}^2.$$

The triangle BAC in like manner gives,

$$\overline{AC}^2+\overline{AB}^2 \asymp 2\overline{AQ}^2+2\overline{QC}^2.$$

Taking the first of these equals from the second, and observing that the triangles APC, APB, being right-angled at P, give

$$\overline{AC}^2-\overline{PC}^2 \asymp \overline{AP}^2, \text{ and } \overline{AB}^2-\overline{PB}^2 \asymp \overline{AP}^2,$$

we shall have,

$$\overline{AP}^2+\overline{AP}^2 \asymp 2\overline{AQ}^2-2\overline{PQ}^2.$$

Therefore, by taking the halves of both, we have

$$\overline{AP}^2 \asymp \overline{AQ}^2-\overline{PQ}^2, \text{ or } \overline{AQ}^2 \asymp \overline{AP}^2+\overline{PQ}^2;$$

hence, the triangle APQ is right-angled at P; hence, AP is perpendicular to PQ.

Scholium. Thus, it is evident, not only that a straight line may be perpendicular to all the straight lines which pass through its foot, in a plane, but that it always must be so, whenever it is perpendicular to two straight lines drawn in the plane: hence, a line and plane may fulfil the conditions of the first definition.

Cor. 1. The perpendicular AP is shorter than any oblique line AQ; therefore, it measures the shortest distance from the point A to the plane MN.

Cor. 2. At a given point P, on a plane, it is impossible to erect more than one perpendicular to the plane; for, if there could be two perpendiculars at the same point P, draw through these two perpendiculars a plane, whose section with the plane MN is PQ; then these two perpendiculars would be both perpendicular to the line PQ, at the same point, which is impossible (B. I., P. 14, C.)

It is also impossible to let fall from a given point, out of a plane, two perpendiculars to that plane; for, if AP, AQ, be two such perpendiculars, the triangle APQ will have two right angles APQ, AQP, which is impossible (B. I., P. 25, C. 3).

PROPOSITION V. THEOREM.

If, from a point without a plane, a perpendicular be drawn to the plane, and oblique lines be drawn to its different points:

1st. *The oblique lines which meet the plane at points equally distant from the foot of the perpendicular, are equal:*

2d *Of two oblique lines which meet the plane at unequal distances, the one passing through the remote point is the longer.*

Let AP be perpendicular to the plane MN; AB, AC, AD, oblique lines intercepting the equal distances PB, PC, PD, and AE a line intercepting the larger distance PE: then will $AB=AC=AD$; and AE will be greater than AD.

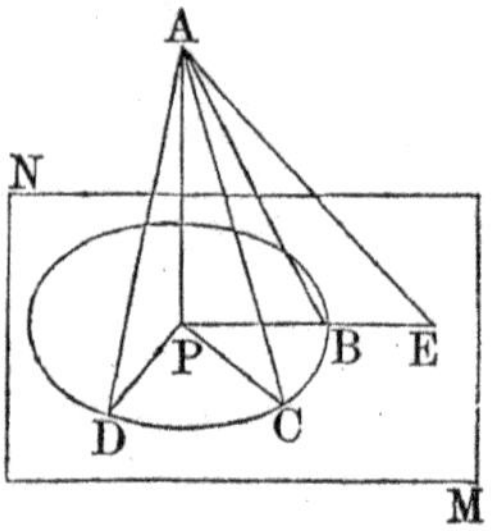

For, the angles APB, APC, APD, being right angles, and the distances PB, PC, PD, equal to each other, the triangles APB, APC, APD, have in each an equal angle contained by two equal sides: therefore they are equal (B. I., P. 5); hence, the hypothenuses, or the oblique lines AB, AC, AD, are equal to each other.

Again, since the distance PE is greater than PD, or its equal PB, the oblique line AE is greater than AB, or its equal AD (B. 1, P. 15).

Cor. All the equal oblique lines, AB, AC, AD, &c., terminate in the circumference BCD, described from P, the foot of the perpendicular, as a centre; therefore, a point A being given out of a plane, the point P at which the perpendicular let fall from A would meet that plane, may be found by marking upon that plane three points, B, C, D, equally distant from the point A, and then finding the centre of the circle which passes through these points; this centre will be P, the point sought.

Scholium. The angle ABP is called the *inclination of the oblique line AB to the plane MN*; which inclination is evidently equal with respect to all such lines AB, AC, AD, as make equal angles with the perpendicular; for, all the triangles ABP, ACP, ADP, &c., are equal to each other.

PROPOSITION VI. THEOREM.

If from the foot of a perpendicular a line be drawn at right angles to any line of a plane, and the point of intersection be joined with any point of the perpendicular, this last line will be perpendicular to the line of the plane.

Let AP be perpendicular to the plane NM, and PD perpendicular to BC; join D with any point of the perpendicular, as A; then will AD also be perpendicular to BC.

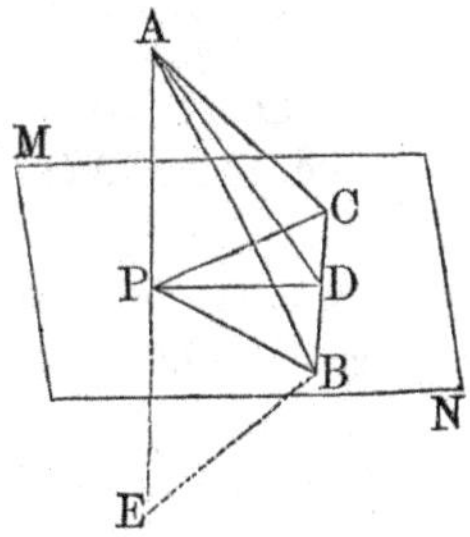

Take $DB = DC$, and draw PB, PC, AB, AC. Now, since DB is equal to DC, the oblique line PB is equal to PC (B. 1, P. 5): and since PB is equal to PC, the oblique line AB is equal to AC (P. 5); therefore, the line AD has two of its points A and D equally distant from the extremities B and C; therefore, AD is a perpendicular to BC, at its middle point D (B. I., P. 16, C.)

Cor. It is evident, likewise, that BC is perpendicular to the plane of the triangle APD, since it is perpendicular to the two straight lines AD, PD of that plane (P. 4).

Scholium 1. The two lines AE, BC, afford an instance of two lines which are not parallel, and yet do not meet, because they are not situated in the same plane. The shortest distance between these lines is the straight line PD, which is at once perpendicular to the line AP and to the line BC. The distance PD is the shortest distance between them: because, if we join any other two points, such as A and B, we shall have $AB>AD$, $AD>PD$; therefore, still more, $AB>PD$.

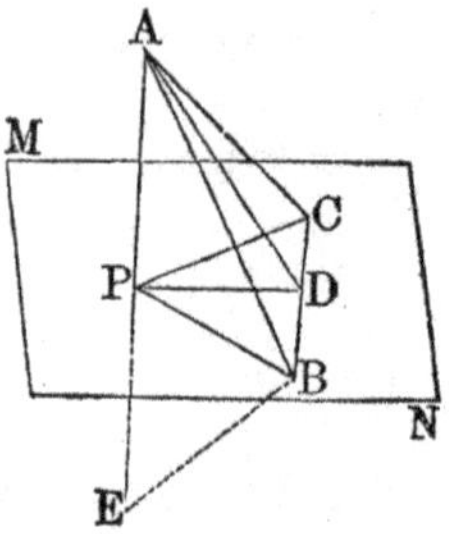

Scholium 2. The two lines AE, CB, though not situated in the same plane, are conceived as forming a right angle with each other; because AE and the line drawn through any one of its points parallel to BC, would make with each other a right angle. In the same manner, AB, PD, which represent any two straight lines not situated in the same plane, are supposed to form with each other the same angle, as would be formed by AB and a straight line drawn through any point of AB, parallel to PD.

PROPOSITION VII. THEOREM.

If one of two parallel lines be perpendicular to a plane, the other will also be perpendicular to the same plane.

Let ED, AP, be two parallel lines; if AP is perpendicular to the plane NM, then will ED be also perpendicular to it.

For, through the parallels AP, DE, pass a plane; its intersection with the plane MN will be PD; in the plane MN draw BD perpendicular to PD, and then draw AD.

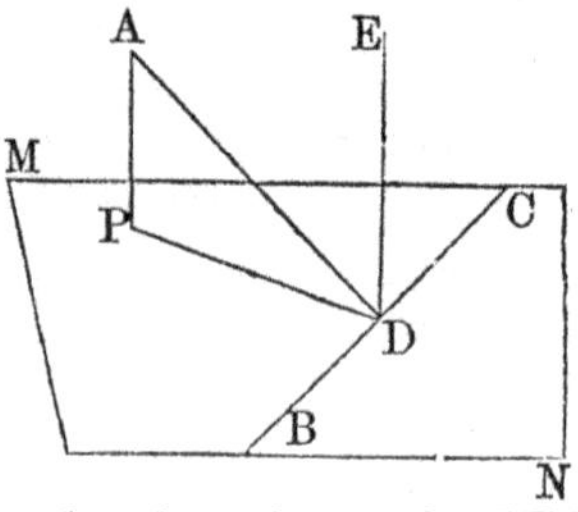

Now, BD is perpendicular to the plane $APDE$ (P. 6, C.) therefore, the angle BDE is a right angle; but the angle EDP is also a right angle, since AP is perpendicular to PD, and DE parallel to AP (B. I., P. 20, C. 1); therefore, the line DE is perpendicular to the two straight lines DP, DB; consequently it is perpendicular to their plane MN (P. 4).

Cor. 1. Conversely: if the straight lines AP, DE, are perpendicular to the same plane MN, they will be parallel. For, if they be not parallel, draw, through the point D, a line parallel to AP, this parallel will be perpendicular to the plane MN, therefore, through the same point D more than one perpendicular will be erected to the same plane, which is impossible (P. 4, C. 2).

Cor. 2. Two lines A and B, parallel to a third C, are parallel to each other; for, conceive a plane perpendicular to the line C; the lines A and B, being parallel to C, are perpendicular to this plane; therefore, by the preceding corollary, they are parallel to each other.

The three parallels are supposed not to be in the same plane; otherwise the proposition would be already proved. (B. I., P. 22).

PROPOSITION VIII. THEOREM.

If a straight line is parallel to a line of a plane, it is parallel to the plane.

Let the straight line AB be parallel to the line CD of the plane NM; then will it be parallel to the plane NM.

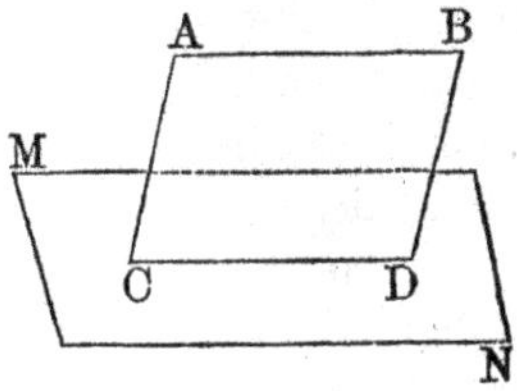

For, if the line AB, which lies in the plane $ABDC$, could meet the plane MN, it could only be in some point of the line CD, the common intersection of the two planes; but the line AB cannot meet CD, since they are parallel (B. I., D. 16): hence, it will not meet the plane MN; therefore, it is parallel to that plane (D. 2).

PROPOSITION IX. THEOREM.

Two planes which are perpendicular to the same straight line are parallel to each other.

Let the planes MN, PQ, be perpendicular to the line AB, then will they be parallel.

For, if they can meet any where, let O be one of their common points, and draw OA, OB. Now, the line AB, which is perpendicular to the plane MN, is perpendicular to the straight line OA, drawn through its foot in that plane (D. 1); for the same reason AB is perpendicular to BO; therefore, there are two perpendiculars, OA and OB, let fall from the same point O, upon the same straight line, which is impossible (B. I., P. 14); therefore, the planes MN, PQ, cannot meet each other; consequently, they are parallel.

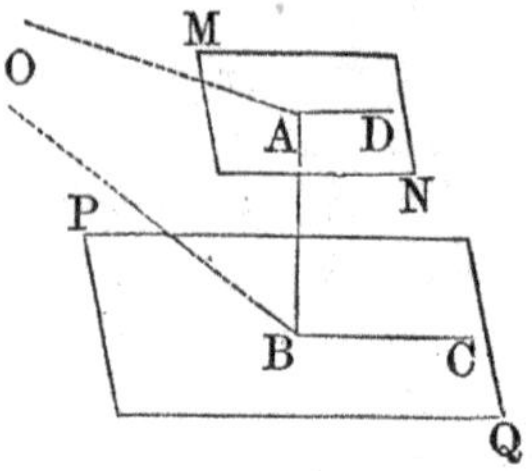

PROPOSITION X. THEOREM.

If a plane cut two parallel planes, the lines of intersection will be parallel.

Let the parallel planes NM, QP, be intersected by the plane EH; then will the lines of intersection EF, GH, be parallel.

For, if the lines EF, GH, lying in the same plane, were not parallel, they would meet each other when prolonged; and then the planes MN, PQ, in which those lines lie, would also meet; and hence, the planes would not be parallel, which is contrary to the hypothesis.

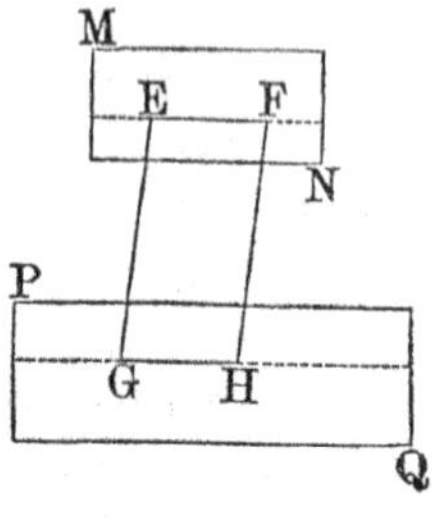

PROPOSITION XI. THEOREM.

If two planes are parallel, a straight line which is perpendicular to one, is also perpendicular to the other.

Let MN, PQ, be two parallel planes, and let AB be perpendicular to the plane NM; then will it also be perpendicular to QP.

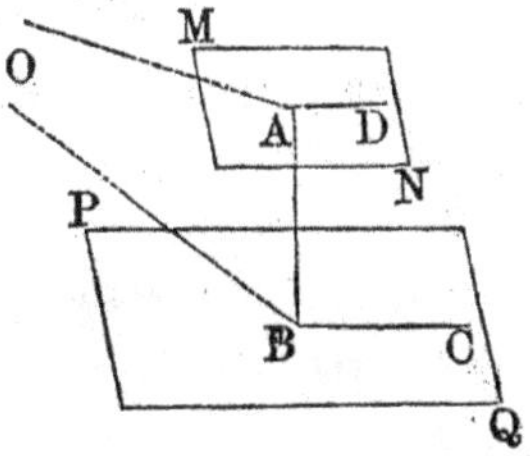

For, draw any line BC in the plane PQ, and through the lines AB and BC, pass a plane ABC, intersecting the plane MN in AD; the intersection AD is parallel to BC (P. 10). But the line AB, being perpendicular to the plane MN, is perpendicular to the straight line AD (D. 1); therefore, also, to its parallel BC (B. I., P. 20, C. 1); hence, the line AB being perpendicular to any line BC, drawn through its foot in the plane PQ, is perpendicular to that plane (D. 1).

PROPOSITION XII. THEOREM.

All parallels included between two parallel planes are equal.

Let MN, PQ, be two parallel planes, and HF, GE, two parallel lines: then will $GE=HF$.

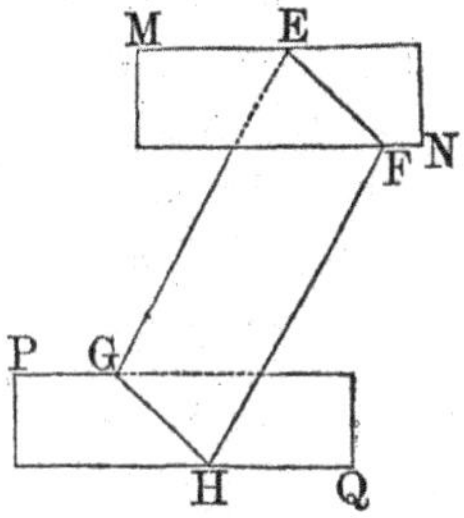

For, through the parallels GE, HF, draw the plane $EGHF$, intersecting the parallel planes in EF and GH. The intersections EF, GH, are parallel to each other (P. 10); and since GE, HF are parallel, the figure $EGHF$ is a parallelogram; consequently, $EG=FH$ (B. I., P. 28).

Cor. Hence, it follows, that *two parallel planes are everywhere equidistant.* For, suppose EG to be perpendicular to the plane PQ; then, the parallel FH is also perpendicular to it (P. 7), and the two parallels are likewise perpendicular to the plane MN (P. 11); and being parallel, they are equal, as shown by the proposition.

PROPOSITION XIII. THEOREM.

If two angles, not situated in the same plane, have their sides parallel and lying in the same direction, these angles will be equal and their planes will be parallel.

Let the angles CAE and DBF, have the side AC parallel to BD, and lying in the same direction: also, AE parallel to BF, and lying in the same direction; then will the angles CAE and DBF be equal, and their planes parallel.

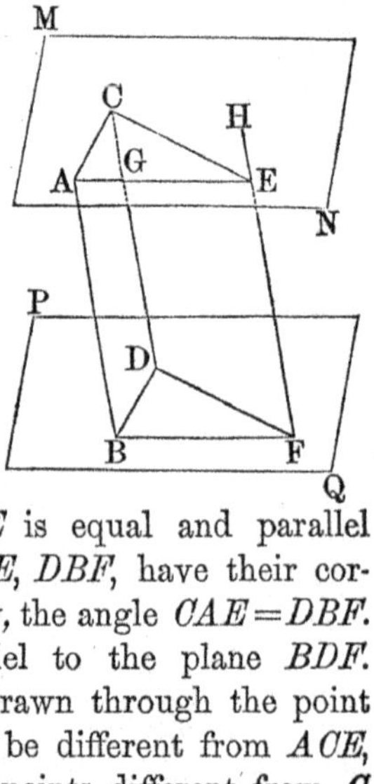

For, take AC and BD equal to each other, and also $AE=BF$; and draw CE, DF, AB, CD, EF. Since AC is equal and parallel to BD, the figure $ABDC$ is a parallelogram (B. I., P. 30); therefore, CD is equal and parallel to AB. For a similar reason, EF is equal and parallel to AB; hence, also, CD is equal and parallel to EF (P. 7, C. 2); hence, the figure $DFEC$ is a parallelogram, and the side CE is equal and parallel to DF; therefore, the triangles CAE, DBF, have their corresponding sides equal; consequently, the angle $CAE=DBF$.

Again, the plane ACE is parallel to the plane BDF. For, if not, suppose a plane to be drawn through the point A, parallel to BDF. If this plane be different from ACE, it will meet the lines CD, EF, in points different from C and E, for instance in G and H; then, the three lines BA, DG, FH, will be equal (P. 12), and each equal to AB: but the lines AB, CD, EF, are already known to be equal; hence, $DC=DG$, and $HF=FE$, which is absurd; hence, the plane ACE is parallel to BDF.

Cor. If two parallel planes MN, PQ, are met by two other planes $CABD$, $EABF$, the angles CAE, DBF, formed by the intersections of the parallel planes are equal; for, the intersection AC is parallel to BD, and AE to BF (P. 10); therefore, the angle $CAE=DBF$.

PROPOSITION XIV. THEOREM.

If three straight lines, not situated in the same plane, are equal and parallel, the triangles formed by joining the extremities of these lines will be equal, and their planes parallel.

Let *AB*, *CD*, *EF*, be three equal and parallel lines.

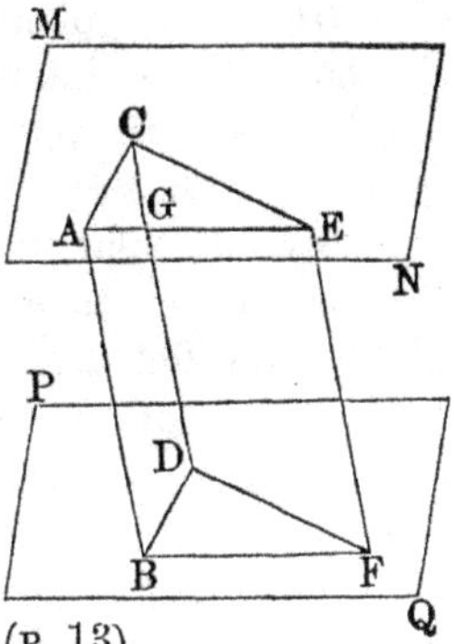

Since *AB* is equal and parallel to *CD*, the figure *ABDC* is a parallelogram; hence, the side *AC* is equal and parallel to *BD* (B. I., P. 30). For a like reason, the sides *AE*, *BF*, are equal and parallel, as also *CE*, *DF*; hence, the two triangles *ACE*, *BDF*, have their sides equal, and are therefore equal (B. I., P. 10); and as their sides are parallel and lie in the same directions, their planes are parallel (P. 13).

PROPOSITION XV. THEOREM.

If two straight lines be cut by three parallel planes, they will be divided proportionally.

Suppose the line *AB* to meet the parallel planes *MN*, *PQ*, *RS*, at the points *A*, *E*, *B*; and the line *CD* to meet the same planes at the points *C*, *F*, *D*: then

$$AE : EB :: CF : FD.$$

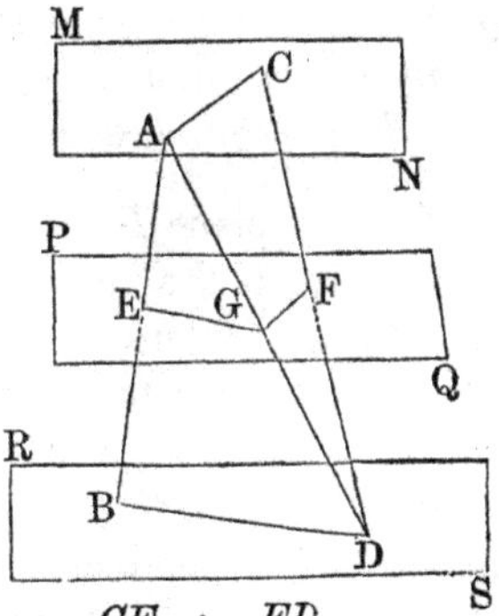

Draw *AD* meeting the plane *PQ* in *G*, and draw *AC*, *EG*, *GF*, *BD*. Since the parallel planes *PQ*, *RS*, are cut by the third plane *BAD*, the intersections *BD* and *EG* are parallel (P. 10): and we have

$$AE : EB :: AG : GD.$$

and the intersections *AC*, *GF*, being parallel,

$$AG : GD :: CF : FD;$$

hence (B. II., P. 4, C.), $AE : EB :: CF : FD.$

PROPOSITION XVI. THEOREM.

If a line is perpendicular to a plane, every plane passed through the perpendicular, is also perpendicular to the plane.

Let AP be perpendicular to the plane NM; then will every plane passing through AP be perpendicular to NM.

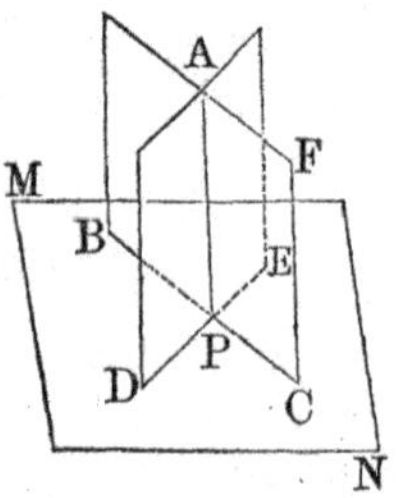

Let BF be any plane passing through AP, and BC its intersection with the plane MN. In the plane MN, draw DP perpendicular to BP: then the line AP, being perpendicular to the plane MN, is perpendicular to each of the two straight lines BC, DE. Now, since AP and DE are both perpendicular to the common intersection BC, the angle which they form will measure the angle between the planes (D. 4): but the angle APD, or APE, is a right angle: hence, the two planes are perpendicular to each other.

Scholium. When three straight lines, such as AP, BP, DP, are perpendicular to each other, any two may be regarded as determining a plane, and the three will determine three planes. Now, each line is perpendicular to the plane of the other two, and the three planes are perpendicular to each other.

PROPOSITION XVII. THEOREM.

If two planes are perpendicular to each other, a line drawn in one of them perpendicular to their common intersection, will be perpendicular to the other plane.

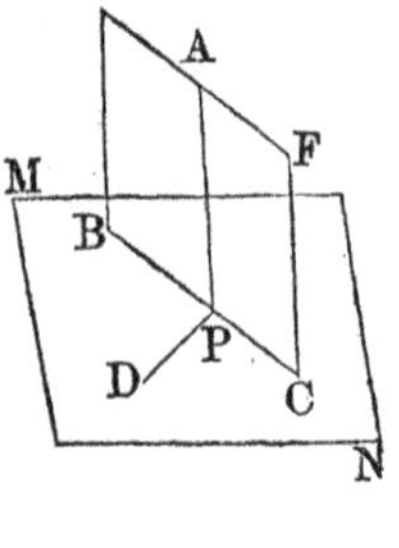

Let the plane BA be perpendicular to NM; then, if the line AP be perpendicular to the intersection BC, it will also be perpendicular to the plane NM.

For, in the plane MN, draw PD perpendicular to PB; then, because the planes are perpendicular, the angle APD is a right angle (D. 4); therefore, the line

AP is perpendicular to the two straight lines PB, PD, passing through its foot; therefore, it is perpendicular to their plane MN (P. 4).

Cor. If the plane BA is perpendicular to the plane MN, and if at a point P of the common intersection we erect a perpendicular to the plane MN, that perpendicular will be in the plane BA. For, let us suppose it will not, then, in the plane BA draw AP perpendicular to PB, the common intersection, and this AP at the same time, is perpendicular to the plane MN, by the theorem; therefore at the same point P there are two perpendiculars to the plane MN, one out of the plane BA, and one in it, which is impossible (P. 4, C. 2).

PROPOSITION XVIII. THEOREM.

If two planes which cut each other are perpendicular to a third plane, their common intersection is also perpendicular to that plane.

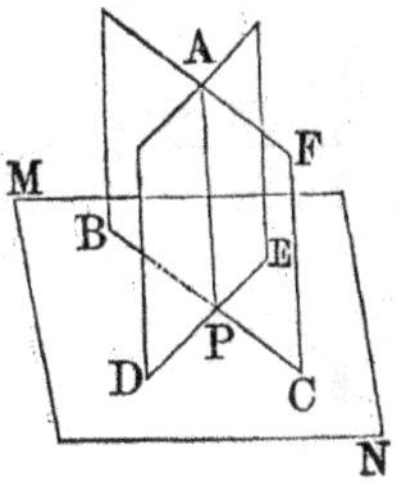

Let the planes BA, DA, be perpendicular to NM; then will their intersection AP be perpendicular to NM.

For, at the point P, erect a perpendicular to the plane MN; that perpendicular must be at once in the plane AB and in the plane AD (P, 17, C.); therefore, it is their common intersection AP.

PROPOSITION XIX. THEOREM.

The sum of either two of the plane angles which include a triedral angle, is greater than the third.

The proposition requires demonstration only when the plane angle, which is compared with the sum of the two others, is greater than either of them. Therefore, suppose the triedral angle S to be formed by the three plane angles ASB, ASC, BSC, and that the angle ASB is the greatest; we are to show that $ASB < ASC + BSC$.

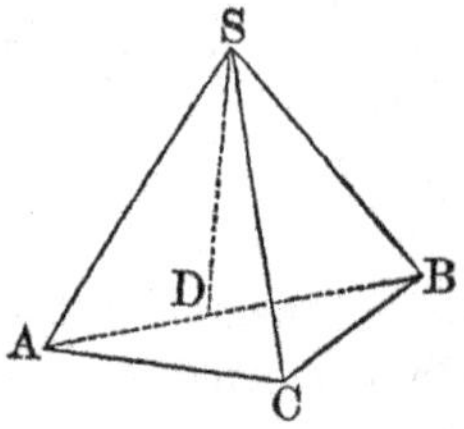

In the plane ASB make the angle $BSD=BSC$, and draw the straight line ADB at pleasure; then make $SC=SD$, and draw AC, BC.

The two sides BS, SD, are equal to the two BS, SC, and the angle $BSD=BSC$; therefore, the triangles BSD, BSC, are equal (B. I., P. 5); hence, $BD=BC$. But $AB<AC+BC$; taking BD from the one side, and from the other its equal BC, there remains $AD<AC$. The two sides AS, SD, are equal to the two AS, SC; the third side AD is less than the third side AC; therefore, the angle $ASD<ASC$ (B. I., P. 9, C.) Adding $BSD=BSC$, we have

$$ASD+BSD, \text{ or } ASB<ASC+BSC.$$

PROPOSITION XX. THEOREM.

The sum of the plane angles which include any polyedral angle is less than four right angles.

Let S be the vertex of a polyedral angle bounded by the faces BSC, CSD, DSE, ESA, ASB; then will the sum of the plane angles about S be less than four right angles.

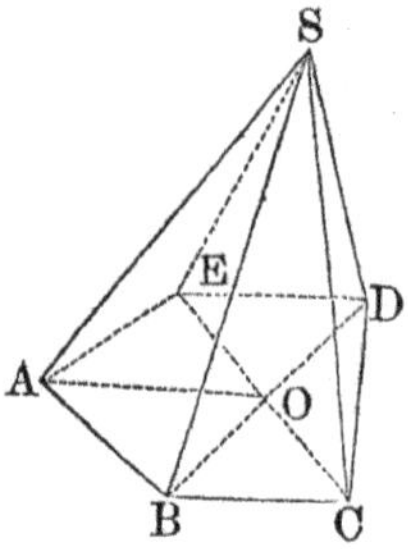

For, let the polyedral angle be cut by any plane AD, intersecting the edges in the points A, B, C, D, E, and the faces in the lines AB, BC, CD, DE, EA. From any point of this plane, as O, draw the straight lines OA, OB, OC, OD, OE.

We thus form two sets of triangles, one set having a common vertex S, the other having a common vertex O, and both having the common bases AB, BC, CD, DE, EA. Now, in the set which has the common vertex S, the sum of all the angles is equal to the sum of all the plane angles which comprise the polyedral angle whose vertex is S, together with the sum of all the angles at the bases: viz.: SAB, SBA, SBC, &c.; and the entire sum is equal to twice as many right angles as there are triangles. In the set whose common vertex is O, the sum of all the angles is equal to the four right angles about O, together with the interior angles of the polygon, and this sum is equal to twice as many right angles as there are triangles. Since the number of triangles, in each set, is the same, it follows that these sums are equal. But in the triedral angle whose vertex is B, $ABS+SBC>ABC$ (P. 19), and the like may be shown at each of the other vertices, C, D, E, A: hence, the sum of the angles at the bases, in the triangles whose common vertex is S, is greater than the sum of the angles at the bases, in the set whose common vertex is O: therefore, the sum of the vertical angles about S is less than the sum of the angles about O: that is, less than four right angles.

Scholium. This demonstration is founded on the supposition that the polyedral angle is convex, or that the plane of no one face produced can ever meet the polyedral angle; if it were otherwise, the sum of the plane angles would no longer be limited, and might be of any magnitude.

PROPOSITION XXI. THEOREM.

If two triedral angles are included by plane angles which are equal each to each, the planes of the equal angles are equally inclined to each other.

Let S and T be the vertices of two triedral angles, and let the angle $ASC=DTF$, the angle $ASB=DTE$, and the angle $BSC=ETF$; then will the inclination of the planes ASC, ASB, be equal to that of the planes DTF, DTE.

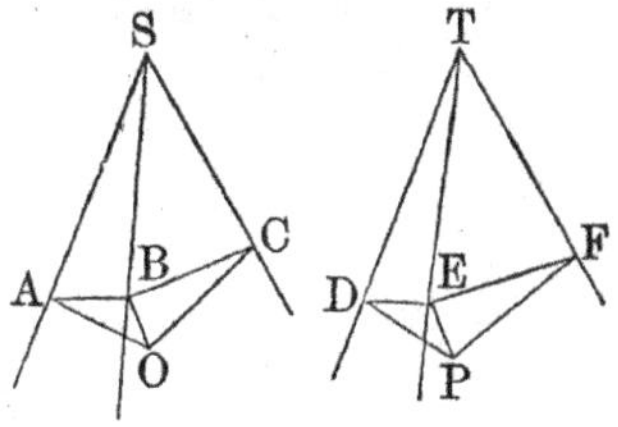

For, having taken SB at pleasure, draw BO perpendicular to the plane ASC; from the point O, where the perpendicular meets the plane, draw OA, OC, perpendicular to SA, SC; draw AB, BC. Next take $TE=SB$; draw EP perpendicular to the plane DTF; from the point P draw PD, PF, perpendicular respectively to TD, TF; lastly, draw DE and EF.

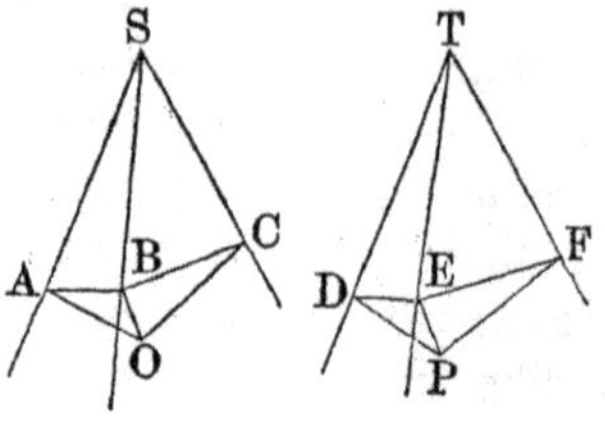

The triangle SAB, is right-angled at A, and the triangle TDE at D (P. 6): and since the angle $ASB=DTE$, we have $SBA=TED$. Moreover, since $SB=TE$, the triangle SAB is equal to the triangle TDE; therefore, $SA=TD$, and $AB=DE$.

In like manner, it may be shown, that $SC=TF$, and $BC=EF$. That proved, the quadrilateral $ASCO$ is equal to the quadrilateral $DTFP$: for, place the angle ASC upon its equal DTF; because $SA=TD$, and $SC=TF$, the point A will fall on D, and the point C on F; and, at the same time, AO, which is perpendicular to SA, will fall on DP, which is perpendicular to TD, and, in like manner, OC on PF; wherefore, the point O will fall on the point P, and hence, AO is equal to DP.

But the triangles AOB, DPE, are right-angled at O and P; the hypothenuse $AB=DE$, and the side $AO=DP$. hence, those triangles are equal (B. I., P. 17); and, consequently, the angle $OAB=PDE$. But the angle OAB measures the inclination of the two faces ASB, ASC; and the angle PDE measures that of the two faces DTE, DTF; hence, those two inclinations are equal to each other.

Scholium 1. It must, however, be observed, that the angle A of the right-angled triangle AOB is properly the inclination of the two planes ASB, ASC, only when the perpendicular BO falls on the same side of SA, with SC; for, if it fell on the other side, the angle of the two planes would be obtuse, and the obtuse angle together with the angle A of the triangle OAB would make two right angles. But in the same case, the angle of the two planes TDE, TDF, would also be obtuse, and the obtuse angle together with the angle D of the triangle DPE, would make two right angles; and the angle A being thus always equal to the angle D, it would follow that the inclination of the two planes ASB, ASC, must be equal to that of the two planes TDE, TDF.

Scholium 2. If two triedral angles are included by three

plane angles, respectively equal to each other, and if, at the same time, the equal or homologous angles are *disposed in the same order*, the two triedral angles will coincide when applied the one to the other, and consequently, are equal (A. 14).

For, we have already seen that the quadrilateral *SAOC* may be placed upon its equal *TDPF*; thus, placing *SA* upon *TD*, *SC* falls upon *TF*, and the point *O* upon the point *P*. But because the triangles *AOB*, *DPE*, are equal, *OB*, perpendicular to the plane *ASC*, is equal to *PE*, perpendicular to the plane *TDF*; besides, these perpendiculars lie in the same direction; therefore, the point *B* will fall upon the point *E*, the line *SB* upon *TE*, and the two angles will wholly coincide.

Scholium 3. The triedral angles will not be equal, unless the equal plane angles are *arranged in the same manner*. For, if they were *arranged in an inverse order*, or, what is the same, if the perpendiculars *OB*, *PE*, instead of lying in the same direction with regard to the planes *ASC*, *DTF*, lay in opposite directions, then it would be impossible to make these triedral angles coincide the one with the other. The theorem would not, however, on this account, be less true, viz.: that the faces containing the equal angles must be equally inclined to each other; so that the two triedral angles would be equal in all their constituent parts, without, however, admitting of superposition. This sort of equality, which is not absolute, or such as admits of superposition, ought to be distinguished by a particular name: we shall call it, *equality by symmetry*.

Thus, those two triedral angles, which are formed by faces respectively equal to each other, but disposed in an inverse order, will be called *triedral angles equal by symmetry*, or simply *symmetrical angles*.

BOOK VII.

POLYEDRONS.

DEFINITIONS.

1. A POLYEDRON is a volume bounded by polygons. The bounding polygons are called *faces* of the polyedron; and the straight line in which any two adjacent faces meet each other, is called an *edge* of the polyedron.

2. A PRISM is a polyedron in which two of the faces are equal polygons, having their homologous sides parallel: all the other faces are parallelograms.

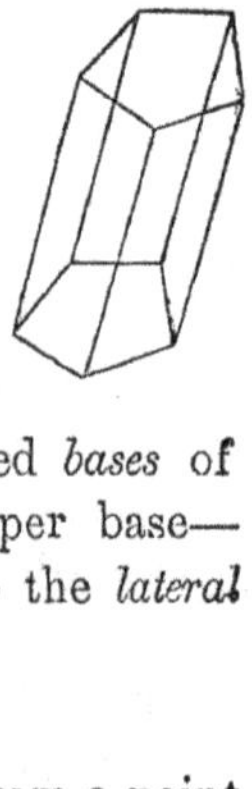

3. The equal and parallel polygons are called *bases* of the prism—the one the lower, the other the upper base—and the parallelograms taken together, make up the *lateral* or *convex surface* of the prism.

4. The ALTITUDE of a prism is a line drawn from a point in one base, perpendicular to the plane of the other.

5. A right prism is one whose edges are perpendicular to the planes of the bases. Each edge is then equal to the altitude of the prism. In every other case, the prism is *oblique*, and each edge is greater than the altitude.

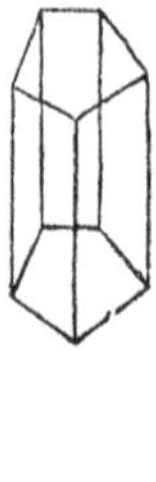

6. A TRIANGULAR PRISM is one whose bases are tri angles: a *quadrangular prism* is one whose bases are quadrilaterals: a *pentangular prism* is one whose bases are pentagons: a *hexangular prism* is one whose bases are hexagons, &c.

7. A PARALLELOPIPEDON is a prism whose bases are parallelograms.

8. A RECTANGULAR PARALLELOPIPEDON is one whose faces are all rectangles. When the faces are squares, it is called a *cube*, or *regular hexaedron*.

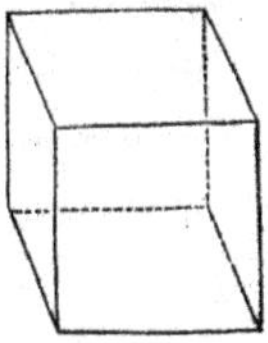

9. A PYRAMID is a volume bounded by a polygon, and by triangles meeting at a common point, called the *vertex*. The polygon is called the *base* of the pyramid, and the triangles, taken together, the *convex*, or *lateral* surface. The pyramid, like the prism, takes different names, according to the form of its base: thus, it may be triangular, quadrangular, pentangular, &c.

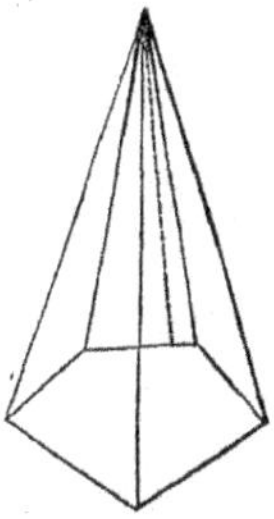

10. The ALTITUDE of a pyramid is the perpendicular let fall from the vertex on the plane of the base.

11. A RIGHT PYRAMID is one whose base is a regular polygon, and in which the perpendicular let fall from the vertex upon the base passes through the centre of the base. This perpendicular is then called the *axis* of the pyramid.

12. The SLANT HEIGHT of a right pyramid, is the perpendicular let fall from the vertex to either side of the polygon which forms the base.

13. If a pyramid is cut by a plane parallel to its base, forming a second base, the part lying between the bases, is called a *frustum of a pyramid*, or *truncated pyramid*.

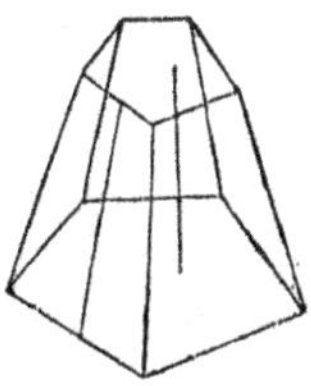

14. The *altitude* of a frustum is a perpendicular drawn from any point of one base to the other; and the *slant height*, is that portion of the slant height of the pyramid intercepted between the bases of the frustum.

15. A *diagonal* of a polyedron is a line joining the vertices of any two of its angles, not in the same face.

16. *Similar polyedrons* are those whose polyedral angles are equal, each to each, and which are bounded by the same number of similar faces.

17. Parts which are like placed, in similar polyedrons, whether faces, edges, or angles, are called *homologous*.

18. A *regular polyedron* is one whose faces are equal and regular polygons. Its polyedral angles are equal.

PROPOSITION I. THEOREM.

The convex surface of a right prism is equal to the perimeter of either base multiplied by its altitude.

Let $ABCDE\text{-}K$ be a right prism: then will its convex surface be equal to

$$(AB+BC+CD+DE+EA)\times AF.$$

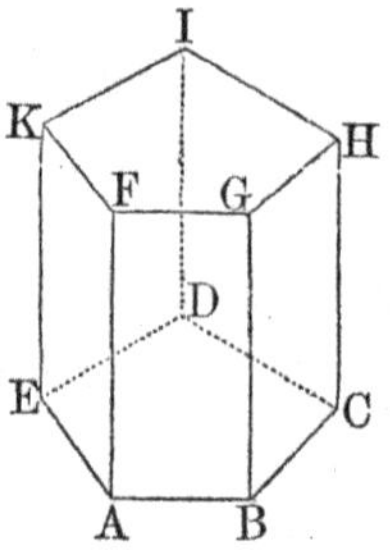

For, the convex surface is equal to the sum of all the rectangles AG, BH, CI, DK, EF, which compose it. Now, the altitudes AF, BG, CH, &c., of the rectangles, are equal to the altitude of the prism, and the area of each rectangle is equal to its base multiplied by its altitude (B. IV., P. 5). Hence, the sum of these rectangles, or the convex surface of the prism, is equal to

$$(AB+BC+CD+DE+EA)\times AF;$$

that is, to the perimeter of the base of the prism multiplied by the altitude.

Cor. If two right prisms have the same altitude, their convex surfaces are to each other as the perimeters of their bases.

PROPOSITION II. THEOREM.

In every prism, the sections formed by parallel planes, are equal polygons.

Let the prism AH be intersected by the parallel planes NP, SV; then are the polygons $NOPQR$, $STVXY$, equal.

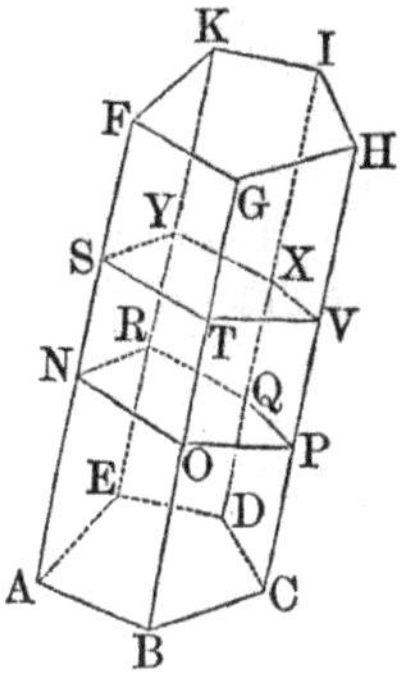

For, the sides ST, NO, are parallel, being the intersections of two parallel planes with a third plane $ABGF$; these same sides, ST, NO, are included between the parallels NS, OT, which are edges of the prism: hence, NO is equal to ST. For like reasons, the sides OP, PQ, QR, &c., of the section $NOPQR$, are equal to the sides TV, VX, XY, &c., of the section $STVXY$, each to each; and since the equal sides are at the same time parallel, it follows that the angles NOP, OPQ, &c., of the first section, are equal to the angles STV, TVX, &c., of the second, each to each (B. VI., P. 13). Hence, the two sections $NOPQR$, $STVXY$, are equal polygons.

Cor. Every section of a prism, parallel to the bases, is equal to either base.

PROPOSITION III. THEOREM.

If a pyramid be cut by a plane parallel to its base:

1*st. The edges and the altitude will be divided proportionally:*

2*d. The section will be a polygon similar to the base.*

Let the pyramid $S\text{-}ABCDE$, of which SO is the altitude be cut by the plane $abcde$; then will

$$Sa : SA :: So : SO,$$

and the same for the other edges; and the polygon $abcde$, will be similar to the base $ABCDE$.

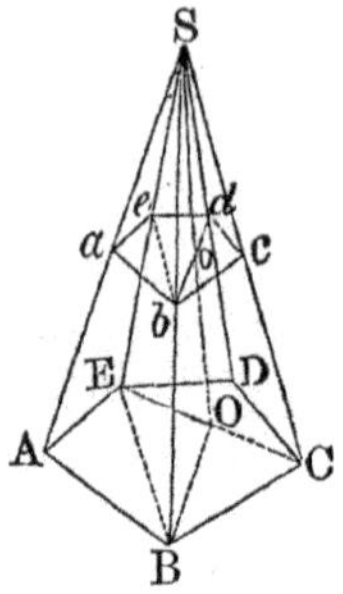

First. Since the planes ABC, abc, are parallel, their intersections AB, ab, by the third plane SAB, are also parallel (B. VI., P. 10); hence, the triangles SAB, Sab, are similar (B. IV., P. 21), and we have

$$SA : Sa :: SB : Sb;$$

for a like reason, we have

$$SB : Sb :: SC : Sc;$$

and so on. Hence, the edges SA, SB, SC, &c., are cut proportionally in a, b, c, &c. The altitude SO is likewise cut in the same proportion, at the point o; for BO and bo are parallel, therefore, we have

$$SO : So :: SB : Sb.$$

Secondly. Since ab is parallel to AB, bc to BC, cd to CD, &c., the angle abc is equal to ABC, the angle bcd to BCD, and so on (B. VI., P. 13). Also, by reason of the similar triangles SAB, Sab, we have

$$AB : ab :: SB : Sb;$$

and by reason of the similar triangles SBC, Sbc, we have

$$SB : Sb :: BC : bc;$$

hence, $$AB : ab :: BC : bc;$$

we might likewise have

$$BC : bc :: CD : cd,$$

and so on. Hence, the polygons $ABCDE$, $abcde$ have their angles equal, each to each, and their sides, taken in the same order, proportional; hence, they are similar (B. IV., D. 1).

Cor. 1. Let $S\text{-}ABCDE$, $S\text{-}XYZ$, be two pyramids, having a common vertex and their bases in the same plane; if these pyramids are cut by a plane parallel to the plane of their bases, *the sections, $abcde$, xyz, will be to each other as the bases $ABCDE$, XYZ.*

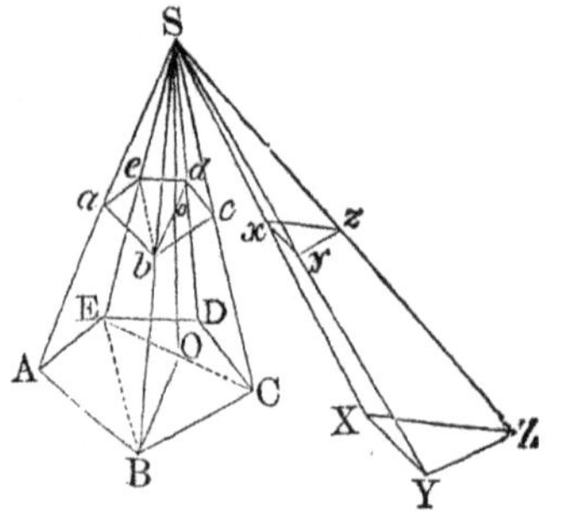

For, the polygons $ABCDE$, $abcde$, being similar, their surfaces are as the squares of the homologous sides AB, ab; that is, B. IV., P. 27),

$$ABCDE : abcde :: \overline{AB}^2 : \overline{ab}^2.$$

but, $$AB : ab :: SA : Sa;$$

hence, $$ABCDE : abcde :: \overline{SA}^2 : \overline{Sa}^2.$$

For a like reason,

$$XYZ : xyz :: \overline{SX}^2 : \overline{Sx}^2.$$

But since abc and xyz are in one plane, we have likewise (B. VI., P. 15),

$$SA : Sa :: SX : Sx;$$

hence, $$ABCDE : abcde :: XYZ : xyz;$$

therefore, the sections $abcde$, xyz, are to each other as the bases $ABCDE$, XYZ.

Cor. 2. If the bases $ABCDE$, XYZ, are equivalent, any sections $abcde$, xyz, made at equal distances from the bases, are also equivalent.

PROPOSITION IV. THEOREM.

The convex surface of a right pyramid is equal to the perimeter of its base multiplied by half the slant height.

Let S be the vertex, $ABCDE$ the base, and SF the slant height of a right pyramid; then the convex surface is equal to $\frac{1}{2} SF \times (AB + BC + CD + DE + EA)$.

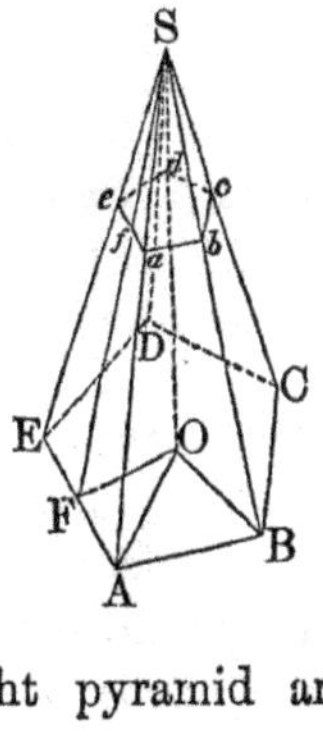

For, since the pyramid is right, the point O, in which the axis meets the base, is the centre of the polygon $ABCDE$ (D. 11); hence, the lines OA, OB, OC, &c., drawn to the vertices of the base, are equal.

In the right-angled triangles SAO, SBO, the bases and perpendiculars are equal: hence, the hypothenuses are equal: and it may be proved in the same way, that all the edges of the right pyramid are equal. The triangles, therefore, which form the convex surface of the prism are all equal to each other. But the area of either of these triangles, as ESA, is equal to its base EA, multiplied by half the perpendicular SF, which is the slant height of the pyramid: hence, the area of all the triangles, or the convex surface of the pyramid, is equal to the perimeter of the base multiplied by half the slant height.

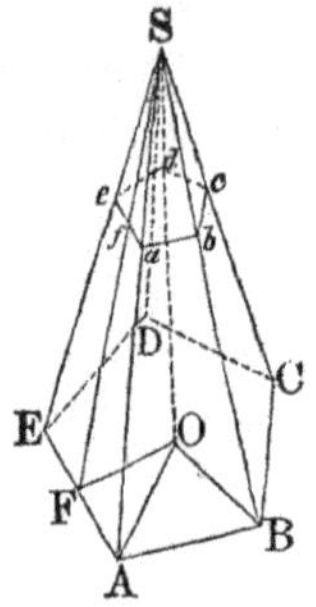

Cor. The convex surface of the frustum of a right pyramid is equal to half the sum of the perimeters of its upper and lower bases multiplied by its slant height.

For, since the section $abcde$ is similar to the base (P. 3), and since the base $ABCDE$ is a regular polygon (D. 11), it follows that the sides ea, ab, bc, cd, and de, are all equal to each other. Hence, the convex surface of the frustum $ABCDE$-d is composed of the equal trapezoids $EAae$, $ABba$, &c., and the perpendicular distance between the parallel sides of either of these trapezoids is equal to Ff, the slant height of the frustum. But the area of either of the trapezoids, as $AEea$, is equal to $\frac{1}{2}(EA+ea) \times Ff$ (B. IV., P. 7): hence, the area of all of them, or the convex surface of the frustum, is equal to half the sum of the perimeters of the upper and lower bases multiplied by the slant height.

PROPOSITION V. THEOREM.

If the three faces which include a triedral angle of a prism are equal to the three faces which include a triedral angle of a second prism, each to each, and are like placed, the two prisms are equal.

Let B and b be the vertices of two triedral angles included by faces respectively equal to each other, and similarly placed; then will the prism $ABCDE$-K be equal to the prism $abcde$-k.

For, place the base $abcde$ upon the equal base $ABCDE$;

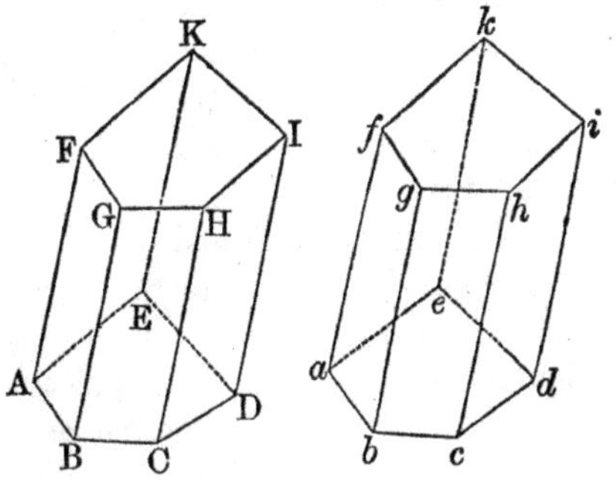

then, since the triedral angles at b and B are equal, the parallelogram bh will coincide with BH, and the parallelogram bf with BF. But the two upper bases being equal to their corresponding lower bases, are equal to each other, and consequently, will coincide: hence, hi will coincide with HI, ik with IK, kf with KF; and therefore, the lateral faces of the prisms will coincide: hence, the two prisms coinciding throughout, are equal (A. 14).

Cor. Two right prisms, which have equal bases and equal altitudes, are equal. For, since the side AB is equal to ab, and the altitude BG to bg, the rectangle $ABGF$ is equal to $abgf$; so also, the rectangle $BGHC$ is equal to $bghc$; and thus the three faces, which include the triedral angle B, are equal to the three which include the triedral angle b, each to each. Hence, the two prisms are equal.

PROPOSITION VI. THEOREM.

In every parallelopipedon, the opposite faces are equal and parallel.

Let $ABCD$ be a parallelopipedon, then will its opposite faces be equal and parallel.

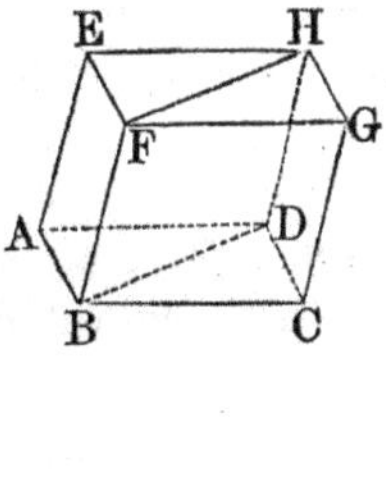

For, the bases $ABCD$, $EFGH$, are equal parallelograms, and have their planes parallel (D. 7). It remains only to show, that the same is true of any two opposite lateral faces, such as $BCGF$, $ADHE$.

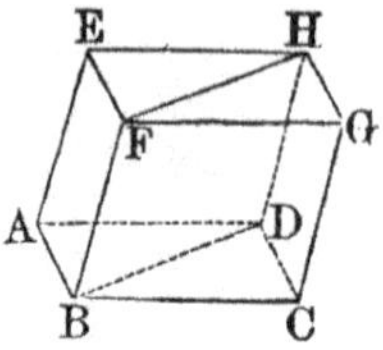

Now, BC is equal and parallel to AD, because the base $ABCD$ is a parallelogram; and since the lateral faces are also parallelograms, BF is equal and parallel to AE, and the like may be shown for the sides FG and EH, CG and DH; hence, the angle CBF is equal to the angle DAE, and the planes DAE, CBF, are parallel (B. VI., P. 13); and the parallelogram $BCGF$, is equal to the parallelogram $ADHE$. In the same way, it may be shown that the opposite parallelograms $ABFE$, $DCGH$, are equal and parallel.

Cor. 1. Since the parallelopipedon is a volume bounded by six faces, of which any two lying opposite to each other, are equal and parallel, it follows that any face and the one opposite to it, may be assumed as the bases of the parallelopipedon.

Cor. 2. *The diagonals of a parallelopipedon bisect each other.* For, suppose two diagonals BH, DF, to be drawn through opposite vertices. Draw also BD, FH. Then, since BF is equal and parallel to DH, the figure $BDHF$ is a parallelogram; hence, the diagonals BH, DF, mutually bisect each other at E (B. I., P. 31). In like manner, it may be shown that the diagonal BH and any other diagonal bisect each other; hence, the four diagonals mutually bisect each other, in a common point. If the six faces are equal to each other, this point may be regarded as the centre of the parallelopipedon.

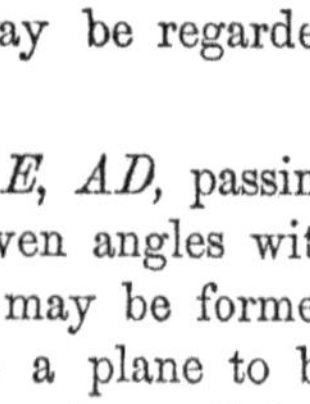

Scholium. If three straight lines AB, AE, AD, passing through the same point A, and making given angles with each other, are known, a parallelopipedon may be formed on these lines. For this purpose, conceive a plane to be passed through the extremity of each line, and parallel to the plane of the other two, that is, through the point B pass a plane parallel to DAE, through D a plane parallel to BAE, and through E a plane parallel to BAD. The mutual intersections of these planes will form the edges of the parallelopipedon required.

PROPOSITION VII. THEOREM.

If a plane be passed through the opposite diagonal edges of a parallelopipedon, it will divide the parallelopipedon into two equivalent triangular prisms.

Let the parallelopipedon *ABCD-H* be divided by the plane *BDHF*, passing through the opposite edges *BF*, *DH*: then will the triangular prism *ABD-H*, be equivalent to the triangular prism *BCD-H*.

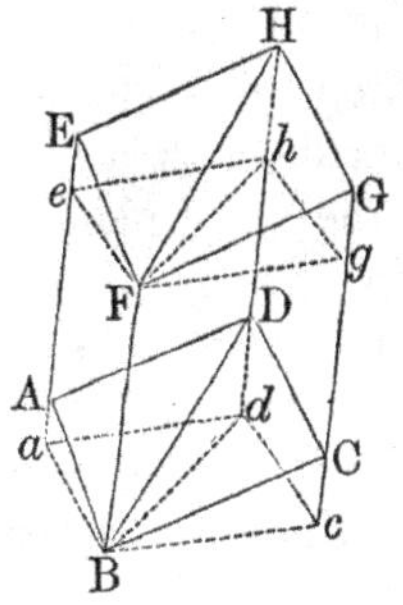

For, through the vertices *B* and *F*, pass the planes *Bcda*, *Fghe*, at right angles to the edge *BF*, the former cutting the three other edges of the parallelopipedon prolonged in the points *c*, *d*, *a*, the latter in the points *g*, *h*, *e*.

Now, the sections *Bcda*, *Fghe*, are equal parallelograms. For, the cutting planes being perpendicular to the same straight line *BF*, are parallel (B. VI., P. 9): hence, the sections are equal (P. 2); and they are parallelograms because *Ba*, *cd*, two opposite sides of the same section, are formed by the meeting of a plane *aBcd*, with two parallel planes *ABFE*, *DCGH* (B. VI., P. 10). For a similar reason *Bc* and *ad* are parallel; hence, the figures are equal parallelograms.

For a like reason the figure *aBFe* is a parallelogram; so also, are *BcgF*, *cghd*, *adhe*, the other lateral faces of the volume *aBcd-h*; hence, that volume is a prism (D. 2), and that prism is right, since the edge *BF* is perpendicular to its bases.

But the right prism *aBcd-h* is divided by the plane *BH* into two equal right prisms *aBd-h*, *Bcd-h*; for, the bases *aBd*, *Bcd*, are equal, being halves of the same parallelogram, and since the prisms have the common altitude *BF*, they are equal (P. 5, C.)

It is now to be proved that the oblique triangular prism *ABD-H* is equivalent to the right triangular prism *aBd-h*. Since these prisms have a common part *ABD-h*, it will only be necessary to prove that the remaining parts,

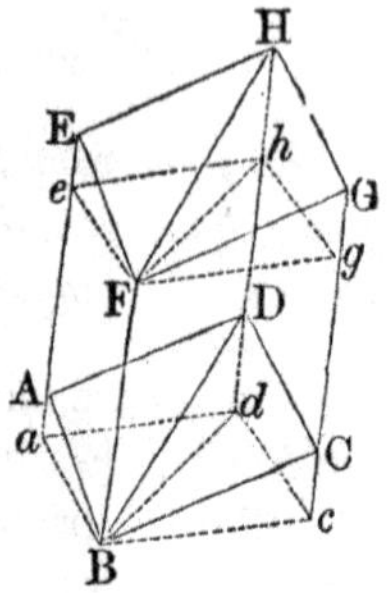

namely, the volumes $aBd\text{-}D$, $eFh\text{-}H$, are equivalent. Since $ABFE$, $aBFe$, are parallelograms, the sides AE, ae, are each equal to BF; hence, they are equal to each other; and taking away the common part Ae, there remains $Aa=Ee$. In the same manner it may be proved that $Dd=Hh$.

To bring about the superposition of the two volumes, $eFh\text{-}H$, $aBd\text{-}D$, let the base eFh be placed on the equal base aBd—the point e falling on a, the point h on d: the edges eE, hH, will then coincide with aA, dD, since all the edges are perpendicular to the same plane $aBcd$. Hence, the two solids will coincide exactly with each other; consequently, the oblique prism $ABD\text{-}H$ is equivalent to the right prism $aBd\text{-}h$. In the same manner, it may be shown that the oblique prism $BCD\text{-}H$ is equivalent to the right prism $Bcd\text{-}h$. But the two right prisms have been proved equal: hence, the two triangular prisms $ABD\text{-}H$, $BCD\text{-}H$, being equivalent to equal right prisms, are equivalent to each other.

Cor. Every triangular prism $ABD\text{-}H$ is half the parallelopipedon AG, having the same triedral angel A, and the same edges AB, AD, AE.

PROPOSITION VIII. THEOREM.

If two parallelopipedons have a common lower base, and their upper bases in the same plane and between the same parallels, they are equivalent.

Let the parallelopipedons AG, AL, have the common base $ABCD$, and their upper bases EG, IL, in the same plane, and between the same parallels EK, HL; then will they be equivalent.

There may be three cases, according as EI is greater than, equal to, or less than EF; but the demonstration, for each case, is the same.

We will show, in the first place, that the triangular prisms $AIE\text{-}H$, $BKF\text{-}G$ are equal. Since EF and IK are

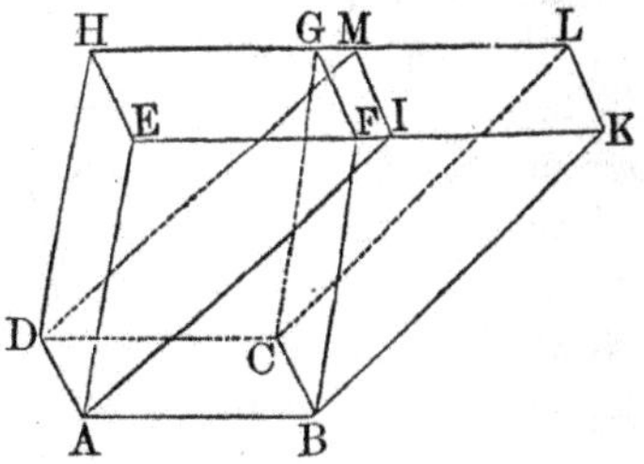

each equal to AB (B. I., P. 28), they are equal to each other. Add FI to each, and we have

$$EI = FK:$$

and since the angle AEF is equal to BFK (B. I., P. 20, C. 3); the triangle AEI is equal to the triangle BFK (B. I., P. 5). Again, since EI is equal to FK, and EH equal and parallel to FG, the parallelogram EM is equal to the parallelogram FL (B. I., P. 28, C. 2): also, the parallelogram AH is equal to the parallelogram CF (P. 6): hence, the three faces which include the polyedral angle at E are respectively equal to the three which include the polyedral angle at F, and being like placed, the triangular prism $AIE\text{-}H$ is equal to the triangular prism $BKF\text{-}G$ (P. 5).

But, if the triangular prism $AIE\text{-}H$ be taken away from the solid AL, there will remain the parallelopipedon $ABCD\text{-}M$; and if the equal triangular prism $BKF\text{-}G$ be taken away from the same solid, there will remain the parallelopipedon $ABCD\text{-}H$; hence, the two parallelopipedons $ABCD\text{-}M$, $ABCD\text{-}H$, are equivalent.

PROPOSITION IX. THEOREM.

Two parallelopipedons, having their lower bases equal, and equal altitudes, are equivalent.

Let the parallelopipedons AG, AL, have the common base $ABCD$, and equal altitudes; then will their upper bases, $EFGH$, $IKLM$, be in the same plane; and the two parallelopipedons will be equivalent.

For, let the edges FE, GH, be prolonged, as also, KL and IM, till, by their intersections, they form the parallelogram $NOPQ$, in the plane of the upper bases: this parallelogram will be equal to either of the bases IL, EG. For, the upper bases IL, EG, being each equal to the common base AC, are equal to each other. But OP which is equal to FG, is also equal to KL, and ON is equal to *KI*, being between the same parallels: hence, the parallelogram *NP* is equal to *IL* or *EG* (B. I., P. 28, C. 2).

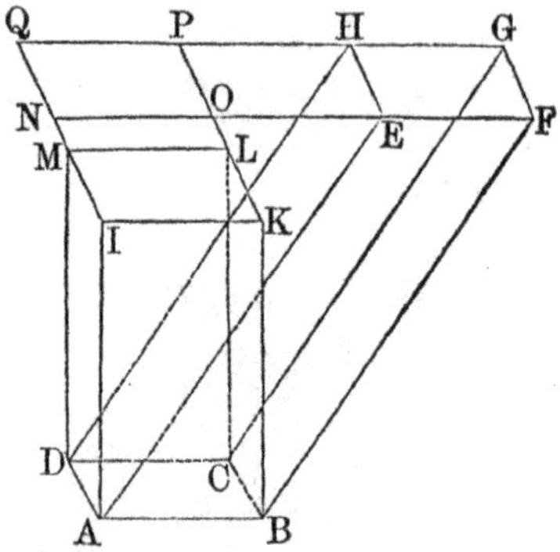

Now, if a third parallelopipedon be conceived, having for its lower base the parallelogram *ABCD*, and for its upper base *NOPQ*, this third parallelopipedon will be equivalent to the parallelopipedon *AG*, since they have the same lower base, and their upper bases lie in the same plane and between the same parallels, *QG*, *NF* (P. 8). For a like reason, this third parallelopipedon will also be equivalent to the parallelopipedon *AL*; hence, the two parallelopipedons *AG*, *AL*, which have equal bases and equal altitudes, are equivalent.

PROPOSITION X. THEOREM.

Any oblique parallelopipedon may be transformed into an equivalent rectangular parallelopipedon having an equal altitude and an equivalent base.

Let *ABCD-H* be any parallelopipedon.

From the vertices *A*, *B*, *C*, *D*, draw *AI*, *BK*, *CL*, *DM*, perpendicular to the plane of the lower base, and equal to the altitude of *AG*: there will thus be formed the parallelopipedon *AL* equivalent to *AG* (P. 9), and having its lateral faces *AK*, *BL*, &c., rectangles. Now, if the base *ABCD* is a rectangle, *AL* will be a rectangular parallelopipedon

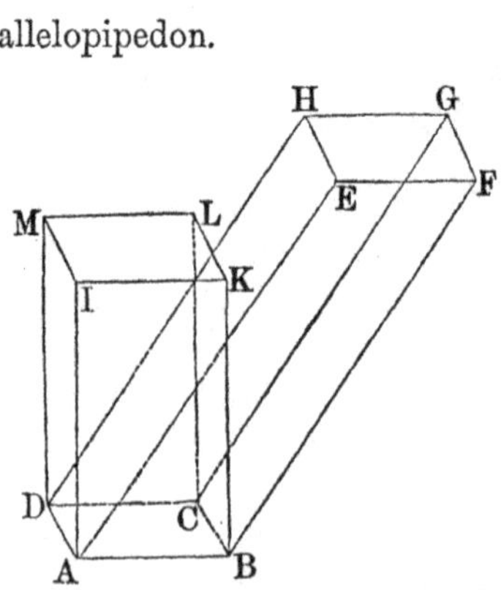

equivalent to AG, and consequently, the parallelopipedon required.

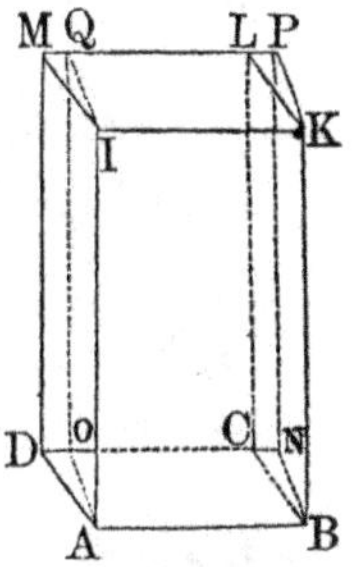

But if $ABCD$ is not a rectangle, draw AO and BN perpendicular to DC, and OQ and NP perpendicular to the base; we shall then have, a rectangular parallelopipedon $ABNO$-Q: for, by construction, the bases $ABNO$, and $IKPQ$, are rectangles; so also, are the lateral faces, the edges AI, OQ, &c., being perpendicular to the plane of the base; hence, the volume AP is a rectangular parallellopipedon. But the two parallelopipedons AP, AL, may be conceived as having the same base $ABKI$, and the same altitude AO: hence, the parallelopipedon AG, which was at first changed into an equivalent parallelopipedon AL, is now changed into an equivalent rectangular parallelopipedon AP, having the same altitude AI, and a base $ABNO$ equivalent to the base $ABCD$.

PROPOSITION XI. THEOREM.

Two rectangular parallelopipedons, which have equal bases, are to each other as their altitudes.

Let the parallelopipedons AG, AL, have the common base BD, then will they be to each other as their altitudes AE, AI.

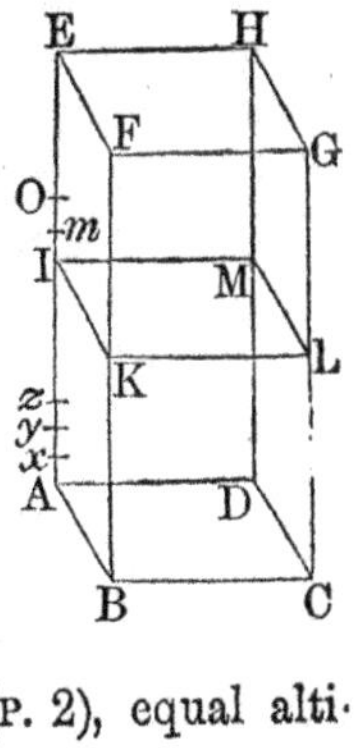

First. Suppose the altitudes AE, AI, to be to each other as two whole numbers, as 15 is to 8, for example. Divide AE into 15 equal parts, whereof AI will contain 8; and through x, y, z, &c., the points of division, pass planes parallel to the common base. These planes will divide the solid AG into 15 parallelopipedons, all equal to each other, because they have equal bases and equal altitudes—equal bases, since every section $KLMI$, parallel to the base $ABCD$, is equal to that base (P. 2), equal altitudes, because the altitudes are the equal divisions, Ax, xy, yz, &c. But of those 15 equal parallelopipedons, 8 are contained in AL; hence, the volume AG is to the volume AL as 15 is to 8, or generally, as the altitude AE is to the altitude AI.

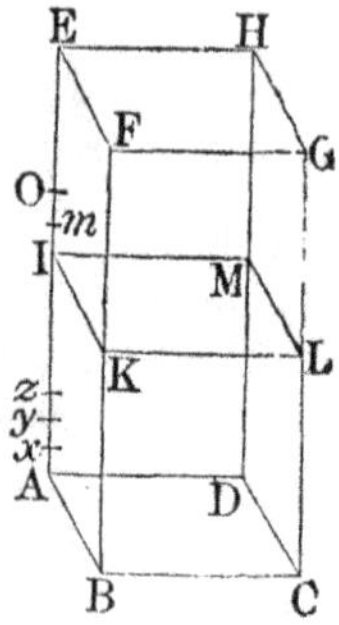

Second. If the ratio of AE to AI cannot be expressed exactly in numbers, it may still be shown, that we shall have

$$vol.\ AG \ : \ vol.\ AL \ :: \ AE \ : \ AI.$$

For, if this proportion is not correct, suppose we have,

$$vol.\ AG \ : \ vol.\ AL \ :: \ AE \ : \ AO \text{ greater than } AI.$$

Divide AE into equal parts, such that each shall be less than OI; there will be at least one point of division m, between O and I. Let P denote the parallelopipedon, whose base is $ABCD$, and altitude Am; since the altitudes AE, Am, are to each other as two whole numbers, we have

$$vol.\ AG \ : \ P \ :: \ AE \ : \ Am.$$

But by hypothesis, we have

$$vol.\ AG \ : \ vol.\ AL \ :: \ AE \ : \ AO;$$

therefore (B. II., P. 4),

$$vol.\ AL \ : \ P \ :: \ AO \ : \ Am.$$

But AO is greater than Am; hence, if the proportion is correct, the volume AL must be greater than P. On the contrary, however, it is less: therefore, AO cannot be greater than AI. By the same mode of reasoning, it may be shown that the fourth term cannot be less than AI; therefore, it is equal to AI: hence, rectangular parallelopipedons having equal bases, are to each other as their altitudes.

PROPOSITION XII. THEOREM.

Two rectangular parallelopipedons, having equal altitudes, are to each other as their bases.

Let the parallelopipedons AG, AK, have the same altitude AE; then will they be to each other as their bases AC, AN.

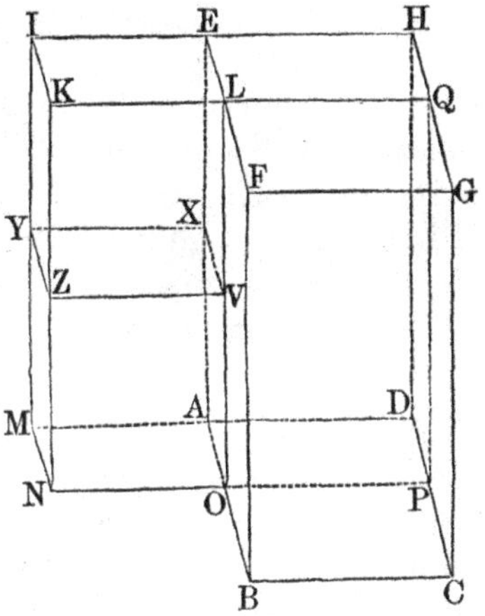

For, having placed the two volumes by the side of each other, as the figure represents, prolong the plane $NKLO$ till it meets the plane $DCGH$ in PQ; we thus have a third parallelopipedon AQ, which may be compared with each of the parallelopipedons AG, AK. The two volumes AG, AQ, having the same base $ADHE$ are to each other as their altitudes AB, AO: in like manner, the two volumes AQ, AK, having the same base $AOLE$, are to each other as their altitudes AD, AM. Hence, we have

$$vol.\ AG : vol.\ AQ :: AB : AO;$$

also, $$vol.\ AQ : vol.\ AK :: AD : AM.$$

Multiplying together the corresponding terms of these proportions, and omitting, in the result, the common multiplier $vol.\ AQ$; we shall have

$$vol.\ AG : vol.\ AK :: AB \times AD : AO \times AM.$$

But $AB \times AD$ represents the area of the base $ABCD$; and $AO \times AM$ represents the area of the base $AMNO$; hence, two rectangular parallelopipedons having equal altitudes, are to each other as their bases.

PROPOSITION XIII. THEOREM.

Any two rectangular parallelopipedons are to each other as the products of their bases by their altitudes; that is, as the products of their three dimensions.

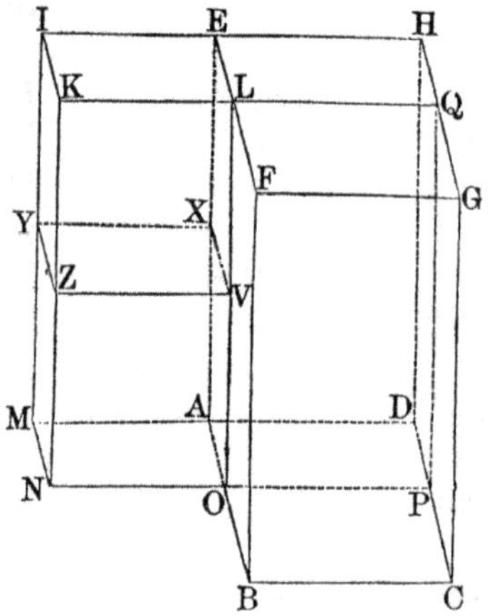

Having placed the two volumes AG, AZ, so that their faces have the common angle BAE, produce the planes necessary for completing the third parallelopipedon AK, which will have an equal altitude with the parallelopipedon AG. By the last proposition, we have

$$vol.\ AG \ :\ vol.\ AK\ ::\ ABCD\ :\ AMNO.$$

But the two parallelopipedons AK, AZ, having the same base NA, are to each other as their altitudes AE, AX; hence, we have,

$$vol.\ AK\ :\ vol.\ AZ\ ::\ AE\ :\ AX.$$

Multiplying together the corresponding terms of these proportions, and omitting in the result the common multiplier *vol.* AK; we shall have,

$$vol.\ AG\ :\ vol.\ AZ\ ::\ ABCD\times AE\ :\ AMNO\times AX.$$

Instead of the bases $ABCD$ and $AMNO$, put $AB\times AD$ and $AO\times AM$, and we shall have,

$$vol.\ AG\ :\ vol.\ AZ\ ::\ AB\times AD\times AE\ :\ AO\times AM\times AX;$$

hence, any two rectangular parallelopipedons are to each other, as the products of their three dimensions.

Scholium 1. The magnitude of a volume, when measured, is called its *contents;* and this word is exclusively employed to designate the measure of a volume: thus, we say the contents of a rectangular parallelopipedon are equal to the product of its base by its altitude, or to the product of its three dimensions

In order to comprehend the nature of this measurement, it is necessary to consider, that the number of linear units in one dimension of the base multiplied by the number of linear units in the other dimension of the base, will give the number of superficial units in the base of the parallelopipedon (B. IV., P. 4, S.) For each unit in height, there are evidently, as many units of volume as there are superficial units in the base. Therefore, the number of superficial units in the altitude, gives the number of units of volume in the parallelopipedon.

If then, we assume as the unit of measure, the cube whose edge is equal to the linear unit, the contents will be expressed numerically, by the number of times which the volume contains its unit of measure.

Scholium 2. As the three dimensions of the cube are equal, if the edge is 1, the contents are denoted by $1 \times 1 \times 1 = 1$: if the edge is 2, by $2 \times 2 \times 2 = 8$; if the edge is 3, by $3 \times 3 \times 3 = 27$; and so on. Hence, if the edges of a series of cubes are to each other as the numbers 1, 2, 3, &c., the cubes themselves, or their contents, are as the numbers 1, 8, 27, &c. Hence it is, that in arithmetic, the cube of a number is the name given to a product which results from three equal factors.

If it were proposed to find a cube, double of a given cube, we should have 1 to the cube root of 2, as the edge of the given cube to the edge of the required cube. Now, by a geometrical construction, it is easy to find the square root of 2 ; but the cube root of it cannot be found, by the operations of elementary geometry, which are limited to the employment of the straight line and circle.

Owing to the difficulty of this solution, the problem of the *duplication of the cube* became celebrated among the ancient geometers, as well as that of the *trisection of an angle*, which is a problem nearly of the same species. The solutions of these problems have, however, long since been discovered ; and though less simple than the constructions of elementary geometry, they are not, on that account, less rigorous or less satisfactory.

PROPOSITION XIV. THEOREM.

The contents of a parallelopipedon, and generally of any prism, are equal to the product of its base by its altitude.

First. Any parallelopipedon is equivalent to a rectangular parallelopipedon, having an equal altitude and an equivalent base (P. 10). But, the contents of a rectangular parallelopipedon are equal to its base multiplied by its height; hence, the contents of any parallelopipedon are equal to the product of its base by its altitude.

Second. Any triangular prism is half a parallelopipedon so constructed as to have an equal altitude and a double base (P. 7). But the contents of the parallelopipedon are equal to its base multiplied by its altitude; hence, that of the triangular prism is also equal to the product of its base, which is half that of the parallelopipedon, multiplied into its altitude.

Third. Any prism may be divided into as many triangular prisms of the same altitude, as there are triangles formed by drawing diagonals from a common vertex in the polygon which constitutes its base. But the contents of each triangular prism are equal to its base multiplied by its altitude; and since the altitudes are equal, it follows that the sum of all the triangular prisms must be equal to the sum of all the triangles which constitute their bases, multiplied by the common altitude.

Hence, the contents of any polygonal prism, are equal to the product of its base by its altitude.

Cor. Since any two prisms are to each other as the products of their bases and altitudes, if the altitudes be equal, they will be to each other as their bases simply; hence, *two prisms of the same altitude are to each other as their bases.* For a like reason, *two prisms having equivalent bases are to each other as their altitudes.*

PROPOSITION XV. THEOREM.

Two triangular pyramids, having equivalent bases and equal altitudes, are equivalent, or equal in volume.

Let *S-ABC*, *S-abc*, be two such pyramids; let their equivalent bases *ABC*, *abc*, be situated in the same plane, and let *AT* be their common altitude: then will they be equivalent.

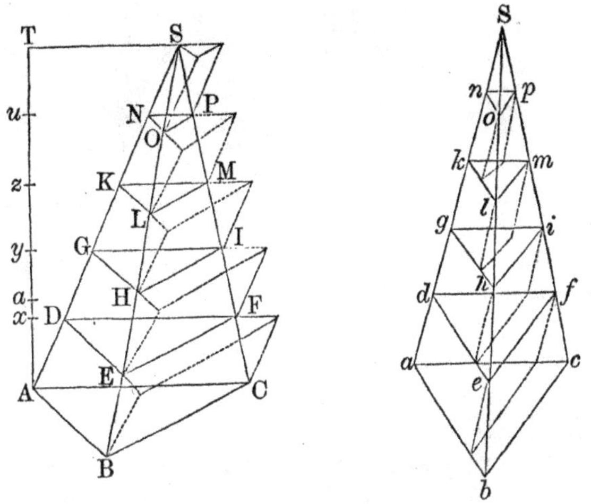

For, if these pyramids are not equivalent, let *S-abc* be the smaller; and suppose *Aa* to be the altitude of a prism which, having *ABC* for its base, is equal to their difference.

Divide the altitude *AT* into equal parts *Ax*, *xy*, *yz*, &c., each less than *Aa*, and let *k* denote one of those parts; through the points of division pass planes parallel to the planes of the bases; the corresponding sections formed by these planes in the two pyramids are respectively equivalent, namely, *DEF* to *def*, *GHI* to *ghi*, &c. (P. 3, C. 2).

This being done, upon the triangles *ABC*, *DEF*, *GHI*, &c., taken as bases, construct exterior prisms having for edges the parts *AD*, *DG*, *GK*, &c., of the edge *SA*; in like manner, on bases *def*, *ghi*, *klm*, &c., in the second pyramid, construct interior prisms, having for edges the correspond-

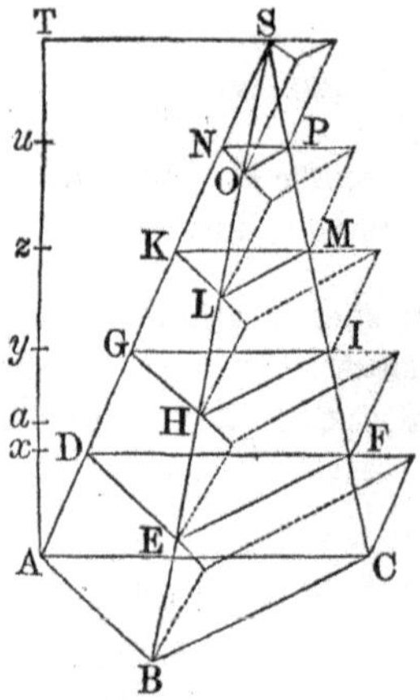

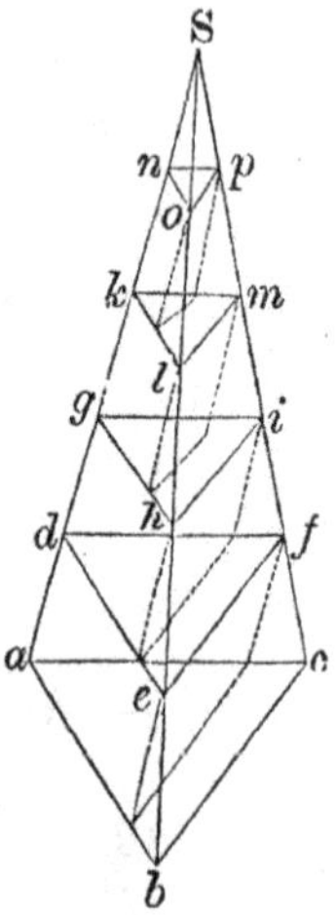

ing parts of *Sa*. It is plain, that the sum of all the exterior prisms of the pyramid *S-ABC* is greater than this pyramid; and also, that the sum of all the interior prisms of the pyramid *S-abc* is less than this pyramid. Hence, the difference, between the sum of all the exterior prisms of one pyramid, and the sum of all the interior prisms of the other, is greater than the difference between the two pyramids themselves.

Now, beginning with the bases, the second exterior prism *EFD-G*, is equivalent to the first interior prism *efd-a*, because they have the same altitude *k*, and their bases *EFD*, *efd*, are equivalent; for a like reason, the third exterior prism *HIG-K*, and the second interior prism *hig-d* are equivalent; the fourth exterior and the third interior; and so on, to the last in each series. Hence, all the exterior prisms of the pyramid *S-ABC*, excepting the first prism *BCA-D*, have equivalent corresponding ones in the interior prisms of the pyramid *S-abc*: hence, the prism *BCA-D*, is the difference between the sum of all the exterior prisms of the pyramid *S-ABC*, and the sum of the interior prisms of the pyramid *S-abc*. But the difference between these two sets of prisms has already been proved to be greater than that between the two pyramids; which latter difference we supposed to be equal to the prism *BCA-a*: hence, the prism BCA-D, should be greater than the prism BCA-a. But in reality it is less; for they have the same base ABC, and the altitude Ax of the first is less than the altitude Aa of the second. Hence, the supposed inequality between the two pyramids cannot exist; therefore, the two pyramids S-ABC, S-abc, having equal altitudes and equivalent bases, are themselves equivalent.

PROPOSITION XVI. THEOREM.

Any triangular prism may be divided into three equivalent triangular pyramids.

Let ABC-DEF be a triangular prism; then may it be divided into three equivalent triangular pyramids.

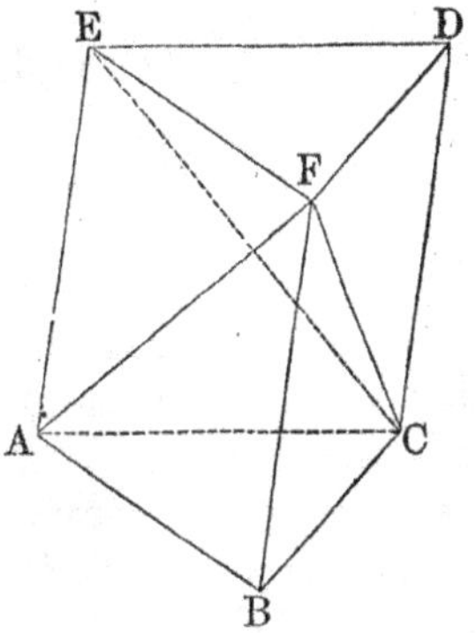

Cut off the pyramid F-ABC from the prism, by the plane FAC; there will remain the solid F-$ACDE$, which may be considered as a quadrangular pyramid, whose vertex is F, and whose base is the parallelogram $ACDE$. Draw the diagonal CE; and pass the plane FCE, which will cut the quadrangular pyramid into two triangular pyramids F-ACE, F-CDE. These two triangular pyramids have for their common altitude the perpendicular let fall from F, on the plane $ACDE$; they have equal bases; for the triangles ACE, CDE, are halves of the same parallelogram; hence, the two pyramids F-ACE, F-CDE, are equivalent (P. 15). But the pyramid F-CDE, and the pyramid F-ABC, have equal bases ABC, DEF; they have also the same altitude, namely, the distance between the parallel planes ABC, DEF; hence, the two pyramids are equivalent. Now, the pyramid F-CDE, has already been proved equivalent to F-ACE; hence, the three pyramids F-ABC, F-CDE, F-ACE, which compose the prism, are all equivalent.

Cor. 1. Every triangular pyramid is a third part of a

triangular prism, which has an equivalent base and an equal altitude.

Cor. 2. The volume of a triangular pyramid is equal to a third part of the product of its base by its altitude.

PROPOSITION XVII. THEOREM.

The contents of every pyramid are equal to a third part of the product of its base by its altitude.

Let *S-ABCDE* be a pyramid: then will its contents be equal to one-third of the product of the base *ABCDE* by the altitude *SO*.

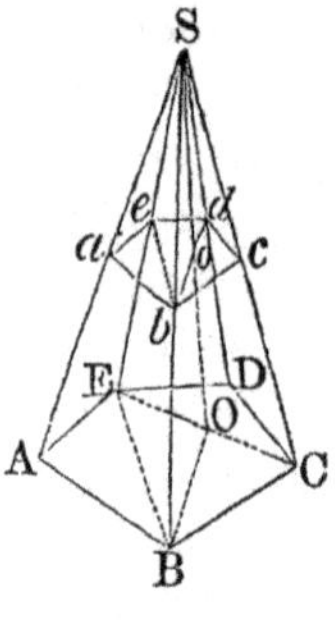

Pass the planes *SEB*, *SEC*, through the vertex *S*, and the diagonals *EB*, *EC*; the polygonal pyramid *S-ABCDE* will then be divided into several triangular pyramids, all having the same altitude *SO*. But each of these pyramids is measured by the product of its base *ABE*, *BCE*, *CDE*, by a third part of its altitude *SO* (P. 16, C. 2); hence, the sum of these triangular pyramids, or the polygonal pyramid *S-ABCDE* is measured by the sum of the triangles *ABE*, *BCE*, *CDE*, or the polygon *ABCDE*, multiplied by one-third of *SO*; hence, every pyramid is measured by a third part of the product of its base by its altitude.

Cor. 1. Every pyramid is the third part of a prism which has the same base and the same altitude.

Cor. 2. Two pyramids having the same altitude are to each other as their bases.

Cor. 3. Two pyramids having equivalent bases are to each other as their altitudes.

Cor. 4. Pyramids are to each other as the products of their bases by their altitudes.

Scholium. The contents of any polyedron may be computed, by dividing it into pyramids; and this division may be accomplished in various ways. One of the simplest is to pass all the planes of division through the vertex of the same polyedral angle; in that case, there will be formed as many pyramids as the polyedron has faces, less those faces which bound the polyedral angle whence the planes of division proceed.

PROPOSITION XVIII. THEOREM.

The contents of the frustum of a pyramid are equal to that of three pyramids having for their common altitude the altitude of the frustum, and for bases the lower base of the frustum, the upper base, and a mean proportional between the two bases.

Let *ABCDE-e* be the frustum of a pyramid: then will its contents be equal to that of three pyramids having the common altitude of the frustum, and for bases the polygons *ABCDE*, *abcde*, and a mean proportional between them. Let *T-FGH* be a triangular pyramid having the same altitude, and an equivalent base with the pyramid *S-ABCDE*. These two pyramids are equivalent (P. 17, C. 3).

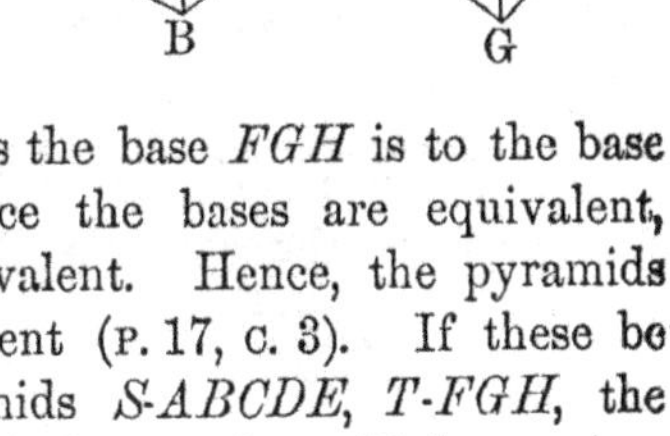

Now, if we regard their bases as situated in the same plane; the plane of the section *abcd*, will form in the triangular pyramid a section *fgh*, at the same distance above the common plane of the bases; and, therefore, the section *fgh* will be to the section *abcde*, as the base *FGH* is to the base *ABCDE* (P. 3, C. 1): and since the bases are equivalent, the sections will also be equivalent. Hence, the pyramids *S-abcde*, *T-fgh* will be equivalent (P. 17, C. 3). If these be taken from the entire pyramids *S-ABCDE*, *T-FGH*, the frustums *ABCDE-e*, *FGH-h* which remain, will be equivalent: hence, if the proposition is true, in the single case of the frustum of a triangular pyramid, it is true in every other.

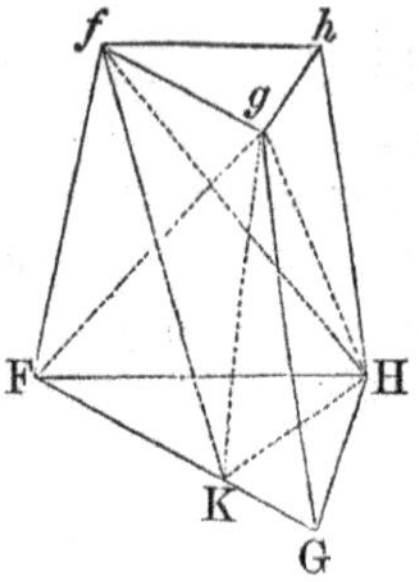

Let $FGH\text{-}h$ be the frustum of a triangular pyramid. Through the three points, F, g, H, pass the plane FgH; it cuts off from the frustum the triangular pyramid $g\text{-}FGH$. This pyramid has for its base the lower base FGH of the frustum; its altitude is equal to that of the frustum, because the vertex g lies in the plane of the upper base fgh.

This pyramid being cut off, there remains the quadrangular pyramid $g\text{-}fhHF$, whose vertex is g, and base $fhHF$. Pass the plane gfH through the three points f, g, H; it divides the quadrangular pyramid into two triangular pyramids $g\text{-}fFH$, $g\text{-}fhH$. The latter has for its base the upper base gfh of the frustum; and for its altitude, the altitude of the frustum, because its vertex H lies in the lower base. Thus we already know two of the three pyramids which compose the frustum.

It remains to examine the third pyramid $g\text{-}FfH$. Now, if gK be drawn parallel to fF, and if we conceive a new pyramid $K\text{-}fFH$, having K for its vertex and fFH for its base, these two pyramids have the same base HfF; they also have the same altitude, because their vertices g and K lie in the line gK, parallel to Ff, and consequently, parallel to the plane of the base: hence, these pyramids are equivalent (P. 17, C. 3). But the pyramid $K\text{-}fFH$ may be regarded as having FKH for its base, and its vertex at f: its altitude is then the same as that of the frustum. We are now to show that the base FKH is a mean proportional between the bases FGH and fgh. The triangles FHK, fgh, have the angle $F=f$; hence (B. IV., P. 24),

$$FHK \; : \; fgh \; :: \; FK \times FH \; : \; fg \times fh;$$

but because of the parallels, $FK=fg$,

$$FHK \; : \; fgh \; :: \; FH \; : \; fh.$$

We have also,

$$FHG \; : \; FHK \; :: \; FG \; : \; FK, \text{ or } fg$$

But the similar triangles FGH, fgh, give

$$FG : fg :: FH : fh;$$

hence, $$FGH : FHK :: FHK : fgh;$$

that is, the base FHK is a mean proportional between the two bases FGH, fgh. Hence, the contents of the frustum of a triangular pyramid are equal to that of three pyramids whose common altitude is that of the frustum, and whose bases are the lower base of the frustum, the upper base, and a mean proportional between the two bases.

PROPOSITION XIX. THEOREM.

Similar triangular prisms are to each other as the cubes of their homologous edges.

Let CBD-P, cbd-p, be two similar triangular prisms, and BC, bc, two homologous edges: then will the prism CBD-P be to the prism cbd-p, as $\overline{BC}^3$ to $\overline{bc}^3$.

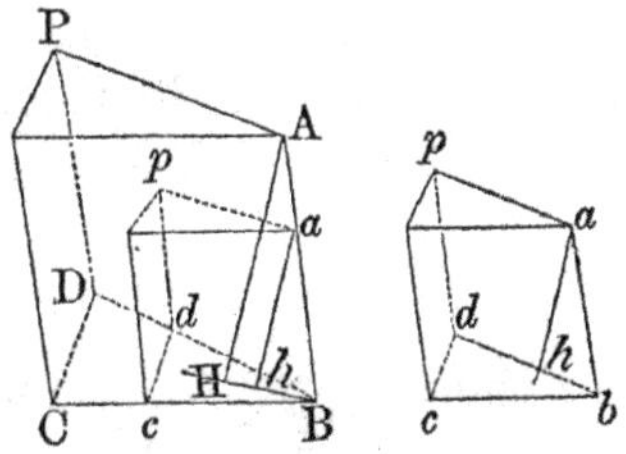

For, since the prisms are similar, the homologous angles B and b are equal, and the faces which bound them are similar (D. 16). Hence, if these triedral angles be applied, the one to the other, the angles cbd will coincide with CBD, the edge ba with BA, and the prism cbd-p will take the position Bcd-p. From A draw AH perpendicular to the common base of the prisms: then will the plane BAH be perpendicular to the plane of the common base (B. VI., P. 16). Through a, in the plane BAH, draw ah perpendicular to BH: then will ah also be perpendicular to the base BDC (B. VI., P. 17); and AH, ah will be the altitudes of the two prisms.

Since the bases CBD, cbd, are similar, we have (B. IV., P. 25),

$$\text{base } CBD : \text{base } cbd :: \overline{CB}^2 : \overline{cb}^2.$$

Now, because of the similar triangles ABH, aBh, and of the similar parallelograms AC, ac, we have

$$AH : ah :: AB : ab :: CB : cb;$$

hence, multiplying together the corresponding terms, we have

$$\text{base } CBD \times AH : \text{base } cbd \times ah :: \overline{CB}^3 : \overline{cb}^3.$$

But the solidity of a prism is equal to the base multiplied by the altitude (P. 14); hence,

$$\text{prism } BCD\text{-}P : \text{prism } bcd\text{-}p :: \overline{BC}^3 : \overline{bc}^3,$$

or as the cubes of any other of their homologous edges.

Cor. Whatever be the bases of similar prisms, the prisms are to each other as the cubes of their homologous edges.

For, since the prisms are similar, their bases are similar polygons (D. 16); and these similar polygons may each be divided into the same number of similar triangles, similarly placed (B. IV., P. 26); therefore, each prism may be divided into the same number of triangular prisms, having their faces similar and like placed; hence, their polyedral angles are equal (B. VI., P. 21, S. 2); and consequently, the triangular prisms are similar (D. 16). But these triangular prisms are to each other as the cubes of their homologous edges, and being like parts of the polygonal prisms, their sums, that is, the polygonal prisms, are to each other as the cubes of their homologous edges.

PROPOSITION XX. THEOREM.

Two similar pyramids are to each other as the cubes of their homologous edges.

For, since the pyramids are similar, the homologous polyedral angles at the vertices are equal (D. 16). Hence, the polyedral angles at the vertices may be made to coincide, or the two pyramids may be so placed as to have the polyedral angle S common.

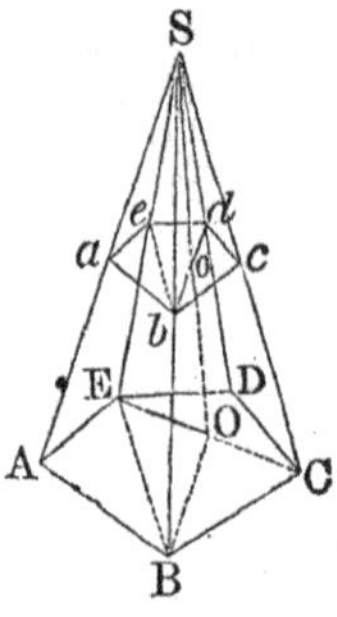

In that position the bases $ABCDE$, $abcde$, are parallel; for, the homologous faces being similar, the angle Sab is equal to SAB, and Sbc to SBC; hence, the plane ABC, is parallel to the plane abc (B. VI., P. 13). This being proved, let SO be drawn from the vertex S, perpendicular to the plane ABC, and let o, be the point where this perpendicular pierces the plane abc: from what has already been shown, we have (P. 3),

$$SO : So :: SA : Sa :: AB : ab;$$

and consequently,

$$\tfrac{1}{3}SO : \tfrac{1}{3}So :: AB : ab.$$

But the bases $ABCDE$, $abcde$, being similar figures, we have (B. IV., P. 27),

$$ABCDE : abcde :: \overline{AB}^2 : \overline{ab}^2;$$

multiply the corresponding terms of these two proportions, there results,

$$ABCDE \times \tfrac{1}{3}SO : abcde \times \tfrac{1}{3}So :: \overline{AB}^3 : \overline{ab}^3.$$

Now, $ABCDE \times \frac{1}{3}SO$ measures the solidity of the pyramid S-$ABCDE$, and $abcde \times \frac{1}{3}So$ measures that of the pyramid S-$abcde$ (P. 17); hence, two similar pyramids are to each other as the cubes of their homologous edges.

GENERAL SCHOLIUMS.

1. The chief propositions of this Book relating to the volumes of polyedrons, may be expressed in algebraical terms, and so recapitulated in the briefest manner possible.

2. Let B represent the base of a *prism*, H its altitude, and V the volume or contents; then,

$$V = B \times H.$$

3. Let B represent the base of a *pyramid*, H its altitude, and V the volume or contents; then,

$$V = B \times \tfrac{1}{3}H.$$

4. Let H represent the altitude of the *frustum of a pyramid*, having the parallel bases A and B; $\sqrt{A \times B}$ is the mean proportional between those bases; then,

$$V = \tfrac{1}{3}H(A + B + \sqrt{A \times B})$$

5. In fine, let P and p represent the *contents of two similar prisms or pyramids;* A and a, two homologous edges: then,

$$P : p :: A^3 : a^3.$$

BOOK VIII.

THE THREE ROUND BODIES.

DEFINITIONS.

1. A CYLINDER is a volume which may be generated by the revolution of a rectangle *ABCD*, turning about the immovable side *AB*.

In this movement, the sides *AD, BC*, continuing always perpendicular to *AB*, describe the equal circles *DHP, CGQ*, which are called the *bases of the cylinder;* the side *CD*, describing, at the same time, the *convex surface.*

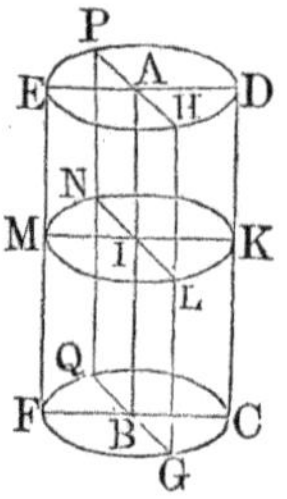

The immovable line *AB* is called the *axis of the cylinder.*

Every section *MNKL*, made in the cylinder, by a plane, at right angles to the axis, is a circle equal to either of the bases. For, whilst the rectangle *ABCD* turns about *AB*, the line *KI*, perpendicular to *AB*, describes a circle, equal to the base, and this circle is nothing else than the section made by a plane, perpendicular to the axis at the point *I*.

Every section *QPHG*, made by a plane passing through the axis, is a rectangle double the generating rectangle *ABCD*.

2. SIMILAR CYLINDERS are those whose axes are proportional to the radii of their bases: hence, they are generated by similar rectangles (B. IV., D. 1).

3. If, in the circle $ABCDE$, which forms the base of a cylinder, a polygon $ABCDE$ be inscribed, and a right prism, constructed on this base, and equal in altitude to the cylinder; then, the prism is said to be *inscribed in the cylinder*, and the cylinder to be *circumscribed about the prism.*

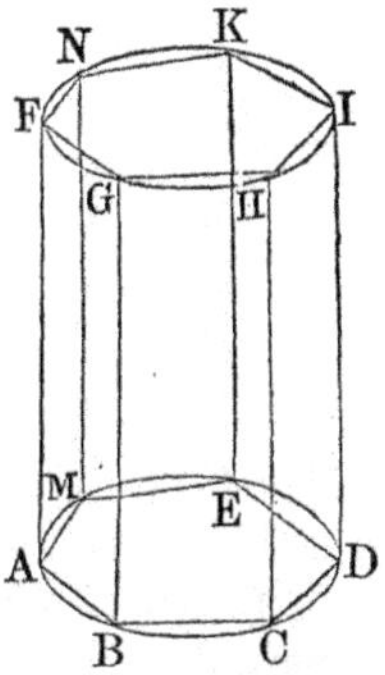

The edges AF, BG, CH, &c., of the prism, being perpendicular to the plane of the base, are contained in the convex surface of the cylinder; hence, the prism and the cylinder touch one another along these edges.

4. In like manner, if $ABCD$ is a polygon, circumscribed about the base of a cylinder, a right prism constructed on this base, and equal in altitude to the cylinder, is said to be *circumscribed about the cylinder*, and the cylinder to be *inscribed in the prism.*

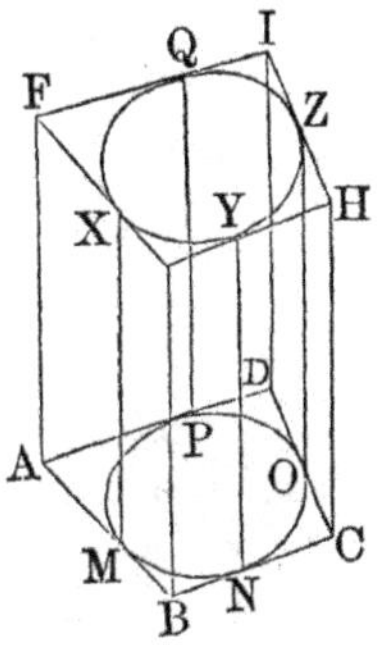

Let M, N, &c., be the points of contact in the sides AB, BC, &c.; and through the points M, N, &c., let MX, NY, &c., be drawn perpendicular to the plane of the base: these perpendiculars will then lie both in the surface of the cylinder, and in that of the circumscribed prism; hence, they will be their lines of contact.

5. A CONE is a volume which may be generated by the revolution of a right-angled triangle SAB, turning about the immovable side SA.

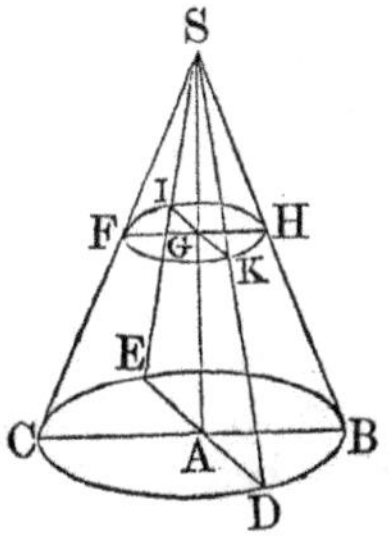

In this movement, the side AB describes a circle $BDCE$, called the *base of the cone;* the hypothenuse SB describes the *convex surface of the cone.*

The point S is called the *vertex of the cone*, SA the *axis*, or the *altitude*, and SB the *slant height.*

Every section $HKFI$, made by a

plane, at right angles to the axis, is a circle. Every section *EDS*, made by a plane passing through the axis, is an isosceles triangle, double the generating triangle *SAB*.

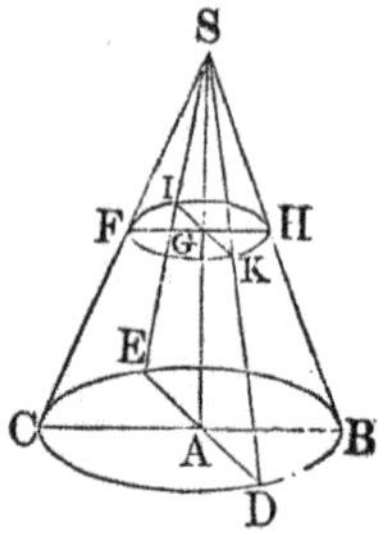

6. If, from the cone *S-CDB*, the cone *S-FKH* be cut off by a plane parallel to the base, the remaining part *CFHB* is called a *truncated* cone, or the frustum of a cone.

The frustum may be generated by the revolution of the trapezoid *ABHG*, turning about the side *AG*. The immovable line *AG* is called the *axis*, or *altitude of the frustum*, the circles *BDC*, *HFK*, are its *bases*, and *BH* its *slant height*.

7. Similar Cones are those whose axes are proportional to the radii of their bases: hence, they are generated by similar right-angled triangles (B. IV., D. 1).

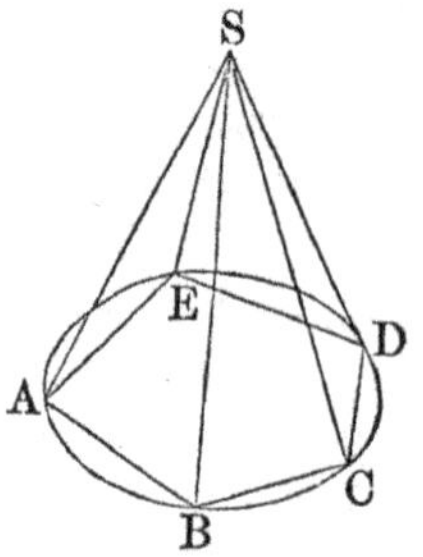

8. If, in the circle *ABCDE*, which forms the base of a cone, any polygon *ABCDE* is inscribed, and from the vertices *A*, *B*, *C*, *D*, *E*, lines are drawn to *S*, the vertex of the cone, these lines may be regarded as the edges of a pyramid whose base is the polygon *ABCDE* and vertex *S*. The edges of this pyramid are in the convex surface of the cone, and the pyramid is said to be *inscribed* in the cone. The cone is also said to be *circumscribed* about the pyramid.

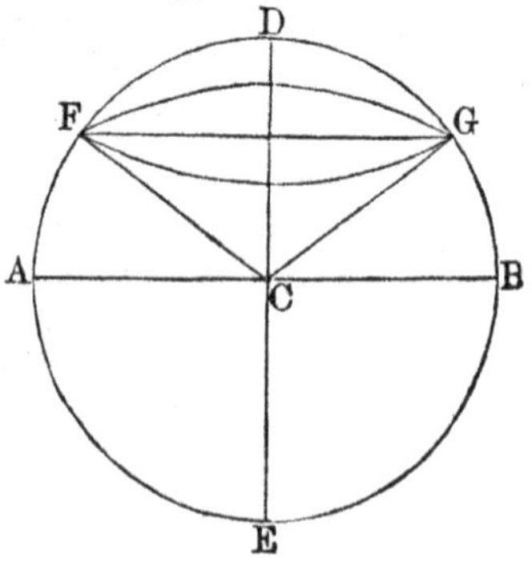

9. The Sphere is a volume terminated by a curved surface, all the points of which are equally distant from a point within, called the *centre*.

The sphere may be generated by the revolution of a semicircle *DAE*, about its diameter *DE*: for, the surface described in this movement, by the semicircumference DAE, will have all its points equally distant from its centre C.

10. Whilst the semicircle DAE, revolving round its diameter DE, describes the sphere, any circular sector, as DCF, or FCA, describes a volume, called a *spherical sector.*

11. The *radius of a sphere* is a straight line drawn from the centre to any point of the surface; the *diameter* or *axis* is a line passing through the centre, and terminated, on both sides, by the surface.

All the radii of a sphere are equal; all the diameters are equal, and each is double the radius.

12. It will be shown (P. 7,) that every section of a sphere, made by a plane, is a circle: this granted, a *great circle* is a section which passes through the centre; a *small circle*, is one which does not pass through the centre.

13. *A plane* is *tangent* to a sphere, when it has but one point in common with the surface.

14. A *zone* is the portion of the surface of the sphere included between the circumferences of two parallel circles, which form its *bases.* If the plane of one of these circles becomes tangent to the sphere, the zone will have only a single base.

15. A *spherical segment* is the portion of the solid sphere, included between two parallel circles which form its bases. If the plane of one of these circles becomes tangent to the sphere, the segment will have only a single base.

16. The *altitude of a zone*, or *of a segment*, is the distance between the planes of the two parallel circles, which form the bases of the zone or segment.

17. The Cylinder, the Cone, and the Sphere, are the *three round bodies* treated of in the Elements of Geometry.

PROPOSITION I. THEOREM.

The convex surface of a cylinder is equal to the circumference of its base multiplied by its altitude.

Let CA be the radius of the base of a cylinder, and H its altitude; denote the circumference whose radius is CA by *circ.* CA: then will the convex surface of the cylinder be equal to *circ.* $CA \times H$.

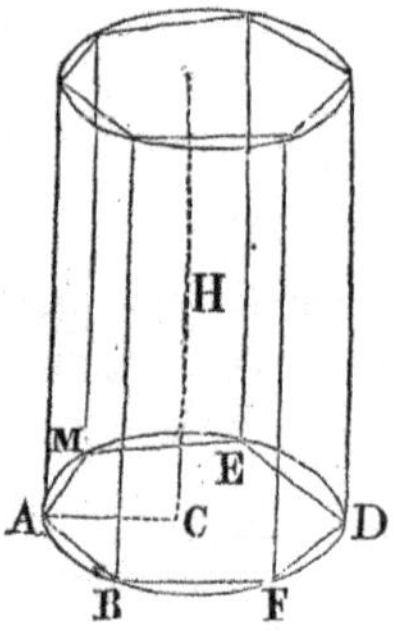

Inscribe in the base of the cylinder any regular polygon, $ABFDEM$, and construct on this polygon a right prism having its altitude equal to H, the altitude of the cylinder: this prism will be inscribed in the cylinder. The convex surface of the prism is equal to the perimeter of the polygon, multiplied by the altitude H (B. VII., P. 1). Let now the arcs which are subtended by the sides of the polygon be continually bisected, and the number of sides of the polygon continually doubled: the limit of the perimeter of the polygon is *circ.* CA (B. 5, P. 12, S. 2), and the limit of the convex surface of the prism is the convex surface of the cylinder. But the convex surface of the prism is always equal to the perimeter of its base multiplied by H; hence, *the convex surface of the cylinder is equal to the circumference of its base multiplied by its altitude.*

PROPOSITION II. THEOREM.

The contents of a cylinder are equal to the product of its base by its altitude.

Let CA be the radius of the base of the cylinder, and H the altitude. Let the circle whose radius is CA be denoted by *area* CA: then will the solidity of the cylinder be equal to *area* $CA \times H$.

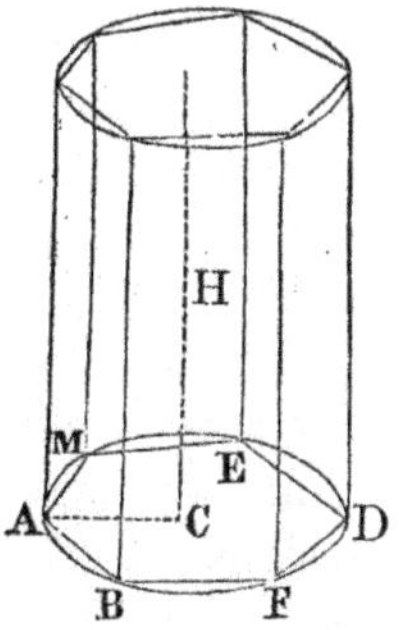

For, inscribe in the base of the cylinder any regular polygon *ABDEM*, and construct on this polygon a right prism having its altitude equal to *H*, the altitude of the cylinder: this prism will be inscribed in the cylinder. The solidity of this prism will be equal to the area of the polygon multiplied by the altitude *H* (B. VII., P. 14).

Let now the number of sides of the polygon be continually increased, as before described; the solidity of each new prism will still be equal to its base multiplied by its altitude: the limit of the polygon is the *area CA*, and the limit of the prisms, the circumscribed cylinder. But the solidity of each new prism is equal to the base multiplied by the altitude: therefore, *the contents of the cylinder are equal to the product of its base by its altitude.*

Cor. 1. Cylinders of equal altitudes are to each other as their bases; and cylinders of equal bases are to each other as their altitudes.

Cor. 2. Similar cylinders are to each other as the cubes of their altitudes, or as the cubes of the radii of their bases. For, the bases are as the squares of their radii (B. V., P. 13); and the cylinders being similar, the radii of their bases are to each other as their altitudes (D. 2); hence, the bases are as the squares of the altitudes; therefore, the bases multiplied by the altitudes, or the cylinders themselves, are as the cubes of the altitudes.

Scholium. Let R denote the radius of a cylinder's base, and H the altitude; then we shall have,

$$\text{surface of base} = \pi \times R^2,$$
$$\text{convex surface} = 2\pi \times R \times H,$$
$$\text{contents} = \pi \times R^2 \times H.$$

PROPOSITION III. THEOREM.

The convex surface of a cone is equal to the circumference of its base, multiplied by half the slant height.

Let the circle $ABCDE$ be the base of a cone, S the vertex, SO the altitude, and SA the slant height: then will the convex surface be equal to *circ.* $OA \times \frac{1}{2}SA$.

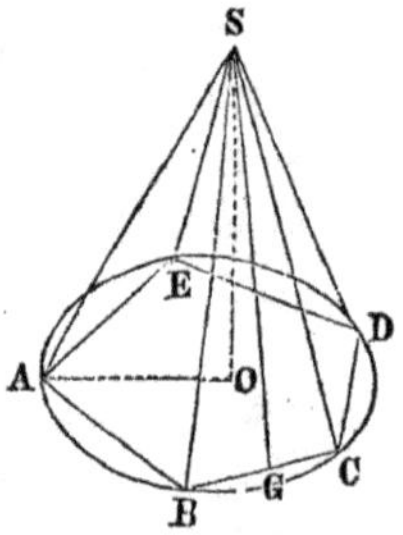

For, inscribe in the base of the cone any regular polygon $ABCDE$, and on this polygon as a base conceive a right pyramid to be constructed, having S for its vertex: this pyramid will be inscribed in the cone.

From S, draw SG perpendicular to one of the sides of the polygon. The convex surface of the inscribed pyramid is equal to the perimeter of the polygon which forms its base, multiplied by half the slant height SG (B. VII., P. 4). Let now the number of sides of the inscribed polygon be continually increased, as before described: the limit of the perimeters of the polygons is *circ.* OA; the limit of the slant height of the pyramids is the slant height of the cone, and the limit of their surfaces, is the convex surface of the circumscribed cone. But the convex surface of each new pyramid is equal to the perimeter of the base multiplied by half the slant height (B. VII., P. 4); hence, *the convex surface of the cone is equal to the circumference of its base multiplied by half its slant height.*

Scholium. Let L denote the slant height, and R the radius of the base: then,

$$\text{convex surface} = 2\pi \times R \times \tfrac{1}{2}L = \pi \times R \times L.$$

PROPOSITION IV. THEOREM.

The convex surface of the frustum of a cone is equal to its slant height, multiplied by half the sum of the circumferences of its bases.

Let *BIA-DE* be a frustum of a cone: then will,

$$\text{convex surface}=AD\times\tfrac{1}{2}(circ.\ OA+circ.\ CD.)$$

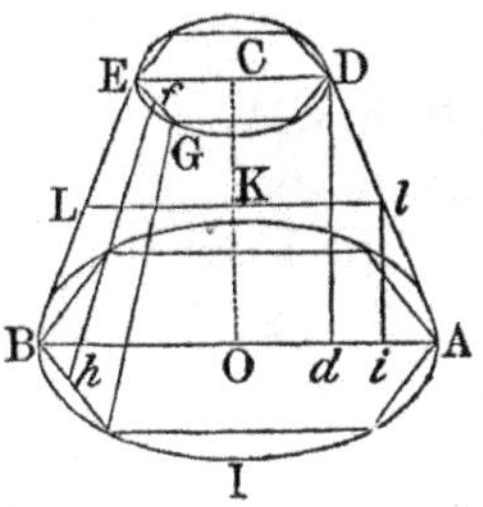

For, inscribe in the bases of the frustum two regular polygons of the same number of sides, and having their sides parallel, each to each. The lines joining the vertices of the corresponding angles may be regarded as the edges of the frustum of a right pyramid inscribed in the frustum of the cone. The convex surface of the frustum of the pyramid is equal to half the sum of the perimeters of its bases multiplied by the slant height *fh* (B. VII., P. 4, C.) Let the number of sides of the inscribed polygons be continually increased as before described: the limits of the perimeters of the polygons are *circ. OA* and *circ. CD*; the limit of the slant height is the slant height of the frustum, and the limit of the convex surface, the convex surface of the frustum; hence, *the convex surface of the frustum of a cone is equal to its slant height multiplied by half the sum of the circumferences of its bases.*

Cor. Through *l*, the middle point of *AD*, draw *lKL* parallel to *AB*, also *li*, *Dd*, parallel to *CO*. Then, since *Al*, *lD*, are equal, *Ai*, *id*, are also equal (B. IV., P. 15, C. 2): hence, *Kl* is equal to $\frac{1}{2}(OA+CD)$. But since the circumferences of circles are to each other as their radii (B. V., P. 13),

$$circ.\ Kl=\tfrac{1}{2}(circ.\ OA+circ.\ CD);$$

therefore, *the convex surface of the frustum of a cone is equal to its slant height multiplied by the circumference of a section at equal distances from the two bases.*

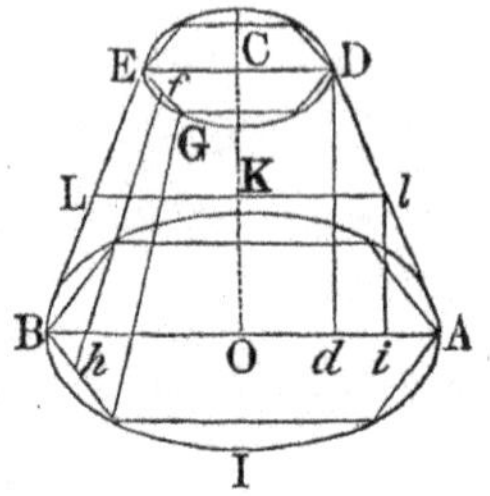

Scholium 1. If from the middle point l and the two extremities A and D, of a line AD, lying wholly on one side of the line OC, the perpendiculars DC, lK, and AO, be drawn, and then the line AD be revolved around OC, we shall have

surf. described by $AD = AD \times \frac{1}{2}(circ.\ OA + circ.\ CD)$
that is, $= AD \times circ.\ Kl.$

For, it is evident that the surface described by AD is that of the frustum of a cone, having OA and CD for the radii of its bases.

Scholium 2. The measure found above applies equally to the case when the point D falls at C, and the surface becomes that of a cone; and to the case in which AD becomes parallel to OC, and the surface becomes that of a cylinder. In the first case, CD is nothing: in the second, it is equal to OA.

PROPOSITION V. THEOREM.

The contents of a cone are equal to its base multiplied by a third of its altitude.

Let SO be the altitude of a cone, OA the radius of its base, and let the area of the base be designated by *area* OA; then will,

$$\text{contents} = area\ OA \times \tfrac{1}{3}SO.$$

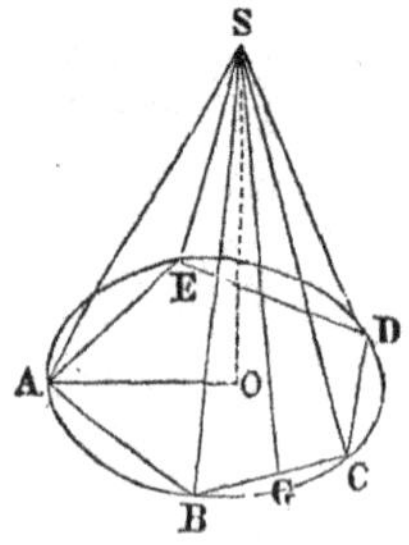

Inscribe in the base of the cone any regular polygon $ABCDE$, and join the vertices A, B, C, &c., with the vertex S of the cone: then will there be inscribed in the cone a right pyramid having the same vertex as the cone, and having for its base the polygon $ABCDE$. The contents of this pyramid will be equal to its base multiplied by one-third of its altitude (B. VII., P. 17).

Let the arcs be bisected and the number of sides of the polygon be continually increased: the limit of the polygons will be the *area OA*, and the limit of the pyramids will be the cone whose vertex is S: hence, *the contents of the cone are equal to its base multiplied by a third of its altitude.*

Cor. 1. A cone is the third of a cylinder having the same base and the same altitude; whence it follows,

1. That cones of equal altitudes are to each other as their bases.

2. That cones of equal bases are to each other as their altitudes;

3. That similar cones are as the cubes of the diameters of their bases, or as the cubes of their altitudes.

Cor. 2. The contents of a cone are equal to the contents of a pyramid having an equivalent base and the same altitude.

Scholium. Let R denote the radius of a cone's base, H its altitude, and V the contents; then,

$$V = \tfrac{1}{3}\pi \times R^2 \times H.$$

PROPOSITION VI. THEOREM.

The contents of the frustum of a cone is equal to the sum of the contents of three cones whose common altitude is the altitude of the frustum, and whose bases are, the lower base of the frustum, the upper base of the frustum, and a mean proportional between them.

Let $AEB\text{-}CD$ be the frustum of a cone, and OP its altitude; then will its contents be equivalent to

$$\tfrac{1}{3}\pi \times OP \times (\overline{OB}^2 + \overline{PC}^2 + OB \times PC).$$

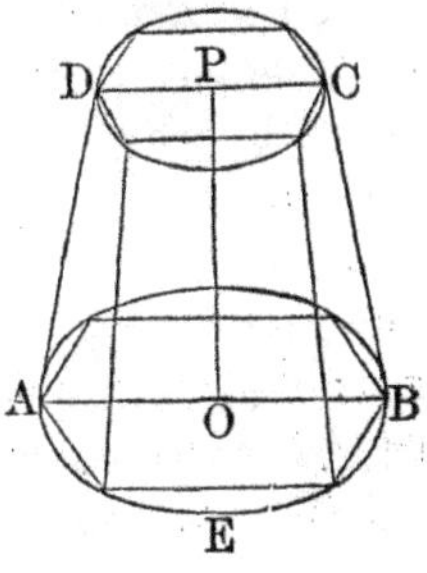

For, inscribe in the lower and upper bases two regular polygons having the same number of sides, and having their sides parallel, each to each. Join the vertices of the corresponding angles, and there will then be inscribed in the frustum of the cone, the frustum of a regular pyramid. The contents of the frustum of this pyramid will be equivalent to three pyramids having the common altitude of the frustum, and for bases, the lower base of the frustum, the upper base of the frustum, and a mean proportional between them (B. VII., P. 18).

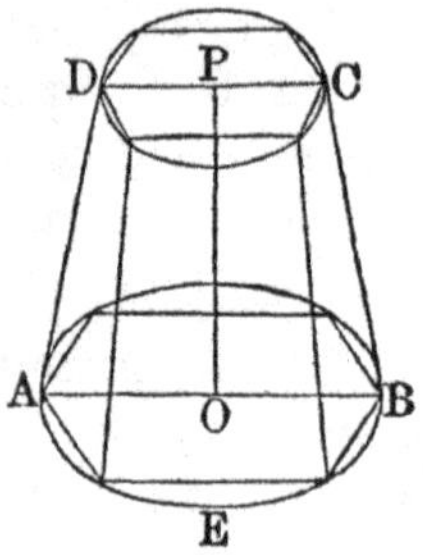

Let the number of sides of the inscribed polygons be continually doubled by the methods before described: the limits of the polygons will be, *area* OB and *area* PC; and the limit of the frustums of the pyramids will be the frustum of the cone: the expression for the contents will then become:

of the first pyramid,	$\frac{1}{3}OP\times\overline{OB}^2\times\pi$,
of the second	$\frac{1}{3}OP\times\overline{PC}^2\times\pi$,
of the third	$\frac{1}{3}OP\times OB\times PC\times\pi$.

hence, the contents of the frustum of the cone are equivalent to

$$\tfrac{1}{3}\pi\times OP\times(\overline{OB}^2+\overline{PC}^2+OB\times PC.)$$

PROPOSITION VII. THEOREM.

Every section of a sphere, made by a plane, is a circle.

Let AMB be any section made by a plane, in the sphere whose centre is C: then will it be a circle.

For, from the point C, draw CO perpendicular to the plane AMB; and different lines CM, CM, to different points of the curve AMB, which terminates the section.

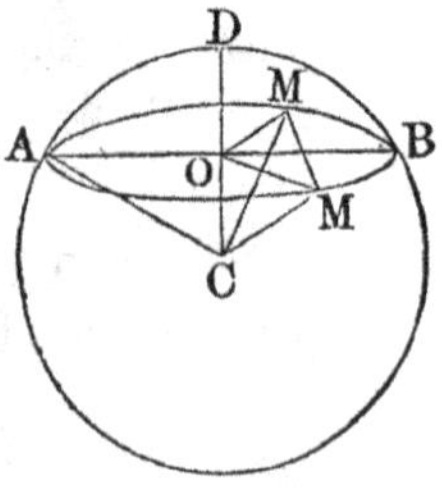

The oblique lines CM, CM, CA, are equal, being radii of the sphere; hence, they pierce the plane AMB at equal distances from the perpendicular CO (B. VI., P. 5, C.); therefore, all the lines OM, OM, OB, are equal; consequently, the section AMB is a circle, whose centre is O.

Cor. 1. If the section pass through the centre of the sphere, its radius will be the radius of the sphere; hence, all great circles are equal.

Cor. 2. Two great circles always bisect each other; for their common intersection, passing through the centre, is a diameter.

Cor. 3. Every great circle divides the sphere and its surface into two equal parts: for, if the two parts were separated and afterwards placed on the common base, with their convexities turned the same way, the two surfaces would exactly coincide, no point of the one being nearer the centre than any point of the other.

Cor. 4. The centre of a small circle, and that of the sphere, are in the same straight line, perpendicular to the plane of the small circle.

Cor. 5. The radius of any small circle is less than the radius of the sphere; and the further its centre is removed from the centre of the sphere, the less is its radius. for, the greater CO is, the less is the chord AB, the diameter of the small circle AMB.

Cor. 6. An arc of a great circle may always be made to pass through any two given points of the surface of the sphere: for, the two given points, and the centre of the sphere make three points, which determine the position of a plane. But if the two given points were at the extremities of a diameter, these two points and the centre would then lie in one straight line, and an infinite number of great circles might be made to pass through the two given points.

Cor. 7. *The distance between any two points on the surface of a sphere is less when measured on the arc of a great circle than when measured on the arc of a small circle.*

For, let A and B be any two points on the surface of a sphere, let ADB be the arc of a great circle, and AMB

the arc of a small circle passing through them, and AB the common chord. Then, since the radius CA is greater than the radius OA, the arc ADB is less than the arc AMB (B. V., P. 17).

PROPOSITION VIII. THEOREM.

Every plane perpendicular to a radius at its extremity is tangent to the sphere.

Let FAG be a plane perpendicular to the radius OA, at its extremity A: then will it be tangent to the sphere.

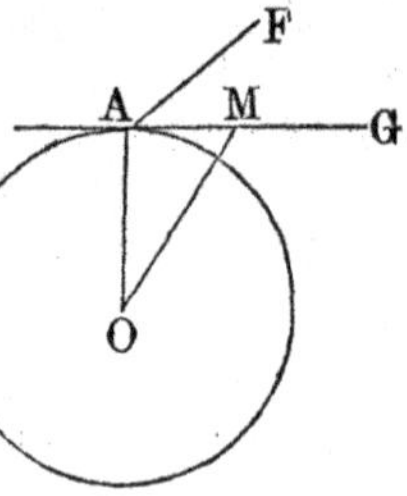

For, assuming any other point M in this plane, draw OA, OM: then the angle OAM is a right angle, and hence, the distance OM is greater than OA: therefore, the point M lies without the sphere; hence, the plane FAG, can have no point but A common to it and the surface of the sphere; consequently, it is a tangent plane (D. 13).

Scholium. In the same way it may be shown, that two spheres are tangent the one to the other, when the distance between their centres is equal to the sum or the difference of their radii; in which case, the centres and the point of contact lie in the same straight line.

PROPOSITION IX. LEMMA.

If a regular semi-polygon be revolved about a line passing through the centre and the vertices of two opposite angles, the surface described by its perimeter will be equal to the axis multiplied by the circumference of the inscribed circle.

Let the regular semi-polygon $ABCDEF$, be revolved about the line AF as an axis: then will the surface described by its perimeter be equal to AF multiplied by the circumference of the inscribed circle.

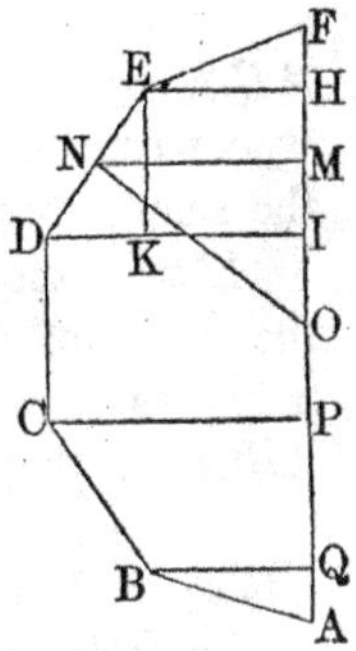

For, from E and D, the extremities of one of the equal sides, let fall the perpendiculars EH, DI, on the axis AF; and from the centre O, draw ON perpendicular to the side DE: ON will be the radius of the inscribed circle (B. V., P. 2). Now, the surface described in the revolution, by any one side of the regular polygon, as DE, has been shown to be equal to $DE \times circ.\ NM$ (P. 4, S. 1). But since the triangles EDK, ONM, are similar (B. IV., P. 21),

$$ED : EK \text{ or } HI :: ON : NM :: circ.\ ON : circ.\ NM;$$

hence, $$ED \times circ.\ NM = HI \times circ.\ ON;$$

and since the like may be shown for each of the other sides, it is plain that the surface described by the entire perimeter is equal to

$$(FH+HI+IP+PQ+QA) \times circ.\ ON = AF \times circ.\ ON.$$

Cor. The surface described by any portion of the perimeter, as EDC, is equal to the distance between the two perpendiculars let fall from its extremities on the axis, multiplied by the circumference of the inscribed circle.

For, the surface described by DE is equal to $HI \times circ.\ ON$, and the surface described by DC is equal to $IP \times circ.\ ON$: hence, the surface described by $ED+DC$, is equal to $(HI+IP) \times circ.\ ON$, or equal to $HP \times circ.\ ON$.

PROPOSITION X. THEOREM.

The surface of a sphere is equal to the product of its diameter by the circumference of a great circle.

Let $ABCDE$ be a semicircle. Inscribe in it a regular semi-polygon, and from the centre O draw OF perpendicular to one of the sides.

Let the semicircle and the semi-polygon be revolved about the common axis AE: the semicircumference $ABCDE$ will describe the surface of a sphere (D. 9); and the perimeter of the semi-polygon will describe a surface which has for its measure $AE \times circ.\ OF$ (P. 9), and this will be true whatever be the number of sides of the semi-polygon.

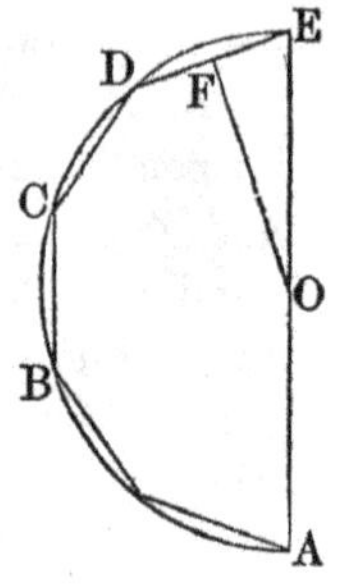

If now, the arcs be continually bisected, the limit of the perimeters of the semi-polygons will be the semicircumference $ABCDE$; the limit of the area described by the perimeter will be surface of the sphere, and the limit of the perpendicular OF will be the radius OE: hence, the surface of the sphere is equal to $AE \times circ.\ OE$.

Cor 1. Since the area of a great circle is equal to the product of its circumference by half the radius, or one-fourth of the diameter (B. V., P. 15), it follows that *the surface of a sphere is equal to four of its great circles*: that is, equal to $4\pi \times \overline{OA}^2$ (B. V., P. 16).

Cor. 2. *The surface of a zone is equal to its altitude multiplied by the circumference of a great circle.*

For, the surface described by any portion of the perimeter of the inscribed polygon, as $BC+CD$, is equal to $EH \times circ.\ OF$ (P. 9, C.): and when we pass to the limit, we have the surface of the zone equal to $EH \times circ.\ OA$.

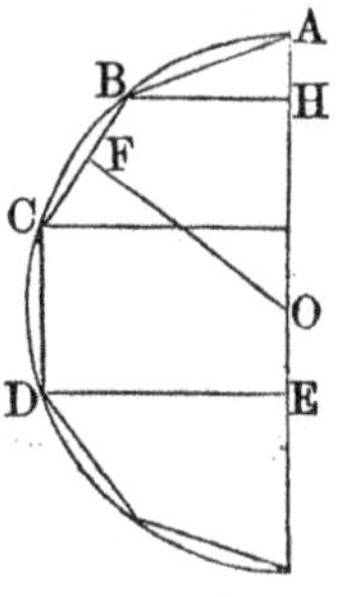

Cor. 3. When the zone has but one base, as the zone described by the arc $ABCD$, its surface will still be equal to the altitude AE multiplied by the circumference of a great circle.

Cor. 4. Two zones, taken in the same sphere or in equal spheres, are to each other as their altitudes; and any zone is to the surface of the sphere as the altitude of the zone is to the diameter of the sphere.

PROPOSITION XI. LEMMA.

If a triangle and a rectangle, having the same base and the same altitude, revolve together about the common base, the volume generated by the triangle is a third part of the cylinder generated by the rectangle.

Let BAC be a triangle, $BFEC$ a rectangle, having the common base BC, about which they are to be revolved.

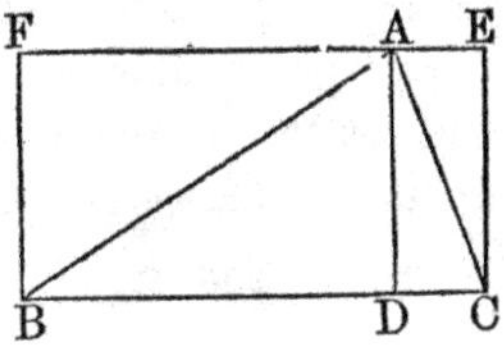

On the axis, let fall the perpendicular AD: then, the cone generated by the triangle BAD is a third part of the cylinder generated by the rectangle $BFAD$ (P. V., C. 1): also, the cone generated by the triangle DAC is a third part of the cylinder generated by the rectangle $DAEC$: hence, the sum of the two cones, or the solid generated by BAC, is a third part of the sum of the cylinders generated by the two rectangles, or a third part of the cylinder generated by the rectangle $BFEC$.

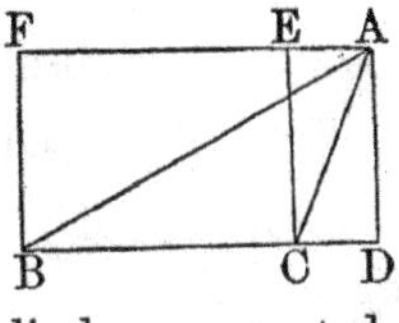

If the perpendicular AD falls without the triangle; the solid generated by CBA is, in that case, the difference of the two cones generated by BAD and CAD; but at the same time, the cylinder generated by $BFEC$, is the difference of the two cylinders generated by $BFAD$ and $CEAD$. Hence, the solid, generated by the revolution of the triangle, is still a third part of the cylinder generated by the revolution of the rectangle having the same base and the same altitude.

Scholium. The circle of which AD is the radius, has for its measure $\pi \times \overline{AD}^2$; hence, $\pi \times \overline{AD}^2 \times BC$ measures the cylinder generated by $BFEC$, and $\frac{1}{3}\pi \times \overline{AD}^2 \times BC$ measures the solid generated by the triangle BAC.

PROPOSITION XII. LEMMA.

The volume generated by the revolution of a triangle revolving about a line in the same plane, and passing through the vertex of one of the angles, is measured by the surface described by the opposite side multiplied by one-third of the perpendicular drawn from the vertex of the angle to the opposite side.

1. Let CAB be a triangle, and CG perpendicular to the side AB; and let this triangle be revolved about the base CB: then,

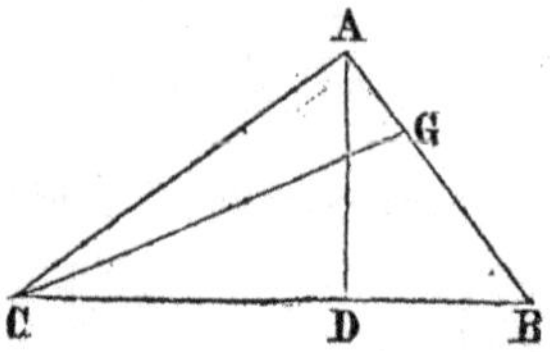

Vol. CAB=Surf. $AB\times\frac{1}{3}CG$.*

Draw AD perpendicular to CB; then (P. XI.)

$$\text{Vol. } CAB=\tfrac{1}{3}\pi\times\overline{AD}^2\times CD+\tfrac{1}{3}\pi\times\overline{AD}^2\times DB=\tfrac{1}{3}\pi\times\overline{AD}^2\times CB.$$

Since CG is perpendicular to AB, we shall have,

$$AD\times CB=CG\times AB,$$

for each product is equal to double the area of the triangle (B. IV., P. 6): Substituting $CG\times AB$ for $AD\times CB$, we have,

$$\text{Vol. } CAB=\tfrac{1}{3}\pi AD\times CG\times AB=\tfrac{1}{3}CG\times\pi\times AD\times AB.$$

But $\pi\times AD\times AB$ is the measure of the convex surface of a cone described by AB (P. 3., SCH.): hence,

$$\text{Vol. } CAB=\text{ Surf. } AB\times\tfrac{1}{3}CG.$$

2. Let us now suppose that the triangle CAB revolves around a right line CD passing through the vertex C. Prolong AB till it intersects the axis at D, and draw CG perpendicular to AB. We shall then have,

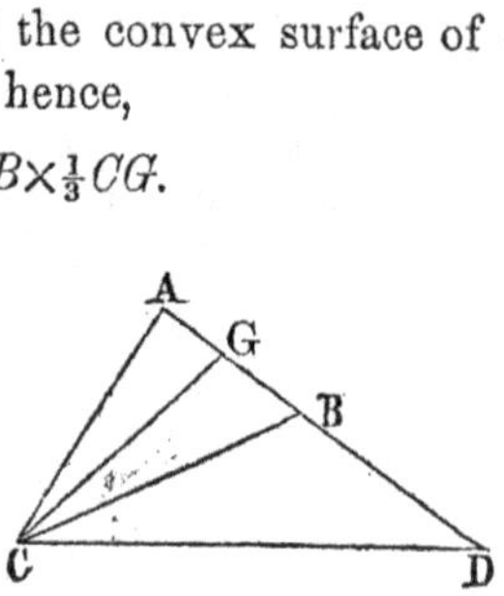

Vol. CAB= Vol. CAD−Vol. CBD. But,

Vol. CAD= Surf. $AD\times\frac{1}{3}CG$; and

Vol. CBD= Surf. $BD\times\frac{1}{3}CG$; hence,

---

* NOTE.—By Vol. CAB, we mean the volume generated by the triangle; and by Surf AB, the surface generated by the line AB.

$$\text{Vol. } CAB = (\text{Surf. } AD - \text{Surf. } BD) \times \tfrac{1}{3} CG,$$
$$= \text{Surf. } AB \times \tfrac{1}{3} CG.$$

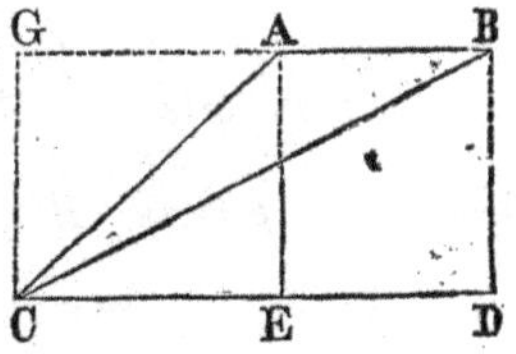

3. In the preceding demonstration, the side AB was supposed to meet the axis CD: let us examine the case when it is parallel to it.

Draw AE and BD perpendicular to the axis CD, and CG perpendicular to the base AB, produced. We shall then have,

$$\text{Vol. } CAB = \text{Vol. } CAE + \text{Vol. } ABDE - \text{Vol. } CBD.$$

But,
$$\text{Vol. } CAE = \tfrac{1}{3}\pi \times \overline{AE}^2 \times CE$$
$$\text{Vol. } ABDE = \pi \times \overline{AE}^2 \times ED$$
$$\text{Vol. } CBD = \tfrac{1}{3}\pi \times \overline{AE}^2 \times CD.$$

Adding the two first equalities, member to member, and then subtracting the third, we have,

$$\text{Vol. } CAB = \pi \overline{AE}^2 (\tfrac{1}{3} CE + ED - \tfrac{1}{3} CD),$$

and as $CD = CE + ED$, we shall have,

$$\text{Vol. } CAB = \pi \overline{AE}^2 \times \tfrac{2}{3}\pi \times ED = \tfrac{1}{3} AE \times 2\pi \times AE \times ED$$
$$= \text{Surf. } AB \times \tfrac{1}{3} CG;$$

which corresponds with the eunciation.

Cor. If the triangle is isosceles, *the volume is measured by two-thirds of π into the square of the perpendicular let fall on the base into the distance between the two perpendiculars let fall from the extremities of the base on the axis.*

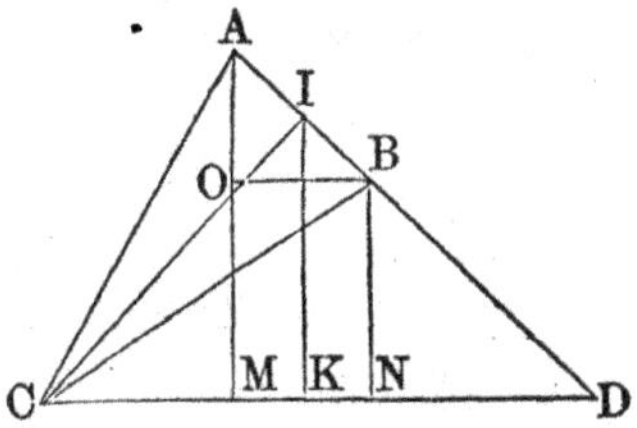

For, when the triangle is isosceles, the perpendicular will pass through I, the middle point of the base, and we shall have,

$$\text{Vol. } CAB = \text{surf. } AB \times \tfrac{1}{3} CI.$$

But (P. IV., SC. 1), Surf. $AB = AB \times \text{circ. } IK$; and

$$\text{circ. } IK = 2\pi IK \text{ (B. V., P. 16); hence,}$$

$$\text{Vol. } CAB = AB \times 2\pi IK \times \tfrac{1}{3}CI = \tfrac{2}{3}\pi AB \times IK \times CI.$$

Having drawn BO parallel, and AM, BN, perpendicular to the base, the triangles AOB, CKI, are similar (B. IV., P. 21);

hence, $AB : BO$ or $MN :: CI : IK$,

which gives, $AB \times IK = MN \times CI$.

Substituting for $AB \times IK$, we have,

$$\text{Vol. } CAB = \tfrac{2}{3}\pi \overline{CI}^2 \times MN.$$

PROPOSITION XIII. LEMMA.

If a regular semi-polygon be revolved about a line passing through its centre and the vertices of two opposite angles, the volume generated will be measured by the surface described by the perimeter into one-third of the apothem.

Let $GDBF$ be a regular semi-polygon, and OI the apothem; then, if this semi-polygon be revolved about GF, the volume generated will have for its measure,

$$\text{Surf. } GDBF \times \tfrac{1}{3}OI.$$

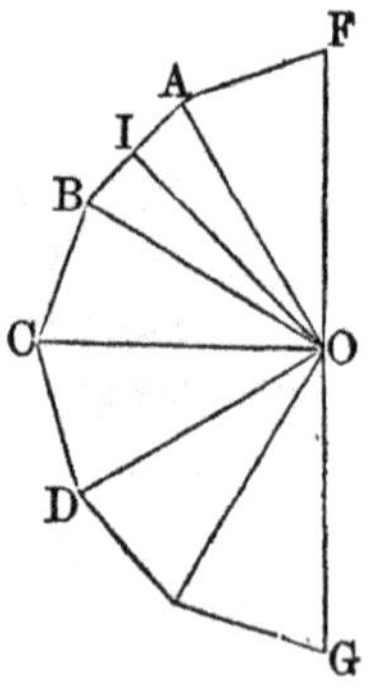

For, since the polygon is regular, the triangles, OFA, OAB, OBC, &c., are isosceles and equal; then, every perpendicular let fall from O on a base, will be equal to the apothem OI.

Now, we have the following measures for the volumes generated by these triangles (P. 12): viz.,

$$\text{Vol. } OFA = \text{Surf. } AF \times \tfrac{1}{3}OI,$$
$$\text{Vol. } OAB = \text{Surf. } AB \times \tfrac{1}{3}OI,$$
$$\text{Vol. } OBC = \text{Surf. } BC \times \tfrac{1}{3}OI,$$

&c. &c. &c.

Hence the entire volume generated by the semi-polygon, is

measured by the sum of all the surfaces generated by the sides multiplied by $\frac{1}{3}OI$: that is,

$$\text{Vol. } GDBF = \text{Surf. } GDBF \times \tfrac{1}{3}OI.$$

PROPOSITION XIV. THEOREM.

The contents of a sphere are equal to its surface multiplied by a third of its radius.

Let O be the centre of a sphere, and OA its radius: then its volume is equal to its surface into one-third of OA: that is,

$$\text{Vol. sphere} = \text{Surf. sphere} \times \tfrac{1}{3}OA.$$

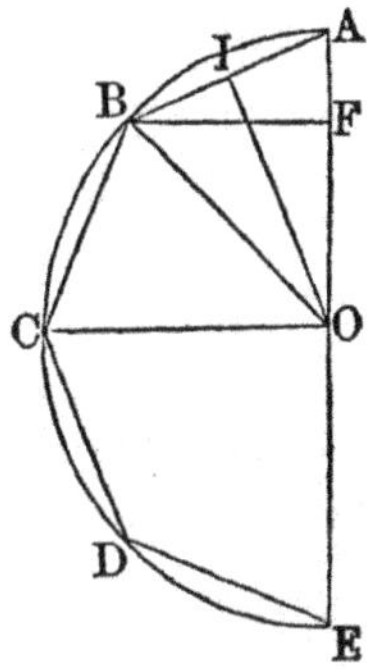

For, inscribe in the semi-circle $ABCDE$ a regular semi-polygon, having any number of sides, and let OI be the apothem of the polygon.

If the semi-circle and semi-polygon be revolved about EA, the semi-circle will generate a sphere, and the semi-polygon a volume, which has for its measure (P. 13),

$$\text{Surf. } ABCDE \times \tfrac{1}{3}OI;$$

and this is true whatever be the number of sides of the semi-polygon. But if the number of sides of the polygon be continually doubled, the limit of the surfaces of the polygons will be the surface of the sphere, and the limit of the volume of the polygons will be the volume of the sphere, and the apothem OI will become the radius OA. Hence, the expression,

$$\text{Vol. } ABCDE = \text{Surf. } ABCDE \times \tfrac{1}{3}OI, \text{ becomes}$$

$$\text{Vol. sphere} = \text{Surf.} \times \tfrac{1}{3}OA.$$

Scholium 1. *The contents of every spherical sector are equal to the zone which forms its base, multiplied by a third of the radius.*

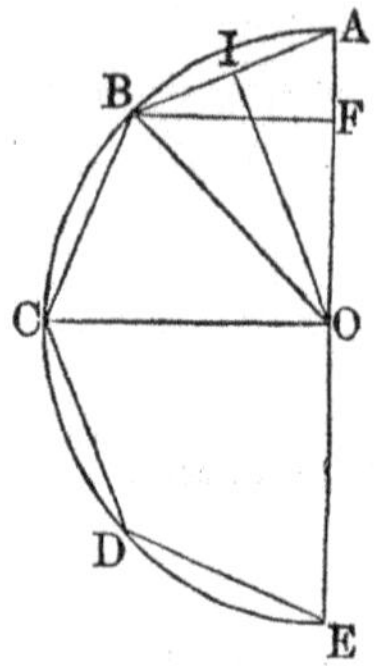

For, the volume generated by any portion of the regular polygon, as the isosceles triangle OAB, is measured by $\frac{2}{3}\pi\overline{OI}^2\times AF$ (P. 12, C.); and when we pass to the limit which is the spherical sector, the expression for this measure becomes $\frac{2}{3}\pi\times\overline{AO}^2\times AF$, which is equal to $2\pi\times AO\times AF\times\frac{1}{3}AO$. But $2\pi\times AO$ is the circumference of a great circle of the sphere (B. V., P. 16), which being multiplied by AF gives the surface of the zone which forms the base of the sector (P. X., C. 2); and the proof is equally applicable to the spherical sector described by the circular sector BOC: hence, *the contents of the spherical sector are equal to the zone which forms its base, multiplied by a third of the radius.*

Scholium 2. Since the surface of a sphere whose radius is R, is expressed by $4\pi\times R^2$ (P. X., C. 1), it follows that the surfaces of spheres are to each other as the squares of their radii; and since their volumes are as their surfaces multiplied by their radii, it follows that *the volumes of spheres are to each other as the cubes of their radii, or as the cubes of their diameters.*

Scholium 3. Let R be the radius of a sphere; its surface will be expressed by $4\pi\times R^2$, and its volume by $4\pi\times R^2\times\frac{1}{3}R$, or $\frac{4}{3}\pi\times R^3$. If the diameter be denoted by D, we shall have $R=\frac{1}{2}D$, and $R^3=\frac{1}{8}D^3$: hence, the volume of the sphere may be expressed by

$$\frac{4}{3}\pi\times\frac{1}{8}D^3=\frac{1}{6}\pi\times D^3.$$

PROPOSITION XV. THEOREM.

The surface of a sphere is to the whole surface of the circumscribed cylinder, including its bases, as 2 is to 3: and the volumes of these two bodies are to each other in the same ratio.

Let $MPNQ$ be a great circle of the sphere; $ABCD$ the

circumscribed square; if the semicircle PMQ and the half square $PADQ$ are at the same time made to revolve about the diameter PQ, the semicircle will generate the sphere, while the half square will generate the cylinder circumscribed about that sphere.

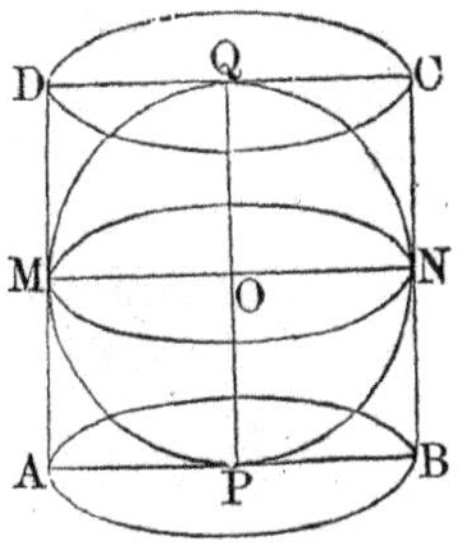

The altitude AD of the cylinder is equal to the diameter PQ; the base of the cylinder is equal to a great circle, since its diameter AB is equal to MN; hence, the convex surface of the cylinder is equal to the circumference of the great circle multiplied by its diameter (P. 1). This measure is the same as that of the surface of the sphere (P. 10); hence, *the surface of the sphere is equal to the convex surface of the circumscribed cylinder.*

But the surface of the sphere is equal to four great circles; hence, the convex surface of the cylinder is also equal to four great circles: and adding the two bases, each equal to a great circle, the total surface of the circumscribed cylinder is equal to six great circles; hence, the surface of the sphere is to the total surface of the circumscribed cylinder, as 4 is to 6, or as 2 is to 3; which is the first branch of the proposition.

In the next place, since the base of the circumscribed cylinder is equal to a great circle of the sphere, and its altitude to the diameter, the volume of the cylinder is equal to a great circle multiplied by its diameter (P. 2). But the volume of the sphere is equal to four great circles multiplied by a third of the radius (P. 14); in other terms, to one great circle multiplied by $\frac{4}{3}$ of the radius, or by $\frac{2}{3}$ of the diameter; hence, the sphere is to the circumscribed cylinder as 2 to 3, and consequently, the volumes of these two bodies are as their surfaces.

Scholium 1. Conceive a polyedron, all of whose faces touch the sphere; this polyedron may be considered as composed of pyramids, each pyramid having for its vertex the centre of the sphere, and for its base one of the polyedron's faces. Now, it is evident that all these pyramids have the radius of the sphere for their common altitude: so that the volume of each pyramid will be equal to one face of the polyedron multiplied by a third of the radius: hence, the volume of the whole polyedron is equal to its surface multiplied by a third of the radius of the inscribed sphere.

It is therefore manifest, that the volumes of polyedrons circumscribed about the sphere, are to each other as their surfaces. Thus, the property, which we have shown to be true with regard to the circumscribed cylinder, is also true with regard to an infinite number of other volumes.

We might likewise have observed, that the surfaces of polygons, circumscribed about a circle, are to each other as their perimeters.

PROPOSITION XVI. THEOREM.

If a circular segment is revolved about a diameter exterior to it, the volume generated is measured by one-sixth of π *into the square of the chord, into the distance between two perpendiculars let fall from the extremities of the arc on the axis.*

Let *DMB* be a circular segment, and *AC* the axis about which it is revolved.

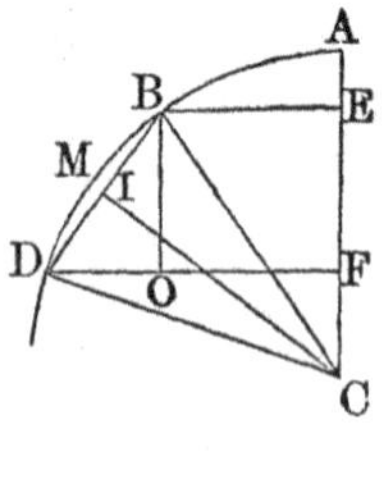

On the axis, let fall the perpendiculars *BE*, *DF*; from the centre *C*, draw *CI* perpendicular to the chord *BD*; also draw the radii *CB*, *CD*.

The volume generated by the sector *CDMB* is measured by $\frac{2}{3}\pi \times \overline{CB}^2 \times EF$ (P. 14, S. 1). The volume generated by the isosceles triangle *CDB* has for its measure $\frac{2}{3}\pi \times \overline{CI}^2 \times EF$ (P. 12, C.); hence, the volume generated by the segment *DMB*, is measured by

$$\tfrac{2}{3}\pi \times EF \times (\overline{CB}^2 - \overline{CI}^2).$$

But in the right-angled triangle CBI, we have (B. IV. P. 8, C.),

$$\overline{CB}^2 - \overline{CI}^2 = \overline{BI}^2 = \tfrac{1}{4}\overline{BD}^2:$$

hence, the volume generated by the segment DMB, has for its measure

$$\tfrac{2}{3}\pi \times EF \times \tfrac{1}{4}\overline{BD}^2 = \tfrac{1}{6}\pi \times \overline{BD}^2 \times EF.$$

Scholium. The volume generated by the segment BMD is to the sphere which has BD for a diameter,

as $\tfrac{1}{6}\pi \times \overline{BD}^2 \times EF$ is to $\tfrac{1}{6}\pi \times \overline{BD}^3$, or as EF to BD.

PROPOSITION XVII. THEOREM.

Every segment of a sphere is equivalent to half the sum of its bases multiplied by its altitude, plus *the contents of a sphere whose diameter is this same altitude.*

Let DMB be the arc of a circle, and DF, BE, perpendiculars let fall on the radius CA: then, if the area $FDMBE$ be revolved about the radius CA it will generate a spherical segment. It is required to find the measure of this segment.

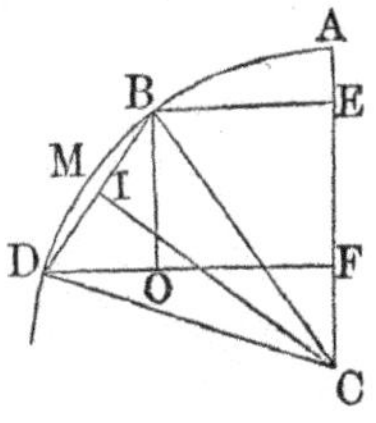

The volume generated by the circular segment DMB is measured by (P. 16)

$$\tfrac{1}{6}\pi \times \overline{BD}^2 \times EF:$$

the frustum of the cone described by the trapezoid $FDBE$ is measured by (P. 6)

$$\tfrac{1}{3}\pi \times EF \times (\overline{BE}^2 + \overline{DF}^2 + BE \times DF):$$

hence, the segment of the sphere, which is the sum of these two volumes, is measured by

$$\tfrac{1}{6}\pi \times EF \times (2\overline{BE}^2 + 2\overline{DF}^2 + 2BE \times DF + \overline{BD}^2).$$

But by drawing BO parallel to EF, we have,

$$DO = DF - BE \text{ and } \overline{DO}^2 = \overline{DF}^2 - 2DF \times BE + \overline{BE}^2;$$

and, $\overline{BD}^2 = \overline{BO}^2 + \overline{DO}^2 = \overline{EF}^2 + \overline{DF}^2 - 2DF \times BE + \overline{BE}^2.$

Substituting this value for $\overline{BD}^2$ in the expression for the contents of the segment, we have,

$\frac{1}{6}\pi\times EF\times(2\overline{BE}^2+2\overline{DF}^2+2BE\times DF+\overline{EF}^2+\overline{DF}^2-2DF\times BE+\overline{BE}^2)$,

equal to $\qquad \frac{1}{6}\pi\times EF\times(3\overline{BE}^2+3\overline{DF}^2+\overline{EF}^2)$;

an expression which may be written in two parts, viz.,

$$EF\times\left(\frac{\pi\times\overline{BE}^2+\pi\times\overline{DF}^2}{2}\right) \text{ and } \frac{1}{6}\pi\times\overline{EF}^3;$$

and these parts correspond with the enunciation.

Cor. If the radius of either base is zero, the segment becomes a spherical segment with a single base; hence, *any spherical segment, with a single base, is equivalent to half the cylinder having the same base and the same altitude*, plus *the sphere of which this altitude is the diameter.*

GENERAL SCHOLIUMS.

1. Let R be the radius of a cylinder's base, H its altitude, and V the measure of the volume: the contents of the cylinder are

$$V=\pi\times R^2\times H.$$

2. Let R be the radius of a cone's base, H its altitude: the contents of the cone are

$$V=\pi\times R^2\times\tfrac{1}{3}H=\tfrac{1}{3}\pi\times R^2\times H.$$

3. Let A and B be the radii of the bases of a frustum of a cone, H its altitude: the contents of the frustum are

$$V=\tfrac{1}{3}\pi\times H\times(A^2+B^2+A\times B).$$

4. Let R be the radius of a sphere; its contents are

$$V=\tfrac{4}{3}\pi\times R^3.$$

5. Let R be the radius of a spherical sector, H the altitude of a zone, which forms its base: the contents of the sector are

$$V=\tfrac{2}{3}\pi\times R^2\times H.$$

6. Let P and Q be the two bases of a spherical segment, H its altitude: the contents of the segment are

$$V=\frac{P+Q}{2}\times H+\tfrac{1}{6}\pi\times H^3.$$

7. If the spherical segment has but one base, its contents are $\qquad V=\tfrac{1}{2}P\times H+\tfrac{1}{6}\pi\times H^3.$

BOOK IX.

SPHERICAL GEOMETRY.

DEFINITIONS.

1. A SPHERICAL TRIANGLE is a portion of the surface of a sphere, bounded by arcs of three great circles.

These arcs are named the *sides* of the triangle, and each is less than a semicircumference. The angles which the planes of the circles make with each other, are the angles of the triangle.

2. A spherical triangle takes the name of *right-angled*, *isosceles*, *equilateral*, in the same cases as a rectilineal triangle.

3. A SPHERICAL POLYGON is a portion of the surface of a sphere bounded by arcs of three or more great circles.

4. A LUNE is a portion of the surface of a sphere included between two semi-circumferences of great circles.

5. A SPHERICAL WEDGE, or UNGULA, is that portion of a sphere, included between two semi-circles passing through the centre.

6. A SPHERICAL PYRAMID is a portion of the sphere, included between three or more planes passing through the centre. The *base* of the pyramid is the portion of the surface of the sphere intercepted by the planes.

7. The POLE OF A CIRCLE is a point on the surface of the sphere, equally distant from every point of the circumference.

PROPOSITION I. THEOREM.

In every spherical triangle, any side is less than the sum of the two other sides.

Let O be the centre of the sphere, and ACB a spherical triangle: then will any side be less than the sum of the two other sides.

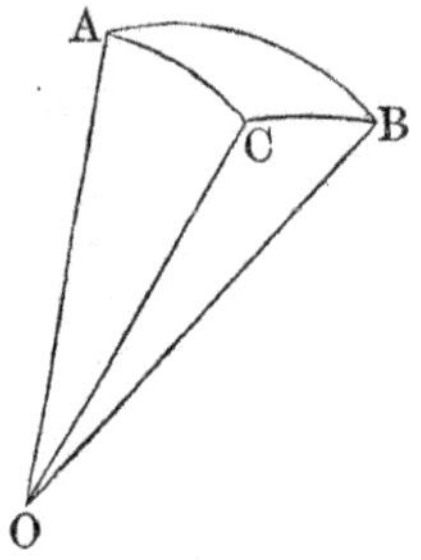

For, draw the radii OA, OB, OC. Conceive the planes AOB, AOC, COB, to be drawn; these planes bound a polyedral angle whose vertex is at the centre O; and the plane angles AOB, AOC, COB, are measured by AB, AC, BC, the sides of the spherical triangle. But each of the three plane angles which bound a polyedral angle is less than the sum of the two other angles (B. VI., P. 19); hence, any side of a spherical triangle is less than the sum of the two other sides.

PROPOSITION II. THEOREM.

The sum of all the sides of any spherical polygon is less than the circumference of a great circle.

Let $ABCDE$ be any spherical polygon, and O the centre of the sphere.

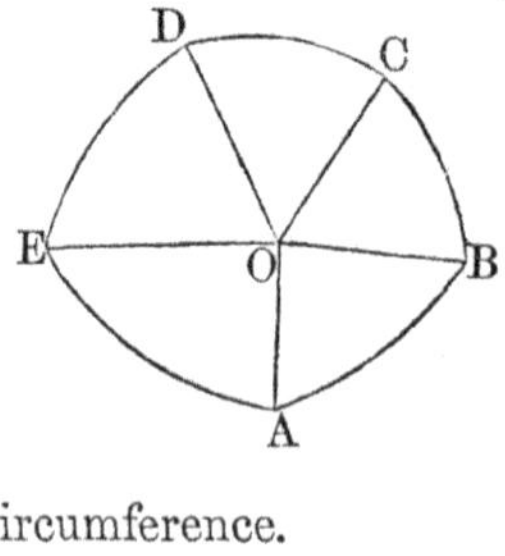

Conceive O to be the vertex of a polyedral angle bounded by the plane angles AOB, BOC, COD, &c. Now, the sum of the plane angles which include a polyedral angle is less than four right angles (B. VI., P. 20); hence, the sum of the sides of any spherical polygon is less than the circumference.

Cor. The sum of the three sides of any spherical triangle is less than the circumference; for, the triangle is a polygon of three sides.

PROPOSITION III. THEOREM.

The poles of a great circle of a sphere are the extremities of that diameter of the sphere which is perpendicular to the circle; and these extremities are also the poles of all small circles parallel to it.

Let *ED* be perpendicular to the great circle *AMB*; then will *E* and *D* be its poles; and they will also be the poles of every parallel small circle *FNG*.

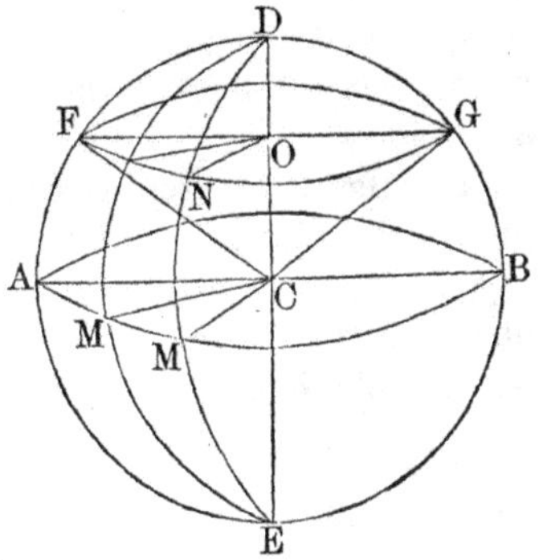

For, *DC* being perpendicular to the plane *AMB*, is perpendicular to all the straight lines *CA, CM, CB*, &c., drawn through its foot in this plane (B. VI., D. 1); hence, all the arcs *DA*, *DM*, *DB*, &c., are quarters of the circumference. So likewise are all the arcs *EA*, *EM*, *EB*, &c.; therefore, the points *D* and *E* are each equally distant from all the points of the circumference *AMB*; hence, they are the poles of that circumference (D. 7).

Again, the radius *DC*, perpendicular to the plane *AMB*, is perpendicular to the parallel *FNG*; hence, it passes through *O*, the centre of the circle *FNG* (B. VIII., P. 7, C. 4); hence, if the chords *DF*, *DN*, *DG*, be drawn, these oblique lines will cut off equal distances measured from *O*; hence, they will be equal (B. VI., P. 5). But, the chords being equal, the arcs are equal; hence, the point *D* is the pole of the small circle *FNG*; and for like reasons, the point *E* is the other pole.

Cor. If through the pole *D* and any point *M*, in the arc of a great circle *AMB*, an arc of another great circle *MD* be drawn, the arc *MD* is a quarter of the circumference, and is called a *quadrant*. This quadrant makes a right angle with the arc *AM*. For, the line *DC* being perpendicular to the plane *AMC*, every plane *DME*, passing through the line *DC* is perpendicular to the plane AMC (B VI., P. 16); hence, the angle of these planes, or the angle AMD is a right angle.

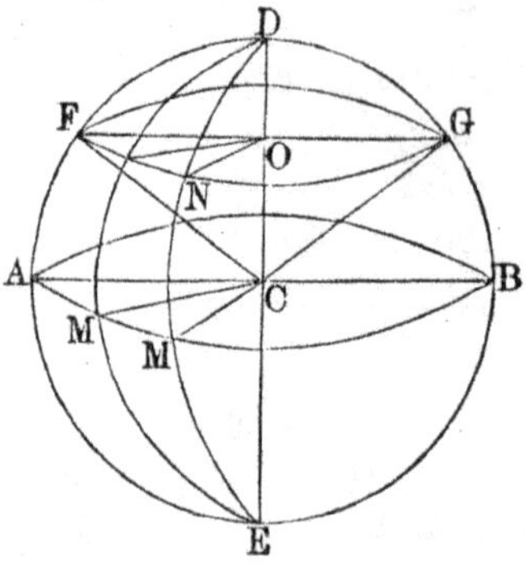

Cor. 2. Conversely: If the distance of the point D from each of the points A and M, in the circumference of a great circle, is equal to a quadrant, the point D is the pole of the arc AM.

For, let C be the centre of the sphere, and draw the radii CD, CA, CM. Since the angles ACD, MCD, are right angles, the line CD is perpendicular to the two straight lines CA, CM; hence, it is perpendicular to their plane (B. VI., P. 4): hence, the point D is the pole of the arc AM.

Scholium. The properties of these poles enable us to describe arcs of a circle on the surface of a sphere, with the same facility as on a plane surface. It is evident, for instance, that by turning the arc DF, or any other line extending to the same distance, round the point D, the extremity F will describe the small circle FNG; and by turning the quadrant DFA round the point D, its extremity A will describe the arc of a great circle AMB.

PROPOSITION IV. THEOREM.

The angle formed by two arcs of great circles, is equal to the angle formed by the tangents to these arcs at their point of intersection. The angle is measured by the arc of a great circle described from the vertex as a pole, and limited by the sides, produced if necessary.

Let the angle BAC be formed by the two arcs AB, AC; then will it be equal to the angle FAG formed by the tangents AF, AG, and be measured by the arc DE of a great circle, described about A as a pole.

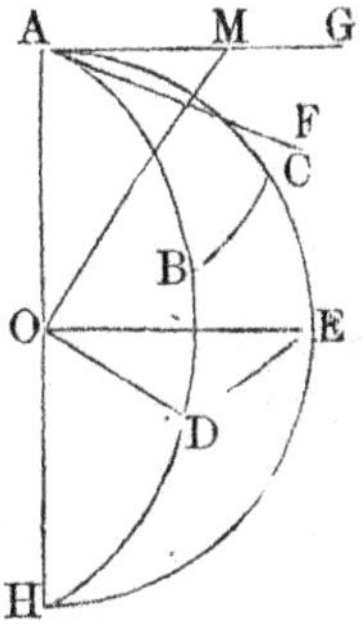

For, the tangent AF, drawn in the plane of the arc AB, is perpendicular to the radius AO; and the tangent AG, drawn in the plane of the arc AC, is perpendicular to the same radius AO. Hence, the angle FAG is equal to the angle contained by the planes $ABDH$, $ACEH$ (B. VI., D. 4); which is that of the arcs AB, AC, and is called the angle BAC.

Again, if the arcs AD and AE are both quadrants, the lines OD, OE, are perpendicular to OA, and the angle DOE is equal to the angle of the planes $ABDH$, $ACEH$; hence, the arc DE is the measure of the angle contained by these planes, or of the angle CAB.

Cor. 1. The angles of spherical triangles may be compared together, by means of the arcs of great circles described from their vertices as poles and included between their sides: hence, it is easy to make an angle of this kind equal to a given angle.

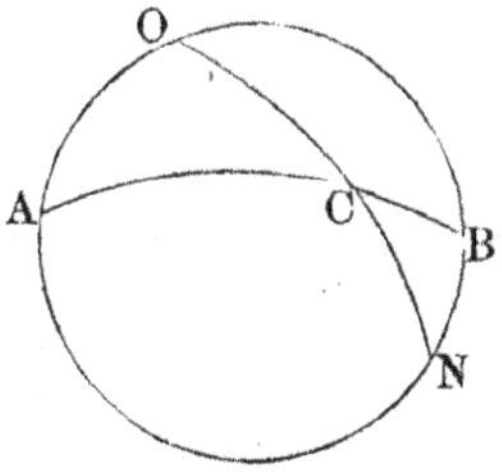

Cor. 2. Vertical angles, such as ACO and BCN are equal; for either of them is still the angle formed by the two planes ACB, OCN.

It is further evident, that, when two arcs ACB, OCN, intersect, the two adjacent angles ACO, OCB, taken together, are equal to two right angles.

PROPOSITION V. THEOREM.

If from the vertices of the three angles of a spherical triangle, as poles, arcs be described forming a spherical triangle; then, the vertices of the angles of this second triangle, will be respectively poles of the sides of the first.

From the vertices A, B, C, as poles, let the arcs EF, FD, ED, be described, forming on the surface of the sphere, the triangle DFE; then will the vertices D, E, and F, be respectively poles of the sides BC, AC, AB.

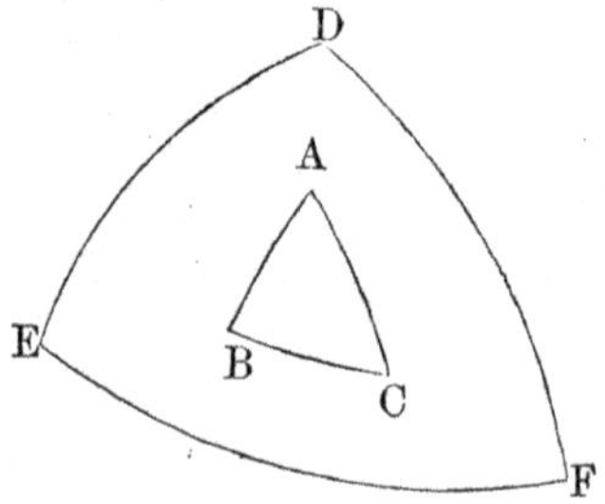

For, the point A being the pole of the arc EF, the distance AE is a quadrant; the point C being the pole of the arc DE, the distance CE is likewise a quadrant: hence, the point E is removed the length of a quadrant from each of the points A and C; hence, it is the pole of the arc AC (P. 3, c. 2). It may be shown by similar reasoning, that D is the pole of the arc BC, and F that of the arc AB.

Scholium. Hence, the triangle ABC may be described by means of DEF, as DEF is described by means of ABC. Triangles so described, are called *polar triangles*, or *supplemental triangles.*

PROPOSITION VI. THEOREM.

The same supposition continuing as in the last Proposition, each angle in one of the triangles, will be measured by a semicircumference, minus *the side lying opposite to it in the other triangle.*

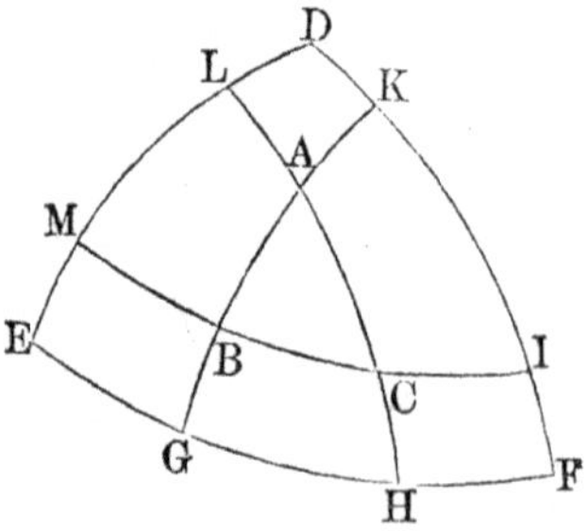

For, produce the sides AB, AC, if necessary, till they meet EF, in G and H. The point A being the pole of the arc GH, the angle A is measured by that arc (P. 4). But, since E is the pole of AH, the arc EH is a quadrant; and since F is the pole of AG, FG is a quadrant: hence, $EH+GF$ is equal to a semicircumference. But, $EH+GF=EF+GH$; hence the arc GH, which measures the angle A, is equal to a semicircumference *minus* the side EF. In like manner, the angle B is measured by $\frac{1}{2}circ.-DF$: the angle C, by $\frac{1}{2}circ.-DE$.

This property is reciprocal in the two triangles, since each of them is described in a similar manner by means of the other. Thus the angle D, for example, of the triangle EDF, is measured by the arc MI; but $MI+BC=MC+BI=\frac{1}{2}circ.$; hence, the arc MI, the measure of D, is equal to $\frac{1}{2}circ.-BC$: the angle E is measured by $\frac{1}{2}circ.-AC$, and the angle F by $\frac{1}{2}circ.-AB$.

Scholium. It must further be observed, that besides the triangle DEF, three others might be formed by the intersection of the three arcs DE, EF, DF. But the proposition is applicable only to the central triangle, which is distinguished from the other three by the circumstance, that the two angles A and D lie on the same side of BC, the two B and E on the same side of AC, and the two C and F on the same side of AB.

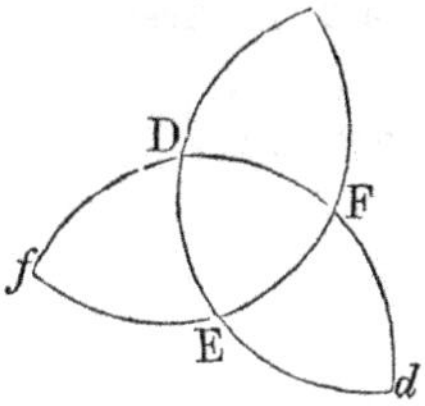

PROPOSITION VII. THEOREM.

If around the vertices of any two angles of a given spherical triangle, as poles, the circumferences of two circles be described which shall pass through the vertex of the third angle of the triangle: if then, through the other point in which these circumferences intersect and the vertices of the first two angles of the triangle, two arcs of great circles be drawn, the triangle thus formed will have all its parts equal to those of the given triangle, each to each.

Let ABC be the given triangle, CED, DFC, the arcs described about A and B as poles; then will the triangles ABC, ADB have all their parts equal each to each.

For, by construction, the side $AD=AC$, $DB=BC$, and AB is common; hence, these two triangles have their *sides* equal, each to each. We are now to show, that the *angles* opposite these equal sides are also equal, each to each.

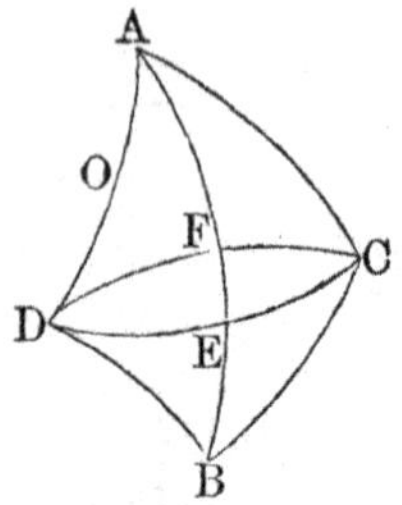

If the centre of the sphere is at O, a triedral angle may be conceived as formed at O by the three plane angles AOB, AOC, BOC; likewise another triedral angle may be conceived as formed by the three plane angles AOB, AOD, BOD. And, because the sides of the triangle ABC are equal to those of the triangle ADB, the plane angles forming the one of these triedral angles, are equal to the plane angles forming the other, each to each: hence, the planes are equally inclined to each other (B. VI., P. 21); and all the angles of the spherical triangle DAB, are respectively equal to those of the triangle CAB, namely, $DAB=BAC$, $DBA=ABC$, and $ADB=ACB$; consequently, the sides and the angles of the triangle ADB, are equal to the sides and the angles of the triangle ACB, each to each.

Scholium. The equality of these triangles is not, however, an *absolute equality*, or one of superposition: for, it would be impossible to apply them to each other, unless they were isosceles. The equality meant here is what we have already named an equality by *symmetry* (B. VI., 21, S. 3); therefore, we shall call the triangles ACB, ADB, *symmetrical triangles.*

PROPOSITION VIII. THEOREM.

Two triangles on the same sphere, or on equal spheres, are equal in all their parts, when two sides and the included angle of the one are equal to two sides and the included angle of the other, each to each.

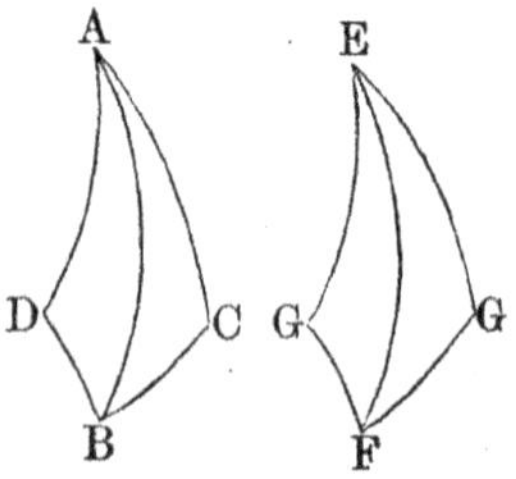

Let ABC, EFG, be two triangles having the side $AB=EF$, the side $AC=EG$, and the angle $BAC=FEG$; then will the two triangles be equal in all their parts.

For, the triangle EFG may be placed on the triangle ABC, or on

ABD symmetrical with ABC, just as two rectilineal triangles are placed upon each other, when they have an equal angle included between equal sides. Hence, all the parts of the triangle EFG are equal to all the parts of the triangle ABC; that is, besides the three parts equal by hypothesis, we have the side $BC=FG$, the angle $ABC=EFG$, and the angle $ACB=EGF$.

PROPOSITION IX. THEOREM.

Two triangles on the same sphere or on equal spheres, are equal in all their parts, when two angles and the included side of the one are equal to two angles and the included side of the other, each to each.

For, one of these triangles, or the triangle symmetrical with it, may be placed on the other, as is done in the corresponding case of rectilineal triangles (B. I., P. 6).

PROPOSITION X. THEOREM.

If two triangles on the same sphere, or on equal spheres, have all their sides equal, each to each, their angles will likewise be equal, each to each, the equal angles lying opposite the equal sides.

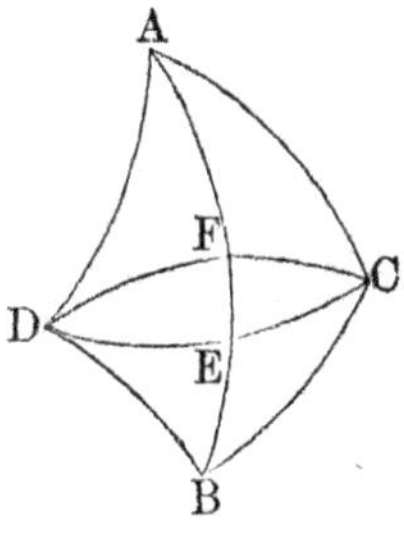

The truth of this proposition is evident from Prop. VII., where it was shown, that with three given sides AB, AC, BC, only two triangles ACB, ABD, can be constructed, and that these triangles will have all their parts equal each to each. Hence, the two triangles, having all their sides respectively equal, must either be absolutely equal, or *symmetrically equal;* in either of which cases, their corresponding angles are equal, and lie opposite to equal sides.

PROPOSITION XI. THEOREM.

In every isosceles spherical triangle, the angles opposite the equal sides are equal; and conversely, if two angles of a spherical triangle are equal, the triangle is isosceles.

First. Suppose the side $AB=AC$; we shall have the angle $C=B$.

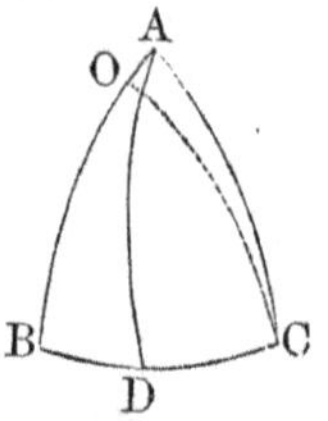

For, if the arc AD be drawn from the vertex A to the middle point D of the base, the two triangles ABD, ACD, will have all the sides of the one respectively equal to the corresponding sides of the other, viz., AD common, $BD=DC$, and $AB=AC$: hence, by the last proposition, their angles will be equal; therefore, $B=C$.

Secondly. Suppose the angle $B=C$; we shall have the side $AC=AB$.

For, if not, let AB be the greater of the two; take $BO=AC$, and draw OC. Then, in the two triangles BOC, BAC, the two sides BO, BC, are equal to the two AC, BC; the angle OBC, contained by the first two is equal to ACB contained by the second two. Hence, the two triangles BOC, ACB, have all their other parts equal (P. 8); hence, the angle $OCB=ABC$: but, by hypothesis, the angle $ABC=ACB$; hence, we have $OCB=ACB$, which is absurd (A. 8); therefore, an absurdity follows if we suppose AB different from AC; hence the sides AB, AC, opposite to the equal angles B and C, are equal.

Scholium. Since, the triangles BAD, DAC, are equal in all their parts (P. 10), the angle $BAD=DAC$, and $BDA=ADC$: consequently, ADB and ADC, are right angles: hence, *the arc drawn from the vertex of an isosceles spherical triangle to the middle of the base, is at right angles to the base and bisects the vertical angle.*

PROPOSITION XII. THEOREM.

In any spherical triangle, the greater side is opposite the greater angle; and conversely, the greater angle is opposite the greater side.

Let the angle A be greater than the angle B, then will BC be greater than AC; and conversely, if BC is greater than AC, then will the angle A be greater than B.

First. Suppose the angle $A>B$; make the angle $BAD=B$; then we shall have $AD=DB$ (P. 11); but $AD+DC$ is greater than AC; hence, putting DB in place of AD, we shall have $DB+DC>AC$, or $BC>AC$.

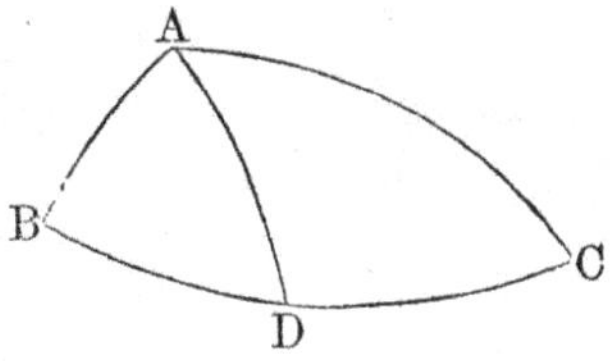

Secondly. If we suppose $BC>AC$, the angle BAC will be greater than ABC. For, if BAC were equal to ABC, we should have $BC=AC$; if BAC were less than ABC, we should then, as has just been shown, find $BC<AC$. Either of these conditions is contrary to the supposition: hence, the angle BAC is greater than ABC.

PROPOSITION XIII. THEOREM.

If two triangles on the same sphere, or on equal spheres, are mutually equiangular, they are also mutually equilateral.

Let A and B be the two given triangles; P and Q their polar triangles.

Since the angles are equal, each to each, in the triangles A and B, the sides are equal each to each, in their polar triangles P and Q (P. 6): but, since the triangles P and Q are mutually equilateral, they must also be mutually equiangular (P. 10); and lastly, the angles being equal, each to each, in the triangles P and Q, it follows that the sides are equal each to each, in their polar triangles A and B.

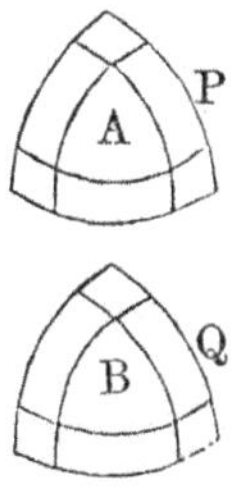

Hence, the mutually equiangular triangles A and B are at the same time, mutually equilateral.

Scholium. This proposition is not applicable to rectilineal triangles; in which equality among the angles indicates only proportionality among the sides. Nor is it difficult to account for the difference, in this respect, between spherical and rectilineal triangles. In the proposition now before us, as well as in the preceding ones, which treat of the comparison of triangles, it is expressly required that the arcs be traced on the same sphere, or on equal spheres. Now, similar arcs are to each other as their radii; hence, on equal spheres, two triangles cannot be similar without being equal. Therefore, it is not strange that equality among the angles should produce equality among the sides.

The case would be different, if the triangles were drawn upon unequal spheres; there, the angles being equal, the triangles would be similar, and the homologous sides would be to each other as the radii of their spheres.

PROPOSITION XIV. THEOREM.

The sum of all the angles, in any spherical triangle, is less than six right angles and greater than two.

For, in the first place, every angle of a spherical triangle is less than two right angles: hence, the sum of the three is less than six right angles.

Secondly, the measure of each angle of a spherical triangle is equal to the semicircumference *minus* the corresponding side of the polar triangle (P. 6); hence, the sum of the three, is measured by the three semicircumferences, *minus* the sum of the sides of the polar triangle. Now, this latter sum is less than a circumference (P. 2, C.); therefore, taking it away from three semicircumferences, the remainder is greater than one semicircumference, which is the measure of two right angles; hence, the sum of the three angles of a spherical triangle is greater than two right angles.

Cor. 1. The sum of the three angles of a spherical triangle is not constant, like that of the angles of a rectilineal triangle, but varies between two right angles and six, without ever reaching either of these limits. Two given angles therefore do not serve to determine the third.

Cor. 2. A spherical triangle may have two, or even three of its angles right angles; also two, or even three of its angles obtuse.

Cor. 3. If the triangle ABC is *bi-rectangular*, in other words, has two right angles B and C, the vertex A is the pole of the base BC; and the sides AB, AC, are quadrants (P. 3, C. 2).

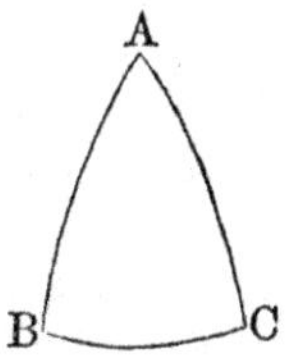

If the angle A is also a right angle, the triangle ABC is *tri-rectangular;* each of its angles is a right angle, and its sides are quadrants. Two tri-rectangular triangles make half a hemisphere, four make a hemisphere, and eight the entire surface of a sphere.

PROPOSITION XV. THEOREM.

The surface of a lune is to the surface of the sphere, as the angle of the lune, to four right angles; or, as the arc which measures that angle, to the circumference.

Let $AMBN$ be a lune, and NCM the angle included between its two great circles: then will its surface be to the surface of the sphere as the angle NCM to four right angles, or as the arc NM to the circumference of a great circle.

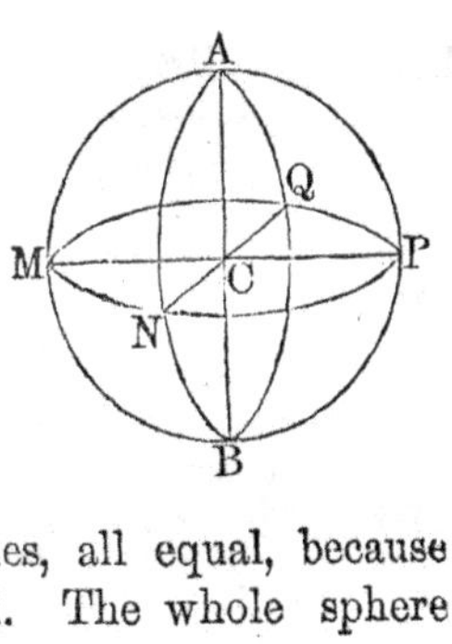

For, suppose the arc MN to be to the circumference $MNPQ$, as some one integer number to another, as 5 to 48, for example. Divide the circumference $MNPQ$, into 48 equal parts, MN will contain 5 of them, and if the pole A were joined with the several points of division, by as many quadrants, we should in the hemisphere $AMNPQ$, have 48 triangles, all equal, because all the corresponding parts are equal. The whole sphere would contain 96 of these triangles, and the lune $AMBNA$, 10 of them; hence, the lune is to the sphere as 10 is to 96, or as 5 to 48; in other words, as the arc MN is to the circumference.

If the arc MN is not commensurable with the circumference, it may still be shown, that the lune is to the sphere as MN to the circumference (B. III., P. 17).

Cor. 1. Two lunes on the same or on equal spheres, are to each other as their respective angles.

Cor. 2. It was shown above, that the whole surface of the sphere is equal to eight tri-rectangular triangles (P. 14, C. 3); hence, if the area of one such triangle be represented by T, the surface of the whole sphere will be expressed by $8T$. This granted, if the right angle be assumed equal to 1, the surface of the lune whose angle is A, will be expressed by $2A \times T$. For,

$$4 : A :: 8T : 2A \times T,$$

in which expression, A represents such a part of unity, as the angle of the lune is of one right angle.

Scholium. The spherical ungula, bounded by the planes AMB, ANB, is to the whole solid sphere, as the angle A is to four right angles. For, the lunes being equal, the spherical ungulas are also equal; hence, two spherical ungulas are to each other, as the angles formed by the planes which bound them.

PROPOSITION XVI. THEOREM.

Two symmetrical spherical triangles are equivalent.

Let ABC, DEF, be two symmetrical triangles, that is to say, two triangles having their sides $AB=DE$, $AC=DF$, $CB=EF$, and yet incapable of superposition: we are to show that the surface ABC is equal to the surface DEF.

Let P be the pole of the small circle passing through the three points A, B, C;* from this point draw the equal

* The circle which passes through the three points A, B, C, or which circumscribes the triangle ABC, can only be a small circle of the sphere; for if it were a great circle, the three sides, AB, BC, AC, would lie in one plane, and the triangle ABC would be reduced to one of its sides.

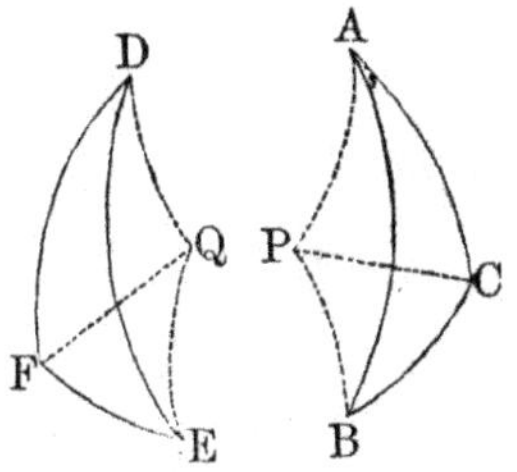

arcs PA, PB, PC (P. 3); at the point F make the angle $DFQ = ACP$, the arc $FQ = CP$; and draw DQ, EQ.

The sides DF, FQ, are equal to the sides AC, CP; the angle $DFQ = ACP$; hence, the two triangles DFQ, ACP, are equal in all their parts (P. 8); consequently, the side $DQ = AP$, and the angle $DQF = APC$.

In the triangles DFE, ABC, the angles DFE, ACB, opposite to the equal sides DE, AB, are equal (P. 10). If the angles DFQ, ACP, which are equal by construction, be taken away from them, there will remain the angle QFE, equal to PCB. The sides QF, FE, are equal to the sides PC, CB; hence, the two triangles FQE, CPB, are equal in all their parts (P. 8); hence, the side $QE = PB$, and the angle $FQE = CPB$.

Now, the triangles DFQ, ACP, which have their sides respectively equal, are at the same time isosceles, and capable of coinciding, when applied the one to the other. For, having placed AC on its equal DF, the equal sides will fall the one on the other, and thus the two triangles will exactly coincide: hence, they are equal; and the surface $DQF = APC$. For a like reason, the surface $FQE = CPB$, and the surface $DQE = APB$; hence we have,

$$DQF + FQE - DQE \approx APC + CPB - APB,$$

or,

$$DFE \approx ABC;$$

hence, the two symmetrical triangles ABC, DEF, are equal in surface.

Scholium. The poles P and Q might lie within triangles ABC, DEF: in which case it would be requisite to add the three triangles DQF, FQE, DQE, together, in order to make up the triangle DEF; and in like manner, to add the three triangles APC, CPB, APB, together, in order to make up the triangle ABC: in all other respects, the demonstration and the result would be the same.

PROPOSITION XVII. THEOREM.

If the circumferences of two great circles intersect each other on the surface of a hemisphere, the sum of the opposite triangles thus formed, is equivalent to the surface of a lune whose angle is equal to the angle formed by the circles.

Let the circumferences *AOB*, *COD*, intersect on the surface of a hemisphere; then will the opposite triangles *AOC*, *BOD*, be equivalent to the lune whose angle is *BOD*.

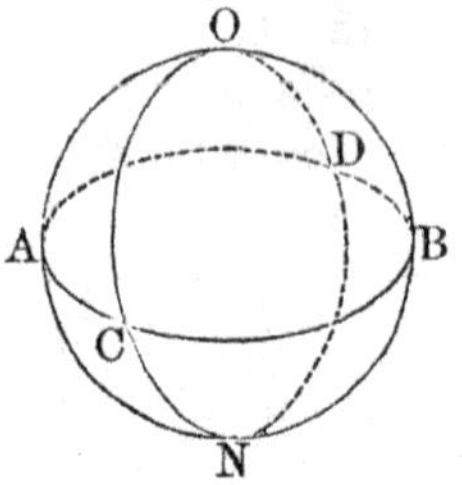

For, produce the arcs *OB*, *OD*, on the other hemisphere, till they meet in *N*. Now, since *AOB* and *OBN* are semicircumferences, if we take away the common part *OB*, we shall have $BN=AO$. For a like reason, we have $DN=CO$, and $BD=AC$. Hence, the two triangles *AOC*, *BDN*, have their three sides respectively equal: they are therefore symmetrical; hence, they are equal in surface (P. 16). But the sum of the triangles *BDN*, *BOD*, is equivalent to the lune *OBNDO*, whose angle is *BOD*: hence, $AOC+BOD$ is equivalent to the lune whose angle is *BOD*.

Scholium. It is likewise evident, that the two spherical pyramids, which have the triangles *AOC*, *BOD*, for bases, are together equivalent to the spherical ungula whose angle is *BOD*.

PROPOSITION XVIII. THEOREM.

The surface of a spherical triangle is equal to the excess of the sum of its three angles above two right angles, multiplied by the tri-rectangular triangle.

Let *ABC* be any spherical triangle: then will its surface be equal to

$$(A+B+C-2)\times T.$$

For, produce its sides till they meet the great circle *DEFG*, drawn at pleasure, without the triangle. By the last theorem, the two triangles *ADE*, *AGH*, are together

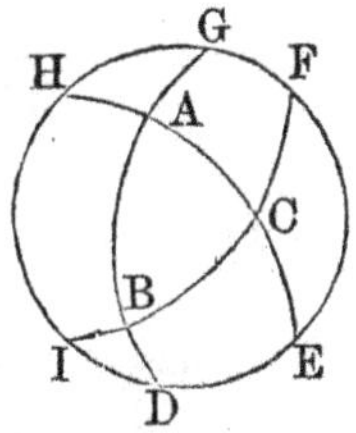

equivalent to the lune whose angle is A, and which is measured by $2A\times T$ (P. 15, C. 2). Hence, we have $ADE+AGH=2A\times T$; and, for a like reason, $BGF+BID=2B\times T$, and $CIH+CFE=2C\times T$. But the sum of these six triangles exceeds the hemisphere by twice the triangle ABC, and the hemisphere is represented by $4T$: therefore, twice the triangle ABC, is equivalent to

$$2A\times T+2B\times T+2C\times T-4T;$$

and, consequently,

$$ABC \approx (A+B+C-2)\times T;$$

hence, every spherical triangle is measured by the sum of its three angles *minus* two right angles, multiplied by the tri-rectangular triangle.

Scholium 1. When we speak of the *spherical angles*, we regard the right angle as unity, and compare the sum of the three angles with this standard. Hence, however many right angles there may be in the sum of the three angles minus two right angles, just so many tri-rectangular triangles, will the proposed triangle contain. If the angles, for example, are each equal to $\frac{4}{3}$ of a right angle, the sum of the three angles is equal to 4 right angles; and this sum, minus two right angles, is represented by 4—2, or 2; therefore, the surface of the triangle is equal to two tri-rectangular triangles, or to the fourth part of the surface of the entire sphere.

Scholium 2. The same proportion which exists between the spherical triangle ABC, and the tri-rectangular triangle, exists also between the spherical pyramid which has ABC for its base, and the tri-rectangular pyramid. The triedral angle of the pyramid is to the triedral angle of the tri-rectangular pyramid, as the triangle ABC to the tri-rectangular triangle. From these relations, the following consequences are deduced.

First. Two triangular spherical pyramids are to each other as their bases: and since a polygonal pyramid may always be divided into a certain number of triangular pyramids, it follows that any two spherical pyramids are to each other, as the polygons which form their bases.

Second. The polyedral angles at the vertices of these pyramids, are also as their bases; hence, for comparing any two polyedral angles, we have merely to place their vertices at the centres of two equal spheres; the angles are to each other as the spherical polygons intercepted between their faces.

The vertical angle of the tri-rectangular pyramid is formed by three planes at right angles to each other: this angle, which may be called a *right polyedral angle*, will serve as a very natural unit of measure for all other polyedral angles. If, for example, the area of the triangle is $\frac{3}{4}$ of the tri-rectangular triangle, the corresponding triedral angle is also $\frac{3}{4}$ of the right polyedral angle.

PROPOSITION XIX. THEOREM.

The surface of a spherical polygon is equal to the excess of the sum of all its angles, over two right angles taken as many times as there are sides in the polygon less two, multiplied by the tri-rectangular triangle.

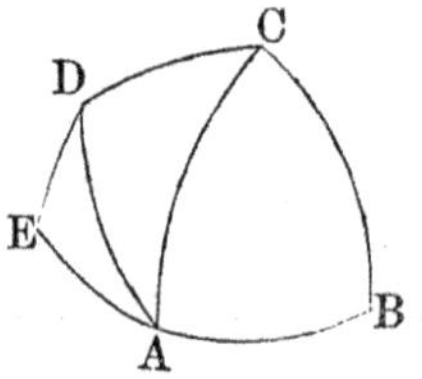

Let $ABCDE$ be a spherical polygon.

From one of the vertices A, let diagonals AC, AD, be drawn to the other vertices; the polygon $ABCDE$ will be divided into as many triangles less two, as it has sides.

Now, the surface of each triangle is equal to the sum of all its angles less two right angles, into the tri-rectangular triangle. The sum of the angles of all the triangles is the same as that of all the angles of the polygon; hence, the surface of the polygon is equal to the sum of all its angles, diminished by twice as many right angles as it has sides less two, into the tri-rectangular triangle.

Scholium. Let s be the sum of all the angles of a spherical polygon, n the number of its sides, and T the tri-rectangular triangle; the right angle being taken as unity, the surface of the polygon will be equal to

$$\left(s-2\ (n-2,)\right)\times T=(s-2n+4)\times T.$$

APPENDIX.

NOTE A.—Page 22.

A Demonstration is a train of logical arguments brought to a conclusion. The bases or premises of a demonstration, are definitions, axioms, propositions previously established, and hypotheses. The arguments are the links which connect the premises, logically, with the conclusion or ultimate truth to be proved.

In Geometry we employ two kinds of demonstration—the Direct, and the Indirect or the method involving the Reductio ad absurdum.

These are also called Positive and Negative Demonstrations. In the direct method, the premises are definitions, axioms, and previous propositions; and by a process of logical argumentation, the magnitudes of which something is to be proved, are shown to bear the mark by which that may always be inferred, or, in other words, are shown to fall under some definition, axiom, or proposition, previously laid down. The direct demonstration may be divided into two classes:

1st. Where the argument depends on superposition—that is, on the coincidence of magnitudes when applied the one to the other: and

2dly. Where it depends on addition and subtraction, or immediately on principles previously laid down.

The indirect method rests on a hypothesis. This hypothesis is combined in a process of logical argumentation, with definitions, axioms, and previous propositions, until a conclusion is obtained, which agrees or disagrees with some known truth. Now, if the conclusion so deduced, is excluded from the truths previously established, that is, if it is opposed to any of them, then it follows that the hypothesis, leading to a result contradictory to such truth, must be false. In the indirect demonstration, therefore, the *conclusion* is compared with the truths known antecedently to the proposition in question; if it disagrees with any of them, the hypothesis is false.

We have examples of the first class of the direct demonstration in the reasoning which establishes Propositions V. and VI.—and of the second class in that which establishes Propositions I. and IV. We have also examples of the indirect method in the demonstrations of Propositions II. and III.

It is often supposed, though erroneously, that the indirect demonstration is less conclusive and satisfactory than the direct. This impression is simply the result of a want of proper analysis. For example: in the demonstration of Proposition II. we propose to prove "that two straight lines having two points in common coincide throughout their whole extent." Now, it is evident that they either coincide or separate. If they separate, they must separate at some point, as C. But the *supposition* or *hypothesis* of their separating at this point, involves the conclusion, that a *part is equal to the whole,* which is contrary to Axiom 8, and therefore untrue: Hence, they do not separate, and *therefore,* they coincide. Similar remarks apply to all indirect demonstrations.

In both kinds of demonstrations the premises and conclusion agree: that is, they are both true or both false, the reasoning or argument in both being supposed strictly logical.

For a more full discussion of this subject, see Davies' Logic of Mathematics.

THE REGULAR POLYEDRONS.

A REGULAR POLYEDRON is one whose faces are all equal regular polygons, and whose polyedral angles are all equal to each other.

1. The TETRAEDRON, or *regular pyramid*, is a volume bounded by four equal equilateral triangles.

2. The HEXAEDRON, or *Cube*, is a volume bounded by six equal squares.

3. The OCTAEDRON, is a volume bounded by eight equal equilateral triangles.

4. The DODECAEDRON, is a volume bounded by twelve equal and regular pentagons.

5. The ICOSAEDRON is a volume bounded by twenty equal equilateral triangles.

First. If the faces are equilateral triangles, polyedrons may be constructed bounded by such triangles and will have polyedral angles contained either by three, four or five of them: hence arise three regular polyedral bodies, viz: the *tetraedron*, the *octaedron*, and the *icosaedron*, and no others can be constructed with equilateral triangles. For, each angle of an equilateral triangle being equal to a third part of two right, six such angles about the vertex of a polyedral angle would be equal to four right angles, which is impossible (B. VI., P. 20,

Secondly. If the faces are squares, their angles may be arranged by threes: hence, results the *hexaedron*, or *cube*. Four angles of a square are equal to four right angles, and cannot form a polyedral angle.

Thirdly. In fine, if the faces are regular pentagons, their angles likewise may be arranged by threes: the regular *dodecaedron* will result.

We can proceed no farther: three angles of a regular hexagon are equal to four right angles; three of a heptagon are greater.

Hence, there can only be five regular polyedrons; three formed with equilateral triangles, one with squares, and one with pentagons.

CONSTRUCTION OF THE TETRAEDRON.

Let *ABC* be the equilateral triangle which is to form one face of the tetraedron. At the point *O*, the centre of this triangle, erect *OS* perpendicular to the plane *ABC*; terminate this perpendicular in *S*, so that $AS = AB$; draw *SB*, *SC*; the pyramid *S-ABC* is the tetraedron required.

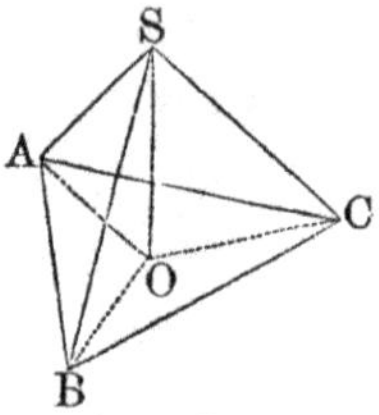

For, by reason of the equal distances *OA*, *OB*, *OC*, the oblique lines *SA*, *SB*, *SC*, cut off equal distances estimated from the foot of the perpendicular *SO*, and consequently are equal (B. VI., P. 5). One of them $SA = AB$; hence, the four faces of the pyramid *S-ABC*, are triangles, equal to the given triangle *ABC*. The triedral angles of this pyramid are all equal, because each of them is bounded by three equal plane angles (B. VI., P. 21, S. 2); hence, this pyramid is a regular tetraedron.

CONSTRUCTION OF THE HEXAEDRON.

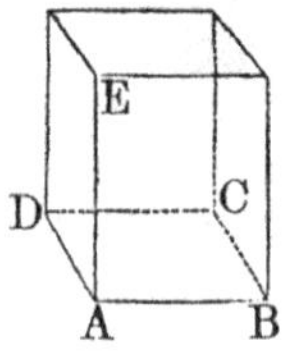

Let *ABCD* be a given square. On the base *ABCD*, construct a right prism whose altitude *AE* shall be equal to the side *AB*. The faces of this prism will evidently be equal squares; and its triedral angles all equal, each being formed with three equal faces: hence, this prism is a regular hexaedron or cube.

The following propositions can be easily proved.

1. Any regular polyedron may be divided into as many right pyramids as the polyedron has faces; the common vertex of these pyramids will be the centre of the polye-

dron; and at the same time, that of an inscribed and of a circumscribed sphere.

2. The solidity of a regular polyedron is equal to its surface multiplied by a third part of the radius of the inscribed sphere.

3. Two regular polyedrons of the same name, are two similar solids, and their homologous dimensions are proportional; hence, the radii of the inscribed or the circumscribed spheres are to each other as the edges of the polyedrons.

4. If a regular polyedron be inscribed in a sphere, the planes drawn from the centre, through the different edges, will divide the surface of the sphere into as many spherical polygons, all equal and similar, as the polyedron has faces.

APPLICATION OF ALGEBRA

TO THE

SOLUTION OF GEOMETRICAL PROBLEMS.

A PROBLEM is a question which requires a solution. A geometrical problem is one, in which certain parts of a geometrical figure are given or known, from which it is required to determine certain other parts.

When it is proposed to solve a geometrical problem by means of Algebra, the given parts are represented by the first letters of the alphabet, and the required parts by the final letters. The geometrical relations which subsist between the known and required parts furnish the equations of the problem. The solution of these equations, when so formed, gives the solution of the problem.

No general rule can be given for forming the equations. The equations must be independent of each other, and their number equal to that of the unknown quantities introduced (Alg., Art. 103). Experience, and a careful examination of all the conditions, whether explicit or implicit (Alg., Art. 94), will serve as guides in stating the questions; to which may be added the following general directions.

1st. Draw a figure which shall represent all the given parts, and all the required parts. Then draw such other lines as will enable us to establish the necessary relations between them. If an angle is given, it is generally best to let fall a perpendicular that shall lie opposite to it; and this perpendicular, if possible, should be drawn from the extremity of a given side.

2d. When two lines or quantities are connected in the same way with other parts of the figure or problem, it is in general, not best to use either of them separately; but to use their sum, their difference, their product, their quotient, or perhaps another line of the figure with which they are alike connected.

3d. When the area, or perimeter of a figure, is given, it is sometimes best to assume another figure similar to that proposed, having one of its sides equal to unity, or some other known quantity. A comparison of the two figures will often give a required part. We will add the following problems.*

PROBLEM I.

In a right-angled triangle BAC, having given the base BA, and the sum of the hypothenuse and perpendicular, it is required to find the hypothenuse and perpendicular.

Put $BA = c = 3$, $BC = x$, $AC = y$, and the sum of the hypothenuse and perpendicular equal to $s = 9$.

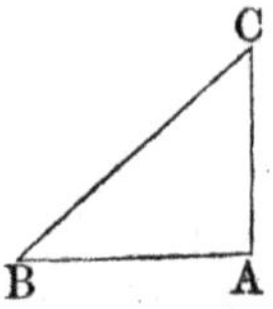

Then, $x + y = s = 9,$

and (B. IV., P. 11), $x^2 = y^2 + c^2.$

From 1st equ: $x = s - y,$

and $x^2 = s^2 - 2sy + y^2.$

By subtracting, $0 = s^2 - 2sy - c^2,$

or, $2sy = s^2 - c^2;$

hence, $y = \dfrac{s^2 - c^2}{2s} = 4 = AC.$

Therefore, $x + 4 = 9$, or $x = 5 = BC.$

---

* The following problems are selected from Hutton's Application of Algebra to Geometry; and the examples in Mensuration, from his treatise on that subject.

PROBLEM II.

In a right-angled triangle, having given the hypothenuse, and the sum of the base and perpendicular, to find these two sides.

Put $BC = a = 5$, $BA = x$, $AC = y$, and the sum of the base and perpendicular $= s = 7$.

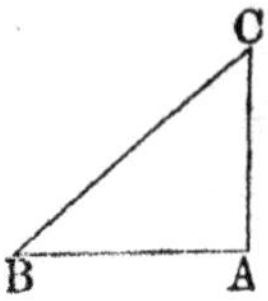

Then, $x + y = s = 7$,

and $x^2 + y^2 = a^2$.

From first equation, $x = s - y$,

or, $x^2 = s^2 - 2sy + y^2$;

Hence, $y^2 = a^2 - s^2 + 2sy - y^2$,

or, $2y^2 - 2sy = a^2 - s^2$;

or, $y^2 - sy = \frac{a^2 - s^2}{2}$.

By completing the square $y^2 - sy + \frac{1}{4}s^2 = \frac{1}{2}a^2 - \frac{1}{4}s^2$,

or, $y = \frac{1}{2}s \pm \sqrt{\frac{1}{2}a^2 - \frac{1}{4}s^2} = 4$ or 3.

Hence, $x = \frac{1}{2}s \mp \sqrt{\frac{1}{2}a^2 - \frac{1}{4}s^2} = 3$ or 4.

PROBLEM III.

In a rectangle, having given the diagonal and perimeter, to find the sides.

Let $ABCD$ be the proposed rectangle.
Put $AC = d = 10$, the perimeter $= 2a = 28$, or $AB + BC = a = 14$: also put $AB = x$, and $BC = y$.

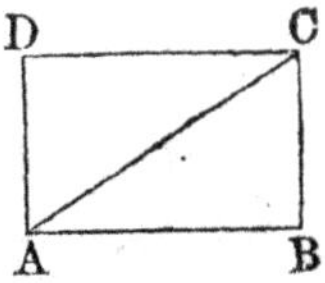

Then, $x^2 + y^2 = d^2$,

and $x + y = a$.

From which equations we obtain,

$$y = \tfrac{1}{2}a \pm \sqrt{\tfrac{1}{2}d^2 - \tfrac{1}{4}a^2} = 8 \text{ or } 6,$$

and $$x = \tfrac{1}{2}a \mp \sqrt{\tfrac{1}{2}d^2 - \tfrac{1}{4}a^2} = 6 \text{ or } 8.$$

PROBLEM IV.

Having given the base and perpendicular of a triangle, to find the side of an inscribed square.

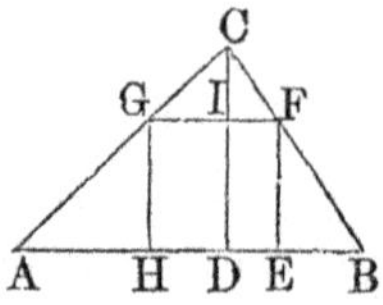

Let ABC be the triangle, and $HEFG$ the inscribed square. Put $AB = b$, $CD = a$, and HE or $GH = x$: then $CI = a - x$.

We have by similar triangles

$$AB : CD :: GF : CI,$$

or, $$b : a :: x : a - x.$$

Hence, $$ab - bx = ax,$$

or, $$x = \frac{ab}{a+b} = \text{the side of the inscribed square;}$$

which, therefore, depends only on the base and altitude of the triangle.

PROBLEM V.

In an equilateral triangle, having given the lengths of the three perpendiculars drawn from a point within, on the three sides: to determine the sides of the triangle.

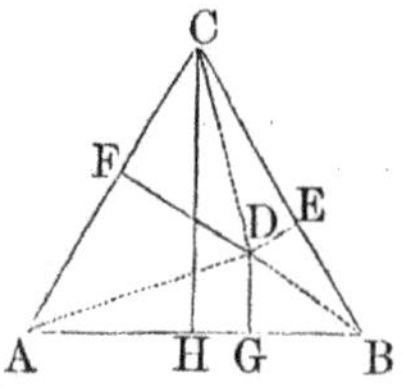

Let ABC be an equilateral triangle: DG, DE and DF the given perpendiculars let fall from D on the sides. Draw DA, DB, DC, to the vertices of the angles, and let fall the perpendicular CH on the base. Let $DG = a$, $DE = b$, and $DF = c$: put one of the equal sides $AB = 2x$; hence, $AH = x$, and $CH = \sqrt{AC^2 - AH^2} = \sqrt{4x^2 - x^2} = \sqrt{3x^2} = x\sqrt{3}$.

Now, since the area of a triangle is equal to half its base into the altitude, (B. IV., P. 6),

$$\tfrac{1}{2}AB \times CH = x \times x\sqrt{3} = x^2\sqrt{3} = \text{triangle } ACB,$$
$$\tfrac{1}{2}AB \times DG = x \times a \quad = ax \quad = \text{triangle } ADB,$$
$$\tfrac{1}{2}BC \times DE = x \times b \quad = bx \quad = \text{triangle } BCD,$$
$$\tfrac{1}{2}AC \times DF = x \times c \quad = cx \quad = \text{triangle } ACD$$

But the last three triangles make up, and are consequently equal to, the first;

hence, $$x^2\sqrt{3} = ax + bx + cx = x(a + b + c);$$

or, $$x\sqrt{3} = a + b + c:$$

therefore, $$x = \frac{a + b + c}{\sqrt{3}}.$$

REMARK. Since the perpendicular CH is equal to $x\sqrt{3}$, it is consequently equal $a + b + c$: that is, the perpendicular let fall from either angle of an equilateral triangle on the opposite side, is equal to the sum of the three perpendiculars let fall from any point within the triangle on the sides respectively.

PROBLEM VI.—In a right-angled triangle, having given the base and the difference between the hypothenuse and perpendicular, to find the sides.

PROBLEM VII.—In a right-angled triangle, having given the hypothenuse, and the difference between the base and perpendicular, to determine the triangle.

PROBLEM VIII.—Having given the area of a rectangle inscribed in a given triangle; to determine the sides of the rectangle.

PROBLEM IX.—In a triangle, having given the ratio of the two sides, together with both the segments of the base made by a perpendicular from the vertical angle; to determine the triangle.

PROBLEM X.—In a triangle, having given the base, the sum of the two other sides, and the length of a line drawn from the vertical angle to the middle of the base; to find the sides of the triangle.

PROBLEM XI.—In a triangle, having given the two sides about the vertical angle, together with the line bisecting that angle and terminating in the base: to find the base.

PROBLEM XII.—To determine a right-angled triangle, having given the lengths of two lines drawn from the acute angles to the middle of the opposite sides.

PROBLEM XIII.—To determine a right-angled triangle, having given the perimeter and the radius of the inscribed circle.

PROBLEM XIV.—To determine a triangle, having given the base, the perpendicular, and the ratio of the two sides.

PROBLEM XV.—To determine a right-angled triangle, having given the hypothenuse, and the side of the inscribed square.

PROBLEM XVI.—To determine the radii of three equal circles, described within and tangent to, a given circle, and also tangent to each other.

PROBLEM XVII.—In a right-angle triangle, having given the perimeter and the perpendicular let fall from the right angle on the hypothenuse, to determine the triangle.

PROBLEM XVIII.—To determine a right-angled triangle, having given the hypothenuse and the difference of two lines drawn from the two acute angles to the centre of the inscribed circle.

PROBLEM XIX.—To determine a triangle, having given the base, the perpendicular, and the difference of the two other sides.

PROBLEM XX.—To determine a triangle, having given the base, the perpendicular, and the rectangle of the two sides.

PROBLEM XXI.—To determine a triangle, having given the lengths of three lines drawn from the three angles to the middle of the opposite sides.

PROBLEM XXII.—In a triangle, having given the three sides, to find the radius of the inscribed circle.

PROBLEM XXIII.—To determine a right-angled triangle, having given the side of the inscribed square, and the radius of the inscribed circle.

PROBLEM XXIV.—To determine a right-angled triangle, having given the hypothenuse and radius of the inscribed circle.

PROBLEM XXV.—To determine a triangle, having given the base, the line bisecting the vertical angle, and the diameter of the circumscribing circle.

INTRODUCTION

TO

PLANE TRIGONOMETRY.

OF LOGARITHMS.

1. *The logarithm of a number is the exponent of the power to which it is necessary to raise a fixed number, in order to produce the first number.*

This fixed number is called the *base* of the system, and may be any number except 1: in the common system, 10 is assumed as the base.

2. If we form those powers of 10, which are denoted by entire exponents, we shall have,

$$10^0 = 1, \quad 10^1 = 10, \quad 10^3 = 1000,$$
$$10^2 = 100, \quad 10^4 = 10000, \text{ \&c., \&c.}$$

From the above table, it is plain, that 0, 1, 2, 3, 4, &c., are respectively the logarithms of 1, 10, 100, 1000, 10000, &c.; we also see, that the logarithm of any number between 1 and 10, is greater than 0, and less than 1: thus,

$$\log 2 = 0.301030.$$

The logarithm of any number greater than 10, and less than 100, is greater than 1, and less than 2: thus,

$$\log 50 = 1.698970.$$

The logarithm of any number greater than 100, and less than 1000, is greater than 2, and less than 3: thus,

$$\log 126 = 2.100371, \text{ \&c.}$$

If the above principles be extended to other numbers, it will appear, that the logarithm of any number, not an exact power of ten, is made up of two parts, *an entire* and a *decimal part.* The *entire part* is called the *characteristic of the logarithm,* and is always *one less* than the number of places of figures in the given number.

3. The principal use of logarithms, is to abridge numerical computations.

Let M denote any number, and let its logarithm be denoted by m, also let N denote a second number whose logarithm is n; then, from the definition, we shall have,

$$10^m = M \quad . \quad . \quad . \quad (1). \qquad 10^n = N \quad . \quad . \quad . \quad (2).$$

Multiplying equations (1) and (2), member by member, we have,

$$10^{m+n} = M \times N; \text{ or, } m + n = \log (M \times N); \text{ hence,}$$

The sum of the logarithms of any two numbers, is equal to the logarithm of their product.

4. Dividing equation (1) by equation (2), member by member, we have,

$$10^{m-n} = \frac{M}{N}; \text{ or, } m - n = \log \frac{M}{N}; \text{ hence,}$$

The logarithm of the quotient of two numbers, is equal to the logarithm of the dividend diminished by the logarithm of the divisor.

5. Since the logarithm of 10 is 1, *the logarithm of the product of any number by* 10, *will be greater by* 1 *than the logarithm of that number* (Art. 3); also, *the logarithm of the quotient of any number divided by* 10, *will be less by* 1 *than the logarithm of that number* (Art. 4).

Similarly, it may be shown that if any number be multiplied by one hundred, the logarithm of the product will be greater by 2 than the logarithm of that number; and if any number be divided by one hundred, the logarithm of the quotient will be less by 2 than the logarithm of that number, and so on.

EXAMPLES.

log 327	is	2.514548
log 32.7	"	1.514548
log 3.27	"	0.514548
log .327	"	$\bar{1}.514548$
log .0327	"	$\bar{2}.514548$

From the above examples, we see, that in a mixed number, that is, one composed of an entire and decimal part, we may change the place of the decimal point without changing the decimal part of the logarithm; but *the characteristic is diminished by* 1 *for every place that the decimal point is removed to the left.*

The *characteristic* in the logarithm of a decimal, is negative, and is, numerically, 1 greater than the number of ciphers immediately after the decimal point. The negative sign extends only to the characteristic, and is written over it, as in the examples given above.

TABLE OF LOGARITHMS.

6. A table of logarithms, is a table in which are written the logarithms of all numbers between 1 and some given number. The logarithms of all numbers between 1 and 10,000 are given in the annexed table. Since rules have been given for determining the characteristics of logarithms by simple inspection, it has not been deemed necessary to write the characteristics in the table, the decimal part only being given. The characteristic, however, is given for all numbers less than 100.

The left hand column of each page of the table, is the column of numbers, and is designated by the letter N; the logarithms of these numbers are placed opposite them on the same horizontal line. The last column on each page, headed D, shows the difference between the logarithms of two consecutive numbers. This difference is found by subtracting the logarithm under the column headed 4, from the one in the column headed 5, in the same horizontal line, and is nearly a mean of the differences of any two consecutive logarithms on this line.

To find, from the Table, the Logarithm of any Number.

7. If the number is less than 100, look on the first page of the table, in the column of numbers under N, until the number is found: the number opposite is the logarithm sought: thus,

$$\log 9 = 0.954243.$$

When the Number is greater than 100, *and less than* 10,000.

8. Find, in the column of numbers, the first three figures of the given number. Then pass across the page along a horizontal line until you come into the column under the fourth figure of the given number: at this place, there are four figures of the required logarithm, to which, two figures taken from the column marked 0, are to be prefixed.

If the four figures already found stand opposite a row of six figures in the column marked 0, the two left hand figures of the six, are the two to be prefixed; but if they stand opposite a row of only four figures, you ascend the column till you find a row of six figures; the two left hand figures of this row are the two to be prefixed. If you then prefix to the decimal part thus found, the characteristic, you will have the logarithm sought: thus,

$$\log\ 8979 = 3.953228$$
$$\log .08979 = \bar{2}.953228$$

If, however, in passing back from the four figures first found, to the 0 column, *any dots be met with,* the two figures to be prefixed must be taken from the horizontal line directly below: thus,

$$\log\ 3098 = 3.491081$$
$$\log\ 30.98 = 1.491081$$

If the logarithm falls at a place where the dots occur, 0 must be written for each dot, and the two figures to be prefixed are, as before, taken from the line below: thus,

$$\log\ 2188 = 3.340047$$
$$\log .2188 = \bar{1}.340047$$

When the Number exceeds 10,000.

9. The characteristic is determined by the rules already given. To find the decimal part of the logarithm:

Place a decimal point after the fourth figure from the left hand, converting the given number into a whole number and decimal. Find the logarithm of the entire part by the rule just given, then take from the right hand column of the page, under D, the number on the same horizontal line with the logarithm, and multiply it by the decimal part; add the product thus obtained to the logarithm already found, and the sum will be the logarithm sought, very nearly.

NOTE.—If the decimal part of the product exceeds .5, let 1 be added to the entire part; if it is less than .5, the decimal part of the product is neglected.

EXAMPLE.

1. To find the logarithm of the number 672887.

The characteristic is 5; placing a decimal point after the fourth figure from the left, we have 6728.87. The decimal part of the log 6728 is .827886, and the corresponding number in the column D is 65; then $65 \times .87 = 56.55$, and since the decimal part exceeds .5, we have 57 to be added to .827886, which gives .827943:

hence, $\log\ 672887 = 5.827943$

Similarly, $\log .0672887 = \bar{2}.827943$

The last rule has been deduced under the supposition that the differences of the numbers are proportional to the differences of their logarithms, which is sufficiently exact within the narrow limits considered.

In the above example, 65 is the difference between the logarithm of 672900 and the logarithm of 672800; that is, it is the difference between the logarithms of two numbers which differ by 100.

We have then the proportion,

$$100 : 87 :: 65 : 56.55;$$

hence, 56.55 is the number to be added to the logarithm before found.

To find, from the Table, the Number corresponding to a given Logarithm.

10. Search in the columns of logarithms for the decimal part of the given logarithm: if it cannot be found in the table, take out the number corresponding to the next less logarithm, and set it aside. Subtract this less logarithm from the given logarithm, and annex to the remainder as many zeros as may be necessary, and divide this result by the corresponding number taken from the column marked D, continuing the division as long as desirable: annex the quotient to the number set aside. Point off, from the left hand, as many integral figures as there are units in the characteristic of the given logarithm increased by 1; the result is the required number.

If the characteristic is negative, the number will be entirely decimal, and the number of zeros to be placed at the left of the number found from the table, will be equal to the number of units in the characteristic diminished by 1.

This rule, like its converse, is founded on the supposition that the differences of the logarithms are proportional to the differences of their numbers, within narrow limits.

EXAMPLE.

1. Find the number corresponding to the logarithm 3.233568.

The decimal part of the given logarithm is - - -	.233568
The next less logarithm of the table is - - - - - -	.233504
and its corresponding number 1712.	
Their difference is - - - - - - - - - - - - - -	64
Tabular difference - - - - - - - - - -	253)6400000(25
Hence, the number sought - - - - 1712.25.	

The number corresponding to the logarithm $\bar{3}.233568$ is .00171225.

2. What is the number corresponding to the logarithm $\bar{2}.785407$?
Ans. .06101084.

3. What is the number corresponding to the logarithm $\bar{1}.846741$?
Ans. .702653.

MULTIPLICATION BY LOGARITHMS.

11. When it is required to multiply numbers by means of their logarithms, we first find, from the table, the logarithms of the numbers to be multiplied; we next add these logarithms together, and their sum is the logarithm of the product of the numbers (Art. 3).

The term *sum* is to be understood in its algebraic sense; therefore, if any of the logarithms have negative characteristics, the difference between their sum and the sum of the positive characteristics, is to be taken; the sign of the remainder is that of the greater sum.

EXAMPLES.

1. Multiply 23.14 by 5.062.

$$\begin{array}{lr} & \log 23.14 = 1.364363 \\ & \log 5.062 = \underline{0.704322} \\ \text{Product, } 117.1347 \quad . \quad . \quad . & \underline{2.068685} \end{array}$$

2. Multiply 3.902, 597.16, and 0.0314728 together.

$$\begin{array}{lr} & \log \quad 3.902 = 0.591287 \\ & \log \quad 597.16 = 2.776091 \\ & \log 0.0314728 = \underline{\bar{2}.497936} \\ \text{Product, } 73.3354 \quad . \quad . \quad . & \underline{1.865314} \end{array}$$

Here, the $\bar{2}$ cancels the $+\ 2$, and the 1 carried from the decimal part is set down.

3. Multiply 3.586, 2.1046, 0.8372, and 0.0294, together.

$$\begin{array}{lr} & \log \quad 3.586 = 0.554610 \\ & \log \quad 2.1046 = 0.323170 \\ & \log \quad 0.8372 = \bar{1}.922829 \\ & \log \quad 0.0294 = \underline{\bar{2}.468347} \\ \text{Product, } 0.1857615 \quad . \quad . \quad . & \underline{\bar{1}.268956} \end{array}$$

In this example, the 2, carried from the decimal part, cancels $\bar{2}$, and there remains $\bar{1}$, which is set down.

DIVISION OF NUMBERS BY LOGARITHMS.

12. When it is required to divide numbers by means of their logarithms, we have only to recollect, that the subtraction of logarithms corresponds to the division of their numbers (Art. 4). Hence,

if we find the logarithm of the dividend, and from it subtract the logarithm of the divisor, the remainder will be the logarithm of the quotient.

NOTE.—This additional caution may be added. The difference of the logarithms, as here used, means the *algebraic difference;* so that, if the logarithm of the divisor have a negative characteristic, its sign must be changed to positive, after diminishing it by the unit, if any, carried in the subtraction from the decimal part of the logarithm. Or, if the characteristic of the logarithm of the dividend is negative, it must be treated as a negative number.

EXAMPLES.

1. To divide 24163 by 4567.

$$\begin{array}{lr} \log 24163 = & 4.383151 \\ \log 4567 = & 3.659631 \\ \hline \text{Quotient, } 5.29078 \ldots & 0.723520 \end{array}$$

2. To divide 0.06314 by .007241.

$$\begin{array}{lr} \log 0.06314 = & \bar{2}.800305 \\ \log 0.007241 = & \bar{3}.859799 \\ \hline \text{Quotient, } 8.7198 \ldots & 0.940506 \end{array}$$

Here, 1 carried from the decimal part to the $\bar{3}$, changes it to $\bar{2}$, which being taken from $\bar{2}$, leaves 0 for the characteristic.

3. To divide 37.149 by 523.76.

$$\begin{array}{lr} \log 37.149 = & 1.569947 \\ \log 523.76 = & 2.719133 \\ \hline \text{Quotient, } 0.0709274 \ldots & \bar{2}.850814 \end{array}$$

4. To divide 0.7438 by 12.9476.

$$\begin{array}{lr} \log 0.7438 = & \bar{1}.871456 \\ \log 12.9476 = & 1.112189 \\ \hline \text{Quotient, } 0.057447 \ldots & \bar{2}.759267 \end{array}$$

Here, the 1 taken from $\bar{1}$, gives $\bar{2}$ for a result, as set down.

ARITHMETICAL COMPLEMENT.

13. The *Arithmetical complement* of a logarithm is the number which remains after subtracting the logarithm from 10.

Thus, if we have the log 9.274687, then,

$$10 - 9.274687 = 0.725313,$$

Hence, 0.725313 is the arithmetical complement of 9.274687.

14. We will now show that, *the difference between two logarithms is truly found, by adding to the first logarithm the arithmetical complement of the logarithm to be subtracted, and then diminishing the sum by* 10.

Let $a =$ the first logarithm,

$b =$ the logarithm to be subtracted,

and $c = 10 - b =$ the arithmetical complement of b.

Now the difference between the two logarithms will be expressed by $a - b$.

But, from the equation, $c = 10 - b$, we have

$$c - 10 = -b;$$

hence, if we place for $-b$ its value, we shall have

$$a - b = a + c - 10,$$

which agrees with the enunciation.

The arithmetical complement of a logarithm may be written directly from the table; thus, *subtract the left hand figure from* 9, *then proceeding to the right, subtract each figure from* 9 *till you reach the last figure, which must be taken from* 10: *this will be the same as taking the logarithm from* 10.

Note.—If the logarithm exceeds 10, its arithmetical complement is found by taking it from the smallest number of exact tens greater than it. Thus, if the logarithm were 15.674523, it would be taken from 20, and its arithmetical complement would be 4.325477. In all cases, the number from which the logarithm is taken is rejected from the sum.

EXAMPLES.

1. From 3.274107 take 2.104729.

By common method.		*By arith. comp.*
3.274107		3.274107
2.104729	its arith. comp.	7.895271
Diff. 1.169378		Sum 1.169378 after sub-

tracting 10.

Hence, to perform division by means of the arithmetical complement, we have the following

RULE.

To the logarithm of the dividend add the arithmetical complement of the logarithm of the divisor: the sum, after subtracting 10, *will be the logarithm of the quotient.*

EXAMPLES.

1. Divide 327.5 by 22.07.

log 327.5	2.515211
log 22.07 arith. comp. . .	8.656198
Quotient, 14.839 . . .	1.171409

2. Divide 0.7438 by 12.9476.

log 0.7438	$\bar{1}$.871456
log 12.9476 arith. comp. . .	8.887811
Quotient, 0.057447 . . .	$\bar{2}$.759267

In this example, the sum of the characteristics is 8, from which, taking 10, the remainder is $\bar{2}$.

3. Divide 37.149 by 523.76.

log 37.149	1.569947
log 523.76 arith. comp. . .	7.280867
Quotient, 0.0709273 . . .	$\bar{2}$.850814

4. Divide 0.875 by 25. *Ans.* 0.035.

5. Find, by logarithms, the 4th term of the proportion,

$$3976 : 7952 :: 5903 : x.$$

log 3976 arith. comp. . .	6.400554
log 7952	3.900476
log 5903	3.771073
log 11806	4.712103

6. Find, by logarithms, the 4th term of the proportion,

$$89721 : 358884 :: 5672 : x.$$

log 89721	arith. comp. . .	5.047106
log 358884	. . . .	5.554954
log 5772	. . . .	3.753736
log 22688	. . . .	4.355796

FINDING THE POWERS AND ROOTS OF NUMBERS BY LOGARITHMS.

15. We have (Art. 3),

$$10^{m} = M.$$

Raising both members of this equation to the nth power, we have,

$$10^{m \times n} = M^{n},$$

in which $m \times n$ is the logarithm of M^{n} (Art. 1): hence,

The logarithm of any power of any number, is equal to the logarithm of the number multiplied by the exponent of the power.

16. Taking the same equation,

$$10^{m} = M,$$

and extracting the nth root of both members, we have,

$$10^{\frac{m}{n}} = M^{\frac{1}{n}},$$

in which $\frac{m}{n}$ is the logarithm of $M^{\frac{1}{n}}$: that is,

The logarithm of the root of any number, is equal to the logarithm of the number divided by the index of the root.

EXAMPLES.

1. What is the 5th power of 9?

Log 9 = 0.954243; 0.954243 × 5 = 4.771215;

number answering to 4.771215 is 59049.

2. What is the 7th power of 8? *Ans.* 2097152.

3. What is the cube root of 4096?

$$\text{Log } 4096 = 3.612360;\ 3.612360 \div 3 = 1.204120;$$

number answering to 1.204120 is 16.

4. What is the 4th root of .00000081?

$$\text{Log } .00000081 = \bar{7}.908485;$$

but, $\bar{7}.908485 = \bar{8} + 1.908485;$

and, $\bar{8}. + 1.908485 \div 4 = \bar{2}.477121,$

the number answering to which is .03, which is the root.

When the characteristic of the logarithm is negative, and not divisible by the index of the root, add to it such a negative number as will make the sum exactly divisible by the index, and then prefix the same number, with a plus sign, to the decimal figures of the logarithm.

5. What is the 6th root of .0432? *Ans.* .592353 +.
6. What is the 7th root of .0004967? *Ans.* .3372969.

GEOMETRICAL CONSTRUCTIONS.

17. Before explaining the method of constructing geometrical problems, we shall describe some of the simpler instruments and their uses.

DIVIDERS.

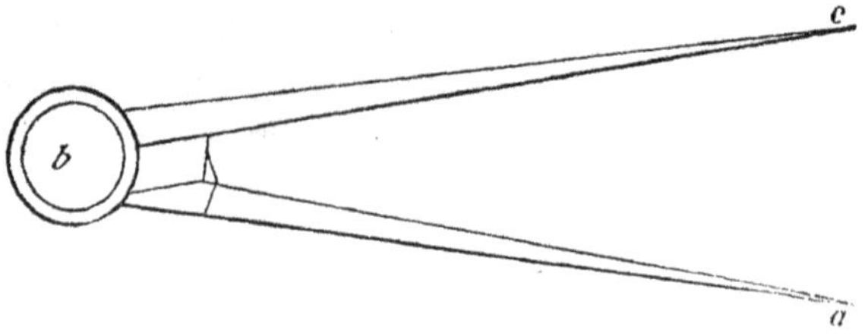

18. The dividers is the most simple and useful of the instruments used for drawing. It consists of two legs *ba*, *bc*, which may be easily turned around a joint at *b*.

One of the principal uses of this instrument is to lay off on a line, a distance equal to a given line.

For example, to lay off on CD a distance equal to AB.

For this purpose, place the forefinger on the joint of the dividers, and set one foot at A: then extend, with the thumb and other fingers, the other leg of the dividers, until its foot reaches the point B. Then raise the dividers, place one foot at C, and mark with the other the distance CE: this will evidently be equal to AB.

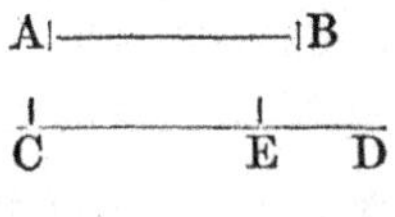

RULER AND TRIANGLE.

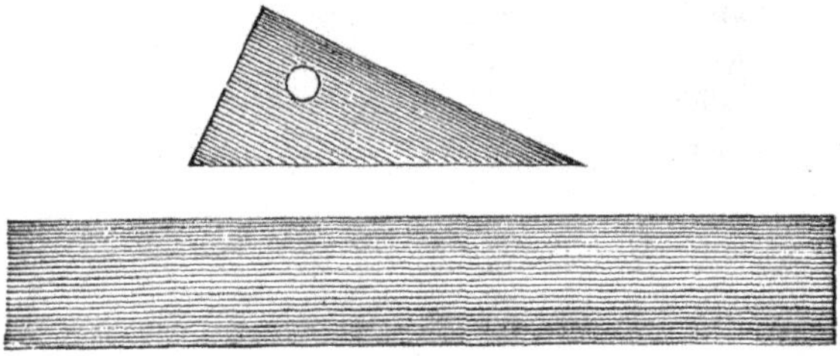

19. A ruler of convenient size, is about twenty inches in length, two inches wide, and a fifth of an inch in thickness. It should be made of a hard material, perfectly straight and smooth.

The hypothenuse of the right-angled triangle, which is used in connection with it, should be about ten inches in length, and it is most convenient to have one of the sides considerably longer than the other. We can solve, with the ruler and triangle, the two following problems.

I. *To draw through a given point a line which shall be parallel to a given line.*

20. Let C be the given point, and AB the given line.

Place the hypothenuse of the triangle against the edge of the ruler, and then place the ruler and triangle on the paper, so that one of the sides of the triangle shall coincide exactly with AB: the triangle being below the line.

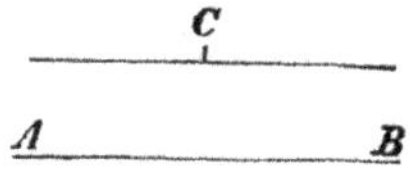

Then, placing the thumb and fingers of the left hand firmly on the ruler, slide the triangle with the other hand along the ruler until the side which coincided with AB reaches the point C. Leaving the thumb of the left hand on the ruler, extend the fingers upon the triangle and hold it firmly, and with the right hand, mark with a pen or pencil, a line through C: this line will be parallel to AB.

II. *To draw through a given point a line which shall be perpendicular to a given line.*

21. Let AB be the given line, and D the given point.

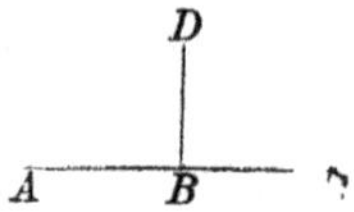

Place the hypothenuse of the triangle against the edge of the ruler, as before. Then place the ruler and triangle so that one of the sides of the triangle shall coincide exactly with the line AB. Then slide the triangle along the ruler until the other side reaches the point D: draw through D a right line, and it will be perpendicular to AB.

SCALE OF EQUAL PARTS.

22. A scale of equal parts is formed by dividing a line of a given length into equal portions.

If, for example, the line ab of a given length, say one inch, be divided into any number of equal parts, as 10, the scale thus formed, is called a scale of ten parts to the inch. The line ab, which is divided, is called the *unit of the scale.* This unit is laid off several times on the left of the divided line, and the points marked 1, 2, 3, &c.

The unit of scales of equal parts, is, in general, either an inch, or an exact part of an inch. If, for example, ab, the unit of the scale, were half an inch, the scale would be one of 10 parts to half an inch, or of 20 parts to the inch.

If it were required to take from the scale a line equal to one inch and six-tenths, place one foot of the dividers at 1 on the left, and extend the other to .6, which marks the sixth of the small divisions: the dividers will then embrace the required distance.

If it were required to take from the scale 2 inches and 9 tenths, place one foot of the dividers at 2 and extend the other to .9; the dividers would then embrace the required distance.

DIAGONAL SCALE OF EQUAL PARTS.

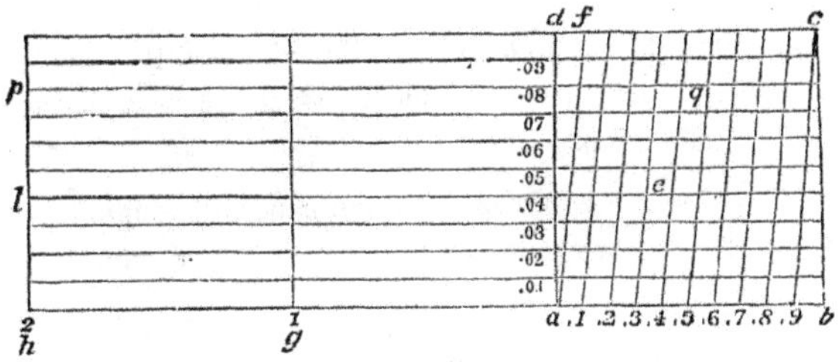

23. This scale is thus constructed. Take *ab* for the unit of the scale, which may be one inch, $\frac{1}{2}$, $\frac{1}{4}$, or $\frac{3}{4}$ of an inch, in length. On *ab* describe the square *abcd.* Divide the sides *ab* and *dc* each into ten equal parts. Draw *af* and the other nine parallels as in the figure.

Produce *ba* to the left, and lay off the unit of the scale any convenient number of times, and mark the points 1, 2, 3, &c. Then, divide the line *ad* into ten equal parts, and through the points of division draw parallels to *ab*, as in the figure.

Now, the small divisions of the line *ab* are each one-tenth (.1) of *ab;* they are, therefore, .1 of *ad*, or .1 of *ag* or *gh.*

If we consider the triangle *adf*, we see that the base *df* is one tenth of *ad*, the unit of the scale. Since the distance from *a* to the first horizontal line above *ab*, is one-tenth of the distance *ad*, it follows that the distance measured on that line between *ad* and *af* is one-tenth of *df;* but since one-tenth of a tenth is a hundredth, it follows that this distance is one hundredth (.01) of the unit of the scale. A like distance measured on the second line will be two hundredths (.02) of the unit of the scale; on the third, .03; on the fourth, .04, &c.

If it were required to take, in the dividers, the unit of the scale, and any number of tenths, place one foot of the dividers at 1, over *g*, and extend the other to that figure between *a* and *b*, which designates the tenths. If two or more units are required, the dividers must be placed on a point of division further to the left.

When units, tenths, and hundredths are required, place one foot of the dividers where the vertical line through the point which designates the units, intersects the line which designates the hundredths: then, extend the dividers to that line between *ad* and *bc* which designates the tenths: the distance so determined will be the one required

For example, to take off the distance 2.34, we place one foot of the dividers at *l*, and extend the other to *e*; and to take off the distance 2.58, we place one foot of the dividers at *p*, and extend the other to *q*.

REMARK I.—If a line is so long that the whole of it cannot be taken from the scale, it must be divided, and the parts of it taken from the scale in succession.

REMARK II.—If a line be given upon the paper, its length can be found by taking it in the dividers and applying it to the scale.

SEMICIRCULAR PROTRACTOR.

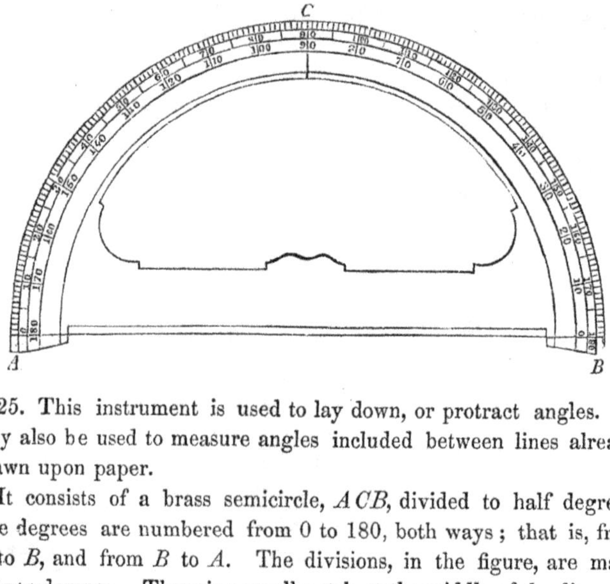

25. This instrument is used to lay down, or protract angles. It may also be used to measure angles included between lines already drawn upon paper.

It consists of a brass semicircle, *ACB*, divided to half degrees. The degrees are numbered from 0 to 180, both ways; that is, from *A* to *B*, and from *B* to *A*. The divisions, in the figure, are made only to degrees. There is a small notch at the middle of the diameter *AB*, which indicates the centre of the protractor.

To lay off an Angle with a Protractor.

25. Place the diameter *AB* on the line, so that the centre shall fall on the angular point. Then count the degrees contained in the given angle from *A* towards *B*, or from *B* towards *A*, and mark the extremity of the arc with a pin. Remove the protractor, and draw a line through the point so marked and the angular point: this line will make, with the given line, the required angle.

PLANE TRIGONOMETRY

TREATED GEOMETRICALLY.

DEFINITIONS.

1. In every plane triangle there are six parts: three sides and three angles. These parts are so related to each other, that when one side and any two other parts are given, the remaining ones can be obtained, either by geometrical construction or by trigonometrical computation.

2. *Plane Trigonometry* explains the methods of computing the unknown parts of a plane triangle, when a sufficient number of the six parts is given.

3. For the purpose of trigonometrical calculation, the circumference of the circle is supposed to be divided into 360 equal parts, called degrees; each degree is supposed to be divided into 60 equal parts, called minutes; and each minute into 60 equal parts, called seconds.

Degrees, minutes, and seconds, are designated respectively, by the characters ° ′ ″. For example, *ten degrees, eighteen minutes, and fourteen seconds,* would be written 10° 18′ 14″.

4. If two lines be drawn through the centre of the circle, at right angles to each other, they will divide the circumference into four equal parts, of 90° each. Every right angle then, as EOA, is measured by an arc of 90°; every acute angle, as BOA, by an arc less than 90°; and every obtuse angle, as FOA, by an arc greater than 90°.

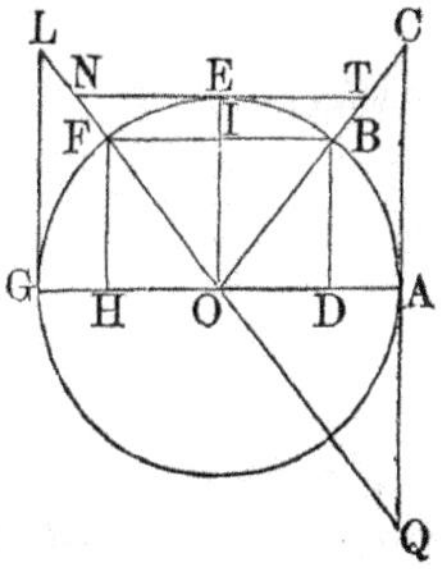

5. The *complement* of an arc is what remains after subtracting the arc from 90°. Thus, the arc EB is the complement of AB. The sum of an arc and its complement is equal to 90°.

6. The *supplement* of an arc is what remains after subtracting the arc from 180°. Thus, GF is the supplement of the arc AEF. The sum of an arc and its supplement is equal to 180°.

7. The *sine* of an arc is the perpendicular let fall from one extremity of the arc on the diameter which passes through the other extremity. Thus, BD is the sine of the arc AB.

8. The *cosine* of an arc is the part of the diameter intercepted between the foot of the sine and centre. Thus, OD is the cosine of the arc AB.

9. The *tangent* of an arc is the line which touches it at one extremity, and is limited by a line drawn through the other extremity and the centre of the circle. Thus, AC is the tangent of the arc AB.

10. The *secant* of an arc is the line drawn from the centre of the circle through one extremity of the arc, and limited by the tangent passing through the other extremity. Thus, OC is the secant of the arc AB.

11. The four lines, BD, OD, AC, OC, depend for their values on the arc AB and the radius OA; they are thus designated:

$$\begin{aligned} &\sin AB \text{ for } BD \\ &\cos AB \text{ for } OD \\ &\tan AB \text{ for } AC \\ &\sec AB \text{ for } OC \end{aligned}$$

12. If ABE be equal to a quadrant, or 90°, then EB will be the complement of AB. Let the lines ET and IB be drawn perpendicular to OE. Then,

ET, the tangent of EB, is called the cotangent of AB;
IB, the sine of EB, is equal to the cosine of AB;
OT, the secant of EB, is called the cosecant of AB.

In general, if A is any arc or angle, we have,

$$\begin{aligned} \cos A &= \sin (90° - A) \\ \cot A &= \tan (90° - A) \\ \operatorname{cosec} A &= \sec (90° - A) \end{aligned}$$

13. If we take an arc, $ABEF$, greater than 90°, its sine will be FH; OH will be its cosine; AQ its tangent, and OQ its secant. But FH is the sine of the arc GF, which is the supplement of AF, and OH is its cosine; hence *the sine of an arc is equal to the sine of its supplement; and the cosine of an arc is equal to the cosine of its supplement.*

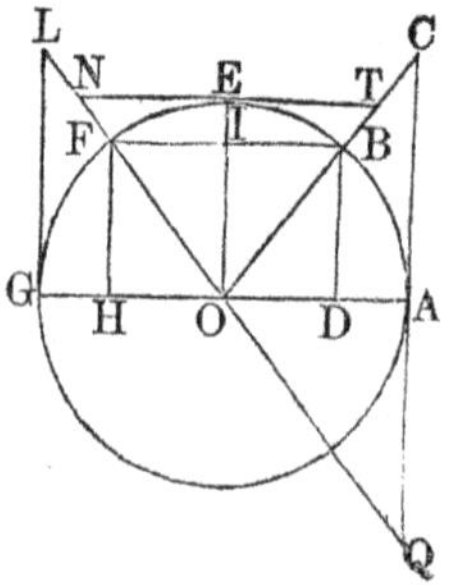

Furthermore, AQ is the tangent of the arc AF, and OQ is its secant: GL is the tangent, and OL the secant of the supplemental arc GF. But since AQ is equal to GL, and OQ to OL, it follows that *the tangent of an arc is equal to the tangent of its supplement; and the secant of an arc is equal to the secant of its supplement.**

TABLE OF NATURAL SINES.

14. Let us suppose, that in a circle of a given radius, the lengths of the sine, cosine, tangent, and cotangent, have been calculated for every minute or second of the quadrant, and arranged in a table; such a table is called a table of sines and tangents. If the radius of the circle is 1, the table is called a table of Natural Sines. A table of Natural Sines, therefore, shows the values of the sines, cosines, tangents, and cotangents of all the arcs of a quadrant, which is divided to minutes or seconds.

If the sines, cosines, tangents, and secants are known for arcs less than 90°, those for arcs which are greater can be found from them. For if an arc is less than 90°, its supplement will be greater than 90°, and the numerical values of these lines are the same for an arc and its supplement. Thus, if we know the sine of 20°, we also know the sine of its supplement, 160°; for the two are equal to each other. The Table of Natural Sines is not given, as it is much easier to make the computations by the Table which we are about to explain.

TABLE OF LOGARITHMIC SINES.

15. In this table are arranged the logarithms of the numerical values of the sines, cosines, tangents, and cotangents of all the arcs of a quadrant, calculated to a radius of 10,000,000,000. The logarithm of this radius is 10. In the first and last horizontal lines of each page, are written the degrees whose sines, cosines, &c., are expressed on the page. The vertical columns on the left and right are columns of minutes.

CASE I.

To find, in the table, the logarithmic sine, cosine, tangent, or cotangent of any given arc or angle.

16. If the angle is less than 45°, look for the degrees in the first horizontal line of the different pages; when the degrees are found,

* These relations are between the *numerical values* of the trigonometrical lines; the algebraic signs, which they have in the different quadrants, are not considered.

descend along the column of minutes, on the left of the page, till you reach the number showing the minutes; then pass along a horizontal line till you come into the column designated, sine, cosine, tangent, or cotangent, as the case may be; the number so indicated is the lagarithm sought. Thus, on page 37, of Tables, for 19° 55′, we find,

sine	19° 55′	9.532312
cos	19° 55′	9.973215
tan	19° 55′	9.559097
cot	19° 55′	10.440903

17. If the angle is greater than 45°, search for the degrees along the bottom line of the different pages: when the number is found, ascend along the column of minutes on the right hand side of the page, till you reach the number expressing the minutes; then pass along a horizontal line into the column designated tang, cot, sine, or cosine, as the case may be: the number so pointed out is the logarithm required.

18. The column designated sine, at the top of the page, is designated by cosine at the bottom; the one designated tang, by cotang, and the one designated cotang, by tang.

The angle found by taking the degrees at the top of the page, and the minutes from the left hand vertical column, is the complement of the angle found by taking the degrees at the bottom of the page, and the minutes from the right hand column on the same horizontal line with the first. Therefore, sine, at the top of the page, should correspond with the cosine, at the bottom; cosine with sine, tang with cotang, and cotang with tang, as in the tables (Art. 12).

If the angle is greater than 90°, we have only to subtract it from 180°, and take the sine, cosine, tangent, or cotangent of the remainder.

The column of the table next to the column of sines, and on the right of it, is designated by the letter *D*. This column is calculated in the following manner:

Opening the table at any page, as 42, the sine of 24° is found to be 9.609313; that of 24° 01′, 9.609597: their difference is 284; this being divided by 60, the number of seconds in a minute, gives 4.73, which is entered in the column *D*.

Now, supposing the increase of the logarithmic sine to be proportional to the increase of the arc, and it is nearly so for 60″, it follows, that 4.73 is the increase of the sine for 1″. Similarly, if the arc were 24° 20′, the increase of the sine for 1″, would be 4.65.

The same remarks are applicable in respect of the column D,

after the column cosine, and of the column D, between the tangents and cotangents. The column *D*, between the columns tangents and cotangents, answers to both these columns.

Now, if it were required to find the logarithmic sine of an arc expressed in degrees, minutes and seconds, we have only to find the degrees and minutes as before; then, multiply the corresponding tabular difference by the seconds, and add the product to the number first found, for the sine of the given arc.

Thus, if we wish the sine of 40° 26′ 28″.

The sine 40° 26′		9.811952
Tabular difference, 2.47 . .		
Number of seconds, 28 . .		
Product,	69.16 to be added	69.16
Gives for the sine of 40° 26′ 28″.		9.812021.

The decimal figures at the right are generally omitted in the last result; but when they exceed five-tenths, the figure on the left of the decimal point is increased by 1; the logarithm obtained is then exact, to within less than one unit of its right hand place.

The tangent of an arc, in which there are seconds, is found in a manner entirely similar. In regard to the cosine and cotangent, it must be remembered, that they increase while the arcs decrease, and decrease as the arcs are increased; consequently, the proportional numbers found for the seconds must be subtracted, not added.

EXAMPLES.

1. To find the cosine of 3° 40′ 40″.

The cosine of 3° 40′ . . .		9.999110
Tabular difference, .13 . .		
Number of seconds, 40 . .		
Product,	5.20 to be subtracted	5.20
Gives for the cosine of 3° 40′ 40″		9.999105.

2. Find the tangent of 37° 28′ 31″.

Ans. 9.884592.

3. Find the cotangent of 87° 57′ 59″.

Ans. 8.550356.

CASE II.

To find the degrees, minutes, and seconds answering to any given logarithmic sine, cosine tangent, or cotangent.

19. Search in the table, in the proper column, and if the number

is found, the degrees will be shown either at the top or bottom of the page, and the minutes in the side column, either at the left or right.

But, if the number cannot be found in the table, take from the table the degrees and minutes answering to the nearest less logarithm, the logarithm itself, and also the corresponding tabular difference. Subtract the logarithm taken from the table from the given logarithm, annex two ciphers to the remainder, and then divide the remainder by the tabular difference: the quotient will be seconds, and is to be connected with the degrees and minutes before found: to be added for the sine and tangent, and subtracted from the cosine and cotangent.

EXAMPLES.

1. Find the arc answering to the sine 9.880054
   Sine 49° 20′, next less in the table, 9.879963
   Tabular difference, 1.81)91.00(50″.

Hence, the arc 49° 20′ 50″ corresponds to the given sine 9.880054.

2. Find the arc whose cotangent is 10.008688
   cot 44° 26′, next less in the table, 10.008591
   Tabular difference, 4.21)97.00(23″

Hence, 44° 26′−23″=44° 25′ 37″ is the arc answering to the given cotangent 10.008688.

3. Find the arc answering to the tangent 9.979110.
   Ans. 43° 37′ 21″.

4. Find the arc answering to cosine 9.944599.
   Ans. 28° 19′ 45″.

20. We shall now demonstrate the principal theorems of Plane Trigonometry.

THEOREM I.

The sides of a plain triangle are proportional to the sines of their opposite angles.

21. Let ABC be a triangle; then will

$$CB : CA :: \sin A : \sin B.$$

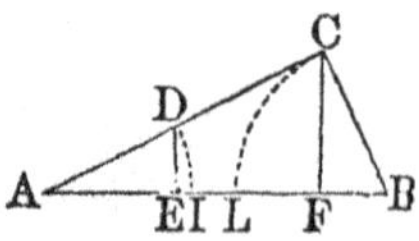

For, with A as a centre, and AD equal to the less side BC, as a radius, describe the arc DI: and with B as a centre and the equal radius BC, describe the arc CL, and draw DE and CF perpendicular to to AB: now DE is the sine of the angle

A, and CF is the sine of B, to the same radius AD or BC. But by similar triangles,

$$AD : DE :: AC : CF.$$

But AD being equal to BC, we have

$$BC : \sin A :: AC : \sin B, \text{ or}$$
$$BC : AC :: \sin A : \sin B.$$

By comparing the sides AB, AC, in a similar manner, we should find,

$$AB : AC :: \sin C : \sin B.$$

THEOREM II.

In any triangle, the sum of the two sides containing either angle, is to their difference, as the tangent of half the sum of the two other angles, to the tangent of half their difference.

22. Let ACB be a triangle : then will

$$AB+AC : AB-AC :: \tan \tfrac{1}{2}(C+B) : \tan \tfrac{1}{2}(C-B).$$

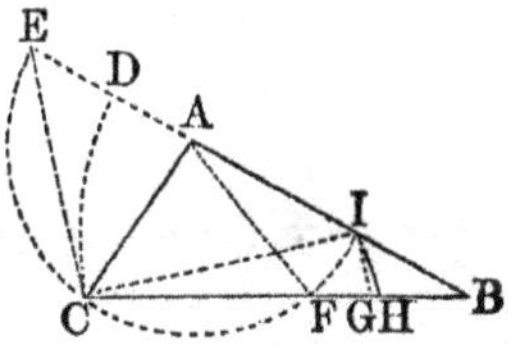

With A as a centre, and a radius AC, the less of the two given sides, let the semicircumference $IFCE$ be described, meeting AB in I, and BA produced, in E. Then, BE will be the sum of the sides, and BI their difference. Draw CI and AF.

Since CAE is an outward angle of the triangle ACB, it is equal to the sum of the inward angles C and B (Bk. I., Prop. XXV., Cor. 6). But the angle CIE being at the circumference, is half the angle CAE at the centre (Bk. III., Prop. XVIII.) ; that is, half the sum of the angles C and B, or equal to $\frac{1}{2}(C+B)$.

The angle $AFC=ACB$, is also equal to $ABC+BAF$; therefore, $BAF=ACB-ABC$.

But, $ICF=\frac{1}{2}(BAF)=\frac{1}{2}(ACB-ABC)$, or $\frac{1}{2}(C-B)$.

With I and C as centres, and the common radius IC, let the arcs CD and IG be described, and draw the lines CE and IH perpendicular to IC. The perpendicular CE will pass through E, the extremity of the diameter IE, since the right angle ICE must be inscribed in a semicircle.

But CE is the tangent of $CIE=\frac{1}{2}(C+B)$; and IH is the tangent of $ICB=\frac{1}{2}(C-B)$, to the common radius CI.

But since the lines CE and IH are parallel, the triangles BHI and BCE are similar, and give the proportion,

$$BE : BI :: CE : IH, \text{ or}$$

by placing for BE and BI, CE and IH, their values, we have

$$AB+AC : AB-AC :: \tan \tfrac{1}{2}(C+B) : \tan \tfrac{1}{2}(C-B).$$

THEOREM III.

In any plane triangle, if a line is drawn from the vertical angle perpendicular to the base, dividing it into two segments; then, the whole base, or sum of the segments, is to the sum of the two other sides, as the difference of those sides to the difference of the segments.

23. Let BAC be a triangle, and AD perpendicular to the base; then will

$$BC : CA+AB :: CA-AB : CD-DB.$$

For, $\overline{AB}^2=\overline{BD}^2+\overline{AD}^2$ (Bk. IV., Prop. XI.);

and $\overline{AC}^2=\overline{DC}^2+\overline{AD}^2$

by subtraction, $\overline{AC}^2-\overline{AB}^2=\overline{CD}^2-\overline{BD}^2$.

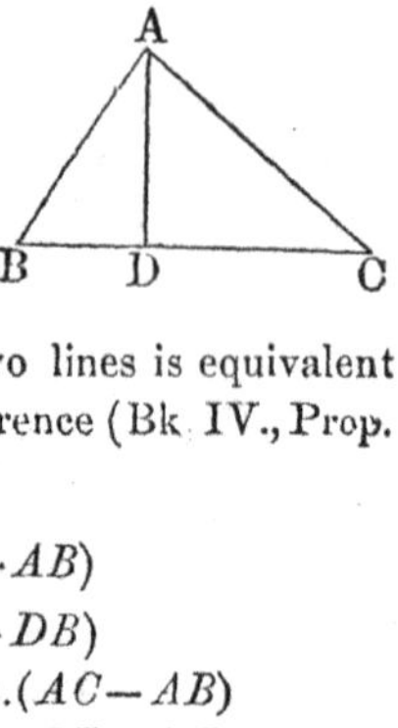

But since the difference of the squares of two lines is equivalent to the rectangle contained by their sum and difference (Bk. IV., Prop. X.), we have,

$$\overline{AC}^2-\overline{AB}^2=(AC+AB).(AC-AB)$$

and $$\overline{CD}^2-\overline{DB}^2=(CD+DB).(CD-DB)$$

therefore, $(CD+DB).(CD-DB)=(AC+AB).(AC-AB)$

hence, $CD+DB : AC+AB :: AC-AB : CD-DB.$

THEOREM IV.

In any right-angled plane triangle, radius is to the tangent of either of the acute angles, as the side adjacent to the side opposite.

24. Let CAB be the proposed triangle, and denote the radius by R: then will

$$R : \tan C :: AC : AB.$$

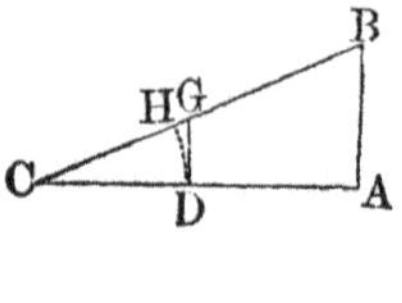

For, with any radius as CD describe the arc DH, and draw the tangent DG.

From the similar triangles CDG and CAB, we have,

$$CD : DG :: CA : AB; \text{ hence,}$$
$$R : \tan C :: CA : AB.$$

By describing an arc with B as a centre, we could show in the same manner that,

$$R : \tan B :: AB : AC.$$

THEOREM V.

In every right-angled triangle, radius is to the cosine of either of the acute angles, as the hypothenuse to the side adjacent.

25. Let ABC be a triangle, right-angled at B; then will,

$$R : \cos A :: AC : AB.$$

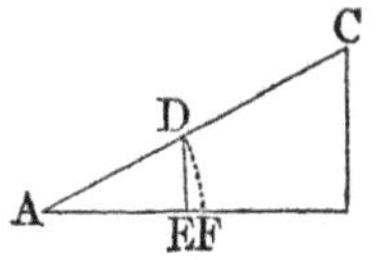

For, from the point A as a centre, with any radius as AD, describe the arc DF, which will measure the angle A, and draw DE perpendicular to AB; then will AE be the cosine of A.

The triangles ADE and ACB, being similar, we have,

$$AD : AE :: AC : AB; \text{ that is,}$$
$$R : \cos A :: AC : AB$$

Remark. The relations between the sides and angles of plane triangles, demonstrated in these five theorems, are sufficient to solve all the cases of Plane Trigonometry. Of the six parts which make up a plane triangle, three must be given, and at least one of these a side, before the others can be determined.

If the three angles only are given, it is plain that an indefinite number of similar triangles may be constructed, the angles of which shall be respectively equal to the angles that are given, and therefore, the sides could not be determined.

Assuming, with this restriction, any three parts of a triangle as given, one of the four following cases will always be presented:

I. When two angles and a side are given.
II. When two sides and an opposite angle are given.
III. When two sides and the included angle are given.
IV. When the three sides are given.

CASE I.

When two angles and a side are given.

26. Add the given angles together, and subtract their sum from 180 degrees. The remaining parts of the triangle can then be found by Theorem I.

EXAMPLES.

1. In a plane triangle, ACB, there are given the angle $A=58°\ 07'$, the angle $B=22°\ 37'$, and the side $AB=408$ yards. Required the other parts.

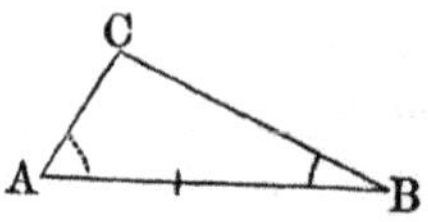

GEOMETRICALLY.

27. Draw an indefinite straight line, AB, and from the scale of equal parts lay off AB equal to 408. Then, at A, lay off an angle equal to $58°\ 07'$, and at B an angle equal to $22°\ 37'$, and draw the lines AC and BC: then will ABC be the triangle required.

The angle C may be measured with the protractor, and when so measured (see page 16), will be found equal to $99°\ 16'$. The sides AC and BC may be measured by referring them to the scale of equal parts (see page 15). We shall find $AC=158.9$ and $BC=351$ yards.

TRIGONOMETRICALLY BY LOGARITHMS.

To the angle . . .	$A=58°\ 07'$
Add the angle . . .	$B=22°\ 37'$
Their sum,	$=80°\ 44'$
taken from . . .	$180°\ 00'$
leaves C	$99°\ 16'$, of which, as it exceeds

90°, we use the supplement $80°\ 44'$.

To find the side BC.

As sin C	$99°\ 16'$	ar. comp.	0.005705
: sin A	$58°\ 07'$	. . . .	9.928972
: : AB	408	. . . .	2.610660
: BC	351.024	(after rejecting 10)	2.545337.

REMARK. The logarithm of the fourth term of a proportion is obtained by adding the logarithm of the second term to that of the third, and subtracting from their sum the logarithm of the first term. But to subtract the first term is the same as to add its arithmetical complement and reject 10 from the sum (page 9, Art. 13): hence, the arithmetical complement of the first term added to the logarithms of the second and third terms, minus ten, will give the logarithm of the fourth term.

To find the side AC.

As sin C	99° 16′	ar. comp.	0.005705
: sin B	22° 37′	. . . .	9.584968
: : AB	408	. . . .	2.610660
: AC	158.976	. . . .	2.201333

2. In a triangle ABC, there are given $A=38°\ 25'$, $B=57°\ 42'$ and $AB=400$: required the remaining parts.

Ans. $C=83°\ 53'$ $BC=249.974$, $AC=340.04$.

CASE II.

When two sides and an opposite angle are given.

28. In a plane triangle, ABC, there are given $AC=216$, $CB=117$, the angle $A=22°\ 37'$, to find the other parts.

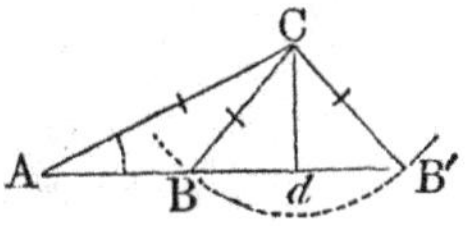

GEOMETRICALLY.

29. Draw an indefinite right line ABB': from any point, as A, draw AC, making $BAC=22°37'$, and make $AC=216$. With C as a centre, and a radius equal to 117, the other given side, describe the arc $B'B$; draw $B'C$ and BC: then will either of the triangles ABC or $AB'C$, answer all the conditions of the question.

TRIGONOMETRICALLY.

To find the angle B.

As BC	117	ar. comp.	7.931814
: AC	216	. . . .	2.334454
: : sin A	22° 37′	. . . .	9.584968
: sin B' 45° 13′ 55″, or ABC 134° 46′ 05″			9.851236

The ambiguity in this, and similar examples, arises in consequence of the first proportion being true for either of the angles ABC, or $AB'C$, which are supplements of each other, and therefore have the same sine (Art. 13). As long as the two triangles exist, the ambiguity will continue. But if the side CB, opposite the given angle, is greater than AC, the arc BB' will cut the line ABB', on the same side of the point A, in but one point, and then there will be only one triangle answering the conditions.

If the side CB is equal to the perpendicular Cd, the arc BB' will be tangent to ABB', and in this case also there will be but one triangle. When CB is less than the perpendicular Cd, the arc BB' will not intersect the base ABB', and in that case, no triangle can be formed, or it will be impossible to fulfill the conditions of the problem.

2. Given two sides of a triangle 50 and 40 respectively, and the angle opposite the latter equal to 32°: required the remaining parts of the triangle.

Ans. If the angle opposite the side 50 is acute, it is equal to 41° 28′ 59″; the third angle is then equal to 106° 31′ 01″, and the third side to 72.368. If the angle opposite the side 50 is obtuse, it is equal to 138° 31′ 01″, the third angle to 9° 28′ 59″, and the remaining side to 12.436.

CASE III.

When the two sides and their included angle are given.

30. Let ABC be a triangle; AB, BC, the given sides, and B the given angle.

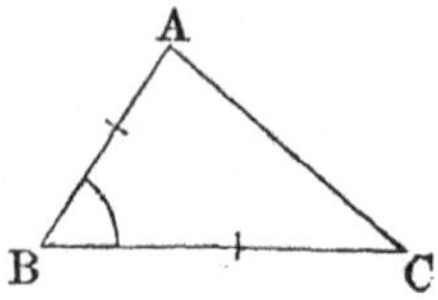

Since B is known, we can find the sum of the two other angles for

$$A+C=180°-B, \text{ and,}$$
$$\tfrac{1}{2}(A+C)=\tfrac{1}{2}(180°-B).$$

We next find half the difference of the angles A and C by Theorem II, viz.,

$$BC+BA \ : \ BC-BA \ :: \ \tan\tfrac{1}{2}(A+C) \ : \ \tan\tfrac{1}{2}(A-C),$$

in which we consider BC greater than BA, and therefore A is greater than C; since the greater angle must be opposite the greater side.

Having found half the difference of A and C, by adding it to the half sum, $\frac{1}{2}(A+C)$, we obtain the greater angle, and by subtracting it from half the sum, we obtain the less. That is,

$$\tfrac{1}{2}(A+C)+\tfrac{1}{2}(A-C)=A, \text{ and,}$$
$$\tfrac{1}{2}(A+C)-\tfrac{1}{2}(A-C)=C.$$

Having found the angles A and C, the third side AC may be found by the proportion,

$$\sin A \ : \ \sin B \ :: \ BC \ : \ AC.$$

EXAMPLES.

1. In the triangle ABC, let $BC=540$, $AB=450$, and the included angle $B=80°$: required the remaining parts.

GEOMETRICALLY.

31. Draw an indefinite right line BC, and from any point, as B, lay off a distance $BC=540$. At B make the angle $CBA=80°$: draw BA, and make the distance $BA=450$; draw AC; then will ABC be the required triangle.

TRIGONOMETRICALLY.

$$BC+BA=540+450=990\text{; and } BC-BA=540-450=90.$$
$$A+C=180°-B=180°-80°=100°, \text{ and therefore,}$$
$$\tfrac{1}{2}(A+C)=\tfrac{1}{2}(100°)=50°.$$

To find $\frac{1}{2}(A-C)$.

As	$BC+BA$	990	ar. comp.	7.004365
:	$BC-BA$	90	. . . .	1.954243
: :	$\tan\frac{1}{2}(A+C)$	50°	. . . .	10.076187
:	$\tan\frac{1}{2}(A-C)$	6° 11′	. . . .	9.034795.

Hence, $50°+6°\ 11'=56°\ 11'=A$; and $50°-6°\ 11'=43°\ 49$ $=C$.

To find the third side AC.

As	$\sin C$	43° 49′	ar. comp.	0.159672
:	$\sin B$	80°	. . . .	9.993351
: :	AB	450	. . . .	2.653213
:	AC	640.082	. . . .	2.806236.

2. Given two sides of a plane triangle, 1686 and 960, and their included angle 128° 04′: required the other parts.

Ans. Angles, 33° 34′ 39″; 18° 21′ 21″; side 2400.

CASE IV.

The three sides of a plane triangle being given, to find the angles.

32. Let fall a perpendicular from the angle opposite the greater side, dividing the given triangle into two right-angled triangles: then find the difference of the segments of the base by Theorem III. Half this difference being added to half the base, gives the greater segment; and, being subtracted from half the base, gives the less segment. Then, since the greater segment belongs to the right-angled triangle having the greater hypothenuse, we have two sides and the right angle of each of two right-angled triangles, to find the acute angles.

EXAMPLES.

1. The sides of a plane triangle being given; viz., $BC=40$, $AC=34$, and $AB=25$: required the angles.

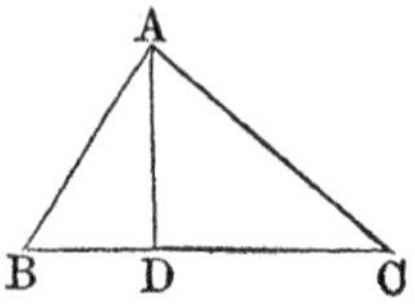

GEOMETRICALLY.

33. With the three given lines as sides construct a triangle. Then measure the angles of the triangle either with the protractor or scale of chords.

TRIGONOMETRICALLY.

As $BC \; : \; AC+AB \; :: \; AC-AB \; : \; CD-BD$,

That is $40 \; : \; 59 \; :: \; 9 \; : \; \frac{59\times 9}{40}=13.275$.

Then $\frac{40+13.275}{2}=26.6375=CD$,

And, $\frac{40-13.275}{2}=13.3625=BD$

In the triangle DAC, to find the angle DAC.

As	AC	34	ar. comp.	8.468521
:	DC	26.6375	. . . .	1.425493
::	sin D	90°	. . . .	10.000000
:	sin DAC	51° 34′ 40″	. . . .	9.894014.

In the triangle BAD, to find the angle BAD.

As	AB	25	ar. comp.	8.602060
:	BD	13.3625	. . . .	1.125887
::	sin D	90°	. . . .	10.000000
:	sin BAD	32° 18′ 35″	. . . .	9.727947.

Hence, $90°-DAC=90°-51° 34' 40''=38° 25' 20''=C$,

and, $90°-BAD=90°-32° 18' 35''=57° 41' 25''=B$,

and, $BAD+DAC=51° 34' 40''+32° 18' 35''=83° 53' 15''$
$=A$.

2. In a triangle, of which the sides are 4, 5, and 6, what are the angles?

Ans. 41° 24′ 35″; 55° 46′ 16″; and 82° 49′ 09″.

SOLUTION OF RIGHT-ANGLED TRIANGLES.

34. The unknown parts of a right-angled triangle may be found by either of the four last cases; or, if two of the sides are given, by means of the property that the square of the hypothenuse is equivalent to the sum of the squares of the two other sides. Or the parts may be found by Theorems IV. and V.

EXAMPLES.

1. In a right-angled triangle BAC, there are given the hypothenuse $BC=250$, and the base $AC=240$: required the other parts.

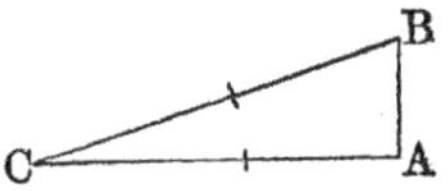

Ans. $B=73° 44' 23''$; $C=16° 15' 37''$; $AB=70.0003$.

2. In a right-angled triangle BAC, there are given $AC=384$, and $B=53° 08'$: required the remaining parts.

Ans. $AB=287.96$; $BC=479.979$; $C=36° 52'$.

3. In a right-angled triangle BAC, there are given $CB=325$ yards, and $C=27° 34'$; required the remaining parts.

Ans. $AB=150.40$ yards, $AC=288.10$ yards, $B=62° 26'$.

4. In a right-angled triangle BAC, there are given $AB=56.293$ feet, $C=54° 27' 39''$, to find the remaining parts.

Ans. $AC=40.2114$, $CB=69.18$ and $B=35° 32' 21''$.

☞ Let the pupil work all the examples under "Application to Heights and Distances," page 77.

ANALYTICAL TRIGONOMETRY.

1. In every triangle, six parts are considered, viz., three angles and three sides. It has been proved in Geometry, that if certain parts of a triangle, either plane or spherical, are given, the remaining parts can be constructed, and the triangle fully determined.

It is found, however, in practice that, on account of the imperfection of the instruments used, as well as want of skill in using them, it is impossible to arrive at a very great degree of accuracy in the construction and measurement of these required parts. It therefore becomes necessary to devise means of accurately computing them.

2. TRIGONOMETRY is that branch of Mathematics which has for its principal object *the explanation of the methods of computing the unknown parts of triangles, when a sufficient number of other parts are known.*

This computation is called *the solution of the triangle.*

Trigonometry consists of two branches, viz., *Plane* and *Spherical.*

PLANE TRIGONOMETRY treats particularly of the solution of plane or rectilineal triangles.

SPHERICAL TRIGONOMETRY treats particularly of the solution of spherical triangles.

3. Before proceeding to the solution of triangles, it will be necessary to demonstrate certain principles and deduce many formulas, which are of great use not only in Trigonometry, but in many other mathematical discussions.

The Division of the Circumference.

4. Angles are usually measured by the arcs of circles included between their sides, these arcs being described from the vertices of the angles as centres, with equal radii. In this treatise, the constant radius of these arcs is taken as *the linear unit of measure*, and is denoted by the number 1. The entire circumference, represented by 2π (π being the representative of the number 3.14159265..), is supposed to be divided into 360 equal parts, each part being called *a degree*, indicated thus, 1°. Each degree is further divided into 60 equal parts called *minutes*, one of which is denoted thus, $1'$; and each minute into 60 equal parts called *seconds*, denoted thus, $1''$; and each second into 60 equal parts called *thirds*, denoted thus, $1'''$; And thus, by a continued division of the thirds into *fourths*, and the fourths into *fifths*, &c., an arc, as small as can be conceived of, can be expressed.

An arc or angle expressed thus,

$$26^\circ \quad 13' \quad 52'' \quad 30''',$$

would be read, twenty-six degrees, thirteen minutes, fifty-two seconds, and thirty-thirds.

It is better, in practice, to express all divisions less than a second, in decimal parts of a second. Thus, the above angle is better written,

$$26^\circ \quad 13' \quad 52.5''.$$

5. The circumference is also divided into four equal parts, by two diameters at right angles to each other, as CA and BD. Each part contains 90°, and is called *a quadrant*.

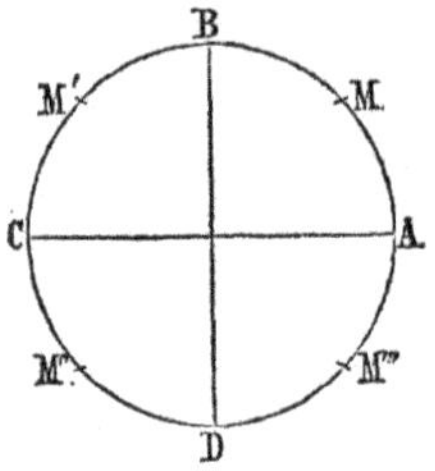

The point A, being taken as the origin, or first point of arcs, AB is the *first* quadrant, BC the *second*, CD the *third*, and DA the *fourth*.

An arc, as AM, beginning at A, estimated in the direction AB, and having its other extremity in AB, is said to be *in the first quadrant*. Hence, all arcs in the first quadrant are less than 90°.

An arc, as AM', having its second extremity in the arc BC, is *in the second quadrant*, and all arcs in the second quadrant are greater than 90°, and less than 180°. In like manner AM'' is in the third, and AM''' in the fourth quadrant.

6. The complement of an angle, or arc, is the remainder after subtracting it from 90°. Thus,

$$90° - 15° = 75°,$$

is the complement of 15°.

$$90° - 115° = -25°,$$

is the complement of 115°, the complement being negative whenever the arc exceeds 90°. The sum of an arc and its complement is always 90°.

7. The supplement of an angle, or arc, is the remainder after subtracting it from 180°. Thus,

$$180° - 35° = 145°, \quad \text{and} \quad 180° - 225° = -45°,$$

are the supplements of 35° and 225°, respectively, the supplement being negative whenever the arc exceeds 180°. The sum of an arc and its supplement is always 180°.

The Circular Functions.

8. The *sine* of an angle, or of its measuring arc, is *the perpendicular distance from the end of the arc to the diameter, passing through its origin.* Thus,

OA being equal to 1, Art. (4),

$MP \quad = \text{sine of } AM;$

$M'P' \quad = \text{sine of } AM';$

$M''P'' \quad = \text{sine of } ABM'';$

$M'''P''' = \text{sine of } ABM'''.$

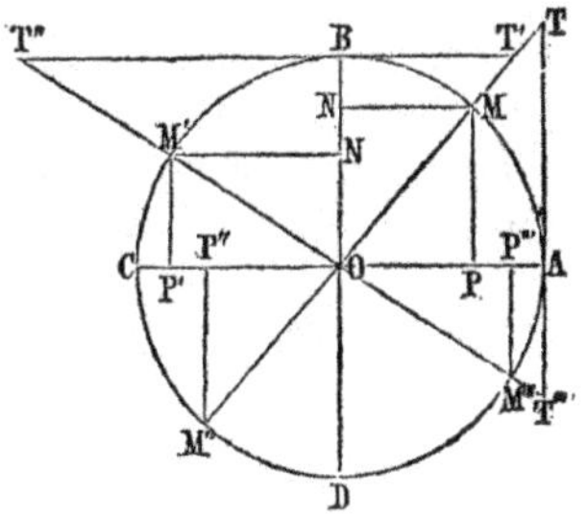

The *cosine* of an arc is *the sine of the complement of the arc.* Thus,

$MN \quad = \text{sine of } MB = \text{cosine of } AM;$

$M'N' = \text{sine of} - BM' = \text{cosine of } AM'$; &c.

From the figure it is obvious, that the cosine of an arc is always equal to the distance from the centre to the foot of the sine. Thus,

$$MN = OP; \qquad M'N' = OP'.$$

9. The *versed sine* of an arc is *the distance, from the origin of the arc to the foot of the sine.* Thus,

$$AP = \text{versed-sine of } AM; \qquad AP'' = \text{versed-sine of } ABM''$$

The *co-versed sine* of an arc is *the versed sine of the complement of the arc.* Thus,

$$BN = \text{co-versed sine of } AM.$$

10. The *tangent* of an arc is *the portion of a straight line touching the arc at its origin, included between the origin and the produced diameter through the end of the arc.* Thus,

$$AT = \text{tangent of } AM; \qquad AT''' = \text{tangent of } ABM'''.$$

The *co-tangent* of an arc is *the tangent of the complement of the arc.* Thus,

$$BT' = \text{co-tangent of } AM; \qquad BT'' = \text{co-tangent of } ABM'$$

11. The *secant* of an arc is *the distance from the centre of the arc to the further extremity of the tangent.* Thus,

$$OT = \text{secant of } AM; \qquad OT''' = \text{secant of } ABM'''.$$

The *co-secant* of an arc is *the secant of the complement of the arc.* Thus,

$$OT' = \text{co-secant of } AM; \qquad OT'' = \text{co-secant of } ABM'.$$

12. The sine, cosine, versed-sine, tangent, &c., are called *functions* of the arc, or *circular functions*, since they are so connected with the arc, that any change in the latter produces a corresponding change in the former.

Elementary Formulas, expressing relations between the Circular Functions.

13. Let a represent any arc, as AM, measuring the angle AOM. Then

$OA = 1$, $MP = \sin\ a$,

$OP = \cos\ a$, $AP = \text{ver-sin}\ a$,

$AT = \tan\ a$, $OT = \sec\ a$.

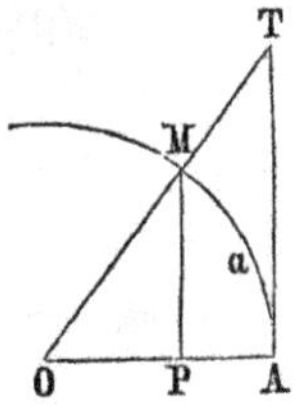

The right angled triangle OPM gives

$$\overline{MP}^2 + \overline{OP}^2 = \overline{OM}^2$$

or substituting for MP, OP and $OM =$ OA, their values as above, we have

$$\sin^2 a + \cos^2 a = 1 \quad . \ . \ . \ . \ . \quad (1).*$$

whence

$$\sin^2 a = 1 - \cos^2 a \ . \ . \ . \ (2); \qquad \cos^2 a = 1 - \sin^2 a \ . \ . \ (3).$$

We have also

$$AP = AO - OP, \quad \text{or,} \quad \text{ver-sin}\ a = 1 - \cos\ a \ . \ . \ . \ (4).$$

Since this formula is true for any value of a, we may substitute $90° - a$ for a, and have

$$\text{ver-sin}\ (90° - a) = 1 - \cos\ (90° - a),$$

or since, (Arts. 8 and 9),

$$\cos\ (90° - a) = \sin\ a, \qquad \text{ver-sin}\ (90° - a) = \text{co-versin}\ a,$$

we have

$$\text{co-versin}\ a = 1 - \sin\ a \ . \ . \ . \ . \ (5).$$

The similar triangles OPM and OAT give the proportion,

---

* Note. The symbols $\sin^2 a$, $\cos^2 a$ indicate *the square of the* sin a, &c.

$$OP : MP :: OA : AT,$$

or

$$\cos a : \sin a :: 1 : \tan a,$$

whence,

$$\tan a = \frac{\sin a}{\cos a} \quad . \quad . \quad . \quad . \quad (6).$$

Substituting $90° - a$ for a, we have

$$\tan (90° - a) = \frac{\sin (90° - a)}{\cos (90° - a)} \quad \text{or,} \quad \cot a = \frac{\cos a}{\sin a} \quad . \quad (7).$$

Multiplying equations (6) and (7), member by member, we have,

$$\tan a \cot a = 1 \quad . \quad . \quad . \quad . \quad (8);$$

or,

$$\tan a = \frac{1}{\cot a} \quad . \quad . \quad . \quad (9). \qquad \cot a = \frac{1}{\tan a} \quad . \quad . \quad . \quad (10).$$

The same similar triangles give the proportion,

$$OP : OM :: OA : OT,$$

or,

$$\cos a : 1 :: 1 : \sec a,$$

whence,

$$\sec a = \frac{1}{\cos a} \quad . \quad . \quad . \quad . \quad (11).$$

Substituting $90° - a$ for a, we have,

$$\sec (90° - a) = \frac{1}{\cos (90° - a)}, \quad \text{or} \quad \text{co-sec}\, a = \frac{1}{\sin a} \quad . \quad . \quad (12).$$

The right angled triangle OAT gives

$$\overline{OT}^2 = \overline{OA}^2 + \overline{AT}^2, \quad \text{or} \quad \sec^2 a = 1 + \tan^2 a \quad . \quad . \quad (13);$$

whence, by the substitution of $90° - a$ for a,

$$\text{co-sec}^2 a = 1 + \cot^2 a \quad . \quad . \quad . \quad (14).$$

14. The formulas of the preceding article are of frequent use, and should be memorized. For convenience of reference they are collected in the following

TABLE I.

1.	$\sin^2 a + \cos^2 a = 1.$	9.	$\tan a = \dfrac{1}{\cot a}.$
2.	$\sin^2 a = 1 - \cos^2 a.$		
3.	$\cos^2 a = 1 - \sin^2 a.$	10.	$\cot a = \dfrac{1}{\tan a}.$
4.	$\text{ver-sin } a = 1 - \cos a.$		
5.	$\text{co-ver sin } a = 1 - \sin a.$	11.	$\sec a = \dfrac{1}{\cos a}.$
6.	$\tan a = \dfrac{\sin a}{\cos a}.$	12.	$\text{co-sec } a = \dfrac{1}{\sin a}.$
7.	$\cot a = \dfrac{\cos a}{\sin a}.$	13.	$\sec^2 a = 1 + \tan^2 a.$
8.	$\tan a \cot a = 1.$	14.	$\text{co-sec}^2 a = 1 + \cot^2 a.$

Algebraic Signs of the Circular Functions.

15. It is a principle of Algebra, that if quantities estimated from a fixed origin, in one direction, are regarded as positive, those estimated from the same origin, in a directly contrary direction, must be regarded as negative. (Davies' Bourdon, Art. 89).

The point A being the origin of arcs, all arcs estimated from this point, along the circumference in the direction $AMBM'$ will be regarded as *positive*.

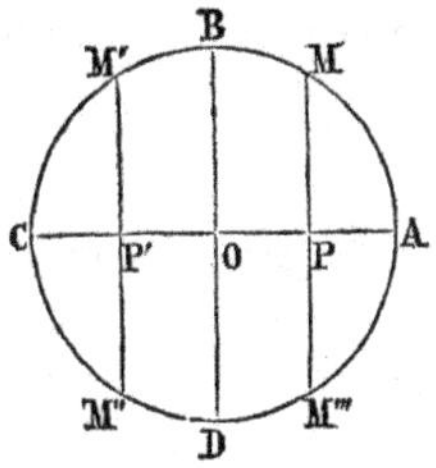

Those estimated from A in the direction $AM'''DM''$ will consequently be *negative*. Thus, if AM, represented by a, contain the same number of degrees as AM''', then

$$AM''' = -AM = -a.$$

16. Likewise, all the circular functions estimated from the horizontal diameter CA, upwards, will be regarded as *positive*. All estimated from the same diameter, downwards, will then be *negative*.

Thus, the sines MP and $M'P'$ of the arcs AM and AM' will be *positive*; $M''P'$ and $M'''P$ will be *negative*; and, in general, the sines of all arcs or angles in *the first and second quadrants will be positive*, and the sines of all arcs or angles in *the third and fourth quadrants will be negative.*

Again, all the circular functions estimated from the vertical diameter DB, to the right, will be regarded as *positive*. Those estimated to the left will then be *negative*.

Thus, OP, the cosine of the arcs AM and $ABCM'''$ is *positive*, while OP', the cosine of the arcs AM' and ABM'' is *negative;* and, in general, the cosines of arcs or angles in *the first and fourth quadrants are positive*, and the cosines of arcs or angles in *the second and third quadrants are negative.*

17. The signs of the other circular functions result, at once, from those of the sine and cosine.

From formulas (4) and (5) of Table I,

$$\text{ver-sin } a = 1 - \cos a, \qquad \text{co-versin } a = 1 - \sin a;$$

since neither the sine nor cosine can exceed the radius or 1, it follows that *the ver-sine and co-versine are always positive.*

18. From formula (6), Table I,

$$\tan a = \frac{\sin a}{\cos a};$$

since $\sin a$ and $\cos a$ have the same signs in the *first* and *third* quadrants, $\tan a$ must there be *positive;* and since they have different signs in the *second* and *fourth* quadrants, $\tan a$ must there be *negative.*

From formula (8),

$$\tan a \cot a = 1;$$

since the second member is positive, $\tan a$ and $\cot a$ must always have the same sign, that is, the co-tangent must also be *positive in the first and third quadrants,* and *negative in the second and fourth.*

19. From formulas (11) and (12),

$$\sec a = \frac{1}{\cos a}, \qquad \text{co-sec } a = \frac{1}{\sin a},$$

we see that the sign of the secant is the same as that of the *cosine,* and the sign of the co-secant, the same as that of the sine, that is. *the secant is positive* in the *first* and *fourth* quadrants, and *negative* in the *second* and *third;* while *the co-secant is positive* in the *first* and *second* quadrants, and *negative* in the *third* and *fourth.*

Changes which take place in the Circular Functions, as the Arc changes.

20. The origin of arcs being at A, the arc at this point is 0, its sine is 0, and its cosine equal to $OA = 1$;
that is,

$$\sin 0 = 0, \qquad \cos 0 = 1.$$

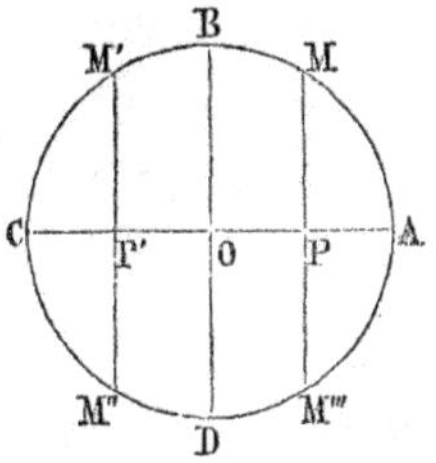

As the arc increases from 0 to 90°, the sine increases from 0 to its greatest value $OB = 1$, and the cosine decreases from 1 to 0; that is,

$$\sin 90^\circ = 1, \qquad \cos 90^\circ = 0.$$

As the arc increases from 90° to 180°, the sine decreases from 1 to 0; the cosine passes through 0, and changes its sign from *plus to minus*, and still decreases, *algebraically*, from 0 to its least value, $- OC = - 1$, and we have

$$\sin 180^\circ = 0, \qquad \cos 180^\circ = -1.$$

As the arc increases from 180° to 270°, the sine passes through 0, and changes its sign from *plus to minus*, and still decreases from 0 to its least value, -1; the cosine increases algebraically from -1 to 0, and we have

$$\sin 270^\circ = -1, \qquad \cos 270^\circ = 0.$$

As the arc increases from 270° to 360°, the sine increases from -1 to 0; the cosine again passes through 0, changes its sign from *minus to plus*, and increases from 0 to its greatest value 1, and we have

$$\sin 360^\circ = 0, \qquad \cos 360^\circ = 1.$$

21. The corresponding changes and values of the other circular functions are deduced from those of the sine and cosine. Thus, from the formulas,

$$\text{ver-sin } a = 1 - \cos a, \qquad \text{co-versin } a = 1 - \sin a,$$

we see that, as the arc increases from 0 to 180°, the versine increases from 0 to its greatest value 2, while the co-versine decreases from 1 to 0, and then increases again to 1. As the arc increases from 180° to 360°, the versine decreases from 2 to its least value 0, while the co-versine increases to its greatest value 2, and then again decreases to 1, and we have

$$\text{versin } 0 = 0, \qquad \text{co-versin } 0 = 1,$$
$$\text{versin } 90^\circ = 1, \qquad \text{co-versin } 90^\circ = 0,$$
$$\text{versin } 180^\circ = 2, \qquad \text{co-versin } 180^\circ = 1,$$
$$\text{versin } 270^\circ = 1, \qquad \text{co-versin } 270^\circ = 2,$$
$$\text{versin } 360^\circ = 0, \qquad \text{co-versin } 360^\circ = 1.$$

22. From the formulas

$$\tan a = \frac{\sin a}{\cos a}, \qquad \cot a = \frac{\cos a}{\sin a},$$

we have

$$\tan 0 = \frac{0}{1} = 0, \qquad \cot 0 = \frac{1}{0} = \infty.$$

As the arc increases from 0 to 90° the tangent increases from 0 to ∞, and the co-tangent decreases from ∞ to 0, and we have

$$\tan 90^\circ = \infty, \qquad \cot 90^\circ = 0.$$

As the arc increases from 90° to 180°, the tangent passes through infinity, and changes its sign from *plus* to *minus*, and then increases, algebraically, to 0. The co-tangent passes through 0, changes its sign from *plus* to *minus*, and decreases to $-\infty$, and we have

$$\tan 180^\circ = 0, \qquad \cot 180^\circ = -\infty.$$

It is thus seen that as the arc increases, *the tangent increases algebraically, while the co-tangent decreases*, and we have

$$\tan 270^\circ = -\infty, \qquad \cot 270^\circ = 0,$$
$$\tan 360^\circ = 0, \qquad \cot 360^\circ = \infty.$$

It should be remarked that there are two exceptions to the principle above enunciated, viz: when the arc changes from its value preceding 90°, to that immediately following, the tangent changes, *at once*, from an infinitely great *positive quantity*, to an infinitely great *negative quantity*; or, in an algebraic sense, changes from its greatest value to its least value; and the same change takes place when the arc passes through 270°.

23. From the formulas

$$\sec a = \frac{1}{\cos a}, \qquad \text{co-sec } a = \frac{1}{\sin a},$$

we see, that as the arc increases from 0, the secant increases from 1 to ∞, at 90°; then changes its sign from + to −, and decreases to − 1, at 180°; and continues to decrease to − ∞, at 270°; then changes its sign from − to +, and increases to 1, at 360°. The co-secant undergoes similar changes, being ∞ when the arc is 0; 1 at 90°; ∞ at 180°; and − 1 at 270°.

24. For convenience of reference, the results of the four preceding articles are arranged in the following

TABLE II.

arc = 0				arc = 180°			
sin	= 0,	cos	= 1.	sin	= 0,	cos	= − 1.
v-sin	= 0,	co-v-sin	= 1.	v-sin	= 2,	co-v-sin	= 1.
tan	= 0,	cot	= ∞	tan	= 0,	cot	= − ∞.
sec	= 1,	co-sec	= ∞.	sec	= − 1,	co-sec	= ∞.
arc = 90°				arc = 270°			
sin	= 1,	cos	= 0.	sin	= − 1,	cos	= 0.
v-sin	= 1,	co-v-sin	= 0.	v-sin	= 1,	co-v-sin	= 2.
tan	= ∞,	cot	= 0.	tan	= − ∞,	cot	= 0.
sec	= ∞,	co-sec	= 1.	sec	= ∞,	co-sec	= − 1.

The circular functions of 360° are all evidently the same as those of 0°.

25. If a represent any arc, as BM', less than 90°, then $AM' = 90° + a$, and

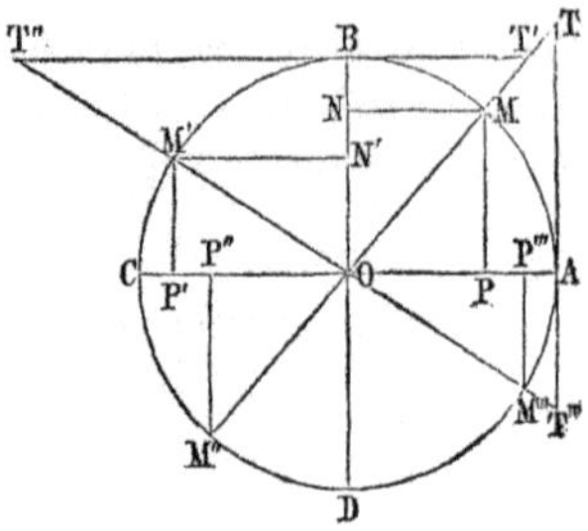

$$M'P' = \sin (90^\circ + a),$$

$$-OP' = \cos (90^\circ + a),$$

$$M'N' = \sin a, \qquad ON' = \cos a,$$

from which it is evident that

$$\sin (90^\circ + a) = \cos a,$$

$$\cos (90^\circ + a) = -\sin a.$$

These values, substituted in the formulas for the tangent, co-tangent, secant and co-secant, give

$$\tan (90^\circ + a) = -\cot a, \qquad \cot (90^\circ + a) = -\tan a,$$

$$\sec (90^\circ + a) = -\text{co-sec}\, a, \qquad \text{co-sec}\, (90^\circ + a) = \sec a.$$

Also, if a represent any arc as CM' less than 90°, then $AM' = 180^\circ - a$, and

$$M'P' = \sin (180^\circ - a), \qquad -OP' = \cos (180^\circ - a),$$

$$M'P' = \sin a, \qquad OP' = \cos a,$$

and we have

$$\sin (180^\circ - a) = \sin a, \qquad \cos (180^\circ - a) = -\cos a,$$

that is: *The sine of an arc is equal to the sine of its supplement*, and *the co-sine of an arc is equal to minus the co-sine of its supplement.*

These values being substituted in the formulas for the tangent, co-tangent, &c., will give corresponding values, for those functions.

In like manner, by the inspection of the figure, and by making the proper substitutions, the tangent, co-tangent, secant and co-secant of the arcs $180^\circ + a$, $270^\circ - a$, $270^\circ + a$, and $360^\circ - a$, can be found. The preceding results are arranged in the following

TABLE III.

arc $= 90 + a$,	arc $= 270° - a$,
$\sin = \cos a$, $\cos = -\sin a$.	$\sin = -\cos a$, $\cos = -\sin a$.
$\tan = -\cot a$, $\cot = -\tan a$.	$\tan = \cot a$, $\cot = \tan a$.
$\sec = -\text{cosec}\, a$, $\text{cosec} = \sec a$.	$\sec = -\text{cosec}\, a$, $\text{cosec} = -\sec a$.
arc $= 180° - a$,	arc $= 270° + a$,
$\sin = \sin a$, $\cos = -\cos a$.	$\sin = -\cos a$, $\cos = \sin a$.
$\tan = -\tan a$, $\cot = -\cot a$.	$\tan = -\cot a$, $\cot = -\tan a$.
$\sec = -\sec a$, $\text{cosec} = \text{cosec}\, a$.	$\sec = \text{cosec}\, a$, $\text{cosec} = -\sec a$.
arc $= 180° + a$,	arc $= 360° - a$,
$\sin = -\sin a$, $\cos = -\cos a$.	$\sin = -\sin a$, $\cos = \cos a$.
$\tan = \tan a$, $\cot = \cot a$.	$\tan = -\tan a$, $\cot = -\cot a$.
$\sec = -\sec a$, $\text{cosec} = -\text{cosec}\, a$.	$\sec = \sec a$, $\text{cosec} = -\text{cosec}\, a$.

This table will be easily memorized, by observing that whenever the question relates to 180° or 360°, the function in the second column has the *same name* as that in the first column; and that whenever the question relates to 90° or 270°, the function in the second column has a *contrary name.* Thus,

$$\tan (180° + a) = \tan a, \qquad \cos (90° + a) = - \sin a.$$

The student will readily prefix the proper algebraic sign to the function in the second column, by recollecting the quadrant in which the first arc ends. Thus,

$$\sin (180° + a) = - \sin a,$$

the arc $180° + a$ being in the third quadrant, its sine must be negative.

By this table the functions of any arc from 90° to 360° can be found in terms of the functions of an arc less than 90°. For instance, the arc 115° gives

$$\sin 115° = \sin (90° + 25°) = \cos 25°.$$

Likewise, the arc 195° gives

$$\tan 195° = \tan (180° + 15°) = \tan 15°;$$

or

$$\tan 195^\circ = \tan (270^\circ - 75^\circ) = \cot 75^\circ.$$

Also,

$$\cot 300^\circ = - \tan 30^\circ.$$

26. If 360° be added any number of times to an arc, the resulting arc will have the same origin and end as the primitive arc. Its different functions will then be the same as those of the primitive arc; thus,

$$\sin (a + n\, 360^\circ) = \sin a, \text{ \&c.}$$

Hence, the functions of any arc greater than 360° may be determined in terms of those of an arc less than 90°, by subtracting 360° from the arc as many times as possible, and then finding the functions of the remainder by Table III. Thus,

$$\sin 950^\circ = \sin (950^\circ - 720^\circ) = \sin 230^\circ = - \sin 50^\circ.$$

27. If AM be any arc denoted by a, then AM''' will be equal to $-a$ (Art. 15), and $M'''P = -MP$, that is,

$$\sin (-a) = -\sin a.$$

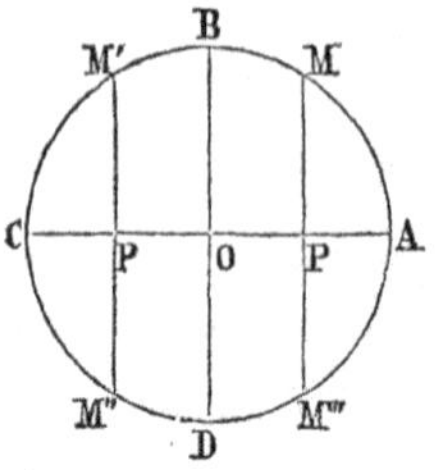

And since OP is the cosine of both arcs, we have

$$\cos (-a) = \cos a.$$

These values being substituted in the formulas for the versine, tangent, &c., give

$$\text{ver-sin} (-a) = \text{ver-sin}\, a, \qquad \text{co-versin} (-a) = 1 + \sin a.$$

$$\tan (-a) = -\tan a, \qquad \cot (-a) = -\cot a.$$

$$\sec (-a) = \sec a, \qquad \text{co-sec} (-a) = -\text{co-sec}\, a.$$

28. We see from the preceding discussion that the functions of all arcs, whether positive or negative, can be readily determined in terms of the functions of positive arcs *less than* 90°. Hence, the various trigonometrical tables contain only positive arcs, and no arcs greater than 90°.

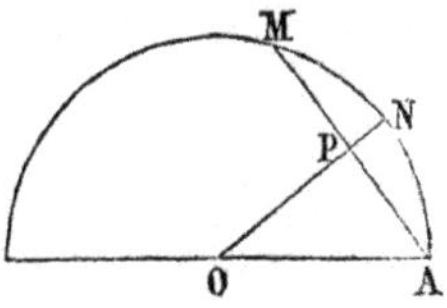

29. If AM be any arc, denoted by $2a$, and OP be drawn perpendicular to its chord MA, it will bisect both arc and chord, and we shall have $MN = a$ and

$$MP = \sin a = \tfrac{1}{2}\, MA\,;$$

that is: *The sine of an arc is equal to one-half the chord of twice the arc.*

If $AM = 60°$, $MN = 30°$, and since we know from Geometry that the chord of $60°$ is the side of the regular inscribed hexagon and equal to the radius $= 1$, we have

$$\sin 30° = \tfrac{1}{2}\,;$$

or: *The sine of* $30°$ *is equal to one-half the radius.*

Also,

$$\sin 30° = \sin (90° - 60°) = \cos 60°\,;$$

hence,

$$\cos 60° = \tfrac{1}{2}.$$

If $AM = 90°$, $MN = 45°$. But the chord AM is then the side of the inscribed square $= \sqrt{2}$; hence,

$$\sin 45° = \tfrac{1}{2}\sqrt{2} = \sqrt{\tfrac{1}{2}}.$$

Also,

$$\sin 45° = \sin (90° - 45°) = \cos 45°\,;$$

hence,

$$\cos 45° = \tfrac{1}{2}\sqrt{2} = \sqrt{\tfrac{1}{2}}.$$

These values being substituted in the formulas 6, 7, 11, 12, Table I, give

$$\tan 45° = 1, \qquad \cot 45° = 1\,;$$

that is: *The tangent and co-tangent of* $45°$ *are each equal to the radius* $= 1$.

$$\sec 45° = \sqrt{2}, \qquad \text{co-sec } 45° = \sqrt{2}.$$

Relations between the Sides, and the Circular Functions of the Angles, of Right-angled Plane Triangles.

30. Let AHB be any right-angled triangle, the right angle being at H, and represent the angles respectively by the letters A, B and H, and the opposite sides by a, b and h. Lay off $AM = 1 =$ the radius, describe the arc MC, and draw MP perpendicular to AH; then

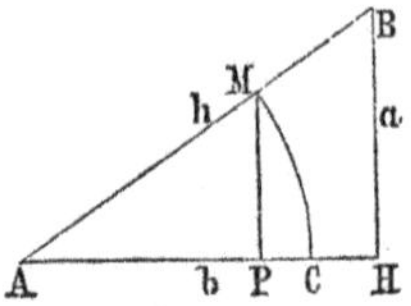

$$MP = \sin A, \qquad AP = \cos A,$$

and from the similar triangles APM and AHB, we have

$$AM : MP :: AB : BH,$$

$$AM : AP :: AB : AH;$$

or,

$$1 : \sin A :: h : a,$$

$$1 : \cos A :: h : b,$$

from which we obtain

$$\sin A = \frac{a}{h} \quad . \quad . \quad . \quad (1), \qquad \cos A = \frac{b}{h} \quad . \quad . \quad . \quad (2)\cdot$$

that is: *The sine of either acute angle* of a right-angled triangle is equal to *the ratio of the hypothenuse to the opposite side.*

Also: *The cosine of either acute angle* is equal to *the ratio of the hypothenuse to the adjacent side.*

From equations (1) and (2), we also have

$$a = h \sin A \quad . \quad . \quad . \quad (3), \qquad b = h \cos A \quad . \quad . \quad . \quad (4);$$

that is: *Either side* of a right-angled triangle is equal to *the hypo thenuse multiplied by the sine of the opposite angle.*

Also: *Either side* is equal to *the hypothenuse multiplied by the cosine of the adjacent angle.*

31. From equations (1) and (2) of the preceding article, by dividing (1) by (2), and then (2) by (1), we obtain

$$\frac{\sin A}{\cos A} = \frac{a}{b}, \qquad \frac{\cos A}{\sin A} = \frac{b}{a},$$

or,

$$\tan A = \frac{a}{b} \quad . \quad . \quad . \quad (5), \qquad \cot A = \frac{b}{a} \quad . \quad . \quad . \quad (6);$$

that is: *The tangent of either acute angle* of a right-angled triangle is equal to *the ratio of the adjacent to the opposite side.*

Also: *The co-tangent of either acute angle* is equal to *the ratio of the opposite to the adjacent side.*

From equations (5) and (6), we have

$$a = b \tan A \quad . \quad . \quad . \quad (7), \qquad b = a \cot A \quad . \quad . \quad . \quad (8);$$

that is: If a be the perpendicular, and b the base of a right-angled triangle, *the perpendicular* is equal *to the base multiplied by the tangent of the angle at the base;* and *the base* is equal *to the perpendicular multiplied by the co-tangent of the angle at the base.*

32. The ratios (1), (2), (5) and (6), of the two preceding articles are important, as all the other relations are deduced at once from them. In fact, these ratios are given, by many writers, as the definitions of the circular functions to which they are respectively equal. All of these formulas should be carefully remembered. To aid in this we arrange them in the following

TABLE IV.

1.	$\sin A = \frac{a}{h}$.	2.	$\cos A = \frac{b}{h}$.
3.	$a = h \sin A$.	4.	$b = h \cos A$.
5.	$\tan A = \frac{a}{b}$.	6.	$\cot A = \frac{b}{a}$.
7.	$a = b \tan A$.	8.	$b = a \cot A$.

Formulas expressing relations between the circular functions of different arcs.

33. Let MCB and BCA be any two angles measured by the arcs MB and BA, represented by a and b, CM being equal to the radius $= 1$. From M draw MP, and MN perpendicular to CA and CB respectively, and through N draw NP' perpendicular, and NL parallel to CA; then

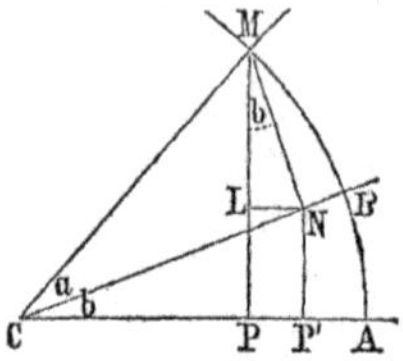

$$MN = \sin a, \qquad CN = \cos a, \qquad MP = \sin (a + b),$$

$$MP = ML + NP' \quad . \quad . \quad . \quad (1).$$

The right-angled triangle $NP'C$ gives, (Art. 30),

$$NP' = CN \sin b = \cos a \sin b;$$

and since the triangle MLN is similar to $NP'C$, the angle $LMN = NCP' = b$, and we have

$$ML = MN \cos b = \sin a \cos b.$$

These values of MP, NP' and ML, being substituted in equation (1), give

$$\sin (a + b) = \sin a \cos b + \cos a \sin b \quad . \quad . \quad . \quad (a);$$

that is: *The sine of the sum of two angles or arcs is equal to the sine of the first into the cosine of the second, plus the cosine of the first into the sine of the second.*

Since the above formula is true for any values of a and b, we may substitute $- b$ for b, and obtain

$$\sin (a - b) = \sin a \cos (- b) + \cos a \sin (- b);$$

but, (Art. 27),

$$\cos (- b) = \cos b \qquad \text{and} \qquad \sin (- b) = - \sin b;$$

hence,

$$\sin (a - b) = \sin a \cos b - \cos a \sin b \quad . \quad . \quad . \quad (b).$$

If in the last formula we substitute $(90° - a)$ for a, we have

$$\sin (90° - a - b) = \sin (90° - a) \cos b - \cos (90° - a) \sin b \ . \ (2);$$

but, (Art. 8),

$$\sin(90^\circ - a - b) = \sin[90^\circ - (a + b)] = \cos(a + b),$$

and

$$\sin(90^\circ - a) = \cos a, \qquad \cos(90^\circ - a) = \sin a;$$

hence, by substitution in equation (2), we have

$$\cos(a + b) = \cos a \cos b - \sin a \sin b \quad . \; . \; . \quad (c).$$

If in this we substitute $-b$ for b, we have

$$\cos(a - b) = \cos a \cos(-b) - \sin a \sin(-b),$$

or,

$$\cos(a - b) = \cos a \cos b + \sin a \sin b \quad . \; . \; . \quad (d).$$

34. If in formula (a) we make $a = b$, we have

$$\sin 2a = 2 \sin a \cos a \quad . \; . \; . \quad (1),$$

a formula giving the value of the sine of *twice an arc* in terms of the sine and cosine of *the arc* itself.

If in formula (c), $a = b$, we have

$$\cos 2a = \cos^2 a - \sin^2 a \quad . \; . \; . \quad (2);$$

or, by substituting first the value of $\cos^2 a$, and then of $\sin^2 a$, as given by formulas (3) and (2) of Table I, we have

$$\cos 2a = 1 - 2 \sin^2 a \quad . \; . \; . \quad (3),$$

$$\cos 2a = 2 \cos^2 a - 1 \quad . \; . \; . \quad (4);$$

whence,

$$\sin a = \sqrt{\frac{1 - \cos 2a}{2}} \;\; . \; . \; (5); \qquad \cos a = \sqrt{\frac{1 + \cos 2a}{2}} \;\; . \; . \; . \; (6).$$

35. If formula (a) be divided, member by member, by (c), we have

$$\frac{\sin(a + b)}{\cos(a + b)} = \frac{\sin a \cos b + \cos a \sin b}{\cos a \cos b - \sin a \sin b},$$

or, dividing both terms of the second member by $\cos a \cos b$, since the first member is equal to the $\tan(a+b)$,

$$\tan(a+b) = \frac{\dfrac{\sin a}{\cos a} + \dfrac{\sin b}{\cos b}}{1 - \dfrac{\sin a}{\cos a}\dfrac{\sin b}{\cos b}};$$

or,

$$\tan(a+b) = \frac{\tan a + \tan b}{1 - \tan a \tan b} \quad . \quad . \quad . \quad (e).$$

If in this, we substitute $-b$ for b, and recollect that $\tan(-b) = -\tan b$, (Art. 27), we have

$$\tan(a-b) = \frac{\tan a - \tan b}{1 + \tan a \tan b} \quad . \quad . \quad . \quad (f).$$

In a similar way, by dividing formula (c) by (a) we obtain

$$\cot(a+b) = \frac{\cot a \cot b - 1}{\cot a + \cot b} \quad . \quad . \quad . \quad (g);$$

and thence, by the substitution of $-b$ for b,

$$\cot(a-b) = \frac{\cot a \cot b + 1}{\cot b - \cot a} \quad . \quad . \quad . \quad (h).$$

36. If in formula (e), $b = a$, it reduces to

$$\tan 2a = \frac{2 \tan a}{1 - \tan^2 a} \quad . \quad . \quad . \quad (1).$$

If $b = 2a$, the same formula reduces to

$$\tan 3a = \frac{\tan a + \tan 2a}{1 - \tan a \tan 2a};$$

or, substituting for $\tan 2a$, its value in (1) and reducing,

$$\tan 3a = \frac{3 \tan a - \tan^3 a}{1 - 3 \tan^2 a} \quad . \quad . \quad . \quad (2).$$

If in formula (g), $b = a$, we obtain by reduction

$$\cot 2a = \tfrac{1}{2} \cot a - \tfrac{1}{2} \tan a \quad . \quad . \quad . \quad (3).$$

By a similar process, we may obtain the tangent and cotanger a, taken any number of times.

37. From formula (8), Table I, we have

$$\tan a \cot a = 1, \qquad \tan b \cot b = 1;$$

whence

$$\tan a \cot a = \tan b \cot b \quad . \; . \; . \quad (1),$$

which gives the proportion

$$\tan a \; : \; \tan b \; :: \; \cot b \; : \; \cot a,$$

or: *The tangents of two arcs are reciprocally proportional to thei cotangents.*

38. If formulas (a) and (b) be first added, member to member and then subtracted, and the same operations be performed upon (c) and (d), we shall obtain,

$$\sin(a+b) + \sin(a-b) = 2 \sin a \cos b;$$

$$\sin(a+b) - \sin(a-b) = 2 \cos a \sin b;$$

$$\cos(a+b) + \cos(a-b) = 2 \cos a \cos b;$$

$$\cos(a-b) - \cos(a+b) = 2 \sin a \sin b.$$

If in these we make

$$a + b = p, \quad \text{and} \quad a - b = q,$$

whence

$$a = \tfrac{1}{2}(p+q), \qquad b = \tfrac{1}{2}(p-q),$$

and then substitute in the above formulas, we obtain

$$\sin p + \sin q = 2 \sin \tfrac{1}{2}(p+q) \cos \tfrac{1}{2}(p-q) \quad . \; . \; . \quad (k);$$

$$\sin p - \sin q = 2 \cos \tfrac{1}{2}(p+q) \sin \tfrac{1}{2}(p-q) \quad . \; . \; . \quad (l);$$

$$\cos p + \cos q = 2 \cos \tfrac{1}{2}(p+q) \cos \tfrac{1}{2}(p-q) \quad . \; . \; . \quad (m);$$

$$\cos q - \cos p = 2 \sin \tfrac{1}{2}(p+q) \sin \tfrac{1}{2}(p-q) \quad . \; . \; . \quad (n).$$

39. If in the above formulas, we make $q = 0$, we have

$$\sin p = 2 \sin \tfrac{1}{2} p \cos \tfrac{1}{2} p \quad . \; . \; . \quad (1);$$

$$1 + \cos p = 2 \cos^2 \tfrac{1}{2} p \quad . \quad . \quad . \quad . \quad . \quad (2);$$

$$1 - \cos p = 2 \sin^2 \tfrac{1}{2} p \quad . \quad . \quad . \quad . \quad . \quad (3).$$

From (3) and (2), respectively, we deduce

$$\sin \tfrac{1}{2} p = \sqrt{\frac{1 - \cos p}{2}}; \qquad \cos \tfrac{1}{2} p = \sqrt{\frac{1 + \cos p}{2}}.$$

Dividing (1) by (2), and then by (3), member by member, we have

$$\frac{\sin p}{1 + \cos p} = \tan \tfrac{1}{2} p \quad . \quad . \quad (4); \qquad \frac{\sin p}{1 - \cos p} = \cot \tfrac{1}{2} p \quad . \quad . \quad (5).$$

Taking the reciprocals of (4) and (5), we also have

$$\frac{1 + \cos p}{\sin p} = \cot \tfrac{1}{2} p \quad . \quad . \quad (6); \qquad \frac{1 - \cos p}{\sin p} = \tan \tfrac{1}{2} p \quad . \quad . \quad (7).$$

40. From formulas (k) and (l), by division, we obtain

$$\frac{\sin p + \sin q}{\sin p - \sin q} = \frac{\sin \frac{1}{2}(p+q) \cos \frac{1}{2}(p-q)}{\cos \frac{1}{2}(p+q) \sin \frac{1}{2}(p-q)} = \frac{\tan \frac{1}{2}(p+q)}{\tan \frac{1}{2}(p-q)} \quad (1);$$

which gives the proportion: *The sum of the sines of two arcs is to their difference, as the tangent of one half the sum of the arcs is to the tangent of one half their difference.*

Also, in like manner, we obtain

$$\frac{\sin p + \sin q}{\cos p + \cos q} = \frac{\sin \frac{1}{2}(p+q) \cos \frac{1}{2}(p-q)}{\cos \frac{1}{2}(p+q) \cos \frac{1}{2}(p-q)} = \tan \tfrac{1}{2}(p+q) \quad (2);$$

$$\frac{\sin p - \sin q}{\cos p + \cos q} = \frac{\sin \frac{1}{2}(p-q) \cos \frac{1}{2}(p+q)}{\cos \frac{1}{2}(p+q) \cos \frac{1}{2}(p-q)} = \tan \tfrac{1}{2}(p-q) \quad (3);$$

$$\frac{\sin p + \sin q}{\sin (p+q)} = \frac{\sin \frac{1}{2}(p+q) \cos \frac{1}{2}(p-q)}{\sin \frac{1}{2}(p+q) \cos \frac{1}{2}(p+q)} = \frac{\cos \frac{1}{2}(p-q)}{\cos \frac{1}{2}(p+q)} \quad (4);$$

$$\frac{\sin p - \sin q}{\sin (p+q)} = \frac{\sin \frac{1}{2}(p-q) \cos \frac{1}{2}(p+q)}{\sin \frac{1}{2}(p+q) \cos \frac{1}{2}(p+q)} = \frac{\sin \frac{1}{2}(p-q)}{\sin \frac{1}{2}(p+q)} \quad (5);$$

$$\frac{\sin (p-q)}{\sin p - \sin q} = \frac{\sin \frac{1}{2}(p-q) \cos \frac{1}{2}(p-q)}{\sin \frac{1}{2}(p-q) \cos \frac{1}{2}(p+q)} = \frac{\cos \frac{1}{2}(p-q)}{\cos \frac{1}{2}(p+q)} \quad (6);$$

all of which give proportions similar to that deduced from formula (1).

Since the second members of (4) and (6) are the same, we have

$$\frac{\sin (p - q)}{\sin p - \sin q} = \frac{\sin p + \sin q}{\sin (p + q)} \quad . \quad . \quad . \quad (7),$$

or

The sine of the difference of two arcs is to the difference of the sines, as the sum of the sines to the sine of the sum.

Introduction of the Radius into Trigonometrical Formulas.

41. In all the formulas of the preceding articles, the radius of the measuring arc having been denoted by the number 1, does not appear in any of their terms. In some cases, particularly in the application of logarithms to the formulas, it is more convenient to denote this radius by a number different from 1. In such cases, it must appear in the formulas. It can readily be introduced by the aid of the principle, that if any circular function be taken in circles with different radii, such functions will be proportional to these radii. Thus,

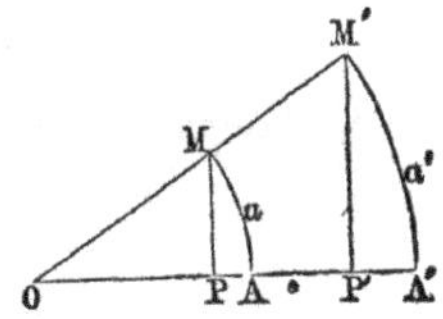

$$MP \ : \ M'P' \ :: \ OM \ : \ OM'.$$

If now

$$OM = 1, \qquad AM = a, \qquad A'M' = a', \qquad OM' = R;$$

then

$$MP = \sin a, \qquad M'P' = \sin a',$$

and we have

$$\sin a \ : \ \sin a' \ :: \ 1 \ : \ R;$$

whence,

$$\sin a = \frac{\sin a'}{R};$$

and in the same way, we shall find any other circular function when the radius is 1, *equal to the corresponding function when the radius is R, divided by R.*

We have then simply to substitute in the preceding formulas for each function its value as above expressed, and the resulting formulas will then express the relations between the functions of the new arc and its radius. Or, since the effect of this substitution is simply to render the formulas homogenous, that is, cause the members and terms to contain the same number of linear dimensions, we may, at once, *either multiply or divide each term by such a power of* R *as will make all the terms of the same degree.* Thus, if we take the formula

$$\tan a = \frac{\sin a}{\cos a},$$

by substitution we obtain

$$\frac{\tan a'}{R} = \frac{\frac{\sin a'}{R}}{\frac{\cos a'}{R}} = \frac{\sin a'}{\cos a'}, \qquad \text{or} \qquad \tan a' = \frac{R \sin a'}{\cos a'} \quad . \quad . \quad (1).$$

Or, if we observe that $\tan a$ is of the first degree, and $\frac{\sin a}{\cos a}$ being the quotient of two expressions of the first degree, is an abstract number, or of the 0 degree, we make the formula homogenous by multiplying the second member by R and obtain the result

$$\tan a = \frac{R \sin a}{\cos a},$$

in which a becomes a' in (1); that is, the arc described with the new radius R. In the formula

$$\tan 2a = \frac{2 \tan a}{1 - \tan^2 a}$$

if the numerator, and first term of the denominator of the second member, be each multiplied by R^2, the numerator will be of the third, and the denominator of the second degree, giving a quotient of the first degree, thus rendering the formula homogenous,

$$\tan 2a = \frac{2 R^2 \tan a}{R^2 - \tan^2 a}.$$

If we divide the second member of formula (l) by R, we have

$$\sin p - \sin q = \frac{2}{R} \sin \tfrac{1}{2}(p - q) \cos \tfrac{1}{2}(p + q),$$

which is homogenous, and in which p and q will represent arcs described with the radius R.

Table of Natural Sines and Cosines.

42. For convenience, in making the various trigonometrical calculations, when the radius is 1, a table is formed, containing the numerical values of the sines and cosines of all the arcs of a quadrant, differing from each other by one minute, the arcs and their functions being so arranged, that if either be given, the others can, at once, be taken from the table.

This table is called a table of *Natural Sines and Cosines*, and is thus constructed.

Since the length of the semi-circumference of a circle whose radius is 1, is equal to the number 3.14159265 . . . , if we divide this number by 10800, the number of minutes in 180°, the quotient will be the length of the arc *one minute* = .0002908882 . . . , and since this arc is so small that it does not differ materially from its sine or tangent, this may be placed in the table as *the sine of one minute.*

Formula (3) of Table I gives

$$\cos 1' = \sqrt{1 - \sin^2 1'} \doteq .9999999577 \quad . \quad . \quad . \quad (1).$$

Having thus determined to a near degree of approximation, the sine and cosine of one minute, we take the first formula of Art. 38 and put it under the form,

$$\sin (a + b) = 2 \sin a \cos b - \sin (a - b),$$

and make in this $b = 1'$, and then in succession,

$$a = 1', \qquad a = 2', \qquad a = 3', \qquad a = 4', \qquad \&c.,$$

and obtain

$$\sin 2' = 2 \sin 1' \cos 1' - \sin 0 = .0005817764 \ldots,$$
$$\sin 3' = 2 \sin 2' \cos 1' - \sin 1' = .0008726646 \ldots$$
$$\sin 4' = 2 \sin 3' \cos 1' - \sin 2' = .0011635526 \ldots$$
$$\sin 5' = \qquad \&c.,$$

thus obtaining the sine of every number of degrees and minutes from 1′ to 45°.

The cosines of the corresponding arcs are then calculated as in equation (1).

Having now the sines and cosines of arcs less than 45°, those of the arcs between 45° and 90°, may be deduced, by considering that the sine of an arc is equal to the cosine of its complement, and the cosine equal to the sine of the complement. Thus,

$$\sin 50^\circ = \sin (90^\circ - 40^\circ) = \cos 40^\circ, \quad \cos 50^\circ = \sin 40^\circ,$$

in which the second members are known from the previous calcula tions.

Columns may be arranged in the tables containing the tangents and cotangents of the different arcs, which are readily found by dividing the sine by the cosine, for the first; and the cosine by the sine, for the second.

The natural secant and co-secant are also found by formulas (11) and (12), Table I.

As the accuracy of the calculation of the sine of any arc, by the above method, depends upon the accuracy of each previous calculation, it would be well to verify the work, by calculating the sines of the degrees separately, (after having found the sines of one and two degrees), by the last proportion of (Art. 40). Thus

$$\sin 1^\circ : \sin 2^\circ - \sin 1^\circ :: \sin 2^\circ + \sin 1^\circ : \sin 3^\circ;$$

$$\sin 2^\circ : \sin 3^\circ - \sin 1^\circ :: \sin 3^\circ + \sin 1^\circ : \sin 4^\circ; \text{ \&c.}$$

Table of Logarithmic Sines, Cosines, &c.

43. As the various calculations in Trigonometry are much facilitated by the application of logarithms, the table of natural sines, &c., is little used. If the logarithms of the numerical values of the sines, &c., as given in the table of natural sines, &c., with the corresponding arcs, were properly arranged in a table, this would constitute a table of logarithmic sines, cosines, tangents, &c. But as a great part of the circular functions, in that table, are less than 1, their common logarithms would be negative, (Davies' Bourdon, Art. 235), which would be inconvenient. The numerical values of these functions are therefore multiplied by the number 10 000,000,000, and the numerical values of the same functions, calculated to a radius of *ten billions*, Art. (41), thus obtained: The common logarithms of these numbers are then properly arranged in a table with

the corresponding arcs, thus constituting the table of logarithmic sines, &c , in common use.

The tables here used for computations are calculated to six decimal places. When a greater degree of accuracy is desired, the tables of Bagay or Callet may well be used.

To explain the use of the tables we take

CASE I.

To find, in the table, the logarithmic sine, cosine, tangent, or cotangent of any given arc or angle.

If the angle is less than 45°, and contains simply degrees and minutes, look for the degrees in the first horizontal line of the different pages: when the degrees are found, descend along the column of minutes, on the left of the page, till you reach the number showing the minutes: then pass along a horizontal line till you come into the column designated, at the top, sine, cosine, tangent, or cotangent, as the case may be: the number so indicated is the logarithm sought. Thus, on page 37, for 19° 55′, we find,

log	sin 19° 55′	. . . .	9.532312
"	cos 19° 55′	. . . .	9.973215
"	tan 19° 55′	. . . .	9.559097
"	cot 19° 55′	. . . .	10.440903

If the angle is greater than 45°, search for the degrees along the bottom line of the different pages: when the number is found, ascend along the column of minutes on the right hand side of the page, till you reach the number expressing the minutes: then pass along a horizontal line into the column designated, at the bottom, tang, cot, sine, or cosine, as the case may be: the number so pointed out is the logarithm required.

The column designated sine, at the top of the page, is designated by cosine at the bottom; the one designated tang, by cotang, and the one designated cotang, by tang.

The angle found by taking the degrees at the top of the page, and the minutes from the left hand vertical column, is the complement of the angle found by taking the degrees at the bottom of the page, and the minutes from the right hand column on the same horizontal line with the first. Therefore, sine, at the top of the page, should correspond with cosine, at the bottom; cosine with sine, tang with cotang, and cotang with tang, as in the tables, Arts. (8 and 10).

If the angle is greater than 90°, we have only to subtract it from 180°, and take the sine, cosine, tangent, or cotangent of the remainder.

In order to obtain the logarithm of any function of an arc, containing a number of seconds, from the tables where the logarithms for the degrees and minutes only are given, there is arranged next to each column of logarithms a second column marked *difference.*

This column is thus calculated. The difference between the logarithms of each arc and the one exceeding it by 1′, is taken. This is divided by 60, and the quotient is, very nearly, the increase or decrease for one second, and this number is placed in the new column opposite the lesser arc. The increase or decrease of the logarithm for any number of seconds will then be obtained by multiplying this tabular difference by the number of seconds.

It should be remarked, that the same column of differences, answers for the logarithmic tangent and cotangent, the reason for which will be seen by applying logarithms to formula (1), (Art. 37). Thus

$$\log.\tan a + \log.\cot a = \log.\tan b + \log.\cot b.$$

$$\log.\tan a - \log.\tan b = \log.\cot b - \log.\cot a,$$

which shows: *That the difference between the logarithms of the tangents of any two consecutive arcs is equal to the difference of the logarithms of the cotangents of the same arcs.*

Now, if it were required to find the logarithmic sine of an arc expressed in degrees, minutes, and seconds, we have only to find it for the degrees and minutes as before; then, multiply the corresponding tabular difference by the seconds, and add the product to the number first found, for the sine of the given arc.

Thus, if we wish the sine of 40° 26′ 28″.

The sine 40° 26′		9.811952
Tabular difference	2.47	
Number of seconds	28	
Product,	69.16 to be added	69.16
Gives for the sine of 40° 26′ 28″.		9.812021.

The decimal figures at the right are generally omitted in the last result; but when they exceed five-tenths, the figure on the left of the decimal point is increased by 1; the logarithm obtained is then exact, to within less than one unit of its right hand place.

The tangent of an arc, in which there are seconds, is found in a manner entirely similar. In regard to the cosine and cotangent, it must be remembered, that they increase while the arcs decrease, and decrease as the arcs are increased; consequently, the proportional numbers found for the seconds, must be subtracted, not added.

EXAMPLES.

1. To find the cosine of 3° 40′ 40″.

The cosine of 3° 40′	9.999110
Tabular difference .13	
Number of seconds 40	
Product, 5.20 to be subtracted	5.20
Gives for the cosine of 3° 40′ 40″	9.999105.

2. Find the tangent of 37° 28′ 31″.

Ans. 9.884592.

3. Find the cotangent of 87° 57′ 59″.

Ans. 8.550356.

CASE II.

To find the degrees, minutes, and seconds answering to any given logarithmic sine, cosine, tangent, or cotangent.

Search in the table, in the proper column, and if the number is found, the degrees will be shown either at the top or bottom of the page, and the minutes in the side column either at the left or right.

But, if the number cannot be found in the table, take from the table the degrees and minutes answering to the nearest less logarithm, the logarithm itself, and also the corresponding tabular difference. Subtract the logarithm taken from the table from the given logarithm, annex two ciphers to the remainder, and then divide the remainder by the tabular difference: the quotient will be seconds, and is to be connected with the degrees and minutes before found: to be added for the sine and tangent, and subtracted for the cosine and cotangent.

EXAMPLES.

1. Find the arc answering to the sine	9.880054
Sine 49° 20′, next less in the table	9.879963
Tabular difference,	1.81)91.00(50″.

Hence, the arc 49° 20′ 50″ corresponds to the given sine 9.880054.

2. Find the arc whose cotangent is	10.008688
cot 44° 26′, next less in the table	10.008591
Tabular difference,	4.21)97.00(23″.

Hence, 44° 26′ — 23″ = 44° 25′ 37″ is the arc answering to the given cotangent 10.008688.

3. Find the arc answering to tangent 9.979110.

Ans. 43° 37′ 21″.

4. Find the arc answering to cosine 9.944599.

Ans. 28° 19′ 45 ′.

ANALYTICAL PLANE TRIGONOMETRY.

44. In every plane, or rectilineal triangle, three parts, one of which must be a side, must be given, to enable us to compute the others. Three angles alone would not suffice, inasmuch as all similar triangles have the three angles of the one equal to the three angles of the other, while their sides are unequal.

We will now deduce certain relations existing between the sides and functions of the angles of a triangle, which will enable us to compute the others, when either of the three parts, with the above limitation, are given.

Relations between the sides and functions of the angles of oblique angled plane triangles.

45. Let ABC be any oblique angled plane triangle, in which the angles are denoted, respectively, by the letters A, B, C, and the sides opposite these angles by a, b, and c.

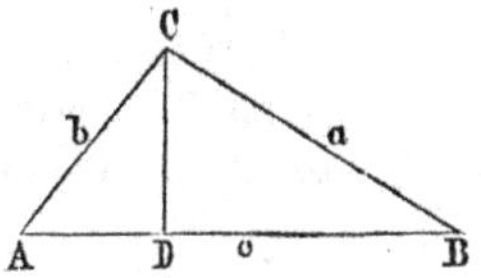

From the vertex C, let fall the perpendicular CD. We then have from the right angled triangles CDB and CDA, Art. (30).

$$CD = a \sin B, \qquad CD = b \sin A;$$

whence,

$$a \sin B = b \sin A,$$

which gives the proportion

$$a \ : \ b \ :: \ \sin A \ : \ \sin B;$$

that is: *In any plane triangle the sides are proportional to the sines of their opposite angles.*

46. If we take the proportion of the preceding article, first by composition, and then by division, we obtain,

$$a + b \ : \ a \ :: \ \sin A + \sin B \ : \ \sin A,$$

$$a - b \ : \ a \ :: \ \sin A - \sin B \ : \ \sin A.$$

Since the consequents of these proportions are the same, we have

$$a + b \ : \ a - b \ :: \ \sin A + \sin B \ : \ \sin A - \sin B;$$

but Art. (40), equation (1),

$$\sin A + \sin B : \sin A - \sin B :: \tan \tfrac{1}{2}(A + B) : \tan \tfrac{1}{2}(A - B);$$

hence,

$$a + b : a - b :: \tan \tfrac{1}{2}(A + B) : \tan \tfrac{1}{2}(A - B);$$

that is: *The sum of any two sides of a plane triangle is to their difference, as the tangent of one-half the sum of their opposite angles, is to the tangent of one-half their difference.*

47. Let ABC be any plane triangle, the angles and sides being denoted as in the preceding article.

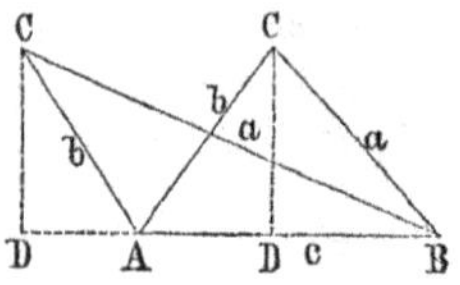

We know from Geometry (Davies' Legendre, Props. 12 and 13, Book IV), that

$$a^2 = b^2 + c^2 \mp 2c\,AD \quad . \ . \ (1);$$

the minus sign being used when the angle A is acute, and the plus sign when it is obtuse.

When the angle is acute, we have from the right-angled triangle ADC Art. (30),

$$AD = b \cos A;$$

and when it is obtuse

$$AD = b \cos CAD.$$

But as CAD is the supplement of A, we have Art. (25),

$$\cos CAD = -\cos A, \qquad \text{and} \qquad AD = -b \cos A.$$

These values of AD being substituted in (1), give in both cases

$$a^2 = b^2 + c^2 - 2bc \cos A;$$

whence,

$$\cos A = \frac{b^2 + c^2 - a^2}{2bc} \quad . \quad . \quad . \quad (2),$$

an important formula, but one to which logarithms cannot be conveniently applied.

If, then, we add to both members the number 1, reduce the second member, and recollect that $1 + \cos A$, in the first member, is equal to $2 \cos^2 \frac{1}{2} A$, equation (2), Art. (39), we have

$$2 \cos^2 \tfrac{1}{2} A = \frac{2bc + b^2 + c^2 - a^2}{2bc}$$

$$= \frac{(b + c)^2 - a^2}{2bc} = \frac{(b + c + a)\ (b + c - a)}{2bc},$$

or

$$\cos^2 \tfrac{1}{2} A = \frac{(b + c + a)\ (b + c - a)}{4bc} \quad . \quad . \quad . \quad (3).$$

If now we place

$$b + c + a = s,$$

we have

$$\frac{b + c + a}{2} = \tfrac{1}{2} s, \qquad \frac{b + c - a}{2} = \tfrac{1}{2} s - a.$$

Substituting these in (3), and extracting the square root, we have

$$\cos \tfrac{1}{2} A = \sqrt{\frac{\frac{1}{2} s\,(\frac{1}{2} s - a)}{bc}} \quad . \quad . \quad . \quad (4),$$

the plus sign only being used, since as A must be less than 180°, $\frac{1}{2} A$ must be less than 90°. From this we see that: *The cosine of half of either angle* of a plane triangle, is equal to *the square root of half the sum of the three sides, into half the sum minus the side opposite the angle, divided by the rectangle of the two adjacent sides.*

If we subtract both members of (2) from the number 1, and recollect that $1 - \cos A$ is equal to $2\sin^2 \frac{1}{2} A$, equation (3), Art. (39), we have

$$2\sin^2 \tfrac{1}{2} A = \frac{2bc - (b^2 + c^2 - a^2)}{2bc}$$

$$= \frac{a^2 - (b - c)^2}{2bc} = \frac{(a + b - c)\,(a - b + c)}{2bc} \quad . \; . \; (5).$$

Placing as before, $a + b + c = s$, we have

$$\frac{a + b - c}{2} = \tfrac{1}{2}s - c, \qquad \frac{a - b + c}{2} = \tfrac{1}{2}s - b.$$

Substituting these in (5), dividing by 2, and extracting the square root, we have

$$\sin \tfrac{1}{2} A = \sqrt{\frac{(\frac{1}{2}s - b)\,(\frac{1}{2}s - c)}{bc}} \quad . \; . \; . \; . \quad (6);$$

that is: *The sine of half of either angle*, of a plane triangle, is equal to *the square root of half the sum of the three sides minus one of the adjacent sides, into half the sum minus the other adjacent side, divided by the rectangle of the two adjacent sides.*

Solution of Right-angled Triangles.

48 Since the right angle of a right-angled triangle is always known; if one side and any other part be given, the triangle may be constructed, or the remaining parts may be accurately computed.

As logarithms are generally used in trigonometrical calculations, it will be necessary, before applying the various formulas previously determined, whenever they are not homogeneous, to introduce into them the radius of the logarithmic tables, the common logarithm of which is 10, Art. (41).

Before proceeding to the computation, the pupil should carefully construct the triangle on some convenient scale, by the rules given in Geometry, and with the instruments already explained.

In the solution of right-angled triangles, *four* different cases may arise. There may be given,

I. The hypothenuse and one acute angle.
II. A side about the right angle and one acute angle.
III. The two sides about the right angle.
IV. The hypothenuse and one other side.

I. *The hypothenuse and either acute angle being given.*

49. Suppose h and A are given. B may be found at once, by subtracting A from 90°.

To compute a, we take equation (3,) Art. (30), after having introduced R, to make it homogeneous, Art. (41).

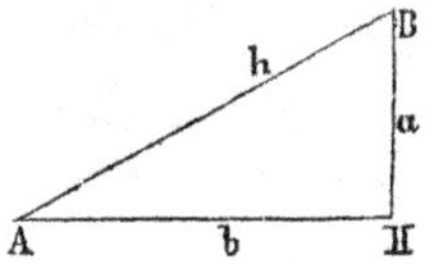

$$a = \frac{h \sin A}{R}$$

from which, by applying logarithms, we obtain

$$\log \sin A + \log h - 10 = \log a \quad . \quad . \quad . \quad . \quad (1),$$

since the arithmetical complement of log R is 0.

The side b may now be computed by either placing B for A and b for a, in the above formula; or by the use of the well known formula

$$b = \sqrt{h^2 - a^2} = \sqrt{(h+a)(h-a)}\ ;$$

whence by the application of logarithms

$$\tfrac{1}{2} \log (h + a) + \tfrac{1}{2} \log (h - a) = \log b \quad . \quad . \quad (2).$$

Example 1. Let $h = 325$ feet, $A = 27° 34'$.

Subtracting A from 90°, we have

$$90° - 27° 34' = 62° 26' = B.$$

Substituting in formula (1)

$$A = 27° 34', \qquad h = 325,$$

we have

+ log sin 27° 34′	. .	9.665375
+ log 325	. . . . . .	2.511883
— 10	. . . . . .	2.177258 = log a,

hence $a = 150.40$ feet.

Substituting in formula (1), B for A and b for a, and then

$$B = 62^\circ\ 26', \qquad h = 325,$$

we have

$+ \log \sin 62^\circ\ 26'$	. . .	9.947665
$+ \log\ 325$	. . . .	2.511883
$-\ 10$	. . . .	$2.459548 = \log b,$

hence $b = 288.10$ feet.

Or by using formula (2), we have

$+ \frac{1}{2} \log (325 + 150.40) = \frac{1}{2} \log 475.40$	. .	1.338529
$+ \frac{1}{2} \log (325 - 150.40) = \frac{1}{2} \log 174.60$	. .	1.121022
		$2.459551 = \log b,$

hence $b = 288.10$ feet, as above.

2. Let $h = 125.7$ yards, $B = 75^\circ\ 12'$.

Ans. $A = 14^\circ\ 48'$; $b = 121.53$*yds.*; $a = 32.11$*yds.*

II. *A side about the right angle and either acute angle being given*

50. Suppose a and A are given. B may be determined as in the last case.

To compute b we take equation (8), Art. (31), first introducing R,

$$b = \frac{a \cot A}{R},$$

whence by the application of logarithms

$$\log \cot A + \log a - 10 = \log b. \quad . \quad . \quad . \quad (1).$$

To obtain h we take equation 3, Art. (30), which after the introduction of R may be put under the form

$$h = \frac{R\ a}{\sin A};$$

whence by the application of logarithms

$$a.c. \log \sin A + \log R + \log a - 10 = \log h;$$

or since $\log R = 10$

$$a.c. \log \sin A + \log a = \log h \quad . \quad . \quad . \quad . \quad (2)$$

Example 1. Let $a = 56.293$ yards, $A = 54° 27' 39''$.

Subtracting A from 90°, we have

$$B = 35° 32' 21''.$$

Substituting in formula (1), the values of A and a, we have

+ log cot 54° 27′ 39″	. . . .	9.853896
+ log 56.293	. . . . .	1.750454
— 10	. . . . .	1.604350 = log *b*.

hence $b = 40.2114$ yards.

Substituting the values of A and a in formula (2), we have

+ *a*. *c*. log sin 54° 27′ 39″	. . . .	0.089527
+ log 56.293	. . . . . .	1.750454
		1.839981 = log *h*

hence $h = 69.18$.

2. Let $a = 125.694$ yards, $A = 81° 15' 07''$.

Ans. $B = 8° 44' 53''$, $b = 19.3418$*yds.* $h = 127.174$*yds.*

III. *The two sides about the right angle being given.*

50.* The two sides a and b being known.

To compute A we take formula (5), of Art. (31), first introducing R,

$$\tan A = \frac{Ra}{b}.$$

Applying logarithms, we have

$$a.c.\log b + \log a = \log \tan A \quad . \quad . \quad . \quad . \quad (1);$$

from which A may be found. Subtracting A from 90°, we shall have B. Or B may be found directly by the equation

$$\tan B = R\frac{b}{a},$$

and the accuracy of the calculation may be verified, by adding A and B together. Their sum should be 90°.

The value of h may be computed from the formula

$$h = \sqrt{a^2 + b^2},$$

or if a and b are large numbers, we may best use equation (1), Art. (30), after placing it under the form

$$h = R\,\frac{a}{\sin A},$$

whence

$$a.\ c.\ \log \sin A + \log a = \log h.$$

Example 1. Let $a = 26$ yards, $b = 15$ yards.

Ans. $A = 60^\circ\ 01'\ 06''$, $B = 29^\circ\ 58'\ 54''$ $h = 30.016$*yds.*

2. Let $a = 347.21$ yards, $b = 1052.29$ yards.

Ans. $A = 18^\circ\ 15'\ 38''$, $B = 71^\circ\ 44'\ 22''$, $h = 1108.09$*yds.*

IV. *The hypothenuse and one other side being given.*

51. Suppose h and a are given.

To compute A, we take equation (1), Art. (30),

$$\sin A = R\,\frac{a}{h};$$

from which we have

$$a.\ c.\ \log h + \log a = \log \sin A;$$

from which A being found and subtracted from 90°, we have the value of B.

To compute b, we use the formula

$$b = \sqrt{h^2 - a^2},$$

as in Case I, Art. (49), or for verification we may use the equation

$$b = \frac{a \cot A}{R},$$

as in Case II.

Example 1. Let $h = 2391.76yds.$ $a = 385.7yds.$

Ans. $A = 9° 16' 48''$, $B = 80° 43' 12''$, $b = 2360.5yds$

The student will have no difficulty in selecting the proper formula to be used, in any of the preceding cases, if he will simply remember that such formula, taken from Table IV, must contain the required and the two given parts only. Before applying logarithms to the formula, the value of the required part should be expressed directly, in terms of the two given parts and the radius.

Solution of Oblique Angled Triangles.

52. In the solution of oblique angled-triangles, four cases also arise, viz.: There may be given

I. *One side and either two angles.*
II. *Two sides and an angle opposite one of them.*
III. *Two sides and their included angle.*
IV. *The three sides.*

All of these cases may be solved by conceiving the triangle to be divided into two right-angled triangles, by a perpendicular drawn from the vertex of one of the angles to the opposite side, the vertex being so chosen that one of the right-angled triangles shall, if possible, contain two of the given parts. It is, however, much more convenient to solve them, directly, by the aid of the proportions and formulas previously deduced.

I. *One side and two angles being given.*

53. Suppose c, A and C are given. By subtracting the sum of the two given angles from 180°, we find the third angle B.

To compute a, we take the proportion, Art. (45),

$$\sin C : \sin A :: c : a;$$

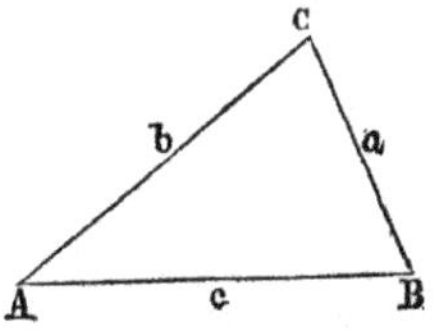

that is: *The sine of the angle opposite the given side is to the sine of the angle opposite the required side, as the given side is to the required side.*

Applying logarithms to the above proportion, using the arithmetical complement of the logarithm of the first term, and deducing the logarithm of the fourth term, we obtain

$$a.c. \log \sin C + \log \sin A + \log c - 10 = \log a \quad . \quad . \quad (1).$$

In the same way b may be found by the proportion,

$$\sin C \ : \ \sin B \ :: \ c \ : \ b,$$

or at once by placing B and b for A and a, respectively, in formula (1).

Example 1. Let $c = 250.4 yds$, $A = 15° \, 19' \, 51''$, $C = 72° \, 44' \, 05''$.

First, subtracting $A + C = 88° \, 03' \, 56''$, from $180°$, we have

$$B = 91° \, 56' \, 04''.$$

Substituting the above values in formula (1), we have

+	a.c. log sin 72° 44′ 05″	. . .	0.020024
+	log sin 15° 19′ 51″	. . .	9.422248
+	log 250.4	. . .	2.398634
−	10	. . .	1.840906 = log a;

hence, $a = 69.327 yds$.

Substituting $B = 91° \, 56' \, 04''$ for A, and b for a, in formula (1), with the above values for C and c, we have

+	a.c. log sin 72° 44′ 05″	. . .	0.020024
+	log sin 91° 56′ 04″	. . .	9.999752
+	log 250.4	. . .	2.398634
−	10	. . .	2.418410 = log b;

hence, $b = 262.066 yds$.

2. Let $c = 400 yds.$, $A = 38° \, 25'$, $B = 57° \, 42'$.

Ans. $C = 83° \, 53'$, $a = 249.974$, $b = 340.04$.

II. *Two sides and an angle opposite one of them being given.*

54. Suppose a, b and A are given,

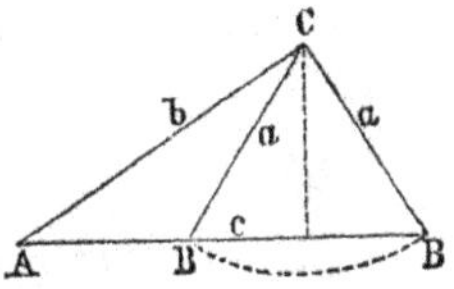

To compute B, we use the proportion,

$$a \ : \ b \ :: \ \sin A \ : \ \sin B;$$

that is: *The side opposite the given angle is to the other given side, as the sine of the given angle, is to the sine of the required angle.*

By the application of logarithms, we have

$$a.c.\log a + \log b + \log \sin A - 10 = \log \sin B \quad . \quad . \quad (1).$$

As the same sine belongs both to an angle and its supplement Art. (25), there will be two values of B which will satisfy equation (1). But it is shown, in Geometry, (Davies' Legendre, Prob. 11, Book III.) that both of these values can be used, only, when *the side opposite the given angle is less than the other given side*, in which case there will be two triangles answering to the given conditions, or *two solutions*, as indicated in the figure, one containing the obtuse angle ABC, and the other the acute angle $AB'C$.

If the side opposite the given angle is greater than the other given side, the acute angle only can be used, and *there will be but one solution*.

Should the side opposite the given angle be just equal to the perpendicular let fall from C on c, the triangle will be right-angled, and *the two solutions become one.*

Should this side be less than the perpendicular *there will be no solution*, and the triangle will be impossible.

The angle B being found, we find C by taking the sum of A and B from 180°, and then find c by the proportion

$$\sin A \ : \ \sin C \ :: \ a \ : \ c.$$

Example 1. Let $a = 367 yds.$ $b = 498 yds.$ $A = 37° \ 44'$

Substituting these values in formula (1), we have

$$\begin{array}{lll} + \ a.c.\log 367 & . \ . \ . \ . & 7.435334 \\ + \quad \log 498 & . \ . \ . \ . & 2.697229 \\ + \quad \log \sin 37° \ 44' & . \ . & 9.786742 \\ - \quad 10 & & \overline{9.919305} = \log \sin B, \end{array}$$

hence

$$B = 56° \ 08' \ 36'', \text{ or } 123° \ 51' \ 24''.$$

Since $a < b$ both of these values must be used, and there will be *two solutions.*

Taking the sum of A and the first value of B from 180°, we have

$$C = 86° \ 07' \ 24''.$$

Taking the sum of A and the second value of B from 180°, we have

$$C = 18° \ 24' \ 36''.$$

Now, computing the value of c as in case I., we find for the first value of C,

$$c = 598.31 \text{ yards.}$$

And for the second value of C,

$$c = 189.38 \text{ yards.}$$

2. Let $a = 27.465$ yards; $b = 13.189$ yards; $A = 18° \ 52' \ 13''$.

Ans. $B = 8° \ 56' \ 05''$, $c = 39.611$ yards; $C = 152° \ 11' \ 42''$.

III. *Two sides and their included angle being given.*

55. Suppose a and b and their included angle C, to be given.

To compute the angles A and B, we first subtract the given angle from 180°, which will give $A + B$. We then take the sum of the two given sides and their difference, and use the proportion, Art. (46).

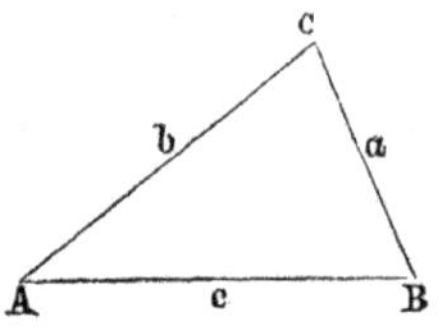

$$a + b \ : \ a - b \ :: \ \tan \tfrac{1}{2} (A + B) \ : \ \tan \tfrac{1}{2} (A - B).$$

By the application of logarithms we have

$$\begin{aligned} &a.c. \log (a + b) + \log (a - b) \\ &+ \log \tan \tfrac{1}{2} (A + B) - 10 = \log \tan \tfrac{1}{2} (A - B) \quad . \ . \quad (1); \end{aligned}$$

from which we find $\frac{1}{2} (A - B)$. Adding this to $\frac{1}{2} (A + B)$ we find the greater angle, A; subtracting it we find the smaller angle B.

The angles being now known, *to compute the remaining side,* we use the proportion, as in case I.,

$$\sin A \ : \ \sin C \ :: \ a \ : \ c.$$

Exam. 1. Let $a = 18.739 yds.$ $b = 7.642 yds.$ $C = 45° 18' 28''$.

$$180° - 45° 18' 28'' = 134° 41' 32'' = A + B.$$

$a + b = 26.381.$ $a - b = 11.097.$ $\frac{1}{2}(A + B) = 67° 20' 46''$.

Substituting these values in formula (1), we have

+	$a. c.$ log 26.381	8.578709
+	log 11.097	1.045207
+	log tan 67° 20′ 46″ .	10.379485
—	10	10.003401 = log tan $\frac{1}{2}(A - B)$;

hence

$$\frac{1}{2}(A - B) = 45° 13' 27'',$$

and

+ 67° 20′ 46″	+ 67° 20′ 46″
+ 45° 13′ 27″	− 45° 13′ 27″
112° 34′ 13″ = A,	22° 07′ 19″ = B.

The side c being computed, as in case I., is found to be

$$c = 14.426 \text{ yards}.$$

2. Let $a = 464.7 yds.$; $b = 289.3 yds.$; $C = 87° 03' 48''$.

Ans. $A = 60° 13' 38''$; $B = 32° 42' 34''$; $c = 534.66 yds.$

IV. *The three Sides being given.*

56. *To compute either angle as A*, we first add the three sides together and take one half their sum, and then use formula (4) of Art. (47), after multiplying the second member by R to render it homogeneous.

$$\cos \tfrac{1}{2} A = R \sqrt{\frac{\frac{1}{2} s (\frac{1}{2} s - a)}{bc}}.$$

Applying logarithms to this, we have

$$\log R + \tfrac{1}{2} (\log \tfrac{1}{2} s + \log (\tfrac{1}{2} s - a)$$
$$+ a.c. \log b + a.c. \log c) - 10 = \log \cos \tfrac{1}{2} A,$$

or since $\log R = 10$, this reduces to

$$\frac{\log \frac{1}{2} s + \log (\frac{1}{2} s - a) + a.c. \log b + a.c. \log c}{2} = \log \cos \tfrac{1}{2} A. \quad (1).$$

In the same way the angles B and C can be computed, and the accuracy of the computation will be tested by taking the sum of the three angles. It should be 180°.

Example 1. Let $a = 71.2 yds.$, $b = 64.8 yds.$, $c = 37.4 yds.$

then

$$\tfrac{1}{2}(a+b+c) = 86.7 = \tfrac{1}{2}s. \quad \tfrac{1}{2}s - a = 15.5.$$

Substituting these with the values of b and c in formula (1), we have

+	log 86.7	1.938019
+	log 15.5	1.190332
+	a.c. log 64.8	8.188425
+	a.c. log 37.4	8.427128
÷	2	19.743904
		9.871952 = log cos $\tfrac{1}{2}A$;

hence,

$$\tfrac{1}{2}A = 41^\circ\ 52'\ 16'' \quad \text{and} \quad A = 83^\circ\ 44'\ 32''.$$

To compute B we put in the above formula (1), b for a, a for b, and B for A, and have, since

$$\tfrac{1}{2}s = 86.7, \qquad \tfrac{1}{2}s - b = 21.9,$$

+	log 86.7	1.938019
+	log 21.9	1.340444
+	a.c. log 71.2	8.147520
+	a.c. log 37.4	8.427128
÷	2	19.853111
		9.926555 = log cos $\tfrac{1}{2}B$;

hence

$$\tfrac{1}{2}B = 32^\circ\ 23'\ 28'' \quad \text{and} \quad B = 64^\circ\ 46'\ 56''$$

In the same way C is found equal to 31° 28′ 30″.

2. Let $a = 425.6 yds.$, $b = 679 yds.$ $c = 1034 yds.$

Ans. $A = 16^\circ\ 6'\ 22''$, $B = 26^\circ\ 16'\ 5''$, $C = 137^\circ\ 37'\ 34''$.

In making all trigonometrical computations, it should be remarked, that each required part of a triangle should, in general, be computed directly from the given parts, as thus, any error which may be made in the computation of one part will not affect the value of any other required part.

Application to Heights and Distances.

57. A *Horizontal Plane* is one which is parallel to the water level.

A plane which is perpendicular to a horizontal plane, is called a *vertical plane.*

All lines parallel to the water level, are called *horizontal lines.*

All lines which are perpendicular to a horizontal plane, are called *vertical lines;* and all lines which are inclined to it, are called *oblique lines.*

A *Horizontal Angle* is one whose sides are horizontal.

A *Vertical Angle* is one, the plane of whose sides is vertical.

An angle of *elevation*, is a vertical angle having one of its sides horizontal, and the inclined side above the horizontal side.

An angle of *depression*, is a vertical angle having one of its sides horizontal, and the inclined side under the horizontal side.

I. *To determine the horizontal distance to a point which is inaccessible by reason of an intervening river.*

58. Let C be the point. Measure along the bank of the river a horizontal base line AB, and select the stations A and B, in such a manner that each can be seen from the other, and the point C from both of them. Then measure the horizontal angles CAB and CBA with an instrument adapted to that purpose.

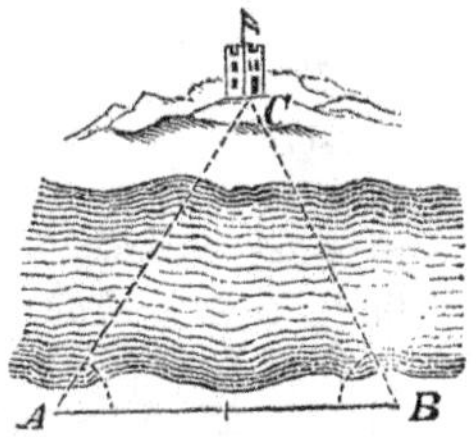

Let us suppose that we have found $AB = 600$ yards,

$$CAB = 57° \ 35', \qquad CBA = 64° \ 51'.$$

$$\text{The angle } C = 180° - (A + B) = 57° \ 34'.$$

The distances AC and BC may now be computed as in Case I Art. (53), and are

$$AC = 643.49 \text{ yards}, \qquad BC = 600.11 \text{ yards}.$$

II. *To determine the altitude of an inaccessible object above a given horizontal plane.*

First Method.

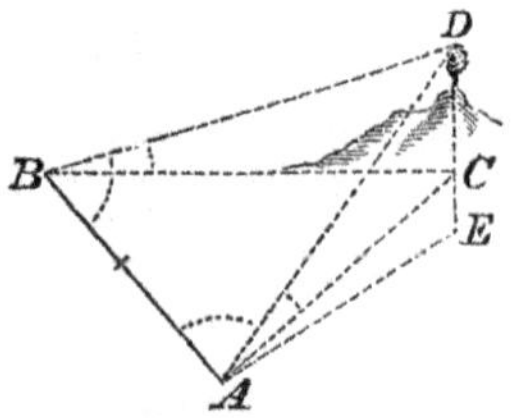

59. Suppose D to be the inaccessible object, and BCA the horizontal plane from which the altitude is to be estimated: then, if we suppose DC to be a vertical line, it will represent the required distance.

Measure any horizontal base line, as BA; and at the extremities B and A, measure the horizontal angles CBA and CAB. Measure also the angle of elevation DBC.

Then in the triangle CBA there will be known, two angles and the side AB; the side BC can therefore be computed. Having found BC, we shall have, in the right-angled triangle DBC, the base BC and the angle at the base, to find the perpendicular DC, which measures the altitude of the point D above the horizontal plane BCA.

Let us suppose that we have found

$$BA = 780 \text{ yards}, \qquad CBA = 41^\circ\ 24';$$
$$CAB = 96^\circ\ 28', \qquad DBC = 10^\circ\ 43'.$$

The horizontal distances BC and AC may be computed as in the preceding article, and are

$$BC = 1155.29 \text{ yards}. \qquad AC = 768.9 \text{ yards}.$$

BC and DBC being known in the right-angled triangle DCB, DC may be computed as in Case II., Art. (50), and is

$$DC = 218.64 \text{ yards}.$$

Remark I. It might, at first, appear, that the solution which we have given, requires that the points B and A should be in the same horizontal plane; but it is entirely independent of such a supposition.

For, the horizontal distance, which is represented by BA, is the same, whether the station A is on the same level with B, above it, or below it. The horizontal angles CAB and CBA are also the same, so long as the point C is in the vertical line DC. Therefore, if the horizontal line through A should cut the vertical line DC, at any point, as E, above or below C, AB would still be the horizontal distance between B and A, and AE, which is equal to AC, would be the horizontal distance between A and C.

If at A, we measure the angle of elevation of the point D, we shall know in the right-angled triangle DAE, the base AE, and the angle at the base; from which the perpendicular DE can be determined.

Let us suppose that we have measured the angle of elevation DAE, and found it equal to $20° 15'$. We then compute DE, as above, and find

$$DE = 283.66 \text{ yards}.$$

Now, since DC is less than DE, it follows that the station B is above the station A. That is,

$$DE - DC = 283.66 - 218.64 = 65.02 = EC,$$

which expresses the vertical distance that the station B is above the station A.

REMARK II. It should be remembered, that the vertical distance which is obtained by the calculation, is estimated from a horizontal line passing through the eye at the time of observation. Hence, the height of the instrument is to be added, in order to obtain the true result.

Second Method.

60. When the nature of the ground will admit of it, measure a base line AB in the direction of the object D. Then measure with the instrument the angles of elevation at A and B.

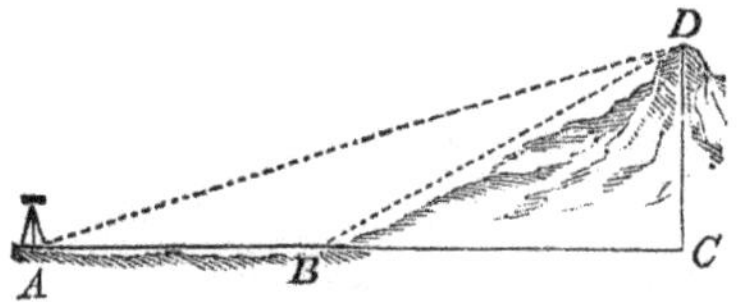

Then, since the outward angle DBC is equal to the sum of the angles A and ADB, it follows that the angle ADB is equal to the difference of the angles of elevation at A and B. Hence, we can find all the parts of the triangle ADB, as in Case I, Art. (53). Having found DB, and knowing the angle DBC, we can find the altitude DC as in Case I, Art. (49).

This method supposes that the stations A and B are on the same horizontal plane, and therefore it can only be used when the line AB is nearly horizontal.

Let us suppose that we have measured the base line and the two angles of elevation, and found

$$AB = 975 yds., \qquad A = 15° \ 36', \qquad DBC = 27° \ 29',$$

we then compute BD and DC and find

$$BD = 1273.3 yds., \qquad DC = 587.61 yds.$$

III. *To determine the perpendicular distance of an object below a given horizontal plane.*

61. Suppose C to be directly over the given object, and A the point through which the horizontal plane is supposed to pass.

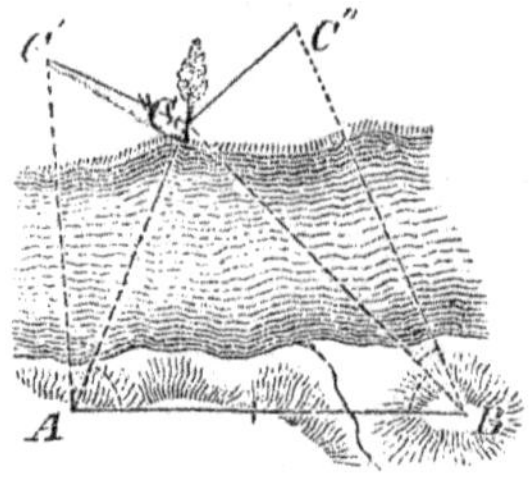

Measure a horizontal base line AB, and at the stations A and B conceive the two horizontal lines AC, BC, to be drawn. The oblique lines from A and B to the object are the hypothenuses of two right-angled triangles, of which AC, BC, are the bases. The perpendiculars of these triangles are the distances from the horizontal lines AC, BC, to the object. If we turn the triangles about their bases AC, BC, until they become horizontal, the object, in the first case, will fall at C', and in the second at C''.

Measure the horizontal angles CAB, CBA, and also the angles of depression $C'AC$, $C''BC$.

Let us suppose that we have found

$$AB = 672 yds. \qquad BAC = 72° \ 29', \qquad ABC = 39° \ 20',$$
$$C'AC = 27° \ 49' \qquad C''BC = 19° \ 10'.$$

Computing AC, BC, CC' and CC'', we find

$$AC = 458.79 \text{ yds.} \qquad BC = 690.28 \text{ yds.}$$
$$CC' = 242.06 \text{ "} \qquad CC'' = 239.93 \text{ "}$$

and

$$CC' - CC'' = 2.13\ yds.,$$

the height of the station A above station B.

Problems.

62.—1. Wanting to know the distance between two inaccessible objects, which lie in a direct level line from the bottom of a tower of 120 feet in height, the angles of depression are measured from the top of the tower, and are found to be, of the nearer 57°, of the more remote 25° 30′ : required the distance between the objects.

Ans. 173.656 feet.

2. In order to find the distance between two trees, A and B, which could not be directly measured because of a pool which occupied the intermediate space, the distances of a third point C from each of them were measured, and also the included angle ACB : it was found that,

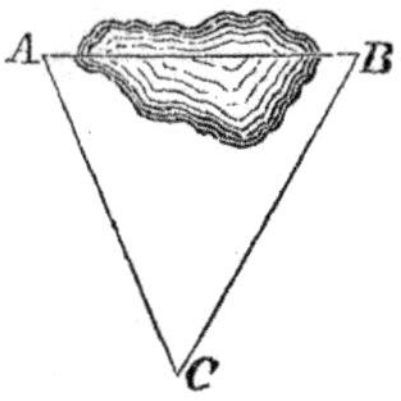

$$CB = 672 \text{ yards}, \qquad CA = 588 \text{ yards}, \qquad ACB = 55° 40'.$$

Required the distance AB. *Ans.* 592.967 yards.

3. Being on a horizontal plane, and wanting to ascertain the height of a tower, standing on the top of an inaccessible hill, there were measured, the angle of elevation of the top of the hill 40°, and of the top of the tower 51° ; then measuring in a direct line 180 feet farther from the hill, the angle of elevation of the top of the tower was 33° 45′; required the height of the tower.

Ans. 83.998 feet.

4. Wanting to know the horizontal distance between two inaccessible objects E and W, the following measurements were made :

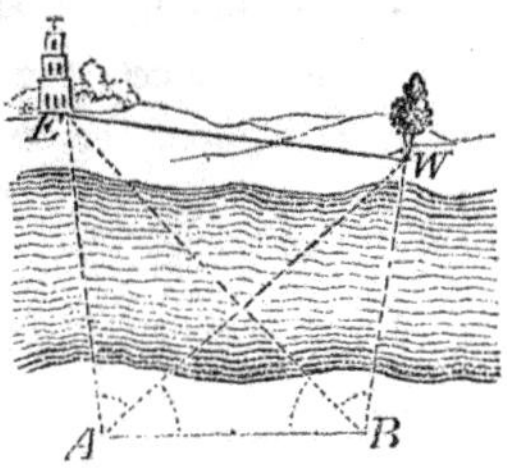

$$AB = 536 \text{ yards}$$
$$BAW = 40° 16'$$
$$WAE = 57° 40'$$
$$ABE = 42° 22'$$
$$EBW = 71° 07'.$$

Required the distance EW. *Ans.* 939.634 yards.

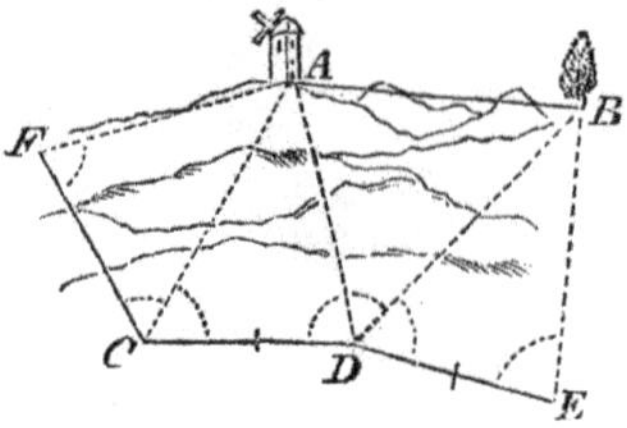

5. Wanting to know the horizontal distance between two inaccessible objects A and B, and not finding any station from which both of them could be seen, two points C and D, were chosen at a distance from each other, equal to 200 yards; from the former of these points A could be seen, and from the latter B, and at each of the points C and D a staff was set up. From C a distance CF was measured, not in the direction DC, equal to 200 yards, and from D a distance DE equal to 200 yards, and the following angles taken:

$AFC = 83°\ 00'$, $BDE = 54°\ 30'$, $ACD = 53°\ 30'$,

$BDC = 156°\ 25'$, $ACF = 54°\ 31'$, $BED = 88°\ 30'$.

Required the distance AB. *Ans.* 345.467 yards.

6. From a station P there can be seen three objects, A, B and C, whose distances from each other are known: viz., $AB = 800$, $AC = 600$, and $BC = 400$ yards. Now, there are measured the horizontal angles,

$APC = 33°\ 45'$ and $BPC = 22°\ 30'$: it is required to find the three distances PA, PC and PB.

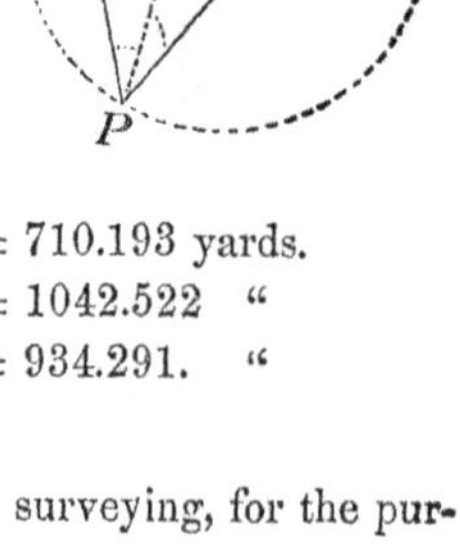

With the three given sides construct the triangle ABC. Then, at A lay off the angle $BAD = 22°\ 30'$, and at B the angle $ABD = 33°\ 45'$, and note D, the point at which the two lines intersect.

Through the points A, D and B describe the circumference of a circle, and through C and D draw the line CDP; the point P in which it intersects the circumference will be the position of the station.

Ans. $\begin{cases} PA = 710.193 \text{ yards.} \\ PC = 1042.522 \text{ "} \\ PB = 934.291. \text{ "} \end{cases}$

This problem is much used in maritime surveying, for the purpose of locating buoys and sounding-boats.

SPHERICAL TRIGONOMETRY.

---

63. The spherical triangles, considered and compared with each other, in Geometry, are regarded as situated upon the surface of the same sphere, and it is there proved that, if *any three* of the six parts of a spherical triangle are given, the triangle may be constructed, and the remaining parts may therefore be measured or computed.

64. Each angle of a spherical triangle is the same as the diedral angle included by the planes of its sides, and is measured by the angle included between two right lines, one in each plane and both perpendicular to their common intersection at the same point. (Davies' Legendre, § 4, Book VI).

If the radius of the sphere be taken equal to 1, each side of the triangle will measure the angle, at the centre, subtended by it.

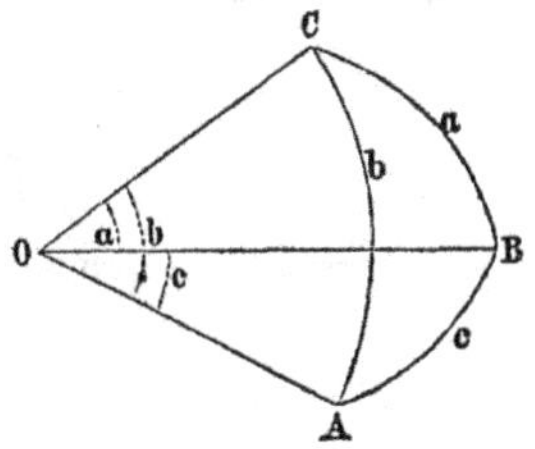

Thus in the triangle ABC, the angle at A is the same as that included between the planes AOC and AOB; and the side a is the measure of the plane angle BOC, O being the centre of the sphere, and OB the radius, equal to 1.

Formulas expressing the relation between the functions of the sides and angles of Spherical Triangles.

65. Let ABC, be any spherical triangle, on the surface of a sphere of which the radius $OB = 1$.

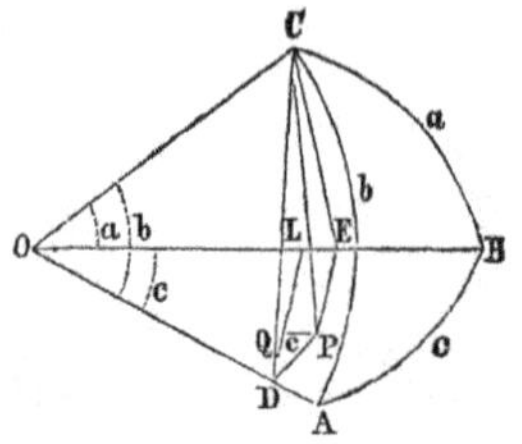

From the vertex C, let fall CP perpendicular to the plane AOB; from P, the foot of this perpendicular, draw PD and PE respectively perpendicular to OA and OB; join CD and CE, these lines will be respectively perpendicular to OA and OB. (Davies' Legendre, Prop. 6, Book VI), and the angles CDP and CEP will be equal to the angles A and B respectively. Draw DL and PQ, the one perpendicular and the other parallel to OB. We then have

$$CE = \sin a, \qquad OE = \cos a, \qquad CD = \sin b, \qquad OD = \cos b.$$

In the right angled triangle CPE, we have, Art. (30),

$$CP = CE \sin CEP = \sin a \sin B \quad . \quad . \quad . \quad (1);$$

and in the right-angled triangle CPD

$$CP = CD \sin CDP = \sin b \sin A \quad . \quad . \quad . \quad (2).$$

Equating these values of CP

$$\sin a \sin B = \sin b \sin A$$

from which results the proportion

$$\sin a \ : \ \sin b \ :: \ \sin A \ : \ \sin B \quad . \quad . \quad . \quad (3).$$

In like manner we may deduce

$$\sin a \ : \ \sin c \ :: \ \sin A \ : \ \sin C \quad . \quad . \quad . \quad (4).$$

$$\sin b \ : \ \sin c \ :: \ \sin B \ : \ \sin C \quad . \quad . \quad . \quad (5).$$

That is, in any spherical triangle, *the sines of the sides are proportional to the sines of their opposite angles.*

66. The construction being the same as in the last article, we have

$$OE = OL + QP \quad . \quad . \quad . \quad (1).$$

In the right angled triangle OLD,

$$OL = OD \cos DOL = \cos b \cos c.$$

The right angled triangle PQD has its sides respectively perpendicular to those of OLD, it is therefore similar to it, and the angle QDP is equal to c, and we have

$$QP = PD \sin QDP = PD \sin c \quad . \quad . \quad . \quad (2).$$

The right angled triangle CPD gives

$$PD = CD \cos CDP = \sin b \cos A;$$

substituting this value in (2), we have

$$QP = \sin b \sin c \cos A;$$

and now substituting these values of OE, OL and QP in (1), we have

$$\cos a = \cos b \cos c + \sin b \sin c \cos A \quad . \quad . \quad . \quad (3).$$

In the same way we may deduce

$$\cos b = \cos a \cos c + \sin a \sin c \cos B \quad . \quad . \quad . \quad (4),$$

$$\cos c = \cos a \cos b + \sin a \sin b \cos C \quad . \quad . \quad . \quad (5);$$

that is: *the cosine of either side of a spherical triangle is equal to the rectangle of the cosines of the other two sides plus the rectangle of the sines of these sides into the cosine of their included angle.*

67. If we represent the angles of the polar triangle of ABC, by A', B' and C', and the sides by a', b' and c', we have from Geometry (Davies' Legendre, Prop. 6, Book IX).

$$a = 180° - A', \qquad b = 180° - B', \qquad c = 180° - C',$$

$$A = 180° - a', \qquad B = 180° - b', \qquad C = 180° - c',$$

Substituting these values in equation (3) of the preceding article, and recollecting, Table III., that

$$\cos(180° - A') = -\cos A', \qquad \sin(180° - B') = \sin B', \text{ \&c.},$$

we have

$$-\cos A' = \cos B' \cos C' - \sin B' \sin C' \cos a',$$

or changing the signs and omitting the dashes, (since the preceding result is true for any triangle),

$$\cos A = \sin B \sin C \cos a - \cos B \cos C \quad . \quad . \quad . \quad (1).$$

In the same way we may deduce

$$\cos B = \sin A \sin C \cos b - \cos A \cos C \quad . \quad . \quad . \quad (2),$$
$$\cos C = \sin A \sin B \cos c - \cos A \cos B \quad . \quad . \quad . \quad (3);$$

that is: *The cosine of either angle of a spherical triangle is equal to the rectangle of the sines of the other two angles into the cosine of their included side, minus the rectangle of the cosines of these angles.*

68. The construction being the same as in Art. (65), we have

$$DL = DQ + PE \quad . \quad . \quad . \quad (1).$$

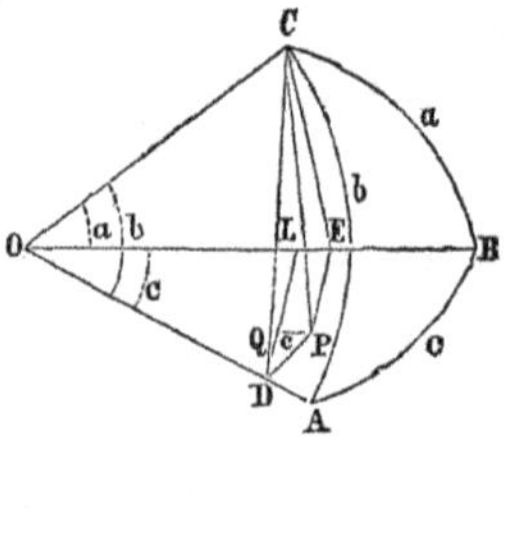

The right-angled triangle OLD gives

$$DL = OD \sin c = \cos b \sin c;$$

and the right-angled triangle PQD,

$$DQ = PD \cos c.$$

From CPE, we have, Art. (31),

$$PE = CP \cot CEP = CP \cot B.$$

Substituting the values of DL, DQ and PE in (1), and dividing both members by $\sin b$, we have

$$\frac{\cos b}{\sin b} \sin c = \frac{PD}{\sin b} \cos c + \frac{CP}{\sin b} \cot B,$$

or, since

$$\frac{PD}{\sin b} = \frac{PD}{CD} = \cos A, \qquad \frac{CP}{\sin b} = \frac{CP}{CD} = \sin A;$$

$$\cot b \sin c = \cos c \cos A + \sin A \cot B \quad . \quad . \quad . \quad (2).$$

In the same way we may deduce

$$\cot a \sin c = \cos c \cos B + \sin B \cot A \quad . \quad . \quad . \quad (3);$$

$$\cot c \sin b = \cos b \cos A + \sin A \cot C \quad . \quad . \quad . \quad (4);$$

that is: *The co-tangent of one side into the sine of another side, is equal to the cosine of the second side into the cosine of their included angle plus the sine of the included angle into the co-tangent of the angle opposite the first side.*

69. From equation (3), Art. (66), we deduce

$$\cos A = \frac{\cos a - \cos b \cos c}{\sin b \sin c} \quad . \quad . \quad . \quad (1).$$

If we add this equation member by member to the number 1, and recollect that $1 + \cos A$, in the first member is equal to $2 \cos^2 \frac{1}{2} A$, Art. (39), and reduce, we have

$$2 \cos^2 \tfrac{1}{2} A = \frac{\sin b \sin c + \cos a - \cos b \cos c}{\sin b \sin c},$$

or, Art. (33),

$$2 \cos^2 \tfrac{1}{2} A = \frac{\cos a - \cos (b + c)}{\sin b \sin c} \quad . \quad . \quad . \quad (2);$$

and since, formula (n), Art. (38),

$$\cos a - \cos (b + c) = 2 \sin \tfrac{1}{2} (a + b + c) \sin \tfrac{1}{2} (b + c - a),$$

equation (2) becomes, after dividing by 2,

$$\cos^2 \tfrac{1}{2} A = \frac{\sin \frac{1}{2} (a + b + c) \sin \frac{1}{2} (b + c - a)}{\sin b \sin c}.$$

If in this we place

$$\tfrac{1}{2} (a + b + c) = \tfrac{1}{2} s, \qquad \text{whence} \qquad \tfrac{1}{2} (b + c - a) = \tfrac{1}{2} s - a,$$

and extract the square root of both members, we have

$$\cos \tfrac{1}{2} A = \sqrt{\frac{\sin \frac{1}{2} s \sin (\frac{1}{2} s - a)}{\sin b \sin c}} \quad . \quad . \quad . \quad (3);$$

that is: *The cosine of one-half of either angle of a spherical triangle is equal to the square root of the sine of one-half the sum of the three sides into the sine of one-half this sum minus the side opposite the angle, divided by the rectangle of the sines of the two adjacent sides.*

70. If we subtract equation (1) of the preceding article, member by member, from the number 1, and recollect that

$$1 - \cos A = 2 \sin^2 \tfrac{1}{2} A,$$

we find, after reduction,

$$\sin \tfrac{1}{2} A = \sqrt{\frac{\sin (\frac{1}{2}s - b) \sin (\frac{1}{2}s - c)}{\sin b \sin c}} \quad . \quad . \quad . \quad (1).$$

71. Dividing the preceding value of $\sin \frac{1}{2} A$ by $\cos \frac{1}{2} A$, we obtain

$$\tan \tfrac{1}{2} A = \sqrt{\frac{\sin (\frac{1}{2}s - b) \sin (\frac{1}{2}s - c)}{\sin \frac{1}{2}s \sin (\frac{1}{2}s - a)}}.$$

72. If the angles and sides of the polar triangle of ABC be represented as in Art. (67), we have

$$A = 180^\circ - a', \qquad b = 180^\circ - B', \qquad c = 180^\circ - C',$$

$$\tfrac{1}{2}s = 270^\circ - \tfrac{1}{2}(A' + B' + C'), \;\; \tfrac{1}{2}s - a = 90^\circ - \tfrac{1}{2}(B' + C' - A').$$

Substituting these values in (3), Art. (69), and reducing by the aid of the formulas in Table III, we find

$$\sin \tfrac{1}{2} a' = \sqrt{\frac{- \cos \frac{1}{2}(A' + B' + C') \cos \frac{1}{2}(B' + C' - A')}{\sin B' \sin C'}}.$$

Placing

$$\tfrac{1}{2}(A' + B' + C') = \tfrac{1}{2}S; \quad \text{whence,} \quad \tfrac{1}{2}(B' + C' - A') = \tfrac{1}{2}S - A'.$$

Substituting and omitting the dashes, we have

$$\sin \tfrac{1}{2} a = \sqrt{\frac{- \cos \frac{1}{2}S \cos (\frac{1}{2}S - A)}{\sin B \sin C}} \quad . \quad . \quad . \quad (1).$$

In a similar way we may deduce from (1), Art. (70),

$$\cos \tfrac{1}{2}a = \sqrt{\frac{\cos(\frac{1}{2}S - B)\cos(\frac{1}{2}S - C)}{\sin B \sin C}} \quad . \quad . \quad . \quad (2);$$

and thence

$$\tan \tfrac{1}{2}a = \sqrt{\frac{-\cos\frac{1}{2}S\cos(\frac{1}{2}S - A)}{\cos(\frac{1}{2}S - B)\cos(\frac{1}{2}S - C)}} \quad . \quad . \quad . \quad (3).$$

73. From equation (1), Art. (67), we have

$$\cos A + \cos B \cos C = \sin B \sin C \cos a = \sin C \frac{\sin A}{\sin a} \sin b \cos a \quad . \quad (1),$$

since, from proportion (3), Art. (65),

$$\sin B = \frac{\sin A}{\sin a} \sin b.$$

Also, from equation (2), Art. (67),

$$\cos B + \cos A \cos C = \sin A \sin C \cos b = \sin C \frac{\sin A}{\sin a} \sin a \cos b \quad . \quad (2).$$

Adding (1) and (2) and dividing by $\sin C$, we obtain

$$(\cos A + \cos B)\frac{1 + \cos C}{\sin C} = \frac{\sin A}{\sin a} \sin(a + b) \quad . \quad . \quad (3).$$

The proportion,

$$\sin A \; : \; \sin B \; : : \; \sin a \; : \; \sin b,$$

taken first by composition, and then by division, gives

$$\sin A + \sin B = \frac{\sin A}{\sin a}(\sin a + \sin b) \quad . \quad . \quad . \quad (4),$$

$$\sin A - \sin B = \frac{\sin A}{\sin a}(\sin a - \sin b) \quad . \quad . \quad . \quad (5).$$

Dividing (4) and (5), in succession, by (3), we obtain

$$\frac{\sin A + \sin B}{\cos A + \cos B} \times \frac{\sin C}{1 + \cos C} = \frac{\sin a + \sin b}{\sin (a + b)} \quad . \quad . \quad . \quad . \quad (6);$$

$$\frac{\sin A - \sin B}{\cos A + \cos B} \times \frac{\sin C}{1 + \cos C} = \frac{\sin a - \sin b}{\sin (a + b)} \quad . \quad . \quad . \quad (7).$$

But by formulas (2) and (4), Art. (40), and formula (6), Art. (39), equation (6) becomes

$$\tan \tfrac{1}{2} (A + B) = \cot \tfrac{1}{2} C \frac{\cos \frac{1}{2} (a - b)}{\cos \frac{1}{2} (a + b)} \quad . \quad . \quad . \quad . \quad (8),$$

and by the similar formulas (3) and (5) of Art. (40), equation (7) becomes

$$\tan \tfrac{1}{2} (A - B) = \cot \tfrac{1}{2} C \frac{\sin \frac{1}{2} (a - b)}{\sin \frac{1}{2} (a + b)} \quad . \quad . \quad . \quad . \quad (9).$$

These last two formulas give the proportions, known as *the first set of Napier's Analogies.*

$$\cos \tfrac{1}{2} (a + b) : \cos \tfrac{1}{2} (a - b) :: \cot \tfrac{1}{2} C : \tan \tfrac{1}{2} (A + B),$$
$$\sin \tfrac{1}{2} (a + b) : \sin \tfrac{1}{2} (a - b) :: \cot \tfrac{1}{2} C : \tan \tfrac{1}{2} (A - B).$$

If in these we substitute the values of a, b, C, A and B, in terms of the corresponding parts of the polar triangle, as expressed in Art. (67), we obtain

$$\cos \tfrac{1}{2} (A + B) : \cos \tfrac{1}{2} (A - B) :: \tan \tfrac{1}{2} c : \tan \tfrac{1}{2} (a + b),$$
$$\sin \tfrac{1}{2} (A + B) : \sin \tfrac{1}{2} (A - B) :: \tan \tfrac{1}{2} c : \tan \tfrac{1}{2} (a - b),$$

the second set of Napier's Analogies.

Formulas relating particularly to right-angled spherical triangles.

74. Let ABC be any right angled spherical triangle, the right angle being at A. If in formula (3), Art. (66),

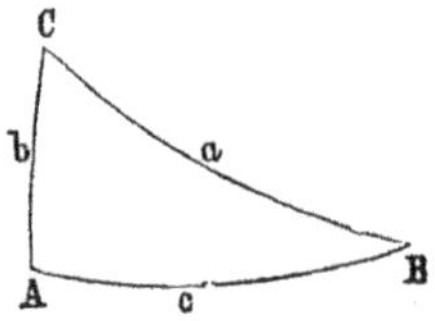

$$\cos a = \cos b \cos c + \sin b \sin c \cos A,$$

we make $A = 90°$, then $\cos A = 0$, and we have

$$\cos a = \cos b \cos c \quad . \quad . \quad (1);$$

that is: *The cosine of the hypothenuse is equal to the rectangle of the cosines of the other two sides.*

If in formula (1), Art. (67),

$$\cos A = \sin B \sin C \cos a - \cos B \cos C,$$

we make $A = 90°$, $\cos A = 0$, and we deduce

$$\sin B \sin C \cos a = \cos B \cos C;$$

whence

$$\cos a = \frac{\cos B \cos C}{\sin B \sin C} = \cot B \cot C \quad . \quad . \quad . \quad . \quad (2).$$

From proportion (3), Art. (65), we have

$$\sin B = \frac{\sin b}{\sin a} \sin A.$$

If in this we make $A = 90°$, then $\sin A = 1$, and

$$\sin B = \frac{\sin b}{\sin a} \quad . \quad . \quad . \quad . \quad (3).$$

From this it also follows that

$$\sin C = \frac{\sin c}{\sin a} \quad . \quad . \quad . \quad . \quad (4).$$

If in formula (3), Art. (67),

$$\cos C = \sin A \sin B \cos c - \cos A \cos B,$$

we make $A = 90°$, $\sin A = 1$, $\cos A = 0$, and

$$\cos C = \sin B \cos c, \qquad \text{or,} \qquad \sin B = \frac{\cos C}{\cos c} \quad . \quad . \quad . \quad . \quad (5).$$

Also

$$\sin C = \frac{\cos B}{\cos b} \quad . \quad . \quad . \quad . \quad (6).$$

If in formula (3), Art. (68),

$$\cot a \sin c = \cos c \cos B + \sin B \cot A,$$

we make $A = 90°$, then $\cot A = 0$, and

$$\cot a \sin c = \cos c \cos B,$$

or

$$\cos B = \cot a \frac{\sin c}{\cos c} = \cot a \tan c,$$

or

$$\cos B = \frac{\tan c}{\tan a} \quad . \quad . \quad . \quad . \quad . \quad (7).$$

Also

$$\cos C = \frac{\tan b}{\tan a} \quad . \quad . \quad . \quad . \quad . \quad (8).$$

If in formula (2), Art. (68),

$$\cot b \sin c = \cos c \cos A + \sin A \cot B,$$

we make $A = 90°$, then

$$\cot b \sin c = \cot B,$$

or,

$$\tan B = \frac{\tan b}{\sin c} \quad . \quad . \quad . \quad . \quad . \quad (9).$$

Also

$$\tan C = \frac{\tan c}{\sin b} \quad . \quad . \quad . \quad . \quad (10).$$

75. The formulas of the preceding article are analogous to the corresponding formulas in plane triangles, Table IV., and as they are of great use in the solution of right-angled triangles, and should be committed to memory, we arrange them in

TABLE V.

1.	$\cos a = \cos b \cos c.$	2.	$\cos a = \cot B \cot C.$
3.	$\sin B = \frac{\sin b}{\sin a}.$	4.	$\sin C = \frac{\sin c}{\sin a}.$
5.	$\sin B = \frac{\cos C}{\cos c}.$	6.	$\sin C = \frac{\cos B}{\cos b}.$
7.	$\cos B = \frac{\tan c}{\tan a}.$	8.	$\cos C = \frac{\tan b}{\tan a}.$
9.	$\tan B = \frac{\tan b}{\sin c}.$	10.	$\tan C = \frac{\tan c}{\sin b}.$

Two parts of a spherical triangle are said to be of *the same species* when they are both less than 90°, or both greater than 90°; and of *different species* when one is less and the other greater than 90°.

From the formulas in the above table, we deduce the following important properties of right angled spherical triangles.

First. From formula (1), we see if $a < 90°$, cos a will be positive, and cos b and cos c will have the same sign, and b and c be both less, or both greater than 90°. Also if $a > 90°$, cos b and cos c must have different signs, and b and c be one less and the other greater than 90°; that is: *If the hypothenuse be less than* 90°, *the other two sides will be of the same species; if the hypothenuse be greater than* 90° *these sides will be of different species*, and the converse.

Second. In the same way we see from formula (2), that: *If the hypothenuse be less than* 90°, *the two oblique angles will be of the same species; and if the hypothenuse be greater than* 90°, *these angles will be of different species.*

Third. From formula (1) we also see, that, since cos b and cos c are both less than 1, their product will be less than either, that is, cos a will be numerically less than either cos b or cos c. But if cos $a <$ cos b and $<$ cos c, a must differ less from 90° than b or c; hence: *The hypothenuse must differ less from* 90° *than either of the other two sides.*

Fourth. Formula (3) may be placed under the form

$$\sin b = \sin a \sin B,$$

in which we see that sin b must be less than sin B, since sin $a < 1$. But if sin $b <$ sin B, numerically, b must differ more from 90° than B; hence: *Either side about the right angle must differ more from* 90° *than its opposite angle.*

Fifth. In formula (5), B being less than 180°, sin B is always positive, hence cos C and cos c must have the same sign, that is: *A side and its opposite angle must be of the same species.*

Sixth. From formula (7) we see that if $B < 90°$, tan c and tan a will have the same sign; if $B > 90°$ they will have contrary signs, that is: *If either oblique angle is less than* 90° *the adjacent side and hypothenuse will be of the same species; if either angle be greater than* 90° *the adjacent side and hypothenuse will be of different species.*

Napier's Circular Parts.

76. In every right-angled spherical triangle, *the two sides* adjacent to the right angle, *the complement* of the hypothenuse, and *the complements* of the two oblique angles, are called *circular parts*.

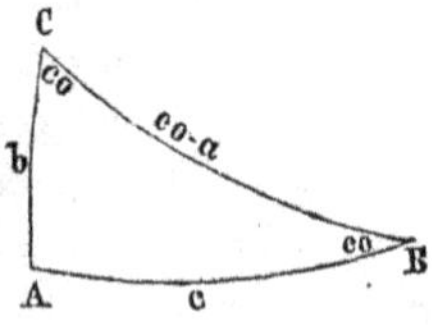

If any *three* of these *five parts* are considered, it will be seen that they will be so situated, that one will either be *adjacent* to the other two; or *opposite* to them, that is, separated from both of them by the two parts which are not considered. The right angle not being a circular part does not separate the parts b and c. Thus, comp. a is adjacent to the two parts comp. B and comp. C, and separated from the parts b and c.

The part which is thus adjacent to the two others, or opposite to them, is called *the middle part*. The two others are called *extremes*, and are either both *adjacent* or both *opposite*.

77. Formulas (1) and (2) of Table V, give two different values for the $\cos a$. From formulas (3) and (10) we deduce two values for $\sin b$, and from formulas (6) and (7), two values for $\cos B$, which may be written thus,

1. $\cos a = \cos b \cos c$, 2. $\cos a = \cot B \cot C$.

3. $\sin b = \sin a \sin B$, 4. $\sin b = \tan c \cot C$.

5. $\cos B = \cos b \sin C$, 6. $\cos B = \cot a \tan c$.

From which may be determined the hypothenuse, either side and either oblique angle, when the other parts of the right-angled triangle are known.

Equations (1), (3) and (5) may be otherwise written,

1. $\sin(\text{comp. } a) = \cos b \cos c$,

3. $\sin b = \cos(\text{comp. } a) \cos(\text{comp. } B)$,

5. $\sin(\text{comp. } B) = \cos b \cos(\text{comp. } C)$;

whence results the following property of the circular parts, viz.: *The sine of the middle part is equal to the rectangle of the cosines of the opposite parts.*

Equations (2), (4) and (6) may also be written,

$$2.\quad \sin(\text{comp. } a) = \tan(\text{comp. } B)\tan(\text{comp. } C),$$
$$4.\quad \sin b = \tan c \tan(\text{comp. } C),$$
$$6.\quad \sin(\text{comp. } B) = \tan(\text{comp. } a)\tan c;$$

that is: *The sine of the middle part is equal to the rectangle of the tangents of the adjacent parts.*

These two principles are called Napier's rules for the solution of right-angled spherical triangles.

Solution of Right-angled Spherical Triangles.

78. In a right-angled spherical triangle, the right angle is always known. If, therefore, either two of the other parts are given, the triangle may be constructed, and the remaining parts computed.

Six different cases may arise. There may be given,

I. The hypothenuse and one side.
II. The hypothenuse and one oblique angle.
III. The two sides about the right angle.
IV. One side and its adjacent angle.
V. One side and its opposite angle.
VI. The two oblique angles.

All of these cases may be solved by the aid of the formulas in Table V, or by the use of the principles given in the preceding article. As these principles are easily remembered and conveniently applied to each case, we will take the latter method.

As in Plane Trigonometry, before applying logarithms to the formulas, the radius of the table of logarithmic sines, &c., must be introduced, or the formulas made homogeneous, Art. (41).

I. *The hypothenuse and one side being given.*

79. Let a and b be given.

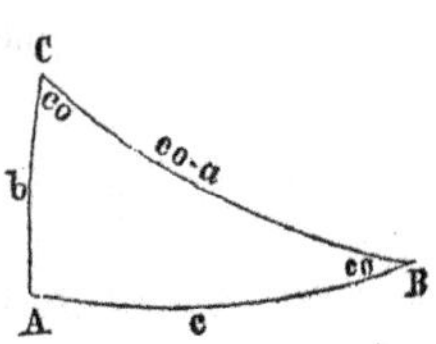

To compute c. The circular parts considered will then be *comp. a*, b and c, *comp. a* being the middle part and the extremes *opposite*, we have from the first of Napier's rules,

$$\cos a = \cos b \cos c, \qquad \text{or} \qquad \cos c = \frac{R \cos a}{\cos b},$$

after introducing the radius. Applying logarithms,

$$\log \cos c = a.c.\log \cos b - 10 + \log \cos a + \log R,$$

or

$$\log \cos c = a.c.\log \cos b + \log \cos a \quad . \quad . \quad . \quad (1),$$

which will give but one value for c, and this will be less or greater than 90°, according as a and b are of the same or different species. First principle, Art. (75).

To compute B. The circular parts considered will be *comp.* a, b and *comp.* B, b is the middle part and the extremes are *opposite.* The same rule as above gives

$$\sin b = \sin a \sin B, \qquad \text{or} \qquad \sin B = \frac{R \sin b}{\sin a},$$

whence, by the application of logarithms,

$$\log \sin B = a.c.\log \sin a + \log \sin b \quad . \quad . \quad . \quad (2),$$

which will give two values of B, supplements of each other. One only can be used, and there will be but one solution, since B must be of the same species as b. Fifth principle, Art. (75).

To compute C. The circular parts considered will be *comp* a, b and *comp.* C. The latter will be the middle part and the extremes *adjacent.* The second of Napier's rules gives

$$\cos C = \frac{\cot a \tan b}{R}.$$

Applying logarithms we obtain

$$\log \cos C = \log \cot a + \log \tan b - 10 \quad . \quad . \quad . \quad (3),$$

which gives but one value of C, and this will be of the same species as c above determined.

Example. Let $a = 105° \, 17' \, 29''$, $b = 38° \, 47' \, 11''$.

To compute c. Substitute these values in (1) and we have

$$\begin{array}{lll} + \ a.c.\log\cos\ 38^\circ\ 47'\ 11'' & \ldots & 0.108192 \\ + \qquad \log\cos\ 105^\circ\ 17'\ 29'' & \ldots & 9.421157 \\ & & \overline{9.529349} = \log\cos c, \end{array}$$

hence,

$$c = 109^\circ\ 46'\ 32'',$$

since a and b are of different species.

To compute B. Substitute the above values of a and b in formula (2), and we have

$$\begin{array}{lll} + \ a.c.\log\sin\ 105^\circ\ 17'\ 29'' & \ldots & 0.015654 \\ + \qquad \log\sin\ 38^\circ\ 47'\ 11'' & \ldots & 9.796865 \\ & & \overline{9.812519} = \log\sin B\ ; \end{array}$$

hence $B = 40^\circ\ 29'\ 50''$ being of the same species as b.

To compute C. Substitute the above values of a and b in formula (3), and we obtain

$$\begin{array}{llll} + \log\cot & 105^\circ\ 17'\ 29'' & \ldots & 9.436811 \\ + \log\tan & 38^\circ\ 47'\ 11'' & \ldots & 9.905055 \\ - & 10 & & \overline{9.341866} = \log\cos C, \end{array}$$

hence $C = 102^\circ\ 41'\ 33''$, since $c > 90^\circ$.

80. By the application of the same rules each of the other five cases may be solved. We give an example of each case.

2. Let $a = 86^\circ\ 51'$, $\qquad B = 18^\circ\ 03'\ 32''$.

Ans. $b = 18^\circ\ 01'\ 50''$, $\quad c = 86^\circ\ 41'\ 14''$, $\quad C = 88^\circ\ 58'\ 25''$.

3. Let $b = 155^\circ\ 27'\ 54''$, $\quad c = 29^\circ\ 46'\ 08''$.

Ans. $a = 142^\circ\ 09'\ 13''$, $\quad B = 137^\circ\ 24'\ 21''$, $\quad C = 54^\circ\ 01'\ 16''$.

4. Let $c = 73^\circ\ 41'\ 35''$, $\quad B = 99^\circ\ 17'\ 33''$.

Ans. $a = 92^\circ\ 42'\ 17''$, $\quad b = 99^\circ\ 40'\ 30''$, $\quad C = 73^\circ\ 54'\ 47''$.

5. Let $b = 115^\circ\ 20'$, $\quad B = 91^\circ\ 01'\ 47''$.

$$\textit{Ans. } a = \begin{cases} 64^\circ\ 41'\ 11'', \\ 115^\circ\ 18'\ 49'', \end{cases} \quad c = \begin{cases} 177^\circ\ 49'\ 27'', \\ 2^\circ\ 10'\ 33'', \end{cases} \quad C = \begin{cases} 177^\circ\ 35'\ 36''. \\ 2^\circ\ 24'\ 24'' \end{cases}$$

6. Let $B = 47° \ 13' \ 43''$, $C = 126° \ 40' \ 24''$.

Ans. $a = 133° \ 32' \ 26''$, $b = 32° \ 08' \ 56''$, $c = 144° \ 27' \ 03''$.

Solution of Quadrantal Triangles.

81. *A quadrantal triangle is a spherical triangle having one of its sides equal to* 90°.

Let $A'B'C'$ be a quadrantal triangle having the side $a' = 90°$. Then for the polar triangle ABC we have

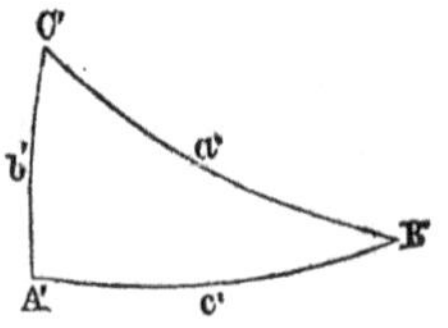

$$A = 180° - a', \quad B = 180° - b',$$

$$a = 180° - A', \quad b = 180° - B',$$

$$C = 180° - c', \quad c = 180° - C'.$$

Since $a' = 90°$, $A = 90°$ and the polar triangle ABC will be a right-angled triangle.

If either two parts of the quadrantal triangle be given, the corresponding parts in the polar triangle become known by the above equations, and the remaining parts may be calculated as in the preceding articles. The values thus deduced being substituted in the above equations, will give the unknown parts of the given quadrantal triangle.

Example. Let $B' = 75° \ 42'$, $c' = 18° \ 37'$;
then

$$b = 104° \ 18' \quad C = 161° \ 23'.$$

from which a, c and B may be computed as in case IV., Art. (78), and these being found, A', C' and b' may be at once deduced, and the quadrantal triangle thus completely solved. We thus find

$$A' = 103° \ 34' \ 49''; \quad C' = 18° \ 04' \ 40''; \quad b' = 85° \ 28' \ 39''.$$

Solution of Oblique-angled Spherical Triangles.

82. Before proceeding to the solution of practical examples of oblique-angled spherical triangles, it is of importance to remember the following principles, which are of great assistance, not only in

enabling us to verify the accuracy of our computations, but also in determining whether a part or all the values computed are true solutions of the case under consideration.

I. *In every spherical triangle considered, each part is less than* 180°.

II. *The sum of the sides is less than* 360°.

III. *The sum of the angles is greater than* 180° *and less than* 540°.

IV. *The greater side is opposite the greater angle, and the reverse.*

V. *Each side is less than the sum of the other two.*

VI. By the third of the above principles, we have

$$A+B+C>180^\circ,$$

whence

$$A>180^\circ-(B+C).$$

If $B+C$ exceeds 180°, we have from the polar triangle of ABC, by the fifth principle,

$$a'<b'+c',$$

or

$$180^\circ-A<180^\circ-B+180^\circ-C,$$

$$-A<180^\circ-(B+C),$$

$$A>B+C-180^\circ,$$

that is: *Each angle is greater than the difference between* 180° *and the sum of the other two.*

VII. By formula (4), Art. (66),

$$\cos b=\cos a\cos c+\sin a\sin c\cos B;$$

whence

$$\cos B=\frac{\cos b-\cos a\cos c}{\sin a\sin c}.$$

If $\cos b>\cos a$ numerically, then since $\cos c<1$ we have

$$\cos b>\cos a\cos c,$$

and the sign of the numerator of the value of $\cos B$ will be the same as that of $\cos b$, and since the denominator is positive, the sign of $\cos B$ will be the same as that of $\cos b$, that is, B and b will be of the same species. But if $\cos b$ is numerically greater than $\cos a$, b differs more from 90° than a, that is: *A side which differs more from* 90° *than another side is of the same species as its opposite angle.*

VIII. From formula (2), Art. (67), we have

$$\cos b = \frac{\cos B + \cos A \cos C}{\sin A \sin C},$$

in which, if $\cos B > \cos A$, numerically, the sign of $\cos b$ must be the same as that of $\cos B$, and b and B must be of the same species. But if $\cos B > \cos A$, B differs more from 90° than A, that is: *An angle which differs more from 90° than another angle, must be of the same species as its opposite side.*

IX. In every spherical triangle, since two of the sides must differ more from 90° than the third side, *there must be, at least, two sides which are of the same species as their opposite angles and the reverse.*

X. The first of Napier's Analogies, Art. (73), gives

$$\cos \tfrac{1}{2}(a + b) \tan \tfrac{1}{2}(A + B) = \cot \tfrac{1}{2} C \cos \tfrac{1}{2}(a - b).$$

The second member of this equation being positive, since $\frac{1}{2} C$ and $\frac{1}{2}(a - b)$ are each less than 90°, the two factors in the first member must have the same sign, that is $\frac{1}{2}(a + b)$ and $\frac{1}{2}(A + B)$ must be of the same species; hence if $\frac{1}{2}(a + b)$ is less than, equal to or greater than 90°, $\frac{1}{2}(A + B)$ will be the same, or: *If the sum of either two sides is less than, equal to or greater than* 180°, *the sum of their opposite angles will be the same.*

83. In the solution of oblique angled triangles six different cases may arise: viz., there may be given,

I. Two sides and an angle opposite one of them.
II. Two angles and a side opposite one of them.
III. Two sides and their included angle.
IV. Two angles and their included side.
V. The three sides.
VI. The three angles.

I. *Two sides and an angle opposite one of them being given.*

84. Let ABC be the triangle, in which a, b and A are given.

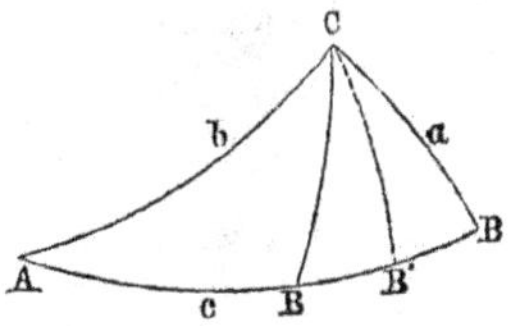

To compute the angle B, we have the proportion,

$$\sin a \ : \ \sin b \ :: \ \sin A \ : \ \sin B;$$

that is: *The sine of the side opposite the given angle is to the sine of the other given side, as the sine of the given angle is to the sine of the required angle.* By the application of logarithms we have

$$a.c.\log\sin a + \log\sin b + \log\sin A - 10 = \log\sin B \quad . \quad . \quad (1),$$

an equation which will give two different values of B, the supplements of each other.

To ascertain when these values will give one solution to the triangle, and when two, we remark, first, that in accordance with principle VII, of Art. (82), if b differs more from 90° than a, it must be of the same species as B; that is, *If the side opposite the required angle differs more from* 90° *than the other given side, there can be but one solution*, and we use that value of B which is of the same species as b.

If b *differs less from* 90° *than a*, then $\cos a > \cos b$, and in the expression

$$\cos B = \frac{\cos b - \cos a \cos c}{\sin a \sin c},$$

c may have two values such as to give two different values of $\cos B$ equal with contrary signs, corresponding to the values of $\sin B$ deduced above, and *there will be two solutions* provided

$$\sin a > \sin b \ \sin A.$$

For if

$$\sin a = \sin b \ \sin A,$$

then, since by Art. (65),

$$\sin b \ \sin A = \sin a \ \sin B,$$

we must have

$$\sin a = \sin a \ \sin B,$$

which can only be satisfied when $\sin B = 1$, and $B = 90°$. The two solutions then unite in one, giving the right-angled triangle $AB'C$.

If a and b are so given that

$$\sin a < \sin b \sin A,$$

then as above we must have

$$\sin a < \sin a \sin B,$$

which is impossible, since, except in the above case, $\sin B < 1$. There can, then, in this case, be no solution.

Hence, *if the side opposite the required angle differs less from* 90° *than the other given side, there will be two solutions, one solution, or no solution, according as the sine of the latter side is greater than, equal to, or less than the sine of its opposite angle multiplied by the sine of the former side.*

If a and b are so given that the side opposite the given angle differs more from 90° than the other given side, and is not of the same species as its opposite angle, the triangle cannot exist, and there can be *no solution.* Principle VIII, Art. (82).

The angle B being determined, we *compute* C by the first of Napier's analogies, Art. (73), taken by inversion,

$$\cos \tfrac{1}{2}(a-b) \ : \ \cos \tfrac{1}{2}(a+b) \ :: \ \tan \tfrac{1}{2}(A+B) \ : \ \cot \tfrac{1}{2} C;$$

whence,

$$a.c.\log \cos \tfrac{1}{2}(a-b) + \log \cos \tfrac{1}{2}(a+b) + \log \tan \tfrac{1}{2}(A+B) - 10 = \log \cot \tfrac{1}{2} C \quad . \quad . \quad . \quad (2).$$

To compute c we now take the proportion,

$$\sin A \ : \ \sin C \ :: \ \sin a \ : \ \sin c \quad . \quad . \quad . \quad (3),$$

which will give two values of c. That one only can be used which is in accordance with the principles of Art, (82).

Example 1. Let

$$a = 43^\circ\ 27'\ 36'', \qquad b = 82^\circ\ 58'\ 17'', \qquad A = 29^\circ\ 32'\ 29''.$$

Substituting these values in formula (1), we have

$$
\begin{array}{llll}
+ & a.c.\log\sin\ 43^\circ\ 27'\ 36'' & \ldots & 0.162508 \\
+ & \log\sin\ 82^\circ\ 58'\ 17'' & \ldots & 9.996724 \\
+ & \log\sin\ 29^\circ\ 32'\ 29'' & \ldots & 9.692893 \\
- & 10 & & \overline{9.852125} = \log\sin B;
\end{array}
$$

hence, $B = 45^\circ\ 21'\ 01''$, or $134^\circ\ 38'\ 59''$, since b differs less from 90° than a, and there will be *two solutions.*

Taking first, $B = 45^\circ\ 21'\ 01''$, *to compute* C, we substitute the values of a, b and B in formula (2), and obtain, since

$$\tfrac{1}{2}(a+b) = 63^\circ\ 12'\ 56'',\quad \tfrac{1}{2}(a-b) = 19^\circ\ 45'\ 20''$$

and

$$\tfrac{1}{2}(A+B) = 37^\circ\ 26'\ 45'',$$

$$
\begin{array}{llll}
+ & a.c.\log\cos\ 19^\circ\ 45'\ 20'' & \ldots & 0.026344 \\
+ & \log\cos\ 63^\circ\ 12'\ 56'' & \ldots & 9.653825 \\
+ & \log\tan\ 37^\circ\ 26'\ 45'' & \ldots & 9.884130 \\
- & 10 & & \overline{9.564299} = \log\cot\tfrac{1}{2}C;
\end{array}
$$

hence, $C = 139^\circ\ 43'\ 30''$.

To compute c we use the proportion (3), and have

$$
\begin{array}{llll}
+ & a.c.\log\sin\ 29^\circ\ 32'\ 29'' & \ldots & 0.307107 \\
+ & \log\sin\ 139^\circ\ 43'\ 30'' & \ldots & 9.810539 \\
+ & \log\sin\ 43^\circ\ 27'\ 36'' & \ldots & 9.837492 \\
- & 10 & & \overline{9.955138} = \log\sin c;
\end{array}
$$

hence, $c = 115^\circ\ 35'\ 48''$, since $C > B$, c must be greater than b, in accordance with principle IV, Art. (82).

In the same way the values of C and c for the second value of B may be computed, viz.,

$$C = 32^\circ\ 20'\ 28'',\quad c = 48^\circ\ 16'\ 18''.$$

2. Let $a = 97^\circ\ 35'$, $b = 27^\circ\ 8'\ 22''$, $A = 40^\circ\ 51'\ 18''$.

Ans. $B = 17^\circ\ 31'\ 9''$, $C = 144^\circ\ 48'\ 10''$, $c = 119^\circ\ 08'\ 25''$.

II. *Two angles and a side opposite one of them being given.*

85. Let ABC be the triangle in which A, B and the side a are given. To compute b, we take the proportion,

$$\sin A \; : \; \sin B \; :: \; \sin a \; : \; \sin b$$

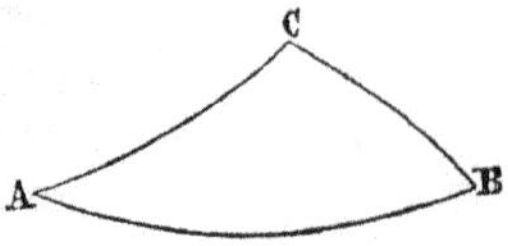

that is, *the sine of the angle opposite the given side is to the sine of the other given angle, as the sine of the given side is to the sine of the required side.*

By the application of logarithms,

$$a.c.\log\sin A + \log\sin B + \log\sin a - 10 = \log\sin b \quad . \; . \; . \quad (1)$$

which will give two values for b. To ascertain when these values give only one solution, and when two, we remark first, that, by principle VIII., Art. (82), if the angle B differs more from 90° than A, then B and b must be of the same species and there can be but one solution; that is: *If the angle opposite the required side differs more from* 90° *than the other given angle there will be but one solution*, and we use that value of b which is of the same species as B.

If B differs less from 90° *than A*, then $\cos A > \cos B$, and in the expression

$$\cos b = \frac{\cos B + \cos A \cos C}{\sin A \sin C},$$

C may have two values, such as to give two different values of cos ! equal with contrary signs, corresponding with the two values of $\sin b$ deduced above, and *there will be two solutions*, provided

$$\sin A > \sin B \sin a.$$

For if

$$\sin A = \sin B \sin a,$$

then since

$$\sin B \sin a = \sin b \sin A,$$

we have

$$\sin A = \sin b \sin A,$$

which can only be the case when $\sin b = 1$ and $b = 90°$, and the two solutions unite in one, giving a quadrantal triangle.

If

$$\sin A < \sin B \sin a,$$

then

$$\sin A < \sin b \sin A,$$

which cannot be, and there can be *no solution;* hence: *If the angle opposite the required side differs less from* 90° *than the other given angle, there will be two solutions, one or none,* according as the sine of the latter angle is greater than, equal to, or less than the sine of its opposite side into the sine of the former angle.

The solution will also be impossible when A and B are so given that A differs more from 90° than B, and is not of the same species as a. Principle VIII., Art. (82).

The side b being now known, we compute c by the third of Napier's analogies, taken by inversion, thus

$$\cos \tfrac{1}{2}(A - B) : \cos \tfrac{1}{2}(A + B) :: \tan \tfrac{1}{2}(a + b) : \tan \tfrac{1}{2} c \quad (2);$$

and then the angle C may be computed by the proportion

$$\sin a : \sin c :: \sin A : \sin C. \quad . \quad . \quad . \quad . \quad (3).$$

Example 1. Let $A = 95° 16'$, $B = 80° 42' 10''$, $a = 57° 38'$.

Substituting these values in formula (1), we have

$$\begin{array}{lll} + \ a.c. & \log \sin 95° 16' \quad . \quad . \quad . \quad . & 0.001837 \\ + & \log \sin 80° 42' 10'' \quad . \quad . \quad . & 9.994257 \\ + & \log \sin 57° 38' \quad . \quad . \quad . \quad . & 9.926671 \\ - & \quad 10 & \overline{9.922765} = \log \sin b; \end{array}$$

hence $b = 56° 49' 57''$, this being of the same species as B, and there being but one solution, since B differs more from 90° than A.

To compute c we substitute for A, B and b their values in proportion (2). By the application of logarithms we have

$$\begin{array}{lll} + \ a.c. & \log \cos 7° 16' 55'' \quad . \quad . \quad . & 0.003517 \\ + & \log \cos 87° 59' 05'' \quad . \quad . \quad . & 8.546124 \\ + & \log \tan 57° 13' 58'' \quad . \quad . \quad . & 10.191352 \\ - & \quad 10 & \overline{8.740993} = \log \tan \tfrac{1}{2} c: \end{array}$$

hence, $c = 6° 18' 18''$.

To compute C, we use proportion (3) and obtain

$$\begin{array}{lll} + \ a.c. & \log \sin 57° 38' \quad . \quad . \quad . \quad . & 0.073329 \\ + & \log \sin 6° 18' 18'' \quad . \quad . \quad . & 9.040685 \\ + & \log \sin 95° 16' \quad . \quad . \quad . \quad . & 9.998163 \\ - & \quad 10 & \overline{9.112177} = \log \sin C, \end{array}$$

hence $C = 7° 26' 21''$, since c differs more from 90° than a. Principle VII., Art. (82).

2. Let $A = 50° 12'$, $B = 58° 8'$, $a = 62° 42'$.

Ans. $b = 79° 12' 10''$, $c = 119° 03' 26''$, $C = 130° 54' 28''$,

or $b = 100° 47' 50''$, $c = 152° 14' 18''$, $C = 156° 15' 06''$.

III. *Two sides and their included angle being given.*

86. Let ABC be the triangle in which a, b and C are given.

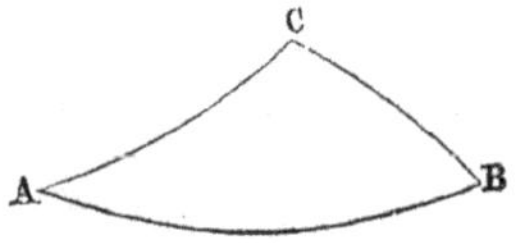

To compute A and B, we take the first set of Napier's analogies, supposing b to be the smaller side.

$$\cos \tfrac{1}{2}(a+b) : \cos \tfrac{1}{2}(a-b) :: \cot \tfrac{1}{2} C : \tan \tfrac{1}{2}(A+B) \quad . . (1),$$

$$\sin \tfrac{1}{2}(a+b) : \sin \tfrac{1}{2}(a-b) :: \cot \tfrac{1}{2} C : \tan \tfrac{1}{2}(A-B) \quad . . (2).$$

By the application of logarithms to these proportions we obtain

$$\tfrac{1}{2}(A+B) \quad \text{and} \quad \tfrac{1}{2}(A-B).$$

Adding these values we obtain A. Subtracting the second from the first we obtain B.

If $\frac{1}{2}(a+b) = 90°$ then also $\frac{1}{2}(A+B) = 90°$ Principle X., Art. (82).

To compute c we may use the proportion

$$\sin \tfrac{1}{2}(A-B) : \sin \tfrac{1}{2}(A+B) :: \tan \tfrac{1}{2}(a-b) : \tan \tfrac{1}{2} c \quad . . (3),$$

or otherwise

$$\sin A : \sin C :: \sin a : \sin c \quad . . . . (4).$$

The solution will always be possible whenever the given parts are in accordance with principle I., Art. (82).

Example 1. Let $a = 62° 38'$, $b = 10° 13' 19''$, $C = 150° 24' 12''$

In this case

$\frac{1}{2}(a+b) = 36° 25' 29''$, $\frac{1}{2}(a-b) = 26° 12' 20''$, $\frac{1}{2} C = 75° 12'$ ..

Substituting these values in proportion (1), and applying logarithms, we have

$+ a.c.$	log cos 36° 25′ 39″	. .	0.094415
+	log cos 26° 12′ 20″	. .	9.952897
+	log cot 75° 12′ 06″	. .	9.421901
—	10		9.469213 = log tan $\frac{1}{2}(A+B)$;

hence, $\frac{1}{2}(A+B) = 16° 24' 51''$.

Substituting the same values in proportion (2), &c., we have

$+ a.c.$	log sin 36° 25′ 39″	. .	0.226356
+	log sin 26° 12′ 20″	. .	9.645022
+	log cot 75° 12′ 06″	. .	9.421901
—	10		9.293279 = log tan $\frac{1}{2}(A-B)$.

hence $\frac{1}{2}(A-B) = 11° 06' 53''$.

Adding this to the value of $\frac{1}{2}(A+B)$, and then subtracting it, we have

$$A = 27° 31' 44'', \quad B = 5° 17' 58''.$$

Computing c by proportion (3) we have

$+ a.c.$	log sin 11° 06′ 53″	. .	0.714952
+	log sin 16° 24′ 51″	. .	9.451139
+	log tan 26° 12′ 20″	. .	9.692125
—	10		9.858216 = log tan $\frac{1}{2}c$;

hence $c = 71° 37' 06''$.

2. Let $a = 68° 46' 02''$, $b = 37° 10'$, $C = 39° 23'$.

Ans. $A = 120° 59' 47''$, $B = 33° 45' 03''$, $c = 43° 37' 38''$.

IV. *Two angles and their included side being given.*

87. ABC being the triangle, let A, B and c be given, B being the smaller angle.

To compute a and b, we take the second set of Napier's Analogies,

$$\cos\tfrac{1}{2}(A+B) : \cos\tfrac{1}{2}(A-B) :: \tan\tfrac{1}{2}c : \tan\tfrac{1}{2}(a+b) \quad . \ (1),$$

$$\sin\tfrac{1}{2}(A+B) : \sin\tfrac{1}{2}(A-B) :: \tan\tfrac{1}{2}c : \tan\tfrac{1}{2}(a-b) \quad . \ (2).$$

from which a and b may be determined as A and B were determined in the preceding article.

If $\frac{1}{2}(A+B) = 90°$, then $\frac{1}{2}(a+b)=90°$. Principle X., Art. (82).

To compute C, we may use the proportion

$$\sin\tfrac{1}{2}(a-b) : \sin\tfrac{1}{2}(a+b) :: \tan\tfrac{1}{2}(A-B) : \cot\tfrac{1}{2}C \quad . \; . \quad (3)$$

or otherwise

$$\sin a \; : \; \sin c \; :: \; \sin A \; : \; \sin C \quad . \; . \; . \quad (4),$$

and the solution is always possible when the given parts are in accordance with principle I.

Ex. 1. Let $A = 81° \, 38' \, 20''$, $B = 70° \, 09' \, 38''$, $c = 59° \, 16' \, 22''$.

Ans. $a = 70° \, 04' \, 17''$, $b = 63° \, 21' \, 27''$, $C = 64° \, 46' \, 24''$.

2. Let $A = 34° \, 15' \, 03''$, $B = 42° \, 15' \, 13''$, $c = 76° \, 35' \, 36''$.

Ans. $a = 40° \, 0' \, 10''$, $b = 50° \, 10' \, 30''$, $C = 121° \, 36' \, 12''$.

88. It will be observed that, in each of the two preceding cases, one of the required parts may be computed by using either one of the proportions (3) or (4). It will be found, however, that the results obtained from these proportions will frequently differ by several seconds. This discrepancy is due to the fact that the logarithmic sines of arcs, differing but little from 90°, change very little as the arc changes, and that arcs differing by several seconds often have the same logarithmic sine. A very slight error in the computation, caused by the omission of the decimal places to the right of those used, may, for such arcs, cause an error of several seconds.

The same is true for the logarithmic cosines of arcs differing little from 0.

The student should, therefore, as far as possible, in his computations, avoid the use of these logarithms.

V. *The three sides being given.*

89. Let ABC be the triangle in which a, b and c are given.

To compute either angle as A, we take the formula of Art. (69), after introducing the radius R,

$$\cos \tfrac{1}{2} A = R\sqrt{\frac{\sin \frac{1}{2} s \sin (\frac{1}{2} s - a)}{\sin b \ \sin c}}.$$

By the application of logarithms to this, we have

$$\log R + \tfrac{1}{2}[\log \sin \tfrac{1}{2} s + \log \sin (\tfrac{1}{2} s - a)$$
$$+ a.c.\log \sin b + a.c.\log \sin c - 20] = \log \cos \tfrac{1}{2} A,$$

or, since $\log R = 10 = \frac{1}{2} 20$,

$$\tfrac{1}{2}[\log \sin \tfrac{1}{2} s + \log \sin (\tfrac{1}{2} s - a)$$
$$+ a.c.\log \sin b + a.c.\log \sin c] = \log \cos \tfrac{1}{2} A \quad . \quad . \quad (1).$$

In the same way we may find B and C, and the solution is always possible when the given sides fulfil the requirements of principles I, II and V, Art. (82).

Example 1. Let $a = 74° 23'$, $b = 35° 46' 14''$, $c = 100° 39'$.

Substituting these values in formula (1), we have, since

$\frac{1}{2} s = 105° 24' 07''$, and $\frac{1}{2} s - a = 31° 01' 07''$,

+	log sin 105° 24′ 07″	. . .	9.984116
+	log sin 31° 01′ 07″	. . .	9.712074
+ a.c.	log sin 35° 46′ 14″	. . .	0.233185
+ a.c.	log sin 100° 39′	. . .	0.007546
÷	2		)19.936921
			9.968460 = log cos ½ A;

hence, $A = 43° 08' 46''$.

To compute B, we put B for A, b for a, and a for b, in formula (1), and have, since $\frac{1}{2} s - b = 69° 37' 53''$,

+	log sin 105° 24′ 07″	. . .	9.984116
+	log sin 69° 37′ 53″	. . .	9.971958
+ a.c.	log sin 74° 23′	. . .	0.016336
+ a.c.	log sin 100° 39′	. . .	0.007546
÷	2		)19.979956
			9.989978 = log cos ½ B;

hence, $B = 24° 31' 26''$.

To compute C, we put C for A, c for a, and a for c, in formula (1), and have, since $\frac{1}{2}s - c = 4° 45' 07''$.

$+$	log sin 105° 24′ 07″	. . .	9.984116
$+$	log sin 4° 45′ 07″	. . .	8.918250
$+ a.c.$	log sin 74° 23′	. . .	0.016336
$+ a.c.$	log sin 35° 46′ 14″	. . .	0.233185
$\div$	2		)19.151887
			9.575943 $= \log \cos \frac{1}{2} C$;

hence, $C = 135° 44' 50''$.

2. Let $a = 56° 40'$, $b = 83° 13'$, $c = 114° 30'$.

Ans. $A = 48° 31' 18''$, $B = 62° 55' 44''$, $C = 125° 18' 56''$.

VI. *The three angles being given.*

90. If A, B and C are given, to compute either side, as a, we take formula (2), Art. (72),

$$\cos \tfrac{1}{2} a = R \sqrt{\frac{\cos(\frac{1}{2} S - B) \cos(\frac{1}{2} S - C)}{\sin B \sin C}};$$

from which by the application of logarithms as in the preceding article, we obtain

$$\tfrac{1}{2} [\log \cos (\tfrac{1}{2} S - B) + \log \cos (\tfrac{1}{2} S - C)$$
$$+ a.c. \log \sin B + a.c. \log \sin C] = \log \cos \tfrac{1}{2} a.$$

From which a may be computed, and in the same way both of the other sides, and the solution is always possible when the given angles conform to principles I, II and VI.

Example 1. Let

$A = 48° 30'$, $B = 125° 20'$, $C = 62° 54'$.

Ans. $a = 56° 39' 30''$, $b = 114° 29' 58''$, $c = 83° 12' 06''$.

2. Let $A = 109° 55' 42''$, $B = 116° 38' 33''$, $C = 120° 43' 37''$.

Ans. $a = 98° 21' 40''$, $b = 109° 50' 22''$, $c = 115° 13' 28''$.

MENSURATION OF SURFACES.

1. MENSURATION is that branch of mathematics which embraces every operation employed in determining the measures of all the geometrical magnitudes.

We determine the area, or contents of a surface, by finding how many times the given surface contains some other surface, assumed as the unit of measure. Thus, when we say that a square yard contains 9 square feet, we should understand that one square foot is taken as the unit of measure, and that this unit is contained 9 times in the square yard.

2. The most convenient unit of measure for a given surface, is a square whose side is the linear unit. Thus, if the linear dimensions are expressed in feet, it will be most convenient to express the area in square feet; if the linear dimensions are yards, it will be most convenient to express the area in square yards, &c.

3. We have already seen, that the term, rectangle or product of two lines, designates the rectangle constructed on the lines as sides (B. IV., P. 4, S. 2); and that the numerical value of this product expresses the number of times which the rectangle contains its unit of measure.

4. To find the area or contents of a square, a rectangle, or a parallelogram.

Multiply the base by the altitude, and the product will be the area or contents (B. IV., P. 5).

Ex. 1. To find the area of a parallelogram, the base being 12.25, and the altitude 8.5. *Ans.* 104.125.

2. What is the area of a square whose side is 204.3 feet?
Ans. 41738.49 *sq. ft.*

3. What are the contents, in square yards, of a rectangle whose base is 66.3 feet, and altitude 33.3 feet? *Ans.* 245.31 *sq. ft.*

4. To find the area of a rectangular board, whose length is $12\frac{1}{2}$ feet, and breadth 9 inches. *Ans.* $9\frac{3}{8}$ *sq. ft.*

5. To find the number of square yards of painting in a parallelogram, whose base is 37 feet, and altitude 5 feet 3 inches. *Ans.* $21\frac{7}{12}$.

5. To find the area of a triangle.

CASE I.

When the base and altitude are given.

Multiply the base by the altitude, and take half the product. Or, *multiply one of these dimensions by half the other* (B. IV., P. 6).

Ex. 1. To find the area of a triangle, whose base is 625, and altitude 520 feet. *Ans.* 162500 *sq. ft.*

2. To find the number of square yards in a triangle, whose base is 40, and altitude 30 feet. *Ans.* $66\frac{2}{3}$.

3. To find the number of square yards in a triangle, whose base is 49, and altitude $25\frac{1}{4}$ feet. *Ans.* 68.7361.

CASE II.

6. When two sides and their included angle are given.

Add together the logarithms of the two sides and the logarithmic sine of their included angle; from this sum subtract the logarithm of the radius, which is 10, *and the remainder will be the logarithm of double the area of the triangle. Find, from the table, the number answering to this logarithm, and divide it by* 2; *the quotient will be the required area.*

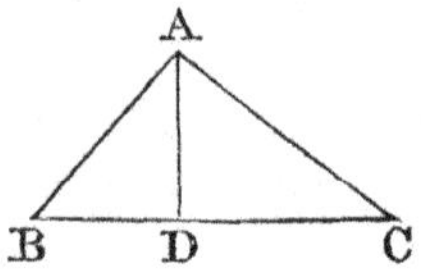

Let BAC be a triangle, in which there are given BA, BC, and the included angle B. From the vertex A, draw AD perpendicular to the base BC, and represent the area of the triangle by Q. Then (Trig. Th. I.),

$$R : \sin B :: BA : AD;$$

hence,

$$AD = \frac{BA \times \sin B}{R}.$$

But,

$$Q = \frac{BC \times AD}{2} \text{ (Art. 5)};$$

hence, by substituting for AD its value, we have,

$$Q = \frac{BC \times BA \times \sin B}{2R}, \text{ or } 2Q = \frac{BC \times BA \times \sin B}{R}.$$

Taking the logarithm of both members, we have,

$$\log 2Q = \log BC + \log BA + \log \sin B - \log R,$$

which proves the rule as enunciated.

Ex. 1. What is the area of a triangle whose sides are, $BC = 125.81$, $BA = 57.65$, and the included angle $B = 57° 25'$?

Then, $\log 2Q = \begin{cases} + \log BC & 125.81 & 2.090715 \\ + \log BA & 57.65 & 1.760799 \\ + \log \sin B & 57° 25' & 9.925626 \\ - \log R & . \quad . & -10. \end{cases}$

$\log 2Q$ 3.786140

and $2Q = 6111.4$, or $Q = 3055.7$, the required area.

2. What is the area of a triangle whose sides are 30 and 40, and their included angle 28° 57'? *Ans.* 290.427.

3. What is the number of square yards in a triangle of which the sides are 25 feet and 21.25 feet, and their included angle 45°?

Ans. 20.8694.

CASE III.

7. When the three sides are known.

1. *Add the three sides together, and take half their sum:*
2. *From this half-sum subtract each side separately:*
3. *Multiply together the half-sum and each of the three remainders, and the product will be the square of the area of the triangle. Then, extract the square root of this product, for the required area:* or,
4. *After having obtained the three remainders, add together the logarithm of the half-sum and the logarithms of the respective remainders, and divide their sum by 2: the quotient will be the logarithm of the area.*

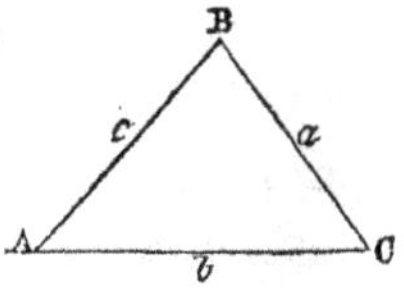

Let ABC be a triangle: and denote the area by Q: then, by the last case, we have,

$$Q = \tfrac{1}{2}bc \times \sin A.$$

But, we have (Plane Trig., Art. 78),

$$\sin A = 2 \sin \tfrac{1}{2} A \cos \tfrac{1}{2} A;$$

hence,
$$Q = bc \sin \tfrac{1}{2} A \cos \tfrac{1}{2} A.$$

By substituting in this equation the values of $\sin \frac{1}{2} A$, and $\cos \frac{1}{2} A$, found in Art. 47, Plane Trigonometry, we obtain,

$$Q = \sqrt{\tfrac{1}{2}s(\tfrac{1}{2}s - a)(\tfrac{1}{2}s - b)(\tfrac{1}{2}s - c)}.$$

Ex. 1. To find the area of a triangle whose three sides 20, 30, and 40.

20	45	45	45 half-sum.
30	20	30	40
40	25 1st rem.	15 2d rem.	5 3d rem.
2)90			
45 half-sum.			

Then, $$45 \times 35 \times 15 \times 5 = 84375;$$

the square root of which is 290.4737, the required area.

2. How many square yards of plastering are there in a triangle whose sides are 30, 40, and 50 feet? *Ans.* $66\frac{2}{3}$.

8. To find the area of a trapezoid.

Add together the two parallel sides: then multiply their sum by the altitude of the trapezoid, and half the product will be the required area (B. IV., P. 7).

Ex. 1. In a trapezoid, the parallel sides are 750 and 1225, and the perpendicular distance between them is 1540: what is the area? *Ans.* 152075.

2. How many square feet are contained in a plank, whose length is 12 feet 6 inches, the breadth at the greater end 15 inches, and at the lesser end 11 inches? *Ans.* $13\frac{13}{24}$ *sq. ft.*

3. How many square yards are there in a trapezoid, whose parallel sides are 240 feet, 320 feet, and altitude 66 feet? *Ans.* $2053\frac{1}{3}$.

9. To find the area of a quadrilateral.

Join two of the angles by a diagonal, dividing the quadrilateral into two triangles. Then, from each of the other angles let fall a perpendicular on the diagonal: then multiply the diagonal by half the sum of the two perpendiculars, and the product will be the area.

Ex. 1. What is the area of the quadrilateral *ABCD*, the diagonal *AC* being 42, and the perpendicular *Dg*, *Bb*, equal to 18 and 16 feet? *Ans.* 714 *sq. ft.*

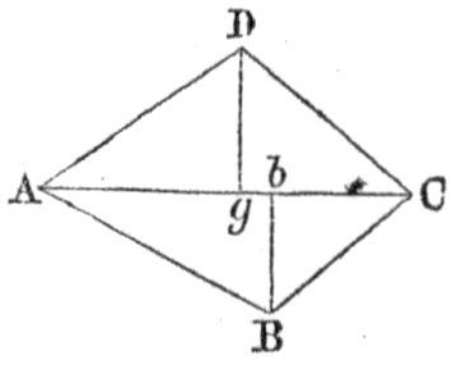

2. How many square yards of paving are there in the quadrilateral whose diagonal is 65 feet, and the two perpendiculars let fall on it 28 and $33\frac{1}{2}$ feet? *Ans.* $222\frac{1}{12}$.

10. To find the area of an irregular polygon.

Draw diagonals dividing the proposed polygon into trapezoids and triangles. Then find the areas of these figures separately, and add them together for the contents of the whole polygon.

Ex. 1. Let it be required to determine the contents of the polygon $ABCDE$, having five sides.

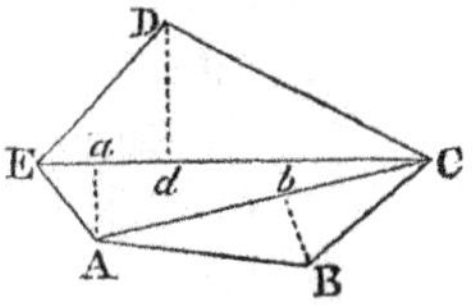

Let us suppose that we have measured the diagonals and perpendiculars, and found $AC = 36.21$, $EC = 39.11$, $Bb = 4$, $Dd = 7.26$, $Aa = 4.18$: required the area. *Ans.* 296.1292.

11. To find the area of a long and irregular figure, bounded on one side by a right line.

1. *At the extremities of the right line, measure the perpendicular breadths of the figure; then divide the line into any number of equal parts, and measure the breadth at each point of division.*
2. *Add together the intermediate breadths and half the sum of the extreme ones: then multiply this sum by one of the equal parts of the base line: the product will be the required area, very nearly.*

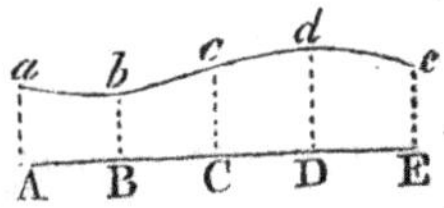

Let $AEea$ be an irregular figure, having for its base the right line AE. Divide AE into equal parts, and at the points of division A, B, C, D, and E, erect the perpendiculars Aa, Bb, Cc, Dd, Ee, to the base line AE, and designate them respectively by the letters a, b, c, d, and e.

Then, the area of the trapezoid $ABba = \frac{a+b}{2} \times AB$,

the area of the trapezoid $BCcb = \frac{b+c}{2} \times BC$,

the area of the trapezoid $CDdc = \frac{c+d}{2} \times CD$,

and the area of the trapezoid $DEed = \frac{d+e}{2} \times DE$;

hence, their sum, or the area of the whole figure, is equal to

$$\left(\frac{a+b}{2} + \frac{b+c}{2} + \frac{c+d}{2} + \frac{d+e}{2}\right) \times AB,$$

since AB, BC, &c., are equal to each other. But this sum is also equal to

$$\left(\frac{a}{2} + b + c + d + \frac{e}{2}\right) \times AB,$$

which corresponds with the enunciation of the rule.

Ex. 1. The breadths of an irregular figure at five equi-distant places being 8.2, 7.4, 9.2, 10.2, and 8.6, and the length of the base 40 : required the area.

$$\begin{array}{r} 8.2 \\ \underline{8.6} \\ 2)\underline{16.8} \\ 8.4 \text{ mean of the extremes.} \\ 7.4 \\ 9.2 \\ \underline{10.2} \\ \underline{35.2} \text{ sum.} \end{array} \qquad \begin{array}{r} 4)\underline{40} \\ 10 \text{ one of the equal parts.} \\ \\ 35.2 \text{ sum.} \\ \underline{10} \\ 352 = \text{area.} \end{array}$$

2. The length of an irregular figure being 84, and the breadths at six equidistant places 17.4, 20.6, 14.2, 16.5, 20.1, and 24.4 : what is the area ? *Ans.* 1550.64.

12. To find the area of a regular polygon.

Multiply half the perimeter of the polygon by the apothem, or perpendicular let fall from the centre on one of the sides, and the product will be the area required (B. V., P. 8).

REMARK I.—The following is the manner of determining the perpendicular, when one side and the number of sides of the regular polygon are known :

First, divide 360 degrees by the number of sides of the polygon, and the quotient will be the angle at the centre ; that is, the angle subtended by one of the equal sides. Divide this angle by 2, and half the angle at the centre will then be known.

Now, the line drawn from the centre to an angle of the polygon, the perpendicular let fall on one of the equal sides, and half this side, form a right-angled triangle, in which there are known the base, which is half the side of the polygon, and the angle at the vertex. Hence, the perpendicular can be determined.

Ex. 1. To find the area of a regular hexagon, whose sides are 20 feet each.

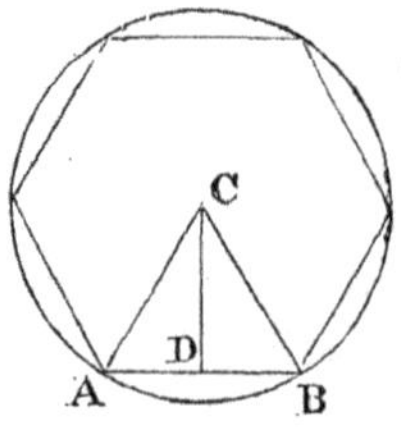

$$\begin{array}{l} 6)\underline{360°} \\ \quad \underline{60°} = ACB, \text{ the angle at the centre.} \\ \quad \underline{30°} = ACD, \text{ half the angle at centre.} \end{array}$$

Also, $CAD = 90° - ACD = 60°$;

and, $AD = 10.$

Then, $CD = AD \times \tan A = 10 \times \tan 60^\circ$ (Trig. Art. 31).

$$\begin{array}{lrl} + \log 10 \quad . \quad . \quad . & 1.000000 & \qquad P \\ + \log \tan 60^\circ \quad . & \underline{10.238561} & \\ - 10 & 1.238561 & = \log CD\,; \end{array}$$

hence, $CD = 17.3205.$

Perimeter $= 120$, and half the perimeter $= 60$.

Then, $60 \times 17.3205 = 1039.23$, the area.

2. What is the area of an octagon whose side is 20?

Ans. 1931.36886.

REMARK II.—The area of a regular polygon of any number of sides may also be easily calculated by the following method:

Let the side of each of the regular polygons be denoted by 1, and let the area of each be calculated and arranged in the following

TABLE.

NAMES.	SIDES.	AREAS.	NAMES.	SIDES.	AREAS.
Triangle,	3	0.4330127	Octagon,	8	4.8284271
Square,	4	1.0000000	Nonagon,	9	6.1818242
Pentagon,	5	1.7204774	Decagon,	10	7.6942088
Hexagon,	6	2.5980762	Undecagon,	11	9.3656399
Heptagon,	7	3.6339124	Dodecagon,	12	11.1961524

Now, since the areas of simple polygons are to each other as the squares of their homologous sides (B. IV., P. 27), we have,

$$1^2 \;:\; \text{any side squared} \;::\; \text{tabular area} \;:\; \text{required area.}$$

Hence, to find the area of any regular polygon,

1. *Square the side of the polygon:*
2. *Then multiply that square by the tabular area set opposite the polygon of the same number of sides, and the product will be the required area.*

Ex. 1. What is the area of a regular hexagon, whose side is 20?

$$20^2 = 400, \quad \text{tabular area} = 2.5980762.$$

Hence, $2.5980762 \times 400 = 1039.2304800$, as before.

2. To find the area of a pentagon whose side is 25.

Ans. 1075.298375.

3. To find the area of a decagon whose side is 20.

Ans. 3077.68352.

13. To find the circumference of a circle, when the diameter is given; or the diameter, when the circumference is given.

Multiply the diameter by 3.1416, *and the product will be the circumference; or, divide the circumference by* 3.1416, *and the quotient will be the diameter.*

It is shown (B. V., P. 16, S. 1), that the circumference of a circle whose diameter is 1, is 3.1415926, or 3.1416, nearly. But, since the circumferences of circles are to each other as their radii or diameters, we have, by calling the diameter of the second circle d,

$$1 : d :: 3.1416 : \text{circumference};$$

hence, $$d \times 3.1416 = \text{circumference}.$$

Hence, also, $$d = \frac{\text{circumference}}{3.1416}.$$

Ex. 1. What is the circumference of a circle whose diameter is 25? *Ans.* 78.54.

2. If the diameter of the earth is 7921 miles, what is the circumference? *Ans.* 24884.6136.

3. What is the diameter of a circle whose circumference is 11652.1904? *Ans.* 37.09.

4. What is the diameter of a circle whose circumference is 6850? *Ans.* 2180.41.

14. To find the length of an arc of a circle containing any number of degrees.

Multiply the number of degrees in the given arc by 0.0087266, *and the product by the diameter of the circle.*

For, since the circumference of a circle whose diameter is 1, is 3.1416, it follows, that if 3.1416 be divided by 360, the quotient will be the length of an arc of 1 degree; that is, $\frac{3.1416}{360} = 0.0087266$ = arc of one degree, to the diameter 1. If this be multiplied by the number of degrees in a given arc, the product will be the length of that arc in the circle whose diameter is 1. If this product be then multiplied by the diameter of any circle, the product will be the length of the arc in that circle.

REMARK.—When the arc contains degrees and minutes, reduce the minutes to the decimal of a degree, which is done by dividing them by 60.

Ex. 1. To find the length of an arc of 30 degrees, the diameter being 18 feet. *Ans.* 4.712364.

2. To find the length of an arc of 12° 10′ or $12\frac{1}{6}$°, the diameter being 20 feet. *Ans.* 2.123472.

3. What is the length of an arc of 10° 15′, or $10\frac{1}{4}$°, in a circle whose diameter is 68? *Ans.* 6.082396.

15. To find the area of a circle.

1. *Multiply the circumference by half the radius* (B. V., P. 15). Or,
2. *Multiply the square of the radius by* 3.1416 (B. V., P. 16).

Ex. 1. To find the area of a circle whose diameter is 10, and circumference 31.416. *Ans.* 78.54.

2. Find the area of a circle whose diameter is 7, and circumference 21.9912. *Ans.* 38.4846.

3. How many square yards in a circle whose diameter is $3\frac{1}{2}$ feet? *Ans.* 1.069016.

4. What is the area of a circle whose circumference is 12 feet? *Ans.* 11.4595.

16. To find the area of a sector of a circle.

1. *Multiply the arc of the sector by half the radius* (B. V., P. 15, C). Or,
2. *Compute the area of the whole circle: then say, as* 360 *degrees is to the degrees in the arc of the sector, so is the area of the whole circle to the area of the sector.*

Ex. 1. To find the area of a circular sector whose arc contains 18 degrees, the diameter of the circle being 3 feet. *Ans.* 0.35343.

2. To find the area of a sector whose arc is 20 feet, the radius being 10. *Ans.* 100.

3. Required the area of a sector whose arc is 147° 29′, and radius 25 feet. *Ans.* 804.3986.

17. To find the area of a segment of a circle.

1. *Find the area of the sector having the same arc, by the last problem:*
2. *Find the area of the triangle formed by the chord of the segment and the two radii of the sector:*
3. *Then add these two together, for the answer, when the segment is greater than a semicircle, and subtract the triangle from the sector, when it is less.*

Ex. 1. To find the area of the segment ACB, its chord AB being 12, and the radius EA, 10 feet.

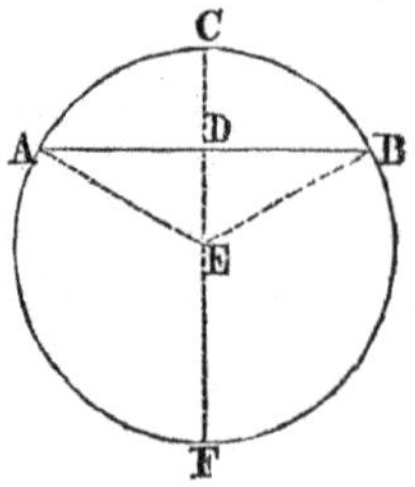

As EA	10 arith. comp.	9.000000
: AD	6	0.778151
: : sin D	90°	10.000000
: sin AED	36° 52′ = 36.87	9.778151
	2	
	73.74 = the degrees in the arc ACB.	

Then, 0.0087266 × 73.74 × 20 = 12.87 = arc ABC, nearly.
5
64.35 = area $EACB$.

Again, $\sqrt{EA^2 - AD^2} = \sqrt{100 - 36} = \sqrt{64} = 8 = ED$;

and, 6 × 8 = 48 = the area of the triangle EAB.

Hence, sect. $EACB - EAB = 64.35 - 48 = 16.35 = ACB$.

2. Find the area of the segment whose height is 18, the diameter of the circle being 50. *Ans.* 636.4834.

3. Required the area of the segment whose chord is 16, the diameter being 20. *Ans.* 44.764.

18. To find the area of a circular ring; that is, the area included between the circumference of two circles which have a common centre.

1. *Take the difference between the areas of the two circles:* Or,
2. *Subtract the square of the less radius from the square of the greater, and multiply the remainder by* 3.1416.

For, the area of the larger is . . . . $R^2\pi$,
and of the smaller . . . . $r^2\pi$.
Their difference, or the area of the ring, is . . . $(R^2 - r^2)\pi$.

Ex. 1. The diameters of two concentric circles being 10 and 6, required the area of the ring contained between their circumferences. *Ans.* 50.2656.

2. What is the area of the ring, when the diameters of the circles are 10 and 20? *Ans.* 235.62.

MENSURATION OF VOLUMES.

---

1. MENSURATION OF VOLUMES is divided into two parts:

First. To measure the contents of their surfaces; and,
Second. To measure the contents of their volumes.

2. We have already seen, that the unit of measure for every plane surface is a square whose side is the unit of length.

A curved line, when expressed by numbers, is also referred to a unit of length, and its numerical value is the number of times which the line contains its unit. If, then, we suppose the linear unit to be reduced to a right line, and a square constructed on this line, this square will be the unit of measure for curved surfaces.

3. The unit of volume is a cube, the face of which is equal to the superficial unit in which the surface of the volume is estimated, and the edge is equal to the linear unit in which the linear dimensions of the volume are expressed (B. VII., P. 13, S. 1).

The following is a table for the measurement of volume:

1728	cubic inches	= 1	cubic foot.
27	cubic feet	= 1	cubic yard.
$4492\frac{1}{8}$	cubic feet	= 1	cubic rod

OF POLYEDRONS, OR, SURFACES BOUNDED BY PLANES.

4. To find the surface of a right prism.

Multiply the perimeter of the base by the altitude, and the product will be the convex surface (B. VII., P. 1). *To this add the area of the two bases, if the entire surface is required.*

Ex. 1. To find the surface of a cube, the length of each side being 20 feet. *Ans.* 2400 *sq. ft.*

2. To find the whole surface of a triangular prism, whose base is an equilateral triangle, having each of its sides equal to 18 inches, and altitude 20 feet. *Ans.* 91.949 *sq. ft.*

3. What must be paid for lining a rectangular cistern with lead, at 2*d*. a pound, the thickness of the lead being such as to require 7*lbs*. for each square foot of surface; the inner dimensions of the cistern being as follows, viz.: the length 3 feet 2 inches, the breadth 2 feet 8 inches, and the depth 2 feet 6 inches? *Ans.* 2*l.* 3*s.* 10$\frac{5}{9}$*d.*

5. To find the surface of a right pyramid.

Multiply the perimeter of the base by half the slant height, and the product will be the convex surface (B. VII., P. 4): *to this add the area of the base, when the entire surface is required.*

Ex. 1. To find the convex surface of a right triangular pyramid, the slant height being 20 feet, and each side of the base 3 feet.

Ans. 90 *sq. ft.*

2. What is the entire surface of a right pyramid, whose slant height is 15 feet, and the base a pentagon, of which each side is 25 feet? *Ans.* 2012.798 *sq. ft.*

6. To find the convex surface of the frustum of a right pyramid.

Multiply the half sum of the perimeters of the two bases by the slant height of the frustum, and the product will be the convex surface (B. VII., P. 4, C).

Ex. 1. How many square feet are there in the convex surface of the frustum of a square pyramid, whose slant height is 10 feet, each side of the lower base 3 feet 4 inches, and each side of the upper base 2 feet 2 inches? *Ans.* 110 *sq. ft.*

2. What is the convex surface of the frustum of an heptagonal pyramid whose slant height is 55 feet, each side of the lower base 8 feet, and each side of the upper base 4 feet? *Ans.* 2310 *sq. ft.*

7. To find the contents of a prism.

1. *Find the area of the base.*
2. *Multiply the area of the base by the altitude, and the product will be the contents of the prism* (B. VII., P. XIV).

Ex. 1. What are the contents of a cube whose side is 24 inches?

Ans. 13824 *cu. in.*

2. How many cubic feet in a block of marble, of which the length is 3 feet 2 inches, breadth 2 feet 8 inches, and height or thickness 2 feet 6 inches? *Ans.* 21$\frac{1}{9}$.

3. How many gallons of water, ale measure, will a cistern contain, whose dimensions are the same as in the last example. *Ans.* $129\frac{17}{47}$.

4. Required the contents of a triangular prism, whose height is 10 feet, and the three sides of its triangular base 3, 4, and 5 feet. *Ans.* 60.

8. To find the contents of a pyramid.

Multiply the area of the base by one-third of the altitude, and the product will be the contents (B. VII., P. 17).

Ex. 1. Required the contents of a square pyramid, each side of its base being 30, and the altitude 25. *Ans.* 7500.

2. To find the contents of a triangular pyramid, whose altitude is 30, and each side of the base 3 feet. *Ans.* 38.9711 *cu. ft.*

3. To find the contents of a triangular pyramid, its altitude being 14 feet 6 inches, and the three sides of its base 5, 6, and 7 feet. *Ans.* 71.0352 *cu. ft.*

4. What are the contents of a pentagonal pyramid, its altitude being 12 feet, and each side of its base 2 feet? *Ans.* 27.5276 *cu. ft.*

5. What are the contents of an hexagonal pyramid, whose altitude is 6.4 feet, and each side of its base 6 inches? *Ans.* 1.38564 *cu. ft.*

9. To find the contents of the frustum of a pyramid.

Add together the areas of the two bases of the frustum, and a mean proportional between them, and then multiply the sum by one-third of the altitude (B. VII., P. 18).

Ex. 1. To find the number of cubic feet in a piece of timber, whose bases are squares, each side of the lower base being 15 inches, and each side of the upper base 6 inches, the altitude being 24 feet. *Ans.* 19.5.

2. Required the contents of a pentagonal frustum, whose altitude is 5 feet, each side of the lower base 18 inches, and each side of the upper base 6 inches. *Ans.* 9.31925 *cu. ft.*

DEFINITIONS.

10. A WEDGE is a solid bounded by five planes: viz., a rectangle, $ABCD$, called the base of the wedge; two trapezoids $ABHG$, $DCHG$, which are called the sides of the wedge, and which intersect each other in the edge GH; and the two triangles GDA, HCB, which are called the ends of the wedge.

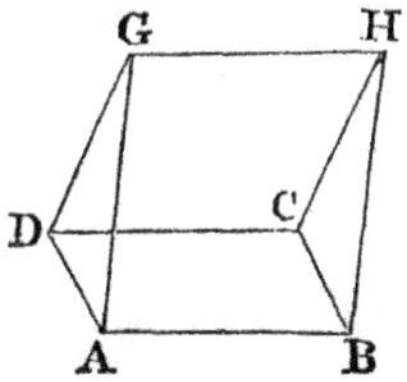

When AB, the length of the base, is equal to GH, the trapezoids $ABHG$, $DCHG$, become parallelograms, and the wedge is then one-half the parallelopipedon described on the base $ABCD$, and having the same altitude with the wedge.

The altitude of the wedge is the perpendicular let fall from any point of the line GH, on the base $ABCD$.

11. A Rectangle Prismoid is a volume resembling the frustum of a quadrangular pyramid. The upper and lower bases are rectangles, having their corresponding sides parallel, and the convex surface is made up of four trapezoids. The altitude of the prismoid is the perpendicular distance between its bases.

TO FIND THE CONTENTS OF THE WEDGE.

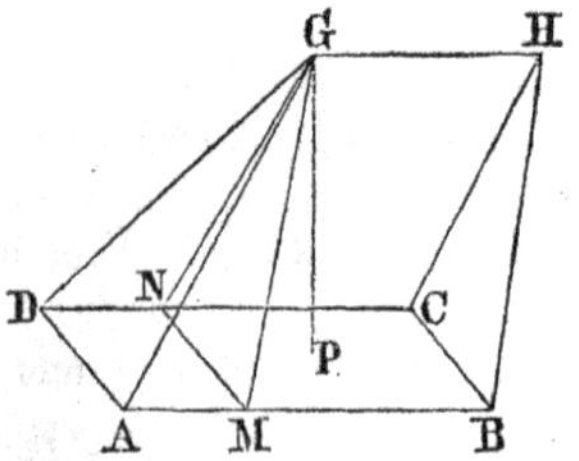

Let $L = AB$, the length of the base, $l = GH$, the length of the edge, $b = BC$, the breadth of the base, $h = PG$, the altitude of the wedge.

Then, $L - l = AB - GH = AM$.

Suppose AB, the length of the base, to be equal to GH, the length of the edge, the volume will then be equal to half the parallelopipedon, having the same base and the same altitude (B. VII., P. 7). Hence, the volume will be equal to $\frac{1}{2}blh$ (B. VII., P. 14).

If the length of the base is greater than that of the edge, let a section MNG be made parallel to the end BCH. The wedge will then be divided into the triangular prism $BCH\text{-}G$, and the quadrangular pyramid $G\text{-}AMND$.

Then, the volume of the prism, $= \frac{1}{2}bhl$;

the volume of the pyramid $= \frac{1}{3}bh(L - l)$;

and their sum,

$$\tfrac{1}{2}bhl + \tfrac{1}{3}bh(L-l) = \tfrac{1}{6}bh3l + \tfrac{1}{6}bh2L - \tfrac{1}{6}bh2l = \tfrac{1}{6}bh(2L + l).$$

If the length of the base is less than the length of the edge, the volume of the wedge will be equal to the difference between the prism and pyramid, and we shall have for the volume of the wedge,

$$\tfrac{1}{2}bhl - \tfrac{1}{3}bh(l - L) = \tfrac{1}{6}bh3l - \tfrac{1}{6}bh2l + \tfrac{1}{6}bh2L = \tfrac{1}{6}bh(2L + l).$$

Ex. 1. If the base of a wedge is 40 by 20 feet, the edge 35 feet, and the altitude 10 feet, what are the contents? *Ans.* 3833.33 *cu. ft.*

2. The base of a wedge being 18 feet by 9, the edge 20 feet, and the altitude 6 feet, what are the contents? *Ans.* 504 *cu. ft.*

12. To find the contents of a rectangular prismoid.

Add together the areas of the two bases and four times the area of a parallel section at equal distances from the bases: then multiply the sum by one-sixth of the altitude.

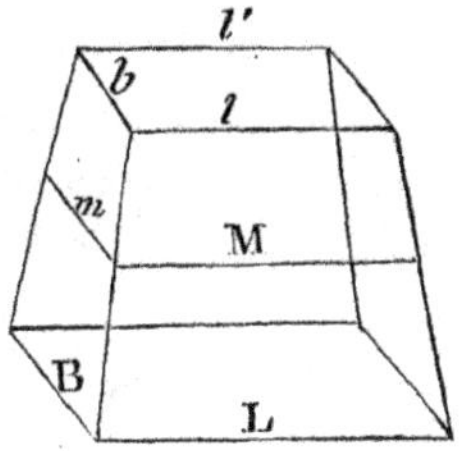

Let L and B denote the length and breadth of the lower base, l and b the length and breadth of the upper base, M and m the length and breadth of the section equidistant from the bases, and h the altitude of the prismoid.

Through the diagonal edges L and l' let a plane be passed, and it will divide the prismoid into two wedges, having for bases, the bases of the prismoid, and for edges the lines L and $l' = l$.

The contents of these wedges, and consequently, of the prismoid, are

$$\tfrac{1}{6}Bh(2L + l) + \tfrac{1}{6}bh(2l + L) = \tfrac{1}{6}h(2BL + Bl + 2bl + bL)$$

$$= \tfrac{1}{6}h(BL + Bl + bL + bl + BL + bl).$$

But, since M is equally distant from L and l, we have,

$$2M = L + l, \quad \text{and} \quad 2m = B + b;$$

hence, $4Mm = (L + l) \times (B + b) = BL + Bl + bL + bl.$

Substituting $4Mm$ for its value, in the preceding equation, we have for the contents,

$$\tfrac{1}{6}h(BL + bl + 4Mm).$$

REMARK.—This rule may be applied to any prismoid whatever. For, whatever be the form of the bases, there may be inscribed in each the same number of rectangles, and the number of these rectangles may be made so great that their sum in each base will differ from that base, by less than any assignable quantity. Now, if on these rectangles, rectangular prismoids be constructed, their sum will differ from the given prismoid by less than any assignable quantity; hence, the rule is general.

Ex. 1. One of the bases of a rectangular prismoid is 25 feet by 20, the other 15 feet by 10, and the altitude 12 feet; required the contents. *Ans.* 3700 *cu. ft.*

2. What are the contents of a stick of hewn timber, whose ends are 30 inches by 27, and 24 inches by 18, its length being 24 feet?
Ans. 102 *cu. ft.*

OF THE MEASURES OF THE THREE ROUND BODIES.

13. To find the surface of a cylinder.

Multiply the circumference of the base by the altitude, and the product will be the convex surface (B. VIII. P. 1). *To this add the areas of the two bases, when the entire surface is required.*

Ex. 1. What is the convex surface of a cylinder, the diameter of whose base is 20, and whose altitude is 50? *Ans.* 3141.6.

2. Required the entire surface of a cylinder, whose altitude is 20 feet, and the diameter of its base 2 feet. *Ans.* 131.9472 *sq. ft.*

14. To find the convex surface of a cone.

Multiply the circumference of the base by half the slant height (B. VIII., P. 3); *and to this product add the area of the base, if the entire surface is required.*

Ex. 1. Required the convex surface of a cone, whose slant height is 50 feet, and the diameter of its base 8½ feet? *Ans.* 667.59 *sq. ft.*

2. Required the entire surface of a cone, whose slant height is 36, and the diameter of its base 18 feet. *Ans.* 1272.348 *sq. ft.*

15. To find the surface of a frustum of a cone.

Multiply the slant height of the frustum by half the sum of the circumference of the two bases, for the convex surface (B. VIII. P. 4); *and to this product add the areas of the two bases, if the entire surface is required.*

Ex. 1. To find the convex surface of the frustum of a cone, the slant height of the frustum being 12½ feet, and the circumferences of the bases 8.4 feet and 6 feet. *Ans.* 90 *cu. ft.*

2. To find the entire surface of the frustum of a cone, the slant height being 16 feet, and the radii of the bases 3 feet and 2 feet.
Ans. 292.1688 *cu. ft.*

16. To find the contents of a cylinder.

Multiply the area of the base by the altitude (B. VIII., P. 2).

Ex. 1. Required the contents of a cylinder whose altitude is 12 feet, and the diameter of its base 15 feet. *Ans.* 2120.58 *cu. ft.*

2. Required the contents of a cylinder whose altitude is 20 feet, and the circumference of whose base is 5 feet 6 inches.

Ans. 48.144 *cu. ft.*

17. To find the contents of a cone.

Multiply the area of the base by the altitude, and take one-third of the product (B. VIII., P. 5).

Ex. 1. Required the contents of a cone whose altitude is 27 feet, and the diameter of the base 10 feet. *Ans.* 706.86 *cu. ft.*

2. Required the contents of a cone whose altitude is $10\frac{1}{2}$ feet, and the circumference of its base 9 feet. *Ans.* 22.56 *cu. ft.*

18. To find the contents of a frustum of a cone.

Add together the areas of the two bases and a mean proportional between them, and then multiply the sum by one third of the altitude (B. VIII., P. 6).

Ex. 1. To find the contents of the frustum of a cone, the altitude being 18, the diameter of lower base 8, and that of the upper base 4.

Ans. 527.7888.

2. What are the contents of the frustum of a cone, the altitude being 25, the circumference of the lower base 20, and that of the upper base 10? *Ans.* 464.216.

3. If a cask, which is composed of two equal conic frustums joined together at their larger bases, have its bung diameter 28 inches, the head diameter 20 inches, and the length 40 inches, how many gallons of wine will it contain, there being 231 cubic inches in a gallon?

Ans. 79.0613.

19. To find the surface of a spherical zone.

Multiply the altitude of the zone by the circumference of a great circle of the sphere, and the product will be the surface (B. VIII., P. 10, C. 2).

Ex. 1. The diameter of a sphere being 42 inches, what is the convex surface of a zone whose altitude is 9 inches.

Ans. 1187.5248 *sq. in.*

2. If the diameter of a sphere is $12\frac{1}{2}$ feet, what will be the surface of a zone whose altitude is 2 feet? *Ans.* 78.54 *sq. ft*

20. To find the contents of a sphere.

1. *Multiply the surface by one-third of the radius* (B. VIII., P. 14). Or,
2. *Cube the diameter and multiply the number thus found by* $\frac{1}{6}\pi$: *that is, by* 0.5236 (B. VIII., P. 14, S. 3).

Ex. 1. What are the contents of a sphere whose diameter is 12? *Ans.* 904.7808.

2. What are the contents of the earth, if the mean diameter b taken equal to 7918.7 miles. *Ans.* 259992792083 *cu. miles.*

21. To find the contents of a spherical segment.

Find the areas of the two bases, and multiply their sum by half the height of the segment; to this product add the contents of a sphere whose diameter is equal to the height of the segment (B. VIII., P. 17)

REMARK.—When the segment has but one base, the other is to be considered equal to 0 (B. VIII., D. 15).

Ex. 1. What are the contents of a spherical segment, the diameter of the sphere being 40, and the distances from the centre to the bases 16 and 10? *Ans.* 4297.7088.

2. What are the contents of a spherical segment with one base the diameter of the sphere being 8, and the altitude of the segment 2 feet? *Ans.* 41.888.

3. What are the contents of a spherical segment with one base, the diameter of the sphere being 20, and the altitude of the segment 9 feet? *Ans.* 1781.2872.

22. To find the contents of a spherical triangle.

1. *Compute the surface of the sphere on which the triangle is formed, and divide it by* 8; *the quotient will be the surface of the tri-rectangular triangle.*
2. *Add the three angles together; from their sum subtract* 180°, *and divide the remainder by* 90°: *then multiply the tri-rectangular triangle by this quotient, and the product will be the surface of the triangle* (B. IX., P. 18).

Ex. 1. Required the contents of a triangle described on a sphere, whose diameter is 30 feet, the angles being 140°, 92°, and 68°.

Ans. 471.24 *sq. ft.*

2. Required the contents of a triangle described on a sphere of 20 feet diameter, the angles being 120° each. *Ans.* 314.16 *sq. ft.*

23. To find the contents of a spherical polygon.

1. *Find the tri-rectangular triangle as before.*
2. *From the sum of all the angles take the product of two right angles by the number of sides less two. Divide the remainder by* 90°, *and multiply the tri-rectangular triangle by the quotient: the product will be the surface of the polygon* (B. IX., P. 19).

Ex. 1. What are the contents of a polygon of seven sides, described on a sphere whose diameter is 17 feet, the sum of the angles being 1080? *Ans.* 226.98.

2. What are the contents of a regular polygon of eight sides, described on a sphere whose diameter is 30, each angle of the polygon being 140°? *Ans.* 157.08 *cu. ft.*

OF THE REGULAR POLYEDRONS.

24. In determining the contents of the regular polyedrons, it becomes necessary to know, for each of them, the angle contained between any two of the adjacent faces. The determination of this angle involves the following property of a regular polygon, viz.:

Half the diagonal which joins the extremities of two adjacent sides of a regular polygon, is equal to the side of the polygon multiplied by the cosine of the angle which is obtained by dividing 360° *by twice the number of sides: the radius being equal to* 1.

For, let $ABCDE$ be any regular polygon. Draw the diagonal AC, and from the centre F, draw FG perpendicular to AB. Draw also, AF, FB; the latter will be perpendicular to the diagonal AC, and will bisect it at H (B. III., P. 6, S).

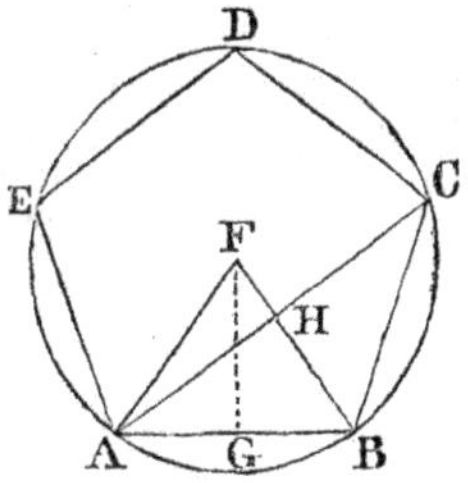

Let the number of sides of the polygon be designated by n: then,

$$AFB = \frac{360°}{n}, \quad \text{and} \quad AFG = CAB = \frac{360°}{2n}.$$

But, in the right-angled triangle ABH, we have,

$$AH = AB \cos A = AB \cos \frac{360^\circ}{2n} \text{ (Trig., Art. 30).}$$

REMARK I.—When the polygon in question is the equilateral triangle, the diagonal becomes a side, and consequently, half the diagonal becomes half a side of the triangle.

REMARK II.—The perpendicular $BH = AB \sin \dfrac{360^\circ}{2n}$.

25. To determine the angle included between two adjacent faces of either of the regular polyedrons, let us suppose a plane to be passed perpendicular to the axis of a polyedron angle, and through the vertices of the polyedral angles which lie adjacent. This plane will intersect the convex surface of the polyedron in a regular polygon; the number of sides of this polygon will be equal to the number of planes which meet at the vertex of either of the polyedral angles, and each side will be a diagonal of one of the equal faces of the polyedron.

Let D be the vertex of a polyedral angle, CD the intersection of two adjacent faces, and $ACBH$ the section made in the convex surface of the polyedron by a plane perpendicular to the axis through D.

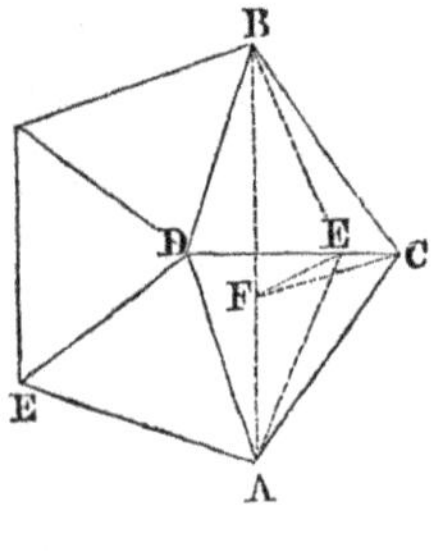

Draw any diagonal of this section, as AB. Then, through AB let a plane be drawn perpendicular to CD, produced, if necessary, and suppose AE, BE, to be the lines in which this plane intersects the adjacent faces. Draw EF perpendicular to AB: then will AEB be the angle included between the adjacent faces, and AEF will be half that angle, which we will represent by $\frac{1}{2}A$.

Then, if we denote by n the number of faces which meet at the vertex of the polyedral angle, and by m the number of sides of each face, we shall have, from what has already been shown,

$$BF = BC \cos \frac{360^\circ}{2n}, \quad \text{and} \quad EB = BC \sin \frac{360^\circ}{2m}.$$

But, $\quad \dfrac{BF}{EB} = \sin FEB = \sin \frac{1}{2}A$, to the radius 1.

Hence,
$$\sin \tfrac{1}{2}A = \frac{\cos \frac{360^\circ}{2n}}{\sin \frac{360^\circ}{2m}}.$$

This formula gives, for the diedral angle formed by any two adjacent faces of the

Tetraedron, ...	70° 31′ 42″
Hexaedron, ...	90°
Octaedron, ...	109° 28′ 18″
Dodecaedron, . . .	116° 33′ 54″
Icosaedron, ...	138° 11′ 23″

Having thus found the diedral angle included between any two adjacent faces, we can easily calculate the perpendicular let fall from the centre of the polyedron on one of its faces, when the faces themselves are known.

The following table shows the contents of surface and volume of the regular polyedrons, when the edges are equal to 1 :

A TABLE OF REGULAR POLYEDRONS WHOSE EDGES ARE 1.

NAMES.	NO. OF FACES.	SURFACE.	VOLUMES.
Tetraedron, . .	4 . .	1.7320508 . .	0.1178513
Hexaedron, . .	6 . .	6.0000000 . .	1.0000000
Octaedron, . .	8 . .	3.4641016 . .	0.4714045
Dodecaedron, .	12 . .	20.6457288 . .	7.6631189
Icosaedron, . .	20 . .	8.6602540 . .	2.1816950

26. To find the contents of a regular polyedron.

1. *Multiply the surface by one-third of the perpendicular let fall from the centre on one of the faces, and the product will be the contents.*

Or, 2. *Multiply the cube of one of the edges by the contents of a similar polyedron whose edge is* 1.

The first rule results from the division of the polyedron into as many equal pyramids as it has faces, having their common vertex at the centre of the polyedron. The second is proved by considering that two regular polyedrons, having the same number of faces, may be divided into an equal number of similar pyramids, and that the sum of the pyramids which make up one of the polyedrons will be to the sum of the pyramids which make up the other polyedron, as a pyramid of the first sum to a pyramid of the second (B. II., P. 10); that is, as the cubes of their homologous edges (B. VII., P. 20); that is, as the cubes of the edges of the polyedrons.

Ex. 1. What are the contents of a tetraedron whose edge is 15?
Ans. 397.75.

2. What are the contents of a hexaedron whose edge is 12?
Ans. 1728.

3. What are the contents of a octaedron whose edge is 20?
Ans. 3771.236.

4. What are the contents of a dodecaedron whose edge is 25?
Ans. 119736.2328.

5. What are the contents of an icosaedron whose edge is 20?
Ans. 17453.56.

A TABLE

OF

LOGARITHMS OF NUMBERS

FROM 1 TO 10,000.

N.	Log.	N.	Log.	N.	Log.	N.	Log.
1	0·000000	26	1·414973	51	1·707570	76	1·880814
2	0·301030	27	1·431364	52	1·716003	77	1·886491
3	0·477121	28	1·447158	53	1·724276	78	1·892095
4	0·602060	29	1·462398	54	1·732394	79	1·897627
5	0·698970	30	1·477121	55	1·740363	80	1·903090
6	0·778151	31	1·491362	56	1·748188	81	1·908485
7	0·845098	32	1·505150	57	1·755875	82	1·913814
8	0·903090	33	1·518514	58	1·763428	83	1·919078
9	0·954243	34	1·531479	59	1·770852	84	1·924279
10	1·000000	35	1·544068	60	1·778151	85	1·929419
11	1·041393	36	1·556303	61	1·785330	86	1·934498
12	1·079181	37	1·568202	62	1·792392	87	1·939519
13	1·113943	38	1·579784	63	1·799341	88	1·944483
14	1·146128	39	1·591065	64	1·806181	89	1·949390
15	1·176091	40	1·602060	65	1·812913	90	1·954243
16	1·204120	41	1·612784	66	1·819544	91	1·959041
17	1·230449	42	1·623249	67	1·826075	92	1·963788
18	1·255273	43	1·633468	68	1·832509	93	1·968483
19	1·278754	44	1·643453	69	1·838849	94	1·973128
20	1·301030	45	1·653213	70	1·845098	95	1·977724
21	1·322219	46	1·662758	71	1·851258	96	1·982271
22	1·342423	47	1·672098	72	1·857333	97	1·986772
23	1·361728	48	1·681241	73	1·863323	98	1·991226
24	1·380211	49	1·690196	74	1·869232	99	1·995635
25	1·397940	50	1·698970	75	1·875061	100	2·000000

REMARK. In the following table, in the nine right hand columns of each page, where the first or leading figures change from 9's to 0's, points or dots are introduced instead of the 0's, to catch the eye, and to indicate that from thence the two figures of the Logarithm to be taken from the second column, stand in the next line below.

N.	0	1	2	3	4	5	6	7	8	9	D.
100	000000	0434	0868	1301	1734	2166	2598	3029	3461	3891	432
101	4321	4751	5181	5609	6038	6466	6894	7321	7748	8174	428
102	8600	9026	9451	9876	•300	•724	1147	1570	1993	2415	424
103	012837	3259	3680	4100	4521	4940	5360	5779	6197	6616	419
104	7033	7451	7868	8284	8700	9116	9532	9947	•361	•775	416
105	021189	1603	2016	2428	2841	3252	3664	4075	4486	4896	412
106	5306	5715	6125	6533	6942	7350	7757	8164	8571	8978	408
107	9384	9789	•195	•600	1004	1408	1812	2216	2619	3021	404
108	033424	3826	4227	4628	5029	5430	5830	6230	6629	7028	400
109	7426	7825	8223	8620	9017	9414	9811	•207	•602	•998	396
110	041393	1787	2182	2576	2969	3362	3755	4148	4540	4932	393
111	5323	5714	6105	6495	6885	7275	7664	8053	8442	8830	389
112	9218	9606	9993	•380	•766	1153	1538	1924	2309	2694	386
113	053078	3463	3846	4230	4613	4996	5378	5760	6142	6524	382
114	6905	7286	7666	8046	8426	8805	9185	9563	9942	•320	379
115	060698	1075	1452	1829	2206	2582	2958	3333	3709	4083	376
116	4458	4832	5206	5580	5953	6326	6699	7071	7443	7815	372
117	8186	8557	8928	9298	9668	••38	•407	•776	1145	1514	369
118	071882	2250	2617	2985	3352	3718	4085	4451	4816	5182	366
119	5547	5912	6276	6640	7004	7368	7731	8094	8457	8819	363
120	079181	9543	9904	•266	•626	•987	1347	1707	2067	2426	360
121	082785	3144	3503	3861	4219	4576	4934	5291	5647	6004	357
122	6360	6716	7071	7426	7781	8136	8490	8845	9198	9552	355
123	9905	•258	•611	•963	1315	1667	2018	2370	2721	3071	351
124	093422	3772	4122	4471	4820	5169	5518	5866	6215	6562	349
125	6910	7257	7604	7951	8298	8644	8990	9335	9681	••26	346
126	100371	0715	1059	1403	1747	2091	2434	2777	3119	3462	343
127	3804	4146	4487	4828	5169	5510	5851	6191	6531	6871	340
128	7210	7549	7888	8227	8565	8903	9241	9579	9916	•253	338
129	110590	0926	1263	1599	1934	2270	2605	2940	3275	3609	335
130	113943	4277	4611	4944	5278	5611	5943	6276	6608	6940	333
131	7271	7603	7934	8265	8595	8926	9256	9586	9915	•245	330
132	120574	0903	1231	1560	1888	2216	2544	2871	3198	3525	328
133	3852	4178	4504	4830	5156	5481	5806	6131	6456	6781	325
134	7105	7429	7753	8076	8399	8722	9045	9368	9690	••12	323
135	130334	0655	0977	1298	1619	1939	2260	2580	2900	3219	321
136	3539	3858	4177	4496	4814	5133	5451	5769	6086	6403	318
137	6721	7037	7354	7671	7987	8303	8618	8934	9249	9564	315
138	9879	•194	•508	•822	1136	1450	1763	2076	2389	2702	314
139	143015	3327	3639	3951	4263	4574	4885	5196	5507	5818	311
140	146128	6438	6748	7058	7367	7676	7985	8294	8603	8911	309
141	9219	9527	9835	•142	•449	•756	1063	1370	1676	1982	307
142	152288	2594	2900	3205	3510	3815	4120	4424	4728	5032	305
143	5336	5640	5943	6246	6549	6852	7154	7457	7759	8061	303
144	8362	8664	8965	9266	9567	9868	•168	•469	•769	1068	301
145	161368	1667	1967	2266	2564	2863	3161	3460	3758	4055	299
146	4353	4650	4947	5244	5541	5838	6134	6430	6726	7022	297
147	7317	7613	7908	8203	8497	8792	9086	9380	9674	9968	295
148	170262	0555	0848	1141	1434	1726	2019	2311	2603	2895	293
149	3186	3478	3769	4060	4351	4641	4932	5222	5512	5802	291
150	176091	6381	6670	6959	7248	7536	7825	8113	8401	8689	289
151	8977	9264	9552	9839	•126	•413	•699	•985	1272	1558	287
152	181844	2129	2415	2700	2985	3270	3555	3839	4123	4407	285
153	4691	4975	5259	5542	5825	6108	6391	6674	6956	7239	283
154	7521	7803	8084	8366	8647	8928	9209	9490	9771	••51	281
155	190332	0612	0892	1171	1451	1730	2010	2289	2567	2846	279
156	3125	3403	3681	3959	4237	4514	4792	5069	5346	5623	278
157	5899	6176	6453	6729	7005	7281	7556	7832	8107	8382	276
158	8657	8932	9206	9481	9755	••29	•303	•577	•850	1124	274
159	201397	1670	1943	2216	2488	2761	3033	3305	3577	3848	272
N.	0	1	2	3	4	5	6	7	8	9	D.

N.	0	1	2	3	4	5	6	7	8	9	D.
160	204120	4391	4663	4934	5204	5475	5746	6016	6286	6556	271
161	6826	7096	7365	7634	7904	8173	8441	8710	8979	9247	269
162	9515	9783	••51	•319	•586	•853	1121	1388	1654	1921	267
163	212188	2454	2720	2986	3252	3518	3783	4049	4314	4579	266
164	4844	5109	5373	5638	5902	6166	6430	6694	6957	7221	264
165	7484	7747	8010	8273	8536	8798	9060	9323	9585	9846	262
166	220108	0370	0631	0892	1153	1414	1675	1936	2196	2456	261
167	2716	2976	3236	3496	3755	4015	4274	4533	4792	5051	259
168	5309	5568	5826	6084	6342	6600	6858	7115	7372	7630	258
169	7887	8144	8400	8657	8913	9170	9426	9682	9938	•193	256
170	230449	0704	0960	1215	1470	1724	1979	2234	2488	2742	254
171	2996	3250	3504	3757	4011	4264	4517	4770	5023	5276	253
172	5528	5781	6033	6285	6537	6789	7041	7292	7544	7795	252
173	8046	8297	8548	8799	9049	9299	9550	9800	••50	•300	250
174	240549	0799	1048	1297	1546	1795	2044	2293	2541	2790	249
175	3038	3286	3534	3782	4030	4277	4525	4772	5019	5266	248
176	5513	5759	6006	6252	6499	6745	6991	7237	7482	7728	246
177	7973	8219	8464	8709	8954	9198	9443	9687	9932	•176	245
178	250420	0664	0908	1151	1395	1638	1881	2125	2368	2610	243
179	2853	3096	3338	3580	3822	4064	4306	4548	4790	5031	242
180	255273	5514	5755	5996	6237	6477	6718	6958	7198	7439	241
181	7679	7918	8158	8398	8637	8877	9116	9355	9594	9833	239
182	260071	0310	0548	0787	1025	1263	1501	1739	1976	2214	238
183	2451	2688	2925	3162	3399	3636	3873	4109	4346	4582	237
184	4818	5054	5290	5525	5761	5996	6232	6467	6702	6937	235
185	7172	7406	7641	7875	8110	8344	8578	8812	9046	9279	234
186	9513	9746	9980	•213	•446	•679	•912	1144	1377	1609	233
187	271842	2074	2306	2538	2770	3001	3233	3464	3696	3927	232
188	4158	4389	4620	4850	5081	5311	5542	5772	6002	6232	230
189	6462	6692	6921	7151	7380	7609	7838	8067	8296	8525	229
190	278754	8982	9211	9439	9667	9895	•123	•351	•578	•806	228
191	281033	1261	1488	1715	1942	2169	2396	2622	2849	3075	227
192	3301	3527	3753	3979	4205	4431	4656	4882	5107	5332	226
193	5557	5782	6007	6232	6456	6681	6905	7130	7354	7578	225
194	7802	8026	8249	8473	8696	8920	9143	9366	9589	9812	223
195	290035	0257	0480	0702	0925	1147	1369	1591	1813	2034	222
196	2256	2478	2699	2920	3141	3363	3584	3804	4025	4246	221
197	4466	4687	4907	5127	5347	5567	5787	6007	6226	6446	220
198	6665	6884	7104	7323	7542	7761	7979	8198	8416	8635	219
199	8853	9071	9289	9507	9725	9943	•161	•378	•595	•813	218
200	301030	1247	1464	1681	1898	2114	2331	2547	2764	2980	217
201	3196	3412	3628	3844	4059	4275	4491	4706	4921	5136	216
202	5351	5566	5781	5996	6211	6425	6639	6854	7068	7282	215
203	7496	7710	7924	8137	8351	8564	8778	8991	9204	9417	213
204	9630	9843	••56	•268	•481	•693	•906	1118	1330	1542	212
205	311754	1966	2177	2389	2600	2812	3023	3234	3445	3656	211
206	3867	4078	4289	4499	4710	4920	5130	5340	5551	5760	210
207	5970	6180	6390	6599	6809	7018	7227	7436	7646	7854	209
208	8063	8272	8481	8689	8898	9106	9314	9522	9730	9938	208
209	320146	0354	0562	0769	0977	1184	1391	1598	1805	2012	207
210	322219	2426	2633	2839	3046	3252	3458	3665	3871	4077	206
211	4282	4488	4694	4899	5105	5310	5516	5721	5926	6131	205
212	6336	6541	6745	6950	7155	7359	7563	7767	7972	8176	204
213	8380	8583	8787	8991	9194	9398	9601	9805	•••8	•211	203
214	330414	0617	0819	1022	1225	1427	1630	1832	2034	2236	202
215	2438	2640	2842	3044	3246	3447	3649	3850	4051	4253	202
216	4454	4655	4856	5057	5257	5458	5658	5859	6059	6260	201
217	6460	6660	6860	7060	7260	7459	7659	7858	8058	8257	200
218	8456	8656	8855	9054	9253	9451	9650	9849	••47	•246	199
219	340444	0642	0841	1039	1237	1435	1632	1830	2028	2225	198

N. 0 1 2 3 4 5 6 7 8 9 D.

N.	0	1	2	3	4	5	6	7	8	9	D.
220	342423	2620	2817	3014	3212	3409	3606	3802	3999	4196	197
221	4392	4589	4785	4981	5178	5374	5570	5766	5962	6157	196
222	6353	6549	6744	6939	7135	7330	7525	7720	7915	8110	195
223	8305	8500	8694	8889	9083	9278	9472	9666	9860	••54	194
224	350248	0442	0636	0829	1023	1216	1410	1603	1796	1989	193
225	2183	2375	2568	2761	2954	3147	3339	3532	3724	3916	193
226	4108	4301	4493	4685	4876	5068	5260	5452	5643	5834	192
227	6026	6217	6408	6599	6790	6981	7172	7363	7554	7744	191
228	7935	8125	8316	8506	8696	8886	9076	9266	9456	9646	190
229	9835	••25	•215	•404	•593	•783	•972	1161	1350	1539	189
230	361728	1917	2105	2294	2482	2671	2859	3048	3236	3424	188
231	3612	3800	3988	4176	4363	4551	4739	4926	5113	5301	188
232	5488	5675	5862	6049	6236	6423	6610	6796	6983	7169	187
233	7356	7542	7729	7915	8101	8287	8473	8659	8845	9030	186
234	9216	9401	9587	9772	9958	•143	•328	•513	•698	•883	185
235	371068	1253	1437	1622	1806	1991	2175	2360	2544	2728	184
236	2912	3096	3280	3464	3647	3831	4015	4198	4382	4565	184
237	4748	4932	5115	5298	5481	5664	5846	6029	6212	6394	183
238	6577	6759	6942	7124	7306	7488	7670	7852	8034	8216	182
239	8398	8580	8761	8943	9124	9306	9487	9668	9849	••30	181
240	380211	0392	0573	0754	0934	1115	1296	1476	1656	1837	181
241	2017	2197	2377	2557	2737	2917	3097	3277	3456	3636	180
242	3815	3995	4174	4353	4533	4712	4891	5070	5249	5428	179
243	5606	5785	5964	6142	6321	6499	6677	6856	7034	7212	178
244	7390	7568	7746	7923	8101	8279	8456	8634	8811	8989	178
245	9166	9343	9520	9698	9875	••51	•228	•405	•582	•759	177
246	390935	1112	1288	1464	1641	1817	1993	2169	2345	2521	176
247	2697	2873	3048	3224	3400	3575	3751	3926	4101	4277	176
248	4452	4627	4802	4977	5152	5326	5501	5676	5850	6025	175
249	6199	6374	6548	6722	6896	7071	7245	7419	7592	7766	174
250	397940	8114	8287	8461	8634	8808	8981	9154	9328	9501	173
251	9674	9847	••20	•192	•365	•538	•711	•883	1056	1228	173
252	401401	1573	1745	1917	2089	2261	2433	2605	2777	2949	172
253	3121	3292	3464	3635	3807	3978	4149	4320	4492	4663	171
254	4834	5005	5176	5346	5517	5688	5858	6029	6199	6370	171
255	6540	6710	6881	7051	7221	7391	7561	7731	7901	8070	170
256	8240	8410	8579	8749	8918	9087	9257	9426	9595	9764	169
257	9933	•102	•271	•440	•609	•777	•946	1114	1283	1451	169
258	411620	1788	1956	2124	2293	2461	2629	2796	2964	3132	168
259	3300	3467	3635	3803	3970	4137	4305	4472	4639	4806	167
260	414973	5140	5307	5474	5641	5808	5974	6141	6308	6474	167
261	6641	6807	6973	7139	7306	7472	7638	7804	7970	8135	166
262	8301	8467	8633	8798	8964	9129	9295	9460	9625	9791	165
263	9956	•121	•286	•451	•616	•781	•945	1110	1275	1439	165
264	421604	1788	1933	2097	2261	2426	2590	2754	2918	3082	164
265	3246	3410	3574	3737	3901	4065	4228	4392	4555	4718	164
266	4882	5045	5208	5371	5534	5697	5860	6023	6186	6349	163
267	6511	6674	6836	6999	7161	7324	7486	7648	7811	7973	162
268	8135	8297	8459	8621	8783	8944	9106	9268	9429	9591	162
269	9752	9914	••75	•236	•398	•559	•720	•881	1042	1203	161
270	431364	1525	1685	1846	2007	2167	2328	2488	2649	2809	161
271	2969	3130	3290	3450	3610	3770	3930	4090	4249	4409	160
272	4569	4729	4888	5048	5207	5367	5526	5685	5844	6004	159
273	6163	6322	6481	6640	6798	6957	7116	7275	7433	7592	159
274	7751	7909	8067	8226	8384	8542	8701	8859	9017	9175	158
275	9333	9491	9648	9806	9964	•122	•279	•437	•594	•752	158
276	440909	1066	1224	1381	1538	1695	1852	2009	2166	2323	157
277	2480	2637	2793	2950	3106	3263	3419	3576	3732	3889	157
278	4045	4201	4357	4513	4669	4825	4981	5137	5293	5449	156
279	5604	5760	5915	6071	6226	6382	6537	6692	6848	7003	155
N.	0	1	2	3	4	5	6	7	8	9	D.

N.	0	1	2	3	4	5	6	7	8	9	D.
280	447158	7313	7468	7623	7778	7933	8088	8242	8397	8552	155
281	8706	8861	9015	9170	9324	9478	9633	9787	9941	••95	154
282	450249	0403	0557	0711	0865	1018	1172	1326	1479	1633	154
283	1786	1940	2093	2247	2400	2553	2706	2859	3012	3165	153
284	3318	3471	3624	3777	3930	4082	4235	4387	4540	4692	153
285	4845	4997	5150	5302	5454	5606	5758	5910	6062	6214	152
286	6366	6518	6670	6821	6973	7125	7276	7428	7579	7731	152
287	7882	8033	8184	8336	8487	8638	8789	8940	9091	9242	151
288	9392	9543	9694	9845	9995	•146	•296	•447	•597	•748	151
289	460898	1048	1198	1348	1499	1649	1799	1948	2098	2248	150
290	462398	2548	2697	2847	2997	3146	3296	3445	3594	3744	150
291	3893	4042	4191	4340	4490	4639	4788	4936	5085	5234	149
292	5383	5532	5680	5829	5977	6126	6274	6423	6571	6719	149
293	6868	7016	7164	7312	7460	7608	7756	7904	8052	8200	148
294	8347	8495	8643	8790	8938	9085	9233	9380	9527	9675	148
295	9822	9969	•116	•263	•410	•557	•704	•851	•998	1145	147
296	471292	1438	1585	1732	1878	2025	2171	2318	2464	2610	146
297	2756	2903	3049	3195	3341	3487	3633	3779	3925	4071	146
298	4216	4362	4508	4653	4799	4944	5090	5235	5381	5526	146
299	5671	5816	5962	6107	6252	6397	6542	6687	6832	6976	145
300	477121	7266	7411	7555	7700	7844	7989	8133	8278	8422	145
301	8566	8711	8855	8999	9143	9287	9431	9575	9719	9863	144
302	480007	0151	0294	0438	0582	0725	0869	1012	1156	1299	144
303	1443	1586	1729	1872	2016	2159	2302	2445	2588	2731	143
304	2874	3016	3159	3302	3445	3587	3730	3872	4015	4157	143
305	4300	4442	4585	4727	4869	5011	5153	5295	5437	5579	142
306	5721	5863	6005	6147	6289	6430	6572	6714	6855	6997	142
307	7138	7280	7421	7563	7704	7845	7986	8127	8269	8410	141
308	8551	8692	8833	8974	9114	9255	9396	9537	9677	9818	141
309	9958	••99	•239	•380	•520	•661	•801	•941	1081	1222	140
310	491362	1502	1642	1782	1922	2062	2201	2341	2481	2621	140
311	2760	2900	3040	3179	3319	3458	3597	3737	3876	4015	139
312	4155	4294	4433	4572	4711	4850	4989	5128	5267	5406	139
313	5544	5683	5822	5960	6099	6238	6376	6515	6653	6791	139
314	6930	7068	7206	7344	7483	7621	7759	7897	8035	8173	138
315	8311	8448	8586	8724	8862	8999	9137	9275	9412	9550	138
316	9687	9824	9962	••99	•236	•374	•511	•648	•785	•922	137
317	501059	1196	1333	1470	1607	1744	1880	2017	2154	2291	137
318	2427	2564	2700	2837	2973	3109	3246	3382	3518	3655	136
319	3791	3927	4063	4199	4335	4471	4607	4743	4878	5014	136
320	505150	5286	5421	5557	5693	5828	5964	6099	6234	6370	136
321	6505	6640	6776	6911	7046	7181	7316	7451	7586	7721	135
322	7856	7991	8126	8260	8395	8530	8664	8799	8934	9068	135
323	9203	9337	9471	9606	9740	9874	•••9	•143	•277	•411	134
324	510545	0679	0813	0947	1081	1215	1349	1482	1616	1750	134
325	1883	2017	2151	2284	2418	2551	2684	2818	2951	3084	133
326	3218	3351	3484	3617	3750	3883	4016	4149	4282	4414	133
327	4548	4681	4813	4946	5079	5211	5344	5476	5609	5741	133
328	5874	6006	6139	6271	6403	6535	6668	6800	6932	7064	132
329	7196	7328	7460	7592	7724	7855	7987	8119	8251	8382	132
330	518514	8646	8777	8909	9040	9171	9303	9434	9566	9697	131
331	9828	9959	••90	•221	•353	•484	•615	•745	•876	1007	131
332	521138	1269	1400	1530	1661	1792	1922	2053	2183	2314	131
333	2444	2575	2705	2835	2966	3096	3226	3356	3486	3616	130
334	3746	3876	4006	4136	4266	4396	4526	4656	4785	4915	130
335	5045	5174	5304	5434	5563	5693	5822	5951	6081	6210	129
336	6339	6469	6598	6727	6856	6985	7114	7243	7372	7501	129
337	7630	7759	7888	8016	8145	8274	8402	8531	8660	8788	129
338	8917	9045	9174	9302	9430	9559	9687	9815	9943	••72	128
339	530200	0328	0456	0584	0712	0840	0968	1096	1223	1351	128
N.	0	1	2	3	4	5	6	7	8	9	D.

N.	0	1	2	3	4	5	6	7	8	9	D.
340	531479	1607	1734	1862	1990	2117	2245	2372	2500	2627	128
341	2754	2882	3009	3136	3264	3391	3518	3645	3772	3899	127
342	4026	4153	4280	4407	4534	4661	4787	4914	5041	5167	127
343	5294	5421	5547	5674	5800	5927	6053	6180	6306	6432	126
344	6558	6685	6811	6937	7063	7189	7315	7441	7567	7693	126
345	7819	7945	8071	8197	8322	8448	8574	8699	8825	8951	126
346	9076	9202	9327	9452	9578	9703	9829	9954	••79	•204	125
347	540329	0455	0580	0705	0830	0955	1080	1205	1330	1454	125
348	1579	1704	1829	1953	2078	2203	2327	2452	2576	2701	125
349	2825	2950	3074	3199	3323	3447	3571	3696	3820	3944	124
350	544068	4192	4316	4440	4564	4688	4812	4936	5060	5183	124
351	5307	5431	5555	5678	5802	5925	6049	6172	6296	6419	124
352	6543	6666	6789	6913	7036	7159	7282	7405	7529	7652	123
353	7775	7898	8021	8144	8267	8389	8512	8635	8758	8881	123
354	9003	9126	9249	9371	9494	9616	9739	9861	9984	•106	123
355	550228	0351	0473	0595	0717	0840	0962	1084	1206	1328	122
356	1450	1572	1694	1816	1938	2060	2181	2303	2425	2547	122
357	2668	2790	2911	3033	3155	3276	3398	3519	3640	3762	121
358	3883	4004	4126	4247	4368	4489	4610	4731	4852	4973	121
359	5094	5215	5336	5457	5578	5699	5820	5940	6061	6182	121
360	556303	6423	6544	6664	6785	6905	7026	7146	7267	7387	120
361	7507	7627	7748	7868	7988	8108	8228	8349	8469	8589	120
362	8709	8829	8948	9068	9188	9308	9428	9548	9667	9787	120
363	9907	••26	•146	•265	•385	•504	•624	•743	•863	•982	119
364	561101	1221	1340	1459	1578	1698	1817	1936	2055	2174	119
365	2293	2412	2531	2650	2769	2887	3006	3125	3244	3362	119
366	3481	3600	3718	3837	3955	4074	4192	4311	4429	4548	119
367	4666	4784	4903	5021	5139	5257	5376	5494	5612	5730	118
368	5848	5966	6084	6202	6320	6437	6555	6673	6791	6909	118
369	7026	7144	7262	7379	7497	7614	7732	7849	7967	8084	118
370	568202	8319	8436	8554	8671	8788	8905	9023	9140	9257	117
371	9374	9491	9608	9725	9842	9959	••76	•193	•309	•426	117
372	570543	0660	0776	0893	1010	1126	1243	1359	1476	1592	117
373	1709	1825	1942	2058	2174	2291	2407	2523	2639	2755	116
374	2872	2988	3104	3220	3336	3452	3568	3684	3800	3915	116
375	4031	4147	4263	4379	4494	4610	4726	4841	4957	5072	116
376	5188	5303	5419	5534	5650	5765	5880	5996	6111	6226	115
377	6341	6457	6572	6687	6802	6917	7032	7147	7262	7377	115
378	7492	7607	7722	7836	7951	8066	8181	8295	8410	8525	115
379	8639	8754	8868	8983	9097	9212	9326	9441	9555	9669	114
380	579784	9898	••12	•126	•241	•355	•469	•583	•697	•811	114
381	580925	1039	1153	1267	1381	1495	1608	1722	1836	1950	114
382	2063	2177	2291	2404	2518	2631	2745	2858	2972	3085	114
383	3199	3312	3426	3539	3652	3765	3879	3992	4105	4218	113
384	4331	4444	4557	4670	4783	4896	5009	5122	5235	5348	113
385	5461	5574	5686	5799	5912	6024	6137	6250	6362	6475	113
386	6587	6700	6812	6925	7037	7149	7262	7374	7486	7599	112
387	7711	7823	7935	8047	8160	8272	8384	8496	8608	8720	112
388	8832	8944	9056	9167	9279	9391	9503	9615	9726	9838	112
389	9950	••61	•173	•284	•396	•507	•619	•730	•842	•953	112
390	591065	1176	1287	1399	1510	1621	1732	1843	1955	2066	111
391	2177	2288	2399	2510	2621	2732	2843	2954	3064	3175	111
392	3286	3397	3508	3618	3729	3840	3950	4061	4171	4282	111
393	4393	4503	4614	4724	4834	4945	5055	5165	5276	5386	110
394	5496	5606	5717	5827	5937	6047	6157	6267	6377	6487	110
395	6597	6707	6817	6927	7037	7146	7256	7366	7476	7586	110
396	7695	7805	7914	8024	8134	8243	8353	8462	8572	8681	110
397	8791	8900	9009	9119	9228	9337	9446	9556	9665	9774	109
398	9883	9992	•101	•210	•319	•428	•537	•646	•755	•864	109
399	600973	1082	1191	1299	1408	1517	1625	1734	1843	1951	109
N.	0	1	2	3	4	5	6	7	8	9	D.

N.	0	1	2	3	4	5	6	7	8	9	D.
400	602060	2169	2277	2386	2494	2603	2711	2819	2928	3036	108
401	3144	3253	3361	3469	3577	3686	3794	3902	4010	4118	108
402	4226	4334	4442	4550	4658	4766	4874	4982	5089	5197	108
403	5305	5413	5521	5628	5736	5844	5951	6059	6166	6274	108
404	6381	6489	6596	6704	6811	6919	7026	7133	7241	7348	107
405	7455	7562	7669	7777	7884	7991	8098	8205	8312	8419	107
406	8526	8633	8740	8847	8954	9061	9167	9274	9381	9488	107
407	9594	9701	9808	9914	••21	•128	•234	•341	•447	•554	107
408	610660	0767	0873	0979	1086	1192	1298	1405	1511	1617	106
409	1723	1829	1936	2042	2148	2254	2360	2466	2572	2678	106
410	612784	2890	2996	3102	3207	3313	3419	3525	3630	3736	106
411	3842	3947	4053	4159	4264	4370	4475	4581	4686	4792	106
412	4897	5003	5108	5213	5319	5424	5529	5634	5740	5845	105
413	5950	6055	6160	6265	6370	6476	6581	6686	6790	6895	105
414	7000	7105	7210	7315	7420	7525	7629	7734	7839	7943	105
415	8048	8153	8257	8362	8466	8571	8676	8780	8884	8989	105
416	9093	9198	9302	9406	9511	9615	9719	9824	9928	••32	104
417	620136	0240	0344	0448	0552	0656	0760	0864	0968	1072	104
418	1176	1280	1384	1488	1592	1695	1799	1903	2007	2110	104
419	2214	2318	2421	2525	2628	2732	2835	2939	3042	3146	104
420	623249	3353	3456	3559	3663	3766	3869	3973	4076	4179	103
421	4282	4385	4488	4591	4695	4798	4901	5004	5107	5210	103
422	5312	5415	5518	5621	5724	5827	5929	6032	6135	6238	103
423	6340	6443	6546	6648	6751	6853	6956	7058	7161	7263	103
424	7366	7468	7571	7673	7775	7878	7980	8082	8185	8287	102
425	8389	8491	8593	8695	8797	8900	9002	9104	9206	9308	102
426	9410	9512	9613	9715	9817	9919	••21	•123	•224	•326	102
427	630428	0530	0631	0733	0835	0936	1038	1139	1241	1342	102
428	1444	1545	1647	1748	1849	1951	2052	2153	2255	2356	101
429	2457	2559	2660	2761	2862	2963	3064	3165	3266	3367	101
430	633468	3569	3670	3771	3872	3973	4074	4175	4276	4376	100
431	4477	4578	4679	4779	4880	4981	5081	5182	5283	5383	100
432	5484	5584	5685	5785	5886	5986	6087	6187	6287	6388	100
433	6488	6588	6688	6789	6889	6989	7089	7189	7290	7390	100
434	7490	7590	7690	7790	7890	7990	8090	8190	8290	8389	99
435	8489	8589	8689	8789	8888	8988	9088	9188	9287	9387	99
436	9486	9586	9686	9785	9885	9984	••84	•183	•283	•382	99
437	640481	0581	0680	0779	0879	0978	1077	1177	1276	1375	99
438	1474	1573	1672	1771	1871	1970	2069	2168	2267	2366	99
439	2465	2563	2662	2761	2860	2959	3058	3156	3255	3354	99
440	643453	3551	3650	3749	3847	3946	4044	4143	4242	4340	98
441	4439	4537	4636	4734	4832	4931	5029	5127	5226	5324	98
442	5422	5521	5619	5717	5815	5913	6011	6110	6208	6306	98
443	6404	6502	6600	6698	6796	6894	6992	7089	7187	7285	98
444	7383	7481	7579	7676	7774	7872	7969	8067	8165	8262	98
445	8360	8458	8555	8653	8750	8848	8945	9043	9140	9237	97
446	9335	9432	9530	9627	9724	9821	9919	••16	•113	•210	97
447	650308	0405	0502	0599	0696	0793	0890	0987	1084	1181	97
448	1278	1375	1472	1569	1666	1762	1859	1956	2053	2150	97
449	2246	2343	2440	2536	2633	2730	2826	2923	3019	3116	97
450	653213	3309	3405	3502	3598	3695	3791	3888	3984	4080	96
451	4177	4273	4369	4465	4562	4658	4754	4850	4946	5042	96
452	5138	5235	5331	5427	5523	5619	5715	5810	5906	6002	96
453	6098	6194	6290	6386	6482	6577	6673	6769	6864	6960	96
454	7056	7152	7247	7343	7438	7534	7629	7725	7820	7916	96
455	8011	8107	8202	8298	8393	8488	8584	8679	8774	8870	95
456	8965	9060	9155	9250	9346	9441	9536	9631	9726	9821	95
457	9916	••11	•106	•201	•296	•391	•486	•581	•676	•771	95
458	660865	0960	1055	1150	1245	1339	1434	1529	1623	1718	95
459	1813	1907	2002	2096	2191	2286	2380	2475	2569	2663	95
N.	0	1	2	3	4	5	6	7	8	9	D.

N.	0	1	2	3	4	5	6	7	8	9	D.
460	662758	2852	2947	3041	3135	3230	3324	3418	3512	3607	94
461	3701	3795	3889	3983	4078	4172	4266	4360	4454	4548	94
462	4642	4736	4830	4924	5018	5112	5206	5299	5393	5487	94
463	5581	5675	5769	5862	5956	6050	6143	6237	6331	6424	94
464	6518	6612	6705	6799	6892	6986	7079	7173	7266	7360	94
465	7453	7546	7640	7733	7826	7920	8013	8106	8199	8293	93
466	8386	8479	8572	8665	8759	8852	8945	9038	9131	9224	93
467	9317	9410	9503	9596	9689	9782	9875	9967	••60	•153	93
468	670246	0339	0431	0524	0617	0710	0802	0895	0988	1080	93
469	1173	1265	1358	1451	1543	1636	1728	1821	1913	2005	93
470	672098	2190	2283	2375	2467	2560	2652	2744	2836	2929	92
471	3021	3113	3205	3297	3390	3482	3574	3666	3758	3850	92
472	3942	4034	4126	4218	4310	4402	4494	4586	4677	4769	92
473	4861	4953	5045	5137	5228	5320	5412	5503	5595	5687	92
474	5778	5870	5962	6053	6145	6236	6328	6419	6511	6602	92
475	6694	6785	6876	6968	7059	7151	7242	7333	7424	7516	91
476	7607	7698	7789	7881	7972	8063	8154	8245	8336	8427	91
477	8518	8609	8700	8791	8882	8973	9064	9155	9246	9337	91
478	9428	9519	9610	9700	9791	9882	9973	••63	•154	•245	91
479	680336	0426	0517	0607	0698	0789	0879	0970	1060	1151	91
480	681241	1332	1422	1513	1603	1693	1784	1874	1964	2055	90
481	2145	2235	2326	2416	2506	2596	2686	2777	2867	2957	90
482	3047	3137	3227	3317	3407	3497	3587	3677	3767	3857	90
483	3947	4037	4127	4217	4307	4396	4486	4576	4666	4756	90
484	4845	4935	5025	5114	5204	5294	5383	5473	5563	5652	90
485	5742	5831	5921	6010	6100	6189	6279	6368	6458	6547	89
486	6636	6726	6815	6904	6994	7083	7172	7261	7351	7440	89
487	7529	7618	7707	7796	7886	7975	8064	8153	8242	8331	89
488	8420	8509	8598	8687	8776	8865	8953	9042	9131	9220	89
489	9309	9398	9486	9575	9664	9753	9841	9930	••19	•107	89
490	690196	0285	0373	0462	0550	0639	0728	0816	0905	0993	89
491	1081	1170	1258	1347	1435	1524	1612	1700	1789	1877	88
492	1965	2053	2142	2230	2318	2406	2494	2583	2671	2759	88
493	2847	2935	3023	3111	3199	3287	3375	3463	3551	3639	88
494	3727	3815	3903	3991	4078	4166	4254	4342	4430	4517	88
495	4605	4693	4781	4868	4956	5044	5131	5219	5307	5394	88
496	5482	5569	5657	5744	5832	5919	6007	6094	6182	6269	87
497	6356	6444	6531	6618	6706	6793	6880	6968	7055	7142	87
498	7229	7317	7404	7491	7578	7665	7752	7839	7926	8014	87
499	8101	8188	8275	8362	8449	8535	8622	8709	8796	8883	87
500	698970	9057	9144	9231	9317	9404	9491	9578	9664	9751	87
501	9838	9924	••11	••98	•184	•271	•358	•444	•531	•617	87
502	700704	0790	0877	0963	1050	1136	1222	1309	1395	1482	86
503	1568	1654	1741	1827	1913	1999	2086	2172	2258	2344	86
504	2431	2517	2603	2689	2775	2861	2947	3033	3119	3205	86
505	3291	3377	3463	3549	3635	3721	3807	3893	3979	4065	86
506	4151	4236	4322	4408	4494	4579	4665	4751	4837	4922	86
507	5008	5094	5179	5265	5350	5436	5522	5607	5693	5778	86
508	5864	5949	6035	6120	6206	6291	6376	6462	6547	6632	85
509	6718	6803	6888	6974	7059	7144	7229	7315	7400	7485	85
510	707570	7655	7740	7826	7911	7996	8081	8166	8251	8336	85
511	8421	8506	8591	8676	8761	8846	8931	9015	9100	9185	85
512	9270	9355	9440	9524	9609	9694	9779	9863	9948	••33	85
513	710117	0202	0287	0371	0456	0540	0625	0710	0794	0879	85
514	0963	1048	1132	1217	1301	1385	1470	1554	1639	1723	84
515	1807	1892	1976	2060	2144	2229	2313	2397	2481	2566	84
516	2650	2734	2818	2902	2986	3070	3154	3238	3323	3407	84
517	3491	3575	3659	3742	3826	3910	3994	4078	4162	4246	84
518	4330	4414	4497	4581	4665	4749	4833	4916	5000	5084	84
519	5167	5251	5335	5418	5502	5586	5669	5753	5836	5920	84
N.	0	1	2	3	4	5	6	7	8	9	D.

N.	0	1	2	3	4	5	6	7	8	9	D.
520	716003	6087	6170	6254	6337	6421	6504	6588	6671	6754	83
521	6838	6921	7004	7088	7171	7254	7338	7421	7504	7587	83
522	7671	7754	7837	7920	8003	8086	8169	8253	8336	8419	83
523	8502	8585	8668	8751	8834	8917	9000	9083	9165	9248	83
524	9331	9414	9497	9580	9663	9745	9828	9911	9994	••77	83
525	720159	0242	0325	0407	0490	0573	0655	0738	0821	0903	83
526	0986	1068	1151	1233	1316	1398	1481	1563	1646	1728	82
527	1811	1893	1975	2058	2140	2222	2305	2387	2469	2552	82
528	2634	2716	2798	2881	2963	3045	3127	3209	3291	3374	82
529	3456	3538	3620	3702	3784	3866	3948	4030	4112	4194	82
530	724276	4358	4440	4522	4604	4685	4767	4849	4931	5013	82
531	5095	5176	5258	5340	5422	5503	5585	5667	5748	5830	82
532	5912	5993	6075	6156	6238	6320	6401	6483	6564	6646	82
533	6727	6809	6890	6972	7053	7134	7216	7297	7379	7460	81
534	7541	7623	7704	7785	7866	7948	8029	8110	8191	8273	81
535	8354	8435	8516	8597	8678	8759	8841	8922	9003	9084	81
536	9165	9246	9327	9408	9489	9570	9651	9732	9813	9893	81
537	9974	••55	•136	•217	•298	•378	•459	•540	•621	•702	81
538	730782	0863	0944	1024	1105	1186	1266	1347	1428	1508	81
539	1589	1669	1750	1830	1911	1991	2072	2152	2233	2313	81
540	732394	2474	2555	2635	2715	2796	2876	2956	3037	3117	80
541	3197	3278	3358	3438	3518	3598	3679	3759	3839	3919	80
542	3999	4079	4160	4240	4320	4400	4480	4560	4640	4720	80
543	4800	4880	4960	5040	5120	5200	5279	5359	5439	5519	80
544	5599	5679	5759	5838	5918	5998	6078	6157	6237	6317	80
545	6397	6476	6556	6635	6715	6795	6874	6954	7034	7113	80
546	7193	7272	7352	7431	7511	7590	7670	7749	7829	7908	79
547	7987	8067	8146	8225	8305	8384	8463	8543	8622	8701	79
548	8781	8860	8939	9018	9097	9177	9256	9335	9414	9493	79
549	9572	9651	9731	9810	9889	9968	••47	•126	•205	•284	79
550	740363	0442	0521	0600	0678	0757	0836	0915	0994	1073	79
551	1152	1230	1309	1388	1467	1546	1624	1703	1782	1860	79
552	1939	2018	2096	2175	2254	2332	2411	2489	2568	2647	79
553	2725	2804	2882	2961	3039	3118	3196	3275	3353	3431	78
554	3510	3588	3667	3745	3823	3902	3980	4058	4136	4215	78
555	4293	4371	4449	4528	4606	4684	4762	4840	4919	4997	78
556	5075	5153	5231	5309	5387	5465	5543	5621	5699	5777	78
557	5855	5933	6011	6089	6167	6245	6323	6401	6479	6556	78
558	6634	6712	6790	6868	6945	7023	7101	7179	7256	7334	78
559	7412	7489	7567	7645	7722	7800	7878	7955	8033	8110	78
560	748188	8266	8343	8421	8498	8576	8653	8731	8808	8885	77
561	8963	9040	9118	9195	9272	9350	9427	9504	9582	9659	77
562	9736	9814	9891	9968	••45	•123	•200	•277	•354	•431	77
563	750508	0586	0663	0740	0817	0894	0971	1048	1125	1202	77
564	1279	1356	1433	1510	1587	1664	1741	1818	1895	1972	77
565	2048	2125	2202	2279	2356	2433	2509	2586	2663	2740	77
566	2816	2893	2970	3047	3123	3200	3277	3353	3430	3506	77
567	3583	3660	3736	3813	3889	3966	4042	4119	4195	4272	77
568	4348	4425	4501	4578	4654	4730	4807	4883	4960	5036	76
569	5112	5189	5265	5341	5417	5494	5570	5646	5722	5799	76
570	755875	5951	6027	6103	6180	6256	6332	6408	6484	6560	76
571	6636	6712	6788	6864	6940	7016	7092	7168	7244	7320	76
572	7396	7472	7548	7624	7700	7775	7851	7927	8003	8079	76
573	8155	8230	8306	8382	8458	8533	8609	8685	8761	8836	76
574	8912	8988	9063	9139	9214	9290	9366	9441	9517	9592	76
575	9668	9743	9819	9894	9970	••45	•121	•196	•272	•347	75
576	760422	0498	0573	0649	0724	0799	0875	0950	1025	1101	75
577	1176	1251	1326	1402	1477	1552	1627	1702	1778	1853	75
578	1928	2003	2078	2153	2228	2303	2378	2453	2529	2604	75
579	2679	2754	2829	2904	2978	3053	3128	3203	3278	3353	75
N.	0	1	2	3	4	5	6	7	8	9	D.

N.	0	1	2	3	4	5	6	7	8	9	D.
580	763428	3503	3578	3653	3727	3802	3877	3952	4027	4101	75
581	4176	4251	4326	4400	4475	4550	4624	4699	4774	4848	75
582	4923	4998	5072	5147	5221	5296	5370	5445	5520	5594	75
583	5669	5743	5818	5892	5966	6041	6115	6190	6264	6338	74
584	6413	6487	6562	6636	6710	6785	6859	6933	7007	7082	74
585	7156	7230	7304	7379	7453	7527	7601	7675	7749	7823	74
586	7898	7972	8046	8120	8194	8268	8342	8416	8490	8564	74
587	8638	8712	8786	8860	8934	9008	9082	9156	9230	9303	74
588	9377	9451	9525	9599	9673	9746	9820	9894	9968	••42	74
589	770115	0189	0263	0336	0410	0484	0557	0631	0705	0778	74
590	770852	0926	0999	1073	1146	1220	1293	1367	1440	1514	74
591	1587	1661	1734	1808	1881	1955	2028	2102	2175	2248	73
592	2322	2395	2468	2542	2615	2688	2762	2835	2908	2981	73
593	3055	3128	3201	3274	3348	3421	3494	3567	3640	3713	73
594	3786	3860	3933	4006	4079	4152	4225	4298	4371	4444	73
595	4517	4590	4663	4736	4809	4882	4955	5028	5100	5173	73
596	5246	5319	5392	5465	5538	5610	5683	5756	5829	5902	73
597	5974	6047	6120	6193	6265	6338	6411	6483	6556	6629	73
598	6701	6774	6846	6919	6992	7064	7137	7209	7282	7354	73
599	7427	7499	7572	7644	7717	7789	7862	7934	8006	8079	72
600	778151	8224	8296	8368	8441	8513	8585	8658	8730	8802	72
601	8874	8947	9019	9091	9163	9236	9308	9380	9452	9524	72
602	9596	9669	9741	9813	9885	9957	••29	•101	•173	•245	72
603	780317	0389	0461	0533	0605	0677	0749	0821	0893	0965	72
604	1037	1109	1181	1253	1324	1396	1468	1540	1612	1684	72
605	1755	1827	1899	1971	2042	2114	2186	2258	2329	2401	72
606	2473	2544	2616	2688	2759	2831	2902	2974	3046	3117	72
607	3189	3260	3332	3403	3475	3546	3618	3689	3761	3832	71
608	3904	3975	4046	4118	4189	4261	4332	4403	4475	4546	71
609	4617	4689	4760	4831	4902	4974	5045	5116	5187	5259	71
610	785330	5401	5472	5543	5615	5686	5757	5828	5899	5970	71
611	6041	6112	6183	6254	6325	6396	6467	6538	6609	6680	71
612	6751	6822	6893	6964	7035	7106	7177	7248	7319	7390	71
613	7460	7531	7602	7673	7744	7815	7885	7956	8027	8098	71
614	8168	8239	8310	8381	8451	8522	8593	8663	8734	8804	71
615	8875	8946	9016	9087	9157	9228	9299	9369	9440	9510	71
616	9581	9651	9722	9792	9863	9933	•••4	••74	•144	•215	70
617	790285	0356	0426	0496	0567	0637	0707	0778	0848	0918	70
618	0988	1059	1129	1199	1269	1340	1410	1480	1550	1620	70
619	1691	1761	1831	1901	1971	2041	2111	2181	2252	2322	70
620	792392	2462	2532	2602	2672	2742	2812	2882	2952	3022	70
621	3092	3162	3231	3301	3371	3441	3511	3581	3651	3721	70
622	3790	3860	3930	4000	4070	4139	4209	4279	4349	4418	70
623	4488	4558	4627	4697	4767	4836	4906	4976	5045	5115	70
624	5185	5254	5324	5393	5463	5532	5602	5672	5741	5811	70
625	5880	5949	6019	6088	6158	6227	6297	6366	6436	6505	69
626	6574	6644	6713	6782	6852	6921	6990	7060	7129	7198	69
627	7268	7337	7406	7475	7545	7614	7683	7752	7821	7890	69
628	7960	8029	8098	8167	8236	8305	8374	8443	8513	8582	69
629	8651	8720	8789	8858	8927	8996	9065	9134	9203	9272	69
630	799341	9409	9478	9547	9616	9685	9754	9823	9892	9961	69
631	800029	0098	0167	0236	0305	0373	0442	0511	0580	0648	69
632	0717	0786	0854	0923	0992	1061	1129	1198	1266	1335	69
633	1404	1472	1541	1609	1678	1747	1815	1884	1952	2021	69
634	2089	2158	2226	2295	2363	2432	2500	2568	2637	2705	69
635	2774	2842	2910	2979	3047	3116	3184	3252	3321	3389	68
636	3457	3525	3594	3662	3730	3798	3867	3935	4003	4071	68
637	4139	4208	4276	4344	4412	4480	4548	4616	4685	4753	68
638	4821	4889	4957	5025	5093	5161	5229	5297	5365	5433	68
639	5501	5569	5637	5705	5773	5841	5908	5976	6044	6112	68
N.	0	1	2	3	4	5	6	7	8	9	D.

N.	0	1	2	3	4	5	6	7	8	9	D.
640	806180	6248	6316	6384	6451	6519	6587	6655	6723	6790	68
641	6858	6926	6994	7061	7129	7197	7264	7332	7400	7467	68
642	7535	7603	7670	7738	7806	7873	7941	8008	8076	8143	68
643	8211	8279	8346	8414	8481	8549	8616	8684	8751	8818	67
644	8886	8953	9021	9088	9156	9223	9290	9358	9425	9492	67
645	9560	9627	9694	9762	9829	9896	9964	••31	••98	•165	67
646	810233	0300	0367	0434	0501	0569	0636	0703	0770	0837	67
647	0904	0971	1039	1106	1173	1240	1307	1374	1441	1508	67
648	1575	1642	1709	1776	1843	1910	1977	2044	2111	2178	67
649	2245	2312	2379	2445	2512	2579	2646	2713	2780	2847	67
650	812913	2980	3047	3114	3181	3247	3314	3381	3448	3514	67
651	3581	3648	3714	3781	3848	3914	3981	4048	4114	4181	67
652	4248	4314	4381	4447	4514	4581	4647	4714	4780	4847	67
653	4913	4980	5046	5113	5179	5246	5312	5378	5445	5511	66
654	5578	5644	5711	5777	5843	5910	5976	6042	6109	6175	66
655	6241	6308	6374	6440	6506	6573	6639	6705	6771	6838	66
656	6904	6970	7036	7102	7169	7235	7301	7367	7433	7499	66
657	7565	7631	7698	7764	7830	7896	7962	8028	8094	8160	66
658	8226	8292	8358	8424	8490	8556	8622	8688	8754	8820	66
659	8885	8951	9017	9083	9149	9215	9281	9346	9412	9478	66
660	819544	9610	9676	9741	9807	9873	9939	•••4	••70	•136	66
661	820201	0267	0333	0399	0464	0530	0595	0661	0727	0792	66
662	0858	0924	0989	1055	1120	1186	1251	1317	1382	1448	66
663	1514	1579	1645	1710	1775	1841	1906	1972	2037	2103	65
664	2168	2233	2299	2364	2430	2495	2560	2626	2691	2756	65
665	2822	2887	2952	3018	3083	3148	3213	3279	3344	3409	65
666	3474	3539	3605	3670	3735	3800	3865	3930	3996	4061	65
667	4126	4191	4256	4321	4386	4451	4516	4581	4646	4711	65
668	4776	4841	4906	4971	5036	5101	5166	5231	5296	5361	65
669	5426	5491	5556	5621	5686	5751	5815	5880	5945	6010	65
670	826075	6140	6204	6269	6334	6399	6464	6528	6593	6658	65
671	6723	6787	6852	6917	6981	7046	7111	7175	7240	7305	65
672	7369	7434	7499	7563	7628	7692	7757	7821	7886	7951	65
673	8015	8080	8144	8209	8273	8338	8402	8467	8531	8595	64
674	8660	8724	8789	8853	8918	8982	9046	9111	9175	9239	64
675	9304	9368	9432	9497	9561	9625	9690	9754	9818	9882	64
676	9947	••11	••75	•139	•204	•268	•332	•396	•460	•525	64
677	830589	0653	0717	0781	0845	0909	0973	1037	1102	1166	64
678	1230	1294	1358	1422	1486	1550	1614	1678	1742	1806	64
679	1870	1934	1998	2062	2126	2189	2253	2317	2381	2445	64
680	832509	2573	2637	2700	2764	2828	2892	2956	3020	3083	64
681	3147	3211	3275	3338	3402	3466	3530	3593	3657	3721	64
682	3784	3848	3912	3975	4039	4103	4166	4230	4294	4357	64
683	4421	4484	4548	4611	4675	4739	4802	4866	4929	4993	64
684	5056	5120	5183	5247	5310	5373	5437	5500	5564	5627	63
685	5691	5754	5817	5881	5944	6007	6071	6134	6197	6261	63
686	6324	6387	6451	6514	6577	6641	6704	6767	6830	6894	63
687	6957	7020	7083	7146	7210	7273	7336	7399	7462	7525	63
688	7588	7652	7715	7778	7841	7904	7967	8030	8093	8156	63
689	8219	8282	8345	8408	8471	8534	8597	8660	8723	8786	63
690	838849	8912	8975	9038	9101	9164	9227	9289	9352	9415	63
691	9478	9541	9604	9667	9729	9792	9855	9918	9981	••43	63
692	840106	0169	0232	0294	0357	0420	0482	0545	0608	0671	63
693	0733	0796	0859	0921	0984	1046	1109	1172	1234	1297	63
694	1359	1422	1485	1547	1610	1672	1735	1797	1860	1922	63
695	1985	2047	2110	2172	2235	2297	2360	2422	2484	2547	62
696	2609	2672	2734	2796	2859	2921	2983	3046	3108	3170	62
697	3233	3295	3357	3420	3482	3544	3606	3669	3731	3793	62
698	3855	3918	3980	4042	4104	4166	4229	4291	4353	4415	62
699	4477	4539	4601	4664	4726	4788	4850	4912	4974	5036	62
N.	0	1	2	3	4	5	6	7	8	9	D.

N.	0	1	2	3	4	5	6	7	8	9	D.
700	845098	5160	5222	5284	5346	5408	5470	5532	5594	5656	62
701	5718	5780	5842	5904	5966	6028	6090	6151	6213	6275	62
702	6337	6399	6461	6523	6585	6646	6708	6770	6832	6894	62
703	6955	7017	7079	7141	7202	7264	7326	7388	7449	7511	62
704	7573	7634	7696	7758	7819	7881	7943	8004	8066	8128	62
705	8189	8251	8312	8374	8435	8497	8559	8620	8682	8743	62
706	8805	8866	8928	8989	9051	9112	9174	9235	9297	9358	61
707	9419	9481	9542	9604	9665	9726	9788	9849	9911	9972	61
708	850033	0095	0156	0217	0279	0340	0401	0462	0524	0585	61
709	0646	0707	0769	0830	0891	0952	1014	1075	1136	1197	61
710	851258	1320	1381	1442	1503	1564	1625	1686	1747	1809	61
711	1870	1931	1992	2053	2114	2175	2236	2297	2358	2419	61
712	2480	2541	2602	2663	2724	2785	2846	2907	2968	3029	61
713	3090	3150	3211	3272	3333	3394	3455	3516	3577	3637	61
714	3698	3759	3820	3881	3941	4002	4063	4124	4185	4245	61
715	4306	4367	4428	4488	4549	4610	4670	4731	4792	4852	61
716	4913	4974	5034	5095	5156	5216	5277	5337	5398	5459	61
717	5519	5580	5640	5701	5761	5822	5882	5943	6003	6064	61
718	6124	6185	6245	6306	6366	6427	6487	6548	6608	6668	60
719	6729	6789	6850	6910	6970	7031	7091	7152	7212	7272	60
720	857332	7393	7453	7513	7574	7634	7694	7755	7815	7875	60
721	7935	7995	8056	8116	8176	8236	8297	8357	8417	8477	60
722	8537	8597	8657	8718	8778	8838	8898	8958	9018	9078	60
723	9138	9198	9258	9318	9379	9439	9499	9559	9619	9679	60
724	9739	9799	9859	9918	9978	••38	••98	•158	•218	•278	60
725	860338	0398	0458	0518	0578	0637	0697	0757	0817	0877	60
726	0937	0996	1056	1116	1176	1236	1295	1355	1415	1475	60
727	1534	1594	1654	1714	1773	1833	1893	1952	2012	2072	60
728	2131	2191	2251	2310	2370	2430	2489	2549	2608	2668	60
729	2728	2787	2847	2906	2966	3025	3085	3144	3204	3263	60
730	863323	3382	3442	3501	3561	3620	3680	3739	3799	3858	59
731	3917	3977	4036	4096	4155	4214	4274	4333	4392	4452	59
732	4511	4570	4630	4689	4748	4808	4867	4926	4985	5045	59
733	5104	5163	5222	5282	5341	5400	5459	5519	5578	5637	59
734	5696	5755	5814	5874	5933	5992	6051	6110	6169	6228	59
735	6287	6346	6405	6465	6524	6583	6642	6701	6760	6819	59
736	6878	6937	6996	7055	7114	7173	7232	7291	7350	7409	59
737	7467	7526	7585	7644	7703	7762	7821	7880	7939	7998	59
738	8056	8115	8174	8233	8292	8350	8409	8468	8527	8586	59
739	8644	8703	8762	8821	8879	8938	8997	9056	9114	9173	59
740	869232	9290	9349	9408	9466	9525	9584	9642	9701	9760	59
741	9818	9877	9935	9994	••53	•111	•170	•228	•287	•345	59
742	870404	0462	0521	0579	0638	0696	0755	0813	0872	0930	58
743	0989	1047	1106	1164	1223	1281	1339	1398	1456	1515	58
744	1573	1631	1690	1748	1806	1865	1923	1981	2040	2098	58
745	2156	2215	2273	2331	2389	2448	2506	2564	2622	2681	58
746	2739	2797	2855	2913	2972	3030	3088	3146	3204	3262	58
747	3321	3379	3437	3495	3553	3611	3669	2727	3785	3844	58
748	3902	3960	4018	4076	4134	4192	4250	4308	4366	4424	58
749	4482	4540	4598	4656	4714	4772	4830	4888	4945	5003	58
750	875061	5119	5177	5235	5293	5351	5409	5466	5524	5582	58
751	5640	5698	5756	5813	5871	5929	5987	6045	6102	6160	58
752	6218	6276	6333	6391	6449	6507	6564	6622	6680	6737	58
753	6795	6853	6910	6968	7026	7083	7141	7199	7256	7314	58
754	7371	7429	7487	7544	7602	7659	7717	7774	7832	7889	58
755	7947	8004	8062	8119	8177	8234	8292	8349	8407	8464	57
756	8522	8579	8637	8694	8752	8809	8866	8924	8981	9039	57
757	9096	9153	9211	9268	9325	9383	9440	9497	9555	9612	57
758	9669	9726	9784	9841	9898	9956	••13	••70	•127	•185	57
759	880242	0299	0356	0413	0471	0528	0585	0642	0699	0756	57
N.	0	1	2	3	4	5	6	7	8	9	D.

N.	0	1	2	3	4	5	6	7	3	9	D.
760	880814	0871	0928	0985	1042	1099	1156	1213	1271	1328	57
761	1385	1442	1499	1556	1613	1670	1727	1784	1841	1898	57
762	1955	2012	2069	2126	2183	2240	2297	2354	2411	2468	57
763	2525	2581	2638	2695	2752	2809	2866	2923	2980	3037	57
764	3093	3150	3207	3264	3321	3377	3434	3491	3548	3605	57
765	3661	3718	3775	3832	3888	3945	4002	4059	4115	4172	57
766	4229	4285	4342	4399	4455	4512	4569	4625	4682	4739	57
767	4795	4852	4909	4965	5022	5078	5135	5192	5248	5305	57
768	5361	5418	5474	5531	5587	5644	5700	5757	5813	5870	57
769	5926	5983	6039	6096	6152	6209	6265	6321	6378	6434	56
770	886491	6547	6604	6660	6716	6773	6829	6885	6942	6998	56
771	7054	7111	7167	7223	7280	7336	7392	7449	7505	7561	56
772	7617	7674	7730	7786	7842	7898	7955	8011	8067	8123	56
773	8179	8236	8292	8348	8404	8460	8516	8573	8629	8685	56
774	8741	8797	8853	8909	8965	9021	9077	9134	9190	9246	56
775	9302	9358	9414	9470	9526	9582	9638	9694	9750	9806	56
776	9862	9918	9974	••30	••86	•141	•197	•253	•309	•365	56
777	890421	0477	0533	0589	0645	0700	0756	0812	0868	0924	56
778	0980	1035	1091	1147	1203	1259	1314	1370	1426	1482	56
779	1537	1593	1649	1705	1760	1816	1872	1928	1983	2039	56
780	892095	2150	2206	2262	2317	2373	2429	2484	2540	2595	56
781	2651	2707	2762	2818	2873	2929	2985	3040	3096	3151	56
782	3207	3262	3318	3373	3429	3484	3540	3595	3651	3706	56
783	3762	3817	3873	3928	3984	4039	4094	4150	4205	4261	55
784	4316	4371	4427	4482	4538	4593	4648	4704	4759	4814	55
785	4870	4925	4980	5036	5091	5146	5201	5257	5312	5367	55
786	5423	5478	5533	5588	5644	5699	5754	5809	5864	5920	55
787	5975	6030	6085	6140	6195	6251	6306	6361	6416	6471	55
788	6526	6581	6636	6692	6747	6802	6857	6912	6967	7022	55
789	7077	7132	7187	7242	7297	7352	7407	7462	7517	7572	55
790	897627	7682	7737	7792	7847	7902	7957	8012	8067	8122	55
791	8176	8231	8286	8341	8396	8451	8506	8561	8615	8670	55
792	8725	8780	8835	8890	8944	8999	9054	9109	9164	9218	55
793	9273	9328	9383	9437	9492	9547	9602	9656	9711	9766	55
794	9821	9875	9930	9985	••39	••94	•149	•203	•258	•312	55
795	900367	0422	0476	0531	0586	0640	0695	0749	0804	0859	55
796	0913	0968	1022	1077	1131	1186	1240	1295	1349	1404	55
797	1458	1513	1567	1622	1676	1731	1785	1840	1894	1948	54
798	2003	2057	2112	2166	2221	2275	2329	2384	2438	2492	54
799	2547	2601	2655	2710	2764	2818	2873	2927	2981	3036	54
800	903090	3144	3199	3253	3307	3361	3416	3470	3524	3578	54
801	3633	3687	3741	3795	3849	3904	3958	4012	4066	4120	54
802	4174	4229	4283	4337	4391	4445	4499	4553	4607	4661	54
803	4716	4770	4824	4878	4932	4986	5040	5094	5148	5202	54
804	5256	5310	5364	5418	5472	5526	5580	5634	5688	5742	54
805	5796	5850	5904	5958	6012	6066	6119	6173	6227	6281	54
806	6335	6389	6443	6497	6551	6604	6658	6712	6766	6820	54
807	6874	6927	6981	7035	7089	7143	7196	7250	7304	7358	54
808	7411	7465	7519	7573	7626	7680	7734	7787	7841	7895	54
809	7949	8002	8056	8110	8163	8217	8270	8324	8378	8431	54
810	908485	8539	8592	8646	8699	8753	8807	8860	8914	8967	54
811	9021	9074	9128	9181	9235	9289	9342	9396	9449	9503	54
812	9556	9610	9663	9716	9770	9823	9877	9930	9984	••37	53
813	910091	0144	0197	0251	0304	0358	0411	0464	0518	0571	53
814	0624	0678	0731	0784	0838	0891	0944	0998	1051	1104	53
815	1158	1211	1264	1317	1371	1424	1477	1530	1584	1637	53
816	1690	1743	1797	1850	1903	1956	2009	2063	2116	2169	53
817	2222	2275	2328	2381	2435	2488	2541	2594	2647	2700	53
818	2753	2806	2859	2913	2966	3019	3072	3125	3178	3231	53
819	3284	3337	3390	3443	3496	3549	3602	3655	3708	3761	53
N.	0	1	2	3	4	5	6	7	8	9	D.

N.	0	1	2	3	4	5	6	7	8	9	D.
820	913814	3867	3920	3973	4026	4079	4132	4184	4237	4290	53
821	4343	4396	4449	4502	4555	4608	4660	4713	4766	4819	53
822	4872	4925	4977	5030	5083	5136	5189	5241	5294	5347	53
823	5400	5453	5505	5558	5611	5664	5716	5769	5822	5875	53
824	5927	5980	6033	6085	6138	6191	6243	6296	6349	6401	53
825	6454	6507	6559	6612	6664	6717	6770	6822	6875	6927	53
826	6980	7033	7085	7138	7190	7243	7295	7348	7400	7453	53
827	7506	7558	7611	7663	7716	7768	7820	7873	7925	7978	52
828	8030	8083	8135	8188	8240	8293	8345	8397	8450	8502	52
829	8555	8607	8659	8712	8764	8816	8869	8921	8973	9026	52
830	919078	9130	9183	9235	9287	9340	9392	9444	9496	9549	52
831	9601	9653	9706	9758	9810	9862	9914	9967	••19	••71	52
832	920123	0176	0228	0280	0332	0384	0436	0489	0541	0593	52
833	0645	0697	0749	0801	0853	0906	0958	1010	1062	1114	52
834	1166	1218	1270	1322	1374	1426	1478	1530	1582	1634	52
835	1686	1738	1790	1842	1894	1946	1998	2050	2102	2154	52
836	2206	2258	2310	2362	2414	2466	2518	2570	2622	2674	52
837	2725	2777	2829	2881	2933	2985	3037	3089	3140	3192	52
838	3244	3296	3348	3399	3451	3503	3555	3607	3658	3710	52
839	3762	3814	3865	3917	3969	4021	4072	4124	4176	4228	52
840	924279	4331	4383	4434	4486	4538	4589	4641	4693	4744	52
841	4796	4848	4899	4951	5003	5054	5106	5157	5209	5261	52
842	5312	5364	5415	5467	5518	5570	5621	5673	5725	5776	52
843	5828	5879	5931	5982	6034	6085	6137	6188	6240	6291	51
844	6342	6394	6445	6497	6548	6600	6651	6702	6754	6805	51
845	6857	6908	6959	7011	7062	7114	7165	7216	7268	7319	51
846	7370	7422	7473	7524	7576	7627	7678	7730	7781	7832	51
847	7883	7935	7986	8037	8088	8140	9191	8242	8293	8345	51
848	8396	8447	8498	8549	8601	8652	8703	8754	8805	8857	51
849	8908	8959	9010	9061	9112	9163	9215	9266	9317	9368	51
850	929419	9470	9521	9572	9623	9674	9725	9776	9827	9879	51
851	9930	9981	••32	••83	•134	•185	•236	•287	•338	•389	51
852	930440	0491	0542	0592	0643	0694	0745	0796	0847	0898	51
853	0949	1000	1051	1102	1153	1204	1254	1305	1356	1407	51
854	1458	1509	1560	1610	1661	1712	1763	1814	1865	1915	5-
855	1966	2017	2068	2118	2169	2220	2271	2322	2372	2423	51
856	2474	2524	2575	2626	2677	2727	2778	2829	2879	2930	51
857	2981	3031	3082	3133	3183	3234	3285	3335	3386	3437	51
858	3487	3538	3589	3639	3690	3740	3791	3841	3892	3943	51
859	3993	4044	4094	4145	4195	4246	4296	4347	4397	4448	51
860	934498	4549	4599	4650	4700	4751	4801	4852	4902	4953	50
861	5003	5054	5104	5154	5205	5255	5306	5356	5406	5457	50
862	5507	5558	5608	5658	5709	5759	5809	5860	5910	5960	50
863	6011	6061	6111	6162	6212	6262	6313	6363	6413	6463	50
864	6514	6564	6614	6665	6715	6765	6815	6865	6916	6966	50
865	7016	7066	7117	7167	7217	7267	7317	7367	7418	7468	50
866	7518	7568	7618	7668	7718	7769	7819	7869	7919	7969	50
867	8019	8069	8119	8169	8219	8269	8320	8370	8420	8470	50
868	8520	8570	8620	8670	8720	8770	8820	8870	8920	8970	50
869	9020	9070	9120	9170	9220	9270	9320	9369	9419	9469	50
870	939519	9569	9619	9669	9719	9769	9819	9869	9918	9968	50
871	940018	0068	0118	0168	0218	0267	0317	0367	0417	0467	50
872	0516	0566	0616	0666	0716	0765	0815	0865	0915	0964	50
873	1014	1064	1114	1163	1213	1263	1313	1362	1412	1462	50
874	1511	1561	1611	1660	1710	1760	1809	1859	1909	1958	50
875	2008	2058	2107	2157	2207	2256	2306	2355	2405	2455	50
876	2504	2554	2603	2653	2702	2752	2801	2851	2901	2950	50
877	3000	3049	3099	3148	3198	3247	3297	3346	3396	3445	59
878	3495	3544	3593	3643	3692	3742	3791	3841	3890	3939	59
879	3989	4038	4088	4137	4186	4236	4285	4335	4384	4433	59
N.	0	1	2	3	4	5	6	7	8	9	D.

N.	0	1	2	3	4	5	6	7	8	9	D.
880	944483	4532	4581	4631	4680	4729	4779	4828	4877	4927	49
881	4976	5025	5074	5124	5173	5222	5272	5321	5370	5419	49
882	5469	5518	5567	5616	5665	5715	5764	5813	5862	5912	49
883	5961	6010	6059	6108	6157	6207	6256	6305	6354	6403	49
884	6452	6501	6551	6600	6649	6698	6747	6796	6845	6894	49
885	6943	6992	7041	7090	7140	7189	7238	7287	7336	7385	49
886	7434	7483	7532	7581	7630	7679	7728	7777	7826	7875	49
887	7924	7973	8022	8070	8119	8168	8217	8266	8315	8364	49
888	8413	8462	8511	8560	8609	8657	8706	8755	8804	8853	49
889	8902	8951	8999	9048	9097	9146	9195	9244	9292	9341	49
890	949390	9439	9488	9536	9585	9634	9683	9731	9780	9829	49
891	9878	9926	9975	••24	••73	•121	•170	•219	•267	•316	49
892	950365	0414	0462	0511	0560	0608	0657	0706	0754	0803	49
893	0851	0900	0949	0997	1046	1095	1143	1192	1240	1289	49
894	1338	1386	1435	1483	1532	1580	1629	1677	1726	1775	49
895	1823	1872	1920	1969	2017	2066	2114	2163	2211	2260	48
896	2308	2356	2405	2453	2502	2550	2599	2647	2696	2744	48
897	2792	2841	2889	2938	2986	3034	3083	3131	3180	3228	48
898	3276	3325	3373	3421	3470	3518	3566	3615	3663	3711	48
899	3760	3808	3856	3905	3953	4001	4049	4098	4146	4194	48
900	954243	4291	4339	4387	4435	4484	4532	4580	4628	4677	48
901	4725	4773	4821	4869	4918	4966	5014	5062	5110	5158	48
902	5207	5255	5303	5351	5399	5447	5495	5543	5592	5640	48
903	5688	5736	5784	5832	5880	5928	5976	6024	6072	6120	48
904	6168	6216	6265	6313	6361	6409	6457	6505	6553	6601	48
905	6649	6697	6745	6793	6840	6888	6936	6984	7032	7080	48
906	7128	7176	7224	7272	7320	7368	7416	7464	7512	7559	48
907	7607	7655	7703	7751	7799	7847	7894	7942	7990	8038	48
908	8086	8134	8181	8229	8277	8325	8373	8421	8468	8516	48
909	8564	8612	8659	8707	8755	8803	8850	8898	8946	8994	48
910	959041	9089	9137	9185	9232	9280	9328	9375	9423	9471	48
911	9518	9566	9614	9661	9709	9757	9804	9852	9900	9947	48
912	9995	••42	••90	•138	•185	•233	•280	•328	•376	•423	48
913	960471	0518	0566	0613	0661	0709	0756	0804	0851	0899	48
914	0946	0994	1041	1089	1136	1184	1231	1279	1326	1374	47
915	1421	1469	1516	1563	1611	1658	1706	1753	1801	1848	47
916	1895	1943	1990	2038	2085	2132	2180	2227	2275	2322	47
917	2369	2417	2464	2511	2559	2606	2653	2701	2748	2795	47
918	2843	2890	2937	2985	3032	3079	3126	3174	3221	3268	47
919	3316	3363	3410	3457	3504	3552	3599	3646	3693	3741	47
920	963788	3835	3882	3929	3977	4024	4071	4118	4165	4212	47
921	4260	4307	4354	4401	4448	4495	4542	4590	4637	4684	47
922	4731	4778	4825	4872	4919	4966	5013	5061	5108	5155	47
923	5202	5249	5296	5343	5390	5437	5484	5531	5578	5625	47
924	5672	5719	5766	5813	5860	5907	5954	6001	6048	6095	47
925	6142	6189	6236	6283	6329	6376	6423	6470	6517	6564	47
926	6611	6658	6705	6752	6799	6845	6892	6939	6986	7033	47
927	7080	7127	7173	7220	7267	7314	7361	7408	7454	7501	47
928	7548	7595	7642	7688	7735	7782	7829	7875	7922	7969	47
929	8016	8062	8109	8156	8203	8249	8296	8343	8390	8436	47
930	968483	8530	8576	8623	8670	8716	8763	8810	8856	8903	47
931	8950	8996	9043	9090	9136	9183	9229	9276	9323	9369	47
932	9416	9463	9509	9556	9602	9649	9695	9742	9789	9835	47
933	9882	9928	9975	••21	••68	•114	•161	•207	•254	•300	47
934	970347	0393	0440	0486	0533	0579	0626	0672	0719	0765	46
935	0812	0858	0904	0951	0997	1044	1090	1137	1183	1229	46
936	1276	1322	1369	1415	1461	1508	1554	1601	1647	1693	46
937	1740	1786	1832	1879	1925	1971	2018	2064	2110	2157	46
938	2203	2249	2295	2342	2388	2434	2481	2527	2573	2619	46
939	2666	2712	2758	2804	2851	2897	2943	2989	3035	3082	46
N.	0	1	2	3	4	5	6	7	8	9	D.

N.	0	1	2	3	4	5	6	7	8	9	D.
940	973128	3174	3220	3266	3313	3359	3405	3451	3497	3543	46
941	3590	3636	3682	3728	3774	3820	3866	3913	3959	4005	46
942	4051	4097	4143	4189	4235	4281	4327	4374	4420	4466	46
943	4512	4558	4604	4650	4696	4742	4788	4834	4880	4926	46
944	4972	5018	5064	5110	5156	5202	5248	5294	5340	5386	46
945	5432	5478	5524	5570	5616	5662	5707	5753	5799	5845	46
946	5891	5937	5983	6029	6075	6121	6167	6212	6258	6304	46
947	6350	6396	6442	6488	6533	6579	6625	6671	6717	6763	46
948	6808	6854	6900	6946	6992	7037	7083	7129	7175	7220	46
949	7266	7312	7358	7403	7449	7495	7541	7586	7632	7678	46
950	977724	7769	7815	7861	7906	7952	7998	8043	8089	8135	46
951	8181	8226	8272	8317	8363	8409	8454	8500	8546	8591	46
952	8637	8683	8728	8774	8819	8865	8911	8956	9002	9047	46
953	9093	9138	9184	9230	9275	9321	9366	9412	9457	9503	46
954	9548	9594	9639	9685	9730	9776	9821	9867	9912	9958	46
955	980003	0049	0094	0140	0185	0231	0276	0322	0367	0412	45
956	0458	0503	0549	0594	0640	0685	0730	0776	0821	0867	45
957	0912	0957	1003	1048	1093	1139	1184	1229	1275	1320	45
958	1366	1411	1456	1501	1547	1592	1637	1683	1728	1773	45
959	1819	1864	1909	1954	2000	2045	2090	2135	2181	2226	45
960	982271	2316	2362	2407	2452	2497	2543	2588	2633	2678	45
961	2723	2769	2814	2859	2904	2949	2994	3040	3085	3130	45
962	3175	3220	3265	3310	3356	3401	3446	3491	3536	3581	45
963	3626	3671	3716	3762	3807	3852	3897	3942	3987	4032	45
964	4077	4122	4167	4212	4257	4302	4347	4392	4437	4482	45
965	4527	4572	4617	4662	4707	4752	4797	4842	4887	4932	45
966	4977	5022	5067	5112	5157	5202	5247	5292	5337	5382	45
967	5426	5471	5516	5561	5606	5651	5696	5741	5786	5830	45
968	5875	5920	5965	6010	6055	6100	6144	6189	6234	6279	45
969	6324	6369	6413	6458	6503	6548	6593	6637	6682	6727	45
970	986772	6817	6861	6906	6951	6996	7040	7085	7130	7175	45
971	7219	7264	7309	7353	7398	7443	7488	7532	7577	7622	45
972	7666	7711	7756	7800	7845	7890	7934	7979	8024	8068	45
973	8113	8157	8202	8247	8291	8336	8381	8425	8470	8514	45
974	8559	8604	8648	8693	8737	8782	8826	8871	8916	8960	45
975	9005	9049	9094	9138	9183	9227	9272	9316	9361	9405	45
976	9450	9494	9539	9583	9628	9672	9717	9761	9806	9850	44
977	9895	9939	9983	••28	••72	•117	•161	•206	•250	•294	44
978	990339	0383	0428	0472	0516	0561	0605	0650	0694	0738	44
979	0783	0827	0871	0916	0960	1004	1049	1093	1137	1182	44
980	991226	1270	1315	1359	1403	1448	1492	1536	1580	1625	44
981	1669	1713	1758	1802	1846	1890	1935	1979	2023	2067	44
982	2111	2156	2200	2244	2288	2333	2377	2421	2465	2509	44
983	2554	2598	2642	2686	2730	2774	2819	2863	2907	2951	44
984	2995	3039	3083	3127	3172	3216	3260	3304	3348	3392	44
985	3436	3480	3524	3568	3613	3657	3701	3745	3789	3833	44
986	3877	3921	3965	4009	4053	4097	4141	4185	4229	4273	44
987	4317	4361	4405	4449	4493	4537	4581	4625	4669	4713	44
988	4757	4801	4845	4889	4933	4977	5021	5065	5108	5152	44
989	5196	5240	5284	5328	5372	5416	5460	5504	5547	5591	44
990	995635	5679	5723	5767	5811	5854	5898	5942	5986	6030	44
991	6074	6117	6161	6205	6249	6293	6337	6380	6424	6468	44
992	6512	6555	6599	6643	6687	6731	6774	6818	6862	6906	44
993	6949	6993	7037	7080	7124	7168	7212	7255	7299	7343	44
994	7386	7430	7474	7517	7561	7605	7648	7692	7736	7779	44
995	7823	7867	7910	7954	7998	8041	8085	8129	8172	8216	44
996	8259	8303	8347	8390	8434	8477	8521	8564	8608	8652	44
997	8695	8739	8782	8826	8869	8913	8956	9000	9043	9087	44
998	9131	9174	9218	9261	9305	9348	9392	9435	9479	9522	44
999	9565	9609	9652	9696	9739	9783	9826	9870	9913	9957	43
N.	0	1	2	3	4	5	6	7	8	9	D.

A TABLE

OF

LOGARITHMIC

SINES AND TANGENTS

FOR EVERY

DEGREE AND MINUTE

OF THE QUADRANT.

REMARK. The minutes in the left-hand column of each page, increasing downwards, belong to the degrees at the top; and those increasing upwards, in the right-hand column, belong to the degrees below.

M.	Sine	D.	Cosine	D.	Tang.	D.	Cotang.	
0	0·000000		10·000000		0·000000		Infinite.	60
1	6·463726	5017·17	000000	·00	6·463726	5017·17	13·536274	59
2	764756	2934·85	000000	·00	764756	2934·83	235244	58
3	940847	2082·31	000000	·00	940847	2082·31	059153	57
4	7·065786	1615·17	000000	·00	7·065786	1615·17	12·934214	56
5	162696	1319·68	000000	·00	162696	1319·69	837304	55
6	241877	1115·75	9·999999	·01	241878	1115·78	758122	54
7	308824	966·53	999999	·01	308825	996·53	691175	53
8	366816	852·54	999999	·01	366817	852·54	633183	52
9	417968	762·63	999999	·01	417970	762·63	582030	51
10	463725	689·88	999998	·01	463727	689·88	536273	50
11	7·505118	629·81	9·999998	·01	7·505120	629·81	12·494880	49
12	542906	579·36	999997	·01	542909	579·33	457091	48
13	577668	536·41	999997	·01	577672	536·42	422328	47
14	609853	499·38	999996	·01	609857	499·39	390143	46
15	639816	467·14	999996	·01	639820	467·15	360180	45
16	667845	438·81	999995	·01	667849	438·82	332151	44
17	694173	413·72	999995	·01	694179	413·73	305821	43
18	718997	391·35	999994	·01	719004	391·36	280997	42
19	742477	371·27	999993	·01	742484	371·28	257516	41
20	764754	353·15	999993	·01	764761	351·36	235239	40
21	7·785943	336·72	9·999992	·01	7·785951	336·73	12·214049	39
22	806146	321·75	999991	·01	806155	321·76	193845	38
23	825451	308·05	999990	·01	825460	308·06	174540	37
24	843934	295·47	999989	·02	843944	295·49	156056	36
25	861662	283·88	999988	·02	861674	283·90	138326	35
26	878695	273·17	999988	·02	878708	273·18	121292	34
27	895085	263·23	999987	·02	895099	263·25	104901	33
28	910879	253·99	999986	·02	910894	254·01	089106	32
29	926119	245·38	999985	·02	926134	245·40	073866	31
30	940842	237·33	999983	·02	940858	237·35	059142	30
31	7·955082	229·80	9·999982	·02	7·955100	229·81	12·044900	29
32	968870	222·73	999981	·02	968889	222·75	031111	28
33	982233	216·08	999980	·02	982253	216·10	017747	27
34	995198	209·81	999979	·02	995219	209·83	004781	26
35	8·007787	203·90	999977	·02	8·007809	203·92	11·992191	25
36	020021	198·31	999976	·02	020045	198·33	979955	24
37	031919	193·02	999975	·02	031945	193·05	968055	23
38	043501	188·01	999973	·02	043527	188·03	956473	22
39	054781	183·25	999972	·02	054809	183·27	945191	21
40	065776	178·72	999971	·02	065806	178·74	934194	26
41	8·076500	174·41	9·999969	·02	8·076531	174·44	11·923469	19
42	086965	170·31	999968	·02	086997	170·34	913003	18
43	097183	166·39	999966	·02	097217	166·42	902783	17
44	107167	162·65	999964	·03	107202	162·68	892797	16
45	116926	159·08	999963	·03	116963	159·10	883037	15
46	126471	155·66	999961	·03	126510	155·68	873490	14
47	135810	152·38	999959	·03	135851	152·41	864149	13
48	144953	149·24	999958	·03	144996	149·27	855004	12
49	153907	146·22	999955	·03	153952	146·27	846048	11
50	162681	143·33	999954	·03	162727	143·36	837273	10
51	8·171280	140·54	9·999952	·03	8·171328	140·57	11·828672	9
52	179713	137·86	999950	·03	179763	137·90	820237	8
53	187985	135·29	999948	·03	188036	135·32	811964	7
54	196102	132·80	999946	·03	196156	132·84	803844	6
55	204070	130·41	999944	·03	204126	130·44	795874	5
56	211895	128·10	999942	·04	211953	128·14	788047	4
57	219581	125·87	999940	·04	219641	125·90	780359	3
58	227134	123·72	999938	·04	227195	123·76	772805	2
59	234557	121·64	999936	·04	234621	121·68	765379	1
60	241855	119·63	999934	·04	241921	119·67	758079	0
	Cosine	D.	Sine		Cotang.	D.	Tang.	M.

M.	Sine	D.	Cosine	D.	Tang.	D.	Cotang.	
0	8.241855	119.63	9.999934	.04	8.241921	119.67	11.758079	60
1	249033	117.68	999932	.04	249102	117.72	750898	59
2	256094	115.80	999929	.04	256165	115.84	743835	58
3	263042	113.98	999927	.04	263115	114.02	736885	57
4	269881	112.21	999925	.04	269956	112.25	730044	56
5	276614	110.50	999922	.04	276691	110.54	723309	55
6	283243	108.83	999920	.04	283323	108.87	716677	54
7	289773	107.21	999918	.04	289856	107.26	710144	53
8	296207	105.65	999915	.04	296292	105.70	703708	52
9	302546	104.13	999913	.04	302634	104.18	697366	51
10	308794	102.66	999910	.04	308884	102.70	691116	50
11	8.314904	101.22	9.999907	.04	8.315046	101.26	11.684954	49
12	321027	99.82	999905	.04	321122	99.87	678878	48
13	327016	98.47	999902	.04	327114	98.51	672886	47
14	332924	97.14	999899	.05	333025	97.19	666975	46
15	338753	95.86	999897	.05	338856	95.90	661144	45
16	344504	94.60	999894	.05	344610	94.65	655390	44
17	350181	93.38	999891	.05	350289	93.43	649711	43
18	355783	92.19	999888	.05	355895	92.24	644105	42
19	361315	91.03	999885	.05	361430	91.08	638570	41
20	366777	89.90	999882	.05	366895	89.95	633105	40
21	8.372171	88.80	9.999879	.05	8.372292	88.85	11.627708	39
22	377499	87.72	999876	.05	377622	87.77	622378	38
23	382762	86.67	999873	.05	382889	86.72	617111	37
24	387962	85.64	999870	.05	388092	85.70	611908	36
25	393101	84.64	999867	.05	393234	84.70	606766	35
26	398179	83.66	999864	.05	398315	83.71	601685	34
27	403199	82.71	999861	.05	403338	82.76	596662	33
28	408161	81.77	999858	.05	408304	81.82	591696	32
29	413068	80.86	999854	.05	413213	80.91	586787	31
30	417919	79.96	999851	.06	418068	80.02	581932	30
31	8.422717	79.09	9.999848	.06	8.422869	79.14	11.577131	29
32	427462	78.23	999844	.06	427618	78.30	572382	28
33	432156	77.40	999841	.06	432315	77.45	567685	27
34	436800	76.57	999838	.06	436962	76.63	563038	26
35	441394	75.77	999834	.06	441560	75.83	558440	25
36	445941	74.99	999831	.06	446110	75.05	553890	24
37	450440	74.22	999827	.06	450613	74.28	549387	23
38	454893	73.46	999823	.06	455070	73.52	544930	22
39	459301	72.73	999820	.06	459481	72.79	540519	21
40	463665	72.00	999816	.06	463849	72.06	536151	20
41	8.467985	71.29	9.999812	.06	8.468172	71.35	11.531828	19
42	472263	70.60	999809	.06	472454	70.66	527546	18
43	476498	69.91	999805	.06	476693	69.98	523307	17
44	480693	69.24	999801	.06	480892	69.31	519108	16
45	484848	68.59	999797	.07	485050	68.65	514950	15
46	488963	67.94	999793	.07	489170	68.01	510830	14
47	493040	67.31	999790	.07	493250	67.38	506750	13
48	497078	66.69	999786	.07	497293	66.76	502707	12
49	501080	66.08	999782	.07	501298	66.15	498702	11
50	505045	65.48	999778	.07	505267	65.55	494733	10
51	8.508974	64.89	9.999774	.07	8.509200	64.96	11.490800	9
52	512867	64.31	999769	.07	513098	64.39	486902	8
53	516726	63.75	999765	.07	516961	63.82	483039	7
54	520551	63.19	999761	.07	520790	63.26	479210	6
55	524343	62.64	999757	.07	524586	62.72	475414	5
56	528102	62.11	999753	.07	528349	62.18	471651	4
57	531828	61.58	999748	.07	532080	61.65	467920	3
58	535523	61.06	999744	.07	535779	61.13	464221	2
59	539186	60.55	999740	.07	539447	60.62	460553	1
60	542819	60.04	999735	.07	543084	60.12	456916	0
	Cosine	D.	Sine		Cotang.	D.	Tang	

M.	Sine	D.	Cosine	D.	Tang.	D.	Cotang.	
0	8·542819	60·04	9·999735	·07	8·543084	60·12	11·456916	60
1	546422	59·55	999731	·07	546691	59·62	453309	59
2	549995	59·06	999726	·07	550268	59·14	449732	58
3	553539	58·58	999722	·08	553817	58·66	446183	57
4	557054	58·11	999717	·08	557336	58·19	442664	56
5	560540	57·65	999713	·08	560828	57·73	439172	55
6	563999	57·19	999708	·08	564291	57·27	435709	54
7	567431	56·74	999704	·08	567727	56·82	432273	53
8	570836	56·30	999699	·08	571137	56·38	428863	52
9	574214	55·87	999694	·08	574520	55·95	425480	51
10	577566	55·44	999689	·08	577877	55·52	422123	50
11	8·580892	55·02	9·999685	·08	8·581208	55·10	11·418792	49
12	584193	54·60	999680	·08	584514	54·68	415486	48
13	587469	54·19	999675	·08	587795	54·27	412205	47
14	590721	53·79	999670	·08	591051	53·87	408949	46
15	593948	53·39	999665	·08	594283	53·47	405717	45
16	597152	53·00	999660	·08	597492	53·08	402508	44
17	600332	52·61	999655	·08	600677	52·70	399323	43
18	603489	52·23	999650	·08	603839	52·32	396161	42
19	606623	51·86	999645	·09	606978	51·94	393022	41
20	609734	51·49	999640	·09	610094	51·58	389906	40
21	8·612823	51·12	9·999635	·09	8·613189	51·21	11·386811	39
22	615891	50·76	999629	·09	616262	50·85	383738	38
23	618937	50·41	999624	·09	619313	50·50	380687	37
24	621962	50·06	999619	·09	622343	50·15	377657	36
25	624965	49·72	999614	·09	625352	49·81	374648	35
26	627948	49·38	999608	·09	628340	49·47	371660	34
27	630911	49·04	999603	·09	631308	49·13	368692	33
28	633854	48·71	999597	·09	634256	48·80	365744	32
29	636776	48·39	999592	·09	637184	48·48	362816	31
30	639680	48·06	999586	·09	640093	48·16	359907	30
31	8·642563	47·75	9·999581	·09	8·642982	47·84	11·357018	29
32	645428	47·43	999575	·09	645853	47·53	354147	28
33	648274	47·12	999570	·09	648704	47·22	351296	27
34	651102	46·82	999564	·09	651537	46·91	348463	26
35	653911	46·52	999558	·10	654352	46·61	345648	25
36	656702	46·22	999553	·10	657149	46·31	342851	24
37	659475	45·92	999547	·10	659928	46·02	340072	23
38	662230	45·63	999541	·10	662689	45·73	337311	22
39	664968	45·35	999535	·10	665433	45·44	334567	21
40	667689	45·06	999529	·10	668160	45·26	331840	20
41	8·670393	44·79	9·999524	·10	8·670870	44·88	11·329130	19
42	673080	44·51	999518	·10	673563	44·61	326437	18
43	675751	44·24	999512	·10	676239	44·34	323761	17
44	678405	43·97	999506	·10	678900	44·17	321100	16
45	681043	43·70	999500	·10	681544	43·80	318456	15
46	683665	43·44	999493	·10	684172	43·54	315828	14
47	686272	43·18	999487	·10	686784	43·28	313216	13
48	688863	42·92	999481	·10	689381	43·03	310619	12
49	691438	42·67	999475	·10	691963	42·77	308037	11
50	693998	42·42	999469	·10	694529	42·52	305471	10
51	8·696543	42·17	9·999463	·11	8·697081	42·28	11·302919	9
52	699073	41·92	999456	·11	699617	42·03	300383	8
53	701589	41·68	999450	·11	702139	41·79	297861	7
54	704090	41·44	999443	·11	704646	41·55	295354	6
55	706577	41·21	999437	·11	707140	41·32	292860	5
56	709049	40·97	999431	·11	709618	41·08	290382	4
57	711507	40·74	999424	·11	712083	40·85	287917	3
58	713952	40·51	999418	·11	714534	40·62	285465	2
59	716383	40·29	999411	·11	716972	40·40	283028	1
60	718800	40·06	999404	·11	719396	40·17	280604	0
	Cosine	D.	Sine		Cotang.	D.	Tang.	M.

M.	Sine	D.	Cosine	D.	Tang.	D.	Cotang.	
0	8·718800	40·06	9·999404	·11	8·719396	40·17	11·280604	60
1	721204	39·84	999398	·11	721806	39·95	278194	59
2	723595	39·62	999391	·11	724204	39·74	275796	58
3	725972	39·41	999384	·11	726588	39·52	273412	57
4	728337	39·19	999378	·11	728959	39·30	271041	56
5	730688	38·98	999371	·11	731317	39·09	268683	55
6	733027	38·77	999364	·12	733663	38·89	266337	54
7	735354	38·57	999357	·12	735996	38·68	264004	53
8	737667	38·36	999350	·12	738317	38·48	261683	52
9	739969	38·16	999343	·12	740626	38·27	259374	51
10	742259	37·96	999336	·12	742922	38·07	257078	50
11	8·744536	37·76	9·999329	·12	8·745207	37·87	11·254793	49
12	746802	37·56	999322	·12	747479	37·68	252521	48
13	749055	37·37	999315	·12	749740	37·49	250260	47
14	751297	37·17	999308	·12	751989	37·29	248011	46
15	753528	36·98	999301	·12	754227	37·10	245773	45
16	755747	36·79	999294	·12	756453	36·92	243547	44
17	757955	36·61	999286	·12	758668	36·73	241332	43
18	760151	36·42	999279	·12	760872	36·55	239128	42
19	762337	36·24	999272	·12	763065	36·36	236935	41
20	764511	36·06	999265	·12	765246	36·18	234754	40
21	8·766675	35·88	9·999257	·12	8·767417	36·00	11·232583	39
22	768828	35·70	999250	·13	769578	35·83	230422	38
23	770970	35·53	999242	·13	771727	35·65	228273	37
24	773101	35·35	999235	·13	773866	35·48	226134	36
25	775223	35·18	999227	·13	775995	35·31	224005	35
26	777333	35·01	999220	·13	778114	35·14	221886	34
27	779434	34·84	999212	·13	780222	34·97	219778	33
28	781524	34·67	999205	·13	782320	34·80	217680	32
29	783605	34·51	999197	·13	784408	34·64	215592	31
30	785675	34·31	999189	·13	786486	34·47	213514	30
31	8·787736	34·18	9·999181	·13	8·788554	34·31	11·211446	29
32	789787	34·02	999174	·13	790613	34·15	209387	28
33	791828	33·86	999166	·13	792662	33·99	207338	27
34	793859	33·70	999158	·13	794701	33·83	205299	26
35	795881	33·54	999150	·13	796731	33·68	203269	25
36	797894	33·39	999142	·13	798752	33·52	201248	24
37	799897	33·23	999134	·13	800763	33·37	199237	23
38	801892	33·08	999126	·13	802765	33·22	197235	22
39	803876	32·93	999118	·13	804758	33·07	195242	21
40	805852	32·78	999110	·13	806742	32·92	193258	20
41	8·807819	32·63	9·999102	·13	8·808717	32·78	11·191283	19
42	809777	32·49	999094	·14	810683	32·62	189317	18
43	811726	32·34	999086	·14	812641	32·48	187359	17
44	813667	32·19	999077	·14	814589	32·33	185411	16
45	815599	32·05	999069	·14	816529	32·19	183471	15
46	817522	31·91	999061	·14	818461	32·05	181539	14
47	819436	31·77	999053	·14	820384	31·91	179616	13
48	821343	31·63	999044	·14	822298	31·77	177702	12
49	823240	31·49	999036	·14	824205	31·63	175795	11
50	825130	31·35	999027	·14	826103	31·50	173897	10
51	8·827011	31·22	9·999019	·14	8·827992	31·36	11·172008	9
52	828884	31·08	999010	·14	829874	31·23	170126	8
53	830749	30·95	999002	·14	831748	31·10	168252	7
54	832607	30·82	998993	·14	833613	30·96	166387	6
55	834456	30·69	998984	·14	835471	30·83	164529	5
56	836297	30·56	998976	·14	837321	30·70	162679	4
57	838130	30·43	998967	·15	839163	30·57	160837	3
58	839956	30·30	998958	·15	840998	30·45	159002	2
59	841774	30·17	998950	·15	842825	30·32	157175	1
60	843585	30·00	998941	·15	844644	30·19	155356	0
	Cosine	D.	Sine		Cotang.	D.	Tang.	M.

(86 DEGREES.)

M.	Sine	D.	Cosine	D.	Tang.	D.	Cotang.	
0	8·843585	30·05	9·998941	·15	8·844644	30·19	11·155356	60
1	845387	29·92	998932	·15	846455	30·07	153545	59
2	847183	29·80	998923	·15	848260	29·95	151740	58
3	848971	29·67	998914	·15	850057	29·82	149943	57
4	850751	29·55	998905	·15	851846	29·70	148154	56
5	852525	29·43	998896	·15	853628	29·58	146372	55
6	854291	29·31	998887	·15	855403	29·46	144597	54
7	856049	29·19	998878	·15	857171	29·35	142829	53
8	857801	29·07	998869	·15	858932	29·23	141068	52
9	859546	28·96	998860	·15	860686	29·11	139314	51
10	861283	28·84	998851	·15	862433	29·00	137567	50
11	8·863014	28·73	9·998841	·15	8·864173	28·88	11·135827	49
12	864738	28·61	998832	·15	865906	28·77	134094	48
13	866455	28·50	998823	·16	867632	28·66	132368	47
14	868165	28·39	998813	·16	869351	28·54	130649	46
15	869868	28·28	998804	·16	871064	28·43	128936	45
16	871565	28·17	998795	·16	872770	28·32	127230	44
17	873255	28·06	998785	·16	874469	28·21	125531	43
18	874938	27·95	998776	·16	876162	28·11	123838	42
19	876615	27·86	998766	·16	877849	28·00	122151	41
20	878285	27·73	998757	·16	879529	27·89	120471	40
21	8·879949	27·63	9·998747	·16	8·881202	27·79	11·118798	39
22	881607	27·52	998738	·16	882869	27·68	117131	38
23	883258	27·42	998728	·16	884530	27·58	115470	37
24	884903	27·31	998718	·16	886185	27·47	113815	36
25	886542	27·21	998708	·16	887833	27·37	112167	35
26	888174	27·11	998699	·16	889476	27·27	110524	34
27	889801	27·00	998689	·16	891112	27·17	108888	33
28	891421	26·90	998679	·16	892742	27·07	107258	32
29	893035	26·80	998669	·17	894366	26·97	105634	31
30	894643	26·70	998659	·17	895984	26·87	104016	30
31	8·896246	26·60	9·998649	·17	8·897596	26·77	11·102404	29
32	897842	26·51	998639	·17	899203	26·67	100797	28
33	899432	26·41	998629	·17	900803	26·58	099197	27
34	901017	26·31	998619	·17	902398	26·48	097602	26
35	902596	26·22	998609	·17	903987	26·38	096013	25
36	904169	26·12	998599	·17	905570	26·29	094430	24
37	905736	26·03	998589	·17	907147	26·20	092853	23
38	907297	25·93	998578	·17	908719	26·10	091281	22
39	908853	25·84	998568	·17	910285	26·01	089715	21
40	910404	25·75	998558	·17	911846	25·92	088154	20
41	8·911949	25·66	9·998548	·17	8·913401	25·83	11·086599	19
42	913488	25·56	998537	·17	914951	25·74	085049	18
43	915022	25·47	998527	·17	916495	25·65	083505	17
44	916550	25·38	998516	·18	918034	25·56	081966	16
45	918073	25·29	998506	·18	919568	25·47	080432	15
46	919591	25·20	998495	·18	921096	25·38	078904	14
47	921103	25·12	998485	·18	922619	25·30	077381	13
48	922610	25·03	998474	·18	924136	25·21	075864	12
49	924112	24·94	998464	·18	925649	25·12	074351	11
50	925609	24·86	998453	·18	927156	25·03	072844	10
51	8·927100	24·77	9·998442	·18	8·928658	24·95	11·071342	9
52	928587	24·69	998431	·18	930155	24·86	069845	8
53	930068	24·60	998421	·18	931647	24·78	068353	7
54	931544	24·52	998410	·18	933134	24·70	066866	6
55	933015	24·43	998399	·18	934616	24·61	065384	5
56	934481	24·35	998388	·18	936093	24·53	063907	4
57	935942	24·27	998377	·18	937565	24·45	062435	3
58	937398	24·19	998366	·18	939032	24·37	060968	2
59	938850	24·11	998355	·18	940494	24·30	059506	1
60	940296	24·03	998344	·18	941952	24·21	058048	0
	Cosine	D.	Sine		Cotang.	D.	Tang.	M.

M.	Sine	D.	Cosine	D.	Tang.	D.	Cotang.	
0	8·940296	24·03	9·998344	·19	8·941952	24·21	11·058048	60
1	941738	23·94	998333	·19	943404	24·13	056596	59
2	943174	23·87	998322	·19	944852	24·05	055148	58
3	944606	23·79	998311	·19	946295	23·97	053705	57
4	946034	23·71	998300	·19	947734	23·90	052266	56
5	947456	23·63	998289	·19	949168	23·82	050832	55
6	948874	23·55	998277	·19	950597	23·74	049403	54
7	950287	23·48	998266	·19	952021	23·66	047979	53
8	951696	23·40	998255	·19	953441	23·60	046559	52
9	953100	23·32	998243	·19	954856	23·51	045144	51
10	954499	23·25	998232	·19	956267	23·44	043733	50
11	8·955894	23·17	9·998220	·19	8·957674	23·37	11·042326	49
12	957284	23·10	998209	·19	959075	23·29	040925	48
13	958670	23·02	998197	·19	960473	23·23	039527	47
14	960052	22·95	998186	·19	961866	23·14	038134	46
15	961429	22·88	998174	·19	963255	23·07	036745	45
16	962801	22·80	998163	·19	964639	23·00	035361	44
17	964170	22·73	998151	·19	966019	22·93	033981	43
18	965534	22·66	998139	·20	967394	22·86	032606	42
19	966893	22·59	998128	·20	968766	22·79	031234	41
20	968249	22·52	998116	·20	970133	22·71	029867	40
21	8·969600	22·44	9·998104	·20	8·971496	22·65	11·028504	39
22	970947	22·38	998092	·20	972855	22·57	027145	38
23	972289	22·31	998080	·20	974209	22·51	025791	37
24	973628	22·24	998068	·20	975560	22·44	024440	36
25	974962	22·17	998056	·20	976906	22·37	023094	35
26	976293	22·10	998044	·20	978248	22·30	021752	34
27	977619	22·03	998032	·20	979586	22·23	020414	33
28	978941	21·97	998020	·20	980921	22·17	019079	32
29	980259	21·90	998008	·20	982251	22·10	017749	31
30	981573	21·83	997996	·20	983577	22·04	016423	30
31	8·982883	21·77	9·997985	·20	8·984899	21·97	11·015101	29
32	984189	21·70	997972	·20	986217	21·91	013783	28
33	985491	21·63	997959	·20	987532	21·84	012468	27
34	986789	21·57	997947	·20	988842	21·78	011158	26
35	988083	21·50	997935	·21	990149	21·71	009851	25
36	989374	21·44	997922	·21	991451	21·65	008549	24
37	990660	21·38	997910	·21	992750	21·58	007250	23
38	991943	21·31	997897	·21	994045	21·52	005955	22
39	993222	21·25	997885	·21	995337	21·46	004663	21
40	994497	21·19	997872	·21	996624	21·40	003376	20
41	8·995768	21·12	9·997860	·21	8·997908	21·34	11·002092	19
42	997036	21·06	997847	·21	999188	21·27	000812	18
43	998299	21·00	997835	·21	9·000465	21·21	10·999535	17
44	999560	20·94	997822	·21	001738	21·15	998262	16
45	9·000816	20·87	997809	·21	003007	21·09	996993	15
46	002069	20·82	997797	·21	004272	21·03	995728	14
47	003318	20·76	997784	·21	005534	20·97	994466	13
48	004563	20·70	997771	·21	006792	20·91	993208	12
49	005805	20·64	997758	·21	008047	20·85	991953	11
50	007044	20·58	997745	·21	009298	20·80	990702	10
51	9·008278	20·52	9·997732	·21	9·010546	20·74	10·989454	9
52	009510	20·46	997719	·21	011790	20·68	988210	8
53	010737	20·40	997706	·21	013031	20·62	986969	7
54	011962	20·34	997693	·22	014268	20·56	985732	6
55	013182	20·29	997680	·22	015502	20·51	984498	5
56	014400	20·23	997667	·22	016732	20·45	983268	4
57	015613	20·17	997654	·22	017959	20·40	982041	3
58	016824	20·12	997641	·22	019183	20·33	980817	2
59	018031	20·06	997628	·22	020403	20·28	979597	1
60	019235	20·00	997614	·22	021620	20·23	978380	0
	Cosine	D.	Sine		Cotang.	D.	Tang.	M.

(84 DEGREES.)

M.	Sine	D.	Cosine	D.	Tang.	D.	Cotang.	
0	9·019235	20·00	9·997614	·22	9·021620	20·23	10·978380	60
1	020435	19·95	997601	·22	022834	20·17	977166	59
2	021632	19·89	997588	·22	024044	20·11	975956	58
3	022825	19·84	997574	·22	025251	20·06	974749	57
4	024016	19·78	997561	·22	026455	20·00	973545	56
5	025203	19·73	997547	·22	027655	19·95	972345	55
6	026386	19·67	997534	·23	028852	19·90	971148	54
7	027567	19·62	997520	·23	030046	19·85	969954	53
8	028744	19·57	997507	·23	031237	19·79	968763	52
9	029918	19·51	997493	·23	032425	19·74	967575	51
10	031089	19·47	997480	·23	033609	19·69	966391	50
11	9·032257	19·41	9·997466	·23	9·034791	19·64	10·965209	49
12	033421	19·36	997452	·23	035969	19·58	964031	48
13	034582	19·30	997439	·23	037144	19·53	962856	47
14	035741	19·25	997425	·23	038316	19·48	961684	46
15	036896	19·20	997411	·23	039485	19·43	960515	45
16	038048	19·15	997397	·23	040651	19·38	959349	44
17	039197	19·10	997383	·23	041813	19·33	958187	43
18	040342	19·05	997369	·23	042973	19·28	957027	42
19	041485	18·99	997355	·23	044130	19·23	955870	41
20	042625	18·94	997341	·23	045284	19·18	954716	40
21	9·043762	18·89	9·997327	·24	9·046434	19·13	10·953566	39
22	044895	18·84	997313	·24	047582	19·08	952418	38
23	046026	18·79	697299	·24	048727	19·03	951273	37
24	047154	18·75	997285	·24	049869	18·98	950131	36
25	048279	18·70	997271	·24	051008	18·93	948992	35
26	049400	18·65	997257	·24	052144	18·89	947856	34
27	050519	18·60	997242	·24	053277	18·84	946723	33
28	051635	18·55	997228	·24	054407	18·79	945593	32
29	052749	18·50	997214	·24	055535	18·74	944465	31
30	053859	18·45	997199	·24	056659	18·70	943341	30
31	9·054966	18·41	9·997185	·24	9·057781	18·65	10·942219	29
32	056071	18·36	997170	·24	058900	18·60	941100	28
33	057172	18·31	997156	·24	060016	18·55	939984	27
34	058271	18·27	997141	·24	061130	18·51	938870	26
35	059367	18·22	997127	·24	062240	18·46	937760	25
36	060460	18·17	997112	·24	063348	18·42	936652	24
37	061551	18·13	997098	·24	064453	18·37	935547	23
38	062639	18·08	997083	·25	065556	18·33	934444	22
39	063724	18·04	997068	·25	066655	18·28	933345	21
40	064806	17·99	997053	·25	067752	18·24	932248	20
41	9·065885	17·94	9·997039	·25	9·068846	18·19	10·931154	19
42	066962	17·90	997024	·25	069938	18·15	930062	18
43	068036	17·86	997009	·25	071027	18·10	928973	17
44	069107	17·81	996994	·25	072113	18·06	927887	16
45	070176	17·77	996979	·25	073197	18·02	926803	15
46	071242	17·72	996964	·25	074278	17·97	925722	14
47	072306	17·68	996949	·25	075356	17·93	924644	13
48	073366	17·63	996934	·25	076432	17·89	923568	12
49	074424	17·59	996919	·25	077505	17·84	922495	11
50	075480	17·55	996904	·25	078576	17·80	921424	10
51	9·076533	17·50	9·996889	·25	9·079644	17·76	10·920356	9
52	077583	17·46	996874	·25	080710	17·72	919290	8
53	078631	17·42	996858	·25	081773	17·67	918227	7
54	079676	17·38	996843	·25	082833	17·63	917167	6
55	080719	17·33	996828	·25	083891	17·59	916109	5
56	081759	17·29	996812	·26	084947	17·55	915053	4
57	082797	17·25	996797	·26	086000	17·51	914000	3
58	083832	17·21	996782	·26	087050	17·47	912950	2
59	084864	17·17	996766	·26	088098	17·43	911902	1
60	085894	17·13	996751	·26	089144	17·38	910856	0
	Cosine	D.	Sine		Cotang.	D.	Tang.	M.

(83 DEGREES.)

M.	Sine	D.	Cosine	D.	Tang.	D.	Cotang.	
0	9·085894	17·13	9·996751	·26	9·089144	17·38	10·910856	60
1	086922	17·09	996735	·26	090187	17·34	909813	59
2	087947	17·04	996720	·26	091228	17·30	908772	58
3	088970	17·00	996704	·26	092266	17·27	907734	57
4	089990	16·96	996688	·26	093302	17·22	906698	56
5	091008	16·92	996673	·26	094336	17·19	905664	55
6	092024	16·88	996657	·26	095367	17·15	904633	54
7	093037	16·84	996641	·26	096395	17·11	903605	53
8	094047	16·80	996625	·26	097422	17·07	902578	52
9	095056	16·76	996610	·26	098446	17·03	901554	51
10	096062	16·73	996594	·26	099468	16·99	900532	50
11	9·097065	16·68	9·996578	·27	9·100487	16·95	10·899513	49
12	098066	16·65	996562	·27	101504	16·91	898496	48
13	099065	16·61	996546	·27	102519	16·87	897481	47
14	100062	16·57	996530	·27	103532	16·84	896468	46
15	101056	16·53	996514	·27	104542	16·80	895458	45
16	102048	16·49	996498	·27	105550	16·76	894450	44
17	103037	16·45	996482	·27	106556	16·72	893444	43
18	104025	16·41	996465	·27	107559	16·69	892441	42
19	105010	16·38	996449	·27	108560	16·65	891440	41
20	105992	16·34	996433	·27	109559	16·61	890441	40
21	9·106973	16·30	9·996417	·27	9·110556	16·58	10·889444	39
22	107951	16·27	996400	·27	111551	16·54	888449	38
23	108927	16·23	996384	·27	112543	16·50	887457	37
24	109901	16·19	996368	·27	113533	16·46	886467	36
25	110873	16·16	996351	·27	114521	16·43	885479	35
26	111842	16·12	996335	·27	115507	16·39	884493	34
27	112809	16·08	996318	·27	116491	16·36	883509	33
28	113774	16·05	996302	·28	117472	16·32	882528	32
29	114737	16·01	996285	·28	118452	16·29	881548	31
30	115698	15·97	996269	·28	119429	16·25	880571	30
31	9·116656	15·94	9·996252	·28	9·120404	16·22	10·879596	29
32	117613	15·90	996235	·28	121377	16·18	878623	28
33	118567	15·87	996219	·28	122348	16·15	877652	27
34	119519	15·83	996202	·28	123317	16·11	876683	26
35	120469	15·80	996185	·28	124284	16·07	875716	25
36	121417	15·76	996168	·28	125249	16·04	874751	24
37	122362	15·73	996151	·28	126211	16·01	873789	23
38	123306	15·69	996134	·28	127172	15·97	872828	22
39	124248	15·66	996117	·28	128130	15·94	871870	21
40	125187	15·62	996100	·28	129087	15·91	870913	20
41	9·126125	15·59	9·996083	·29	9·130041	15·87	10·869959	19
42	127060	15·56	996066	·29	130994	15·84	869006	18
43	127993	15·52	996049	·29	131944	15·81	868056	17
44	128925	15·49	996032	·29	132893	15·77	867107	16
45	129854	15·45	996015	·29	133839	15·74	866161	15
46	130781	15·42	995998	·29	134784	15·71	865216	14
47	131706	15·39	995980	·29	135726	15·67	864274	13
48	132630	15·35	995963	·29	136667	15·64	863333	12
49	133551	15·32	995946	·29	137605	15·61	862395	11
50	134470	15·29	995928	·29	138542	15·58	861458	10
51	9·135387	15·25	9·995911	·29	9·139476	15·55	10·860524	9
52	136303	15·22	995894	·29	140409	15·51	859591	8
53	137216	15·19	995876	·29	141340	15·48	858660	7
54	138128	15·16	995859	·29	142269	15·45	857731	6
55	139037	15·12	995841	·29	143196	15·42	856804	5
56	139944	15·09	995823	·29	144121	15·39	855879	4
57	140850	15·06	995806	·29	145044	15·35	854956	3
58	141754	15·03	995788	·29	145966	15·32	854034	2
59	142655	15·00	995771	·29	146885	15·29	853115	1
60	143555	14·96	995753	·29	147803	15·26	852197	0
	Cosine	D.	Sine		Cotang.	D.	Tang.	M.

(82 DEGREES.)

M.	Sine	D.	Cosine	D.	Tang.	D.	Cotang.	
0	9·143555	14·96	9·995753	·30	9·147803	15·26	10·852197	60
1	144453	14·93	995735	·30	148718	15·23	851282	59
2	145349	14·90	995717	·30	149632	15·20	850368	58
3	146243	14·87	995699	·30	150544	15·17	849456	57
4	147136	14·84	995681	·30	151454	15·14	848546	56
5	148026	14·81	995664	·30	152363	15·11	847637	55
6	148915	14·78	995646	·30	153269	15·08	846731	54
7	149802	14·75	995628	·30	154174	15·05	845826	53
8	150686	14·72	995610	·30	155077	15·02	844923	52
9	151569	14·69	995591	·30	155978	14·99	844022	51
10	152451	14·66	995573	·30	156877	14·96	843123	50
11	9·153330	14·63	9·995555	·30	9·157775	14·93	10·842225	49
12	154208	14·60	995537	·30	158671	14·90	841329	48
13	155083	14·57	995519	·30	159565	14·87	840435	47
14	155957	14·54	995501	·31	160457	14·84	839543	46
15	156830	14·51	995482	·31	161347	14·81	838653	45
16	157700	14·48	995464	·31	162236	14·79	837764	44
17	158569	14·45	995446	·31	163123	14·76	836877	43
18	159435	14·42	995427	·31	164008	14·73	835992	42
19	160301	14·39	995409	·31	164892	14·70	835108	41
20	161164	14·36	995390	·31	165774	14·67	834226	40
21	9·162025	14·33	9·995372	·31	9·166654	14·64	10·833346	39
22	162885	14·30	995353	·31	167532	14·61	832468	38
23	163743	14·27	995334	·31	168409	14·58	831591	37
24	164600	14·24	995316	·31	169284	14·55	830716	36
25	165454	14·22	995297	·31	170157	14·53	829843	35
26	166307	14·19	995278	·31	171029	14·50	828971	34
27	167159	14·16	995260	·31	171899	14·47	828101	33
28	168008	14·13	995241	·32	172767	14·44	827233	32
29	168856	14·10	995222	·32	173634	14·42	826366	31
30	169702	14·07	995203	·32	174499	14·39	825501	30
31	9·170547	14·05	9·995184	·32	9·175362	14·36	10·824638	29
32	171389	14·02	995165	·32	176224	14·33	823776	28
33	172230	13·99	995146	·32	177084	14·31	822916	27
34	173070	13·96	995127	·32	177942	14·28	822058	26
35	173908	13·94	995108	·32	178799	14·25	821201	25
36	174744	13·91	995089	·32	179655	14·23	820345	24
37	175578	13·88	995070	·32	180508	14·20	819492	23
38	176411	13·86	995051	·32	181360	14·17	818640	22
39	177242	13·83	995032	·32	182211	14·15	817789	21
40	178072	13·80	995013	·32	183059	14·12	816941	20
41	9·178900	13·77	9·994993	·32	9·183907	14·09	10·816093	19
42	179726	13·74	994974	·32	184752	14·07	815248	18
43	180551	13·72	994955	·32	185597	14·04	814403	17
44	181374	13·69	994935	·32	186439	14·02	813561	16
45	182196	13·66	994916	·33	187280	13·99	812720	15
46	183016	13·64	994896	·33	188120	13·96	811880	14
47	183834	13·61	994877	·33	188958	13·93	811042	13
48	184651	13·59	994857	·33	189794	13·91	810206	12
49	185466	13·56	994838	·33	190629	13·89	809371	11
50	186280	13·53	994818	·33	191462	13·86	808538	10
51	9·187092	13·51	9·994798	·33	9·192294	13·84	10·807706	9
52	187903	13·48	994779	·33	193124	13·81	806876	8
53	188712	13·46	994759	·33	193953	13·79	806047	7
54	189519	13·43	994739	·33	194780	13·76	805220	6
55	190325	13·41	994719	·33	195606	13·74	804394	5
56	191130	13·38	994700	·33	196430	13·71	803570	4
57	191933	13·36	994680	·33	197253	13·69	802747	3
58	192734	13·33	994660	·33	198074	13·66	801926	2
59	193534	13·30	994640	·33	198894	13·64	801106	1
60	194332	13·28	994620	·33	199713	13·61	800287	0
	Cosine	D.	Sine		Cotang.	D.	Tang.	M.

(81 DEGREES.)

M.	Sine	D.	Cosine	D.	Tang.	D.	Cotang.	
0	9·194332	13·28	9·994620	·33	9·199713	13·61	10·800287	60
1	195129	13·26	994600	·33	200529	13·59	799471	59
2	195925	13·23	994580	·33	201345	13·56	798655	58
3	196719	13·21	994560	34	202159	13·54	797841	57
4	197511	13·18	994540	·34	202971	13·52	797029	56
5	198302	13·16	994519	·34	203782	13·49	796218	55
6	199091	13·13	994499	·34	204592	13·47	795408	54
7	199879	13·11	994479	·34	205400	13·45	794600	53
8	200666	13·08	994459	·34	206207	13·42	793793	52
9	201451	13·06	994438	·34	207013	13·40	792987	51
10	202234	13·04	994418	·34	207817	13·38	792183	50
11	9·203017	13·01	9·994397	·34	9·208619	13·35	10·791381	49
12	203797	12·99	994377	·34	209420	13·33	790580	48
13	204577	12·96	994357	·34	210220	13·31	789780	47
14	205354	12·94	994336	·34	211018	13·28	788982	46
15	206131	12·92	994316	·34	211815	13·26	788185	45
16	206906	12·89	994295	·34	212611	13·24	787389	44
17	207679	12·87	994274	·35	213405	13·21	786595	43
18	208452	12·85	994254	·35	214198	13·19	785802	42
19	209222	12·82	994233	·35	214989	13·17	785011	41
20	209992	12·80	994212	·35	215780	13·15	784220	40
21	9·210760	12·78	9·994191	·35	9·216568	13·12	10·783432	39
22	211526	12·75	994171	·35	217356	13·10	782644	38
23	212291	12·73	994150	·35	218142	13·08	781858	37
24	213055	12·71	994129	·35	218926	13·05	781074	36
25	213818	12·68	994108	·35	219710	13·03	780290	35
26	214579	12·66	994087	·35	220492	13·01	779508	34
27	215338	12·64	994066	·35	221272	12·99	778728	33
28	216097	12·61	994045	·35	222052	12·97	777948	32
29	216854	12·59	994024	·35	222830	12·94	777170	31
30	217609	12·57	994003	·35	223606	12·92	776394	30
31	9·218363	12·55	9·993981	·35	9·224382	12·90	10·775618	29
32	219116	12·53	993960	·35	225156	12·88	774844	28
33	219868	12·50	993939	·35	225929	12·86	774071	27
34	220618	12·48	993918	·35	226700	12·84	773300	26
35	221367	12·46	993896	·36	227471	12·81	772529	25
36	222115	12·44	993875	·36	228239	12·79	771761	24
37	222861	12·42	993854	·36	229007	12·77	770993	23
38	223606	12·39	993832	·36	229773	12·75	770227	22
39	224349	12·37	993811	·36	230539	12·73	769461	21
40	225092	12·35	993789	·36	231302	12·71	768698	20
41	9·225833	12·33	9·993768	·36	9·232065	12·69	10·767935	19
42	226573	12·31	993746	·36	232826	12·67	767174	18
43	227311	12·28	993725	·36	233586	12·65	766414	17
44	228048	12·26	993703	·36	234345	12·62	765655	16
45	228784	12·24	993681	·36	235103	12·60	764897	15
46	229518	12·22	993660	·36	235859	12·58	764141	14
47	230252	12·20	993638	·36	236614	12·56	763386	13
48	230984	12·18	993616	·36	237368	12·54	762632	12
49	231714	12·16	993594	·37	238120	12·52	761880	11
50	232444	12·14	993572	·37	238872	12·50	761128	10
51	9·233172	12·12	9·993550	·37	9·239622	12·48	10·760378	9
52	233899	12·09	993528	·37	240371	12·46	759629	8
53	234625	12·07	993506	·37	241118	12·44	758882	7
54	235349	12·05	993484	·37	241865	12·42	758135	6
55	236073	12·03	993462	·37	242610	12·40	757390	5
56	236795	12·01	993440	·37	243354	12·38	756646	4
57	237515	11·99	993418	·37	244097	12·36	755903	3
58	238235	11·97	993396	·37	244839	12·34	755161	2
59	238953	11·95	993374	·37	245579	12·32	754421	1
60	239670	11·93	993351	·37	246319	12·30	753681	0
	Cosine	D.	Sine		Cotang.	D.	Tang.	M.

(80 DEGREES.)

M.	Sine	D.	Cosine	D.	Tang.	D.	Cotang.	
0	9·239670	11·93	9·993351	·37	9·246319	12·30	10·753681	60
1	240386	11·91	993329	·37	247057	12·28	752943	59
2	241101	11·89	993307	·37	247794	12·26	752206	58
3	241814	11·87	993285	·37	248530	12·24	751470	57
4	242526	11·85	993262	·37	249264	12·22	750736	56
5	243237	11·83	993240	·37	249998	12·20	750002	55
6	243947	11·81	993217	·38	250730	12·18	749270	54
7	244656	11·79	993195	·38	251461	12·17	748539	53
8	245363	11·77	993172	·38	252191	12·15	747809	52
9	246069	11·75	993149	·38	252920	12·13	747080	51
10	246775	11·73	993127	·38	253648	12·11	746352	50
11	9·247478	11·71	9·993104	·38	9·254374	12·09	10·745626	49
12	248181	11·69	993081	·38	255100	12·07	744900	48
13	248883	11·67	993059	·38	255824	12·05	744176	47
14	249583	11·65	993036	·38	256547	12·03	743453	46
15	250282	11·63	993013	·38	257269	12·01	742731	45
16	250980	11·61	992990	·38	257990	12·00	742010	44
17	251677	11·59	992967	·38	258710	11·98	741290	43
18	252373	11·58	992944	·38	259429	11·96	740571	42
19	253067	11·56	992921	·38	260146	11·94	739854	41
20	253761	11·54	992898	·38	260863	11·92	739137	40
21	9·254453	11·52	9·992875	·38	9·261578	11·90	10·738422	39
22	255144	11·50	992852	·38	262292	11·89	737708	38
23	255834	11·48	992829	·39	263005	11·87	736995	37
24	256523	11·46	992806	·39	263717	11·85	736283	36
25	257211	11·44	992783	·39	264428	11·83	735572	35
26	257898	11·42	992759	·39	265138	11·81	734862	34
27	258583	11·41	992736	·39	265847	11·79	734153	33
28	259268	11·39	992713	·39	266555	11·78	733445	32
29	259951	11·37	992690	·39	267261	11·76	732739	31
30	260633	11·35	992666	·39	267967	11·74	732033	30
31	9·261314	11·33	9·992643	·39	9·268671	11·72	10·731329	29
32	261994	11·31	992619	·39	269375	11·70	730625	28
33	262673	11·30	992596	·39	270077	11·69	729923	27
34	263351	11·28	992572	·39	270779	11·67	729221	26
35	264027	11·26	992549	·39	271479	11·65	728521	25
36	264703	11·24	992525	·39	272178	11·64	727822	24
37	265377	11·22	992501	·39	272876	11·62	727124	23
38	266051	11·20	992478	·40	273573	11·60	726427	22
39	266723	11·19	992454	·40	274269	11·58	725731	21
40	267395	11·17	992430	·40	274964	11·57	725036	20
41	9·268065	11·15	9·992406	·40	9·275658	11·55	10·724342	19
42	268734	11·13	992382	·40	276351	11·53	723649	18
43	269402	11·11	992359	·40	277043	11·51	722957	17
44	270069	11·10	992335	·40	277734	11·50	722266	16
45	270735	11·08	992311	·40	278424	11·48	721576	15
46	271400	11·06	992287	·40	279113	11·47	720887	14
47	272064	11·05	992263	·40	279801	11·45	720199	13
48	272726	11·03	992239	·40	280488	11·43	719512	12
49	273388	11·01	992214	·40	281174	11·41	718826	11
50	274049	10·99	992190	·40	281858	11·40	718142	10
51	9·274708	10·98	9·992166	·40	9·282542	11·38	10·717458	9
52	275367	10·96	992142	·40	283225	11·36	716775	8
53	276024	10·94	992117	·41	283907	11·35	716093	7
54	276681	10·92	992093	·41	284588	11·33	715412	6
55	277337	10·91	992069	·41	285268	11·31	714732	5
56	277991	10·89	992044	·41	285947	11·30	714053	4
57	278644	10·87	992020	·41	286624	11·28	713376	3
58	279297	10·86	991996	·41	287301	11·26	712699	2
59	279948	10·84	991971	·41	287977	11·25	712023	1
60	280599	10·82	991947	·41	288652	11·23	711348	0
	Cosine	D.	Sine		Cotang.	D.	Tang.	M.

(79 DEGREES.)

M.	Sine	D.	Cosine	D.	Tang.	D.	Cotang.	
0	9·280599	10·82	9·991947	·41	9·288652	11·23	10·711348	60
1	281248	10·81	991922	·41	289326	11·22	710674	59
2	281897	10·79	991897	·41	289999	11·20	710001	58
3	282544	10·77	991873	·41	290671	11·18	709329	57
4	283190	10·76	991848	·41	291342	11·17	708658	56
5	283836	10·74	991823	·41	292013	11·15	707987	55
6	284480	10·72	991799	·41	292682	11·14	707318	54
7	285124	10·71	991774	·42	293350	11·12	706650	53
8	285766	10·69	991749	·42	294017	11·11	705983	52
9	286408	10·67	991724	·42	294684	11·09	705316	51
10	287048	10·66	991699	·42	295349	11·07	704651	50
11	9·287687	10·64	9·991674	·42	9·296013	11·06	10·703987	49
12	288326	10·63	991649	·42	296677	11·04	703323	48
13	288964	10·61	991624	·42	297339	11·03	702661	47
14	289600	10·59	991599	·42	298001	11·01	701999	46
15	290236	10·58	991574	·42	298662	11·00	701338	45
16	290870	10·56	991549	·42	299322	10·98	700678	44
17	291504	10·54	991524	·42	299980	10·96	700020	43
18	292137	10·53	991498	·42	300638	10·95	699362	42
19	292768	10·51	991473	·42	301295	10·93	698705	41
20	293399	10·50	991448	·42	301951	10·92	698049	40
21	9·294029	10·48	9·991422	·42	9·302607	10·90	10·697393	39
22	294658	10·46	991397	·42	303261	10·89	696739	38
23	295286	10·45	991372	·43	303914	10·87	696086	37
24	295913	10·43	991346	·43	304567	10·86	695433	36
25	296539	10·42	991321	·43	305218	10·84	694782	35
26	297164	10·40	991295	·43	305869	10·83	694131	34
27	297788	10·39	991270	·43	306519	10·81	693481	33
28	298412	10·37	991244	·43	307168	10·80	692832	32
29	299034	10·36	991218	·43	307815	10·78	692185	31
30	299655	10·34	991193	·43	308463	10·77	691537	30
31	9·300276	10·32	9·991167	·43	9·309109	10·75	10·690891	29
32	300895	10·31	991141	·43	309754	10·74	690246	28
33	301514	10·29	991115	·43	310398	10·73	689602	27
34	302132	10·28	991090	·43	311042	10·71	688958	26
35	302748	10·26	991064	·43	311685	10·70	688315	25
36	303364	10·25	991038	·43	312327	10·68	687673	24
37	303979	10·23	991012	·43	312967	10·67	687033	23
38	304593	10·22	990986	·43	313608	10·65	686392	22
39	305207	10·20	990960	·43	314247	10·64	685753	21
40	305819	10·19	990934	·44	314885	10·62	685115	20
41	9·306430	10·17	9·990908	·44	9·315523	10·61	10·684477	19
42	307041	10·16	990882	·44	316159	10·60	683841	18
43	307650	10·14	990855	·44	316795	10·58	683205	17
44	308259	10·13	990829	·44	317430	10·57	682570	16
45	308867	10·11	990803	·44	318064	10·55	681936	15
46	309474	10·10	990777	·44	318697	10·54	681303	14
47	310080	10·08	990750	·44	319329	10·53	680671	13
48	310685	10·07	990724	·44	319961	10·51	680039	12
49	311289	10·05	990697	·44	320592	10·50	679408	11
50	311893	10·04	990671	·44	321222	10·48	678778	10
51	9·312495	10·03	9·990644	·44	9·321851	10·47	10·678149	9
52	313097	10·01	990618	·44	322479	10·45	677521	8
53	313698	10·00	990591	·44	323106	10·44	676894	7
54	314297	9·98	990565	·44	323733	10·43	676267	6
55	314897	9·97	990538	·44	324358	10·41	675642	5
56	315495	9·96	990511	·45	324983	10·40	675017	4
57	316092	9·94	990485	·45	325607	10·39	674393	3
58	316689	9·93	990458	·45	326231	10·37	673769	2
59	317284	9·91	990431	·45	326853	10·36	673147	1
60	317879	9·90	990404	·45	327475	10·35	672525	0
	Cosine	D.	Sine		Cotang.	D.	Tang.	M.

(78 DEGREES.)

M.	Sine	D.	Cosine	D.	Tang.	D.	Cotang.	
0	9·317879	9·90	9·990404	·45	9·327474	10·35	10·672526	60
1	318473	9·88	990378	·45	328095	10·33	671905	59
2	319066	9·87	990351	·45	328715	10·32	671285	58
3	319658	9·86	990324	·45	329334	10·30	670666	57
4	320249	9·84	990297	·45	329953	10·29	670047	56
5	320840	9·83	990270	·45	330570	10·28	669430	55
6	321430	9·82	990243	·45	331187	10·26	668813	54
7	322019	9·80	990215	·45	331803	10·25	668197	53
8	322607	9·79	990188	·45	332418	10·24	667582	52
9	323194	9·77	990161	·45	333033	10·23	666967	51
10	323780	9·76	990134	·45	333646	10·21	666354	50
11	9·324366	9·75	9·990107	·46	9·334259	10·20	10·665741	49
12	324950	9·73	990079	·46	334871	10·19	665129	48
13	325534	9·72	990052	·46	335482	10·17	664518	47
14	326117	9·70	990025	·46	336093	10·16	663907	46
15	326700	9·69	989997	·46	336702	10·15	663298	45
16	327281	9·68	989970	·46	337311	10·13	662689	44
17	327862	9·66	989942	·46	337919	10·12	662081	43
18	328442	9·65	989915	·46	338527	10·11	661473	42
19	329021	9·64	989887	·46	339133	10·10	660867	41
20	329599	9·62	989860	·46	339739	10·08	660261	40
21	9·330176	9·61	9·989832	·46	9·340344	10·07	10·659656	39
22	330753	9·60	989804	·46	340948	10·06	659052	38
23	331329	9·58	989777	·46	341552	10·04	658448	37
24	331903	9·57	989749	·47	342155	10·03	657845	36
25	332478	9·56	989721	·47	342757	10·02	657243	35
26	333051	9·54	989693	·47	343358	10·00	656642	34
27	333624	9·53	989665	·47	343958	9·99	656042	33
28	334195	9·52	989637	·47	344558	9·98	655442	32
29	334766	9·50	989609	·47	345157	9·97	654843	31
30	335337	9·49	989582	·47	345755	9·96	654245	30
31	9·335906	9·48	9·989553	·47	9·346353	9·94	10·653647	29
32	336475	9·46	989525	·47	346949	9·93	653051	28
33	337043	9·45	989497	·47	347545	9·92	652455	27
34	337610	9·44	989469	·47	348141	9·91	651859	26
35	338176	9·43	989441	·47	348735	9·90	651265	25
36	338742	9·41	989413	·47	349329	9·88	650671	24
37	339306	9·40	989384	·47	349922	9·87	650078	23
38	339871	9·39	989356	·47	350514	9·86	649486	22
39	340434	9·37	989328	·47	351106	9·85	648894	21
40	340996	9·36	989300	·47	351697	9·83	648303	20
41	9·341558	9·35	9·989271	·47	9·352287	9·82	10·647713	19
42	342119	9·34	989243	·47	352876	9·81	647124	18
43	342679	9·32	989214	·47	353465	9·80	646535	17
44	343239	9·31	989186	·47	354053	9·79	645947	16
45	343797	9·30	989157	·47	354640	9·77	645360	15
46	344355	9·29	989128	·48	355227	9·76	644773	14
47	344912	9·27	989100	·48	355813	9·75	644187	13
48	345469	9·26	989071	·48	356398	9·74	643602	12
49	346024	9·25	989042	·48	356982	9·73	643018	11
50	346579	9·24	989014	·48	357566	9·71	642434	10
51	9·347134	9·22	9·988985	·48	9·358149	9·70	10·641851	9
52	347687	9·21	988956	·48	358731	9·69	641269	8
53	348240	9·20	988927	·48	359313	9·68	640687	7
54	348792	9·19	988898	·48	359893	9·67	640107	6
55	349343	9·17	988869	·48	360474	9·66	639526	5
56	349893	9·16	988840	·48	361053	9·65	638947	4
57	350443	9·15	988811	·49	361632	9·63	638368	3
58	350992	9·14	988782	·49	362210	9·62	637790	2
59	351540	9·13	988753	·49	362787	9·61	637213	1
60	352088	9·11	988724	·49	363364	9·60	636636	0
	Cosine	D.	Sine		Cotang.	D.	Tang.	M.

M.	Sine	D.	Cosine	D.	Tang.	D.	Cotang.	
0	9·352088	9·11	9·988724	·49	9·363364	9·60	10·636636	60
1	352635	9·10	988695	·49	363940	9·59	636060	59
2	353181	9·09	988666	·49	364515	9·58	635485	58
3	353726	9·08	988636	·49	365090	9·57	634910	57
4	354271	9·07	988607	·49	365664	9·55	634336	56
5	354815	9·05	988578	·49	366237	9·54	633763	55
6	355358	9·04	988548	·49	366810	9·53	633190	54
7	355901	9·03	988519	·49	367382	9·52	632618	53
8	356443	9·02	988489	·49	367953	9·51	632047	52
9	356984	9·01	988460	·49	368524	9·50	631476	51
10	357524	8·99	988430	·49	369094	9·49	630906	50
11	9·358064	8·98	9·988401	·49	9·369663	9·48	10·630337	49
12	358603	8·97	988371	·49	370232	9·46	629768	48
13	359141	8·96	988342	·49	370799	9·45	629201	47
14	359678	8·95	988312	·50	371367	9·44	628633	46
15	360215	8·93	988282	·50	371933	9·43	628067	45
16	360752	8·92	988252	·50	372499	9·42	627501	44
17	361287	8·91	988223	·50	373064	9·41	626936	43
18	361822	8·90	988193	·50	373629	9·40	626371	42
19	362356	8·89	988163	·50	374193	9·39	625807	41
20	362889	8·88	988133	·50	374756	9·38	625244	40
21	9·363422	8·87	9·988103	·50	9·375319	9·37	10·624681	39
22	363954	8·85	988073	·50	375881	9·35	624119	38
23	364485	8·84	988043	·50	376442	9·34	623558	37
24	365016	8·83	988013	·50	377003	9·33	622997	36
25	365546	8·82	987983	·50	377563	9·32	622437	35
26	366075	8·81	987953	·50	378122	9·31	621878	34
27	366604	8·80	987922	·50	378681	9·30	621319	33
28	367131	8·79	987892	·50	379239	9·29	620761	32
29	367659	8·77	987862	·50	379797	9·28	620203	31
30	368185	8·76	987832	·51	380354	9·27	619646	30
31	9·368711	8·75	9·987801	·51	9·380910	9·26	10·619090	29
32	369236	8·74	987771	·51	381466	9·25	618534	28
33	369761	8·73	987740	·51	382020	9·24	617980	27
34	370285	8·72	987710	·51	382575	9·23	617425	26
35	370808	8·71	987679	·51	383129	9·22	616871	25
36	371330	8·70	987649	·51	383682	9·21	616318	24
37	371852	8·69	987618	·51	384234	9·20	615766	23
38	372373	8·67	987588	·51	384786	9·19	615214	22
39	372894	8·66	987557	·51	385337	9·18	614663	21
40	373414	8·65	987526	·51	385888	9·17	614112	20
41	9·373933	8·64	9·987496	·51	9·386438	9·15	10·613562	19
42	374452	8·63	987465	·51	386987	9·14	613013	18
43	374970	8·62	987434	·51	387536	9·13	612464	17
44	375487	8·61	987403	·52	388084	9·12	611916	16
45	376003	8·60	987372	·52	388631	9·11	611369	15
46	376519	8·59	987341	·52	389178	9·10	610822	14
47	377035	8·58	987310	·52	389724	9·09	610276	13
48	377549	8·57	987279	·52	390270	9·08	609730	12
49	378063	8·56	987248	·52	390815	9·07	609185	11
50	378577	8·54	987217	·52	391360	9·06	608640	10
51	9·379089	8·53	9·987186	·52	9·391903	9·05	10·608097	9
52	379601	8·52	987155	·52	392447	9·04	607553	8
53	380113	8·51	987124	·52	392989	9·03	607011	7
54	380624	8·50	987092	·52	393531	9·02	606469	6
55	381134	8·49	987061	·52	394073	9·01	605927	5
56	381643	8·48	987030	·52	394614	9·00	605386	4
57	382152	8·47	986998	·52	395154	8·99	604846	3
58	382661	8·46	986967	·52	395694	8·98	604306	2
59	383168	8·45	986936	·52	396233	8·97	603767	1
60	383675	8·44	986904	·52	396771	8·96	603229	0
	Cosine	D.	Sine		Cotang.	D.	Tang.	M.

M.	Sine	D.	Cosine	D.	Tang.	D.	Cotang.	
0	9·383675	8·44	9·986904	·52	9·396771	8·96	10·603229	60
1	384182	8·43	986873	·53	397309	8·96	602691	59
2	384687	8·42	986841	·53	397846	8·95	602154	58
3	385192	8·41	986809	·53	398383	8·94	601617	57
4	385697	8·40	986778	·53	398919	8·93	601081	56
5	386201	8·39	986746	·53	399455	8·92	600545	55
6	386704	8·38	986714	·53	399990	8·91	600010	54
7	387207	8·37	986683	·53	400524	8·90	599476	53
8	387709	8·36	986651	·53	401058	8·89	598942	52
9	388210	8·35	986619	·53	401591	8·88	598409	51
10	388711	8·34	986587	·53	402124	8·87	597876	50
11	9·389211	8·33	9·986555	·53	9·402656	8·86	10·597344	49
12	389711	8·32	986523	·53	403187	8·85	596813	48
13	390210	8·31	986491	·53	403718	8·84	596282	47
14	390708	8·30	986459	·53	404249	8·83	595751	46
15	391206	8·28	986427	·53	404778	8·82	595222	45
16	391703	8·27	986395	·53	405308	8·81	594692	44
17	392199	8·26	986363	·54	405836	8·80	594164	43
18	392695	8·25	986331	·54	406364	8·79	593636	42
19	393191	8·24	986299	·54	406892	8·78	593108	41
20	393685	8·23	986266	·54	407419	8·77	592581	40
21	9·394179	8·22	9·986234	·54	9·407945	8·76	10·592055	39
22	394673	8·21	986202	·54	408471	8·75	591529	38
23	395166	8·20	986169	·54	408997	8·74	591003	37
24	395658	8·19	986137	·54	409521	8·74	590479	36
25	396150	8·18	986104	·54	410045	8·73	589955	35
26	396641	8·17	986072	·54	410569	8·72	589431	34
27	397132	8·17	986039	·54	411092	8·71	588908	33
28	397621	8·16	986007	·54	411615	8·70	588385	32
29	398111	8·15	985974	·54	412137	8·69	587863	31
30	398600	8·14	985942	·54	412658	8·68	587342	30
31	9·399088	8·13	9·985909	·55	9·413179	8·67	10·586821	29
32	399575	8·12	985876	·55	413699	8·66	586301	28
33	400062	8·11	985843	·55	414219	8·65	585781	27
34	400549	8·10	985811	·55	414738	8·64	585262	26
35	401035	8·09	985778	·55	415257	8·64	584743	25
36	401520	8·08	985745	·55	415775	8·63	584225	24
37	402005	8·07	985712	·55	416293	8·62	583707	23
38	402489	8·06	985679	·55	416810	8·61	583190	22
39	402972	8·05	985646	·55	417326	8·60	582674	21
40	403455	8·04	985613	·55	417842	8·59	582158	20
41	9·403938	8·03	9·985580	·55	9·418358	8·58	10·581642	19
42	404420	8·02	985547	·55	418873	8·57	581127	18
43	404901	8·01	985514	·55	419387	8·56	580613	17
44	405382	8·00	985480	·55	419901	8·55	580099	16
45	405862	7·99	985447	·55	420415	8·55	579585	15
46	406341	7·98	985414	·56	420927	8·54	579073	14
47	406820	7·97	985380	·56	421440	8·53	578560	13
48	407299	7·96	985347	·56	421952	8·52	578048	12
49	407777	7·95	985314	·56	422463	8·51	577537	11
50	408254	7·94	985280	·56	422974	8·50	577026	10
51	9·408731	7·94	9·985247	·56	9·423484	8·49	10·576516	9
52	409207	7·93	985213	·56	423993	8·48	576007	8
53	409682	7·92	985180	·56	424503	8·48	575497	7
54	410157	7·91	985146	·56	425011	8·47	574989	6
55	410632	7·90	985113	·56	425519	8·46	574481	5
56	411106	7·89	985079	·56	426027	8·45	573973	4
57	411579	7·88	985045	·56	426534	8·44	573466	3
58	412052	7·87	985011	·56	427041	8·43	572959	2
59	412524	7·86	984978	·56	427547	8·43	572453	1
60	412996	7·85	984944	·56	428052	8·42	571948	0
	Cosine	D.	Sine		Cotang.	D.	Tang.	M.

M.	Sine	D.	Cosine	D.	Tang.	D.	Cotang.	
0	9·412996	7·85	9·984944	·57	9·428052	8·42	10·571948	60
1	413467	7·84	984910	·57	428557	8·41	571443	59
2	413938	7·83	984876	·57	429062	8·40	570938	58
3	414408	7·83	984842	·57	429566	8·39	570434	57
4	414878	7·82	984808	·57	430070	8·38	569930	56
5	415347	7·81	984774	·57	430573	8·38	569427	55
6	415815	7·80	984740	·57	431075	8·37	568925	54
7	416283	7·79	984706	·57	431577	8·36	568423	53
8	416751	7·78	984672	·57	432079	8·35	567921	52
9	417217	7·77	984637	·57	432580	8·34	567420	51
10	417684	7·76	984603	·57	433080	8·33	566920	50
11	9·418150	7·75	9·984569	·57	9·433580	8·32	10·566420	49
12	418615	7·74	984535	·57	434080	8·32	565920	48
13	419079	7·73	984500	·57	434579	8·31	565421	47
14	419544	7·73	984466	·57	435078	8·30	564922	46
15	420007	7·72	984432	·58	435576	8·29	564424	45
16	420470	7·71	984397	·58	436073	8·28	563927	44
17	420933	7·70	984363	·58	436570	8·28	563430	43
18	421395	7·69	984328	·58	437067	8·27	562933	42
19	421857	7·68	984294	·58	437563	8·26	562437	41
20	422318	7·67	984259	·58	438059	8·25	561941	40
21	9·422778	7·67	9·984224	·58	9·438554	8·24	10·561446	39
22	423238	7·66	984190	·58	439048	8·23	560952	38
23	423697	7·65	984155	·58	439543	8·23	560457	37
24	424156	7·64	984120	·58	440036	8·22	559964	36
25	424615	7·63	984085	·58	440529	8·21	559471	35
26	425073	7·62	984050	·58	441022	8·20	558978	34
27	425530	7·61	984015	·58	441514	8·19	558486	33
28	425987	7·60	983981	·58	442006	8·19	557994	32
29	426443	7·60	983946	·58	442497	8·18	557503	31
30	426899	7·59	983911	·58	442988	8·17	557012	30
31	9·427354	7·58	9·983875	·58	9·443479	8·16	10·556521	29
32	427809	7·57	983840	·59	443968	8·16	556032	28
33	428263	7·56	983805	·59	444458	8·15	555542	27
34	428717	7·55	983770	·59	444947	8·14	555053	26
35	429170	7·54	983735	·59	445435	8·13	554565	25
36	429623	7·53	983700	·59	445923	8·12	554077	24
37	430075	7·52	983664	·59	446411	8·12	553589	23
38	430527	7·52	983629	·59	446898	8·11	553102	22
39	430978	7·51	983594	·59	447384	8·10	552616	21
40	431429	7·50	983558	·59	447870	8·09	552130	20
41	9·431879	7·49	9·983523	·59	9·448356	8·09	10·551644	19
42	432329	7·49	983487	·59	448841	8·08	551159	18
43	432778	7·48	983452	·59	449326	8·07	550674	17
44	433226	7·47	983416	·59	449810	8·06	550190	16
45	433675	7·46	983381	·59	450294	8·06	549706	15
46	434122	7·45	983345	·59	450777	8·05	549223	14
47	434569	7·44	983309	·59	451260	8·04	548740	13
48	435016	7·44	983273	·60	451743	8·03	548257	12
49	435462	7·43	983238	·60	452225	8·02	547775	11
50	435908	7·42	983202	·60	452706	8·02	547294	10
51	9·436353	7·41	9·983166	·60	9·453187	8·01	10·546813	9
52	436798	7·40	983130	·60	453668	8·00	546332	8
53	437242	7·40	983094	·60	454148	7·99	545852	7
54	437686	7·39	983058	·60	454628	7·99	545372	6
55	438129	7·38	983022	·60	455107	7·98	544893	5
56	438572	7·37	982986	·60	455586	7·97	544414	4
57	439014	7·36	982950	·60	456064	7·96	543936	3
58	439456	7·36	982914	·60	456542	7·96	543458	2
59	439897	7·35	982878	·60	457019	7·95	542981	1
60	440338	7·34	982842	·60	457496	7·94	542504	0
	Cosine	D.	Sine		Cotang.	D.	Tang.	M.

M.	Sine	D.	Cosine	D.	Tang.	D.	Cotang.	
0	9·440338	7·34	9·982842	·60	9·457496	7·94	10·542504	60
1	440778	7·33	982805	·60	457973	7·93	542027	59
2	441218	7·32	982769	·61	458449	7·93	541551	58
3	441658	7·31	982733	·61	458925	7·92	541075	57
4	442096	7·31	982696	·61	459400	7·91	540600	56
5	442535	7·30	982660	·61	459875	7·90	540125	55
6	442973	7·29	982624	·61	460349	7·90	539651	54
7	443410	7·28	982587	·61	460823	7·89	539177	53
8	443847	7·27	982551	·61	461297	7·88	538703	52
9	444284	7·27	982514	·61	461770	7·88	538230	51
10	444720	7·26	982477	·61	462242	7·87	537758	50
11	9·445155	7·25	9·982441	·61	9·462714	7·86	10·537286	49
12	445590	7·24	982404	·61	463186	7·85	536814	48
13	446025	7·23	982367	·61	463658	7·85	536342	47
14	446459	7·23	982331	·61	464129	7·84	535871	46
15	446893	7·22	982294	·61	464599	7·83	535401	45
16	447326	7·21	982257	·61	465069	7·83	534931	44
17	447759	7·20	982220	·62	465539	7·82	534461	43
18	448191	7·20	982183	·62	466008	7·81	533992	42
19	448623	7·19	982146	·62	466476	7·80	533524	41
20	449054	7·18	982109	·62	466945	7·80	533055	40
21	9·449485	7·17	9·982072	·62	9·467413	7·79	10·532587	39
22	449915	7·16	982035	·62	467880	7·78	532120	38
23	450345	7·16	981998	·62	468347	7·78	531653	37
24	450775	7·15	981961	·62	468814	7·77	531186	36
25	451204	7·14	981924	·62	469280	7·76	530720	35
26	451632	7·13	981886	·62	469746	7·75	530254	34
27	452060	7·13	981849	·62	470211	7·75	529789	33
28	452488	7·12	981812	·62	470676	7·74	529324	32
29	452915	7·11	981774	·62	471141	7·73	528859	31
30	453342	7·10	981737	·62	471605	7·73	528395	30
31	9·453768	7·10	9·981699	·63	9·472068	7·72	10·527932	29
32	454194	7·09	981662	·63	472532	7·71	527468	28
33	454619	7·08	981625	·63	472995	7·71	527005	27
34	455044	7·07	981587	·63	473457	7·70	526543	26
35	455469	7·07	981549	·63	473919	7·69	526081	25
36	455893	7·06	981512	·63	474381	7·69	525619	24
37	456316	7·05	981474	·63	474842	7·68	525158	23
38	456739	7·04	981436	·63	475303	7·67	524697	22
39	457162	7·04	981399	·63	475763	7·67	524237	21
40	457584	7·03	981361	·63	476223	7·66	523777	20
41	9·458006	7·02	9·981323	·63	9·476683	7·65	10·523317	19
42	458427	7·01	981285	·63	477142	7·65	522858	18
43	458848	7·01	981247	·63	477601	7·64	522399	17
44	459268	7·00	981209	·63	478059	7·63	521941	16
45	459688	6·99	981171	·63	478517	7·63	521483	15
46	460108	6·98	981133	·64	478975	7·62	521025	14
47	460527	6·98	981095	·64	479432	7·61	520568	13
48	460946	6·97	981057	·64	479889	7·61	520111	12
49	461364	6·96	981019	·64	480345	7·60	519655	11
50	461782	6·95	980981	·64	480801	7·59	519199	10
51	9·462199	6·95	9·980942	·64	9·481257	7·59	10·518743	9
52	462616	6·94	980904	·64	481712	7·58	518288	8
53	463032	6·93	980866	·64	482167	7·57	517833	7
54	463448	6·93	980827	·64	482621	7·57	517379	6
55	463864	6·92	980789	·64	483075	7·56	516925	5
56	464279	6·91	980750	·64	483529	7·55	516471	4
57	464694	6·90	980712	·64	483982	7·55	516018	3
58	465108	6·90	980673	·64	484435	7·54	515565	2
59	465522	6·89	980635	·64	484887	7·53	515113	1
60	465935	6·88	980596	·64	485339	7·53	514661	0
	Cosine	D.	Sine		Cotang.	D.	Tang.	M.

M.	Sine	D.	Cosine	D.	Tang.	D.	Cotang.	
0	9·465935	6·88	9·980596	·64	9·485339	7·55	10·514661	60
1	466348	6·88	980558	·64	485791	7·52	514209	59
2	466761	6·87	980519	·65	486242	7·51	513758	58
3	467173	6·86	980480	·65	486693	7·51	513307	57
4	467585	6·85	980442	·65	487143	7·50	512857	56
5	467996	6·85	980403	·65	487593	7·49	512407	55
6	468407	6·84	980364	·65	488043	7·49	511957	54
7	468817	6·83	980325	·65	488492	7·48	511508	53
8	469227	6·83	980286	·65	488941	7·47	511059	52
9	469637	6·82	980247	·65	489390	7·47	510610	51
10	470046	6·81	980208	·65	489838	7·46	510162	50
11	9·470455	6·80	9·980169	·65	9·490286	7·46	10·509714	49
12	470863	6·80	980130	·65	490733	7·45	509267	48
13	471271	6·79	980091	·65	491180	7·44	508820	47
14	471679	6·78	980052	·65	491627	7·44	508373	46
15	472086	6·78	980012	·65	492073	7·43	507927	45
16	472492	6·77	979973	·65	492519	7·43	507481	44
17	472898	6·76	979934	·66	492965	7·42	507035	43
18	473304	6·76	979895	·66	493410	7·41	506590	42
19	473710	6·75	979855	·66	493854	7·40	506146	41
20	474115	6·74	979816	·66	494299	7·40	505701	40
21	9·474519	6·74	9·979776	·66	9·494743	7·40	10·505257	39
22	474923	6·73	979737	·66	495186	7·39	504814	38
23	475327	6·72	979697	·66	495630	7·38	504370	37
24	475730	6·72	979658	·66	496073	7·37	503927	36
25	476133	6·71	979618	·66	496515	7·37	503485	35
26	476536	6·70	979579	·66	496957	7·36	503043	34
27	476938	6·69	979539	·66	497399	7·36	502601	33
28	477340	6·69	979499	·66	497841	7·35	502159	32
29	477741	6·68	979459	·66	498282	7·34	501718	31
30	478142	6·67	979420	·66	498722	7·34	501278	30
31	9·478542	6·67	9·979380	·66	9·499163	7·33	10·500837	29
32	478942	6·66	979340	·66	499603	7·33	500397	28
33	479342	6·65	979300	·67	500042	7·32	499958	27
34	479741	6·65	979260	·67	500481	7·31	499519	26
35	480140	6·64	979220	·67	500920	7·31	499080	25
36	480539	6·63	979180	·67	501359	7·30	498641	24
37	480937	6·63	979140	·67	501797	7·30	498203	23
38	481334	6·62	979100	·67	502235	7·29	497765	22
39	481731	6·61	979059	·67	502672	7·28	497328	21
40	482128	6·61	979019	·67	503109	7·28	496891	20
41	9·482525	6·60	9·978979	·67	9·503546	7·27	10·496454	19
42	482921	6·59	978939	·67	503982	7·27	496018	18
43	483316	6·59	978898	·67	504418	7·26	495582	17
44	483712	6·58	978858	·67	504854	7·25	495146	16
45	484107	6·57	978817	·67	505289	7·25	494711	15
46	484501	6·57	978777	·67	505724	7·24	494276	14
47	484895	6·56	978736	·67	506159	7·24	493841	13
48	485289	6·55	978696	·68	506593	7·23	493407	12
49	485682	6·55	978655	·68	507027	7·22	492973	11
50	486075	6·54	978615	·68	507460	7·22	492540	10
51	9·486467	6·53	9·978574	·68	9·507893	7·21	10·492107	9
52	486860	6·53	978533	·68	508326	7·21	491674	8
53	487251	6·52	978493	·68	508759	7·20	491241	7
54	487643	6·51	978452	·68	509191	7·19	490809	6
55	488034	6·51	978411	·68	509622	7·19	490378	5
56	488424	6·50	978370	·68	510054	7·18	489946	4
57	488814	6·50	978329	·68	510485	7·18	489515	3
58	489204	6·49	978288	·68	510916	7·17	489084	2
59	489593	6·48	978247	·68	511346	7·16	488654	1
60	489982	6·48	978206	·68	511776	7·16	488224	0
	Cosine	D.	Sine	D.	Cotang.	D.	Tang.	M.

(72 DEGREES.)

M.	Sine	D.	Cosine	D.	Tang.	D.	Cotang.	
0	9·489982	6·48	9·978206	·68	9·511776	7·16	10·488224	60
1	490371	6·48	978165	·68	512206	7·16	487794	59
2	490759	6·47	978124	·68	512635	7·15	487365	58
3	491147	6·46	978083	·69	513064	7·14	486936	57
4	491535	6·46	978042	·69	513493	7·14	486507	56
5	491922	6·45	978001	·69	513921	7·13	486079	55
6	492308	6·44	977959	·69	514349	7·13	485651	54
7	492695	6·44	977918	·69	514777	7·12	485223	53
8	493081	6·43	977877	·69	515204	7·12	484796	52
9	493466	6·42	977835	·69	515631	7·11	484369	51
10	493851	6·42	977794	·69	516057	7·10	483943	50
11	9·494236	6·41	9·977752	·69	9·516484	7·10	10·483516	49
12	494621	6·41	977711	·69	516910	7·09	483090	48
13	495005	6·40	977669	·69	517335	7·09	482665	47
14	495388	6·39	977628	·69	517761	7·08	482239	46
15	495772	6·39	977586	·69	518185	7·08	481815	45
16	496154	6·38	977544	·70	518610	7·07	481390	44
17	496537	6·37	977503	·70	519034	7·06	480966	43
18	496919	6·37	977461	·70	519458	7·06	480542	42
19	497301	6·36	977419	·70	519882	7·05	480118	41
20	497682	6·36	977377	·70	520305	7·05	479695	40
21	9·498064	6·35	9·977335	·70	9·520728	7·04	10·479272	39
22	498444	6·34	977293	·70	521151	7·03	478849	38
23	498825	6·34	977251	·70	521573	7·03	478427	37
24	499204	6·33	977209	·70	521995	7·03	478005	36
25	499584	6·32	977167	·70	522417	7·02	477583	35
26	499963	6·32	977125	·70	522838	7·02	477162	34
27	500342	6·31	977083	·70	523259	7·01	476741	33
28	500721	6·31	977041	·70	523680	7·01	476320	32
29	501099	6·30	976999	·70	524100	7·00	475900	31
30	501476	6·29	976957	·70	524520	6·99	475480	30
31	9·501854	6·29	9·976914	·70	9·524939	6·99	10·475061	29
32	502231	6·28	976872	·71	525359	6·98	474641	28
33	502607	6·28	976830	·71	525778	6·98	474222	27
34	502984	6·27	976787	·71	526197	6·97	473803	26
35	503360	6·26	976745	·71	526615	6·97	473385	25
36	503735	6·26	976702	·71	527033	6·96	472967	24
37	504110	6·25	976660	·71	527451	6·96	472549	23
38	504485	6·25	976617	·71	527868	6·95	472132	22
39	504860	6·24	976574	·71	528285	6·95	471715	21
40	505234	6·23	976532	·71	528702	6·94	471298	20
41	9·505608	6·23	9·976489	·71	9·529119	6·93	10·470881	19
42	505981	6·22	976446	·71	529535	6·93	470465	18
43	506354	6·22	976404	·71	529950	6·93	470050	17
44	506727	6·21	976361	·71	530366	6·92	469634	16
45	507099	6·20	676318	·71	530781	6·91	469219	15
46	507471	6·20	976275	·71	531196	6·91	468804	14
47	507843	6·19	976232	·72	531611	6·90	468389	13
48	508214	6·19	976189	·72	532025	6·90	467975	12
49	508585	6·18	976146	·72	532439	6·89	467561	11
50	508956	6·18	976103	·72	532853	6·89	467147	10
51	9·509326	6·17	9·976060	·72	9·533266	6·88	10·466734	9
52	509696	6·16	976017	·72	533679	6·88	466321	8
53	510065	6·16	975974	·72	534092	6·87	465908	7
54	510434	6·15	975930	·72	534504	6·87	465496	6
55	510803	6·15	975887	·72	534916	6·86	465084	5
56	511172	6·14	975844	·72	535328	6·86	464672	4
57	511540	6·13	975800	·72	535739	6·85	464261	3
58	511907	6·13	975757	·72	536150	6·85	463850	2
59	512275	6·12	975714	·72	536561	6·84	463439	1
60	512642	6·12	975670	·72	536972	6·84	463028	0
	Cosine	D.	Sine	D.	Cotang.	D.	Tang.	M.

(71 DEGREES.)

M.	Sine	D.	Cosine	D.	Tang.	D.	Cotang.	
0	9·512642	6·12	9·975670	·73	9·536972	6·84	10·463028	60
1	513009	6·11	975627	·73	537382	6·83	462618	59
2	513375	6·11	975583	·73	537792	6·83	462208	58
3	513741	6·10	975539	·73	538202	6·82	461798	57
4	514107	6·09	975496	·73	538611	6·82	461389	56
5	514472	6·09	975452	·73	539020	6·81	460980	55
6	514837	6·08	975408	·73	539429	6·81	460571	54
7	515202	6·08	975365	·73	539837	6·80	460163	53
8	515566	6·07	975321	·73	540245	6·80	459755	52
9	515930	6·07	975277	·73	540653	6·79	459347	51
10	516294	6·06	975233	·73	541061	6·79	458939	50
11	9·516657	6·05	9·975189	·73	9·541468	6·78	10·458532	49
12	517020	6·05	975145	·73	541875	6·78	458125	48
13	517382	6·04	975101	·73	542281	6·77	457719	47
14	517745	6·04	975057	·73	542688	6·77	457312	46
15	518107	6·03	975013	·73	543094	6·76	456906	45
16	518468	6·03	974969	·74	543499	6·76	456501	44
17	518829	6·02	974925	·74	543905	6·75	456095	43
18	519190	6·01	974880	·74	544310	6·75	455690	42
19	519551	6·01	974836	·74	544715	6·74	455285	41
20	519911	6·00	974792	·74	545119	6·74	454881	40
21	9·520271	6·00	9·974748	·74	9·545524	6·73	10·454476	39
22	520631	5·99	974703	·74	545928	6·73	454072	38
23	520990	5·99	974659	·74	546331	6·72	453669	37
24	521349	5·98	974614	·74	546735	6·72	453265	36
25	521707	5·98	974570	·74	547138	6·71	452862	35
26	522066	5·97	974525	·74	547540	6·71	452460	34
27	522424	5·96	974481	·74	547943	6·70	452057	33
28	522781	5·96	974436	·74	548345	6·70	451655	32
29	523138	5·95	974391	·74	548747	6·69	451253	31
30	523495	5·95	974347	·75	549149	6·69	450851	30
31	9·523852	5·94	9·974302	·75	9·549550	6·68	10·450450	29
32	524208	5·94	974257	·75	549951	6·68	450049	28
33	524564	5·93	974212	·75	550352	6·67	449648	27
34	524920	5·93	974167	·75	550752	6·67	449248	26
35	525275	5·92	974122	·75	551152	6·66	448848	25
36	525630	5·91	974077	·75	551552	6·66	448448	24
37	525984	5·91	974032	·75	551952	6·65	448048	23
38	526339	5·90	973987	·75	552351	6·65	447649	22
39	526693	5·90	973942	·75	552750	6·65	447250	21
40	527046	5·89	973897	·75	553149	6·64	446851	20
41	9·527400	5·89	9·973852	·75	9·553548	6·64	10·446452	19
42	527753	5·88	973807	·75	553946	6·63	446054	18
43	528105	5·88	973761	·75	554344	6·63	445656	17
44	528458	5·87	973716	·76	554741	6·62	445259	16
45	528810	5·87	973671	·76	555139	6·62	444861	15
46	529161	5·86	973625	·76	555536	6·61	444464	14
47	529513	5·86	973580	·76	555933	6·61	444067	13
48	529864	5·85	973535	·76	556329	6·60	443671	12
49	530215	5·85	973489	·76	556725	6·60	443275	11
50	530565	5·84	973444	·76	557121	6·59	442879	10
51	9·530915	5·84	9·973398	·76	9·557517	6·59	10·442483	9
52	531265	5·83	973352	·76	557913	6·59	442087	8
53	531614	5·82	973307	·76	558308	6·58	441692	7
54	531963	5·82	973261	·76	558702	6·58	441298	6
55	532312	5·81	973215	·76	559097	6·57	440903	5
56	532661	5·81	973169	·76	559491	6·57	440509	4
57	533009	5·80	973124	·76	559885	6·56	440115	3
58	533357	5·80	973078	·76	560279	6·56	439721	2
59	533704	5·79	973032	·77	560673	6·55	439327	1
60	534052	5·78	972986	·77	561066	6·55	438934	0
	Cosine	D.	Sine	D.	Cotang.	D.	Tang.	M.

(70 DEGREES.)

M.	Sine	D.	Cosine	D.	Tang.	D.	Cotang.	
0	9·534052	5·78	9·972986	·77	9·561066	6·55	10·438934	60
1	534399	5·77	972940	·77	561459	6·54	438541	59
2	534745	5·77	972894	·77	561851	6·54	438149	58
3	535092	5·77	972848	·77	562244	6·53	437756	57
4	535438	5·76	972802	·77	562636	6·53	437364	56
5	535783	5·76	972755	·77	563028	6·53	436972	55
6	536129	5·75	972709	·77	563419	6·52	436581	54
7	536474	5·74	972663	·77	563811	6·52	436189	53
8	536818	5·74	972617	·77	564202	6·51	435798	52
9	537163	5·73	972570	·77	564592	6·51	435408	51
10	537507	5·73	972524	·77	564983	6·50	435017	50
11	9·537851	5·72	9·972478	·77	9·565373	6·50	10·434627	49
12	538194	5·72	972431	·78	565763	6·49	434237	48
13	538538	5·71	972385	·78	566153	6·49	433847	47
14	538880	5·71	972338	·78	566542	6·49	433458	46
15	539223	5·70	972291	·78	566932	6·48	433068	45
16	539565	5·70	972245	·78	567320	6·48	432680	44
17	539907	5·69	972198	·78	567709	6·47	432291	43
18	540249	5·69	972151	·78	568098	6·47	431902	42
19	540590	5·68	972105	·78	568486	6·46	431514	41
20	540931	5·68	972058	·78	568873	6·46	431127	40
21	9·541272	5·67	9·972011	·78	9·569261	6·45	10·430739	39
22	541613	5·67	971964	·78	569648	6·45	430352	38
23	541953	5·66	971917	·78	570035	6·45	429965	37
24	542293	5·66	971870	·78	570422	6·44	429578	36
25	542632	5·65	971823	·78	570809	6·44	429191	35
26	542971	5·65	971776	·78	571195	6·43	428805	34
27	543310	5·64	971729	·79	571581	6·43	428419	33
28	543649	5·64	971682	·79	571967	6·42	428033	32
29	543987	5·63	971635	·79	572352	6·42	427648	31
30	544325	5·63	971588	·79	572738	6·42	427262	30
31	9·544663	5·62	9·971540	·79	9·573123	6·41	10·426877	29
32	545000	5·62	971493	·79	573507	6·41	426493	28
33	545338	5·61	971446	·79	573892	6·40	426108	27
34	545674	5·61	971398	·79	574276	6·40	425724	26
35	546011	5·60	971351	·79	574660	6·39	425340	25
36	546347	5·60	971303	·79	575044	6·39	424956	24
37	546683	5·59	971256	·79	575427	6·39	424573	23
38	547019	5·59	971208	·79	575810	6·38	424190	22
39	547354	5·58	971161	·79	576193	6·38	423807	21
40	547689	5·58	971113	·79	576576	6·37	423424	20
41	9·548024	5·57	9·971066	·80	9·576958	6·37	10·423041	19
42	548359	5·57	971018	·80	577341	6·36	422659	18
43	548693	5·56	970970	·80	577723	6·36	422277	17
44	549027	5·56	970922	·80	578104	6·36	421896	16
45	549360	5·55	970874	·80	578486	6·35	421514	15
46	549693	5·55	970827	·80	578867	6·35	421133	14
47	550026	5·54	970779	·80	579248	6·34	420752	13
48	550359	5·54	970731	·80	579629	6·34	420371	12
49	550692	5·53	970683	·80	580009	6·34	419991	11
50	551024	5·53	970635	·80	580389	6·33	419611	10
51	9·551356	5·52	9·970586	·80	9·580769	6·33	10·419231	9
52	551687	5·52	970538	·80	581149	6·32	418851	8
53	552018	5·52	970490	·80	581528	6·32	418472	7
54	552349	5·51	970442	·80	581907	6·32	418093	6
55	552680	5·51	970394	·80	582286	6·31	417714	5
56	553010	5·50	970345	·81	582665	6·31	417335	4
57	553341	5·50	970297	·81	583043	6·30	416957	3
58	553670	5·49	970249	·81	583422	6·30	416578	2
59	554000	5·49	970200	·81	583800	6·29	416200	1
60	554329	5·48	970152	·81	584177	6·29	415823	0
	Cosine	D.	Sine	D.	Cotang.	D.	Tang.	M.

M.	Sine	D.	Cosine	D.	Tang.	D.	Cotang.	
0	9·554329	5·48	9·970152	·81	9·584177	6·29	10·415823	60
1	554658	5·48	970103	·81	584555	6·29	415445	59
2	554987	5·47	970055	·81	584932	6·28	415068	58
3	555315	5·47	970006	·81	585309	6·28	414691	57
4	555643	5·46	969957	·81	585686	6·27	414314	56
5	555971	5·46	969909	·81	586062	6·27	413938	55
6	556299	5·45	969860	·81	586439	6·27	413561	54
7	556626	5·45	969811	·81	586815	6·26	413185	53
8	556953	5·44	969762	·81	587190	6·26	412810	52
9	557280	5·44	969714	·81	587566	6·25	412434	51
10	557606	5·43	969665	·81	587941	6·25	412059	50
11	9·557932	5·43	9·969616	·82	9·588316	6·25	10·411684	49
12	558258	5·43	969567	·82	588691	6·24	411309	48
13	558583	5·42	969518	·82	589066	6·24	410934	47
14	558909	5·42	969469	·82	589440	6·23	410560	46
15	559234	5·41	969420	·82	589814	6·23	410186	45
16	559558	5·41	969370	·82	590188	6·23	409812	44
17	559883	5·40	969321	·82	590562	6·22	409438	43
18	560207	5·40	969272	·82	590935	6·22	409065	42
19	560531	5·39	969223	·82	591308	6·22	408692	41
20	560855	5·39	969173	·82	591681	6·21	408319	40
21	9·561178	5·38	9·969124	·82	9·592054	6·21	10·407946	39
22	561501	5·38	969075	·82	592426	6·20	407574	38
23	561824	5·37	969025	·82	592798	6·20	407202	37
24	562146	5·37	968976	·82	593170	6·19	406829	36
25	562468	5·36	968926	·83	593542	6·19	406458	35
26	562790	5·36	968877	·83	593914	6·18	406086	34
27	563112	5·36	968827	·83	594285	6·18	405715	33
28	563433	5·35	968777	·83	594656	6·18	405344	32
29	563755	5·35	968728	·83	595027	6·17	404973	31
30	564075	5·34	968678	·83	595398	6·17	404602	30
31	9·564396	5·34	9·968628	·83	9·595768	6·17	10·404232	29
32	564716	5·33	968578	·83	596138	6·16	403862	28
33	565036	5·33	968528	·83	596508	6·16	403492	27
34	565356	5·32	968479	83	596878	6·16	403122	26
35	565676	5·32	968429	·83	597247	6·15	402753	25
36	565995	5·31	968379	·83	597616	6·15	402384	24
37	566314	5·31	968329	·83	597985	6·15	402015	23
38	566632	5·31	968278	·83	598354	6·14	401646	22
39	566951	5·30	968228	·84	598722	6·14	401278	21
40	567269	5·30	968178	·84	599091	6·13	400909	20
41	9·567587	5·29	9·968128	·84	9·599459	6·13	10·400541	19
42	567904	5·29	968078	·84	599827	6·13	400173	18
43	568222	5·28	968027	·84	600194	6·12	399806	17
44	568539	5·28	967977	·84	600562	6·12	399438	16
45	568856	5·28	967927	·84	600929	6·11	399071	15
46	569172	5·27	967876	·84	601296	6·11	398704	14
47	569488	5·27	967826	·84	601662	6·11	398338	13
48	569804	5·26	967775	·84	602029	6·10	397971	12
49	570120	5·26	967725	·84	602395	6·10	397605	11
50	570435	5·25	967674	·84	602761	6·10	397239	10
51	9·570751	5·25	9·967624	·84	9·603127	6·09	10·396873	9
52	571066	5·24	967573	·84	603493	6·09	396507	8
53	571380	5·24	967522	·85	603858	6·09	396142	7
54	571695	5·23	967471	·85	604223	6·08	395777	6
55	572009	5·23	967421	·85	604588	6·08	395412	5
56	572323	5·23	967370	·85	604953	6·07	395047	4
57	572636	5·22	967319	·85	605317	6·07	394683	3
58	572956	5·22	967268	·85	605682	6·07	394318	2
59	573263	5·21	967217	·85	606046	6·06	393954	1
60	573575	5·21	967166	·85	606410	6·06	393590	0
	Cosine	D.	Sine	D.	Cotang.	D.	Tang.	M.

(68 DEGREES.)

M.	Sine	D.	Cosine	D.	Tang.	D.	Cotang.	
0	9·573575	5·21	9·967166	·85	9·606410	6·06	10·393590	60
1	573888	5·20	967115	·85	606773	6·06	393227	59
2	574200	5·20	967064	·85	607137	6·05	392863	58
3	574512	5·19	967013	·85	607500	6·05	392500	57
4	574824	5·19	966961	·85	607863	6·04	392137	56
5	575136	5·19	966910	·85	608225	6·04	391775	55
6	575447	5·18	966859	·85	608588	6·04	391412	54
7	575758	5·18	966808	·85	608950	6·03	391050	53
8	576069	5·17	966756	·86	609312	6·03	390688	52
9	576379	5·17	966705	·86	609674	6·03	390326	51
10	576689	5·16	966653	·86	610036	6·02	389964	50
11	9·576999	5·16	9·966602	·86	9·610397	6·02	10·389603	49
12	577309	5·16	966550	·86	610759	6·02	389241	48
13	577618	5·15	966499	·86	611120	6·01	388880	47
14	577927	5·15	966447	·86	611480	6·01	388520	46
15	578236	5·14	966395	·86	611841	6·01	388159	45
16	578545	5·14	966344	·86	612201	6·00	387799	44
17	578853	5·13	966292	·86	612561	6·00	387439	43
18	579162	5·13	966240	·86	612921	6·00	387079	42
19	579470	5·13	966188	·86	613281	5·99	386719	41
20	579777	5·12	966136	·86	613641	5·99	386359	40
21	9·580085	5·12	9·966085	·87	9·614000	5·98	10·386000	39
22	580392	5·11	966033	·87	614359	5·98	385641	38
23	580699	5·11	965981	·87	614718	5·98	385282	37
24	581005	5·11	965928	·87	615077	5·97	384923	36
25	581312	5·10	965876	·87	615435	5·97	384565	35
26	581618	5·10	965824	·87	615793	5·97	384207	34
27	581924	5·09	965772	·87	616151	5·96	383849	33
28	582229	5·09	965720	·87	616509	5·96	383491	32
29	582535	5·09	965668	·87	616867	5·96	383133	31
30	582840	5·08	965615	·87	617224	5·95	382776	30
31	9·583145	5·08	9·965563	·87	9·617582	5·95	10·382418	29
32	583449	5·07	965511	·87	617939	5·95	382061	28
33	583754	5·07	965458	·87	618295	5·94	381705	27
34	584058	5·06	965406	·87	618652	5·94	381348	26
35	584361	5·06	965353	·88	619008	5·94	380992	25
36	584665	5·06	965301	·88	619364	5·93	380636	24
37	584968	5·05	965248	·88	619721	5·93	380279	23
38	585272	5·05	965195	·88	620076	5·93	379924	22
39	585574	5·04	965143	·88	620432	5·92	379568	21
40	585877	5·04	965090	·88	620787	5·92	379213	20
41	9·586179	5·03	9·965037	·88	9·621142	5·92	10·378858	19
42	586482	5·03	964984	·88	621497	5·91	378503	18
43	586783	5·03	964931	·88	621852	5·91	378148	17
44	587085	5·02	964879	·88	622207	5·90	377793	16
45	587386	5·02	964826	·88	622561	5·90	377439	15
46	587688	5·01	964773	·88	622915	5·90	377085	14
47	587989	5·01	964719	·88	623269	5·89	376731	13
48	588289	5·01	964666	·89	623623	5·89	376377	12
49	588590	5·00	964613	·89	623976	5·89	376024	11
50	588890	5·00	964560	·89	624330	5·88	375670	10
51	9·589190	4·99	9·964507	·89	9·624683	5·88	10·375317	9
52	589489	4·99	964454	·89	625036	5·88	374964	8
53	589789	4·99	964400	·89	625388	5·87	374612	7
54	590088	4·98	964347	·89	625741	5·87	374259	6
55	590387	4·98	964294	·89	626093	5·87	373907	5
56	590686	4·97	964240	·89	626445	5·86	373555	4
57	590984	4·97	964187	·89	626797	5·86	373203	3
58	591282	4·97	964133	·89	627149	5·86	372851	2
59	591580	4·96	964080	·89	627501	5·85	372499	1
60	591878	4·96	964026	·89	627852	5·85	372148	0
	Cosine	D.	Sine	D.	Cotang.	D.	Tang.	M.

(67 DEGREES.)

M.	Sine	D.	Cosine	D.	Tang.	D.	Cotang.	
0	9·591878	4·96	9·964026	·89	9·627852	5·85	10·372148	60
1	592176	4·95	963972	·89	628203	5·85	371797	59
2	592473	4·95	963919	·89	628554	5·85	371446	58
3	592770	4·95	963865	·90	628905	5·84	371095	57
4	593067	4·94	963811	·90	629255	5·84	370745	56
5	593363	4·94	963757	·90	629606	5·83	370394	55
6	593659	4·93	963704	·90	629956	5·83	370044	54
7	593955	4·93	963650	·90	630306	5·83	369694	53
8	594251	4·93	963596	·90	630656	5·83	369344	52
9	594547	4·92	963542	·90	631005	5·82	368995	51
10	594842	4·92	963488	·90	631355	5·82	368645	50
11	9·595137	4·91	9·963434	·90	9·631704	5·82	10·368296	49
12	595432	4·91	963379	·90	632053	5·81	367947	48
13	595727	4·91	963325	·90	632401	5·81	367599	47
14	596021	4·90	963271	·90	632750	5·81	367250	46
15	596315	4·90	963217	·90	633098	5·80	366902	45
16	596609	4·89	963163	·90	633447	5·80	366553	44
17	596903	4·89	963108	·91	633795	5·80	366205	43
18	597196	4·89	963054	·91	634143	5·79	365857	42
19	597490	4·88	962999	·91	634490	5·79	365510	41
20	597783	4·88	962945	·91	634838	5·79	365162	40
21	9·598075	4·87	9·962890	·91	9·635185	5·78	10·364815	39
22	598368	4·87	962836	·91	635532	5·78	364468	38
23	598660	4·87	962781	·91	635879	5·78	364121	37
24	598952	4·86	962727	·91	636226	5·77	363774	36
25	599244	4·86	962672	·91	636572	5·77	363428	35
26	599536	4·85	962617	·91	636919	5·77	363081	34
27	599827	4·85	962562	·91	637265	5·77	362735	33
28	600118	4·85	962508	·91	637611	5·76	362389	32
29	600409	4·84	962453	·91	637956	5·76	362044	31
30	600700	4·84	962398	·92	638302	5·76	361698	30
31	9·600990	4·84	9·962343	·92	9·638647	5·75	10·361353	29
32	601280	4·83	962288	·92	638992	5·75	361008	28
33	601570	4·83	962233	·92	639337	5·75	360663	27
34	601860	4·82	962178	·92	639682	5·74	360318	26
35	602150	4·82	962123	·92	640027	5·74	359973	25
36	602439	4·82	962067	·92	640371	5·74	359629	24
37	602728	4·81	962012	·92	640716	5·73	359284	23
38	603017	4·81	961957	·92	641060	5·73	358940	22
39	603305	4·81	961902	·92	641404	5·73	358596	21
40	603594	4·80	961846	·92	641747	5·72	358253	20
41	9·603882	4·80	9·961791	·92	9·642091	5·72	10·357909	19
42	604170	4·79	961735	·92	642434	5·72	357566	18
43	604457	4·79	961680	·92	642777	5·72	357223	17
44	604745	4·79	961624	·93	643120	5·71	356880	16
45	605032	4·78	961569	·93	643463	5·71	356537	15
46	605319	4·78	961513	·93	643806	5·71	356194	14
47	605606	4·78	961458	·93	644148	5·70	355852	13
48	605892	4·77	961402	·93	644490	5·70	355510	12
49	606179	4·77	961346	·93	644832	5·70	355168	11
50	606465	4·76	961290	·93	645174	5·69	354826	10
51	9·606751	4·76	9·961235	·93	9·645516	5·69	10·354484	9
52	607036	4·76	961179	·93	645857	5·69	354143	8
53	607322	4·75	961123	·93	646199	5·69	353801	7
54	607607	4·75	961067	·93	646540	5·68	353460	6
55	607892	4·74	961011	·93	646881	5·68	353119	5
56	608177	4·74	960955	·93	647222	5·68	352778	4
57	608461	4·74	960899	·93	647562	5·67	352438	3
58	608745	4·73	960843	·94	647903	5·67	352097	2
59	609029	4·73	960786	·94	648243	5·67	351757	1
60	609313	4·73	960730	·94	648583	5·66	351417	0
	Cosine	D.	Sine	D.	Cotang.	D.	Tang.	M.

M.	Sine	D.	Cosine	D.	Tang.	D.	Cotang.	
0	9·609313	4·73	9·960730	·94	9·648583	5·66	10·351417	60
1	609597	4·72	960674	·94	648923	5·66	351077	59
2	609880	4·72	960618	·94	649263	5·66	350737	58
3	610164	4·72	960561	·94	649602	5·66	350398	57
4	610447	4·71	960505	·94	649942	5·65	350058	56
5	610729	4·71	960448	·94	650281	5·65	349719	55
6	611012	4·70	960392	·94	650620	5·65	349380	54
7	611294	4·70	960335	·94	650959	5·64	349041	53
8	611576	4·70	960279	·94	651297	5·64	348703	52
9	611858	4·69	960222	·94	651636	5·64	348364	51
10	612140	4·69	960165	·94	651974	5·63	348026	50
11	9·612421	4·69	9·960109	·95	9·652312	5·63	10·347688	49
12	612702	4·68	960052	·95	652650	5·63	347350	48
13	612983	4·68	959995	·95	652988	5·63	347012	47
14	613264	4·67	959938	·95	653326	5·62	346674	46
15	613545	4·67	959882	·95	653663	5·62	346337	45
16	613825	4·67	959825	·95	654000	5·62	346000	44
17	614105	4·66	959768	·95	654337	5·61	345663	43
18	614385	4·66	959711	·95	654674	5·61	345326	42
19	614665	4·66	959654	·95	655011	5·61	344989	41
20	614944	4·65	959596	·95	655348	5·61	344652	40
21	9·615223	4·65	9·959539	·95	9·655684	5·60	10·344316	39
22	615502	4·65	959482	·95	656020	5·60	343980	38
23	615781	4·64	959425	·95	656356	5·60	343644	37
24	616060	4·64	959368	·95	656692	5·59	343308	36
25	616338	4·64	959310	·96	657028	5·59	342972	35
26	616616	4·63	959253	·96	657364	5·59	342636	34
27	616894	4·63	959195	·96	657699	5·59	342301	33
28	617172	4·62	959138	·96	658034	5·58	341966	32
29	617450	4·62	959081	·96	658369	5·58	341631	31
30	617727	4·62	959023	·96	658704	5·58	341296	30
31	9·618004	4·61	9·958965	·96	9·659039	5·58	10·340961	29
32	618281	4·61	958908	·96	659373	5·57	340627	28
33	618558	4·61	958850	·96	659708	5·57	340292	27
34	618834	4·60	958792	·96	660042	5·57	339958	26
35	619110	4·60	958734	·96	660376	5·57	339624	25
36	619386	4·60	958677	·96	660710	5·56	339290	24
37	619662	4·59	958619	·96	661043	5·56	338957	23
38	619938	4·59	958561	·96	661377	5·56	338623	22
39	620213	4·59	958503	·97	661710	5·55	338290	21
40	620488	4·58	958445	·97	662043	5·55	337957	20
41	9·620763	4·58	9·958387	·97	9·662376	5·55	10·337624	19
42	621038	4·57	958329	·97	662709	5·54	337291	18
43	621313	4·57	958271	·97	663042	5·54	336958	17
44	621587	4·57	958213	·97	663375	5·54	336625	16
45	621861	4·56	958154	·97	663707	5·54	336293	15
46	622135	4·56	958096	·97	664039	5·53	335961	14
47	622409	4·56	958038	·97	664371	5·53	335629	13
48	622682	4·55	957979	·97	664703	5·53	335297	12
49	622956	4·55	957921	·97	665035	5·53	334965	11
50	623229	4·55	957863	·97	665366	5·52	334634	10
51	9·623502	4·54	9·957804	·97	9·665697	5·52	10·334303	9
52	623774	4·54	957746	·98	666029	5·52	333971	8
53	624047	4·54	957687	·98	666360	5·51	333640	7
54	624319	4·53	957628	·98	666691	5·51	333309	6
55	624591	4·53	957570	·98	667021	5·51	332979	5
56	624863	4·53	957511	·98	667352	5·51	332648	4
57	625135	4·52	957452	·98	667682	5·50	332318	3
58	625406	4·52	957393	·98	668013	5·50	331987	2
59	625677	4·52	957335	·98	668343	5·50	331657	1
60	625948	4·51	957276	·98	668672	5·50	331328	0
	Cosine	D.	Sine	D.	Cotang.	D.	Tang.	M.

(65 DEGREES.)

M.	Sine	D.	Cosine	D.	Tang.	D.	Cotang.	
0	9·625948	4·51	9·957276	·98	9·668673	5·50	10·331327	60
1	626219	4·51	957217	·98	669002	5·49	330998	59
2	626490	4·51	957158	·98	669332	5·49	330668	58
3	626760	4·50	957099	·98	669661	5·49	330339	57
4	627030	4·50	957040	·98	669991	5·48	330009	56
5	627300	4·50	956981	·98	670320	5·48	329680	55
6	627570	4·49	956921	·99	670649	5·48	329351	54
7	627840	4·49	956862	·99	670977	5·48	329023	53
8	628109	4·49	956803	·99	671306	5·47	328694	52
9	628378	4·48	956744	·99	671634	5·47	328366	51
10	628647	4·48	956684	·99	671963	5·47	328037	50
11	9·628916	4·47	9·956625	·99	9·672291	5·47	10·327709	49
12	629185	4·47	956566	·99	672619	5·46	327381	48
13	629453	4·47	956506	·99	672947	5·46	327053	47
14	629721	4·46	956447	·99	673274	5·46	326726	46
15	629989	4·46	956387	·99	673602	5·46	326398	45
16	630257	4·46	956327	·99	673929	5·45	326071	44
17	630524	4·46	956268	·99	674257	5·45	325743	43
18	630792	4·45	956208	1·00	674584	5·45	325416	42
19	631059	4·45	956148	1·00	674910	5·44	325090	41
20	631326	4·45	956089	1·00	675237	5·44	324763	40
21	9·631593	4·44	9·956029	1·00	9·675564	5·44	10·324436	39
22	631859	4·44	955969	1·00	675890	5·44	324110	38
23	632125	4·44	955909	1·00	676216	5·43	323784	37
24	632392	4·43	955849	1·00	676543	5·43	323457	36
25	632658	4·43	955789	1·00	676869	5·43	323131	35
26	632923	4·43	955729	1·00	677194	5·43	322806	34
27	633189	4·42	955669	1·00	677520	5·42	322480	33
28	633454	4·42	955609	1·00	677846	5·42	322154	32
29	633719	4·42	955548	1·00	678171	5·42	321829	31
30	633984	4·41	955488	1·00	678496	5·42	321504	30
31	9·634249	4·41	9·955428	1·01	9·678821	5·41	10·321179	29
32	634514	4·40	955368	1·01	679146	5·41	320854	28
33	634778	4·40	955307	1·01	679471	5·41	320529	27
34	635042	4·40	955247	1·01	679795	5·41	320205	26
35	635306	4·39	955186	1·01	680120	5·40	319880	25
36	635570	4·39	955126	1·01	680444	5·40	319556	24
37	635834	4·39	955065	1·01	680768	5·40	319232	23
38	636097	4·38	955005	1·01	681092	5·40	318908	22
39	636360	4·38	954944	1·01	681416	5·39	318584	21
40	636623	4·38	954883	1·01	681740	5·39	318260	20
41	9·636886	4·37	9·954823	1·01	9·682063	5·39	10·317937	19
42	637148	4·37	954762	1·01	682387	5·39	317613	18
43	637411	4·37	954701	1·01	682710	5·38	317290	17
44	637673	4·37	954640	1·01	683033	5·38	316967	16
45	637935	4·36	954579	1·01	683356	5·38	316644	15
46	638197	4·36	954518	1·02	683679	5·38	316321	14
47	638458	4·36	954457	1·02	684001	5·37	315999	13
48	638720	4·35	954396	1·02	684324	5·37	315676	12
49	638981	4·35	954335	1·02	684646	5·37	315354	11
50	639242	4·35	954274	1·02	684968	5·37	315032	10
51	9·639503	4·34	9·954213	1·02	9·685290	5·36	10·314710	9
52	639764	4·34	954152	1·02	685612	5·36	314388	8
53	640024	4·34	954090	1·02	685934	5·36	314066	7
54	640284	4·33	954029	1·02	686255	5·36	313745	6
55	640544	4·33	953968	1·02	686577	5·35	313423	5
56	640804	4·33	953906	1·02	686898	5·35	313102	4
57	641064	4·32	953845	1·02	687219	5·35	312781	3
58	641324	4·32	953783	1·02	687540	5·35	312460	2
59	641584	4·32	953722	1·03	687861	5·34	312139	1
60	641842	4·31	953660	1·03	688182	5·34	311818	0
	Cosine	D.	Sine	D.	Cotang.	D.	Tang.	M.

(64 DEGREES.)

M.	Sine	D.	Cosine	D.	Tang.	D.	Cotang.	
0	9·641842	4·31	9·953660	1·03	9·688182	5·34	10·311818	60
1	642101	4·31	953599	1·03	688502	5·34	311498	59
2	642360	4·31	953537	1·03	688823	5·34	311177	58
3	642618	4·30	953475	1·03	689143	5·33	310857	57
4	642877	4·30	953413	1·03	689463	5·33	310537	56
5	643135	4·30	953352	1·03	689783	5·33	310217	55
6	643393	4·30	953290	1·03	690103	5·33	309897	54
7	643650	4·29	953228	1·03	690423	5·33	309577	53
8	643908	4·29	953166	1·03	690742	5·32	309258	52
9	644165	4·29	953104	1·03	691062	5·32	308938	51
10	644423	4·28	953042	1·03	691381	5·32	308619	50
11	9·644680	4·28	9·952980	1·04	9·691700	5·31	10·308300	49
12	644936	4·28	952918	1·04	692019	5·31	307981	48
13	645193	4·27	952855	1·04	692338	5·31	307662	47
14	645450	4·27	952793	1·04	692656	5·31	307344	46
15	645706	4·27	952731	1·04	692975	5·31	307025	45
16	645962	4·26	952669	1·04	693293	5·30	306707	44
17	646218	4·26	952606	1·04	693612	5·30	306388	43
18	646474	4·26	952544	1·04	693930	5·30	306070	42
19	646729	4·25	952481	1·04	694248	5·30	305752	41
20	646984	4·25	952419	1·04	694566	5·29	305434	40
21	9·647240	4·25	9·952356	1·04	9·694883	5·29	10·305117	39
22	647494	4·24	952294	1·04	695201	5·29	304799	38
23	647749	4·24	952231	1·04	695518	5·29	304482	37
24	648004	4·24	952168	1·05	695836	5·29	304164	36
25	648258	4·24	952106	1·05	696153	5·28	303847	35
26	648512	4·23	952043	1·05	696470	5·28	303530	34
27	648766	4·23	951980	1·05	696787	5·28	303213	33
28	649020	4·23	951917	1·05	697103	5·28	302897	32
29	649274	4·22	951854	1·05	697420	5·27	302580	31
30	649527	4·22	951791	1·05	697736	5·27	302264	30
31	9·649781	4·22	9·951728	1·05	9·698053	5·27	10·301947	29
32	650034	4·22	951665	1·05	698369	5·27	301631	28
33	650287	4·21	951602	1·05	698685	5·26	301315	27
34	650539	4·21	951539	1·05	699001	5·26	300999	26
35	650792	4·21	951476	1·05	699316	5·26	300684	75
36	651044	4·20	951412	1·05	699632	5·26	300368	24
37	651297	4·20	951349	1·06	699947	5·26	300053	23
38	651549	4·20	951286	1·06	700263	5·25	299737	22
39	651800	4·19	951222	1·06	700578	5·25	299422	21
40	652052	4·19	951159	1·06	700893	5·25	299107	20
41	9·652304	4·19	9·951096	1·06	9·701208	5·24	10·298792	19
42	652555	4·18	951032	1·06	701523	5·24	298477	18
43	652806	4·18	950968	1·06	701837	5·24	298163	17
44	653057	4·18	950905	1·06	702152	5·24	297848	16
45	653308	4·18	950841	1·06	702466	5·24	297534	15
46	653558	4·17	950778	1·06	702780	5·23	297220	14
47	653808	4·17	950714	1·06	703095	5·23	206905	13
48	654059	4·17	950650	1·06	703409	5·23	296591	12
49	654309	4·16	950586	1·06	703723	5·23	296277	11
50	654558	4·16	950522	1·07	704036	5·22	295964	10
51	9·654808	4·16	9·950458	1·07	9·704350	5·22	10·295650	9
52	655058	4·16	950394	1·07	704663	5·22	295337	8
53	655307	4·15	950330	1·07	704977	5·22	295023	7
54	655556	4·15	950266	1·07	705290	5·22	294710	6
55	655805	4·15	950202	1·07	705603	5·21	294397	5
56	656054	4·14	950138	1·07	705916	5·21	294084	4
57	656302	4·14	950074	1·07	706228	5·21	293772	3
58	656551	4·14	950010	1·07	706541	5·21	293459	2
59	656799	4·13	949945	1·07	706854	5·21	293146	1
60	657047	4·13	949881	1·07	707166	5·20	292834	0
	Cosine	D.	Sine	D.	Cotang.	D.	Tang.	M.

M.	Sine	D.	Cosine	D.	Tang.	D.	Cotang.	
0	9·657047	4·13	9·949881	1·07	9·707166	5·20	10·292834	60
1	657295	4·13	949816	1·07	707478	5·20	292522	59
2	657542	4·12	949752	1·07	707790	5·20	292210	58
3	657790	4·12	949688	1·08	708102	5·20	291898	57
4	658037	4·12	949623	1·08	708414	5·19	291586	56
5	658284	4·12	949558	1·08	708726	5·19	291274	55
6	658531	4·11	949494	1·08	709037	5·19	290963	54
7	658778	4·11	949429	1·08	709349	5·19	290651	53
8	659025	4·11	949364	1·08	709660	5·19	290340	52
9	659271	4·10	949300	1·08	709971	5·18	290029	51
10	659517	4·10	949235	1·08	710282	5·18	289718	50
11	9·659763	4·10	9·949170	1·08	9·710593	5·18	10·289407	49
12	660009	4·09	949105	1·08	710904	5·18	289096	48
13	660255	4·09	949040	1·08	711215	5·18	288785	47
14	660501	4·09	948975	1·08	711525	5·17	288475	46
15	660746	4·09	948910	1·08	711836	5·17	288164	45
16	660991	4·08	948845	1·08	712146	5·17	287854	44
17	661236	4·08	948780	1·09	712456	5·17	287544	43
18	661481	4·08	948715	1·09	712766	5·16	287234	42
19	661726	4·07	948650	1·09	713076	5·16	286924	41
20	661970	4·07	948584	1·09	713386	5·16	286614	40
21	9·662214	4·07	9·948519	1·09	9·713696	5·16	10·286304	39
22	662459	4·07	948454	1·09	714005	5·16	285995	38
23	662703	4·06	948388	1·09	714314	5·15	285686	37
24	662946	4·06	948323	1·09	714624	5·15	285376	36
25	663190	4·06	948257	1·09	714933	5·15	285067	35
26	663433	4·05	948192	1·09	715242	5·15	284758	34
27	663677	4·05	948126	1·09	715551	5·14	284449	33
28	663920	4·05	948060	1·09	715860	5·14	284140	32
29	664163	4·05	947995	1·10	716168	5·14	283832	31
30	664406	4·04	947929	1·10	716477	5·14	283523	30
31	9·664648	4·04	9·947863	1·10	9·716785	5·14	10·283215	29
32	664891	4·04	947797	1·10	717093	5·13	282907	28
33	665133	4·03	947731	1·10	717401	5·13	282599	27
34	665375	4·03	947665	1·10	717709	5·13	282291	26
35	665617	4·03	947600	1·10	718017	5·13	281983	25
36	665859	4·02	947533	1·10	718325	5·13	281670	24
37	666100	4·02	947467	1·10	718633	5·12	281367	23
38	666342	4·02	947401	1·10	718940	5·12	281060	22
39	666583	4·02	947335	1·10	719248	5·12	280752	21
40	666824	4·01	947269	1·10	719555	5·12	280445	20
41	9·667065	4·01	9·947203	1·10	9·719862	5·12	10·280138	19
42	667305	4·01	947136	1·11	720169	5·11	279831	18
43	667546	4·01	947070	1·11	720476	5·11	279524	17
44	667786	4·00	947004	1·11	720783	5·11	279217	16
45	668027	4·00	946937	1·11	721089	5·11	278911	15
46	668267	4·00	946871	1·11	721396	5·11	278604	14
47	668506	3·99	946804	1·11	721702	5·10	278298	13
48	668746	3·99	946738	1·11	722009	5·10	277991	12
49	668986	3·99	946671	1·11	722315	5·10	277685	11
50	669225	3·99	946604	1·11	722621	5·10	277379	10
51	9·669464	3·98	9·946538	1·11	9·722927	5·10	10·277073	9
52	669703	3·98	946471	1·11	723232	5·09	276768	8
53	669942	3·98	946404	1·11	723538	5·09	276462	7
54	670181	3·97	946337	1·11	723844	5·09	276156	6
55	670419	3·97	946270	1·12	724149	5·09	275851	5
56	670658	3·97	946203	1·12	724454	5·09	275546	4
57	670896	3·97	946136	1·12	724759	5·08	275241	3
58	671134	3·96	946069	1·12	725065	5·08	274935	2
59	671372	3·96	946002	1·12	725369	5·08	274631	1
60	671609	3·96	945935	1·12	725674	5·08	274326	0
	Cosine	D.	Sine	D.	Cotang.	D.	Tang.	M.

(62 DEGREES.)

M.	Sine	D.	Cosine	D.	Tang.	D.	Cotang.	
0	9·671609	3·96	9·945935	1·12	9·725674	5·08	10·274326	60
1	671847	3·95	945868	1·12	725979	5·08	274021	59
2	672084	3·95	945800	1·12	726284	5·07	273716	58
3	672321	3·95	945733	1·12	726588	5·07	273412	57
4	672558	3·95	945666	1·12	726892	5·07	273108	56
5	672795	3·94	945598	1·12	727197	5·07	272803	55
6	673032	3·94	945531	1·12	727501	5·07	272499	54
7	673268	3·94	945464	1·13	727805	5·06	272195	53
8	673505	3·94	945396	1·13	728109	5·06	271891	52
9	673741	3·93	945328	1·13	728412	5·06	271588	51
10	673977	3·93	945261	1·13	728716	5·06	271284	50
11	9·674213	3·93	9·945193	1·13	9·729020	5·06	10·270980	49
12	674448	3·92	945125	1·13	729323	5·05	270677	48
13	674684	3·92	945058	1·13	729626	5·05	270374	47
14	674919	3·92	944990	1·13	729929	5·05	270071	46
15	675155	3·92	944922	1·13	730233	5·05	269767	45
16	675390	3·91	944854	1·13	730535	5·05	269465	44
17	675624	3·91	944786	1·13	730838	5·04	269162	43
18	675859	3·91	944718	1·13	731141	5·04	268859	42
19	676094	3·91	944650	1·13	731444	5·04	268556	41
20	676328	3·90	944582	1·14	731746	5·04	268254	40
21	9·676562	3·90	9·944514	1·14	9·732048	5·04	10·267952	39
22	676796	3·90	944446	1·14	732351	5·03	267649	38
23	677030	3·90	944377	1·14	732653	5·03	267347	37
24	677264	3·89	944309	1·14	732955	5·03	267045	36
25	677498	3·89	944241	1·14	733257	5·03	266743	35
26	677731	3·89	944172	1·14	733558	5·03	266442	34
27	677964	3·88	944104	1·14	733860	5·02	266140	33
28	678197	3·88	944036	1·14	734162	5·02	265838	32
29	678430	3·88	943967	1·14	734463	5·02	265537	31
30	678663	3·88	943899	1·14	734764	5·02	265236	30
31	9·678895	3·87	9·943830	1·14	9·735066	5·02	10·264934	29
32	679128	3·87	943761	1·14	735367	5·02	264633	28
33	679360	3·87	943693	1·15	735668	5·01	264332	27
34	679592	3·87	943624	1·15	735969	5·01	264031	26
35	679824	3·86	943555	1·15	736269	5·01	263731	25
36	680056	3·86	943486	1·15	736570	5·01	263430	24
37	680288	3·86	943417	1·15	736871	5·01	263129	23
38	680519	3·85	943348	1·15	737171	5·00	262829	22
39	680750	3·85	943279	1·15	737471	5·00	262529	21
40	680982	3·85	943210	1·15	737771	5·00	262229	20
41	9·681213	3·85	9·943141	1·15	9·738071	5·00	10·261929	19
42	681443	3·84	943072	1·15	738371	5·00	261629	18
43	681674	3·84	943003	1·15	738671	4·99	261329	17
44	681905	3·84	942934	1·15	738971	4·99	261029	16
45	682135	3·84	942864	1·15	739271	4·99	260729	15
46	682365	3·83	942795	1·16	739570	4·99	260430	14
47	682595	3·83	942726	1·16	739870	4·99	260130	13
48	682825	3·83	942656	1·16	740169	4·99	259831	12
49	683055	3·83	942587	1·16	740468	4·98	259532	11
50	683284	3·82	942517	1·16	740767	4·98	259233	10
51	9·683514	3·82	9·942448	1·16	9·741066	4·98	10·258934	9
52	683743	3·82	942378	1·16	741365	4·98	258635	8
53	683972	3·82	942308	1·16	741664	4·98	258336	7
54	684201	3·81	942239	1·16	741962	4·97	258038	6
55	684430	3·81	942169	1·16	742261	4·97	257739	5
56	684658	3·81	942099	1·16	742559	4·97	257441	4
57	684887	3·80	942029	1·16	742858	4·97	257142	3
58	685115	3·80	941959	1·16	743156	4·97	256844	2
59	685343	3·80	941889	1·17	743454	4·97	256546	1
60	685571	3·80	941819	1·17	743752	4·96	256248	0
	Cosine	D.	Sine	D.	Cotang.	D.	Tang.	M.

(61 DEGREES.)

M.	Sine	D.	Cosine	D.	Tang.	D.	Cotang.	
0	9·685571	3·80	9·941819	1·17	9·743752	4·96	10·256248	60
1	685799	3·79	941749	1·17	744050	4·96	255950	59
2	686027	3·79	941679	1·17	744348	4·96	255652	58
3	686254	3·79	941609	1·17	744645	4·96	255355	57
4	686482	3·79	941539	1·17	744943	4·96	255057	56
5	686709	3·78	941469	1·17	745240	4·96	254760	55
6	686936	3·78	941398	1·17	745538	4·95	254462	54
7	687163	3·78	941328	1·17	745835	4·95	254165	53
8	687389	3·78	941258	1·17	746132	4·95	253868	52
9	687616	3·77	941187	1·17	746429	4·95	253571	51
10	687843	3·77	941117	1·17	746726	4·95	253274	50
11	9·688069	3·77	9·941046	1·18	9·747023	4·94	10·252977	49
12	688295	3·77	940975	1·18	747319	4·94	252681	48
13	688521	3·76	940905	1·18	747616	4·94	252384	47
14	688747	3·76	940834	1·18	747913	4·94	252087	46
15	688972	3·76	940763	1·18	748209	4·94	251791	45
16	689198	3·76	940693	1·18	748505	4·93	251495	44
17	689423	3·75	940622	1·18	748801	4·93	251199	43
18	689648	3·75	940551	1·18	749097	4·93	250903	42
19	689873	3·75	940480	1·18	749393	4·93	250607	41
20	690098	3·75	940409	1·18	749689	4·93	250311	40
21	9·690323	3·74	9·940338	1·18	9·749985	4·93	10·250015	39
22	690548	3·74	940267	1·18	750281	4·92	249719	38
23	690772	3·74	940196	1·18	750576	4·92	249424	37
24	690996	3·74	940125	1·19	750872	4·92	249128	36
25	691220	3·73	940054	1·19	751167	4·92	248833	35
26	691444	3·73	939982	1·19	751462	4·92	248538	34
27	691668	3·73	939911	1·19	751757	4·92	248243	33
28	691892	3·73	939840	1·19	752052	4·91	247948	32
29	692115	3·72	939768	1·19	752347	4·91	247653	31
30	692339	3·72	939697	1·19	752642	4·91	247358	30
31	9·692562	3·72	9·939625	1·19	9·752937	4·91	10·247063	29
32	692785	3·71	939554	1·19	753231	4·91	246769	28
33	693008	3·71	939482	1·19	753526	4·91	246474	27
34	693231	3·71	939410	1·19	753820	4·90	246180	26
35	693453	3·71	939339	1·19	754115	4·90	245885	25
36	693676	3·70	939267	1·20	754409	4·90	245591	24
37	693898	3·70	939195	1·20	754703	4·90	245297	23
38	694120	3·70	939123	1·20	754997	4·90	245003	22
39	694342	3·70	939052	1·20	755291	4·90	244709	21
40	694564	3·69	938980	1·20	755585	4·89	244415	20
41	9·694786	3·69	9·938908	1·20	9·755878	4·89	10·244122	19
42	695007	3·69	938836	1·20	756172	4·89	243828	18
43	695229	3·69	938763	1·20	756465	4·89	243535	17
44	695450	3·68	938691	1·20	756759	4·89	243241	16
45	695671	3·68	938619	1·20	757052	4·89	242948	15
46	695892	3·68	938547	1·20	757345	4·88	242655	14
47	696113	3·68	938475	1·20	757638	4·88	242362	13
48	696334	3·67	938402	1·21	757931	4·88	242069	12
49	696554	3·67	938330	1·21	758224	4·88	241776	11
50	696775	3·67	938258	1·21	758517	4·88	241483	10
51	9·696995	3·67	9·938185	1·21	9·758810	4·88	10·241190	9
52	697215	3·66	938113	1·21	759102	4·87	240898	8
53	697435	3·66	938040	1·21	759395	4·87	240605	7
54	697654	3·66	937967	1·21	759687	4·87	240313	6
55	697874	3·66	937895	1·21	759979	4·87	240021	5
56	698094	3·65	937822	1·21	760272	4·87	239728	4
57	698313	3·65	937749	1·21	760564	4·87	239436	3
58	698532	3·65	937676	1·21	760856	4·86	239144	2
59	698751	3·65	937604	1·21	761148	4·86	238852	1
60	698970	3·64	937531	1·21	761439	4·86	238561	0
	Cosine	D.	Sine	D.	Cotang.	D.	Tang.	M.

M.	Sine	D.	Cosine	D.	Tang.	D.	Cotang.	
0	9·698970	3·64	9·937531	1·21	9·761439	4·86	10·238561	60
1	699189	3·64	937458	1·22	761731	4·86	238269	59
2	699407	3·64	937385	1·22	762023	4·86	237977	58
3	699626	3·64	937312	1·22	762314	4·86	237686	57
4	699844	3·63	937238	1·22	762606	4·85	237394	56
5	700062	3·63	937165	1·22	762897	4·85	237103	55
6	700280	3·63	937092	1·22	763188	4·85	236812	54
7	700498	3·63	937019	1·22	763479	4·85	236521	53
8	700716	3·63	936946	1·22	763770	4·85	236230	52
9	700933	3·62	936872	1·22	764061	4·85	235939	51
10	701151	3·62	936799	1·22	764352	4·84	235648	50
11	9·701368	3·62	9·936725	1·22	9·764643	4·84	10·235357	49
12	701585	3·62	936652	1·23	764933	4·84	235067	48
13	701802	3·61	936578	1·23	765224	4·84	234776	47
14	702019	3·61	936505	1·23	765514	4·84	234486	46
15	702236	3·61	936431	1·23	765805	4·84	234195	45
16	702452	3·61	936357	1·23	766095	4·84	233905	44
17	702669	3·60	936284	1·23	766385	4·83	233615	43
18	702885	3·60	936210	1·23	766675	4·83	233325	42
19	703101	3·60	936136	1·23	766965	4·83	233035	41
20	703317	3·60	936062	1·23	767255	4·83	232745	40
21	9·703533	3·59	9·935988	1·23	9·767545	4·83	10·232455	39
22	703749	3·59	935914	1·23	767834	4·83	232166	38
23	703964	3·59	935840	1·23	768124	4·82	231876	37
24	704179	3·59	935766	1·24	768413	4·82	231587	36
25	704395	3·59	935692	1·24	768703	4·82	231297	35
26	704610	3·58	935618	1·24	768992	4·82	231008	34
27	704825	3·58	935543	1·24	769281	4·82	230719	33
28	705040	3·58	935469	1·24	769570	4·82	230430	32
29	705254	3·58	935395	1·24	769860	4·81	230140	31
30	705469	3·57	935320	1·24	770148	4·81	229852	30
31	9·705683	3·57	9·935246	1·24	9·770437	4·81	10·229563	29
32	705898	3·57	935171	1·24	770726	4·81	229274	28
33	706112	3·57	935097	1·24	771015	4·81	228985	27
34	706326	3·56	935022	1·24	771303	4·81	228697	26
35	706539	3·56	934948	1·24	771592	4·81	228408	25
36	706753	3·56	934873	1·24	771880	4·80	228120	24
37	706967	3·56	934798	1·25	772168	4·80	227832	23
38	707180	3·55	934723	1·25	772457	4·80	227543	22
39	707393	3·55	934649	1·25	772745	4·80	227255	21
40	707606	3·55	934574	1·25	773033	4·80	226967	20
41	9·707819	3·55	9·934499	1·25	9·773321	4·80	10·226679	19
42	708032	3·54	934424	1·25	773608	4·79	226392	18
43	708245	3·54	934349	1·25	773896	4·79	226104	17
44	708458	3·54	934274	1·25	774184	4·79	225816	16
45	708670	3·54	934199	1·25	774471	4·79	225529	15
46	708882	3·53	934123	1·25	774759	4·79	225241	14
47	709094	3·53	934048	1·25	775046	4·79	224954	13
48	709306	3·53	933973	1·25	775333	4·79	224667	12
49	709518	3·53	933898	1·26	775621	4·78	224379	11
50	709730	3·53	933822	1·26	775908	4·78	224092	10
51	9·709941	3·52	9·933747	1·26	9·776195	4·78	10·223805	9
52	710153	3·52	933671	1·26	776482	4·78	223518	8
53	710364	3·52	933596	1·26	776769	4·78	223231	7
54	710575	3·52	933520	1·26	777055	4·78	222945	6
55	710786	3·51	933445	1·26	777342	4·78	222658	5
56	710997	3·51	933369	1·26	777628	4·77	222372	4
57	711208	3·51	933293	1·26	777915	4·77	222085	3
58	711419	3·51	933217	1·26	778201	4·77	221799	2
59	711629	3·50	933141	1·26	778487	4·77	221512	1
60	711839	3·50	933066	1·26	778774	4·77	221226	0
	Cosine	D.	Sine	D.	Cotang.	D.	Tang.	M.

M.	Sine	D.	Cosine	D.	Tang.	D.	Cotang.	
0	9·711839	3·50	9·933066	1·26	9·778774	4·77	10·221226	60
1	712050	3·50	932990	1·27	779060	4·77	220940	59
2	712260	3·50	932914	1·27	779346	4·76	220654	58
3	712469	3·49	932838	1·27	779632	4·76	220368	57
4	712679	3·49	932762	1·27	779918	4·76	220082	56
5	712889	3·49	932685	1·27	780203	4·76	219797	55
6	713098	3·49	932609	1·27	780489	4·76	219511	54
7	713308	3·49	932533	1·27	780775	4·76	219225	53
8	713517	3·48	932457	1·27	781060	4·76	218940	52
9	713726	3·48	932380	1·27	781346	4·75	218654	51
10	713935	3·48	932304	1·27	781631	4·75	218369	50
11	9·714144	3·48	9·932228	1·27	9·781916	4·75	10·218084	49
12	714352	3·47	932151	1·27	782201	4·75	217799	48
13	714561	3·47	932075	1·28	782486	4·75	217514	47
14	714769	3·47	931998	1·28	782771	4·75	217229	46
15	714978	3·47	931921	1·28	783056	4·75	216944	45
16	715186	3·47	931845	1·28	783341	4·75	216659	44
17	715394	3·46	931768	1·28	783626	4·74	216374	43
18	715602	3·46	931691	1·28	783910	4·74	216090	42
19	715809	3·46	931614	1·28	784195	4·74	215805	41
20	716017	3·46	931537	1·28	784479	4·74	215521	40
21	9·716224	3·45	9·931460	1·28	9·784764	4·74	10·215236	39
22	716432	3·45	931383	1·28	785048	4·74	214952	38
23	716639	3·45	931306	1·28	785332	4·73	214668	37
24	716846	3·45	931229	1·29	785616	4·73	214384	36
25	717053	3·45	931152	1·29	785900	4·73	214100	35
26	717259	3·44	931075	1·29	786184	4·73	213816	34
27	717466	3·44	930998	1·29	786468	4·73	213532	33
28	717673	3·44	930921	1·29	786752	4·73	213248	32
29	717879	3·44	930843	1·29	787036	4·73	212964	31
30	718085	3·43	930766	1·29	787319	4·72	212681	30
31	9·718291	3·43	9·930688	1·29	9·787603	4·72	10·212397	29
32	718497	3·43	930611	1·29	787886	4·72	212114	28
33	718703	3·43	930533	1·29	788170	4·72	211830	27
34	718909	3·43	930456	1·29	788453	4·72	211547	26
35	719114	3·42	930378	1·29	788736	4·72	211264	25
36	719320	3·42	930300	1·30	789019	4·72	210981	24
37	719525	3·42	930223	1·30	789302	4·71	210698	23
38	719730	3·42	930145	1·30	789585	4·71	210415	22
39	719935	3·41	930067	1·30	789868	4·71	210132	21
40	720140	3·41	929989	1·30	790151	4·71	209849	20
41	9·720345	3·41	9·929911	1·30	9·790433	4·71	10·209567	19
42	720549	3·41	929833	1·30	790716	4·71	209284	18
43	720754	3·40	929755	1·30	790999	4·71	209001	17
44	720958	3·40	929677	1·30	791281	4·71	208719	16
45	721162	3·40	929599	1·30	791563	4·70	208437	15
46	721366	3·40	929521	1·30	791846	4·70	208154	14
47	721570	3·40	929442	1·30	792128	4·70	207872	13
48	721774	3·39	929364	1·31	792410	4·70	207590	12
49	721978	3·39	929286	1·31	792692	4·70	207308	11
50	722181	3·39	929207	1·31	792974	4·70	207026	10
51	9·722385	3·39	9·929129	1·31	9·793256	4·70	10·206744	9
52	722588	3·39	929050	1·31	793538	4·69	206462	8
53	722791	3·38	928972	1·31	793819	4·69	206181	7
54	722994	3·38	928893	1·31	794101	4·69	205899	6
55	723197	3·38	928815	1·31	794383	4·69	205617	5
56	723400	3·38	928736	1·31	794664	4·69	205336	4
57	723603	3·37	928657	1·31	794945	4·69	205055	3
58	723805	3·37	928578	1·31	795227	4·69	204773	2
59	724007	3·37	928499	1·31	795508	4·68	204492	1
60	724210	3·37	928420	1·31	795789	4·68	204211	0
	Cosine	D.	Sine	D.	Cotang.	D.	Tang.	M.

(58 DEGREES.)

M.	Sine	D.	Cosine	D.	Tang.	D.	Cotang.	
0	9·724210	3·37	9·928420	1·32	9·795789	4·68	10·204211	60
1	724412	3·37	928342	1·32	796070	4·68	203930	59
2	724614	3·36	928263	1·32	796351	4·68	203649	58
3	724816	3·36	928183	1·32	796632	4·68	203368	57
4	725017	3·36	928104	1·32	796913	4·68	203087	56
5	725219	3·36	928025	1·32	797194	4·68	202806	55
6	725420	3·35	927946	1·32	797475	4·68	202525	54
7	725622	3·35	927867	1·32	797755	4·68	202245	53
8	725823	3·35	927787	1·32	798036	4·67	201964	52
9	726024	3·35	927708	1·32	798316	4·67	201684	51
10	726225	3·35	927629	1·32	798596	4·67	201404	50
11	9·726426	3·34	9·927549	1·32	9·798877	4·67	10·201123	49
12	726626	3·34	927470	1·33	799157	4·67	200843	48
13	726827	3·34	927390	1·33	799437	4·67	200563	47
14	727027	3·34	927310	1·33	799717	4·67	200283	46
15	727228	3·34	927231	1·33	799997	4·66	200003	45
16	727428	3·33	927151	1·33	800277	4·66	199723	44
17	727628	3·33	927071	1·33	800557	4·66	199443	43
18	727828	3·33	926991	1·33	800836	4·66	199164	42
19	728027	3·33	926911	1·33	801116	4·66	198884	41
20	728227	3·33	926831	1·33	801396	4·66	198604	40
21	9·728427	3·32	9·926751	1·33	9·801675	4·66	10·198325	39
22	728626	3·32	926671	1·33	801955	4·66	198045	38
23	728825	3·32	926591	1·33	802234	4·65	197766	37
24	729024	3·32	926511	1·34	802513	4·65	197487	36
25	729223	3·31	926431	1·34	802792	4·65	197208	35
26	729422	3·31	926351	1·34	803072	4·65	196928	34
27	729621	3·31	926270	1·34	803351	4·65	196649	33
28	729820	3·31	926190	1·34	803630	4·65	196370	32
29	730018	3·30	926110	1·34	803908	4·65	196092	31
30	730216	3·30	926029	1·34	804187	4·65	195813	30
31	9·730415	3·30	9·925949	1·34	9·804466	4·64	10·195534	29
32	730613	3·30	925868	1·34	804745	4·64	195255	28
33	730811	3·30	925788	1·34	805023	4·64	194977	27
34	731009	3·29	925707	1·34	805302	4·64	194698	26
35	731206	3·29	925626	1·34	805580	4·64	194420	25
36	731404	3·29	925545	1·35	805859	4·64	194141	24
37	731602	3·29	925465	1·35	806137	4·64	193863	23
38	731799	3·29	925384	1·35	806415	4·63	193585	22
39	731996	3·28	925303	1·35	806693	4·63	193307	21
40	732193	3·28	925222	1·35	806971	4·63	193029	20
41	9·732390	3·28	9·925141	1·35	9·807249	4·63	10·192751	19
42	732587	3·28	925060	1·35	807527	4·63	192473	18
43	732784	3·28	924979	1·35	807805	4·63	192195	17
44	732980	3·27	924897	1·35	808083	4·63	191917	16
45	733177	3·27	924816	1·35	808361	4·63	191639	15
46	733373	3·27	924735	1·36	808638	4·62	191362	14
47	733569	3·27	924654	1·36	808916	4·62	191084	13
48	733765	3·27	924572	1·36	809193	4·62	190807	12
49	733961	3·26	924491	1·36	809471	4·62	190529	11
50	734157	3·26	924409	1·36	809748	4·62	190252	10
51	9·734353	3·26	9·924328	1·36	9·810025	4·62	10·189975	9
52	734549	3·26	924246	1·36	810302	4·62	189698	8
53	734744	3·25	924164	1·36	810580	4·62	189420	7
54	734939	3·25	924083	1·36	810857	4·62	189143	6
55	735135	3·25	924001	1·36	811134	4·61	188866	5
56	735330	3·25	923919	1·36	811410	4·61	188590	4
57	735525	3·25	923837	1·36	811687	4·61	188313	3
58	735719	3·24	923755	1·37	811964	4·61	188036	2
59	735914	3·24	923673	1·37	812241	4·61	187759	1
60	736109	3·24	923591	1·37	812517	4·61	187483	0
	Cosine	D.	Sine	D.	Cotang.	D.	Tang.	M.

M.	Sine	D.	Cosine	D.	Tang.	D.	Cotang.	
0	9·736109	3·24	9·923591	1·37	9·812517	4·61	10·187482	60
1	736303	3·24	923509	1·37	812794	4·61	187206	59
2	736498	3·24	923427	1·37	813070	4·61	186930	58
3	736692	3·23	923345	1·37	813347	4·60	186653	57
4	736886	3·23	923263	1·37	813623	4·60	186377	56
5	737080	3·23	923181	1·37	813899	4·60	186101	55
6	737274	3·23	923098	1·37	814175	4·60	185825	54
7	737467	3·23	923016	1·37	814452	4·60	185548	53
8	737661	3·22	922933	1·37	814728	4·60	185272	52
9	737855	3·22	922851	1·37	815004	4·60	184996	51
10	738048	3·22	922768	1·38	815279	4·60	184721	50
11	9·738241	3·22	9·922686	1·38	9·815555	4·59	10·184445	49
12	738434	3·22	922603	1·38	815831	4·59	184169	48
13	738627	8·21	922520	1·38	816107	4·59	183893	47
14	738820	3·21	922438	1·38	816382	4·59	183618	46
15	739013	3·21	922355	1·38	816658	4·59	183342	45
16	739206	3·21	922272	1·38	816933	4·59	183067	44
17	739398	3·21	922189	1·38	817209	4·59	182791	43
18	739590	3·20	922106	1·38	817484	4·59	182516	42
19	739783	3·20	922023	1·38	817759	4·59	182241	41
20	739975	3·20	921940	1·38	818035	4·58	181965	40
21	9·740167	3·20	9·921857	1·39	9·818310	4·58	10·181690	39
22	740359	3·20	921774	1·39	818585	4·58	181415	38
23	740550	3·19	921691	1·39	818860	4·58	181140	37
24	740742	3·19	921607	1·39	819135	4·58	180865	36
25	740934	3·19	921524	1·39	819410	4·58	180590	35
26	741125	3·19	921441	1·39	819684	4·58	180316	34
27	741316	3·19	921357	1·39	819959	4·58	180041	33
28	741508	3·18	921274	1·39	820234	4·58	179766	32
29	741699	3·18	921190	1·39	820508	4·57	179492	31
30	741889	3·18	921107	1·39	820783	4·57	179217	30
31	9·742080	3·18	9·921023	1·39	9·821057	4·57	10·178943	29
32	742271	3·18	920939	1·40	821332	4·57	178668	28
33	742462	3·17	920856	1·40	821606	4·57	178394	27
34	742652	3·17	920772	1·40	821880	4·57	178120	26
35	742842	3·17	920688	1·40	822154	4·57	177846	25
36	743033	3·17	920604	1·40	822429	4·57	177571	24
37	743223	3·17	920520	1·40	822703	4·57	177297	23
38	743413	3·16	920436	1·40	822977	4·56	177023	22
39	743602	3·16	920352	1·40	823250	4·56	176750	21
40	743792	3·16	920268	1·40	823524	4·56	176476	20
41	9·743982	3·16	9·920184	1·40	9·823798	4·56	10·176202	19
42	744171	3·16	920099	1·40	824072	4·56	175928	18
43	744361	3·15	920015	1·40	824345	4·56	175655	17
44	744550	3·15	919931	1·41	824619	4·56	175381	16
45	744739	3·15	919846	1·41	824893	4·56	175107	15
46	744928	3·15	919762	1·41	825166	4·56	174834	14
47	745117	3·15	919677	1·41	825439	4·55	174561	13
48	745306	3·14	919593	1·41	825713	4·55	174287	12
49	745494	3·14	919508	1·41	825986	4·55	174014	11
50	745683	3·14	919424	1·41	826259	4·55	173741	10
51	9·745871	3·14	9·919339	1·41	9·826532	4·55	10·173468	9
52	746059	3·14	919254	1·41	826805	4·55	173195	8
53	746248	3·13	919169	1·41	827078	4·55	172922	7
54	746436	4·13	919085	1·41	827351	4·55	172649	6
55	746624	3·13	919000	1·41	827624	4·55	172376	5
56	746812	3·13	918915	1·42	827897	4·54	172103	4
57	746999	3·13	918830	1·42	828170	4·54	171830	3
58	747187	3·12	918745	1·42	828442	4·54	171558	2
59	747374	3·12	918659	1·42	828715	4·54	171285	1
60	747562	3·12	918574	1·42	828987	4·54	171013	0
	Cosine	D.	Sine	D.	Cotang.	D.	Tang.	M.

(56 DEGREES.)

M.	Sine	D.	Cosine	D.	Tang.	D.	Cotang.	
0	9·747562	3·12	9·918574	1·42	9·828987	4·54	10·171013	60
1	747749	3·12	918489	1·42	829260	4·54	170740	59
2	747936	3·12	918404	1·42	829532	4·54	170468	58
3	748123	3·11	918318	1·42	829805	4·54	170195	57
4	748310	3·11	918233	1·42	830077	4·54	169923	56
5	748497	3·11	918147	1·42	830349	4·53	169651	55
6	748683	3·11	918062	1·42	830621	4·53	169379	54
7	748870	3·11	917976	1·43	830893	4·53	169107	53
8	749056	3·10	917891	1·43	831165	4·53	168835	52
9	749243	3·10	917805	1·43	831437	4·53	168563	51
10	749429	3·10	917719	1·43	831709	4·53	168291	50
11	9·749615	3·10	9·917634	1·43	9·831981	4·53	10·168019	49
12	749801	3·10	917548	1·43	832253	4·53	167747	48
13	749987	3·09	917462	1·43	832525	4·53	167475	47
14	750172	3·09	917376	1·43	832796	4·53	167204	46
15	750358	3·09	917290	1·43	833068	4·52	166932	45
16	750543	3·09	917204	1·43	833339	4·52	166661	44
17	750729	3·09	917118	1·44	833611	4·52	166389	43
18	750914	3·08	917032	1·44	833882	4·52	166118	42
19	751099	3·08	916946	1·44	834154	4·52	165846	41
20	751284	3·08	916859	1·44	834425	4·52	165575	40
21	9·751469	3·08	9·916773	1·44	9·834696	4·52	10·165304	39
22	751654	3·08	916687	1·44	834967	4·52	165033	38
23	751839	3·08	916600	1·44	835238	4·52	164762	37
24	752023	3·07	916514	1·44	835509	4·52	164491	36
25	752208	3·07	916427	1·44	835780	4·51	164220	35
26	752392	3·07	916341	1·44	836051	4·51	163949	34
27	752576	3·07	916254	1·44	836322	4·51	163678	33
28	752760	3·07	916167	1·45	836593	4·51	163407	32
29	752944	3·06	916081	1·45	836864	4·51	163136	31
30	753128	3·06	915994	1·45	837134	4·51	162866	30
31	9·753312	3·06	9·915907	1·45	9·837405	4·51	10·162595	29
32	753495	3·06	915820	1·45	837675	4·51	162325	28
33	753679	3·06	915733	1·45	837946	4·51	162054	27
34	753862	3·05	915646	1·45	838216	4·51	161784	26
35	754046	3·05	915559	1·45	838487	4·50	161513	25
36	754229	3·05	915472	1·45	838757	4·50	161243	24
37	754412	3·05	915385	1·45	839027	4·50	160973	23
38	754595	3·05	915297	1·45	839297	4·50	160703	22
39	754778	3·04	915210	1·45	839568	4·50	160432	21
40	754960	3·04	915123	1·46	839838	4·50	160162	20
41	9·755143	3·04	9·915035	1·46	9·840108	4·50	10·159892	19
42	755326	3·04	914948	1·46	840378	4·50	159622	18
43	755508	3·04	914860	1·46	840647	4·50	159353	17
44	755690	3·04	914773	1·46	840917	4·49	159083	16
45	755872	3·03	914685	1·46	841187	4·49	158813	15
46	756054	3·03	914598	1·46	841457	4·49	158543	14
47	756236	3·03	914510	1·46	841726	4·49	158274	13
48	756418	3·03	914422	1·46	841996	4·49	158004	12
49	756600	3·03	914334	1·46	842266	4·49	157734	11
50	756782	3·02	914246	1·47	842535	4·49	157465	10
51	9·756963	3·02	9·914158	1·47	9·842805	4·49	10·157195	9
52	757144	3·02	914070	1·47	843074	4·49	156926	8
53	757326	3·02	913982	1·47	843343	4·49	156657	7
54	757507	3·02	913894	1·47	843612	4·49	156388	6
55	757688	3·01	913806	1·47	843882	4·48	156118	5
56	757869	3·01	913718	1·47	844151	4·48	155849	4
57	758050	3·01	913630	1·47	844420	4·48	155580	3
58	758230	3·01	913541	1·47	844689	4·48	155311	2
59	758411	3·01	913453	1·47	844958	4·48	155042	1
60	758591	3·01	913365	1·47	845227	4·48	154773	0
	Cosine	D.	Sine	D.	Cotang.	D.	Tang.	M.

M.	Sine	D.	Cosine	D.	Tang.	D.	Cotang.	
0	9·758591	3·01	9·913365	1·47	9·845227	4·48	10·154773	60
1	758772	3·00	913276	1·47	845496	4·48	154504	59
2	758952	3·00	913187	1·48	845764	4·48	154236	58
3	759132	3·00	913099	1·48	846033	4·48	153967	57
4	759312	3·00	913010	1·48	846302	4·48	153698	56
5	759492	3·00	912922	1·48	846570	4·47	153430	55
6	759672	2·99	912833	1·48	846839	4·47	153161	54
7	759852	2·99	912744	1·48	847107	4·47	152893	53
8	760031	2·99	912655	1·48	847376	4·47	152624	52
9	760211	2·99	912566	1·48	847644	4·47	152356	51
10	760390	2·99	912477	1·48	847913	4·47	152087	50
11	9·760569	2·98	9·912388	1·48	9·848181	4·47	10·151819	49
12	760748	2·98	912299	1·49	848449	4·47	151551	48
13	760927	2·98	912210	1·49	848717	4·47	151283	47
14	761106	2·98	912121	1·49	848986	4·47	151014	46
15	761285	2·98	912031	1·49	849254	4·47	150746	45
16	761464	2·98	911942	1·49	849522	4·47	150478	44
17	761642	2·97	911853	1·49	849790	4·46	150210	43
18	761821	2·97	911763	1·49	850058	4·46	149942	42
19	761999	2·97	911674	1·49	850325	4·46	149675	41
20	762177	2·97	911584	1·49	850593	4·46	149407	40
21	9·762356	2·97	9·911495	1·49	9·850861	4·46	10·149139	39
22	762534	2·96	911405	1·49	851129	4·46	148871	38
23	762712	2·96	911315	1·50	851396	4·46	148604	37
24	762889	2·96	911226	1·50	851664	4·46	148336	36
25	763067	2·96	911136	1·50	851931	4·46	148069	35
26	763245	2·96	911046	1·50	852199	4·46	147801	34
27	763422	2·96	910956	1·50	852466	4·46	147534	33
28	763600	2·95	910866	1·50	852733	4·45	147267	32
29	763777	2·95	910776	1·50	853001	4·45	146999	31
30	763954	2·95	910686	1·50	853268	4·45	146732	30
31	9·764131	2·95	9·910596	1·50	9·853535	4·45	10·146465	29
32	764308	2·95	910506	1·50	853802	4·45	146198	28
33	764485	2·94	910415	1·50	854069	4·45	145931	27
34	764662	2·94	910325	1·51	854336	4·45	145664	26
35	764838	2·94	910235	1·51	854603	4·45	145397	25
36	765015	2·94	910144	1·51	854870	4·45	145130	24
37	765191	2·94	910054	1·51	855137	4·45	144863	23
38	765367	2·94	909963	1·51	855404	4·45	144596	22
39	765544	2·93	909873	1·51	855671	4·44	144329	21
40	765720	2·93	909782	1·51	855938	4·44	144062	20
41	9·765896	2·93	9·909691	1·51	9·856204	4·44	10·143796	19
42	766072	2·93	909601	1·51	856471	4·44	143529	18
43	766247	2·93	909510	1·51	856737	4·44	143263	17
44	766423	2·93	909419	1·51	857004	4·44	142996	16
45	766598	2·92	909328	1·52	857270	4·44	142730	15
46	766774	2·92	909237	1·52	857537	4·44	142463	14
47	766949	2·92	909146	1·52	857803	4·44	142197	13
48	767124	2·92	909055	1·52	858069	4·44	141931	12
49	767300	2·92	908964	1·52	858336	4·44	141664	11
50	767475	2·91	908873	1·52	858602	4·43	141398	10
51	9·767649	2·91	9·908781	1·52	9·858868	4·43	10·141132	9
52	767824	2·91	908690	1·52	859134	4·43	140866	8
53	767999	2·91	908599	1·52	859400	4·43	140600	7
54	768173	2·91	908507	1 52	859666	4·43	140334	6
55	768348	2·90	908416	1·53	859932	4·43	140068	5
56	768522	2·90	908324	1·53	860198	4·43	139802	4
57	768697	2·90	908233	1·53	860464	4·43	139536	3
58	768871	2·90	908141	1·53	860730	4·43	139270	2
59	769045	2·90	908049	1·53	860995	4·43	139005	1
60	769219	2·90	907958	1·53	861261	4·43	138739	0
	Cosine	D.	Sine	D.	Cotang.	D.	Tang.	M.

(54 DEGREES.)

M.	Sine	D.	Cosine	D.	Tang.	D.	Cotang.	
0	9·769219	2·90	9·907958	1·53	9·861261	4·43	10·138739	60
1	769393	2·89	907866	1·53	861527	4·43	138473	59
2	769566	2·89	907774	1·53	861792	4·42	138208	58
3	769740	2·89	907682	1·53	862058	4·42	137942	57
4	769913	2·89	907590	1·53	862323	4·42	137677	56
5	770087	2·89	907498	1·53	862589	4·42	137411	55
6	770260	2·88	907406	1·53	862854	4·42	137146	54
7	770433	2·88	907314	1·54	863119	4·42	136881	53
8	770606	2·88	907222	1·54	863385	4·42	136615	52
9	770779	2·88	907129	1·54	863650	4·42	136350	51
10	770952	2·88	907037	1·54	863915	4·42	136085	50
11	9·771125	2·88	9·906945	1·54	9·864180	4·42	10·135820	49
12	771298	2·87	906852	1·54	864445	4·42	135555	48
13	771470	2·87	906760	1·54	864710	4·42	135290	47
14	771643	2·87	906667	1·54	864975	4·41	135025	46
15	771815	2·87	906575	1·54	865240	4·41	134760	45
16	771987	2·87	906482	1·54	865505	4·41	134495	44
17	772159	2·87	906389	1·55	865770	4·41	134230	43
18	772331	2·86	906296	1·55	866035	4·41	133965	42
19	772503	2·86	906204	1·55	866300	4·41	133700	41
20	772675	2·86	906111	1·55	866564	4·41	133436	40
21	9·772847	2·86	9·906018	1·55	9·866829	4·41	10·133171	39
22	773018	2·86	905925	1·55	867094	4·41	132906	38
23	773190	2·86	905832	1·55	867358	4·41	132642	37
24	773361	2·85	905739	1·55	867623	4·41	132377	36
25	773533	2·85	905645	1·55	867887	4·41	132113	35
26	773704	2·85	905552	1·55	868152	4·40	131848	34
27	773875	2·85	905459	1·55	868416	4·40	131584	33
28	774046	2·85	905366	1·56	868680	4·40	131320	32
29	774217	2·85	905272	1·56	868945	4·40	131055	31
30	774388	2·84	905179	1·56	869209	4·40	130794	30
31	9·774558	2·84	9·905085	1·56	9·869473	4·40	10·130527	29
32	774729	2·84	904992	1·56	869737	4·40	130263	28
33	774899	2·84	904898	1·56	870001	4·40	129999	27
34	775070	2·84	904804	1·56	870265	4·40	129735	26
35	775240	2·84	904711	1·56	870529	4·40	129471	25
36	775410	2·83	904617	1·56	870793	4·40	129207	24
37	775580	2·83	904523	1·56	871057	4·40	128943	23
38	775750	2·83	904429	1·57	871321	4·40	128679	22
39	775920	2·83	904335	1·57	871585	4·40	128415	21
40	776090	2·83	904241	1·57	871849	4·39	128151	20
41	9·776259	2·83	9·904147	1·57	9·872112	4·39	10·127888	19
42	776429	2·82	904053	1·57	872376	4·39	127624	18
43	776598	2·82	903959	1·57	872640	4·39	127360	17
44	776768	2·82	903864	1·57	872903	4·39	127097	16
45	776937	2·82	903770	1·57	873167	4·39	126833	15
46	777106	2·82	903676	1·57	873430	4·39	126570	14
47	777275	2·81	903581	1·57	873694	4·39	126306	13
48	777444	2·81	903487	1·57	873957	4·39	126043	12
49	777613	2·81	903392	1·58	874220	4·39	125780	11
50	777781	2·81	903298	1·58	874484	4·39	125516	10
51	9·777950	2·81	9·903203	1·58	9·874747	4·39	10·125253	9
52	778119	2·81	903108	1·58	875010	4·39	124990	8
53	778287	2·80	903014	1·58	875273	4·38	124727	7
54	778455	2·80	902919	1·58	875536	4·38	124464	6
55	778624	2·80	902824	1·58	875800	4·38	124200	5
56	778792	2·80	902729	1·58	876063	4·38	123937	4
57	778960	2·80	902634	1·58	876326	4·38	123674	3
58	779128	2·80	902539	1·59	876589	4·38	123411	2
59	779295	2·79	902444	1·59	876851	4·38	123149	1
60	779463	2·79	902349	1·59	877114	4·38	122886	0
	Cosine	D.	Sine	D.	Tang.	D.	Cotang.	M.

(53 DEGREES.)

M.	Sine	D.	Cosine	D.	Tang.	D.	Cotang.	
0	9·779463	2·79	9·902349	1·59	9·877114	4·38	10·122886	60
1	779631	2·79	902253	1·59	877377	4·38	122623	59
2	779798	2·79	902158	1·59	877640	4·38	122360	58
3	779966	2·79	902063	1·59	877903	4·38	122097	57
4	780133	2·79	901967	1·59	878165	4·38	121835	56
5	780300	2·78	901872	1·59	878428	4·38	121572	55
6	780467	2·78	901776	1·59	878691	4·38	121309	54
7	780634	2·78	901681	1·59	878953	4·37	121047	53
8	780801	2·78	901585	1·59	879216	4·37	120784	52
9	780968	2·78	901490	1·59	879478	4·37	120522	51
10	781134	2·78	901394	1·60	879741	4·37	120259	50
11	9·781301	2·77	9·901298	1·60	9·880003	4·37	10·119997	49
12	781468	2·77	901202	1·60	880265	4·37	119735	48
13	781634	2·77	901106	1·60	880528	4·37	119472	47
14	781800	2·77	901010	1·60	880790	4·37	119210	46
15	781966	2·77	900914	1·60	881052	4·37	118948	45
16	782132	2·77	900818	1·60	881314	4·37	118686	44
17	782298	2·76	900722	1·60	881576	4·37	118424	43
18	782464	2·76	900626	1·60	881839	4·37	118161	42
19	782630	2·76	900529	1·60	882101	4·37	117899	41
20	782796	2·76	900433	1·61	882363	4·36	117637	40
21	9·782961	2·76	9·900337	1·61	9·882625	4·36	10·117375	39
22	783127	2·76	900240	1·61	882887	4·36	117113	38
23	783292	2·75	900144	1·61	883148	4·36	116852	37
24	783458	2·75	900047	1·61	883410	4·36	116590	36
25	783623	2·75	899951	1·61	883672	4·36	116328	35
26	783788	2·75	899854	1·61	883934	4·36	116066	34
27	783953	2·75	899757	1·61	884196	4·36	115804	33
28	784118	2·75	899660	1·61	884457	4·36	115543	32
29	784282	2·74	899564	1·61	884719	4·36	115281	31
30	784447	2·74	899467	1·62	884980	4·36	115020	30
31	9·784612	2·74	9·899370	1·62	9·885242	4·36	10·114758	29
32	784776	2·74	899273	1·62	885503	4·36	114497	28
33	784941	2·74	899176	1·62	885765	4·36	114235	27
34	785105	2·74	899078	1·62	886026	4·36	113974	26
35	785269	2·73	898981	1·62	886288	4·36	113712	25
36	785433	2·73	898884	1·62	886549	4·35	113451	24
37	785597	2·73	898787	1·62	886810	4·35	113190	23
38	785761	2·73	898689	1·62	887072	4·35	112928	22
39	785925	2·73	898592	1·62	887333	4·35	112667	21
40	786089	2·73	898494	1·63	887594	4·35	112406	20
41	9·786252	2·72	9·898397	1·63	9·887855	4·35	10·112145	19
42	786416	2·72	898299	1·63	888116	4·35	111884	18
43	786579	2·72	898202	1·63	888377	4·35	111623	17
44	786742	2·72	898104	1·63	888639	4·35	111361	16
45	786906	2·72	898006	1·63	888900	4·35	111100	15
46	787069	2·72	897908	1·63	889160	4·35	110840	14
47	787232	2·71	897810	1·63	889421	4·35	110579	13
48	787395	2·71	897712	1·63	889682	4·35	110318	12
49	787557	2·71	897614	1·63	889943	4·35	110057	11
50	787720	2·71	897516	1·63	890204	4·34	109796	10
51	9·787883	2·71	9·897418	1·64	9·890465	4·34	10·109535	9
52	788045	2·71	897320	1·64	890725	4·34	109275	8
53	788208	2·71	897222	1·64	890986	4·34	109014	7
54	788370	2·70	897123	1·64	891247	4·34	108753	6
55	788532	2·70	897025	1·64	891507	4·34	108493	5
56	788694	2·70	896926	1·64	891768	4·34	108232	4
57	788856	2·70	896828	1·64	892028	4·34	107972	3
58	789018	2·70	896729	1·64	892289	4·34	107711	2
59	789180	2·70	896631	1·64	892549	4·34	107451	1
60	789342	2·69	896532	1·64	892810	4·34	107190	0
	Cosine	D.	Sine	D.	Cotang.	D.	Tang.	M.

(52 DEGREES.)

M.	Sine	D.	Cosine	D.	Tang.	D.	Cotang.	
0	9·789342	2·69	9·896532	1·64	9·892810	4·34	10·107190	60
1	789504	2·69	896433	1·65	893070	4·34	106930	59
2	789665	2·69	896335	1·65	893331	4·34	106669	58
3	789827	2·69	896236	1·65	893591	4·34	106409	57
4	789988	2·69	896137	1·65	893851	4·34	106149	56
5	790149	2·69	896038	1·65	894111	4·34	105889	55
6	790310	2·68	895939	1·65	894371	4·34	105629	54
7	790471	2·68	895840	1·65	894632	4·33	105368	53
8	790632	2·68	895741	1·65	894892	4·33	105108	52
9	790793	2·68	895641	1·65	895152	4·33	104848	51
10	790954	2·68	895542	1·65	895412	4·33	104588	50
11	9·791115	2·68	9·895443	1·66	9·895672	4·33	10·104328	49
12	791275	2·67	895343	1·66	895932	4·33	104068	48
13	791436	2·67	895244	1·66	896192	4·33	103808	47
14	791596	2·67	895145	1·66	896452	4·33	103548	46
15	791757	2·67	895045	1·66	896712	4·33	103288	45
16	791917	2·67	894945	1·66	896971	4·33	103029	44
17	792077	2·67	894846	1·66	897231	4·33	102769	43
18	792237	2·66	894746	1·66	897491	4·33	102509	42
19	792397	2·66	894646	1·66	897751	4·33	102249	41
20	792557	2·66	894546	1·66	898010	4·33	101990	40
21	9·792716	2·66	9·894446	1·67	9·898270	4·33	10·101730	39
22	792876	2·66	894346	1·67	898530	4·33	101470	38
23	793035	2·66	894246	1·67	898789	4·33	101211	37
24	793195	2·65	894146	1·67	899049	4·32	100951	36
25	793354	2·65	894046	1·67	899308	4·32	100692	35
26	793514	2·65	893946	1·67	899568	4·32	100432	34
27	793673	2·65	893846	1·67	899827	4·32	100173	33
28	793832	2·65	893745	1·67	900086	4·32	099914	32
29	793991	2·65	893645	1·67	900346	4·32	099654	31
30	794150	2·64	893544	1·67	900605	4·32	099395	30
31	9·794308	2·64	9·893444	1·68	9·900864	4·32	10·099136	29
32	794467	2·64	893343	1·68	901124	4·32	098876	28
33	794626	2·64	893243	1·68	901383	4·32	098617	27
34	794784	2·64	893142	1·68	901642	4·32	098358	26
35	794942	2·64	893041	1·68	901901	4·32	098099	25
36	795101	2·64	892940	1·68	902160	4·32	097840	24
37	795259	2·63	892839	1·68	902419	4·32	097581	23
38	795417	2·63	892739	1·68	902679	4·32	097321	22
39	795575	2·63	892638	1·68	902938	4·32	097062	21
40	795733	2·63	892536	1·68	903197	4·31	096803	20
41	9·795891	2·63	9·892435	1·69	9·903455	4·31	10·096545	19
42	796049	2·63	892334	1·69	903714	4·31	096286	18
43	796206	2·63	892233	1·69	903973	4·31	096027	17
44	796364	2·62	892132	1·69	904232	4·31	095768	16
45	796521	2·62	892030	1·69	904491	4·31	095509	15
46	796679	2·62	891929	1·69	904750	4·31	095250	14
47	796836	2·62	891827	1·69	905008	4·31	094992	13
48	796993	2·62	891726	1·69	905267	4·31	094733	12
49	797150	2·61	891624	1·69	905526	4·31	094474	11
50	797307	2·61	891523	1·70	905784	4·31	094216	10
51	9·797464	2·61	9·891421	1·70	9·906043	4·31	10·093957	9
52	797621	2·61	891319	1·70	906302	4·31	093698	8
53	797777	2·61	891217	1·70	906560	4·31	093440	7
54	797934	2·61	891115	1·70	906819	4·31	093181	6
55	798091	2·61	891013	1·70	907077	4·31	092923	5
56	798247	2·61	890911	1·70	907336	4·31	092664	4
57	798403	2·60	890809	1·70	907594	4·31	092406	3
58	798560	2·60	890707	1·70	907852	4·31	092148	2
59	798716	2·60	890605	1·70	908111	4·30	091889	1
60	798872	2·60	890503	1·70	908369	4·30	091631	0
	Cosine	D.	Sine	D.	Cotang.	D.	Tang.	M.

M.	Sine	D.	Cosine	D.	Tang.	D.	Cotang.	
0	9·798872	2·60	9·890503	1·70	9·908369	4·30	10·091631	60
1	799028	2·60	890400	1·71	908628	4·30	091372	59
2	799184	2·60	890298	1·71	908886	4·30	091114	58
3	799339	2·59	890195	1·71	909144	4·30	090856	57
4	799495	2·59	890093	1·71	909402	4·30	090598	56
5	799651	2·59	889990	1·71	909660	4·30	090340	55
6	799806	2·59	889888	1·71	909918	4·30	090082	54
7	799962	2·59	889785	1·71	910177	4·30	089823	53
8	800117	2·59	889682	1·71	910435	4·30	089565	52
9	800272	2·58	889579	1·71	910693	4·30	089307	51
10	800427	2·58	889477	1·71	910951	4·30	089049	50
11	9·800582	2·58	9·889374	1·72	9·911209	4·30	10·088791	49
12	800737	2·58	889271	1·72	911467	4·30	088533	48
13	800892	2·58	889168	1·72	911724	4·30	088276	47
14	801047	2·58	889064	1·72	911982	4·30	088018	46
15	801201	2·58	888961	1·72	912240	4·30	087760	45
16	801356	2·57	888858	1·72	912498	4·30	087502	44
17	801511	2·57	888755	1·72	912756	4·30	087244	43
18	801665	2·57	888651	1·72	913014	4·29	086986	42
19	801819	2·57	888548	1·72	913271	4·29	086729	41
20	801973	2·57	888444	1·73	913529	4·29	086471	40
21	9·802128	2·57	9·888341	1·73	9·913787	4·29	10·086213	39
22	802282	2·56	888237	1·73	914044	4·29	085956	38
23	802436	2·56	888134	1·73	914302	4·29	085698	37
24	802589	2·56	888030	1·73	914560	4·29	085440	36
25	802743	2·56	887926	1·73	914817	4·29	085183	35
26	802897	2·56	887822	1·73	915075	4·29	084925	34
27	803050	2·56	887718	1·73	915332	4·29	084668	33
28	803204	2·56	887614	1·73	915590	4·29	084410	32
29	803357	2·55	887510	1·73	915847	4·29	084153	31
30	803511	2·55	887406	1·74	916104	4·29	083896	30
31	9·803664	2·55	9·887302	1·74	9·916362	4·29	10·083638	29
32	803817	2·55	887198	1·74	916619	4·29	083381	28
33	803970	2·55	887093	1·74	916877	4·29	083123	27
34	804123	2·55	886989	1·74	917134	4·29	082866	26
35	804276	2·54	886885	1·74	917391	4·29	082609	25
36	804428	2·54	886780	1·74	917648	4·29	082352	24
37	804581	2·54	886676	1·74	917905	4·29	082095	23
38	804734	2·54	886571	1·74	918163	4·28	081837	22
39	804886	2·54	886466	1·74	918420	4·28	081580	21
40	805039	2·54	886362	1·75	918677	4·28	081323	20
41	9·805191	2·54	9·886257	1·75	9·918934	4·28	10·081066	19
42	805343	2·53	886152	1·75	919191	4·28	080809	18
43	805495	2·53	886047	1·75	919448	4·28	080552	17
44	805647	2·53	885942	1·75	919705	4·28	080295	16
45	805799	2·53	885837	1·75	919962	4·28	080038	15
46	805951	2·53	885732	1·75	920219	4·28	079781	14
47	806103	2·53	885627	1·75	920476	4·28	079524	13
48	806254	2·53	885522	1·75	920733	4·28	079267	12
49	806406	2·52	885416	1·75	920990	4·28	079010	11
50	806557	2·52	885311	1·76	921247	4·28	078753	10
51	9·806709	2·52	9·885205	1·76	9·921503	4·28	10·078497	9
52	806860	2·52	885100	1·76	921760	4·28	078240	8
53	807011	2·52	884994	1·76	922017	4·28	077983	7
54	807163	2·52	884889	1·76	922274	4·28	077726	6
55	807314	2·52	884783	1·76	922530	4·28	077470	5
56	807465	2·51	884677	1·76	922787	4·28	077213	4
57	807615	2·51	884572	1·76	923044	4·28	076956	3
58	807766	2·51	884466	1·76	923300	4·28	076700	2
59	807917	2·51	884360	1·76	923557	4·27	076443	1
60	808067	2·51	884254	1·77	923813	4·27	076187	0
	Cosine	D.	Sine	D.	Cotang.	D.	Tang.	M.

(50 DEGREES.)

M.	Sine	D.	Cosine	D.	Tang.	D.	Cotang.	
0	9·808067	2·51	9·884254	1·77	9·923813	4·27	10·076187	60
1	808218	2·51	884148	1·77	924070	4·27	075930	59
2	808368	2·51	884042	1·77	924327	4·27	075673	58
3	808519	2·50	883936	1·77	924583	4·27	075417	57
4	808669	2·50	883829	1·77	924840	4·27	075160	56
5	808819	2·50	883723	1·77	925096	4·27	074904	55
6	808969	2·50	883617	1·77	925352	4·27	074648	54
7	809119	2·50	883510	1·77	925609	4·27	074391	53
8	809269	2·50	883404	1·77	925865	4·27	074135	52
9	809419	2·49	883297	1·78	926122	4·27	073878	51
10	809569	2·49	883191	1·78	926378	4·27	073622	50
11	9·809718	2·49	9·883084	1·78	9·926634	4·27	10·073366	49
12	809868	2·49	882977	1·78	926890	4·27	073110	48
13	810017	2·49	882871	1·78	927147	4·27	072853	47
14	810167	2·49	882764	1·78	927403	4·27	072597	46
15	810316	2·48	882657	1·78	927659	4·27	072341	45
16	810465	2·48	882550	1·78	927915	4·27	072085	44
17	810614	2·48	882443	1·78	928171	4·27	071829	43
18	810763	2·48	882336	1·79	928427	4·27	071573	42
19	810912	2·48	882229	1·79	928683	4·27	071317	41
20	811061	2·48	882121	1·79	928940	4·27	071060	40
21	9·811210	2·48	9·882014	1·79	9·929196	4·27	10·070804	39
22	811358	2·47	881907	1·79	929452	4·27	070548	38
23	811507	2·47	881799	1·79	929708	4·27	070292	37
24	811655	2·47	881692	1·79	929964	4·26	070036	36
25	811804	2·47	881584	1·79	930220	4·26	069780	35
26	811952	2·47	881477	1·79	930475	4·26	069525	34
27	812100	2·47	881369	1·79	930731	4·26	069269	33
28	812248	2·47	881261	1·80	930987	4·26	069013	32
29	812396	2·46	881153	1·80	931243	4·26	068757	31
30	812544	2·46	881046	1·80	931499	4·26	068501	30
31	9·812692	2·46	9·880938	1·80	9·931755	4·26	10·068245	29
32	812840	2·46	880830	1·80	932010	4·26	067990	28
33	812988	2·46	880722	1·80	932266	4·26	067734	27
34	813135	2·46	880613	1·80	932522	4·26	067478	26
35	813283	2·46	880505	1·80	932778	4·26	067222	25
36	813430	2·45	880397	1·80	933033	4·26	066967	24
37	813578	2·45	880289	1·81	933289	4·26	066711	23
38	813725	2·45	880180	1·81	933545	4·26	066455	22
39	813872	2·45	880072	1·81	933800	4·26	066200	21
40	814019	2·45	879963	1·81	934056	4·26	065944	20
41	9·814166	2·45	9·879855	1·81	9·934311	4·26	10·065689	19
42	814313	2·45	879746	1·81	934567	4·26	065433	18
43	814460	2·44	879637	1·81	934823	4·26	065177	17
44	814607	2·44	879529	1·81	935078	4·26	064922	16
45	814753	2·44	879420	1·81	935333	4·26	064667	15
46	814900	2·44	879311	1·81	935589	4·26	064411	14
47	815046	2·44	879202	1·82	935844	4·26	064156	13
48	815193	2·44	879093	1·82	936100	4·26	063900	12
49	815339	2·44	878984	1·82	936355	4·26	063645	11
50	815485	2·43	878875	1·82	936610	4·26	063390	10
51	9·815631	2·43	9·878766	1·82	9·936866	4·25	10·063134	9
52	815778	2·43	878656	1·82	937121	4·25	062879	8
53	815924	2·43	878547	1·82	937376	4·25	062624	7
54	816069	2·43	878438	1·82	937632	4·25	062368	6
55	816215	2·43	878328	1·82	937887	4·25	062113	5
56	816361	2·43	878219	1·83	938142	4·25	061858	4
57	816507	2·42	878109	1·83	938398	4·25	061602	3
58	816652	2·42	877999	1·83	938653	4·25	061347	2
59	816798	2·42	877890	1·83	938908	4·25	061092	1
60	816943	2·42	877780	1·83	939163	4·25	060837	0
	Cosine	D.	Sine	D.	Cotang.	D.	Tang.	M.

(49 DEGREES.)

M.	Sine	D.	Cosine	D.	Taug.	D.	Cotang.	
0	9·816943	2·42	9·877780	1·83	9·939163	4·25	10·060837	60
1	817088	2·42	877670	1·83	939418	4·25	060582	59
2	817233	2·42	877560	1·83	939673	4·25	060327	58
3	817379	2·42	877450	1·83	939928	4·25	060072	57
4	817524	2·41	877340	1·83	940183	4·25	059817	56
5	817668	2·41	877230	1·84	940438	4·25	059562	55
6	817813	2·41	877120	1·84	940694	4·25	059306	54
7	817958	2·41	877010	1·84	940949	4·25	059051	53
8	818103	2·41	876899	1·84	941204	4·25	058796	52
9	818247	2·41	876789	1·84	941458	4·25	058542	51
10	818392	2·41	876678	1·84	941714	4·25	058286	50
11	9·818536	2·40	9·876568	1·84	9·941968	4·25	10·058032	49
12	818681	2·40	876457	1·84	942223	4 25	057777	48
13	818825	2·40	876347	1·84	942478	4·25	057522	47
14	818969	2·40	876236	1·85	942733	4·25	057267	46
15	819113	2·40	876125	1·85	942988	4·25	057012	45
16	819257	2·40	876014	1·85	943243	4·25	056757	44
17	819401	2·40	875904	1·85	943498	4·25	056502	43
18	819545	2·39	875793	1·85	943752	4·25	056248	42
19	819689	2·39	875682	1·85	944007	4·25	055993	41
20	819832	2·39	875571	1·85	944262	4·25	055738	40
21	9·819976	2·39	9·875459	1·85	9·944517	4·25	10·055483	39
22	820120	2·39	875348	1·85	944771	4·24	055229	38
23	820263	2·39	875237	1·85	945026	4·24	054974	37
24	820406	2·39	875126	1·86	945281	4·24	054719	36
25	820550	2·38	875014	1·86	945535	4·24	054465	35
26	820693	2·38	874903	1·86	945790	4·24	054210	34
27	820836	2·38	874791	1·86	946045	4·24	053955	33
28	820979	2·38	874680	1·86	946299	4·24	053701	32
29	821122	2·38	874568	1·86	946554	4·24	053446	31
30	821265	2·38	874456	1·86	946808	4·24	053192	30
31	9·821407	2·38	9·874344	1·86	9·947063	4·24	10·052937	29
32	821550	2·38	874232	1·87	947318	4·24	052682	28
33	821693	2·37	874121	1·87	947572	4·24	052428	27
34	821835	2·37	874009	1·87	947826	4·24	052174	26
35	821977	2·37	873896	1·87	948081	4·24	051919	25
36	822120	2·37	873784	1·87	948336	4·24	051664	24
37	822262	2·37	873672	1·87	948590	4·24	051410	23
38	822404	2·37	873560	1·87	948844	4·24	051156	22
39	822546	2·37	873448	1·87	949099	4·24	050901	21
40	822688	2·36	873335	1·87	949353	4·24	050647	20
41	9·822830	2·36	9·873223	1·87	9·949607	4·24	10·050393	19
42	822972	2·36	873110	1·88	949862	4·24	050138	18
43	823114	2·36	872998	1·88	950116	4·24	049884	17
44	823255	2·36	872885	1·88	950370	4·24	049630	16
45	823397	2·36	872772	1·88	950625	4·24	049375	15
46	823539	2·36	872659	1·88	950879	4·24	049121	14
47	823680	2·35	872547	1·88	951133	4·24	048867	13
48	823821	2·35	872434	1·88	951388	4·24	048612	12
49	823963	2·35	872321	1·88	951642	4·24	048358	11
50	824104	2·35	872208	1·88	951896	4·24	048104	10
51	9·824245	2·35	9·872095	1·89	9·952150	4·24	10·047850	9
52	824386	2·35	871981	1·89	952405	4·24	047595	8
53	824527	2·35	871868	1·89	952659	4·24	047341	7
54	824668	2·34	871755	1·89	952913	4·24	047087	6
55	824808	2·34	871641	1·89	953167	4·23	046833	5
56	824949	2·34	871528	1·89	953421	4·23	046579	4
57	825090	2·34	871414	1·89	953675	4·23	046325	3
58	825230	2·34	871301	1·89	953929	4·23	046071	2
59	825371	2·34	871187	1·89	954183	4·23	045817	1
60	825511	2·34	871073	1·90	954437	4·33	045563	0
	Cosine	D.	Sine	D.	Cotang.	D.	Tang.	M.

(48 DEGREES.)

M.	Sine	D.	Cosine	D.	Tang.	D.	Cotang.	
0	9·825511	2·34	9·871073	1·90	9·954437	4·23	10·045563	60
1	825651	2·33	870960	1·90	954691	4·23	045309	59
2	825791	2·33	870846	1·90	954945	4·23	045055	58
3	825931	2·33	870732	1·90	955200	4·23	044800	57
4	826071	2·33	870618	1·90	955454	4·23	044546	56
5	826211	2·33	870504	1·90	955707	4·23	044293	55
6	826351	2·33	870390	1·90	955961	4·23	044039	54
7	826491	2·33	870276	1·90	956215	4·23	043785	53
8	826631	2·33	870161	1·90	956469	4·23	043531	52
9	826770	2·32	870047	1·91	956723	4·23	043277	51
10	826910	2·32	869933	1·91	956977	4·23	043023	50
11	9·827049	2·32	9·869818	1·91	9·957231	4·23	10·042769	49
12	827189	2·32	869704	1·91	957485	4·23	042515	48
13	827328	2·32	869589	1·91	957739	4·23	042261	47
14	827467	2·32	869474	1·91	957993	4·23	042007	46
15	827606	2·32	869360	1·91	958246	4·23	041754	45
16	827745	2·32	869245	1·91	958500	4·23	041500	44
17	827884	2·31	869130	1·91	958754	4·23	041246	43
18	828023	2·31	869015	1·92	959008	4·23	040992	42
19	828162	2·31	868900	1·92	959262	4·23	040738	41
20	828301	2·31	868785	1·92	959516	4·23	040484	40
21	9·828439	2·31	9·868670	1·92	9·959769	4·23	10·040231	39
22	828578	2·31	868555	1·92	960023	4·23	039977	38
23	828716	2·31	868440	1·92	960277	4·23	039723	37
24	828855	2·30	868324	1·92	960531	4·23	039469	36
25	828993	2·30	868209	1·92	960784	4·23	039216	35
26	829131	2·30	868093	1·92	961038	4·23	038962	34
27	829269	2·30	867978	1·93	961291	4·23	038709	33
28	829407	2·30	867862	1·93	961545	4·23	038455	32
29	829545	2·30	867747	1·93	961799	4·23	038201	31
30	829683	2·30	867631	1·93	962052	4·23	037948	30
31	9·829821	2·29	9·867515	1·93	9·962306	4·23	10·037694	29
32	829959	2·29	867399	1·93	962560	4·23	037440	28
33	830097	2·29	867283	1·93	962813	4·23	037187	27
34	830234	2·29	867167	1·93	963067	4·23	036933	26
35	830372	2·29	867051	1·93	963320	4·23	036680	25
36	830509	2·29	866935	1·94	963574	4·23	036426	24
37	830646	2·29	866819	1·94	963827	4·23	036173	23
38	830784	2·29	866703	1·94	964081	4·23	035919	22
39	830921	2·28	866586	1·94	964335	4·23	035665	21
40	831058	2·28	866470	1·94	964588	4·22	035412	20
41	9·831195	2·28	9·866353	1·94	9·964842	4·22	10·035158	19
42	831332	2·28	866237	1·94	965095	4·22	034905	18
43	831469	2·28	866120	1·94	965349	4·22	034651	17
44	831606	2·28	866004	1·95	965602	4·22	034398	16
45	831742	2·28	865887	1·95	965855	4·22	034145	15
46	831879	2·28	865770	1·95	966105	4·22	033891	14
47	832015	2·27	865653	1·95	966362	4·22	033638	13
48	832152	2·27	865536	1·95	966616	4·22	033384	12
49	832288	2·27	865419	1·95	966869	4·22	033131	11
50	832425	2·27	865302	1·95	967123	4·22	032877	10
51	9·832561	2·27	9·865185	1·95	9·967376	4·22	10·032624	9
52	832697	2·27	865068	1·95	967629	4·22	032371	8
53	832833	2·27	864950	1·95	967883	4·22	032117	7
54	832969	2·26	864833	1·96	968136	4·22	031864	6
55	833105	2·26	864716	1·96	968389	4·22	031611	5
56	833241	2·26	864598	1·96	968643	4·22	031357	4
57	833377	2·26	864481	1·96	968896	4·22	031104	3
58	833512	2·26	864363	1·96	969149	4·22	030851	2
59	833648	2·26	864245	1·96	969403	4·22	030597	1
60	833783	2·26	864127	1·96	969656	4·22	030344	0
	Cosine	D.	Sine	D.	Cotang.	D.	Tang.	M.

(47 DEGREES.)

M.	Sine	D.	Cosine	D.	Tang.	D.	Cotang.	
0	9·833783	2·26	9·864127	1·96	9·969656	4·22	10·030344	60
1	833919	2·25	864010	1·96	969909	4·22	030091	59
2	834054	2·25	863892	1·97	970162	4·22	029838	58
3	834189	2·25	863774	1·97	970416	4·22	029584	57
4	834325	2·25	863656	1·97	970669	4·22	029331	56
5	834460	2·25	863538	1·97	970922	4·22	029078	55
6	834595	2·25	863419	1·97	971175	4·22	028825	54
7	834730	2·25	863301	1·97	971429	4·22	028571	53
8	834865	2·25	863183	1·97	971682	4·22	028318	52
9	834999	2·24	863064	1·97	971935	4·22	028065	51
10	835134	2·24	862946	1·98	972188	4·22	027812	50
11	9·835269	2·24	9·862827	1·98	9·972441	4·22	10·027559	49
12	835403	2·24	862709	1·98	972694	4·22	027306	48
13	835538	2·24	862590	1·98	972948	4·22	027052	47
14	835672	2·24	862471	1·98	973201	4·22	026799	46
15	835807	2·24	862353	1·98	973454	4·22	026546	45
16	835941	2·24	862234	1·98	973707	4·22	026293	44
17	836075	2·23	862115	1·98	973960	4·22	026040	43
18	836209	2·23	861996	1·98	974213	4·22	025787	42
19	836343	2·23	861877	1·98	974466	4·22	025534	41
20	836477	2·23	861758	1·99	974719	4·22	025281	40
21	9·836611	2·23	9·861638	1·99	9·974973	4·22	10·025027	39
22	836745	2·23	861519	1·99	975226	4·22	024774	38
23	836878	2·23	861400	1·99	975479	4·22	024521	37
24	837012	2·22	861280	1·99	975732	4·22	024268	36
25	837146	2·22	861161	1·99	975985	4·22	024015	35
26	837279	2·22	861041	1·99	976238	4·22	023762	34
27	837412	2·22	860922	1·99	976491	4·22	023509	33
28	837546	2·22	860802	1·99	976744	4·22	023256	32
29	837679	2·22	860682	2·00	976997	4·22	023003	31
30	837812	2·22	860562	2·00	977250	4·22	022750	30
31	9·837945	2·22	9·860442	2·00	9·977503	4·22	10·022497	29
32	838078	2·21	860322	2·00	977756	4·22	022244	28
33	838211	2·21	860202	2·00	978009	4·22	021991	27
34	838344	2·21	860082	2·00	978262	4·22	021738	26
35	838477	2·21	859962	2·00	978515	4·22	021485	25
36	838610	2·21	859842	2·00	978768	4·22	021232	24
37	838742	2·21	859721	2·01	979021	4·22	020979	23
38	838875	2·21	859601	2·01	979274	4·22	020726	22
39	839007	2·21	859480	2·01	979527	4·22	020473	21
40	839140	2·20	859360	2·01	979780	4·22	020220	20
41	9·839272	2·20	9·859239	2·01	9·980033	4·22	10·019967	19
42	839404	2·20	859119	2·01	980286	4·22	019714	18
43	839536	2·20	858998	2·01	980538	4·22	019462	17
44	839668	2·20	858877	2·01	980791	4·21	019209	16
45	839800	2·20	858756	2·02	981044	4·21	018956	15
46	839932	2·20	858635	2·02	981297	4·21	018703	14
47	840064	2·19	858514	2·02	981550	4·21	018450	13
48	840196	2·19	858393	2·02	981803	4·21	018197	12
49	840328	2·19	858272	2·02	982056	4·21	017944	11
50	840459	2·19	858151	2·02	982309	4·21	017691	10
51	9·840591	2·19	9·858029	2·02	9·982562	4·21	10·017438	9
52	840722	2·19	857908	2·02	982814	4·21	017186	8
53	840854	2·19	857786	2·02	983067	4·21	016933	7
54	840985	2·19	857665	2·03	983320	4·21	016680	6
55	841116	2·18	857543	2·03	983573	4·21	016427	5
56	841247	2·18	857422	2·03	983826	4·21	016174	4
57	841378	2·18	857300	2·03	984079	4·21	015921	3
58	841509	2·18	857178	2·03	984331	4·21	015669	2
59	841640	2·18	857056	2·03	984584	4·21	015416	1
60	841771	2·18	856934	2·03	984837	4·21	015163	0
	Cosine	D.	Sine	D.	Cotang.	D.	Tang.	M.

(46 DEGREES.)

CPSIA information can be obtained
at www.ICGtesting.com
Printed in the USA
LVHW040721020323
740708LV00002B/85

9 783375 148850